Contributions to Jaina Studies

Contributions to Jaina Studies

Jaina Schools & Sects

PETER FLÜGEL

MLBD PUBLICATIONS

Motilal Banarsidass Publications

MOTILAL BANARSIDASS
PUBLICATIONS
4741/23, Ansari Road, Daryaganj, New Delhi - 110002 (India)
Email: mlbd@mlbd.com | sales@mlbd.com
exports@mlbd.com | publications@mlbd.com
Website: www.mlbd.com

Contributions to Jaina Studies
by
Peter Flügel

First Edition Published in 2020

Published in India by Motilal Banarsidass Publications

ISBN : 978-81-94243-83-0 (HB)

Printed and bound in India

Preface

The twelve articles assembled in this first volume of the author's collected papers in Jaina Studies written in English were published as journal articles and book chapters between 1996 and 2016. They are reproduced here in almost identical form, though an attempt was made to eliminate typographical errors and minor mistakes. Three articles which on request were first published without the use of diacritical marks have been changed back to their original format: chapters 2, 6, 11. In a few cases, the biographical data of recently deceased individuals were updated.

The articles address aspects of the history, doctrine, organisation and religious practice of Jaina mendicant orders, sects and schools, following an overview of the contemporary monastic traditions. They are outcomes of a long-term research project, covering a period of over 30 years, on the aniconic or *amūrtipūjaka* Śvetāmbara Jaina traditions, which have been neglected by modern scholarship, and with the notable exception of the Terāpanth and the Śramaṇa Saṅgha, are almost unknown even in India itself. Two articles pertain to the Akrama Vijñāna Mārga, a new syncretistic religious movement, combining Sāṃkhya ontology with Jaina soteriology.

The articles are here republished in a thematic sequence. The original dates and places of publication are: (1) Flügel, P. (ed.) (2006), *Studies in Jaina History and Culture: Disputes and Dialogues.* London: Routledge Advances in Jaina Studies, pp. 312-398; (2) Melton, J.G. & G. Baumann (eds.) (2002), *Religions of the World: A Comprehensive Encyclopedia of Beliefs and Practices.* Santa Barbara: ABC-Clio, pp. 1221-1223; (3) Kimura, T. (ed.) (2014), *Indian and Buddhist Studies in Honor of President Dr. Shouou (Kiyoaki) Okuda in Recognition of his Lifelong Scholarship.* Osaka: Kosei Publishers, pp. 314-333; (4) Caillat, C. & N. Balbir (eds.) (2008), *Jaina Studies.* Delhi: Motilal Banarsidass, pp. 181-

279; (5) *Jaina Studies: Newsletter of the Centre of Jaina Studies* 11(2016) 28-31; (6) Melton, J.G. & G. Baumann (eds.) (2002), *Religions of the World: A Comprehensive Encyclopedia of Beliefs and Practices*. Santa Barbara: ABC-Clio, pp. 1266-1267; (7) *Bulletin D'Études Indiennes* 13 (1996) 117-176; (8) *South Asia Research* 23, 1 (2003) 7-53; (9) Qvarnström, O. (ed.) (2003), *Jainism and Early Buddhism in the Indian Cultural Context: Festschrift in Honour of P.S. Jaini*. Fremont, California: Asian Humanities Press, pp. 167-204; (10) *Jaina Studies: Newsletter of the Centre of Jaina Studies* 4 (2009) 24-29; (11) King, A.S. & J. Brockington (eds.) (2005), *The Intimate Other: Love Divine in the Indic Religions*. New Delhi: Orient Longman, pp. 194-243; (12) *International Journal of Tantric Studies* 7, 1 & 7, 2 (2005) 1-43 & 1-28.

A significant number of the author's publications on the *amūrtipūjaka* traditions are published in German, notably a monograph on the Terāpanth tradition (*Askese und Devotion: Das rituelle System der Terāpanth Śvetāmbara Jaina*. Band I-II. Alt- und Neuindische Studien 56. Dettelbach: Röll Verlag, 2018), and the first four of six instalments of a comprehensive study of the history of the Sthānakavāsī traditions, published under the title 'Protestantische und Post-Protestantische Jaina-Reformbewegungen: Zur Geschichte und Organisation der Sthānakavāsī I-IV' in the *Berliner Indologische Studien* 13-14 (2000) 37-103, 15-17 (2003) 149-240, 18 (2007) 127-206, 20 (2012) 37-124. These publications should be read in conjunction with the articles presented in this volume.

I would like to express my gratitude to Pranav Jain for publishing my English language articles in Jaina Studies with Motilal Banarsidass Publications. Special thanks go to Kanchan Vasudev for preparing the print ready of text and to Manju Arya for preparing the Book of this volume.

Peter Flügel
London, January, 7, 2019

For Ingrid

Contents

1

Demographic Trends in Jaina Monasticism

The study of Jainism as a living religion is still hampered by a lack of reliable sociological and demographic information both on the Jain laity and Jain mendicants.[1] Most empirical studies to date have been thematically oriented or were of an exploratory nature. They were based on the methods advanced by the classical anthropological village studies or on small surveys of a non-representative nature.[2] In both cases, the units of investigation were defined in terms of observer categories[3] which were often created *ad hoc* in the field due to the advantages of snowball sampling under conditions of limited resources. In a paper read at the American Oriental Society Meeting in 1978, at a time when comprehensive field studies had yet to be conducted, the late Kendall Folkert (1993: 156) suggested avoiding the inevitable abstractions of 'general accounts of the Jains' by concentrating on 'the smaller divisions within the tradition' which 'have actually been the basic units of the tradition.' What Folkert had in mind was to study the individual 'schools, sects or orders' (*gaccha*) of the Jain mendicant tradition,[4] rather than 'Jain religious culture' in general.[5] Certainly, not all Jains coalesce around monastic groups, but the majority does so in one way or another.

The investigation of categories which are recognised by the Jains themselves promises indeed to yield testable results of greater accuracy and relevance for the Jain community itself. However, the research programme envisaged by Folkert has yet to be implemented.[6] Despite the pioneering studies of Vilas Sangave (1959/1980) on the social divisions of the Jain lay community and of Muni Uttam Kamal Jain (1975) on the pre-modern history of the religious divisions of the Jain mendicants, most students of Jainism, and indeed most Jains, have still no way of knowing how many independent mendicant orders exist today and how they are organised.[7] The aim of this chapter is to fill this gap and to provide a brief overview of the present schools, orders and sects[8] within both the Śvetāmbara-and the Digambara-denomination[9] and to bring together the available demographic data on the current Jain monastic traditions. A comprehensive description of the Jain lay movements is beyond the scope of this chapter.

Jain laity

Although no studies of the demographic trends in Jain monasticism are currently available, general surveys of the Jain lay community have been produced on the basis of the available census data by Sangave (1959/1980), Sharma (1976) and M.K. Jain (1986). The inclusion of the category 'Jain'[10] into the questionnaire for the Census of India 1881[11] is widely regarded as one of the defining moments for the modern construction of Jainism as an independent 'religion.'[12] It was introduced by the colonial government after Jacobi (1879) proved the historical independence of Jainism from Buddhism, and a number of high court judgements in favour of westernised Jains such Paṇḍit Padmarāja (1886), J.L. Jaini (1916) and C.R. Jain (1926) who were interested in securing a privileged legal status for their community. However, notwithstanding the desire of the educated Jain elite to establish a clear-cut boundary between 'Jainism' and 'Hinduism,' in the census itself many Jains continued to return themselves as 'Hindu.'

A number of explanations have been put forward for this. Amongst them 'enumerators' error' figures most prominently, since local volunteers frequently filled in the census forms themselves on the basis of their own local knowledge.[13] Another interpretation suggests that many respondents were either unable or unwilling to make a distinction between the categories. They may have followed the example of their ancestors who often, in the fear of persecution, maintained an outward conformity with Hinduism (cf. Williams 1983: xix). In other words, they were not so much confronted with the question of 'who they were' (Cohn 1992: 248), but rather how they preferred to be perceived.[14]

Reform orientated Jain intellectuals were highly conscious of the problem of communal self-objectification already by the 1870s, and in response to the low turnout of Jains in 1881 actively embraced the census as a medium of communal self-representation. At the turn of the twentieth century, the leaders of the newly founded Jain Conferences even designed petitions which actively encouraged community members to return themselves as 'Jain' and not as 'Hindu.' They also volunteered to carry out the census in their own communities in an attempt to boost the numbers and hence the importance of the Jain community in the eyes of the colonial government.[15] Demographic growth was generally depicted as a sign of communal progress and used as an argument in contexts of 'democratic' politics of representation.[16] This sentiment is still echoed today in the work of Vilas Sangave (1980) and other Jain intellectuals who lament the fact that, even after a century of communal revival, many Jains keep on regarding themselves and are regarded as Hindus,[17] which 'necessarily vitiates the census figures and obscures the increase or decrease of the Jaina population from census to census' (ibid.: 3).[18]

The debate on whether Jains are culturally 'Hindus' or a 'minority community' wages unabated within the community. Thus far, Jain communalists have failed to establish the Jains 'as a separate social group' (ibid.: 411) against the opposition of many Śvetāmbara *ācāryas*. The majority of the Jain laity retains an ambiguous social identity midway between the Jain mendicant communities and the wider 'Hindu' society. It is therefore not surprising that still no reliable demographic data is available for the Jain laity. Certainly, the Jain community is very small. The official figure generated by the Census of India 1991 was 3,352,706, that is, 0.4 per cent of the Indian population (Vijayanunni 1991: x–xi). The Census of 2001 produced the figure of 4,225,053, also 0.4 per cent of the Indian population (www. censusindia.net). In addition, about 150,000 Jains live outside India, but no mendicants. No data is available on the number of lay followers of particular Jain schools and sects, although some of these may be estimated on the basis of caste directories, in cases where caste and sect membership widely overlap.

Jain mendicants

The rhetoric of numbers, adopted by the Jain lay Conferences, also had a significant influence on the monastic orders, which were put under pressure to compete with each other not only in terms of behavioural purity and education, but also in terms of sheer numbers — in the name of democracy and modernisation.[19] The rhetoric of numbers is not necessarily new, but no documents con-tain-ing information on the actual number of Jain monks and nuns are known before the early-modern period.

There are two exceptions. The Jinacaritra in the so-called Paryuṣaṇa Kalpa Sūtra, which was traditionally attributed to Bhadrabāhu I who is said to have lived *c.*170 or 162 years after Mahāvīra although the Jinacaritra is certainly much younger, tells us that Mahāvīra's four-fold community comprised of

> fourteen thousand Śramaṇas with Indrabhūti at their head; thirty-six thousand nuns with Candanā at their head; one hundred and fifty-nine thousand lay votaries with Saṅkhaṣataka at their head; three hundred and eighteen thousand female lay votaries with Sulasā and Revatī at their head.
>
> (Jinacaritra 136f., in Jacobi 1884: 267f.)

The Sthavirāvalī, or List of the Elders, which is generally attributed to Devarddhi Gaṇi, the fifth century CE redactor of the Śvetāmbara canon, mentions not 14,000, but merely 4,411 monks and gives no total figures for nuns and laity (Sthavirāvalī 1, in Jacobi 1884: 286f.). Both of these accounts, collected in the same compilation, are somewhat mythical, but they clearly depict relatively small communities.[20] The first text pictures a very high proportion of mendicants (1–9.54 laity) and an overwhelming numerical dominance of female ascetics and lay supporters. The prevalence of nuns is all the more remarkable, because, until very recently, neither Buddhist nor Hindu monastic orders had significant, if any, numbers of female ascetics. Even today, Theravāda Buddhist orders in Sri Lanka, Thailand, Burma and Laos do not have fully initiated *bhikkunis.*[21] The second account contains a list of the succession after Mahāvīra, which is corroborated by epigraphical evidence.[22] It mentions only the names of 7 nuns amongst a total of 19 disciples of Nandanabhadra, the seventh elder (*thera*) after Mahāvīra.[23] The corresponding inscription of the first or second century CE, mentions 9 nuns, which Bühler (1890: 321) accepted as 'clear proof that in the first century of our own era the order of female ascetics was well established.'

At the beginning of the twentieth century most lay communities began to publish sporadic demographic information on the numbers of their monks and nuns in community newsletters. However, these newsletters had only a limited circulation. Readily available information on individual monastic communities remained largely inaccessible until the last two decades of the twentieth century, which saw a significant improvement. The person responsible for this is the Sthānakavāsī layman Bābūlāl 'Ujjavala' Jain of Mumbaī. Once an active member of the Akhil Bhāratīya Jain Mahāmaṇḍal, the principal ecumenical forum of the Jain communalists[24] founded in 1899 under the name Jain Young Men's Association but renamed in 1929, he began to compile and publish charts of the *cāturmāsa* residences of all the mendicants of the reformist Sthānakavāsī Śramaṇa Saṅgha from 1979 onwards. The rational was to generate a sense of unity and coordination amongst the followers of the Śramaṇa Saṅgha, which, although nominally governed by only one *ācārya*, is internally subdivided into many local mendicant traditions. The documentation proved to be useful in keeping track of the movements of the almost 1,000 mendicants, which from the time of the foundation of the Śramaṇa Saṅgha in 1952 began to extend their *vihāras* from their traditional strongholds in western and northern India to the entire territory of the new independent state of India.

In 1984, B.U. Jain produced an extended version of the *cāturmās* list, now covering not only the Śramaṇa Saṅgha, but all Sthānakavāsī ascetic and lay communities. In this he was supported by the Śramaṇa Saṅgha *muni* Kanhaiyalāl, the Mūrtipūjaka *paṅnyās* Haras Sāgar, and the Akhil Bhāratīya Samagra Jain Cāturmās Sūcī Prakāśan Pariṣad Bambaī. Finally, in 1986, the first annual Samagra Jain Cāturmāsi Sūcī was published with the intention of providing information on the *cāturmās* residencies of all Jain mendicants.[25] This project was officially endorsed by the great assembly of the Śramaṇa Saṅgha ascetics in Pune in 1987 (AISJC 1987: 19f., B.U. Jain 1987: 71). From this time onwards, the available demographic data of all Jain mendicant communities were published annually, first by the Cāturmās Sūcī Prakāśan Pariṣad 1986–1992, then by the Jain Ektā Mahāmaṇḍal, and last by B.U. Jain himself (SJCS 1987: 67f.).

The following overview of the current divisions of the Jain mendicants, their numbers and main demographic shifts between 1987 and 2002 is to a significant extent based on the data compiled in B.U. Jain's *Cāturmās Sūcī* publications of 1987, 1990, 1996, 1999 and 2002. For want of reliable information, I was not always able to shed light on earlier demographic developments. To my knowledge, only the Śvetāmbara Terā Panth has published complete demographic and biodata going back to the time of its foundation in 1760 (Navratnamal 1981ff.). I was able to locate some useful material on the numbers of Sthānakavāsī mendicants in the early twentieth century, but little on the Mūrtipūjaka and Digambara ascetics. In these instances I had to rely on sporadic information scattered in the secondary literature.

I have rearranged B.U. Jain's data on the Śvetāmbara mendicant orders into a number of tables summarising figures from 1987, 1990, and 1996, with additional information from 1999 and 2002 provided either in the text or in supplementary tables or footnotes. Initially, the figures published by B.U. Jain were not reliable for non-Sthānakavāsī orders, but this has changed with regard to the Śvetāmbara orders. An important lacuna in B.U. Jain's publications is the lack of reliable information on the Digambara ascetics, on which no sound data existed until recently. I have nevertheless cited some of B.U. Jain's fragmentary and inconsistent figures on the Digambaras between 1986 and 2000, because they contribute significantly to our generally meagre knowledge on the Digambara mendicants, whose organisational history is reviewed in greater detail in this chapter. From the year 2000 onwards, reliable information on the Digambara mendicants and *cāturmāsa* places is published annually by A. Jain (2000a, 2000b, 2001) of Indore in form of a brochure which together with D. Śāstrī's (1985) Digambara Jain Sādhu Paricay is the main source on the demography of the Digambara ascetics.

The figures in the available Jain publications rely on credible self-reporting by the different Jain orders. The quality of this data, especially from the Mūrtipūjaka traditions, varies from year to year. In order to compensate for this, B.U. Jain included personal estimates in his summary tables to account for those ascetics for whom no detailed information was supplied to him (B.U. Jain 1996: 37, 27f., n. 1–2, 1999: 382, n. 1–7). By contrast, I only counted those ascetics which were listed individually and not B.U. Jain's considerably higher estimates, which may nevertheless represent a more accurate picture. Another difference concerns the classification of mendicant orders into broader categories. From 1990, B.U. Jain re-classified certain reformist movements, such as Amar Muni's Vīrāyatan, Muni Suśīl Kumār's Arhat Saṅgha and the Nava Terā Panth, under the new category 'independently roaming progressive thinkers who use vehicles' (*pragatiśīl vicārak vāhan vihārī svatantra vicaraṇ karne vāle*). But I continued listing them together with their traditions of origin. A major deficit of the publications of B.U. Jain and A. Jain is the lack of statistical data on the social background of the ascetics, especially on caste, class and region, their initiation age and level of formal education. They also offer no overview of the history and organisation of the mendicant groups. As far as possible, I have supplemented this information from other sources.

In the following tables, the *ācāryas* are also included in the total numbers of *sādhus*. A hyphen indicates that no information is available or means zero. The data is neither complete nor entirely consistent. But, in general, it is reliable and provides the most accurate available information to date.

Mūrtipūjaka

The Mūrtipūjaka mendicants are currently divided into six independent traditions, which emerged between the eleventh and the sixteenth century CE from the *caityavāsin*, or temple-dwelling, Śvetāmbara tradition:[26] (1) the Kharatara Gaccha (1023), (2) the A(ñ)cala Gaccha or Vidhi Pakṣa (1156), (3) the Āgamika- or Tristuti Gaccha (1193) and (4) the Tapā Gaccha (1228), from which (5) the Vimala Gaccha (1495), and (6) the Pārśvacandra Gaccha (1515) separated.[27] The two main reasons for these so-called *gaccha*-reforms were (a) the laxity of the *caityavāsins*, and (b) minor doctrinal differences. Similar reforms within the *gacchas* in the seventeenth century led to the division between *yatis* and *saṁvegī sādhus*. The term *saṁvegī*, upright, was introduced by Upādhyāya Yaśo Vijay (1624–1688) for his own reformist mendicant group, whose tradition was revived in the nineteenth and early twentieth centuries, at a time when most of the previously dominant white-clad *yatis* were replaced by yellow-clad *saṁvegī sādhus*. Today, almost all Mūrtipūjaka mendicant groups are *saṁvegī* orders. With the exception of the Vallabhasūri Samudāya of the Tapā Gaccha, all reverted to wearing white dresses. The orders are independently organised and form the institutional core of distinct sects and schools. At present, no detailed sociological or demographic information is available for most of these monastic traditions, especially for the period before the twentieth century. Two notable exceptions are the studies of the recent history and organisation of the Tapā Gaccha by Cort (1989: 93–112) and of the A(ñ)cala Gaccha by Balbir (2003), both

Figure 1.1 Yati Motī Sāgar of the A(ñ)cala Gaccha in Mumbaī. Photograph by the author, December 2004.

of which are supplemented by the studies of the *paṭṭāvalīs* of both traditions by Śivprasād (2000, 2001). Of the Kharatara Gaccha only the *paṭṭāvalī* of its monastic order and contemporary religious practices of the laity have been studied (Laidlaw 1995, Babb 1996).

The Kharatara Gaccha and the A(ñ)cala Gaccha are the only Mūrtipūjaka traditions which still have a dual system of succession *(paramparā)* of *yatis* and *saṁvegī sādhus*;[28] although there is only one *yati* left in the A(ñ)cala Gaccha (see Figures 1.1 and 1.2).[29] The *sādhus* and *sādhvīs* of the A(ñ)cala Gaccha are nowadays centrally organised under the supervision of only one *ācārya* (*gacchādhipati*) and still[30] constitute one of the largest mendicant orders of the Mūrtipūjaka tradition.[31] By far the largest of the six Mūrtipūjaka *gacchas* is the Tapā Gaccha. According to Darśanavijaya (1933: 67, fn.), it had only 428 members at the end of the fifteenth century. By 2002 this figure had risen to 6,696.[32] Today, the Tapā Gaccha is divided into two branches (*śākhā*), the Vijaya Śākhā and the Sāgara

Śākhā. The *śākhās* are further subdivided into a number of lineages which are currently divided in twenty separate groups, or *samudāyas*, which are named after prominent *ācāryas* of their root lineage, with the *sādhvīs* defined through the male members of the traditions (Cort 1991: 661f.). The origins of the Sāgara Śākhā are opaque. Kañcansāgarsūri *et al.* (1977: 311–76) attribute its beginnings to Hīra Vijaya Sūri (1527–1569), though Śāh (1987: 14, 65, 168) points to the year 1630 in which Ācārya Rāj Sūri (formerly Muni Mukti Sāgar) seceded from the main line of the Tapā Gaccha with the

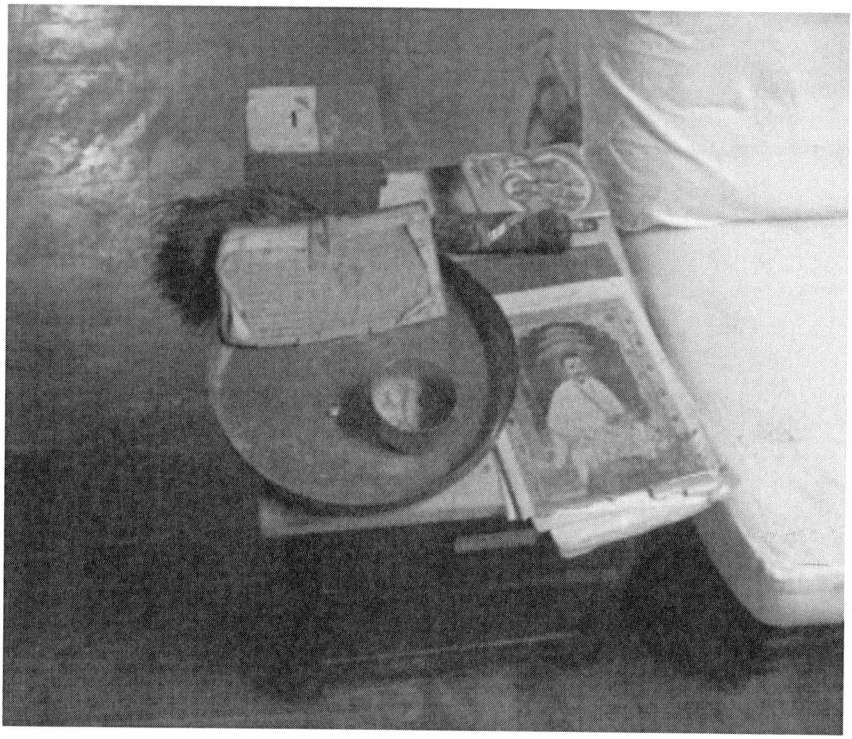

Figure 1.2 Paraphernalia of Yati Moti Sagar. Photograph by the author in Mumbaī, December 2004.

help of the first *nagarśeṭh* of Ahmedabad, Śāntīdās Jhāverī (1585/1590–1659);[33] who in 1660 also sponsored the Ānandjī Kalyāṇjī Trust.[34] According to Dundas (1996: 101, n. 108), this tradition was disrupted in the eighteenth and nineteenth centuries.[35] It was revived in the mid-nineteenth century by Mayā Sāgar with the help of Hemābhāī, another *nagarśeṭh* of Ahmedabad, and of Śeṭh

Haṭhīsiṅha Keśarībhāī (died 1845).[36] After Mayā Sāgar, the tradition split into two *samudāyas*, the two most famous *ācāryas* of which were Buddhi Sāgar Sūri (1874–1925) and the 'Agamoddhāraka' Sāgar Ānand Sūri (1875–1950) respectively. The Vijaya Śākhā emerged apparently in 1657, a date which roughly corresponds to Śāh's (1987) version of the origin of the Sāgar Śākhā, following a succession dispute after the death of Vijay Deva Sūri (1577–1656).[37] In 1999, it was internally subdivided into twenty *samudāyas*.

Cort (1989) observed momentous changes within the Vijaya Śākhā over the last one and a half centuries, as narrated in the histories of the Tapā Gaccha orders by Ratna Prabhā Vijay (1948) and others. First of all, the *yatis*, that is, sedentary ascetics who fulfil ritual and administrative tasks and who do not pledge themselves fully to the observance of the *mahāvratas*, became almost extinct in the twentieth century[38] and were replaced by the reformed *saṁvegī sādhus*, of which apparently only two dozen or so existed in the early nineteenth century:[39]

> In the mid-19th century, several activist *sādhus* reinvigorated the institution of the *saṃvegi sādhu*. Over two-thirds of the over 1,000 *sādhus* in the Tapā Gacch today trace their lineage back to Paññyās Maṇi Vijay Gaṇī (1796–1879), known as Dādā (Grandfather). One of his disciples was the former Sthānakvāsī *sādhu* Muni Buddhi Vijay (1807–1882), known by his Sthānakvāsī name of Buṭerāyjī. He was very active in the Panjab among both mendicants and laity, convincing Sthānakvāsīs of the correctness of the Mūrtipūjak teachings. Among his disciples was the charismatic Ātmārāmjī (1837–1896), who in 1876 in Ahmedabad took a second *dīkṣā* (initiation) as the Mūrtipūjak *saṁvegī sādhu* Ānand Vijay, along with eighteen other Sthānakvāsī *sādhus*, under the leadership of Ātmārāmjī and other similar minded *sādhus*, and later under the umbrella of the Śvetāmbar Mūrtipūjak Conference, a wide-ranging campaign was waged to reform both mendicant and lay practices. As the result of this reform the institution of the *yati* has virtually disappeared from the Mūrtipūjak society.
>
> (Cort 1989: 99f.)

Cort showed that after the disintegration of the *gaddī*-centred *yati*-orders, new decentred patterns emerged, based on demographics, geography and charisma rather than on organisational power and property. It is worthwhile quoting him again at length:

> As the Tapā Gacch has grown, it has subdivided in new ways which shed light on earlier processes of subdivision and *gacch* formation. The former subdivisions, which were based primarily on affiliation with the *gāḍīs* (seats, thrones) of specific *śrīpūjyas*, have disappeared, with the exception of the Vijay-Sāgar *śākhā* distinction, and been replaced by about 15 *samudāys* (literally 'co-arising,' i.e. descendants of the same *sādhu*; here synonymous with *sampradāy*). In general, three interrelated principles accounted for the development of the various *samudāys*: geography, demographics, and charisma. As the number of *sādhus* increased, it became increasingly difficult for one *ācārya* to oversee the large number of *sādhus* under him. Smaller groups of *sādhus* were placed under the direction of other senior *sādhus*, and the sharp increase in the number of the *ācāryas* within the Tapā Gacch in the past several years is directly related to this need for additional supervisory personnel. As the *sādhus* increasingly interacted solely with the lesser *ācārya* rather than the seniormost *ācārya*, a new *samudāy* might evolve.
>
> (Cort 1989: 103f.)

According to Jacobi (in Glasenapp 1925: 342, 352–354), the Tapā Gaccha was in 1913–1914 still ruled by 'a number' of *śrīpūjyas* and, as a whole, comprised 1,200 *sādhus* and *sādhvīs*.[40] Guérinot (1926: 56) reported the existence of '30 sub-divisions' of the Tapā Gaccha at the beginning of the twentieth century, without mentioning any figures, while B.U. Jain (1986) and Cort (1989: 100–105) found only two *śākhās* and altogether 15–17 autonomous groups (*samudāya*). Table 1.1 shows that by 1999 this figure had grown to twenty due to further splits in the dominant Vijaya Śākhā tradition of Prem Sūri, the latest being the separation of Kamal Ratna Sūri from the Ramacandrasūri Samudāya in 1998. Prem Sūri was one of the chief disciples of Buddhi Vijay, the reformer of the *saṁvegī sādhus*, together with Ātmā Rām, Dharma Vijay (1868–1922) and Nīti Sūri (whose lineage further split into the Bhaktisūri- and the Siddhīsūri Samudāya) (Ratna Prabhā Viyay 5, 2 1948: 218). At present, four *samudāyas* trace themselves back to Prem Sūri: the Ramacandrasūri Samudāya, the Kamalaratnasūri Samudāya, the Bhuvanabhānusūri Samudāya and the Amṛtasūri Samudāya. Four *samudāyas* descend directly from Ātmā Rām (Vijay Ānand), the most famous disciple of Buddhi Vijay: the Vallabhasūri Samudāya, the Mohanalāla Samudāya, the Dharmasūri Samudāya and the Śānticandrasūri Samudāya. The Ramacandrasūri Samudāya is the only group which advocates the *be tithi* interpretation of the religious calendar,[41] and has therefore been excluded from many Tapā Gaccha *upāśrayas*. Table 1.1 does not include detailed figures for 1986 (cf. Cort 1989: 491f.), 1999 and 2002, which are appended in the endnotes. But it reflects the group structure of 1999 and shows that at the time the Mūrtipūjaka tradition was divided into some twenty-seven independent monastic groups.

In 1999, the Mūrtipūjaka *gacchas* comprised altogether 6,843 mendicants, 1,489 *sādhus* and 5,354 *sādhvīs*. Amongst them, the Tapā Gaccha was the largest tradition, with 6,027 mendicants, 1,349 *sādhus* and 4,678 *sādhvīs*.[42] The table shows a massive increase in numbers particularly of female ascetics within little more than a decade.[43] It also illustrates the fact, emphasised by Cort (1989: 494, 1991: 661), that occasionally significant population shifts occur within and between *samudāyas*, which – in the absence of centralised *gaddī*-structures – seem to divide and unite like segmentary lineages, under the influence of circumstantial factors. Similar changes cannot be observed at the level of the *gaccha* categories.[44] Commensality between ascetics of different *gacchas* is, for instance, prohibited.[45] Schubring (2000: § 139, p. 252) already noted that *gacchas* are not necessarily actual groups. Mūrtipūjaka *gacchas* are in the first place doctrinal schools and at the same time social categories which may or may not be congruent with organised monastic groups, such as the *samudāyas*. However, doctrinal disputes are also significant for processes of group-formation at the *samudāya* level. A good example is the *ek tithi/be tithi* dispute between Rām Candra Sūri and Bhuvan Bhānu Sūri, which split the Premsūri Samudāya into two main sections in 1986 (Cort 1999: 50f.).

Another important factor influencing processes of fission and fusion are the ways in which *gacchas* and *samudāya*s are organised. Shāntā (1985: 329–331) and Cort (1991) explain population shifts and processes of group segmentation amongst the Tapā Gaccha *samudāyas* mainly with reference to charismatic leadership. Cort emphasises, for instance, the effect of the unusually high numbers of *ācāryas* on the processes of segmentation and the size of Tapā Gaccha *samudāyas*. He explains this effect both with 'internal organisational pressures for the growth of the number of Tapā Gacch *ācāryas* – a growth which has been criticised by many *sādhus* and laity' and with 'the desire of influential laity to have the *sādhu* of whom they are a personal devotee be an *ācārya*' (ibid.: 668, n. 16). But he also notes that a distinction between 'charismatic' *saṁvegī*

Table 1.1 **Mūrtipūjaka *sādhus and sādhvīs* 1987, 1990 and 1996**[46]

Gaccha Samudāya	*Gacchādhipati*[47] *1996*	*Ācārya*			*Cāturmāsa-places*			*Sādhu*			*Sādhvī*			*Total*		
		1987	*1990*	*1996*	*1987*	*1990*	*1996*	*1987*	*1990*	*1996*	*1987*	*1990*	*1996*	*1987*	*1990*	*1996*
1 Tapā Gaccha																
A. Vijaya Śākhā																
Rāmcandrasūri	Mahodaysūri[48]	27	17	28	144	124	131	423	238	265	443	463	520	866	701	785
Kamalratnasūri[49]	—	—	—	—	—	—	—	—	—	—	—	—	—	—	—	—
Bhuvanbhanusūri	Jayghoṣsūri[50]	—	12	9	—	78	80	—	225	232	—	225	210	—	450	442
Amṛtsūri	Jinendrasūri[51]	—	—	1	—	—	6	—	—	5	—	—	21	—	—	26
Nītisūri	Arihantsiddhasūri[52]	4	4	3	94	82	70	61	42	40	312	329	385	373	371	425
Bhaktisūri (Samīvalā)	Premsūri[53]	7	7	6	55	44	36	65	59	48	193	163	195	258	222	243
Siddhisūri (Bāpjī)	Bhadraṅkarsūri[54]	2	4	3	13	54	13	24	28	26	80	373	99	104	401	125
Dharmavijay (Ḍehlāvālā)	Rāmsūri[55]	6	6	6	58	62	67	35	33	29	196	214	220	231	247	249
Nemīsūri	Devsūri[56]	19	18	27	102	93	112	180	189	195	340	362	396	520	551	591
Vallabhsūri	Indradinnsūri[57]	2	2	6	69	57	57	57	60	52	195	210	205	252	270	257
Labdhisūri (Navinsūri)	Jinbhadrasūri[58]	13	12	9	36	39	35	57	56	52	163	177	181	220	233	233
Mohanlālsūri	Cidānandsūri[59]	1	1	1	20	19	17	13	17	19	46	34	23	59	51	42
Dharmasūri (Mohansūri)	Yaśodevsūri[60]	3	4	7	62	50	65	36	34	30	189	200	186	225	234	216

Keśarsūri	Hemprabhasūri[61]	1	3	2	44	41	45	28	26	25	157	162	173	185	188	198
Kanaksūri	Kalāpūrṇsūri[62]	1	1	1	73	72	84	22	24	26	455	379	421	477	403	447
(Vāgaḍvālā)																
Himācalsūri	Panyās Ratnākar[63]	1	1	—	28	23	27	17	16	20	81	75	121	98	91	141
Śanticandrasūri																
Bhāg 1	Bhuvanśekharsūri[64]	2	6	4	21	19	26	41	25	25	62	120	160	103	145	185
Bhāg 2	Jincandrasūri[65]	—	—	2	—	—	21	—	—	12	—	—	109	—	—	121
B. Sāgara Śākhā																
Ānandsāgarsūri	Sūryodaysāgarsūri[66]	3	6	14	116	111	141	114	122	127	583	640	564	697	762	691
Buddhisāgarsūri	Subodhsāgarsūri[67]	6	6	6	34	38	30	58	52	50	95	100	101	153	152	151
Tapā Gaccha altogether		98	110	135	969	1006	1063	1231	1246	1278	3590	4226	4290	4821	5472	5568
2 Vimala Gaccha	Cidānandsūri[68]	1	1	1	8	2	17	9	6	19	20	—	23	29	6	42
3 Añcala Gaccha	Guṇodaysāgarsūri[69]	2	2	2	85	81	84	42	37	39	181	194	213	223	231	252
4 Kharatara Gaccha	Jin Mahodaysāgar[70]	2	1	1	65	64	58	19	22	19	188	192	205	207	214	224
5 Tristuti Gaccha																
Bhāg 1	Jayantsenasūri[71]	2	1	1	22	23	22	32	27	25	57	68	80	89	95	105
Bhāg 2	Hemendrasūri[72]	—	1	1	—	12	14	—	14	16	—	41	48	—	55	64
Bhāg 3	Up.Praśanncandra[73]	—	1	—	—	1	2	—	3	6	—	—	—	—	3	6
6 Pārśvacandra Gaccha[74]	Muni Bhuvancandra	—	—	—	24	29	30	12	12	8	64	68	64	76	80	72
7 Other[75]	Ānanddhansūri etc.	4	1	7	9	2	19	30	6	40	—	—	—	30	6	40
Total		109	118	148	1182	1220	1309	1375	1373	1450	4100	4789	4923	5475	6162	6373

Source: B.U. Jain 1987: 85–165, 1990: 113–184, 1996: 165–304.

sādhus and 'domesticated' *yatis* is not exactly applicable, since even the *saṁvegī sādhus* have a succession of leaders and thus are not 'purely charismatic figures in the Weberian sense' (ibid.: 669, n. 22). Weber (1978) himself categorised Jain monastic orders not as charismatic movements but primarily as 'hierocratic organisations.'[76]

Although some *samudāyas* share the same customary law (*maryādā*),[77] Tapā Gaccha *samudāyas* are generally organised independently, and compete with one another, even within their *śākhās*. As a rule, members of one *samudāya* do not share food with those of another (personal invitations notwithstanding).[78] Each *samudāya* is governed by a *gacchādhipati* or *pramukha ācārya*, head teacher, who is generally determined according to monastic age (*dīkṣā paryāya*) or by consensus, except in the Ramacandrasūri Samudāya, where the *gacchādhipati* ideally selects his own successor.[79] The *gacchādhipati* presides over a varying number of monastic functionaries, including subordinate *ācāryas* with or without administrative duties, who received their title solely because of their academic achievements.[80]

I suspect that the maximum size of Jain monastic groups is primarily a function of their rules and regulations, which mediate between the categories of descent and the imperatives of group integration (Flügel 2003b: 191ff.).[81] Circumstantial factors such as the socio-economic resources of a particular religio-geographic field (*kṣetra*) or charismatic leadership are important in specific cases, particularly on the level of gatherings. But generally, the degree of organisation determines its chances of reproduction over time, the maximum group size and thus the potential geographic influence of a particular monastic order. To put it simply, the better the organisation of a group, the greater its potential size and the greater its size, the greater its potential influence. The three principal dimensions of Śvetāmbara monastic orders are descent, succession and seniority. They can be combined in various ways to produce different types of organisation.

In theory, it should be possible to develop a formula for calculating the ability of different types of organisation to compensate for demographic pressure. Practically, there is an upper limit for the size of groups without formal organisation based solely on the principle of recurrent personal interaction. As a first approximation, the breaking point leading to group fission within the orders of the Vijaya Śākhā can be estimated through simple averages. In 1996, the average group size of the smallest organised units of the Tapā Gaccha *samudāyas*, the itinerant groups or *Saṅghaḍās*, gatherings, was 5.24 at *cāturmāsa*. This figure is not unusual for Śvetāmbara orders. It reflects both religious rules on minimal group sizes as well as socio-economic factors, such as the number and wealth of lay-supporters. Evidently, a large group of alms-collecting ascetics can only stay together at one particular place if provisions are available and if their procurement is carefully organised (with the help of the laity).

Within the Mūrtipūjaka tradition, as a rule, the *Saṅghaḍās* have a fluctuating membership. They comprise the members of one or more categories of ascetics who belong to the lineage of one particular *ācārya*. These are called *parivāras*, or families, and are composed of both *sādhus* and *sādhvīs*. The *parivāras* are co-ordinated by one *pramukha ācārya*, who is the leader of a *gaccha* or a *samudāya*. The majority of the *ācāryas* have no administrative duties, although this varies from group to group, but they possess the qualification for the transformation of their *parivāras* into independent groups. In 1996, the actual average size of a Tapā Gaccha *samudāya* was 278.4 ascetics, distributed, on average, among 53.13 itinerant groups. However, the number of Tapā Gaccha ascetics divided among the total number of *ācāryas* is 41.24, which represented theoretically the lowest average limit of potential group fission between Tapā Gaccha *ācāryas* in 1996. The difference between average actual group sizes and potentially lowest average group size demonstrates the importance of other organisational factors determining group size. But in order to understand, for instance, how the 447 ascetics under the sole leadership of Ācārya Kalāpūrṇ Sūri of the Kanakasūri Samudāya operate as an integral monastic order, further historical and ethnographic research is required. Segmentary lineages can temporarily form very large groups. Nevertheless, it seems that *samudāyas* of such a size are not merely segmentary lineages, but internally highly organised, and divided into subgroups whose membership is not based on descent alone.[82] That the Tapā Gaccha *samudāyas* form distinct monastic orders, whose members share specific rules and regulations (*maryādā*), is evident for instance in the explicit prohibition of sharing meals with members of other *samudāyas*.[83] In fact, most Jain mendicant groups operate on the basis of an internal administrative hierarchy and a rudimentary division of labour. However, further statistical investigation of the correlation of group size and group structure becomes only meaningful if more information on organisational structures and other important variables is available. Complete data and careful theoretical modelling might, in future, lead to reliable predictions of expected group sizes under specified conditions.

Sthānakavāsī

The Sthānakavāsī mendicants are presently divided into twenty six monastic orders. These can be classified according to regional affiliation, doctrinal schools and the lineages descending from one of the five founders of the contemporary traditions, the so-called *pañcmuni*.[84] Three of these founders separated themselves from the now virtually extinct Loṅkā Gaccha *yati* traditions to set up reformed ascetic orders within the aniconic, or non-image worshipping, Jain tradition which originated between 1473 and 1476 after the 'protestant' reforms of the Jain layman Loṅkā (*c.*1415–1489) in Gujarāt:[85] (1) Jīv Rāj (seceded 1551, 1609 or 1629), who apparently canonised the thirty two Śvetāmbara scriptures that are acceptable to the Sthānakavāsīs, established the permanent use of a mouthmask (*muhapattī*), and other principal features shared by all modern-day Sthānakavāsī traditions; (2) Dharma Siṅha (seceded 1628, 1635 or 1644) and (3) Lava (seceded 1637, 1648, 1653–1655 or 1657). Dharma Siṅha was the founder of the Āṭh Koṭi (eighth grade) traditions,[86] and Lava the founder of the Ḍhūṇḍhiyā traditions, which are also known under the name Ṛṣi Sampradāya. (4) The founder of the Bāīs Ṭolā traditions, Dharma Dāsa (seceded 1659, 1560, 1564 or 1665), was originally a member of the lay order of the Ekala Patriya Panth and maybe a follower of Jīv Rāj shortly before Jīv Rāj's death; and (5) Hara (seceded 1668 or 1728), the ancestor of the Sādhu Mārgī traditions, divorced himself either from the Lahaurī Loṅkā Gaccha or from the Ṛṣi Sampradāya.

Doctrinally, Dharma Siṅha's Āṭh Koṭi tradition differs significantly from the other four schools, which disagree only on minor points of interpretation. It is today represented by the Dariyāpurī tradition in Gujarāt and by the two Āṭh Koṭi traditions in Kacch, one of which – the Nānā Pakṣ – is very orthodox. The other Sthānakavāsī traditions are divided along regional lines between the Gujarātī and the non-Gujarātī (North Indian) traditions. The non-Gujarātī traditions are further subdivided into those who joined the reformist Śramaṇa Saṅgha, which was founded in 1952 in a merely partially successful attempt to unite all Sthānakavāsī groups, and those who remained outside or left the Śramaṇa Saṅgha. Both the centralised Śramaṇa Saṅgha and the independent traditions include ascetics from four of the five main Sthānakavāsī traditions which were split into thirty three different organised groups at the beginning of the twentieth century (excluding only the Āṭh Koṭi traditions).

I have written elsewhere on the history and organisation of the aniconic Loṅkā, Sthānakavāsī- and Terā Panth Śvetāmbara traditions.[87] Therefore, I confine myself here to the description of their principal demographic features. Like the Jain Śvetāmbara conference of the Mūrtipūjaka laity, the second All India Sthānakavāsī Jain Conference in Ajmer in 1909 resolved to increase the educational standard and the total number of Sthānakavāsī *ācāryas* in order to raise the competitiveness of the Sthānakavāsīs *vis-à-vis* other Jain traditions (AISJC 1988 II: 8–32). In 1933 in Ajmer, the first assembly of representatives of all the Sthānakavāsī monastic orders decided to unify all traditions under the leadership of one *ācārya*. Finally, the Śramaṇa Saṅgha was created by 22 out of the 30 traditions present at the assembly in 1952 in Sādaṛī in Rājasthān. Table 1.2 shows the regional distribution and the number of ascetics of the Śramaṇa Saṅgha, which is now the largest organised group amongst the Sthānakavāsī mendicants, from 1987–1996.

Although they are nominally under the command of one single *ācārya* (at present: Dr Śiv Muni), the remaining founding traditions continue to operate within the Śramaṇa Saṅgha more or less independently. The official statistics therefore do not tell the whole story. Some mendicant orders never joined the Śramaṇa Saṅgha: for instance, the Jñāna Gaccha. And because of perpetual discord between the founding traditions, many disappointed ascetics, such as Upācārya Gaṇeśīlāl (1890–1963) of the Sādhu Mārgī or Upādhyāya Amar Muni (1901–1992) of the Manoharadāsa Dharmadāsa tradition, subsequently left the Śramaṇa Saṅgha and re-established their own independent groups. Moreover, in May 2003 the Śramaṇa Saṅgha split into two groups, one of which is nominally presided over by the orthodox Pravartaka Umeś Muni, who has however not officially accepted the *ācārya* title in order to avoid further conflict. Table 1.3 shows the independent Sthānakavāsī groups outside Gujarāt (for details see Flügel 2003b).

Table 1.2 **Regional distribution of Śramaṇa Saṅgha *sādhus and sādhvīs* 1987, 1990 and 1996**[a]

States (prānta)	*Ācārya 1996*	*Cāturmāsa-places*			*Sādhu*			*Sādhvī*			*Total*		
		1987	*1990*	*1996*	*1987*	*1990*	*1996*	*1987*	*1990*	*1996*	*1987*	*1990*	*1996*
1 Rājasthān	—	40	42	51	21	42	48	140	164	173	161	206	221
2 Dillī	1	24	22	33	21	12	25	93	105	170	114	117	195
3 Mahārāṣṭra	—	70	55	37	111	42	34	202	184	115	313	22	149
4 Hariyāṇā	—	11	16	25	4	19	12	52	56	107	56	75	119
5 Madhya Pradeś	—	17	32	28	7	21	24	76	63	77	83	84	101
6 Pañjāb	—	26	18	14	38	23	26	49	38	22	87	61	48
8 Uttar Pradeś	—	4	6	8	2	7	13	18	17	30	20	24	43
9 Karṇāṭak	—	2	7	10	—	7	2	7	11	37	7	18	39
10 Āndhra Pradeś	—	2	3	4	2	8	2	4	8	15	6	16	17
11 Tamil Nāḍu	—	5	11	4	—	20	2	21	29	14	21	49	16
12 Paścim Baṅgāl	—	1	—	1	2	—	10	—	—	—	2	—	10
13 Himācal Pradeś	—	—	1	2	—	—	4	—	5	5	—	5	9
14 Gujarāt	—	—	—	3	—	—	2	—	—	6	—	—	8
15 Caṇḍīgaṛh	—	1	2	1	2	3	3	—	4	—	2	7	3
16 Bihār	—	3	2	1	7	3	1	—	—	—	7	3	1
17 Uṛīsā	—	1	—	—	3	—	—	—	—	—	3	—	—
Other	—	—	16	—	—	11	—	—	6	—	—	17	—
Total	1	207	224	222	221	220	208	662	690	771	883	910	979

Source: B.U. Jain 1987: 73f., 1990: 59–60, 1996: 3–38.

Note:
The table is based on the group-by-group accounts listed in B.U. Jain 1996. B.U. Jain did not have accurate information on 'other' Śramaṇa Saṅgha a mendicants in 1996, but cited the total figure of 1,017 mendicants and 230 *cāturmāsa* places. For 1996, he quotes the figure of 208 *munis* (identical figure) and the much higher figure of 809 *sādhvīs*, based on estimates (see ibid.: 37f .).

Table 1.3 ***Sādhus* and *Sādhvīs* of the Independent Sthānakavāsī- Traditions outside Gujarāt 1987, 1990 and 1996**

Sampradāya	*Ācārya/ Gacchādhipati*	*Cāturmāsa-places*			*Sādhu*			*Sādhvī*			*Total*		
		1987	*1990*	*1996*	*1987*	*1990*	*1996*	*1987*	*1990*	*1996*	*1987*	*1990*	*1996*
1 Dharmadās	Mānmuni	8	7	8	6	6	6	19	21	23	25	27	29
2 Jñāngacch I	Campālāl	53	61	72	40	42	47	240	255	306	280	297	353
3 Jaymalgacch	Ācārya Śubhcand	8	9	8	6	5	5	32	31	26	38	36	31
4 Ratnavaṃś	Ācārya Hīrācand	10	9	9	18	16	9	34	35	40	52	51	49
5 Vardhamān V.	Śītalrāj	—	1	1	—	3	2	—	—	—	—	3	2
6 Amarmuni I[a]	Ācārya Sādhvī Candanā	7	9	1	15	13	—	8	9	10	23	22	10
7 Amarmuni II	Ācārya Vimalmuni[b]	—	—	3	—	—	7	—	—	—	—	—	7
8 Māyārām I	Sudarśanlāl	6	6	7	26	25	30	—	—	—	26	25	30
9 Māyārām II	Rāmkṛṣṇa	1	1	1	5	6	9	—	—	—	5	6	9
10 Ṣādhumārgī	Ācārya Nānālāl	49	51	51	46	41	31	211	233	254	257	274	285
11 Śāntikrānti	Śāntimuni[c]	—	—	3	—	—	11	—	—	—	—	—	11
12 Nānakgacch	Ācārya Sohanlāl	4	2	4	4	6	5	15	11	12	19	17	17
13 Hagāmīlāl	Ācārya Abhaykumār	3	3	1	2	2	3	3	3	—	5	5	3
14 Arhat Saṅgh I	Saubhāgyamuni[d]	2	—	2	2	—	6	—	—	—	2	—	6
15 Arhat Saṅgh II	Sādhvī Dr Sādhanā[e]	2	—	3	—	—	—	6	—	8	6	—	8
Other[f]		21	13	15	16	12	15	18	5	18	34	17	33
Total	6	175	172	189	186	177	186	586	603	697	772	780	883

Source: B.U. Jain 1987 II: 23–42, 73f.; 1990 II: 27–53; 1996 II: 39–86, 305f.

Notes:

a Today: Vīrāyatan.

b The group had only two ascetics in 1999 (B.U. Jain 1999: 365).

c The information for 1996 is incomplete.

d The Arhat Saṅgha was founded by Muni Suśīl Kumār. In 1999 it was lead by Yuvācarya Amarandra.

e There is no information for the year 1990.

f This category also comprises mendicants who 'walk alone' (*ekala vihārī*).

Table 1.4 ***Sādhus* and *Sādhvīs* of the Gujarātī Sthānakavāsī-Traditions 1987, 1990 and 1996**

Sampradāya	*Ācārya Gacchādhipati*	*Cāturmāsa-places*			*Sādhu*			*Sādhvī*			*Total*		
		1987	*1990*	*1996*	*1987*	*1990*	*1996*	*1987*	*1990*	*1996*	*1987*	*1990*	*1996*
1 Dariyāpurī Āṭh Koṭi	Ācārya Śāntilāl	26	27	33	14	13	14	107	115	118	121	128	132
2 Kacch Āṭh Koṭi Moṭā Pakṣ	Gādīpati Prāṇalāl	22	25	27	17	17	14	72	72	73	89	89	87
3 Kacch Āṭh Koṭi Nānā Pakṣ	Ācārya Rāghva	14	14	14	23	23	21	32	34	37	55	57	57
4 Khambhāt	Ācārya Kantīrṣi	9	9	11	12	11	9	34	34	37	46	45	46
5 Līmbḍī Cha Koṭi Moṭā Pakṣ	Gādīpati Narsiṅha	56	55	64	18	21	19	216	232	266	234	253	285
6 Līmbḍī Cha Koṭi Nānā Pakṣ	Tapasvī Rāmmuni	17	22	27	9	12	11	98	105	128	107	117	139
7 Goṇḍal Moṭā Pakṣ	Tapasvī Ratilāl	64	68	69	18	19	18	246	231	249	264	250	267
8 Goṇḍal Saṅghāṇī	Narendramuni	5	7	6	1	1	1	29	32	33	30	33	34
9 Barvāḍā	Sardārmuni	6	6	8	6	5	7	11	12	12	17	17	19
10 Boṭād	Navīnmuni	8	10	12	4	4	4	36	36	48	40	40	52
11 Sāyalā	Balbhadramuni	1	1	1	1	2	1	—	—	—	1	2	1
12 Hālārī	Keśabmuni	—	—	2	—	—	2	—	—	4	—	—	6
13 Vardhamān	Nirmalmuni	—	—	2	—	—	1	—	—	6	—	—	7
Other		8	8	3	10	7	3	8	10	4	18	17	7
Total	3	236	252	279	133	135	125	889	913	1014	1022	1048	1139

Source: B.U. Jain 1987: 73f., 1990: 59–60, 1996: 87–140.

Table 1.5 **Sthānakavāsī *sādhus* and *sādhvīs* 1987, 1996 and 1999**

Sampradāya	*Ācārya*			*Cāturmāsa-places*			*Sādhu*			*Sādhvī*			*Total*		
	1987	*1996*	*1999*	*1987*	*1996*	*1999*	*1987*	*1996*	*1999*	*1987*	*1996*	*1999*	*1987*	*1996*	*1999*
Śramaṇsaṅgh	1	1	1	207	222	264	221	208	227	662	771	869	883	979	1096
Independent	5	6	5	181	188	208	186	182	183	586	694	784	772	876	967
Gujarātī	3	3	3	236	279	296	133	125	123	889	1014	1037	1022	1139	1160
Total	9	10	9	624	689	768	540	515	533	2137	2479	2690	2677	2994	3223

Note: Compare B.U. Jain 1987: 73–82, 1996: 143–64, 306f., 1999: 101.

The majority of the Sthānakavāsī traditions in Gujarāt, listed in Table 1.4, descend from Dharma Dāsa and separated themselves in the years after 1788 from the Līmbḍī Dharmadāsa Sampradāya (Chah Koṭi Moṭā Pakṣa). The only surviving Ṛṣi Sampradāya in Gujarāt, the Khambhāt Sampradāya, and the Āṭh Koṭi traditions restrict their activities to Gujarāt and Mumbaī. None of these Gujarātī groups joined the Śramaṇa Saṅgha, which is a Hindī-speaking order or association. They are usually not lead by a selected head, like the independent traditions outside Gujarāt, but by the monk with the highest monastic age, or *dīkṣā paryāya*, who may or may not be called *ācārya*.

The overall number of Sthānakavāsī mendicants is much higher than generally assumed.[88] At the time of the first All India Sthānakavāsī Śramaṇa Sammelan in Ajmer, the total number of mendicants of the then 30 Sthānakavāsī traditions was 1,595, 463 *sādhus* and 1,132 *sādhvīs* (Maṇilāl 1934: 263). This figure had more than doubled by 1999 to altogether 3,223 mendicants, 533 *sādhus* and 2,690 *sādhvīs*, and by the year 2002 had increased further to altogether 3,331 mendicants, 559 *sādhus* and 2,772 *sādhvīs*.[89] In the sixty-six years between 1933 and 1999 the total number of Sthānakavāsī ascetics grew by 102.07%. However, the number of *sādhus* increased merely by 15.19%, while the number of *sādhvīs* expanded by a staggering 137.63%, increasing their share by 12.48% from 70.97% to 83.46%. Table 1.5 shows that the total number of Sthānakavāsī mendicants grew from 1987–1999 by 20.40%. All this growth was generated by an accelerated increase in the number of Sthānakavāsī *sādhvīs* during the last 12 years. At the same time, the absolute number of *sādhus* slightly declined.

The overall growth rate in 1987–1999 was almost twice as high in the Śramaṇa Saṅgha and the independent orders than in Gujarāt (Śramaṇa Saṅgha 24.12%, Independent 25.26%, Gujarātī 13.5%). This can partly be explained by the fact that in 1987 the percentage of *sādhvīs* was already particularly high in Gujarāt (1999: Gujarāt 89.39%, Śramaṇa Saṅgha 79.29%, Independent 81.08%). While the overall share of the *sādhvīs* increased by 3.63%, their growth was higher outside Gujarāt (Śramaṇa Saṅgha 4.32%, Independent 5.17%, Gujarātī 2.4%). It is difficult to say why Gujarātī traditions have a larger percentage of *sādhvīs* in the absence of detailed historical studies. It is not inconceivable that initiations were artificially increased in Gujarāt; since already in 1933, at the Ajmer *sammelan*, an inconclusive debate was held amongst leading monks of the Sthānakavāsīs about a proposal to deliberately increase the number of disciples (Devendramuni 2000: 20).

B.U. Jain does not supply any information on the biodata and on the social background of the mendicants. According to Bordiyā (in Shāntā 1985: 336f.), 30% of the Sthānakavāsī *sādhvīs* were widows in 1975, 16% married and 53% unmarried. The average age of initiation was 10–20 years. Most of the Sthānakavāsī ascetics stem from the Osvāl and Śrīmālī castes in Gujarāt, Rājasthān, Madhya Prades, Mahārāṣṭra and Pañjāb, but also from southern India (Shāntā 1985: 333). In contrast to many other Sthānakavāsī traditions, the Śramaṇa Saṅgha comprises a large number of mendicants recruited from non-Jain castes such as Rājputs, Brāhmaṇas, or Jats particularly in the Pañjāb, while the lay following is almost entirely composed of members of the Osvāl castes, who are almost all Jain by religion. However, by convention, only an Osvāl can become *ācārya*.[90] Like most orders, the Śramaṇa Saṅgha has banned the initiation of children below the age of 8 (*bāla dīkṣā*) and of old people (*vṛddha*) (AISJC 1987: 52).[91] However, the Jñāna Gaccha[92] and the Dariyāpurī Sampradāy set a minumum age of 15 years.[93]

The two largest schools amongst the five principal Sthānakavāsī traditions are at the moment the Bāīs Ṭolā (Dharmadāsa) and the Lavjīṛṣi tradition. Maṇilāl (1934: 211, 233) mentions that before its internal division in 1788, the Mūlacandra Dharmadāsa tradition in Gujarāt comprised about 300 mendicants. In 1933 it had not much more than 334 mendicants. If the figure for 1788 is correct, then little growth occurred in the 150 years between 1788 and 1933.[94]

Groups of more than 100 mendicants are rarely reported before the twentieth century. This may be due to the fact that no reliable figures are available before the nineteenth century, which had generally lower numbers of Jain ascetics than the twentieth century. In 1933, the six largest organised mendicant orders (*Saṅghāṛā* or *Saṅghaḍā*) were the Amarasiṁha Lavjīṛṣi Sampradāya in the Pañjāb (133 mendicants: 73 *sādhus* and 60 *sādhvīs*), the Amolakaṛṣi Lavjīṛṣi Sampradāya in Mālvā (105 mendicants: 24 *sādhus* and 81 *sādhvīs*), the orthodox Rāmaratna Dharmadāsa Jñāna Gaccha in Rājasthān (118 mendicants: 13 *sādhus* and 105 *sādhvīs*), the Jayamala Gaccha of the Bāīs Ṭolā tradition in Rājasthān (103 mendicants: 13 *sādhus* and 99 *sādhvīs*), the Līmbḍī Moṭā Pakṣa of the Bāīs Ṭolā tradition in Gujarāt (94 mendicants: 28 *sādhus* and 66 *sādhvīs*), and the Goṇḍal Moṭā Pakṣa of the Bāīs Ṭolā tradition in Gujarāt (86 mendicants: 20 *sādhus* and 66 *sādhvīs*) (Maṇilāl 1934: 211–262).

A closer look at the gender composition of the mendicant groups in 1933 shows that, with the remarkable exception of the Amarasiṁha tradition and certain sub-groups within the Śramaṇa Saṅgha, all traditions with more than ten mendicants tended to have many more *sādhvīs* than *sādhus* (generally at the rate of 3:1). It also becomes clear that small groups, such as the Manoharadāsa tradition (7 *sādhus*)[95] or the Boṭād and Sāyalā traditions (6 *sādhus* each), were and often are homogeneous male groups.[96]

The principal factor for the emergence of exclusively male groups is schisms. Generally, divisions are only instigated by *sādhus* who initially form small single sex groups which, after a while, may or may not accrete an entourage of *sādhvīs*. The severance of the Terā Panth from the Ragunātha Sampradāya in 1760 is one example. In some cases breakaway groups are formed by both *sādhus* and *sādhvīs*. But even then, *sādhus* are generally the majority.

Larger groups of up to 100 mendicants seem to have emerged more frequently at the end of the nineteenth century with the general revival of Jainism. In response, some groups, such as the influential Amarasiṁha Lavjīṛṣi tradition, re-introduced rudimentary hierocratic structures to prevent the breakup of their communities. Organisation is necessary for the integration of nuns and for the reproduction of a monastic order over time. The need for organisation arises in times of expansion, when the mendicant orders grow and attempt to exert their influence on society as a whole. Organisation is also a major factor determining group size, as indicated earlier. It is symptomatic for an increase in power, not necessarily purity, because it counteracts the segmentary pressures that are systematically generated by the observation of the canonical rules for mendicant-lay interaction. These rules prescribe the itinerary of the ascetics and unmediated face-to-face interaction between guru and disciple, thus impeding the permanent aggregation of large assemblies of ascetics in small towns and villages. Even sizable and well-organised groups are split into smaller itinerant groups of 2–15 and, rarely, up to 70 mendicants, called *Saṅghaḍā* or *parivāra* among the Sthānakavāsīs, to make the observation of the canonical rules of non-violent conduct easier.

Another approach to the processes of group segmentation amongst Jain mendicants follows from network theory. I have outlined this approach in an earlier, yet to be published, paper (Flügel 1991) and restrict myself here to general remarks. As mentioned earlier, the size of sustainable groups depends partly on the number of followers in a given region. Studies in network size have shown that informal personal networks rarely exceed thirty individuals in a modern urban environment: 'In general it appears that there is probably a limit to the number of people with whom an individual might be in direct and regular contact, but as yet there does not seem to be enough empirical evidence available to provide an estimate of what it might be' (Mitchell 1969: 19f.).[97]

By observing the canonical codes of conduct for their itinerary, or *vihāra*, and the collection of alms, or *gocarī*, Jain mendicants are both forced and able to sustain much larger networks of personal, if formal, contacts. In practice, this often requires the keeping of lists of addresses and various other organisational techniques which cannot be detailed here.[98] In other words, while the monastic code of conduct limits the size of mendicant groups, it simultaneously contributes to the widening of the circle of lay contacts. However, even if one accepts that the formalisation of mendicant-lay interactions through the Jain monastic code results in a larger personal network, there seems to be an upper limit of sustainable contacts (a figure which awaits to be calculated). Beyond this limit, both the mendicant order and the mendicant-lay network can only be enlarged with the help of hierocratic organisation. The permutations of this general postulate still await thorough sociological analysis.[99] However, given that schisms privilege male ascetics, it seems that the sustenance of large numbers of female mendicants is predicated on the existence of large and formally organised monastic groups with the capacity of weaving partial individual or *parivāra* networks into aggregate group networks. Historically, the emergence of organised monastic orders amongst the Śvetāmbaras seems to be related to the problem of integrating the principally bilateral structure of descent of nuns and the unilateral structure of descent of monks within a single tradition.[100]

Śvetambara Terā Panth

Systematic research in the history of the Terā Panth began in 1946 under the supervision of Ācārya Tulsī, who commissioned Muni Navratnamal (1921–2004) to collect the biographies of all Terā Panth mendicants and asked his lay followers to submit all family records and personal notes on the movements of the mendicants, since little reliable data can be found in the writings of the early Terā Panth monks. It is due to Muni Navratnamal's meticulous study of these sources, spanning more than five decades, that the Terā Panth offers now almost complete published demographic data on the monastic order and on the individual life-histories of its ascetics from its inception in 1760. During the last four decades an annual census was conducted and published under the title Terāpanth Digdarśan. The demographic statistics extracted from these materials differentiate between region of origin (*deś*), caste (*jāti*), age (*vay*), marital status before initiation: unmarried (*avivāhit*), married (*patnī/patī ko chorkar*), or widowed (*patnī/patī-viyog ke bād*), age at the time of initiation (*navalīg/bālig*), initiation with or without spouse (*sapatnī/patī sahit*), initiation of one spouse after the other (*prāg dīkṣit patnī/patī*), death (*svargavās*), departure (*gaṇ bāhar*), and the name of the initiating *ācārya*. Most of the available data was compiled by Muni Navratnamal (1981 ff.) and published in 26 volumes under the title *Śāsana Samudra*. Slightly different figures are quoted by Muni Budhmal (1995) and in other Terā Panth publications. The statistics of different Terā Panth publications do not always match, but are reliable enough to support general conclusions.

The Terā Panth is governed autocratically by a single *ācārya* who is invested with the constitutional power to select his successor, to initiate all mendicants, to annually rotate the personnel of the itinerant groups, and to determine the number and size of the groups. This administrative technique is unique amongst Jain orders, although the *ācārya* of the Sthānakavāsī Jñāna Gaccha – always the monk with the highest monastic age – also rotates the personnel of the itinerant groups, while most other Sthānakavāsī orders similarly operate with only one *ācārya*. It was devised deliberately to counteract segmentary pressures resulting from the fact that traditionally the members of a *Saṅghaḍā* stayed together for life and automatically developed a distinct group identity and

Table 1.6 **Terā Panth *sādhus* and *sādhvīs* 1987, 1990, 1996 and 1999**

Sampradāya	*Ācārya 1996*	*Cāturmāsa-places*				*Sādhu*				*Sādhvī*				*Total*			
		1987	*1990*	*1996*	*1999*	*1987*	*1990*	*1996*	*1999*	*1987*	*1990*	*1996*	*1999*	*1987*	*1990*	*1996*	*1999*
Terā Panth	Ācārya Tulsī	135	128	123	121	148	149	142	145	559	553	538	543	707	702	681	688
Nava Terā Panth 1[a]	Muni Candanmal	—	—	4	4	—	—	3	3	—	—	7	7	—	—	10	10
Nava Terā Panth 2	Muni Rūpcandra		6	3	2		8	2	2		9	7	7		17	9	9
Nagrāj	Muni Dr Nagrāj			17	1			22	4			32	—			54	4
Total		135	134	147	128	148	157	169	157	559	562	584	557	707	719	754	711

Source: B.U. Jain 1987: 73–82, 1990: 97–106, 1996: 143–64, 306f., 1999: 169, 365f.

Note:

a The Nava Terā Panth was already split in two sections in 1990, but B.U. Jain 1990: 106 did not have any figures. Therefore, numbers for both groups are listed under Rup Candra's section for 1990.

Table 1.7 **Initiations, deaths, departures and total numbers of Terā Panth *sādhus and sādhvīs* 1764–1997**[a]

Ācārya (period of reign)	*Entry*			*Death*			*Exit*			*Total*		
	Sādhu	*Sādhvī*	*Total*	*Sādhu*	*Sādhvī*	*Total*	*Sādhu*	*Sādhvī*	*Total*	*Sadhu*	*Sadhvi*	*All*
1 Bhikṣu (1760–1803)	49	56	105	10	12	22	18	17	35	21	27	48
2 Bhārīmāl (1803–1821)	38	44	82	16	26	42	8	3	11	35	42	77
3 Rāycand (1821–1851)	77	168	245	29	65	94	16	2	18	67	143	210
4 Jītmal (1851–1881)	105	224	329	68	151	219	33	11	44	71	205	276
5 Maghrāj (1881–1892)	36	83	119	25	89	114	9	6	15	71	193	264
6 Māṇaklāl (1892–1897)	16	42	58	10	22	32	5	2	7	72	194	266
7 Ḍālcand (1897–1909)	36	125	161	31	87	118	9	1	10	68	231	299
8 Kālūrām (1909–1936)	155	255	410	49	132	181	35	1	36	139	333	472
9 Tulsī (1936–1997)	257	619	876	143	396	539	119	39	158	144	541	685
Total	769	1616	2385	381	980	1361	252	82	334	688	1909	2597

Note:

a These figures stem from Budhmal 1995: 237, 292, 328, 532 and Navratnamal (personal correspondance 30 April 2000). They refer to the day of death of the *ācāryas* clientele. The centralised system of administration was introduced by Ācārya Bhikṣu (1726–1803) and refined by Ācārya Jītmal (1803–1881). It allowed the Terā Panth to grow both numerically and geographically well beyond the size of an average *samudāya* in the twentieth century. In 1955 the Terā Panth comprised of altogether 660 mendicants (180 *sādhus* and 480 *sādhvīs*), in 1975 of 657 mendicants (151 *sādhus* and 506 *sādhvīs*) and in 1981 of 695 mendicants (164 *sādhus* and 531 *sādhvīs*).[101]

The 1981 figures would have been higher had they not been compiled shortly after the secession of the groups of the Muni Nag Rāj and the Nava Terā Panth, lead by Muni Candan Māl and Muni Rup Candra. The main reason for the constitution of breakaway groups was the controversial introduction of a new intermediary category of novices, called *samaṇa śreṇī*, by Ācārry Tulsī in 1981. The dispute leading to the division focused on the decision to allow these novices to travel abroad and to use modern means of transportation and even money. In this respect, Terā Panth *samaṇas* resemble the *bhaṭṭārakas* of the Digambara and the *yatis* of the Śvetāmbara, which form similar categories midway between the laity and fully initiated mendicants.[102] While orthodox ascetics rejected the innovation, reformist ascetics were disappointed that the reforms did not go far enough.

Initially, the *samaṇa śreṇī* proved to be extremely popular, at least among young females, who were interested in religious education and travel. But the expansion has periodically slowed down. In 1992 the order comprised of 4 *samaṇas* and 51 *samaṇīs*, in 1996 of 4 *samaṇas* and 81 *samaṇīs*, and in 1999 of 4 *samaṇa*s and 80 *samaṇīs*.[103] However, in the meantime the recruitment has been accelerated. Altogether 89 *samaṇīs* existed by 2001, and more than 100 in 2003. The periodical reduction in numbers is a result of the progression of many *samaṇīs* into the order of the *sādhvīs*.

In 1992 the main branch of the Terā Panth had altogether 827 ascetics and novices and apparently more than 300,000 lay followers. At that time, it was one of the largest corporate Jain mendicant groups. If ascetics and novices are taken together, the Terā Panth had also the highest rate of growth of all Śvetāmbara Jain orders between 1987–1999. However, if only the numbers of fully initiated ascetics are taken into account, the growth rate seems to be stagnating. Table 1.6 shows that the main group had 688 members in 1999, 145 *sādhus* and 543 *sādhvīs*, that is, much more than in 1955, particularly if the 23 ascetics of the splinter groups of Muni Dr Nag Rāj and the Nava Terā Panth are taken into account. But the figures confirm the stagnation of the number of fully initiated ascetics between 1987 and 1999. This general trend is underlined by the low recruitment of male novices (*samaṇa*), whose growth has stagnated.

The main expansion of the Terā Panth occurred under Ācārya Kālū Rām (1877–1936) and Ācārya Tulsī (1914–1997) in the first half of the twentieth century, that is, during the Indian struggle for independence and the first decade after independence. Table 1.7 shows that under Kālū Rām's reign both the absolute number of initiations of mendicants and the ratio of female mendicants increased dramatically. Simultaneously, caste exclusivity also increased. Terā Panth mendicants were increasingly recruited only from the Osvāl *jātis*. By contrast, many of the ascetics that were initiated by the first four Terā Panth *ācāryas* between 1760 and 1881 were Agravālas (sometimes Sarāvagīs) and Porvālas, and Maheśvarīs, though Bhikṣu himself was also a Bīsa Osvāl.[104] The recruitment patterns also reflect regional changes. Initially, most of the Terā Panth mendicants came from Mārvāṛ and Mevāṛ. However, after a series of *cāturmāsa* sojourns by Ācārya Jītmal in Lāḍnūṁ and Bīdāsar between 1872 and 1877, the focus of activities shifted towards the Thalī region. From Ācārya Kālū Rām onwards the great majority of Terā Panth ascetics were recruited from the area of the old principality of Bīkāner.[105] Table 1.7 shows the pattern of growth of the Terā Panth, whose *ācāryas* initiated altogether 2597 mendicants between 1760 and 1997.[106]

The table shows that one of the factors contributing to the low number of *sādhus* are secessions or excommunications, which occur much more frequently amongst *sādhus* than amongst *sādhvīs* (cf. Navratnamal 1981 II: 311, 322, III: 273, 291, X: 309, 325). This confirms Balbir's (1983: 42) observation that the disposition to rebel against the autocratic regime of the Terā Panth *ācāryas* is greater amongst male ascetics. The figures show that the number of exclusions was much higher under the regimes of the reformist disciplinarians Jītmal, Kālū Rām and Tulsī.

Goonasekere's (1986: 87ff.) analysis of the recruitment patterns between 1760–1944 shows that, with the exception of the first years after the foundation of the Terā Panth during which the *sādhus* were in the majority, at all times significantly more *sādhvīs* were initiated than *sādhus* (on average 65.97% *sādhvīs* and 34.03% *sādhus*), and that the percentage of female ascetics continually increased. His investigations of the marital status at the time of initiation give further insights into the historical changes taking place within the monastic community. He shows that until 1944 the two dominant categories were 'unmarried men' and 'widows': 49.83% of all *sādhus* were unmarried between 1760–1944, 37.28% widowed, 12.89% married, and altogether 67.77% of the *sādhvīs* – 44.77% of all Terā Panth mendicants – were widows (ibid.: 100f.). Goonasekere explains the different ratio of widows and widowers by the fact that, in contrast to women, men were always permitted to remarry (due to Ācārya Tulsī's reforms widow remarriage is today officially accepted by the Terā Panthīs though it is still despised by the Osvāls). From this he infers the prevailing motives for renunciation: widowhood for women, and impossibility or fear of marriage for men. But he also mentions other socially induced reasons for renunciation, such as infertility, bankruptcy, unhappy marriage, and death of a family member (ibid.: 114f.) – in my experience a very, if not the most, significant external factor, particularly for women, apart from the influence of the monks and nuns, and the alternative to marriage that is offered to women by a well-organised monastic order.[107]

Cort's (1991:660) re-analysis of Goonasekere's data reveals important changes in the marital status of the Terā Panth ascetics. Under Ācārya Bhikṣu (1760–1803) less than 10% of all mendicants were unmarried. However, between 1909 and 1944 all mendicants under Ācārya Kālū Rām and Ācārya Tulsī were unmarried (women: 72.7%, men: 56%). Similar increases in the share of unmarried women amongst the *sādhvīs* had already been observed by Shāntā (1985: 320, 336f., following Bordiyā 1975) for the Sthānakavāsīs and the Kharatara Gaccha, and by Cort (1989b) amongst the Tapā Gaccha *samudāyas*. Cort (1991: 660) rightly concludes that 'P.S. Jaini's (1979: 247, n. 8) statement that most Jain *sādhvīs* are widows needs to be qualified.'

The average age at the time of the initiation has also increased. It is today 18–19 years, compared to 15–16 years some sixty years ago. The significant increase of the age of initiation can be explained by Ācārya Tulsī's reversal of Ācārya Kālū Rām's preference for child initiations (*bāla dīkṣā*). Kālū Rām favoured child initiations in order to reduce the prevalence of widows in the order and to boost the overall number of mendicants.[108] Tulsī, by contrast, was primarily interested in increasing the standard of education. The rising age of initiation is mainly a consequence of his decision to initiate only educated female candidates, given the overall trend towards the initiation of young unmarried women, who seem to prefer the relative independence of monastic life to marriage. One of the reasons for the creation of the *samaṇa* category was to give young women the opportunity to study and thus to qualify themselves for full mendicancy, which nowadays can only be entered by young females after some years as a novice. Usually, girls are not initiated before the age of 20. But there is no such arrangement for boys, who are generally less inclined to join mendicancy. They are trained after initiation.

Initiations of children from the age of 8 and initiations of 45–60 year olds are exceptions today, although they still take place.[109]

Digambara

With the exception of very small traditions, such as the Tāraṇa Svāmī Panth, the Gumāna Panth and the Totā Panth,[110] the overwhelming majority of the Digambaras follow either the Terah Panth, the 'path of thirteen,' or the Bīsa Panth, the 'path of twenty' or both traditions in a non-discriminate manner. In contrast to the aniconic Śvetāmbara Terah Panth, the image-worshipping Digambara Terah Panth – both are also called Terā Panth – was originally not a tradition led by mendicants but a lay movement. It emerged in the sixteenth and seventeenth centuries in North India in protest against the lax and ostentatious conduct of contemporary orange-clad 'Bīsa Panthī' ascetics, the so-called *bhaṭṭārakas*, whose 'modern'[111] monastic lineages evolved from those of the naked *munis* and increasingly replaced them from the thirteenth century onwards.

The precise significance of the distinction between Terah Panthīs and Bīsa Panthīs is not known anymore. Nor do we know much about the history and organisation of the contemporary Digambara ascetics.[112] Most writers associate the beginning of the Terah Panth movement either with Paṇḍit Ṭoḍarmal (1719–1766), an influential Digambara layman of Jaypur, or with Banārsīdās (1586–1643), a merchant and co-founder (*ādiguru*) of the

Adhyātma circle in Āgrā which drew on the mystical philosophy of Ācārya Kunda Kunda to inspire its own version of a non-ascetic lay religiosity that is oriented towards self-realisation through the direct meditative experience of the soul. Yet, the fundamental ideas of both the Adhyātma circle and the Terah Panth movement clearly antedated both Banārsīdās and Ṭoḍarmal.[113] Lath (1981: xxxvi–vii), for instance, points to the influence of the revenue minister of King Akbar, Rājā Ṭoḍarmal (died 1589) in Vārāṇasī and to his younger associate Bāsū Sāh, who introduced Banārsīdās to Digambara mysticism. Cort (2002: 63f.) emphasised the fact that 'we cannot conclude that an interest in Digambar mysticism equates automatically with the Terah Panth emphasis on reforming the Digambar ritual culture' (p. 66). It appears rather that in the sixteenth and seventeenth centuries the trans-sectarian Adhyātma circle in Āgrā and the more ritualistically oriented and more radically anti-*bhaṭṭāraka* Digambara Terah Panth movement around Jaypur constituted distinct though related lay movements, which became indistinguishable only with the waning of the influence of the Adhyātma movement in the eighteenth century and the institutional consolidation of the Terah Panth through the construction of numerous temples in North India.

According to M.U.K. Jain (1975: 137f.), the radical *anti-bhaṭṭāraka* movement was started either in 1528[114] or in the early seventeenth century by Amar Cand, a resident of Sāṅganer near modern Jaypur. The movement first called itself Vidhi Mārga, though its opponents mocked it 'Terah Panth,' the path of (only) thirteen. The second account is corroborated by Lath (1981: xxxix), who points to Amar Siṅgh as the founder of the 'Terah Panth' movement in 1626. The most detailed investigation of the origin of the Terah Panth/Bīsa Panth distinction was undertaken by Nāthūrām Premī (1912, 1957), one of the main sources for M.U. K. Jain and Lath, who identified the oldest confirmed record of the word Terah Panth and of the year 1626 as its date of origin in Paṇḍit Bakhat Rām's eighteenth century work *Buddhivilās* v. 631.[115] He concluded, therefore, that the origin of the Terah Panth must be located in the early seventeenth century. In Premī's (1912/n.d.: 22f.) assessment, the passage refers to the ritualistic Terah Panth and not to the Adhyātma movement, as Cort (2002: 67) argues.[116] Premī (1957) later recorded three versions of the origin of the Terah Panth in the literature of its opponents.[117] All of these point to the pivotal role of the family of Amrā Bhaumsā Godīkā of Sāṅganer: One version can be found in Bakhat Rām's work *Mithyātva Khaṇḍan Nāṭak* of 1764, which describes how Amrā Bhaumsā Godīkā was expelled from the congregation of the *brahmacārī* Amar Cand [*sic*!] because of his ostentatious display of wealth. In turn, he founded his own group which initially had only thirteen (*terah*) members and was therefore mocked as the 'Terah Panth.' The group built a temple apparently with the help of a minister of the king of Amer. A second version is given in a poem called *Kavitt Terāpanthkau* by Cand Kavi. The poem describes how Jodhrāj Godīkā, the son of Amrā Bhaumsā Godīkā, in 1618 – a date which Premī regards as fifty years too early[118] – repeatedly interrupted the sermon of the visiting *bhaṭṭāraka* Narendrakīrti of the Balātkāra Gaṇa Dillī-Jaypur Śākhā of Amer. He was then expelled and founded his own group on the basis of thirteen unreported principles. The third and oldest version goes back to Jodhrāj Godīkā himself who, in his 1667/1669 Hindi translation of Kunda Kunda's *Pravacanasāra*, exploited the homonym of *terah* and *terā* by interpreting *terah panth*, 'path of thirteen,' as *terā panth*, 'your path,' that is, as another term for the 'Jina's path' or the 'right path.'[119] Hence, the Śvetāmbara Terā Panthī ascetics must have borrowed their own identical explanation of the three possible meanings of their name from existing Digambara Terā Panth sources;[120] though M.U.K. Jain (1975: 138) reports that N. Premī elsewhere expressed the view that the name *terā panth* only became current amongst the Digambaras after the founding of the Śvetāmbara 'Terā Panth' in 1760 — a view which may merely reflect the fact that Bakhat Rām's works *Mithyātva Khaṇḍan Nāṭak* and *Buddhivilās* were composed in the year 1764 and 1770.

None of the sources cited by Premī give a clear answer to the question of the significance of the numbers thirteen and twenty in *terah panth* and *bīsa panth*, which may indeed just reflect a superficial claim of superiority by the self-declared 'Bīsa Panthīs' 'since the number 20 exceeds 13 by 7' (Nathmal 1968: 7). The influential twentieth century Terā Panth *paṇḍit* Phūlcand Śāstrī (1985b: 538), a born Parvār, could therefore take the liberty to identify the Terā Panth with the 'orthodox Mūla Saṅgha of Kunda Kunda' and the Bīsa Panth with the 'heterodox Kāṣṭhā Saṅgha';[121] and also to associate the 'pure line' (*śuddhāmnaya*) of the Parvār caste with the tradition of Kunda Kunda (ibid.: 536).[122] Śāstrī could, of course, only identify the entire *bhaṭṭāraka* tradition with the Kāṣṭhā Saṅgha by disregarding the known history of the *muni* and *bhaṭṭāraka* traditions. However, many Terā Panthīs nowadays claim descent from the 'orthodox' Mūla Saṅgha and interpret the words *terā panth* as a designation of the 'right path' shown by the Jinas and Kunda Kunda.[123] The words *bīsa panth*, 'path of twenty,' are in turn polemically depicted as a corruption of *viṣam panth*, 'irregular-' or 'poisonous path' (Śāstrī 1985b: 538),[124] or as a corruption of *viśva panth*, 'universal path' (Glasenapp 1925: 357 for both versions).

Digambara Terā Panth

The Digambara Terā Panthīs are today guided by *paṇḍits*, or lay intellectuals, who are associated with predominantly local religious trusts and temples. There is no unifying organisational framework. About 500–600 Terā Panth *paṇḍits* exist in North India today with strongholds in Jaypur, Āgrā and Vārāṇasī. Most of them teach Jainism only part-time. Although they do respect 'true' Jain mendicants,[125] the Terā Panthīs represent largely a temple-centred form of lay asceticism, whose main doctrinal inspirations derive more from the mystical writings of Ācārya Padmanandin, known as Kunda Kunda (Pkt. Koṇḍa Kunda), than from Bhūtabalī and Puṣpadanta for instance. Their following has recently split between those who accept Kānjī Svāmī's (1889–1980) deterministic interpretation of Kunda Kunda's teachings and those who do not.[126]

Two-thirds of today's Digambaras[127] are said to be Terā Panthīs,[128] who are the predominant Digambara tradition in Rājasthān, Madhya Prades and Uttar Prades, while the Bīsa Panthīs dominate in Mahārāṣṭra, Karṇāṭaka and Keralā, as well as in Tamil Nāḍu and Gujarāt where only few Digambaras are left[129] apart from the followers of Kānjī Svāmī. The reasons for the differential distribution of Terā Panthīs and Bīsa Panthīs have not yet been studied, but there seems to be a clear correlation between caste membership and sectarian affiliation in North India, where, today, most Agravāls and Parvārs are Terā Panthīs and most Khaṇḍelvāls Bīsa Panthīs.[130] However, the majority of the Digambara laity does not consciously differentiate between Terā Panthīs and Bīsa Panthīs *qua* sectarian membership or following, and merely practises local Jain rituals and caste customs.[131] The absence of deep-seated sectarian awareness amongst the Digambara laity in North India[132] – apart from the divide between the followers and the opponents of Kānjī Svāmī[133]

– can be attributed to a number of factors: the extinction of the last North Indian *bhaṭṭāraka* seats in the early twentieth century, the revival of the doctrinally amorphous *muni* traditions, and the lack of organisation not only of the Terā Panth,[134] but of the Digambaras in general whose dearth of inspirational religious leaders in the nineteenth century resulted in the dominance of caste (*jāti*) identities amongst the local Digambara communities (*samāj*) in both North- and South India.[135] Another factor may have been the long-standing cultural influence of Terā Panth practices on the Bīsa Panthīs in North India, whose rituals are less elaborate than those of the Bīsa Panthīs in the South.[136]

Bīsa Panth

In contrast to the Terā Panthīs, who practise a dry *pūjā* and reject the *bhaṭṭārakas*, the Bīsa Panthīs practise *pūjā* with flowers and fruits and support the *bhaṭṭārakas*, who continued the ascetic tradition after the decline of the *munis* in the late medieval period. The reconstruction of the organisational history of the Digambara ascetics is a difficult and not yet fully accomplished task.[137] Carrithers (1990: 154) suspects that the current use of specific designations for monastic lineages or groups is largely fictitious since from the medieval period onwards no independently organised *muni saṅghas* existed besides the *bhaṭṭārakas*. One of the problems is the unclear contextual meaning of the lineage and group categories used by the Digambaras. Muni U.K. Jain (1975: 132) writes that 'Units like Āmnāya, Anvaya, Bali, Samudāya, Saṁgha and Vaṁśa appear to be peculiar to the Digambara section'; though he does not fail to mention the common use of the terms *gaṇa, gaccha, kula* and *śākhā* in both the Digambara and the Śvetāmbara traditions.[138] The difficulty in connecting the influence of the classical Digambara teachings of Umāsvāmī, Guṇadhara, Puṣpadanta and Bhūtabalī, on the one hand, and the mystical tradition of Kunda Kunda, on the other, with specific lines of succession is, at least in part, connected to the problem of clearly identifying enduring organisational units within the relatively unorganised Digambara ascetic lineages. It has only sporadically been observed that the doctrine of Kunda Kunda, who in old inscriptions is generally associated with the Nandi Saṅgha, was more prominent in the Mathurā Gaccha and in certain factions of the Sena Gaṇa.[139]

The nineteenth century *paṭṭāvalīs* of the Sarasvatī Gaccha (Balātkāra Gaṇa Uttara Śākhā), which were translated by Hoernle (1891, 1892), trace the origin of the lineages of the contemporary Digambara *bhaṭṭārakas* to a disciple of Ācārya Bhadrabāhu II, Guptigupta, who is also known under the names of Ardhabalin and Viśākhācārya.[140] Ardhabalin is presented as the last pontiff who was able to keep the monks (*muni*) of the originally undivided Mūla Saṅgha, or root community, together. When he was succeeded, apparently in the year 21 BCE, each of his four chief disciples – Māghanandin, Vṛṣabha called Jinasena, Siṅha and Deva – took over one of the four sub-groups which subsequently developed into independent traditions: the Nandi, the Vṛṣabha- (Sena-), the Siṅha- and the Deva Saṅgha.[141] The oldest sources for this narrative are two inscriptions in Śravaṇabeḷagola dated 1398 and 1432.[142] The later inscription dates the group formation within the Mūla Saṅgha to the latter half of the eight century.[143] Schubring (2000: § 30, p. 63) pointed out the discrepancy between this account and references to a Mūla Saṅgha of a different internal composition of the twelfth to thirteenth centuries, and Dundas (2002: 122) concludes 'that the Mūla Saṅgha gradually became little more than a prestigious but artificial designation, redolent of a long unattainable orthodoxy.'[144]

For the early medieval periods four 'heterodox' Digambara traditions are attested to by Deva Sena's tenth century polemical work *Daṃsanasāra (Darśanasāra)*:[145] the Drāvīḍa-, Kāṣṭhā-, Mathurā- and the Yāpanīya- or Gopya Saṅgha. The four traditions are described as 'heterodox,' because they differed on specific points of doctrine and practice from the 'orthodox' Mūla Saṅgha,[146] which is not mentioned in the text because it was represented by Deva Sena himself (Schubring 2000: § 30, p. 63).[147] The reported dates of origin of these traditions vary in the surviving manuscripts of the Darśanasāra. Hence, the Drāvīḍa Saṅgha may have been founded either in 479 CE,[148] 469 CE,[149] or in 583 CE[150] by Pūjya Pāda's disciple Vajra Nandin in Madurā (Madurai) in South India. The reported reason was a disagreement within the Mūla Saṅgha over the eating of particular plants, bathing in cold water, practising agriculture and trade.[151] The origins of the Kāṣṭhā Saṅgha[152] seem to go back to the seventh or eighth century CE. By the tenth century it was divided into four divisions:[153] the Mathurā Gaccha,[154] Lāḍa Bāgaḍa/ Lāṭa Vargaṭa Gaccha,[155] Bāgaḍa Gaccha[156] and Nandī Taṭa Gaccha.[157]

The Yāpanīya Saṅgha – the only one of the four 'heterodox' traditions which is depicted as a non-Digambara tradition in the academic literature[158] – originated apparently in 648 CE,[159] in 159 CE,[160] or in 148 CE.[161]

In North India the most influential traditions[162] were the Sena Gaṇa[163] and the Balātkāra Gaṇa (Sarasvatī Gaccha)[164] with its ten sub-divisions which were internally further sub-divided: Kārañjā Śākhā,[165] Lātūra Śākhā,[166] Uttara Śākhā,[167] Īḍara Śākhā,[168] Bhānapura Śākhā,[169] Surat Śākhā,[170] Jerahaṭa Śākhā,[171] Dillī-Jaypur Śākhā,[172] Nāgaura Śākhā,[173] and Aṭera Śākhā.[174] Both the Sena Gaṇa and the Balātkāra Gaṇa presented themselves as branches of the 'orthodox' Mūla Saṅgha in a direct line from Kunda Kunda (Padmanandin)'. However, the link appears to be a later construction.[175] The currently available sources point to Ācārya Śrī Candra (r. 1013–1030) as the founder of the Balātkāra Gaṇa.[176]

After the demise of the Yāpanīya- and the Drāvīḍa Saṅgha in the late medieval period, merely a few branches of the Kāṣṭhā Saṅgha – especially the Mathurā Gaccha – and of the Sena Gaṇa, the Balātkāra Gaṇa and the Deśiya Gaṇa of the Mūla Saṅgha remained, and only some sections of the Sena Gaṇa and the Balātkāra Gaṇa survived until today. In the late medieval period the members of most sub-branches of these traditions transformed themselves from naked *munis* to orange-clad *bhaṭṭārakas* with a relaxed code of conduct. These domesticated *bhaṭṭārakas* had only very few disciples, amongst them occasionally nuns (*āryā*),[177] which may be the reason why the term *yati* is rarely used in the Digambara tradition. There is no reliable demographic information available on the *bhaṭṭāraka* traditions, but one can safely assume that the absolute number of both Digambara *munis* and *yatis* was very small during this period. In the first of his planned two volumes on the early *bhaṭṭāraka* traditions, Joharāpurkara (1958: 23) identified the names of only 400 *bhaṭṭārakas* and 165 disciples who were associated with 31 *jātis* and 200 place names in North India between the thirteenth and nineteenth centuries.

Bhaṭṭāraka traditions

The honorific title *bhaṭṭāraka*, 'great lord' or 'learned man,' was given to prominent *ācāryas* and *munis* in the early medieval period (Premī 1912/n.d.: 3ff.). From the late medieval period onwards, the term came to designate the celibate heads of monasteries (*maṭha*)[178] who observe a relaxed set of ascetic vows, which entitles them to wear clothes, to administer monastic property in the name of the *saṅgha* (private property is not permitted), to live permanently in one or more monastery, to use vehicles, to act as heads of the Jain communities and later of Jain castes, etc. To distinguish the two types of *bhaṭṭārakas,* the term *paṭṭācārya* is also used for the latter.[179] Domesticated *bhaṭṭārakas* are not fully initiated mendicants, but occupy an intermediary status between the naked *munis* and the common laity.[180] Technically, they are defined as *kṣullakas* and classified together with the ordinary *kṣullaka*s and *ailakas* as 'superior laymen' (*utkṛṣṭa śrāvaka*) who accept to observe the eleventh *śrāvaka pratimā,* to different degrees, in contrast to the 'basic' (*jaghanya*) and the 'intermediate' (*madhyam*) laity, who must only observe the *pratimās* 1–6 and 1–9 respectively.[181] In practice, *jaghanya śrāvaka*s observe at best the first or *darśana pratimā,* that is the stage of 'right views' combined with vegetarianism. The *barah vratas* or 'twelve vows' of the second or *vrata pratimā* are rarely formally accepted (in toto) by lay Jains, who are reluctant to impose lifelong (*ājīvana*) vows upon themselves, except sometimes in old age.[182] Similarly, the intermediate status is regarded as almost synonymous with the seventh or *brahmacarya pratimā,* the vow of sexual continence which is outwardly marked by wearing a white dress. The eleventh or *uddiṣṭa tyāga pratimā,* which should be practiced by *bhaṭṭārakas,* demands world-renunciation and the observance of a monastic lifestyle, including the begging of food. The *uddiṣṭa tyāga pratimā* is today sub-divided in the stages of the *kṣullaka* and the *ailaka.*[183] The *kṣullaka* (f. *kṣullikā*) or 'junior' (monk) gives up all but two (or three) pieces of cloth of orange colour, while the *ailaka* keeps only a loincloth (*kaupīna*).[184] Both the *kṣullaka*s and *ailakas* are consecrated by a personal guru. At their *dīkṣā* they are both given the three possessions of a Digambara ascetic: peacock feather broom (*piñchī*), scripture (*śāstra*) and water pot (*kamaṇḍalu*).[185] In contrast to the *kṣullaka*s, who may reside with householders, the *ailakas* always stay with the *munis,* and should eat their food, like the *munis,* with 'one hand,' that is the two hands folded into one, but in a seated position. They also have to practice *keśa luñcana,* or the ritual plucking of hair and beard, and silence at night, and are not permitted to use vehicles.[186] For this reason *ailakas* are considered to be superior to *bhaṭṭārakas* although this is disputed some *bhaṭṭārakas* who as the descendants of the original *muni* tradition claim predominance even over the modern *munis* and perform a modified *muni dīkṣā*.

The procedures of selection and the inauguration or *paṭṭābhiṣeka* ceremony of a *bhaṭṭāraka* are different from an ordinary *kṣullaka dīkṣā* which usually precedes it. Nowadays, a *bhaṭṭāraka* is often not chosen by his predecessor, but by a *pañcāyat* or by prominent members of the community, who judge the available candidates according to their attitude, conduct and knowledge. If no suitable successor, a *laghu-nandana* or 'small son' such as a *brahmacārī* or *yati* under training[187] with a good horoscope, is available, the *ācāryas* of the *muni saṅghas* are approached to recommend one of their *kṣullakas* or *ailakas* who could be persuaded to fill the position.[188] If a candidate is accepted by consensus, the *paṭṭābhiṣeka* is organised, in which a Digambara *muni* plays the role of the *dīkṣā-dātā* or giver of initiation. The candidate first renounces his old clothes and his personal name[189] in public and is then given a single orange dress and the traditional title of the occupier of the seat. After taking his vows (at least a lifelong *brahmacarya vrata*), he is blessed with *mantras* and by sprinkled water on his head and then presented with the principal insignia of a *bhaṭṭāraka* – a *piñchī* with a handle made out of silver or gold, an insignia ring, and a metal *kamaṇḍalu*. A *bhaṭṭāraka* also commands ceremonial elephants, litters (*meṇā*), and other symbols of worldly status. Generally, he does not keep money on his own nowadays, but leaves the financial assets of the *maṭha* in the hands of the lay trustees, who will cover all his expenses.[190]

The tradition of domesticated *bhaṭṭārakas* evolved at the beginning of the thirteenth century under Muslim rule from the existing traditions of the naked *munis* who they replaced almost entirely until the revival of the *muni* tradition in the twentieth century. There are three accounts of its origin, all of which emphasise the pioneering role of the Balātkāra Gaṇa: The first account attributes the introduction of the custom of wearing clothes – symbolic of possessions in general – to Ācārya Vasant Kīrti (1174–1207) of the Uttara Śākhā of the Balātkāra Gaṇa, who died only one year after his accession to the seat in Ajmer. According to Śruta Sāgar Sūri, he took the decision to cover himself with a sheet of cotton (*taṭṭī-sādara*) when going for alms in the village of Maṇḍapadurga (Māṇḍalagaṛh) in Rājasthān in reaction to the Muslim rulers' criticism of the custom of walking naked in public.[191]

Other accounts locate the beginning of the practice in the time of Phīroz Śāh (1350–1387), the sultan of Delhi, who desired to meet the guru of the Digambaras.[192] A *paṭṭāvalī* names the seventh *ācārya* of the Uttara Śākhā of the Balātkāra Gaṇa, the miracle working Padma Nandin (born 1318, r. 1328–1393),[193] as the first *bhaṭṭāraka* who put on a loin cloth. It is said that the title of a *bhaṭṭāraka* was conferred on him by a Gujarātī *śrāvaka* who wanted him to consecrate a statue and in this way to transmit to it his miraculous powers (Hoernle 1891: 354). According to an oral tradition, the reason for putting on clothes was Padma Nandin's acceptance of the request by King Muhammad Ghōrī to present himself in a decent manner to his wife who desired to meet him (ibid.: 361).[194]

Under the impact of the Terā Panth reform movement in the sixteenth and seventeenth centuries, most of the *bhaṭṭāraka* seats in North India collapsed. The two last remaining seats in Rājasthān, Mahāvīrji and Pratāpgaṛh, were discontinued in the first and second half of the twentieth century respectively, due to the increasing influence of the 'modern' lay reform movements which criticised the *bhaṭṭārakas* with arguments similar to those of the 'protestant'[195] Digambara reform movements of the sixteenth and seventeenth centuries.[196] Only the southern *bhaṭṭāraka* traditions of the 'Mūla Saṅgha' in Mahārāṣṭra (Sena Gaṇa: Kolhāpura, Nāndaṇī), Karṇāṭaka (Balātkāra Gaṇa: Hūmachā; Deśiya Gaṇa: Kambadahalli/ Nagamaṅgala, Kanakagiri/Maleyur, Kārkala, Mūḍabidrī, Śravaṇabeḷagola; Sena Gaṇa: Narasiṅharājapura) and Tamil Nāḍu (Sena Gaṇa: Melasittamūra (Arahatasugiri); Deśiya Gaṇa: Tiruvannamalai) survived. The institutional pillars of the present-day Bīsa Panth traditions, the twelve[197] surviving *bhaṭṭāraka* seats in Hūmachā,[198] Kambadahalli, Kanakagiri, Kārkala,[199] Kolhāpura,[200] Melasittamūra,[201] Mūḍabidrī,[202] Nāndaṇī,[203] Narasiṅharājapura,[204] Śravaṇabeḷagola,[205] Sondā/Svādī and Tiruvannamalai are all located in the south, and closely connected with individual local castes.[206] The cultivation of exclusive links with the members of specific Jain castes in South India was facilitated by the fact that many of them were founded by *bhaṭṭārakas*,[207] who protected and dominated them for centuries as their religious rulers, or *rājagurus*, who exercised penitential powers. The *bhaṭṭārakas* still initiate and excommunicate their followers and in some cases select their own successor, who is then installed by the members of the respective caste and cannot be removed during his lifetime.[208] In the past, the *bhaṭṭārakas* accumulated large assets in land and artwork and maintained an exclusive monopoly over the surviving manuscripts of the principal sacred scriptures of the Digambaras, the *Kaṣāyapāhuḍa* of Guṇadharācārya and the *Ṣaṭkhaṇḍāgama* of Puṣpadanta and Bhūtabalī, until copies were produced and smuggled out of the *maṭha* of Mūḍabidrī in the early twentieth century.

The exclusivist orientation of the *bhaṭṭārakas* towards the castes which they dominated and to the property of their *saṅgha* proved to be a major obstacle to the ambitions of Jain communalists to unify the Jain community on a national platform during the years of the freedom struggle in the nineteenth and twentieth centuries. *Saṅgha* reforms were imposed on the *bhaṭṭārakas* by the laity, who also increasingly took control of the monastic property from the latter half of the nineteenth century onwards. Much of the landed property was recovered by the state governments through Land Reform Acts.[209] As a consequence, the legal powers which the *bhaṭṭārakas* once held over their followers have now completely disappeared. With the re-establishment of separately organised *saṅghas* of itinerant naked *munis* in the 1920s,[210] who were predominantly recruited from the relatively impoverished agricultural Digambara castes of the Bogāras, Caturthas, Pañcamas and Saitavālas in northern Karṇāṭaka and southern Mahārāṣṭra, even the southern *bhaṭṭārakas* lost much of their worldly and religious influence. They have no disciples amongst the newly established lineages of *munis* and *āryikā*, who are independent and considered to be of a higher religious status.[211] However, they are still consulted as arbiters for conflict resolution, and supervise the conduct of the *upādhyāyas* who conduct the temple rituals in southern India. It is due to the continuing influence of the *bhaṭṭārakas* on the social life of South Indian Jains that their castes tend to be homogenously 'Jain' and that the feeling of 'Jain' social identity, is more prevalent than in mixed Jain-Hindu castes.

The lack of credible mendicant leaders with a national reputation may explain why the desire for social and religious reform was at the time particularly strongly expressed by the Digambara laity in North India. Another factor was the aspiration of some community leaders to bridge the caste divisions, and the economic divide between the poor Digambara agriculturists in the South and the wealthy Digambara (and Śvetāmbara) merchants in the North. The revival of the *munis* came therefore just in time. The *munis* were promoted by the laity as symbols of Digambara unity on a national platform.[212] Particularly the leading members of the Akhil Bhāratvarṣīya Digambara Jain Mahāsabhā and the Khaṇḍelvāla Mahāsabhā[213] associated themselves closely with the new *muni saṅgha.*[214] The reformist Akhil Bhāratvarṣīya Digambara Jain Pariṣad also supported the revival of the *munis* and the unity of all Digambaras, but advocated for social reforms in addition to the religious reforms which were promoted by the *munis.*[215] The association was founded on the 22 January 1923 in Delhi by Champat Rāy Jain (1867–1942), Brahmacārī Sital Prasad Jain (1879–1942) and other reformers from North India who had left the conservative Bhāratvarṣīya Digambara Jain Mahāsabhā, which was established in 1892 in Mathurā under Rājā Lakṣmaṇdās and supported by traditional *bhaṭṭārakas* and *paṇḍits,* who resisted both the publication of the scriptures,[216] and socio-religious reform movements amongst the Digambaras, such as the Dasa Pūjādhikāra Āndolan, the Dasa's Right to Worship Movement.[217] Reportedly, some members of the Mahāsabhā even opposed the independence of the *munis* from the *bhaṭṭārakas.*[218]

History of the modern muni saṅgha

The Digambara *muni* tradition never entirely disappeared, though for the nineteenth century the names of only a handful of *munis* are reported whose precise relationship, if any, with the *bhaṭṭārakas* is still not entirely clear.[219] A Muni Nara Siṅha is reported to have visited the town of Ḍhākā with his disciple Muni Vinay Sāgar in 1870, and another *muni* is reported to have visited Jaypur.[220] In South India, several *munis* lived away from larger settlements on hillsides and in caves, though reliable information on them is difficult to obtain. Amongst them was 'Tapasvī' Muni Candra Kīrti, who was probably born in Guramaṇḍayā, but no detailed information on him is available. At the time, the only *muni* in North India was Candra Sāgar, who was born into the Padmasī family of the Hūmaḍ caste in Phalaṭan (Satārā). He took the *kṣullaka* vow in 1912 in Jinappāsvāmī (Śolāpūr) and a few months later the *mahāvratas* in Jhālarāpāṭan and started to wander as a naked *muni* as far as Āgrā.[221] Muni Anant Kīrti was born in 1883 in Nellikāru (Kārakaḷ) and died untimely on 16 February 1918 in Gvāliyar where, in his memory, an eternal light (*akhaṇḍa jyoti*) is still maintained by his followers.[222] In South India, three additional *munis* existed: Candra Sāgar 'Maṇihalī,' Sana Kumār, and Siddha Sāgar 'Tervāl' (1828–1903),[223] who reportedly self-initiated himself in front of a statue at Sammet Śikhar. In 1921, one Muni Ānand Sāgar lived in Udaypur. It has been reported that he often visited the nearby shrine of Ṛṣabhdeva Keśarīyā.[224]

Although the Digambara mendicants are not organised, most, but not all present-day *munis* trace their lines of descent to 'Caritra Cakravartī' Śānti Sāgar 'Dakṣiṇ' (1872–1955) – not to be confused with his namesake from North India: Muni Śānti Sāgar 'Chāṇī' (1888–1944) – who is 'regarded as having revived the institution of *munis* single-handedly from nearly complete eclipse' (Carrithers 1989: 232). Śānti Sāgar was born on the 26 July 1872 (1929 Āṣāḍh Kṛṣṇa 6) in the village Aināpur-Bhoj in the Belgāṁv District of Karṇāṭaka. His original name was Gauḍā Pāṭīl, and he belonged to a family of farmers of the Caturtha caste. When he was nine years old, he was married to a five year old bride, who died only seven months after the wedding. In 1890, he took the *brahmacarya* vow 'in the presence of a *muni*'[225] on 25 June 1915 (1972 Jyeṣth Śuklā 13), the *kṣullaka* vow from the Digambara '*muni*' Devendra Kīrti;[226] in Uttaragrām, and in 1916 the *ailaka* vow from Muni Akalīk Svāmī (? = Ādi Sāgar 'Aṅkalīkar'), who lived on the Bāhubalī hill near Kumbhoj. He was finally initiated as a *muni* from another '*nirgrantha muni*' on 4 March 1920 in Yarnāl (Yeranāl) in Karṇāṭaka[227] and recognised as an *ācārya* after the initiation of his first disciple, Muni Vīr Sāgar, on 9 October 1924 (1981 Āśvin Śuklā 11) in Sāṅglī. He initiated altogether 18 *munis*, *kṣullakas*, *āryikā* and *kṣullikās*, most of whom accompanied him on his barefoot journeys throughout India.

At the time, roaming naked in the streets of large cities was prohibited (*berok-ṭok*) by the Colonial Government (K.P. Jain 1938: 161f.). In British India and in the Indian princely states (*riyāsat*) wandering naked was an arrestable offence. The *munis* were therefore more numerous in southern India. In 1926, the Commissioner of Kāṭhiyāvāḍ gave permission for Muni Munīdra Sāgar to move lawfully, if he was surrounded by a circle of his devotees, though this restriction was opposed by the Akhil Bhāratīya Jaina Samāj, and a committee was formed to repell it with the argument that according to both British and Indian law, neither the government nor any other ruler or *sampradāya* should interfere in the religious affairs of a particular tradition.[228]

When Ācārya Śānti Sāgar entered Bombay in 1927, the case was still pending. He therefore had to transgress the rule of wandering naked (*nagna muni vihāra*) and to cover his body during his visit to the city (Kāsalīvāl 1992: 35). On the request of the local Seṭh Ghāsīrām Pūnamcand Jauharī, he then lead a communal pilgrimage to the sacred sites of the Digambaras throughout India, to re-establish for the Digambara *munis* the right to roam naked and uninhibited by provincial bound-aries, and to revive the 'true' Digambara religion.[229] On his tour, he was welcomed by the provincial kings of Mahārāṣṭra. In the year 1927–1928, he led the pilgrimage from Bhopāl to the *mahā sammelan* of Digambara *munis* at Mount Śikhar in Bihār,[230] and on to Jabalpur, Lakhnaū, Kānpur, Jhāṁsī, Āgrā, Dhaulapur, Mathurā, Phīrozābād, Eṭā, Hātharas, Alīgaṛh, Hastināpūr, Muzapharnagar, etc. to Delhi, where he spent *cāturmāsa*. He was famously stopped by the police in Delhi for breaking the law by walking naked, but was pardoned because he refused to move from the spot where he was stopped, asking: 'how can I walk back?' After *cāturmāsa*, he went on to Alavar for a *sammelan* of all existing *sādhu gaṇas*, that is, the groups of ascetics which performed mainly *jñāna-dhyāna* and *tapās* rather than the rituals promoted by the *bhaṭṭārakas*, though rituals were not rejected per se. The following six Digambara mendicant groups (*saṅgha*) were present (K.P. Jain 1932: 161f.):

1 Ācārya Śānti Sāgar 'Dakṣiṇ,' with the *munis* Candra Sāgar, Śrut Sāgar, Vīr Sāgar, Nami Sāgar and Jñān Sāgar (6 *munis* altogether).

2 Muni [Ācārya] Śānti Sāgar 'Chāṇī,' with Muni Malli Sāgar, Brahmacārī Phatah Sāgar, and Brahmacārī Lakṣmī Cand (2 *munis* altogether). Śānti Sāgar 'Chāṇī' was born as Kevaldās Jain into a family of the Dasa Humaḍ caste in the village Chāṇī, some 15 km from Ṛṣabhdev Keśariyā in the state of Udaypur. He took the *brahmacarya vrata* on 1 January 1919 at Sammet Śikhara, and a few months later, with permission of the lay community of Gaṛhī in Rājasthān, initiated himself as *kṣullaka* under the name Śānti Sāgar in front of the image of 'Bhagavān Jinendradeva' (due to the absence of *munis* in North India). On 5 September 1922 (*anant caturdaśī*) in the Ādināth temple of Sāgavāṛa he started 'to wear the dress of a Digambara *muni*'

(*Digambara veṣa dhāraṇa*). In 1926, he was installed as an *ācārya* by the Digambara community of Giriḍīha. He converted Ṭhākur Krūrasiṁha of Bhukhiyā (Bāṁsavāṛā) to Jainism, but had fewer disciples than his counterpart in the south.[231]

3 Muni Sūrya Sāgar (9 November 1883 to 14 September 1952), with Ajit Sāgar, Dharma Sāgar and Brahmacārī Bhagavān Dās (3 *munis* altogether). Sūrya Sāgar's birthname was Hajārīmāl and he belonged to the Porvāḍ caste of Jhālarāpāṭan. In 1916 his wife died. He was initiated by Śānti Sāgar 'Chāṇī' first as a *kṣullaka* on the 19 October 1924 in Indore and a few weeks later as a *muni* on the 22 December 1924. In 1928 he was given the *ācārya* epithet from the *samāj*. He initiated at least four male ascetics: Ācārya Vijay Sāgar, Muni Ānand Sāgar, Muni Padma Sāgar, and Kṣullaka Cidānand.[232]

4 'Muni'[Ācārya] Ādi Sāgar, (13 September 1866 to 21 October 1944) with Muni Malli Sāgar and Kṣullaka Sūri Siṁha. 'Mahātapasvī' Ādi Sāgar 'Aṅkalīkar'was born in the village Aṅkali in southern Mahārāṣṭra. He belonged to the Caturtha caste and was named Śiv Gauṛā by his parents. In 1909 he took the *kṣullaka* vow, and in 1913 initiated himself in front of the Jinendra image at Kunthalgiri. He died in 1944 in the village Ūd (Kāsalīvāl 1992: 35, Suśīlā Bai, in Brahmacāriṇī Maināb
āī Jain 1996: iv–x). In the year 1926, his group stayed at Udgāṁv (3 *munis* altogether).

5 Muni Munīdra Sāgar, with the *munis* Devendra Sāgar and Vijay Sāgar. Munīdra Sāgar was born in Lalitpur into the Parvār caste. He was very young in 1927 and spent his previous *cāturmāsa* in Māṁdvī (Sūrat) (3 *munis* altogether).

6 Muni Pāy Sāgar, who restricted his movements to South India (1 *muni*).

In addition, Muni Jñān Sāgar of Khairābād and Muni Ānand Sāgar (and possibly others for which no record is available at the moment) belonged to the Digambara *sādhu gaṇa*. These 21 mendicants were the only naked *munis* who performed *vihāra* at the time.

It seems, though this is a question for further research, that of these six groups only the lineages of Śānti Sāgar 'Dakṣiṇ,' Śānti Sāgar 'Chāṇī,' and of Muni Ādi Sāgar 'Aṅkalīkar' survived. In accordance with the general tendency amongst modern Jains to present a homogenous image of the Jaina community to the outside world, it is often said that doctrinal disagreements are not significant within the tradition of the modern *munis*, only minor differences in lineage and succession. There is, indeed, no clear doctrinal division between the *ācārya saṅghas* with regard to the Terā Panth/Bīsa Panth distinction concerning the latter's use of green vegetables, fruit, worship with lamps (*dīpa pūjā*) or incense (*dhupa*), etc. Effectively, each ascetic follows his own interpretation. However, Ācārya Śānti Sāgar 'Chāṇī' was known for his rejection of the *pañca abhiṣeka* ritual because it is conducted with milk. Instead he advocated for the use of 'pure' water in *abhiṣeka* rituals. He spent one *cāturmāsa* together with Śānti Sāgar 'Dakṣiṇ' in Byāvar, where differences of opinion emerged, since Śānti Sāgar 'Dakṣiṇ' insisted on the Bīsa Panthī view. Śānti Sāgar 'Chāṇī's main line of succession is represented by the *ācāryas* Sūrya Sāgar (1883–1952), Vijay Sāgar, Vimal Sāgar (Bhiṇḍa) (1891–1973), Sumati Sāgar (1917–1994), and Upādhyāya Jñān Sāgar (b. 1957).[233] However, a number of splits occurred due to succession disputes, and several *guru-śiṣya paramparās* exist today.[234]

Doctrinal disagreements were also instrumental for the schisms between the successors of Śānti Sāgar 'Dakṣiṇ,' who after his death on the 20 August 1955 (2012 Bhādrapad Śuklā 2) in Kunthalgiri split into five independent lineages. Four lines were started by Śānti Sāgar's disciples Ācārya Nami Sāgar (1888–1956), Ācārya Pāy Sāgar (1890–1956), Ācārya Sudharma Sāgar (1885–1938) and Ācārya Kunthu Sāgar (1894–1945). However, the dominant line of his successors (*paṭṭadhāra* or *paṭṭādhīśa*) is represented by the *ācāryas* Vīr Sāgar (born 7 June 1876, *kṣullaka* 13 March 1924, *muni* 9 October 1924, *Ācārya* 9 September 1955, died 23 September 1957), Śiv Sāgar (born 1901, *dīkṣā* 7 July 1949, *ācārya* 3 November 1957, died 18 March 1969), Dharma Sāgar (born 11 January 1914, *dīkṣā* 13 December 1951, *ācārya* 24 June 1969, died 22 April 1987),[235] Ajit Sāgar (died 1988),[236] and the present Ācārya Vardhamān Sāgar (*dīkṣā* 24 February 1969), who was chosen by Ajit Sāgar, though the older and much more popular monk Abhinandan Sāgar (*dīkṣā* 29 October 1968) was favoured by the majority of the lay followers.[237] After Ajit Sāgar's death, Abhinandan Sāgar and his teacher Śreyāṁs Sāgar therefore separated themselves from Vardhamān Sāgar and founded their own group which is now headed by Ācārya Abhinandan Sāgar.

A third influential line was started by Ācārya Vīr Sāgar's disciple Muni Jñān Sāgar (*c.*1891–1 June 1973), a Khaṇḍelvāla (Chābṛā) Jain from Sīkar, previously known as the Terā Panth Paṇḍit Bhūrāmal Śāstrī and from 1955 as Kṣullaka Jñānbhūṣaṇ (*dīkṣā dātā: Ācārya Vīr Sāgar*). He was initiated as a *muni* in 1959 in Jaypur by Ācārya Śiv Sāgar but seceded on doctrinal grounds from Śiv Sāgar and his dedicated successor Dharma Sāgar, in 1961 and – though not being recognised as an *ācārya* – initiated Vidyā Sāgar (*dīkṣā* 30 June 1968) in the same Saṃvat year in Ajmer. In turn, he was installed as an *ācārya* by his disciple with the consent of his lay followers on the 7 February 1969 in Nasīrābād and immediately afterwards initiated Muni Vivek Sāgar (*dīkṣā* 7 February 1969 or 8 March 1969). Vidyā Sāgar was born on the 10 October 1946 into a middle-class Aṣṭage family of the Caturtha caste in the village Cikkoḍī-Sadlagā in Belgāṁv.[238] He took the *brahmacarya* vow from Ācārya Deś Bhūṣaṇ in 1967, and *muni dīkṣā* from Ācārya Jñān Sāgar, who appointed him as the new *ācārya* on the 22 November 1972 in Nasīrābād, and immediately afterwards resigned and asked Vidyā Sāgar to bestow upon him the *sallekhanā* vow (M. Jain 2001: 23–26, 494, K.R. Jain 2003: 23–52). After Jñān Sāgar's death in 1973, Vivek Sāgar parted company from Vidyā Sāgar, apparently because the charismatic Vidyā Sāgar was junior to him in physical age, although slightly older in monastic age. But the main reason may have been doctrinal differences. In the group of Vidyā Sāgar, *āryikā* cannot initiate *ailakas*, on behalf of the *ācārya*, on the grounds that the *ailakas* wear only one piece of cloth and therefore deserve a higher status than the *āryikā*, who cover their entire body.[239] This reversal of the traditional hierarchy – *muni, āryikā, ailaka, kṣullaka, kṣullikā* – was a main point of contention between Jñān Sāgar and Ācārya Śiv Sāgar.[240] Other disputes concerned the consumption of 'green' vegetables such as tomatoes, and Jñān Sāgar's refusal to condemn the use of the sacred thread, which is common among the Digambara laity in South India but not practiced north of Karṇāṭaka, which prevented him to become installed as an *ācārya* by Śiv Sāgar. Vidyā Sāgar additionally resolved that *āryikā* should not wear the *piñchī*, the principal status symbol of a Digambara ascetic, during their menses, and that only 'born Jainas' should be able to become *munis.* The highest status for renouncers from non-Jain families amongst his followers is thus the position of an *ailaka* in his group.[241]

A fourth line was started by Ādi Sāgar 'Aṅkalīkar,' who was a contemporary of Śānti Sāgar 'Dakṣiṇ,' and is often presented as his disciple, despite the fact that he was not initiated by him.[242] He was succeeded by Mahāvīr Kīrti (born 1 June 1910, *dīkṣā* 1937, died 6 February 1972) and Vimal Sāgar (born 30 October 1915, *dīkṣā* 19 July 1950, *ācārya* 24 December 1961), who apparently gained the *ācārya* title not through succession but by acclamation of the lay community, especially by the *paṇḍits* Lala Rām Śāstrī and Māṇik Candra Śāstrī.[243] Both Mahāvīr Kīrti and Vimal Sāgar[244] were succeeded by a great number of *ācāryas* who created numerous small groups.[245] Vimal Sāgar's successors were Ācārya Sanmati Sāgar (born 26 January 1939, *dīkṣā* 9 November 1962, *ācārya* 5 March 1972), and the current *ācāryas* Bharat Sāgar (born 7 April 1949, *dīkṣā* 23 November 1972)[246] (who was Vimal Sāgar's *upādhyāya*),[247] Puṣpadanta Sāgar (born 1 January 1952, *dīkṣā* 31 January 1980) (who shifted from Vidyā Sāgar to Vimal Sāgar and teaches an idiosyncratic mixture of Terā Panth and Bīsa Panth views), Nirmal Sāgar (born 10 December 1946, *dīkṣā* 12 July 1967), Sanmati Sāgar 'Tapasvī Samrāṭ,' Vāsu Pūjya Sāgar, Virāg Sāgar, as well as Muni Nirañjan Sāgar, Gaṇinī Vijay Matī, the *kṣullakas* Dhaval Sāgar, Ratna Kīrti, and the *kṣullikā* Siddhānta Matī (A. Jain 2001: 1–34). Amongst Mahāvīr Kīrti's successors were the present Ācārya Sambhav Sāgar and the present '*gaṇadharācārya*' Kunthu Sāgar, who initiated many disciples under new names ending in the suffix *-Nandi*. Some of his disciples parted from him in order to establish themselves as *ācāryas*, *ācāryakalpas*, *upādhyāyas* and *muni*s in their own right – to name only the present *ācāryas* Deva Nandi, Guṇadhara Nandi, Guṇa Nandi, Gupti Nandi, Kanak Nandi, Karma Vijay Nandi (?=self-initiated), Karuṇā Sāgar, and Kumud Nandi, Kuśāgra Nandi, Padma Nandi, Śānti Sāgar 'Korasār Vāle,' the *ācāryakalpas* Karuṇā Nandi and Śruta Nandi, the *ailācārya* Niścay Sāgar, and the *upādhyāya*s Kāma Kumār Nandi Śruta Sāgar. Ācārya Deś Bhūṣaṇ (1908–1987), the politically most influential Digambara *muni* after Śānti Sāgar, was a disciple of Ācārya Jay Kīrti, who may have been associated with Mahāvīr Kīrti, though the link is not clear.[248] He is succeeded by the presently influential *ācārya* Vidyānand 'Rāṣṭrasant' (born 22 April 1925), who also comes from Belgāṁv but has few disciples and resides predominantly in New Delhi, by Ācārya Bāhubalī Sāgar, who separated himself from Vidyānand and by Ācārya Subahu Sāgar, Ācārya Subal Sāgar, Muni Guṇ Bhūṣaṇ, Kṣullaka Vṛṣabh Sena, and Kṣullikā Anant Matī (ibid.).

In 1981, 151 mendicants and representatives of the national Digambara lay associations gathered in Śravaṇabeḷagola in order to witness the *mahāmastakābhiṣeka* ceremony and to overcome the differences between the growing number of Digambara ascetics and lineages by establishing a common institutional framework for the mendicants – the Digambara Jain Muni Pariṣad. Several rules were drafted with the intention of preventing the practice of wandering alone (*ekala vihāra*) and a decline in the standards of conduct (*śithilācāra*). But these resolutions were not implemented and had no effect (Kāsalīvāl 1992: 24).

Though there are no clear-cut divisions among the *munis* with regard to political-ideological and doctrinal orientations, conservative Bīsa Panthī *munis* tend to support the Mahāsabhā, while modern monks such as Ācārya Vidyānand and Ācārya Vidyā Sāgar associate themselves with the Mahāsamiti whose wealthy leadership has a wider support base in North India and tends to support Terā Panth views. The main catalyst for the recent trend towards a conscious doctrinal self-demarcation of Bīsa Panthī and Terā Panthī mendicant groups was the debate on Kānjī Svāmī's idiosyncratic 'Terā Panth' interpretation of Kunda Kunda's philosophy from the early 1960s onwards, which split the Digambaras into two clearly distinguished factions.[249] Beyond the specific context of this dispute, the picture is less clear. There is no exclusive link between Kunda Kunda and the Terā Panth tradition. In the late twentieth century, the Terā Panth *paṇḍit* Phulcand Śāstrī (1985b: 244, 1992: 146) came to the conclusion that the Terā Panth is identical with the *śuddhāmnaya*, the 'pure tradition' of the Mūla Saṅgha Kunda-kundāmnaya Balātkāra Gaṇa Sarasvatī Gaccha,[250] which propagates the *mokṣa mārga* and not – like the Bīsa Panthī *bhaṭṭārakas* (' = Kāṣṭhā Saṅgha') – the ways of living a religious life in the world (*saṃsāra*). The same claim had already been made at the beginning of the century by the Bīsa Panthī Ācārya Śānti Sāgar 'Dakṣiṇ'[251] who, somewhat imaginatively, attributed himself to the line of the 'Mūla Saṅgha' Kundakundāmnaya Nandi Saṅgha Balātkāra Gaṇa Sarasvatī Gaccha (Jñān Matī 1980: 249) – which may have inspired Phūlcand Śāstrī's view. Although few details about his life are known, Ācārya Kunda Kunda (*c.*1–8 CE)[252] is currently regarded by all contemporary Digambara *munis* as their ancestor.[253] According to Anupam Jain,[254] all *munis* derive their descent from the lineage of Kunda

Kunda and Ācārya Śānti Sāgar.[255] However, although the majority belongs to the lineage of Śānti Sāgar 'Dakṣiṇ' and propagates southern, that is Bīsa Panthī, practices, a minority descends from Śānti Sāgar 'Chāṇī,' who rejected the Bīsa Panthī *pañca abhiṣeka* and *devī pūjā* rituals, and from Adi Sāgar 'Aṅkalīkar.'

After the recent death of the influential Ācārya Vimal Sāgar (born 1915), the most prominent *ācāryas* of today are Vidyā Ānand (born 1925), who took the twelve year long *sallekhana* vow in 1999, and the charismatic Vidyā Sāgar. Vidyā Sāgar is renowned and respected for his strict observance of the rules of the Digambara Agamas, and for his emphasis on Jain philosophy rather than on rituals and imposed vows; especially for his single-handed revival of the study of the *Ṣaṭkhaṇḍāgama*. He explicitly favours the Terā Panth view on rituals and speaks out both against the *bhaṭṭārakas* (first on 8 November 1998),[256] and against the followers of the Kānjī Panth. Like his *guru,* Jñān Sāgar, who did not express any objections to the *bhaṭṭārakas,* he also favours the mystical teachings of Kunda Kunda. In contrast to his late rival, the ritualistically oriented Ācārya Vimal Sāgar, who was from a Khaṇḍelvāl business class background and supported the Mahāsabhā, Vidyā Sāgar comes from a South Indian merchant family of modest income and favours the 'liberal' Digambara Mahāsamiti and the Digambara Pariṣad which promote both ritual and social reforms.[257] He explicitly propagates the recognition of the Jains as a 'minority' community, which is now supported by most Digambaras, particularly in the South, where they form homogenous Jain castes. The North Indian Śvetāmbaras and Digambaras, especially those from Gujarāt and Rājasthān, are traditionally self-employed merchants and wealthier than the southern Digambara agriculturalists and petty traders whose preferred route of social advancement tends to be government service. They form predominately mixed Jain–Hindu castes and tend to oppose the minority status for Jains.[258] Vidyā Sāgar is also a strong supporter of the cow protection movement and inspired the formation of a lay organisation called Ahiṁsā Army which is based in Delhi and works for a total ban on the slaughter of cows in India.[259] It is possible that the North Indian cultural environment has influenced Vidyā Sāgar's change of attitude towards the *bhaṭṭārakas* and the Bīsa Panthī tradition in general. He was born in Karṇāṭaka, but recruited most of his disciples in the North, particularly in Madhya Pradeś, where he spends most of his time.

With the notable exception of the strictly anti-monastic Kānjī Panth, the revived *muni* traditions are today respected both by the Terā Panth *paṇḍits*[260] and by the Bīsa Panth *bhaṭṭārakas*, though the contact of the *munis* with either of them is irregular.[261] In fact, the majority of the present-day mendicants attach themselves neither to the Bīsa Panth- nor the Terā Panth Digambara tradition, but act independently and are free to articulate their individual doctrinal interpretations. The widely held view that Digambara ascetics always preferred to impress people 'more by their behaviour than by their church organisation' and 'seemed to favour solitary life' (Deo 1956: 360f.) indirectly supports the claims of the modern *munis* that they are the revivers of the authentic form of Jain monasticism that was introduced by Mahāvīra himself. However, although the Digambaras did not, like the Śvetāmbaras, create elaborate monastic codes of conduct, their *ācāryas* and later their *bhaṭṭārakas* presided over *maṭhas*, or monasteries, which were highly organised manifestations of monastic landlordism.[262] It was monastic property rather than a code of conduct which stabilised the tradition. The long-standing organisational and numerical weakness of the Digambara mendicants from the beginning of Muslim rule may thus be related to the relative success of the *bhaṭṭārakas* as well as the educated laity, whose influence within the Digambara community is reflected in the extensive post-canonical Digambara *Śrāvakācāra* literature, which is partly written by lay intellectuals: 'Digambars seem to have felt more keenly than the Śvetāmbars the need to concretize and systematize the lay doctrine' (Williams 1983: xviii). The strength of the Digambara laity over the last 500 years also explains the leading role of Digambara intellectuals within the twentieth century Jain reform movement. Yet, the increasing influence of the scholars amongst the modern *munis* seems to displace the communal role of the lay intellectual for the time being.

Organisation of the muni Saṅgha

Since the demise of the Drāvīḍa Saṅgha and other regional traditions, and with the ascendancy of the *bhaṭṭārakas* who profess to continue some of these traditions even today, Digambara mendicants are not split into distinct schools and sects anymore. Amongst modern *munis* the popular suffix *-nandi* or *-sāgar* does not indicate sectarian affiliation, only lineage affiliation. Not much is known about the doctrinal and organisational differences between the lineages.

Maybe by using these suffixes some modern *munis* attempt to recapture the symbolic identities (and properties) of old *bhaṭṭāraka* lineages which are now extinct. But our empirical knowledge of Digambara history and sociology is presently not sufficient to answer this question.[263] The lack of a reliable demographic survey of the contemporary Digambara ascetics was lamented by Carrithers (1989), who encountered great difficulties in his attempt to piece together a reasonably accurate ethnographic picture of the Digambara mendicants:

> 'The *munis* as I met them are significantly different from their predecessors, especially those in the nineteenth century. *Munis* are few. They have no central organisation and it is difficult to gather even the most elementary census data concerning them. Jaini (1979: 247, n. 8) estimated that there were only sixty-five *munis* when he was writing, and another sixty novices. An unattributable Hindi newspaper cutting shown to me by the *muni* Vidyānandajī Mahārāj in 1984 estimated the number of *munis* at 100. These numbers have to be understood in relation to the number of Digambar laity. The 1981 Census of India returned about three and a quarter million Jains of whom Jaini estimates a third to be Digambar. On that estimate there is one *muni* for every 11 or 12 thousand Digambars' (ibid.: 221).[264]

Table 1.8 **Digambara ascetics in 2000 and 2001**

Position	*Total number*		*Number of groups*		*Male members*		*Female members*		*All members*	
	2000	*2001*	*2000*	*2001*	*2000*	*2001*	*2000*	*2001*	*2000*	*2001*
Ācārya	51	51	51	51	237	213	122	128	359	341
Ācāryakalpa	4	4	3	4	3	4	1	0	4	4
Ailācārya	3	4	2	2	4	3	0	0	4	3
Bālācārya	1	1	1	1	5	3	8	6	13	9
Upādhyāya	16	20	13	18	22	25	1	0	23	25
Muni	269	305	81	133	147	208	33	23	180	231
Gaṇinī Āryikā	10	8	5	5	2	2	31	31	33	33
Āryikā	312	325	41	67	0	0	162	194	162	194
Ailaka	26	29	10	13	13	15	0	0	13	15
Kṣullaka	80	94	19	35	20	35	0	0	20	35
Kṣullikā	46	63	6	12	0	0	7	12	7	12
Total	818	902	232	341	453	508	365	394	818	902

Source: A. Jain 2000: 1–27, 2001: 1–34.

According to the information on individual ascetics made available by B.U. Jain, the Digambara mendicants were 1987–1996 split into some 175 independent groups, including ascetics who wander alone. But B.U. Jain's figures on the Digambara ascetics are, in his own judgement, unreliable and inconsistent, due to insufficient self-reporting by the Digambara monks.[265] Often, for instance, only the leader of an itinerant group is mentioned and not the total number of group members, which was simply estimated by B.U. Jain (1999: 382, n. 1–7) in his summary figures. However, his lists give some idea of the structure of the Digambara mendicant groups in the decade before the turn of the millennium and a rough estimate of the overall number of ascetics.[266]

A more precise annual *cāturmāsa* list, the *Digambara Jain Sādhu-Sādhvīyoṁ ke Varṣayoga kī Sūcī*, was compiled for the first time for the year 2000 by Anupam Jain of the Tīrthaṅkara Ṛṣabhadeva Jaina Vidvanta Mahāsaṅgha in order to provide information for the laity 'who want to contact different *saṅgha*s' (Letter 25 September 2002). The categories he used to compile complete alphabetical[267] lists of groups (*saṅgha*),[268] names (*sādhu/sādhvī*, etc.), initiating monks (*dīkṣā guru*), and addresses of the monsoon retreats (*cāturmās sthal evaṃ sampark sūtra*) of the Digambara mendicants in the years 2000 and 2001, confirm that the Digambaras effectively treat both nuns (*āryikā*) and novices who observe the eleventh *śrāvaka pratimā*[269] – the *ailakas*,[270] *kṣullakas*, and *kṣullikās* – as members of the ascetic community. The change of status is indicated by the changes of the name at the *kṣullaka/kṣullikā dīkṣā* and the *muni dīkṣā*. *Brahmacārīs* and *brahmacāriṇīs* are not listed in the almanacs of A. Jain and B.U. Jain, because they are considered to be lay ascetics, although they sometimes accompany the wandering ascetics like novices. According to B.U. Jain (2002: 312), there are more than 100 *brahmacārīs* and 300 *brahmacāriṇīs* today amongst the disciples of Vidyā Sāgar alone, and some, though very few, are still under the command of the *bhaṭṭārakas*.

Table 1.8 summarises the data published by A. Jain in 2000–2001. The ranking of the monastic positions (*pada*) adopted by A. Jain indicates that the status of *āryikā* is generally considered to be higher than the status of *ailaka*s and *kṣullaka*s. The status categories *ācāryakalpa, ailācārya*[271] and *bālācārya*[272] designate the most disciplined and learned *munis* and the chosen successor of an *ācārya*, whom he will consult in all important matters regarding the *saṅgha*. With or without the official permission of an *ācārya*, members of all categories can form their own groups (*saṅgha*), which may comprise members from all lower status categories.[273]

There is only one *ācārya* in every *saṅgha*. A Digambara *ācārya* acts independently. He either wanders alone or forms his own ascetic group (*saṅgha*), which usually includes *munis*, *āryikā*, *kṣullakas*, *kṣullikās* and sometimes one or two *ailakas*. In 2001, of altogether 51 *ācāryas*,[274] 14 *ācāryas* wandered alone and 37 lead small groups of 2–25 ascetics. Of the 37 group leaders, 5 wandered with only one other *muni*, 2 with one *āryikā*, 18 led small groups of up to 9 male and/or female ascetics, and only 12 formed groups with 10 or more members (A. Jain 2001: 1–11).

For practical reasons, larger groups are usually sub-divided into smaller units of itinerant ascetics. Even if they belong to the *saṅgha* of one and the same *ācārya*, most *munis* roam alone or in small bands of 2–5 male mendicants who spend their *cāturmāsa* together in one place. *āryikā*, however, should never wander alone and travel always in company of laity. Sometimes they can be found in pairs, or they form larger groups of 4–20 nuns who wander together independently of the monks. However, in most *saṅghas* the members of the central group surrounding the *ācārya* are of mixed gender, and the male and female sub-groups travel and assemble together in public. They also stay at the same location for *cāturmāsa*, but reside in different buildings.[275] In the year 2001, for instance, only 13 of the 37 groups that were led by *ācāryas* were composed entirely of men — notably the groups of the popular *ācāryas* Kunthu Sāgar and Vidyā Sāgar (A. Jain 2001: 1–11).

The large and centrally organised group of Ācārya Vidyā Sāgar is exceptional amongst the contemporary Digambara *saṅghas* because of its size and influence.[276] In the year 2001, 20.8% of all Digambara mendicants were under the control of Vidyā Sāgar. Uniquely, the structure and demographic composition of Vidyā Sāgar's group in the years 2000–2002 can be precisely reconstructed from the accounts of A. Jain (2000b, 2001) and of B.U. Jain (2002: 309–12), who received comprehensive information for this particular Digambara *saṅgha* in the year 2002. Despite its exceptional status, the Vidyāsāgara Saṅgha can serve as a paradigmatic example for the organisation of contemporary Digambara mendicant groups in general. From the year 1999 onwards, B.U. Jain's demographic figures for this *saṅgha* are said to be reliable (B.U. Jain 1996: 323, 1999: 372, n. 2). They show that in 1999 Vidyā Sāgar had 190 disciples and more than 50 *brahmacārīs* and 150 *brahmacāriṇīs* (commonly called *dīdīs*: elder sisters) under his personal command, although the figures do not exactly correspond to the self-reported number of 195 members in 1999 (62 *munis*, 10 *ailakas*, 114 *āryikā*, 9 *kṣullakas*) (Ṭoṅgyā 1999: 8). For 2001, the figure of 188 members (63 *munis*, 10 *ailakas*, 113 *āryikā* and 2 *kṣullakas*) is reported by A. Jain (2001: 9–34). Because of the rapidly increasing membership of this group, the mendicants were distributed into 26 different sub-groups in 1996, 34 in 1999, and 44 in 2001, as reflected in the number of *cāturmāsa* residencies.

In the year 2002, the group had 183 members which were divided into 42 groups: 64 *munis*, 109 *āryikā*, 8 *ailakas* and 2 *kṣullakas* (there are presently no *kṣullikās* in Vidyā Sāgar's *saṅgha*).[277] The *munis* were divided in seventeen units.[278] The majority (37) stayed together with Ācārya Vidyā Sāgar, 9 *munis* formed groups of three, 10 *munis* groups of two and 7 wandered alone. The 3 *kṣullakas* and 6 of the 8 *ailakas* – which are considered to be superior to the *āryikā* in Vidyā Sāgar's order – wandered alone.[279] The *āryikā* were divided into 16 groups of 2–17 members, who roamed independently from the male mendicants. Male and female mendicants never wander together or spend *cāturmāsa* at the same location in order to maintain the reputation of this *saṅgha* for strict standards of conduct (B.U. Jain 2002: 312).[280]

Due to the large number of sub-units, the *saṅgha* commanded a vast geographical sphere of influence, covering Madhya Prades̀ (20 sub-divisions), Mahārāṣṭra (5), Rājasthān (4), Hariyāṇā (2), Uttar Prades̀ (1) and Karṇāṭaka (1). At the same time, almost half of all *munis* and half of all *āryikā* spent *cāturmāsa* together in one single location in Madhya Prades̀ and Mahārāṣṭra respectively.[281] These states are the two main recruitment areas for the Vidyā Sāgar Saṅgha. With few exceptions, all disciples of Ācārya Vidyā Sāgar come from Mahārāṣṭra, Madhya Prades̀ and Uttar Prades̀, although he himself was born in Karṇāṭaka. Similar patterns of a nationwide mission starting from a regional base can be observed amongst the Śvetāmbara Terā Panthīs and amongst other contemporary Jain orders.

As a rule, all Digambara ascetics associated with the *muni saṅgha* are initiated by an *ācārya* or with his permission.[282] Indeed, all members of the Vidyāsāgara Saṅgha today have been initiated by Vidyā Sāgar himself. *Āryikā* are also by rule always initiated by an *ācārya* and should never constitute entirely autonomous orders, although they do not always move around with the *munis*.[283] Within a *saṅgha* led by an *ācārya* the *munis* and *āryikā* remain under the control of the *ācārya* who initiated them. However, though a *gaṇinī* has a lower status than a *muni*, under certain circumstances an *ācārya* will appoint a qualified nun as the leader of all the *āryikā* in his *saṅgha*, while the *munis* remain always under the direct control of the *ācārya*. As amongst most Śvetāmbara orders, in the absence of an *ācārya*, the head of the *āryikā gaṇa*, the *gaṇinī*, will act like an *ācārya* for the *āryikā*.

Sometimes, *gaṇinīs* or *āryikā* are given permission by the *ācārya* to initiate their own female disciples.[284] The lists of A. Jain for the year 2001 show that 4 *gaṇinīs* had initiated altogether 16 *āryikā* and 4 *kṣullikās*, and 4 *āryikās* initiated altogether 8 *āryikā*. There are evidently also male ascetics who performed initiations independently. In 2001, 1 *upādhyāya* and 2 *munis* initiated altogether 6 *āryikā*. One *ailaka*, 7 *kṣullakas*, and one *kṣullikā* were also initiated by various *ācāryakalpas*, *ailācāryas* and *munis* — with or without the permission of an *ācārya*.[285] Occasionally, even self-initiations of *munis* are reported.[286]

The monastic names of the *āryikā* always have the double suffix *-matī matā* at the end. The *gaṇinīs* are called *gaṇinī āryikā śrī* ____ [name] *matī mātā jī*. The *gaṇinī pramukhā* Āryikā Jñān Matī and her namesake Āryikā Jñān Matī (Gujarāt), have each one *kṣullaka* amongst their disciples. However, the *kṣullakas* were not initiated by the *āryikā* themselves but by Ācārya Vimal Sāgar and by Ācārya Ajit Sāgar respectively.[287] According to Shāntā (1985: 514f.) and Balbir (1990: 182f.), the prominent Āryikā Jñān Matī (born 19 October 1933) was initiated by the late Ācārya Deś Bhūṣaṇ. However, D. Śāstrī (1985: 150) points out that only her *kṣullikā dīkṣā* was performed by Deś Bhūṣaṇ in 1953, but her *āryikā dīkṣā* by Ācārya Vīr Sāgar in 1956. After his death, Jñān Matī was associated with the late Ācārya Sumati Sāgar. She now commands her own separate group, which is largely composed of family members but includes also celibate male lay followers (*brahmacārī*) who were personally initiated by her in 1987 — the first event of its kind. Due to health reasons, she stays more or less permanently in her abode in

Hastināpūr, where her followers have built a giant cosmographic model of the continent Jambūdvīpa in concrete.[288] She is closely associated with the Mahāsabhā and with the opponents of the cosmological interpretations of the Kānjī Panth.[289]

Even the largest Digambara *saṅghas* have a flat administrative structure, which confirms that formal organisation does not play a prominent role in Digambara monasticism. The *guru-śiṣya* link alone constitutes the institutional core of the Digambara mendicant traditions. This is reflected in publications such as D. Śāstrī's (1985) *Digambara Jain Sādhu Paricay*, which lists only the immediate disciples of a *muni*, but does not depict any lineages. Of the 37 groups led by *ācāryas*, only 5 comprise another office-holder apart from the *ācārya* himself. The majority of these 5 groups are not even particularly large, which suggests that the titles (2x *upādhyāya*, 2x *ailācārya*, 1 x *gaṇinī*) designate honorary rather than administrative roles. The dedicated successors of an *ācārya*, the *ācāryakalpas*, *ailācāryas* or *yuvācāryas*,[290] *bālācaryas* and *upādhyāyas*, are usually permitted to form their own groups and to initiate their own disciples, while continuing to respect the moral authority of their *dīkṣā guru*. Because of his limited powers, an *ācārya* cannot prevent his disciples leaving, if they are supported by members of the lay communities.[291] Although, in principle, only an *ācārya* can convey the titles of *ācāryakalpa*, *ailācārya*, *bālācarya*, or *upādhyāya* or *gaṇinī* on highly respected monks or nuns,[292] there are several recognised methods for becoming an *ācārya*: either by the choice of the acting *ācārya*, or – if the *ācārya* dies without having determined a successor – by the choice of the *muni saṅgha*[293] and/or the *samāj*, or by the acclamation of a self-selected successor (e.g. the oldest disciple). In practice, the laity always interfere in the decision making process. Often, individual monks sever themselves from their *ācāryas* and simply declare themselves to be *ācāryas* in their own right. However, most *ācāryas*, even those who command their own disciples, remain nominally part of the lineage of their teacher, although 'there is no formal recognition of a line of pupillary succession' (Carrithers 1990: 153). In the absence of clear organisational and disciplinary rules (*maryādā*) – there are no established criteria for initiation and excommunication (which is never practised) – the group structure and the personnel of the peripatetic groups of a Digambara *muni saṅgha* is in perpetual flux. Changes occur not only through temporary visits in other groups for purposes of study, but also through the inflow and outflow of new mendicants from one *saṅgha* to another, and through the deliberate division of a large group into smaller groups for convenience by the *ācāryas*. It is therefore doubtful whether descent constructs are of practical importance beyond the purpose of legitimisation qua tradition. However, the doctrinal differences between the group of Vidyā Sāgar, who promotes idiosyncratic Terā Panth teachings, and the majority of the other Digambara *ācāryas*, sometimes causes the rejection of the *munis* of one lineage by another.

Demographic trends

According to the data collected by A. Jain, the total number of Digambara ascetics increased between 2000 to 2001 by 10.3% or 84 mendicants, within a single year. The category with the greatest increase is the one of the *munis*, who are responsible for the higher growth rate of male rather than female ascetics. In the year 2000, the 450 male ascetics represented 55% of all Digambara ascetics, the 368 female ascetics 45%, and in the year 2001 the 508 male ascetics represented 56.42% and the 394 female ascetics 43.7%. In 2001, the totally 902 ascetics were distributed over 341 groups. The average group size was only 2.65 (*āryikā*: 2.9). However, the average size of the groups (*saṅgha*) of the *ācāryas* was 6.9, which reflects their importance for the organisation of the Digambara ascetics. The fissiparous tendencies of the Digambara ascetics are illustrated by the fact that the groups led by *ācāryas* lost 18 members altogether within one year, whereas the groups led my *munis* and *āryikā* gained 51 and 32 members respectively.

The data published by B.U. Jain (1999: 382) show that the Digambara as a whole have by far the highest growth rate of all Jain mendicant traditions, even if we take into account that the nominal statistical growth largely reflects underreporting in earlier years.[294] Within 12 years, the reported numbers have almost tripled from a total of 363 in 1987 to a total of 960 in 1999. The overall trend has been confirmed by the reliable information of A. Jain for the years 2000–2001. This growth is all the more astonishing considering the fact that one of the first modern *munis*, Ādi Sāgar, who died in 1943, initiated himself as late as 1913. The accelerated increase in numbers started even later, after Śānti Sāgar's death in 1955, when the Digambara laity began to actively encourage the initiation of *munis* (Kāsalīvāl 1992: 35). Two explanations for the revival of the *muni saṅgha* are generally offered by the Digambaras: The abolition of the limitations imposed by both the colonial government and local kings on the free movement of the naked ascetics after Indian Independence, and the lack of any examination of the qualifications of the candidates because of the absence of organisational rules. Critics noted that the artificial increase of numbers due to the unchecked intake resulted in diminishing standards of conduct amongst the *munis*, many of whom joined the mendicant life 'mainly to gain influence and to enrich themselves' and to leave again as they please.[295] This argument is rejected by others, who point out that, if this would be true, then even more initiations would take place. Instead, the inspirational role of family members who became *munis* is highlighted, and the effects of the renaissance of Jain religious education in the last 100 years. Economic factors are generally discredited with reference to the fact that the main recruiting grounds for *munis* in northern Karṇāṭaka and southern Mahārāṣṭra, and elsewhere, have experienced considerable economic growth over the last decades.

The most interesting result of this preliminary demographic analysis of the Digambara mendicants is that the Digambaras are the only contemporary Jain tradition which has more monks than nuns (monks 1986: 86.89%, 1990: 63.38%, 1995: 54.13%, 1998: 54.25% and 1999: 63.54%).[296] Part of the explanation for this must be sought in the Digambara doctrine of the spiritual inferiority of women, which is naturally unappealing for unmarried girls who may perceive monastic life as an alternative to marriage (Jaini 1991: 26). Yet, for all practical purposes, Digambara *āryikā* have more personal freedom than Mūrtipūjaka *sādhvīs*, and their numbers are currently increasing. Another factor may be the lack of institutional structures, which offer protection to nuns.[297]

Jaina mendicants 1987–1999

The total number of Jain mendicants for the period between 1987 and 1999, and the relative size of the four principal mendicant traditions are summarised in Table 1.9 and Table 1.10. According to the figures published by B.U. Jain, 11,737 Jain *sādhus, ailakas, kṣullakas, sādhvīs* and *āryikā* have been counted in 1999. This total is based on confirmed figures only, excluding the personal estimates by B.U. Jain. The real number of mendicants was certainly higher, maybe between 100–300, disregarding *yatis*, *bhaṭṭārakas*, *brahmacārīs* and *brahmacāriṇīs*.

The figures illustrate the continuing numerical dominance of the Mūrtipūjaka ascetics and particularly of the Tapā Gaccha mendicants, who retained more than 50% of the overall share. A look at the summary figures for 1999 and a comparison with those of 1987 shows that the ratios of the main sectarian schools remain relatively stable, considering the significant underreporting of the number of Digambara ascetics before 1996. In 1987, 59.37% of all mendicants were Mūrtipūjakas and 52.28% belonged to the Tapā Gaccha, and in 1999, 58.30% were Mūrtipūjakas and 51.51% belonged to the Tapā Gaccha. The percentages of the Sthānakavāsīs and the Terā Panthīs – whose rapidly increasing number of *samaṇīs* was not taken into account in the statistics – fell slightly; in the case of the Sthānakavāsīs, from 29.03% in 1987 to 27.46% in 1999, and in the case of the Terā Panthīs, from 7.66% in 1987 to 6.06% in 1999. By contrast, the share of the Digambaras rose sharply from 3.94% in 1987 to 8.18% in 1999 for the reasons given earlier.

A comparison of the data from 1987 and 1999 shows that the total number of Jain mendicants has increased from 9,222 in 1987 to 11,737 in 1999.[298] The overall growth rate for the twelve year period 1987–1999 was an astonishing 26.75%: Mūrtipūjaka 24.99%, Sthānakavāsī 20.40%, Terā Panth 0.57% (1987–1996: 6.65%) and Digambara 164.46%. The growth rate would have been even higher if the sharply rising number of novices and lay ascetics had been taken into account.[299]

The accelerated increase in the number of Jain ascetics in recent years contrasts with the slow growth of the Jain population as a whole, which rose between 1981 and 1991 by 4.98%, from 3.193 million to 3.352 million. Apart from the Zoroastrians, the Jains had by far the lowest relative growth rate of all Indian religions (4.42% between 1981 and 1991, 26% between 1991 and 2001), which reduces their share of the total population from 0.48% in 1981 to 0.40% both in 1991 and 2001 (cf. M.K. Jain 1986: 33f., Vijayanunni 1991: x–xi, www.censusindia.net). The divergent growth rates of the mendicants and the lay population indicate an increasing popularity of monastic life for the period under investigation.[300] This is a puzzling fact, especially if one assumes that secularisation and

Table 1.9 **Total number of Jaina *sādhus* and *sādhvīs* 1987, 1990 and 1996**

Sampradāya	*Ācārya*			*Cāturmāsa-places*			*Sādhu/Muni*			*Sādhvī/Āryikā*			*Total*		
	1987	*1990*	*1996*	*1987*	*1990*	*1996*	*1987*	*1990*	*1996*	*1987*	*1990*	*1996*	*1987*	*1990*	*1996*
Mūrtipūjaka	109	118	148	1182	1220	1309	1375	1373	1450	4100	4789	4923	5475	6162	6373
Sthānakavāsī	9	9	10	624	647	689	540	532	515	2137	2206	2479	2677	2738	2994
Terā Panth	1	1	1	135	134	147	148	157	169	559	562	584	707	719	754
Śvetāmbara	119	128	159	1941	2001	2145	2062	2062	2134	6796	7557	7986	8859	9619	10121
Digambara	19	32	36	52	103	125	227	225	326	136	130	213	363	355	539
Total	138	160	195	1993	2104	2270	2289	2287	2460	6932	7687	8199	9222	9974	10660

Note: Compare B.U. Jain 1987: 77, 1990: 59–63.

Table 1.10 **Total number of Jaina *sādhus* and *sādhvīs* 1999**[a]

Sampradāya	*Ācārya*	*Cāturmāsa-places*	*Sādhu/Muni*	*Sādhvī/Aryikā*	*Total*	*%*
Mūrtipūjaka	164	1485	1489	5354	6843	58.30
Sthānakavāsī	9	768	533	2690	3223	27.46
Terā Panth	1	128	154	557	711	6.06
Digambara	40	190	610	350	960	8.18
Total	214	2571	2786	8951	11737	100

Note:
a These figures do not include the three recent splinter groups of the Terā Panth, nor the Sthānakavāsī traditions of Vīrāyatan and the Arhat Saṅgha.

religious decline are two sides of the same coin. Cort (1989: 100, n. 16) remarked that the continuing rise of the numbers of Jain mendicants is a 'quite striking phenomenon . . . given the economic and social status and the degree of Westernisation of Jain society.' If the data is correct, our pre-conceptions need to be revised. Apparently, westernisation and modernisation have not contributed to a decline, but to an increase in the popularity of renunciation amongst Jains.

Reasons for renunciation

How can we explain this? There is no easy answer. One explanation would be to argue that renunciation became more popular as a consequence of the monastic reforms at the beginning of the twentieth century, which improved the standards and therefore the appeal of monastic life. A social psychological perspective, on the other hand, would focus on the function of the institution of renunciation as a socio-cultural defense-mechanism which compensates for the disruptive effects of modernisation and socio-economic change.[301] We can, for instance, observe a strong rise in the number of male mendicants during the struggle for national independence and in the first years after Indian independence, when Gāndhī's influence reached its zenith. During these years, male mendicants in particular were attracted both by the political utility of the cultural symbolism of renunciation for the purpose of social integration and by the social activism of reform-orientated Jain *ācāryas*. But this interpretation does not account for the unprecedented popularity of renunciation in the last two decades.

Another argument points to the recent economic success of the Jain community, which enables it to lose some male workforce and to sustain larger mendicant communities. This point is sometimes raised within the Śvetāmbara Jain community. The absolute number of Jain mendicants is very small, compared to Buddhism which has at least 300,000 fully initiated *bhikkhus* worldwide[302] or Christianity which still has more than 1,000,000 monks and nuns.[303] However, the proportion of mendicants relative to the Jain population as a whole is higher than amongst Buddhists or Christians, and probably always was. In 1990 the ratio was 1 mendicant for every 336 laity (9,974 mendicants: 3,352,706 laity). This extraordinary high ratio of mendicants may indeed be explained in terms of the wealth of the Jain population, which can easily afford to feed such a big mendicant community.

Another explanation is given by Goonasekere (1986: 118f.), who interprets Jain renunciation as an institutionalised protest movement against specific social constraints within the status-conscious *baniya* castes in Western India. Yet, this variant of the deprivation theory which explains the higher proportion of mendicants from families with a relatively lower income from a rural or small town background[304] with reference to economic difficulties and the resulting psychological tensions[305] does not account for the motivation of the monks in his own sample, who cited charismatic attraction to a monk or nun as the main factor. As we have seen, the recent accelerated increase of Digambara *munis* is sometimes explained by members of the Digambara community itself by the lack of disciplinary procedures within the Digambara mendicant orders and by the opportunity for young men from the relatively poor Digambara agricultural castes in South India to increase their status and power by joining one of the *saṅghas.* However, if these were the only reasons, then even more young men would renounce.[306]

The main reason for the rapidly growing popularity of monastic life must be sought amongst the population of male Digambara and female Śvetāmbara renouncers. One of the most interesting findings is the continuing predominance of the male ascetics amongst the Digambara, which reflects the different status of nuns in this tradition. Amongst the Śvetāmbaras, only the Tapā Gaccha Bhuvanabhānusūri Samudāya has – for the said reasons – also more *sādhus* than *sādhvīs.* Śvetāmbara Jainism is unique, because of the

Table 1.11 **Percentage of *sādhvīs* 1987–1999**

Year	*Mūrtipūjaka*	*Sthānakavāsī*	*Terā Panth*	*Digambara*	*Total*
1987	74.88	79.83	79.07	37.46	75.17
1990	77.72	80.57	78.16	36.61	77.07
1996	77.25	82.80	77.45	39.52	76.91
1999	78.24	83.55	78.92	36.46	76.30

institutionalised option of full ordination for women, which is neither offered by Hinduism nor Theravāda Buddhism.[307] Why is the percentage of female Jain mendicants presently rising? A comparison of the percentages of the *sādhvīs* between 1987 and 1999 shows a significant (>3%) increase in the number of female ascetics amongst the Mūrtipūjakas and Sthānakavāsīs, while the ratios of the Terā Panthīs and the Digambaras remained stable for the reasons cited earlier (Table 1.11). Sthānakavāsīs have the highest percentage of female mendicants, most certainly because they allow the greatest degree of freedom for *sādhvīs*, who are permitted to read all scriptures, to preach, and to roam separately. However, the overall ratios between *sādhus* and *sādhvīs* remained not only relatively stable between 75% and 77%, they also roughly corresponded to the percentage of 72% *sādhvīs* quoted in the Kalpa Sūtra.

Social reasons, such as widowhood, unmarritability, high dowry claims amongst higher castes,[308] and other experiences of institutionalised social constraints have been cited already by Bühler and others,[309] in order to account for the consistent popularity of renunciation amongst Jain women. But this does not explain either the absence of female renunciation in similar social groups or recent developments. Reynell (1985: 269) pointed to the rising age of marriage in the Jain communities. Following on from Goonasekera (1986), Cort (1991) diagnosed 'drastic changes in the demographics of Śvetāmbar mendicancy' (ibid.: 659), from 'a situation not unlike the traditional Brāhmaṇical prescription for the *vānaprastha* and *saṅnyāsa āśramas*, the stages of gradual withdrawal and renunciation after the householder (*gṛhastha*) stage of life,' to a pattern in which 'the vast majority of contemporary ascetics are unmarried and take *dīkṣā* before the age of thirty' (ibid.: 660). He sees the improvements in the social world of women as the reason for the declining number of widow mendicants during the twentieth century. He argues that because nowadays most widows are likely to have had children – due to the rise in the age of marriage and rising health standards – they are less inclined to renounce than child widows in the nineteenth century: 'Having to raise the children means that becoming a *sādhvī* is less of a realistic option for a widow. Changing social attitudes towards widows also make it less likely that a Jain widow feels that she has little choice but to become a *sādhvī*' (Cort 1989: 111f.). Therefore, 'becoming a *sādhvī* is now seen as an alternative vocation to that of a housewife' (ibid.).[310]

This theory certainly explains the declining number of widows within the mendicant orders, but not the increasing number of unmarried women. Why should more and more young Jain women become disillusioned with family life under conditions of increasing prosperity and personal freedom? An important factor, which has not been considered thus far, is the significant change in the standard of education of Jain women. One hundred years ago, most Jain women were illiterate. Yet, the last Census of India in 2001 recorded a female literacy rate of 90.6 per cent amongst the Jains – the second highest after the Parsis – while in India as a whole it was only 47 per cent. Contemporary Śvetāmbara women are often born into privileged social groups and increasingly able to enjoy higher education, to choose their husbands within given limits but rarely to give up housework for an independent professional career, unimpaired by customary constraints. Formal education and the experience of an extended period of pre-marital independence often raise expectations which make it difficult for young educated women to re-adjust to the lifestyle of a traditional Jain housewife.

The experience of small freedoms generally increases the desire for more. Yet, monastic life does not offer more individual freedom, but an even more disciplined and restrained way of life. Socio-economic reasons for renunciation are recognised as a matter of fact but not condoned by the Jain scriptures (Ṭhāṇā 712a, 335a, Schubring 2000, § 137) and can only offer a partial explanation to a difficult question. A more complete answer must take into account multiple factors, in particular the motivating role of the Śvetāmbara doctrine of salvation and the opportunity of an alternative lifestyle offered by the existing *sādhvī* traditions themselves, as well as the elevated individual status of a nun in the Jain community. I think the most likely candidate for further exploration is the romantic image of freely roaming female ascetics, who enjoy enhanced conditions of living in reformed and materially well supported mendicant orders which offer opportunities for education and self-development that are still unavailable in traditional family life, which currently catches the imagination of young Jain women,[311] in the same way as men were attracted by the political symbolism of renunciation during the independence struggle.[312]

Concluding remarks

The most interesting result of this study, however preliminary it may be, is the emerging, nearly complete, pattern of the group structure of the current Jain mendicant traditions. The Digambara *muni* tradition is currently divided into some 341 itinerant groups and individuals, who belong to three lineages and maybe a dozen sub-lineages which have a flat administrative structure. However, more than half of all Digambara mendicants were initiated and are supervised by only a handful of *ācāryas.*[313] Although the Digambara tradition has currently no monastic orders, nor clearly identifiable schools and sects, it shows significant organisational and doctrinal faultlines which deserve further investigation. In total, the Śvetāmbara tradition is composed of some 57 independently organised groups: 27 Mūrtipūjaka, 26 Sthānakavāsī and 4 Terā Panth. These independently organised 'orders,' together with their lay followers can be designated as sociological 'sects,' in contrast to doctrinal 'schools,' although some overlap and fluid transitions between the three categories occur. There are, of course, fewer doctrinal schools than orders and sects. The principal schools of the Mūrtipūjakas are the six *gacchas.* The situation amongst the Sthānakavāsīs is more diffuse, since not all of the 5 founding fathers had major doctrinal differences. However, there are at least two broad schools within the Sthānakavāsī movement. On the one hand, those who follow the teachings of Dharma Siṁha, who may have had a significant, though never acknowledged, influence on the Terā Panth *ācārya* Bhikṣu and his idiosyncratic teachings, and, on the other hand, those who follow the teachings of Lava and Dharma Dāsa, who had only minor disagreements. The few globalising mendicant groups on the fringe of the Sthānakavāsī movement, which allow their ascetics to use modern means of transport and travel abroad, represent a new development, and share many attributes with Jain lay movements with the *yati* traditions, and with the disdained mendicants 'who wander alone' (Pkt. *egalla vihārī*), who can always be found on the fringes of the organised Jain ascetic traditions.[314] The use of modern means of transport might in future significantly modify the relationship between group size and size of lay following. However, the use of modern means of communication which, in contrast to the modern means of transport, are now endorsed by most, but not all, mendicant groups, has presently no significant influence on the pattern of recruitment of devotees, which continues to be predicated on regular personal contact between guru and devotee.

Acknowledgement

I am very grateful to Professor Padmanabh S. Jaini for his comments on an earlier version of this study.

Notes

1 Throughout the text, the colloquial 'Jain' rather than 'Jaina' is used, and with the exception of the Sanskritic names of sects and schools and technical Jain terms, proper names are not sanskritised.

2 See the volume *Village India* edited by McKim Marriott in 1955. Survey techniques were first used in Jaina studies by Sangave 1959/1980, whose literature review on the social divisions of the Jains is still the standard reference source. The first book length field studies were the monographs by Mahias 1985 and Shāntā 1985. Regional, subaltern, media, etc. studies have yet to be applied on a larger scale in the emerging field of Jaina studies.

3 'Jains,' 'lay Jains in a particular location,' 'Mūrtipūjaka/ Digambara Jain laity,' 'Jain mendicants,' 'Jain merchants,' 'Jain women,' 'Jain nuns,' etc.

4 Following Schubring 2000: § 139, 252, Folkert 1993: 153, 163 translates the ambivalent terms *gaccha* and its Digambara equivalent *saṅgha* variably as 'school,' 'sect' and 'order.' He defines schools as 'doctrinally' demarcated units, sects as 'modern,' and monastic orders as primarily concerned with issues of 'praxis.' Balbir 2003: 48 focuses only on 'orders' or 'lineages' – the terms are used as synonyms – and dismisses the doctrinal dimension as insignificant with regard to *gacchas*. However, many orders are doctrinally demarcated, as Balbir's study of doctrinal controversies concerning proper praxis shows; and even in the pre-modern period sects existed with and without core monastic orders. For alternative definitions of the terms school, order and sect see Flügel 2000: 77f. and note 8.

5 For a similar research strategy see Banks 1986: 458 and Flügel 1994: 4, 1995–96: 119, n. 4.

6 See also Cort in this volume, p. 261.

7 Sangave's 1959/1980 attempt at conducting a representative survey did not meet sufficient response from the Jain community.

8 It is neither possible nor methodologically desirable to find for every Jain (Indian) term an equivalent analytical term and *vice versa.* I would propose to define Jain schools, orders and sects in the following way (cf. Flügel 2000: 42, n. 9). Doctrinal 'schools' may inform both individuals or (un-) organised religious 'movements' of various types; organised monastic 'orders' contrast with unorganised ascetic groups and ascetics who 'wander alone' (*ekala vihārī*); 'sects' are exclusive groups which either (a) encompass both ascetics and laity, that is the classical four-fold community (*caturvidha saṅgha*) and variations created by added intermediary categories such as the *pañcavidha saṅgha* etc. or by the deliberate exclusion or factual absence of one or more of the four categories, or (b) represent self-conscious lay movements. Corresponding to the distinction between orders and sects is the distinction between the casual 'supporter' of the ascetics, the initiated (through the vow of allegiance) or simply dedicated lay 'follower,' and the born and/or paying 'member' of a sect-specific Jain caste- or community organisation. See Flügel 1994: 404; and Dundas' 2003: 129 for the differentiation between 'affiliation' and 'conversion.' For the distinction between Indian monastic 'orders' and 'sects' which encompass both ascetics and laity see Vallée-Poussin 1918: 716. The peculiar dual organisation of the majority of the contemporary Jain (and other Indian) 'sects,' with monastic orders as a core supported by amorphous lay communities under the spiritual command of the monks, was also highlighted by Max Weber 1920/1978: 207. See Dumont's 1980: 284 distinction between the doctrinal exclusivity of an Indian 'sect' and its social inclusivity. Generally, social categories, organised groups and gatherings need to be distinguished.

9 It seems advisable to distinguish the level of more or less exclusive 'schools,' organised 'sects' and 'movements' from the level of the two principal religious 'denominations' in Jainism which Leumann 1934: 1 called '*Confessionen.*'

10 The use of the word 'Jaina' as a self-designation for both the monastic community and the lay community is a relatively recent one (Böhtlingk and Roth 1861: 132, Flügel 2005: 3f.). In the ancient texts, the words *niggaṃtha* and *niggaṃthī* referred only to Jain monks and nuns, but not to their followers, or *upāsakas* (Jacobi 1879: 5), who were classified as part of the four-fold *saṅgha* only from the late-canonical period onwards by both the Śvetāmbaras (Viyāhapannatti 792b, Ṭhāṇa 281b) and by the early Digambaras (Mūlācāra, Chappāhuḍa, etc.) (Schubring 2000, § 30, § 137).

11 Between 1871 and 1891, the Census of India gradually substituted the initial classification of the Indian population in terms of religion with a dual religion/caste classification: 1871: 'Hindu,' 'Muslim,' 'Other,' 1881: 'religion (caste),' 1891: 'religion (sect),' 'caste (sub-caste)' (Baines 1893: 186f.). 'The . . . change was made in order to get rid of the notion that caste, or social distinction, was not required for Musalmans, Sikhs, Jains, and so on, or was held to be subordinate in any way to sect or religion' (ibid.: 187).

12 Brekke 2002: 129–132, cf. Dundas 2002: 4–6, Flügel 1994: 11–15.

13 'Many Jains have . . . undoubtedly given their religion as Hindoo, and in some cases, though these are not many, I am inclined to think the enumerators have returned as Hindoos persons who really stated their religion to be Jain. As the followers of the Jain creed are generally held and themselves generally claim, to be Hindoos, this is not surprising: nor is this error of importance, for the domestic and social economy of the Jains differ little from the orthodox Hindoo' (Plowden 1883: 23, cf. Kitts, in Plowden 1883: 19f., Baines, in Plowden 1883, III: cvii). See Cohn 1992: 248, Sangave 1980: 3, Dundas 2002: 4–6, Carrithers 2000: 833f.

14 The main reason for the ambiguous self-identification of many Jains is the equivocal nature of the concept 'Hindu' itself.

15 For example, Keshroy 1924, Maṇilāl 1934: 270f., Natarajan 1971 I: 39. The preface of Singh's 1894: 1 report on the census of 1891 in Marwar states that in addition to the questionnaire of the census supervisors and inspectors 'a good many facts were investigated through personal enquiries from trustworthy representatives of various communities.'

16 There is no evidence for the inflated estimates that are frequently quoted in popular Jain publications. Kalidas Nag wrote in his speech to a Jain audience, 'Jainism – A World Religion,' in the *Jaina Gazette* 57, 2–3 (1951): 'You should prepare a census of your own, regardless of the government census, to arrive at a correct conclusion' (ibid.: 35). Earlier attempts to produce community censuses, such as the *Jain Śvetāmbara Directory (Gujarāt)* written in Gujarātī (Jain Śvetāmbara Conference 1909, 1915, 1916), were lacking an integral 'Jain' communal or communitarian perspective. The first Jain Śvetāmbara Directory was produced between 1906 and 1907 in accordance with resolution No. 8 of the *Jain Śvetāmbara Conference* in 1904 which called for the collection of information on the followers of the different Mūrtipūjaka and 'Loṅkāgaccha' Śvetāmbara *gacchas* and *samudāyas* in all districts (*jillā*), sub-districts (*tāluka*) and villages (*gāma*) in India. The book was intended in particular as a travel guide, for instance for pilgrimages (*yātrā*). With the help of local volunteers a questionnaire was distributed by the main coordinators Śobhācand Mohanlāl Śāh and Ḍāhyācand Trībhovan Gāndhī, who listed the following categories: the number of family houses (*kula ghara*), women (*strī*), men (*puruṣa*), caste (*jñāti*), sect (*gaccha*), literacy; and the local

temples (*jina-mandira*), images (*jina-pratimā*), monasteries (*upāśraya*), libraries (*jñāna-bhaṇḍāra*), schools (*pāthśālā*), old books (*pūrvācārya praṇīta grantha*), Jain societies (*sabhā*) and associations (*maṇḍala*). The interesting resulting statistics suffer from imprecise lists of *jñātis* and *gacchas* and problems of inaccurate self-reporting and counting, as the compilers of the first report emphasise (Jain Śvetāmbara Conference 1909: ii–iii). It was probably in response to the Śvetāmbara efforts that the eleventh meeting of the Digambara Jain Mahāsabhā inspired Māṇikcand Hīrācand Jauharī of Bombay to produce between 1907 and 1914 the *Shri Bharatvarshiya Digambara Jain Directory* (Jhaveri 1914) 'for the good of all Digambara Jain brothers.' The ensuing publication contains lists of towns, leading community members, caste, professions, etc. Cf. Sangave 1980: 119–121, 124–130. I am grateful to Yashvant Malaiya, who has pointed this source out to me. Nowadays, excellent self-produced national statistics are available for certain castes, such as the Khaṇḍelvālas, which have a high proportion of Jain members.

17 A Digambara Jain layman told me that the results of the Census of India of 1981 and 1991 in North Indian states were manipulated by 'Hindutva' inspired enumerators who wrote 'Hindu (Jain)' into the forms, even if the answer given was 'Jain.' During the Census of 2001, Jain community leaders started awareness rising campaigns to prevent a recurrence of these practices.

18 The introduction of a question on religious affiliation into the UK-census of 2001 stirred similar sentiments amongst leading members of the Jain community in Britain. For a Hindutva inspired variation of demographic *angst* regarding the outgrowth of the Hindus by the Muslims in India see A.P. Joshi *et al.* 2003.

19 B.U. Jain 1999, for instance, lists the Mūrtipūjaka *samudāyas* according to their size. See Appadurai 1993: 117 on the role of numbers for the colonial 'illusion of bureaucratic control.' The role of numbers (regarding fasts etc.) is even greater in traditional Jainism.

20 Jacobi 1884: 267, n. 1, Schubring 2000 § 22: 44. Sharma 1999: 78f. noted that Ācārya Hemacandra's 12th C. *Triṣaṣṭiśalākāpuruṣacaritra* associates varying numbers of monks, nuns and laity with different Jinas.

21 Cf. Jaini 1991: 25.

22 Plates 13–15 in A. Cunningham's Archaeological Survey Report 20.3, in Bühler 1887: 169.

23 Sthavirāvalī 5, in Jacobi 1884: 289.

24 Sangave now seems to prefer the less charged term 'communitarianism' (personal communication, 2 January 2005).

25 Cort 1989: 491–94 summarised B.U. Jain's demographic data of the Mūrtipūjaka *sādhus* and *sādhvīs* in 1986 in an appendix, but noted

their incompleteness, which was partly rectified by B.U. Jain's subsequent publications.

26 These are the conventional dates. Except in the case of the 'panths,' I have represented the names of monastic orders in their sanskritised form, but proper names in their spoken form.

27 The primary source of information on the origins of these groups is the *Pravacanaparīkṣā* of the sixteenth century Tapā Gaccha *upādhyāya* Dharma Sāgara. For an overview of their history, doctrines and practices see M.U.K. Jain 1975.

28 The *paṭṭāvalīs* of the Kharatara Gaccha and of the Añcala Gaccha were published in many Sanskrit and vernacular editions. They were studied by Klatt 1894 and by Śivprasād 2001. See also Pārśva 1968: 9–21.

29 The *gacchādhipati* of the Añcala Gaccha is presently Śrīpūja Moti Sāgar Sūri (born 1944). See Photographs. The Śvetāmbara Loṅkāgaccha still has one *yati* but no *sādhus*. A notable feature of the *yati* traditions is that they do not have any female members.

30 The surprisingly high figure of more than 3,517 ascetics and a higher proportion of monks than nuns is reported in the Añcala Gaccha *paṭṭāvalī* for the Añcala Gaccha in the year 1180. It is said that Ācārya Āryarakṣita Sūri (1080–1180) initiated '2100 sādhus and 1130 sādhvīs, the ācārya-padam to 12 sādhus, the upādhyāya-padam to 20, the Paṇḍita-padam to 70, the mahattarā-padam to 103 sādhvīs (Samayaśrī and others), the pravartinī-padam to 82 sādhvīs, the total number of sādhus and sādhvīs being 3517' (Klatt 1894: 175). If the figures are true, then a huge number of Jain mendicants must have existed during the heydays of Jainism in the medieval period.

31 The equally centralised Rāmacandrasūri Samudāya of the Tapā Gaccha is the largest order. Balbir 2003: 48f. provides much information on the doctrinal foundation of the Añcala Gaccha, but not on initiation procedures.

32 According to Ācārya Jay Sundar Sūri of the Bhuvanabhānu Samudāya, the last *saṅghācārya* of the Vijaya Śākhā was Ācārya Vijay Prabhā, who commanded. *c.*200–300 ascetics. After him the number of *saṁvegī sādhus* decreased to 20–25 under Buṭerāy in the early nineteenth century (plus 10–15 in the Sāgara Śākhā, and 40–50 in the Vimala Gaccha), while the Tapā Gaccha *yati* orders had more than 1,500 members. Personal communication, Mumbaī 23 October, 2005.

33 Cf. Kañcansāgarsūri *et al.* 1977: 355–61.

34 Desāī 1983 I: 106ff., M. Śāh 1987. The precise origins of the trust are not known, but Śāntīdās Jhāverī was instrumental in institutionalising this influential organisation.

35 Probably only the *saṃvegī sādhu* tradition was interrupted.

36 Kañcansāgarsūri *et al.* 1977.

37 See Paul Dundas' forthcoming book.

38 Only the Kharatara Gaccha and the Añcala Gaccha still have some *yatis*.

39 'In his biography of Nemīsūri, one of the great reformist *ācāryas* of the early twentieth century, Śīlcandravijay 1973: 6 has estimated the number of *saṃvegī sādhus* in the period 1845–1865 to be no more than 25 to 30. While it is not clear if he means only within the Tapā Gacch, or in all the Mūrtipūjak *gacchas*, the number is still very small. He further comments on the low level of scholarly knowledge among these *sādhus*. Thus, the position of the Śvetāmbar *saṃvegī sādhu* in the early nineteenth century was not all that different from the position of the full-fledged *muni*, or *nirvāṇ svāmī*, among the South Indian Digambaras (see Carrithers . . .)' (Cort 1989: 99, n. 14). Unfortunately, the only information we have on the numbers of *yatis* in the nineteenth century are a number of *kṣetrādeśapaṭṭakas* and sporadic evidence in the reports of British colonial officials. A *cāturmāsa* list of 1867 issued by the successor of Ācārya Vijay Devendra Sūri, Ācārya Vijay Dharaṇendra Sūri, for instance, lists 212 monks (figures for nuns are not given) organised into 74 groups of 2 and 14 groups of 4 (Sandesara 1974: 229–233). For the year 1891, Singh 1894: 82 cites the number of 834 '*jātis*' in Marwar (Jodhpura) alone, but gives no figures for the *saṃvegīs*, who 'owe their origin to one Ānand Bimal Sūri' (ibid.: 95). The Jain mendicants in Mārvāṛ were classified as 'devotees' of the 'priests' (*yatis*, *brāhmaṇs*, etc.) and all counted under the label 'Samegi, Dhundia etc.' (ibid.: 85). Their total figure of 2,314 comprises 725 male and 1,589 female mendicants.

40 The *Jain Śvetāmbara Directory* published in 1916 by the reformist Jain Association of India lists some 228 monks, divided into 79 groups, and 203 nuns, divided into 40 groups, apparently belonging to reformed segments of the Tapā Gaccha, including the groups of the *ācāryas* Vijay Kamal Sūri, Vijay Nemī Sūri and Buddhi Sāgar Sūri which were mainly active in Kacch and Mārvāṛ (Jain Śvetāmbara Conference 1916: 18–22).

41 See Cort 1999.

42 In 2002, the total number had increased to 7,541 mendicants, 1,585 *munis* and 5,947 *sādhvīs*. The Tapā Gaccha had 6,696 mendicants, 1,445 *sādhus* and 5,242 *sādhvīs* (cf. ibid.: 70, 305).

43 Jaini 1991: 26 explains the attractiveness of the Tapā Gaccha for women with the 'spiritual equality' offered to Śvetāmbara *sādhvīs*. However, Mūrtipūjaka *sādhvīs* are still not allowed to read certain *āgama*-texts nor to deliver public sermons, a fact which Shāntā 1985: 315, 321f., n. 5, 456 explains by pointing at the high number of *ācāryas*, which limits speaking opportunities.

44 'The *samudāy* is not as formal a grouping as the *gacch*. Mendicants in one *samudāy* will, for a variety of reasons, sometimes travel with mendicants of another *samudāy*. But mendicants do not travel with mendicants of another *gacch*, as that would involve changing some of the details of their daily practices' (Cort 1991: 663). In his later publications, Cort 1999: 44, 2001: 46 supplies enough material for the conjecture that many *samudāyas* have a distinct doctrinal and organisational identity with separate *pañcāṅgas*, rituals and lay support.

45 Shāntā 1985: 329.

46 The use of the sign '-' in the columns indicates cases of separation (cf. Tristuti Gaccha).

47 The names of all *ācāryas* of the Vijaya Śākhā are preceded by the epithet 'Vijaya.' Some *gacchādhipatis* are not *ācāryas* (*sūri*).

48 After his death, Prem Sūri's line split into two *samudāyas*, led by Rām Candra Sūri and Bhuvan Bhānu Sūri respectively. Following Rām Candra Sūri's (1896–1991) death, this *samudāya* was named after him by his successor Mahoday Sūri (died 2002), who was in turn succeeded by Ācārya Hem Bhūṣaṇ Sūri (B.U. Jain 1996: 165–177). Rām Candra Sūri was one of the most influential and orthodox *ācāryas* of the Vijaya Śākhā. He nearly became the leader (*śāsanasamrāṭa* or *adhipatī*) of the entire Tapā Gaccha. Cort 1989: 103, n. 18 quotes demographic data which show that the Dān-Prem Samudāya has grown from 36 *sādhus* in 1944 to 219 *sādhus* in 1975 (Cort had no information on the numbers of *sādhvīs*). By 1999, this tradition had split into four sections, including Śānti Candra Sūri's group, and Vibuddha Prabhā Sūri's group. However, after 1996 the Amṛtasūri Samudāya, lead by Jinendra Sūri, was re-integrated into the Ramacandrasūri Samudāya, which had in all 905 members in 1999, 290 *sādhus* and 615 *sādhvīs*, and 1,138 members in 2002, 310 *munis* and 828 *sādhvīs* (B.U. Jain 1999: 197, 2002: 169). Important particularities, in addition to the *be tithi* doctrine, are the performance of *guru pūjā* in the manner of the *aṣṭaprakārī pūjā* to the body of the *ācārya* Rām Candra Sūri and his statues, and the permission for lay followers to mount Śatruñjaya Hill even during *cāturmāsa* (personal communication).

49 This group separated in 1998 from the Ramacandrasūri Samudāya. It operates mainly in Rājasthān. In 1999 it had 45 mendicants, 23 *sādhus* and 22 *sādhvīs* (B.U. Jain 1999: 325f.).

50 This *samudāya* also derives from Prem Sūri, but was renamed after Bhuvan Bhānu Sūri (1911–1993) who broke with Rām Candra Sūri in 1986 after a dispute on calendrical issues (*ek tithi-be tithi*). See Cort 1999, B.U. Jain 1996: 179–87. Originally, the group was active in Halar, but its main sphere of activity is now Gujarāt and Mahārāṣṭra. In 1999 it had 560 members, 285 *sādhus* and 275 *sādhvīs* (B.U. Jain 1999: 230), in 2002 712 members, 361 *sādhus* and 351 *sādhvīs* (B.U. Jain 2002: 186). It is one of the few contemporary Jain orders which has more

monks than nuns, because Ācārya Prem Sūri objected to the initiation of *sādhvīs*, since their presence would inevitably cause the development of relationships between monks and nuns. One of Prem Sūri's disciples, Ācārya Jaśodev Sūri, successfully criticised this rule, by pointing to the unnecessary problems it creates when entire families want to renounce. Prem Sūri allowed him to start an order of nuns within his tradition, on the condition that he and his successors would be responsible for the supervision of the nuns, of which the main line of *gacchādhipatis* should remain aloof. After the death of Jaśodev Sūri, his successor Rajendra Sūri is now responsible for the *sādhvī* section.

51 This group separated itself in 1995 under Prem Sūri from the tradition of Rām Candra Sūri (whose *guru* was Prem Sūri). In 1999, it was nominally reincorporated into the Ramacandrasūri Sampradāya, but still maintains a separate existence. It is mainly active in Halar, near Jamnagar. In 2002 it had 26 mendicants, 4 *sādhus* and 22 *sādhvīs* (B.U. Jain 2002: 170, cf. 273).

52 Niti Sūri was a pupil of Buddhi Vijay and the teacher of Bhakti Sūri and Siddhi Sūri (Ratna Prabhā Vijay 5, 2 1948–1950: 217f.). In 1999, this group had 465 mendicants, 50 *sādhus* and 415 *sādhvīs* (B.U. Jain 1999: 254), in 2002, 426 mendicants, 40 *sādhus* and 386 *sādhvīs* (B.U. Jain 2002: 211).

53 In 1999, this group had 245 mendicants, 49 *sādhus* and 196 *sādhvīs* (B.U. Jain 1999: 295), the figures for 2002 – 128 mendicants, 46 *sādhus* and 82 *sādhvīs* – are incomplete (B.U. Jain 2002: 250).

54 Figures for the period between 1987 and 1996 are incomplete. In 1999, this group had 384 mendicants, 27 *sādhus* and 357 *sādhvīs* (B.U. Jain 1999: 271), in 2002, 311 mendicants, 31 *sādhus* and 280 *sādhvīs* (B.U. Jain 2002: 227). Today, Ācārya Vijay Arihant Sūri is the head of the order. Apparently, 150 *sādhvīs* joined the Ramacandrasūri Sampradāya (ibid.: 231).

55 Siddhi Sūri (1895–1959) was succeeded by Megh Śrī. One of his pupils was Bhuvan Vijay, the father and *dīkṣā guru* of the influential scholar Muni Jambū Vijay. In 1999, it had 250 mendicants, 30 *sādhus* and 220 *sādhvīs* (B.U. Jain 1999: 289), in 2002, 260 mendicants, 29 *sādhus* and 231 *sādhvīs* (B.U. Jain 2002: 240). The present *gacchādhipati* Rām Sūri has been selected, because he is the *ācārya* with the highest monastic age (ibid.: 246).

56 Dev Sūri's (1911–2002) predecessor was Meru Prabhā Sūri. The present head of the order is Ācārya Suśīl Sūri. In 1999 this group had 543 mendicants, 138 *sādhus* and 405 *sādhvīs* (ibid.: 242), and in 2002, 567 mendicants, 146 *sādhus* and 421 *sādhvīs* (B.U. Jain 1999: 230). It is mainly active in Gujarāt and Rājasthān, and has produced many scholarly monks.

57 Vijay Vallabh Sūri (1870–1954) was one of the most influential reformers of the Tapā Gaccha in the twentieth century and an

important promotor of modern education and social reform. He was initiated in 1886 by Vijay Ānand Sūri (Ātmā Rām). The ascetics of this tradition wear yellow garments, originally to distinguish themselves from the *yatis* who were clad in white. They permit nuns to give public lectures, and use microphones and in big cities flush toilets (in other *samudāyas* the excretions of the mendicants are collected and then flushed away by the laity). They share food with the mendicants of the Keśarasūri and Dharmasūri Samudāyas, who descend from the same lineage. In 1999, this group had 274 mendicants, 54 *sādhus* and 220 *sādhvīs* (B.U. Jain 1999: 277), and in 2002, 295 mendicants, 60 *sādhus* and 235 *sādhvīs* (B.U. Jain 2002: 232). After the death of Vijay Indradinn Sūri (1923–2002), who originated from a tribal group in Gujarāt, Ācārya Vijay Ratnākar Sūri became the head of the order.

58 In 1999, it had 259 mendicants, 57 *sādhus* and 202 *sādhvīs* (B.U. Jain 1999: 284), in 2002, 250 mendicants, 55 *sādhus* and 195 *sādhvīs* (B.U. Jain 2002: 235). Jin Bhadra Sūri died in 1999. His predecessor was Kīrti Candra Sūri, his successor as *gacchādhipati* is Aśok Ratna Sūri (B.U. Jain 1999: 288f.).

59 Mohan Lāl was a pupil of Khānti Viyay, who was a disciple of Buddhi Vijay. He was particularly active in Bombay. In 1999, this group had 44 mendicants, 22 *sādhus* and 22 *sādhvīs* (B.U. Jain 1999: 323), in 2002, 57 mendicants, 26 *sādhus* and 31 *sādhvīs* (B.U. Jain 2002: 272).

60 Vijay Dharma Sūri (1868–1922) was an influential moderniser. He was initiated in 1887 by Vṛddhi Candra Vijay (died 1893), a pupil of Buddhi Vijay, and was succeeded by Vijay Indra Sūri (born 1881). In 1999, this group had 236 mendicants, 33 *sādhus* and 203 *sādhvīs* (B.U. Jain 1999: 302), in 2002, 229 mendicants, 33 *sādhus* and 196 *sādhvīs* (B.U. Jain 2002: 251).

61 Hem Prabhā Sūri's predecessor was Svayam Prabhā Sūri. The figures for 1987–1996 are based partly on estimates. In 1999, this group had 188 mendicants, 14 *sādhus* and 174 *sādhvīs* (B.U. Jain 1999: 309), in 2002, 217 mendicants, 22 *sādhus* and 195 *sādhvīs* (B.U. Jain 2002: 258).

62 Kanak Sūri was the teacher of Catur Vijay, the teacher of Pūṇya Vijay (1895–1971), who inspired the creation of the L. D. Institute in Ahmedabad in 1957. In 1999, this group had 451 mendicants, 29 *sādhus* and 422 *sādhvīs* (B.U. Jain 1999: 262), in 2002, 533 mendicants, 35 *sādhus* and 498 *sādhvīs* (B.U. Jain 2002: 217). After the death of Kalāpūrṇ Sūri in 2002, Ācārya Vijay Kalā Prabhā Sūri became head of the order (*gacchādhipati*), which is also called Kaccha Bāgaṛa Samudāya, because of the regional base of Kanaka Sūri (ibid.: 226).

63 Ratnākar's predecessor was Lakṣmī Sūri. This *samudāya* is predominantly active in Mevāṛ. In 1999, this group had 148 mendicants, 20 *sādhus* and 128 *sādhvīs* (B.U. Jain 1999: 313), in 2002, 153 mendicants, 22 *sādhus* and 131 *sādhvīs* (B.U. Jain 2002: 261).

64 Śānti Candra Sūri was a pupil of Vijay Ānand Sūri (Ātmā Rām). In 1999, this group had approximately 75 mendicants, 25 *sādhus* and 50 *sādhvīs* (B.U. Jain 1999: 322), and in 2002, 165 mendicants, 19 *sādhus* and 146 *sādhvīs* (B.U. Jain 2002: 270). In 2002, Bhuvan Śekhar Sūri died and was succeeded by Ācārya Rajendra Sūri (ibid.: 271).

65 Both the present *ācārya* Som Sundar Sūri and Jin Candra Sūri were initiated by Bhuvan Śekhar Sūri. In 1999, this group reported the figure of 80 mendicants, 8 *sādhus* and 72 *sādhvīs* (B.U. Jain 1999: 320), in 2002, 151 mendicants, 19 *sādhus* and 132 *sādhvīs* (B.U. Jain 2002: 268), but the figures are incomplete.

66 This group was started by Ānand Sāgar Sūri, a bitter opponent of Rām Candra Sūri, the leading monk of the Vijaya Śākhā in the twentieth century (cf. Cort 1999: 43): 'Rāmcandra Sūri (1895–1991) has argued that the scriptures should not be published at all, a view which found many partisans, while the other party followed the view that of Sāgarānanda Sūri (1875–1950), celebrated as the "uplifter of the scriptural tradition" (*āgamoddhāraka*), who advocated the publication of the scriptures but along with the old *Niryukti* and *Vṛtti* commentaries' (Dundas 1996: 90, cf. Banks 1992: 110). The group experienced frequent changes of leadership in the 1980s. In 1986, the leader was Devendra Sāgar, 1987 Cidānand Sāgar, 1990 Darśan Sāgar, who was succeeded by Suryoday Sāgar, and Aśok Sāgar in 2004–2005. The former *sādhu* Citra Bhānu (Candra Prabhā Sāgar), who continues to inspire diaspora Jains in the US and the UK, was a member of this lineage from 1942 to 1970. In 1999, this group had 740 members, 150 *sādhus* and 590 *sādhvīs* (B.U. Jain 1999: 215), in 2002, 956 members, 136 *sādhus* and 820 *sādhvīs* (B.U. Jain 2002: 171). Its main agenda is currently the defence of the scientific accuracy of the canonical Jaina cosmography.

67 Buddhi Sāgar Sūri (1874–1925), a disciple of Ravi Sāgar and one of only four *saṃvegī sādhu ācāryas* in 1913 (Cort 1997: 125), popularised the worship of the protector god Ghaṇṭākarṇa amongst Gujarātī Jains, particularly in Mahudi near Vījāpur (Cort 1989: 406–407, 428–433, 2001: 91, 164–168). He was succeeded by Monogam Sāgar (?), Rudhi Sāgar, and Subodh Sāgar Sūri, who inspired the construction of the *tīrthas* Vījāpur and Mahesāṇā, where the *tīrthaṅkara* Sīmandhara Svāmī is venerated. Ācārya Padma Sāgar Sūri (born 1934), who inspired the construction of the Jain centre at Kobā near Ahmedabad, also belongs to this order. In 1999, this *samudāya* had 135 mendicants, 45 *sādhus* and 90 *sādhvīs* (B.U. Jain 1999: 316); for 2002 the figures are incomplete: 115 mendicants, 45 *sādhus* and 70 *sādhvīs* (B.U. Jain 2002: 264).

68 Cidānand Sūri's predecessor was Ravi Vimal Sūri. He is now succeeded by Pradyumna Vimal Sūri. Figures are based on estimates. In 1999, it had about 51 mendicants, 6 *sādhus* and 45 *sādhvīs* (B.U. Jain 1999: 360), in 2002 approximately 49 mendicants, 4 *sādhus* and

45 *sādhvīs* (B.U. Jain 2002: 304).

69 This *sampradāya*, which is also called Vidhi Pakṣa, is mainly active in Kacch, Hālār and Mumbaī (Jain 1996: 274). In 1999, it had 250 members, 29 *sādhus* and 221 *sādhvīs* (B.U. Jain 1999: 327), in 2002 249 members, 29 *sādhus* and 220 *sādhvīs* (B.U. Jain 2002: 274). For its history see Śivprasād 2001, Balbir 2003.

70 Jin Mahoday Sāgar Sūri's predecessor was Jin Uday Sāgar (died 1996). The current *gacchādhipati* is Upādhyāya Kailaś Sāgar. This *sampradāya* is mainly active in Rājasthān, Mahārāṣṭra, Gujarāt, M.P., Dillī and Mumbaī. In 1999, it had 229 mendicants, 20 *sādhus* and 209 *sādhvīs* (B.U. Jain 1999: 340), in 2002 258 mendicants, 28 *sādhus* and 230 *sādhvīs* (B.U. Jain 2002: 286).

71 Figures are incomplete. In 1999, this group had 118 mendicants, 28 *sādhus* and 90 *sādhvīs* (B.U. Jain 1999: 340), in 2002, 127 mendicants, 27 *sādhus* and 100 *sādhvīs* (B.U. Jain 2002: 293). The *ācārya* position is the only administrative post of this group (B.U. Jain 1999: 252, n.4). In the year 2000, a group of three *sādhus* led by Muni Jay Ānand split off and founded a fourth Tristuti tradition (B.U. Jain 2002: 293). The most famous monk of the Tristuti Gaccha was Rājendra Sūri (1827–1906), who is renown as the composer of the *Abhidhānarājendra Kośa.*

72 In 1999, this group comprised approximately 70 mendicants, 19 *sādhus* and 51 *sādhvīs* (B.U. Jain 1999: 353); in 2002, 73 mendicants, 22 *sādhus* and 51 *sādhvīs* (B.U. Jain 2002: 297).

73 Praśam Candra's predecessor was Labdhi Sūri (1884–1961). In 1999 and 2002, this group consisted of 2 *sādhus* only (B.U. Jain 1999: 361, 2002: 299).

74 Because of a dispute on proper ascetic conduct, this order split from the Tapā Gaccha in 1515 under Sādhu Ratna Sūri (Ratna Prabhā Vijay 5, 2 1948–1950: 134). Although this group is sometimes considered to be part of the Tapā Gaccha, its *sādhus* do not use '*vijaya*' or '*sāgara*' as a suffix or prefix. The group does not have administrative posts and is the only order that is led by two monks: Muni Bhuvan Candra is currently responsible for the region of Kacch and Saurāṣṭra, and Muni Vijay Candra for the region of Mumbaī. Bhuvan Candra's predecessor was Muni Rām Candra. In 1999, this group had 74 mendicants, 9 *sādhus* and 64 *sādhvīs*, though numbers are incomplete (B.U. Jain 1999: 356), in 2002, 68 mendicants, 9 *sādhus* and 59 *sādhvīs* (B.U. Jain 2002: 301).

75 Figures are incomplete. B.U. Jain 1999: 362 estimates a total of 28 *sādhus* for the year 1999, and 16 for the year 2002 (B.U. Jain 2002: 305).

76 Cort's observations are inversely mirrored by R.K. Jain's 1999: 32 distinction between the charismatic 'individualistic, prophet-derived and sect-like character of the Digambara religious field as contrasted

with the group-bound, "priest"-derived and church-like ambience of the Shvetambara religious field'; a distinction which deliberately ignores the institutions of the *bhaṭṭāraka* traditions.

77 Cort 2001: 46 observed that subtle liturgical differences do not exist 'between *samudāys*.' However, according to Muni Mukti Vallab Vijay of the Bhuvanabhānu Samudāya, four different lists of *maryādās* exist within the Tapā Gaccha. A leading monk of the Rāmacandrasūri Samudāya mentioned the figure of 64 differences in the rules and regulations of the *samudāyas*. A number of monks and nuns of other *samudāyas* confirmed these statements (personal communications, December 2004–January 2005). But more research is necessary to map out the details.

78 Only if their *samudāyas* derive from the same lineage food is sometimes shared; for instance between the members of the Vallabhasūri, the Keśarasūri and the Dharmasūri Samudāyas.

79 Personal communication of monks and nuns of the Vallabhasūri Samudāya and of the Rāmacandrasūri Samudāya in January 2005. In his will, Rāmcandra Sūri determined Mahodaya Sūri as his successor. But according to A. Luithle (personal communication, July 2005) the present *gacchādhipati* Hem Bhūṣaṇ Sūri was elected in an assembly of *ācāryas* in 2003 after one year of dispute.

80 Cf. Jacobi 1915: 270, Cort 1991: 669, n. 19.

81 As evidence, the cases of the centralised orders of the Añcala Gaccha, the Ramacandrasūri Samudāya, and the Śvetāmbara Terā Panth may be cited, all of which have a large number of members.

82 The contrast between the principles of pupillary descent and group organisation in Jain monastic traditions has been analysed in Flügel 2003b: 182–193.

83 Personal communication, Ācārya Jay Sundar Sūri, Mumbaī 23 October 2003.

84 The term *sthānakavāsī* in its present meaning became only current in the context of the early twentieth century unification movement of the traditions of the *pañcmuni*.

85 The dates given in the available sources are not matching up. See Flügel 2000: 46–48, in press.

86 See Flügel 2000: 61–68 on the grades of the *sāmāyika* vow.

87 Flügel 1995–1996, 2000, 2003a, 2003b, in press.

88 Jaini 1979: 246f., n. 8 quotes the figure of 847 mendicants for the year 1977. Goonasekere 1986: 27 speaks of about *c.*900 for the year 1983. Cort 1989: 491, 96 calculates altogether 553 ascetics – probably for the year 1986. Shāntā 1985: 332, 341, 489 cites Terā Panth sources for the much higher figure of 1,757 ascetics for the year 1981, which broadly corresponds to Sangave's 1980: 323f. plausible figure of 1,900 Sthānakavāsī mendicants in the year 1946.

89 B.U. Jain 2002: 65f.

90 This is seen as a potential cause of conflict. Personal communication, Ratan Jain, Delhi 16 October 2004.

91 This is in accordance with the scriptures. See Ṭhāṇa 164b, Vav 10.15–17 and the Nisīha Bhāsa. On the issue of child initiation see also Balbir 2001.

92 See Flügel forthcoming.

93 The resolution was taken on the 5–6 December 1932. See Jauharī 1946: 197.

94 Another source informs us that, at the time of Loṅkā's death, the Loṅkā Gaccha had 400 disciples and 800,000 lay followers (Prakāścandra 1998: 32).

95 Manohar Dās was a disciple of Dharma Dās. The two Amarmuni traditions continue his line today.

96 The following figures were given by Maṇilāl (1934) for selected smaller traditions in 1933: Khambhāt Sampradāya (15 mendicants: 6 *sādhus* and 9 *sādhvīs*), Cauthamala (Raghunātha Dharmadāsa) Sampradāya (18 mendicants: 3 *sādhus* and 15 *sādhvīs*), Ratnavaṃśa (Dharmadāsa Sampradāya) (47 mendicants: 9 *sādhus* and 38 *sādhvīs*), Nānā Pṛthvīrāja (Mevāṛa Dharmadāsa Sampradāya) (43 mendicants: 8 *sādhus* and 35 *sādhvīs*), Kaccha Āṭh Koṭi Moṭā Pakṣa (53 mendicants: 22 *sādhus* and 31 *sādhvīs*), Kaccha Āṭh Koṭi Nānā Pakṣa (39 mendicants: 14 *sādhus* and 25 *sādhvīs*), Līmbaḍī Gopāla Sampradāya (26 mendicants: 7 *sādhus* and 19 *sādhvīs*), Goṇḍala Nānā Pakṣa (no *sādhus* and 'some' *sādhvīs*), Barvāḍā Sampradāya (24 mendicants: 4 *sādhus* and 20 *sādhvīs*).

97 The latest findings have been summarised by Degenne and Forsé (1999: 21): 'Acquaintances form the largest, a virtual network that includes everyone the respondent has ever met. The average for this outermost circle is about 5,000 people. The circle of immediate contacts is far smaller. The average respondent has only 100–200 people he can contact to link himself up to a target stranger. She has regular talks with fewer than twenty people per week, subject to variation with age, sex, education and other socio-demographic criteria. Again, real confidants average only three.'

98 It is regarded as a sign of the laxity though if Jain mendicants deliberately maintain contacts, because this contradicts their vow to renounce the world.

99 For a comparable study in the context of Christian monasticism see Sampson 1969. I have collected data for an analysis of a Jain monastic network in the year 2001. See Flügel forthcoming.

100 This argument is outlined in Flügel 2003b: 183.

101 Nair 1970: 6–7 quotes Muni Dhana Rājā's data for 1955 and 1969. Balbir 1983: 40f gives figures for 1975 and 1981. Shāntā 1985: 332, 341, 489 cites a Terā Panth census by Nāhaṭā for 1982. The total number of ascetics in 1983 can be found in Goonasekere 1986: 27, who reproduced historical data from 'a Jain Śvetāmbara Mahāsabhā Publication' (ibid.: 88f.). His tables do not contain information on the composition of the monastic community after 1944, which can be extracted from the volumes edited by Navratnamal 1981ff. and the tables of Balbir 1983: 41, B.U. Jain 1987: 77, 1990: 62–63 and in the annual almanacs of the Terā Panth (e.g. Navratnamal 1991: 28).

102 See Flügel 2003a.

103 Cf. B.U. Jain 1999: 193. New intermediary categories of female novices, or *samaṇera*, are also characteristic for the reformist 'protestant Buddhism.' See Bloss 1987: 13, Kawanami 1990: 20.

104 The change affected the *sādhvīs* first. Under Ācārya Rāy Cand (1821–1851) and Ācārya Jītmal (1851–1881) only 58.44% and 57.1% of all newly initiated *sādhus* were Osvāls, but already 73.8% and 89.3% of all new *sādhvīs*. Under Kālū Rām, 89.7% of newly initiated *sādhus* and 95.3% of *sādhvīs* were Osvāls (Navratnamal 1981 II: 311, 322, III: 273, 291, X: 309, 325). This pattern still prevails. In 1985, 96.98% of the Terā Panth *sādhus* and 94.46% of the *sādhvīs* were Osvāls (Navratnamal XII 1985: 522f.).

105 A percentage of 58.6 of Ācārya Jītmal's ascetics came from Mārvāṛ and Mevāṛ and only 24.9% from the Thalī region. By contrast, only 29.7% of Ācārya Kālū Rām's ascetics were recruited in Mārvāṛ and Mevāṛ, but 60.97% in Thalī. This pattern was perpetuated under Ācārya Tulsī. In 1985, 23.5% of his mendicants came from Mārvāṛ and Mevāṛ and 63.3% from Thalī (*sādhus*: 58.62%, *sādhvīs*: 65.35%) (cf. Navratnamal 1981 II: 311, 322, III: 273, 291, VI: 486, 495, VIII: 348, 356, X: 309, 325, 1985 XII: 522).

106 The average number of initiated ascetics is one of the determinants of the status of an *ācārya*. On average, Bhikṣu initiated 1.13 *sādhus* and 1.3 *sādhvīs* per year, Kālū Rām 5.63 *sādhus* and 9.44 *sādhvīs*, and Tulsī 4.84 *sādhus* and 11.13 *sādhvīs* between 1936 and 1981.

107 For a statistical analysis of the demographic structure of the Terā Panth order and the motives of renunciation in the year 2001 see Flügel forthcoming.

108 While his predecessors initiated on average *c*.20% of minors, Kālū Rām initiated 45.8% under age *sādhus* and 41.5% under age *sādhvīs* (Navratnamal 1981: 309, 325). The Terā Panth has not yet followed the example of the Sthānakavāsī Śramaṇa Saṅgha, which has officially raised the minimum age for initiation for both girls and boys from eight to fourteen.

109 Cf. Balbir 1983: 42, 2001.

110 On the Tāraṇa Svāmī Panth see Cort (in this volume). The Tota

Panth and the Gumāna Panth, an eighteenth century splinter group of the Terā Panth, have not yet been studied systematically. For an overview see Sangave 1980: 51–54.

111 M.U.K. Jain 1975: 94f.

112 The following historical reconstruction is therefore necessary.

113 P. Śāstrī 1985b: 537.

114 No source is given.

115 '*Inhī gach meṁ nīkasau, nūtan terahpanth / solah sai terāsie, so sab jab jānant //631//*' (Bakhatrām, in Premī 1912/n.d.: 22).

116 Cort 2002: 67 lists a reference to Megha Vijaya, who located the origin of the Adhyātma movement in 1623, in an appendix.

117 No original sources of the tradition itself on its origins have been found so far. I follow John Cort's 2002: 52f., 67–69 summary here.

118 Narendra Kīrti of Amer was *bhaṭṭāraka* between 1634 and 1665 (Premī, cited by Cort 2002: 52).

119 P. Śāstrī 1985b: 536, cf. p. 538 found the expression '*terā – bhagavan āp kā panth*' not only in Joghrām (Joghrāj) Godīkā's work, but also in Jñān Cand's work *Śrāvakācāra* and in the Jaypur Paṇḍit Pannālāl's *Terā Panth Khaṇḍan*, where also thirteen practices are listed which the tradition rejected – opposing the use of fruits in *pūjā*, the worship of Padmāvatī and other gods and goddesses, etc. (ibid.: 539). For more references see P. Śāstrī 1992: 146–149.

120 Like the Śvetāmbara Terā Panthīs, the Digambara Terā Panth *paṇḍits* exploit the ambiguity of the word *terā panth*. The two words *terā* and *terah* are homonyms: *terā* means 'your' and *terah* means 'thirteen.' However, it seems the Śvetāmbara Terā Panthīs prefer to interpret 'your' (*terā*) more in the sense of 'the people' rather than 'God.' Cf. Budhmal 1995: 69–76, Flügel 1994–1995: 123, n. 12, cf. p. 122, n. 9. It is likely that this wordplay is a religio-poetic topos that can be found in other traditions as well.

121 He refers to a newly found inscription from 950 CE which identifies the Balātkāra Gaṇa with the Sarasvatī Gaccha and the Mūla Saṅgha: '*vi. saṃvat 1007 māsottamamāse phālgunamāse śuklapakṣe tithau caturthāṃ budhavāre śrīmūlasāṅgha sarasvatīgaccha balātkāragaṇa ṭhākurasī dās pratiṣṭhaṃ*' (in P. Śāstrī 1985b: 535), and – because the word *śuddāmnāya* is used in different contexts both for the Terā Panth and the Balātkāra Gaṇa – concludes elsewhere that they are one: '*terāpanth śuddhāmnaya tathā mūlasaṅgha kundakundāmnaya balātkāragaṇa sarasvatīgaccha ye donoṁ ek haiṁ*' (P. Śāstrī 1992: 146).

122 On the presumed special relationship with the Parvār caste see particularly P. Śāstrī 1992: 114–149.

123 '*kahe jodh aho jin! terāpanth terā hai*' (Joghrām Godīkā, in P. Śāstrī 1985b: 538). See also Paṇḍit Pannālāl cited ibid., and P. Śāstrī 1985b: 536: '*terā – bhagavān āp kā panth.*'

124 '*bīsapanth arthāt viṣampanth – ṭerhāpanth jinmat meṁ mānya nahīṁ*' (Jaina Nibandha Ratnāvalī, in P. Śāstrī 1985b: 538). The word was apparently coined by Jinendra in his *Jñānānand Śrāvakācāra* which is cited by P. Śāstrī with approval (ibid.: 244).

125 Like the Terā Panthīs, the Tāraṇa Panthīs also venerate 'true' ascetics. See Tāraṇa Taraṇa Svāmī 1933, P. Śāstrī 1985c, and J.E. Cort (in this volume).

126 For the two debates between 20 August 1963 and 1 October 1963 in Jaypur on Kānjī Svāmī's theory of *krama-baddha-paryāya*, or sequence-bound-modification, see P. Śāstrī 1967, 1985a, Jaini 1977, Bharill 1980, P.H. Śāstrī 1985. On the divisive disputes amongst the Digambaras after Kānjī Svāmī's death, see R.K. Jain 1999: 101–117.

127 Jhaveri's 1914: 1418–1424 community census counted altogether 450, 584 Digambaras in 1914. For detailed numerical data on Jain castes from this census and the Śvetāmbara Directory of 1909 as well as the Colonial Indian Census see Sangave 1980: 119–121, 124–130.

128 Sangave 1980: 52. This estimate may be too high. According to P.S. Jaini (personal communication), the distinction was totally unknown in South India and is even now rejected by most.

129 Glasenapp 1925: 357, Sangave 1980: 52.

130 Cf. Cort 2002: 62. Earlier, the now extinct 'heterodox' Kāṣṭhā Saṅgha was associated with the Agravāls in Rājasthān (K.C. Jain 1963: 72), and the Mūla Saṅgha, which was dominant in Western India between the fourteenth and the nineteenth century, primarily with the Khaṇḍelvālas (and Parvārs) (ibid.: 73, 103). Both in South India and in North India, close relationships developed between Digambara *gacchas* and certain *jāti*s or *gotras*. An important factor for the success of the Terā Panth amongst specific Digambara caste communities seems to have been the long term absence of the institution of the *bhaṭṭāraka* as a caste guru. Sangave 1980: 318 notes that in the 1950s 'the Hummaḍa Mevāḍā, Narasiṅgapurā, Khaṇḍelvāla, Saitavāla, Chaturtha, Pañchama, Bogāra, Upādhyāya, Vaiśya and Kshatriya castes have their separate *Bhaṭṭārakas* while the Kaṭhanerā, Budhelā, Agravāla, Golāpūrva, Jaisavāla, Nevi and Hummaḍa (from Mahārāshṭra) castes have no *Bhaṭṭāraka* system at all. Besides in some castes like Paravāra, Bannore, Ḍhākaḍa and Bagheravāla the *Bhaṭṭāraka* system was prevalent formerly but now it is extinct.'

131 Glasenapp 1925: 357 reported that the contrast was so big that the followers of one 'sect' do not visit the temples of the other. However, through an unrepresentative survey amongst the Jain laity Sangave 1980: 299 found that 'among the persons who do not know about their divisions the Digambaras form a larger proportion than the Śvetāmbaras. Besides, it has been stated that there are no such

divisions among the Digambaras at present.'

132 'The Bīspanth-Terāpanth division is not found in Karnataka, Tamil Nadu or souther Maharashtra' (Cort 2002: 70, n. 3).

133 R.K. Jain 1999: 89f., 101–117.

134 Cort 2002: 65 contrasts the lack of organisation of the Adhyātma movement with the 'organisational foundation' of the Terā Panth which is still influential. However, the organisational capacity of the local temple- and library trusts of the Terā Panthīs is insignificant compared to the old institutions of the *bhaṭṭāraka* traditions and in particular the (trans-) regionally organised Śvetāmbara sects.

135 Cf. Jhaveri 1914, Sangave 1980: 119ff.

136 Cort 2002: 62.

137 See Deo 1956: 360ff. for a beginning.

138 We have seen that the Sthānakavāsīs also use the terms *samudāya, saṅgha* and *vaṃśa*. According to Hoernle 1891: 342 *āmnāya* – 'succession' – is a synonym of *kula*, as is the term *santāna*. *Anvaya* – 'line' – can also be used as a synonym. Sangave 1980: 299 presents a less convincing picture of the organisational levels of the Digambara *bhaṭṭāraka* traditions (*saṅgha, gaṇa, gaccha, śākhā*) than Joharāpuraka 1958, whose book is still the most detailed study to date.

139 Joharāpurkara 1958: 19 noted that the writings of Kunda Kunda were 'certainly some cause of unease' between some of the late medieval *bhaṭṭārakas* of the Sena Gaṇa. Allegedly, the 52 *paṭṭa* Bhaṭṭāraka Vīr Sena (died 1938) had a great belief in Kunda Kunda's Samayasāra (ibid.: 35, n. 20). Many *paṭṭāvalīs* of the *bhaṭṭāraka* traditions present Kunda Kunda conventionally as their ancestor, for instance the Balātkāra Gaṇa (ibid.: 44, 71, n. 24).

140 Translated by Hoernle 1891: 350f., cf. Hoernle 1892: 59.

141 The third leader of the Nandi Saṅgha was apparently Kunda Kunda (Padma Nandin), who is cited as the ancestor of today's Sarasvatī Gaccha of the Nandi line (*anvaya*) which identifies itself with the Balātkāra Gaṇa of the Mūla Saṅgha and calls itself Kundakundānvaya (Hoernle 1891: 342, 350f.). The early dates for Kunda Kunda have been questioned by Dhaky 1991: 190, and the artificial link to Kunda Kunda by Dundas 2002: 122.

142 Epigraphia Carnatica 2, 77, 82, in Schubring 2000: § 30, p. 63.

143 Schubring 2000: § 30, p. 63 cites in this respect also Indra Nandin's sixteenth century work Nītisāra and the nineteenth century *paṭṭāvalīs* translated by Hoernle 1891, 1892.

144 See M.U.K. Jain 1975: 126–128 for the complex (putative) internal divisions of the Mūla Saṅgha, whose history in South India has not been analysed.

145 Apart from the available inscriptions, *praśastis* and nineteenth century *paṭṭāvalīs*, the two main sources on the history of the Digambara traditions are Deva Sena's Darśanasāra of 933 CE and the Śvetāmbara

monk Guṇa Ratna's fifteenth century commentary to Haribhadra's Ṣaḍdarśanasamuccaya. See the summaries by Glasenapp 1925: 355f., Schubring 2000: § 30, pp. 61–63, Varṇī 1997 I: 317 and Joharāpurkara 1958. A source cited by Delamaine 1827: 414 is the Buddhavilāsa.

146 Rāja Śekhara writes in his *Ṣaḍdarśanasamuccaya* 21–25 (*c.*1350): 'In the Kāṣṭhāsaṅgha, the broom is ordained to be made of the yak's tail. In the Mūlasaṅgha, the brush is made of peacock feathers. The broom has never been an issue in the Mathurā Saṅgha. The Gopyas sweep with peacock feathers; their greeting is "*dharma labha.*" The rest greet with "*dharma vṛddhi.*" The Gopyas declare release for women. The three Saṅghas other than the Gopya declare that women cannot attain it. Neither the other three nor the Gopyas hold that an omniscient takes food. There is no release for one wearing a monk's garb, though he keep the vow well (tr. by Folkert 1993: 363). Schubring 1964: 224 mentions that both the Yāpanīya and the Kāṣṭhā Saṅgha taught that women can reach salvation.

147 The view that the North Indian Kāṣṭhā Saṅgha is 'heterodox' and the Mūla Saṅgha 'orthodox' is nowadays – after the disappearance of the Kāṣṭhā Saṅgha – expressed by Bīsa Panthīs and Terā Panthīs alike, which both claim descent from the Mūla Saṅgha. See P. Śāstrī 1985b.

148 Premī 1912/n.d.: 4, M.U.K. Jain 1975: 130.

149 Schubring 2000: § 30, p. 62.

150 Glasenapp 1925: 355.

151 Cf. Folkert 1993: 161, and Dundas 2002: 122.

152 The tradition was first mentioned in Deva Sena's Darśanasāra. There are two versions of its origins. According to the prevalent version it was founded in the year 753 CE (? Vikram Saṃvat: 696 CE) in the village Nāndeḍ (Nandiyaḍ) in the region of modern Bombay by Ācārya Kumār Sena I of the Pañcastūpa Saṅgha (Kumārasena II lived around 955). Kumār Sena was a reformer who insisted on the observation of the 'sixth *aṇuvrata*,' that is, no consumption of food and drink after dark, and on the performance of atonements in accordance with the Digambara Āgamas. A later and less popular (and convincing) version relates that Ācārya Loha I from the Nandi Saṅgha Balātkāra Gaṇa founded this tradition some 515 years after Mahāvīra. He converted 125,000 members of the Agravāla caste in Agrohā near Hisār, and used wooden (*kāṣṭhā*) images for the *pūjā* ritual (this story contradicts other legends narrating the origins of this caste). The use of wooden images was strongly opposed by the older Digambara traditions, because it begins to rot after being bathed with milk and water during the traditional *pañca kalyāṇaka pūjā*s. The tradition was also known under the name Gopuccha Saṅgha, because the *muni*s used whisks made of the hair of cow tails rather than peacock feathers (Glasenapp 1925: 356, Varṇī 1998 I: 320f.). According to Joharāpurkara (1958: 211), the name Kāṣṭhā Saṅgha derives from the name of a village near Dillī. From the fourteenth

century internal divisions are reported, and at the end of the seventeenth century four distinct branches, such as the older Mathurā Gaccha, were established, with important seats in Ārā (Bihār), Hisār (Hariyāṇā), Sūrat (Gujarāt), Gvāliyar (Madhya Pradeś) and Kārañjā (Mahārāṣṭra) (ibid.: 6f., 210–212). The *ācāryas* and *bhaṭṭārakas* of this tradition produced important literary works (cf. ibid.: 238–247). The Kāṣṭhā Saṅgha seems to have continued at least till the early nineteenth century and maybe into the twentieth century (cf. Glasenapp 1925: 356, Dundas 2002: 124 citing Col. Tod).

153 This is again mentioned in Surendra Kīrti's work *Dānavīra Maṇikcandra* of 1690. See M.U.K. Jain's (1975: 112–126) extensive description of the sub-divisions of this tradition.

154 According to both the *Darśanasāra* (Glasenapp 1925: 356), and the *Subhāṣita Ratnasaṁdoha* of Ācārya Amitagati II (993–1026 CE), the founder of the Mathurā Gaccha was Muni Rām Sena, who became *ācārya* in 896 CE; but he is not mentioned in the *paṭṭāvalī* of the tradition (Varṇī 1998: 321f.). He originally belonged to the Kāṣṭhā Saṅgha and rejected both the use of peacock feather and cow hair whisks (*picchī* or *piñchī*). His tradition was therefore called Niṣpacchaka Saṅgha. He demanded from his disciples the explicit rejection of other *gurus*, and argued that salvation can only be reached through meditation on the true self (*ātmā dhyāna*) following the teaching of Kunda Kunda rather than Bhūtabalī and Puṣpadanta's *Ṣaṭkhaṇḍāgama* (*Darśanapāhuḍa* and *Darśanasāra*, ibid., Schubring 2000: § 30, p. 62). Until its demise sometime in the nineteenth or twentieth century, the main seats of this *gaccha* were in Hisār (Rājasthān), Gvāliyar, and Senāgiri (Madhya Pradeś) (Joharāpurkara 1958: 6f., 238–247). Its followers belonged mainly to the North Indian Agravāla caste (ibid.: 13).

155 Bāgaḍa is a region near Chittor (M.U.K. Jain 1975: 118). Certain branches of the tradition may have predated the formation of the Kāṣṭhā Saṅgha (cf. ibid.: 118–120). It was also called Punnāṭa Gaccha, with reference to its place of origin in Karṇāṭaka, or Lāḍabāgaḍa Gaccha, with reference to its centre in Gujarāt. It is mentioned in inscriptions between the seventh century and fifteenth century and maintained important seats in Masāṛh (East India) and Kārañjā (Mahārāṣṭra) (Joharāpurkara 1958: 6f., 257–262). Its followers belonged mainly to the Baghervāl caste (ibid.: 13).

156 This tradition is mentioned only in two sources of the tenth and fifteenth century (Joharāpurkara 1958: 6f., 263). It apparently re-joined the Lāḍa-Bāgaḍa Gaccha (M.U.K. Jain 1975: 120).

157 This tradition (also: Vidyā Gaṇa and Rāmasena-Anvaya) was founded in the fifteenth century in the village Nandītaṭ – the modern Nāndeḍ/Mumbaī. It came to an end in the early nineteenth century. One of its main seats was Sojitrā in Gujarāt (Joharāpurkara 1958: 6f,

293–299). Its followers belonged mainly to the Hūmaḍa caste (ibid.: 13). The founder of this tradition appears to have been Ratna Kīrti (M.U.K. Jain 1975: 125).

158 See in particular A.N. Upadhye 1933, 1970, 1974. For the subdivisions of the Yāpanīya tradition see M.U.K. Jain 1975: 136.

159 Premī 1912, n.d.: 4, Glasenapp 1925: 356.

160 Upadhye 1933: 225.

161 Schubring 2000: § 30, p. 62, n. 2.

162 The details of the lineage histories in South India have yet to be investigated.

163 The tradition is first mentioned in the *praśasti* of the Uttarapurāṇa of Guṇa Bhadra's disciple Loka Sena (898 CE) and in inscriptions of the ninth century and of the sixteenth century. It started with Candra Sena, Ārya Nandin and the famous scholastic Vīra Sena (816 CE), the author of the Dhavalā Ṭīkā of the Ṣaṭkhaṇḍāgama, and is famous for the many important Digambara philosophers such as Samanta Bhadra and Siddha Sena Divākara in its ranks. It had/has seats in Kārañjā (Akola, Berara) and Kolhāpura (still existing) in Mahārāṣṭra. The tradition was occasionally called Sūrasthagaṇa and may have been popular in Saurāṣṭra during a certain period. The last *bhaṭṭāraka* of this tradition was apparently Vīra Sena, a great believer in Kunda Kunda's Samayasāra, who died sometime between 1850 and 1938 (Joharāpurkar 1958: 6f., 26–38, cf. Upadhye 1948, M.U.K. Jain 1975: 84–88).

164 The tradition is first mentioned in inscriptions of the tenth century, most of them in Karṇāṭaka. Its branches had seats in Ajmer, Bhānpur, Cittauṛ, Jaypur, Jehrahaṭ, Nāgaur (Rājasthān), Aṭer, Gvāliyar, Senāgiri (Mālvā), Īḍar, Sūrat (Gujarāt), Bhānapur, Jherahaṭ, Malakheḍ and its sub-branches Kārañjā and Lātūr (Mahārāṣṭra). See Joharāpurkara 1958: 6f., 44–47, and the lineage diagram p. 209. The seats had special links to particular local castes, such as the Hūmaḍ caste in Sūrat, the Lamecū caste in Aṭer, the Parvār caste in Jerahaṭ and the Khaṇḍelvāla caste in Dillī and Jaypur (ibid.: 12). From the tenth (Śāstrī 1985b: 535) or the fourteenth century (Joharāpurkara 1958: 44) the tradition was known under the names Sarasvatī Gaccha, Vāgeśvāri Gaccha, Bhāratī Gaccha, Śāradā Gaccha. The original name seems to have been Balagāra Gaṇa (ibid.: 44. cf. M.U.K. Jain 1975: 88ff.) and Nandi Saṅgha (Hoernle 1891: 350, 1892: 73). In Kananda Balagāra (*baḷegāra*) means bangle-maker (a caste name) which was transformed into Skt. *balātkāra* or 'force' according to A.N. Upadhye. I am grateful to P.S. Jaini for this information.

165 Joharāpurkara 1958: 71–78. The tradition was established in the late fourteenth/early fifteenth century. The nineteenth and last *paṭṭa* of this branch was Devendra Kīrti, who died in 1916 (ibid.: 76f., n. 29). The Lātūra Śākhā split off this line in 1675 (ibid.: 77). Two *samādhis* have been built for *bhaṭṭārakas* of this tradition (M.U.K.

Jain 1975: 90, n. 80).

166 Joharāpurkara 1958: 86–90. See the picture of Bhaṭṭāraka Viśāl Kīrti (died 1891) and of his successor who was also called Viśāl Kīrti and enthroned in 1914 (ibid.: 89f.). The seat in Lātūra is revered by the Saitavāla Jains (M.U.K. Jain 1975: 94, n. 92). According to Tuschen (1995: 23), it became defunct only recently.

167 This tradition started the *bhaṭṭāraka* tradition by introducing the custom of wearing clothes in public. The main seats of this now defunct line, which was first closely connected with the Bagherväla caste and later with the 'Hūṃbad' and Brāhmaṇ castes were Sūrat etc. in Gujarāt, Ajmer, Dillī and Jaypur. After the death of Padma Nandin in 1493, the Uttara Śākhā branched out into the Īḍar, Sūrat and Dillī-Jaypur Śākhās (Joharāpurkara 1958: 93–96, cf. M.U.K. Jain 1975: 94–96).

168 This tradition was started by Sakal Kīrti. It possesses a famous library in Īḍar. See Joharāpurkara 1958: 153–158, cf. M.U.K. Jain 1975: 102–105.

169 In 1477 the Bhānapura Śākhā split off the Īḍara Śākhā. The last *bhaṭṭāraka* was apparently Devacandra (1730–1748). See Joharāpurkara 1958: 166–168. According to M.U.K. Jain 1975: 105 a splinter group of the tradition still prevailed in South India in 1975 (?).

170 This branch, founded in 1436 by Devendra Kīrti, was closely associated with the Hūmaḍa caste. In 1495 Tribhuvan Kīrti split off and founded the Jerahaṭa Śākhā. See Joharāpurkar 1958: 194–201, 207, cf. M.U.K. Jain 1975: 107–111.

171 This branch, which became defunct early in the seventeenth century, was closely associated with the Parvār caste (Joharāpurkar 1958: 202–209, cf. Varṇī 1998 I: 320f.).

172 After 1514 the tradition split into three branches, two of which are the Nāgaura- and the Aṭera Śākhā. The last *bhaṭṭāraka* of the Dillī-Jaypur line was apparently Candra Kīrti who either died or was installed in 1918 (Joharāpurkara 1958: 109–113). Cort (2002: 62) writes that the last *bhaṭṭāraka*, a Candra Kīrti, died in 1969 and was deliberately not replaced. The Dillī-Jaypur Śākhā was closely related to the Khaṇḍelvāla caste and established special links to the Kachavāhā kings of Amer, where the *bhaṭṭāraka* seat was shifted in the sixteenth century (ibid.: 51, cf. Clémentin-Ojha, forthcoming).

173 In 1524, Ratna Kīrti was appointed as the first head. The last *bhaṭṭāraka* was apparently Devendra Kīrti in the mid-twentieth century (Joharāpurkara 1958: 121–125). Many *bhaṭṭāraka* belonged to the Chābaḍā and Seṭhi sub-castes (M.U.K. Jain 1975: 98–101).

174 This branch splitt off the Uttara Śākhā in 1493 and was closely associated with the Lamecū caste (Joharāpurkara 1958: 132–135, cf. M.U.K. Jain 1975: 101f.).

175 The inscriptions artificially incorporate the names of all famous Digambara *ācāryas* of the past in one lineage.

176 Johārāpurkara 1958: 44.

177 Shāntā 1985: 137f.

178 Until the nineteenth century, the term *bhaṭṭāraka* was used both by Bīsa Panthī Digambaras and Mūrtipūjaka Śvetāmbara *yatis*. Today, it is only used by Bīsa Panthī Digambaras.

179 Personal communication of Bhaṭṭārak Lakṣmī Sena, Kolhāpura 4 January 2005.

180 Sangave 1980: 317–322.

181 The Śvetāmbaras list the *abhrama-varjana pratimā* already on the sixth position, before the *sacitta-tyāga pratimā*, and call the eleventh stage *śramaṇa-bhūta pratimā* (Williams 1963: 173).

182 Williams 1963: 172 notes that the *pratimās* were originally conceived as a progressive sequence rather than as alternative options. Jaini 1979: 185 suggests that originally each *pratimā* may have been practiced only of a limited period of time.

183 Williams 1963: 179 found the first mentioning of this distinction in the eleventh century text Śrāvakadharmadohaka by an unknown Digambara author.

184 Hirālāl Jain's view that the word *ailaka* derives from Skt. *acelaka*, 'unclothed' or 'partially clothed,' was rejected by Williams 1963: 179, n. 5 who pointed out that the *ailaka* is characterised explicitly as *cela-khaṇḍa-dhara* in the twelfth century Vasunandi-Śrāvakacāra edited by H. Jain.

185 If the sources of Williams 1963/1983: 180 are still of influence, then full access to the 'mysteries' of the scriptures is not granted to lay ascetics. The initiation rituals of the (Vimala Saṅgha) Digambara *munis* are detailed in Syādvādmatī 2000: 442–452. Their key ritual elements apart from the acceptance of the respective vows (*vratāropaṇa*) are: the shaving and pulling out of some of the hair (*keśa-luñcana*), change of dress/nakedness (*nāgnya-pradāna*), change of name (*nāma-karaṇa*), ritual giving of the peacock feather broom (*piccha-pradāna*), of the scriptures (*śāstra-pradāna*), and of the water pot (*kamaṇḍalu-pradāna*) (ibid.: 442). The *munis* receive a large broom (*picchī*), and all other (lay) ascetics only a small broom (*picchikā*). For a commented compilation of other textual sources for the Digambara *muni dīkṣā* see Kanaka Nandi 1994: 214–226. On the basis of incomplete information, Carrithers 1990: 153 suspects that there is little evidence for the existence of a *saṅgha* in the Digambara *dīkṣā* rituals: 'there is not even an explicit vow to live in obedience to a guru' and 'no formal recognition of a line of pupillary succession,' nor the passing on of a mantra (ibid.: 155). He argues that the orientation towards the 'aesthetic standard of self-restraint'

is the main element in the transmission of tradition (ibid.: 157). Although his general observation is shared by all modern scholars, mantras of a general nature, oriented toward the veneration of the guru, are prescribed in the *dīkṣā vidhi* texts. For instance: '*ṇamo arahaṃtāṇaṃ. . . atha guruvāvalīṃ paṭhitvā, amukasya amukanāmā tvaṃ śiṣya iti kathayitvā saṃyamādyupakaraṇāni dadyāt*' (Syādvādmatī 2000: 447). One of the mantras used for the inauguration of an *ācārya* is: '*oṃ hrīṃ śrīṃ arhaṃ saḥ ācāryāya namaḥ. ācāryamantra*' (p. 482).

186 Varṇī 1997 I: 468f., II: 188f. Personal communication of Āryikā Muktimatī of the Vimal Sāgar Saṅgha, 22.10.2004, and of the *bhaṭṭārakas* Jina Sena and Lakṣmī Sena, 2–4 January 2005. The rules and regulations cannot be discussed here in detail.

187 *Bhaṭṭārakas* do not have many *śiṣyas* and often ask dedicated followers to send their young sons to take boarding and lodging in their *maṭhas* to receive religious training in addition to their secular school education.

188 This happened in the case of Jina Sena of the Nāndaṇī *maṭha*.

189 Since the generic name is apparently associated with the *bhaṭṭāraka* lineage there are at least three Lakṣmī Senas, of the *maṭhas* in Kolhāpura, Jinākāñcī and Siṅhanagadde (Penagoṇḍa in Andrah Pradeś), amongst the contemporary *bhaṭṭāraka*.

190 According to Premī 1912, n.d.: 27, the *bhaṭṭāraka dīkṣā* is – in principle – similar to a *muni dīkṣā*. The *bhaṭṭāraka* can therefore not be categorised as a layman. The ritual, he writes, is prescribed in an ancient book in the Bhaṇḍār of Īḍar. There it is stated that a layman can only be installed as a *bhaṭṭāraka* when the search for a worthy *muni* has failed. The initiation requires the nakedness of the candidate and the ritual plucking of the hair (*keśa luñcana*). After receiving the *sūri mantra*, the candidate is attributed with the qualities of an *ācārya*, and continues to practise nakedness when he eats his meals and during certain ceremonies: '*is se sāph mālūm hotā hai ki, bhaṭṭārak vāstav meṁ gṛhastha nahīṁ hai, muni tathā ācārya haiṁ*' (ibid.: 28). Joharāpurkar, interviewed by Shāntā 1985: 186, n. 99, emphasised that even today's *bhaṭṭārakas* continue to accept five '*mahāvratas*' (effectively *aṇuvratas*), not only four as often mentioned in the literature, for instance in Flügel 2003a: 8. According to Carrithers 1990: 151, 'the method of succession was derived not from any Jain prescriptions but from the usages of local polity.' This impression is echoed by the views of the *bhaṭṭārakas* Jina Sena and Lakṣmī Sena (personal communication 2–4 January 2004).

191 Śruta Sāgara Sūri's sixteenth century commentary of the Ṣaṭprābhṛta, the Ṣaṭprābhṛtādisaṃgraha 1.24. See Glasenapp 1925: 72, Joharāpurkar 1958: 89 (original passage reproduced), 91, M.U.K. Jain 1975: 94f., Cort 2002: 41.

192 Cort 2002: 41 quotes Bakhatrām Sāh's *Buddhi Vilās* of 1770 as the source of the information that 'Bhaṭṭārak Prabhācandra of Delhi'

[(r. 1253–1327) the predecessor of Padma Nandin (M.U.K. Jain 1975: 95f.)] 'took to wearing a loincloth during the reign of Feroz Śāh Tughluq (1351–1380) at the request of the king.' Cort (ibid.) also cites a discussion of an inscription suggesting the date of 1333. Premī 1912/n.d.: 1f. refers to oral accounts of the events in Delhi. See also Sangave 1980: 269–271, 317–322 and Tuschen 1995: 20f.

193 Dates according to M.U.K. Jain 1975: 95f.

194 According to Bhaṭṭāraka Lakṣmī Sena of Kolhāpura, the name of the first *bhaṭṭāraka* of the Sena Gaṇa was Vidyā Sāgar and the first *maṭhas* were established in Dillī, Kolhāpura, Jinākāñcī (Tamil Nāḍu) and Penagoṇḍa (Andrah Pradeś) – the *maṭhas* of his associates. Personal communication, Kolhāpura 4 January 2005. V. Śāstrī 1932: 5–7 gives the line of succession of Vidyā Sāgar, whose *samādhi* is in Akīvāṭ/ Zilā Cikoḍī. It comprises some *munis*, but ends with Bhaṭṭāraka Vidyā Mān (r. 1904 ff.), whose conduct is unfavourably contrasted with Muni Śānti Sāgar's.

195 Lath 1981: lvi.

196 See Sangave 2001: 136. In 1875–1876, Bühler 1878: 28 visited a *bhaṭṭāraka* in Delhi, who was accompanied by 'ascetics (who are called paṇḍits).' Bühler described the *bhaṭṭārakas* he had met during his travels as 'very ignorant.' This statement was still echoed by Sangave 1980: 321f. 100 years later. See Cort (in this volume p. 299 n.9) on the Canderī seat of Bhaṭṭāraka Devendrakīrti.

197 Personal communication by the Jain Bhavan in Bangalore 31 December 2005 and by Bhaṭṭāraka Jina Sena, Nāndaṇī 2 February 2005, who seems to be the only *bhaṭṭāraka* who currently has a disciple, Brahmacārī Vṛṣabha Sena. According to Tuschen 1997: 23, the seats of Bhaṭṭāraka Viśālakīrti in Lātūr in Mahārāṣṭra (traditionally associated with the Saitavāla caste) and Bhaṭṭāraka Yaśakīrti in Pratāpgaṛh in Rājasthān (traditionally associated with the Narasiṅhapura caste), which are mentioned by Sangave 2001: 135, are now defunct. This would leave only nine *bhaṭṭārakas*. For the names of more than thirty-six old *bhaṭṭāraka* seats see Johарāpurkara 1958: 6f., M.U.K. Jain 1975: 131, Sangave 2001: 134. In addition to the seats that can be linked to specific traditions, Joharāpurkara 1958: 6f. mentions a number of other, now equally defunct, seats in Eastern India (Ārā), Gujarāt (Navasārī, Bhaḍaurī, Khambhāt, Jāmbūsar, Ghoghā), Mālvā (Devgaṛh, Dhārā Nagarī, Lalitpur, Mahuā, Ḍūṅgarpūr, Indaur, Sāgavāḍā, Aṭer) and Mahārāṣṭra (branches in Riddhipur, Bālāpur, Rāmaṭek, Nāndeḍ, Devagiri, Paithan, Śiraḍ, Vaṇṭ, Vairāṭ, Vaphād, Malayakheḍ, Kāryarañjakpur, etc.). There is currently no information on the old seats in the Pañjāb, only on various seats in Dillī. Apart from Meraṭh and Hastināpūr, there are no *bhaṭṭāraka* seats reported from Uttar Pradeś. Sangave 2001: 134 mentions the additional seats of Jehrahaṭ, Keśarīyajī, Mahāvīrjī (Rājasthān), Sonāgiri (Mālvā), Bhānpur, Sojitrā, Kalol (Gujarāt),

Nāgpur, Nāndaṇī (Mahārāṣṭra), Narasiṁharājapura (Karṇāṭaka), Svādī in Sondā (Karṇāṭaka) and Melasittamūra, that is Jinākāñcī (Tamil Nāḍu).

198 The seat was established in the eighth century and belongs to the Mūla Saṅgha Kundakundanvaya Nandi Saṅgha Sarasvatī Gaccha Balātkāra Gaṇa (Tuschen 1997: 28). It is associated with the Bogāra caste (Sangave 1980: 318, 2001: 137) and governed by Bhaṭṭāraka Devendrakīrti.

199 Associated with the Kṣatriya caste (ibid.), and governed by Bhaṭṭāraka Lalitkīrti.

200 Associated with the Pañcama caste (ibid.), and governed by Bhaṭṭāraka Lakṣmī Sena I (I add Roman numbers to distinguish *bhaṭṭārakas* with the same title). The seat has two other *maṭhas* under its administration, in Hosūr-Belgāṁv and Rāybāg, and is associated with the Sena Gaṇa *maṭhas* in Dillī, Jinakāñcī and Penagoṇḍa (Siṁhanagaddī in Narasiṁharājapura). For Lakṣmī Sena's works see for instance Sangave 2003.

201 Also called Jinakāñcī. Associated with the Kṣatriya and Vaiśya castes and governed by Bhaṭṭāraka Lakṣmī Sena III of the Sena Gaṇa (Sangave 2001: 137).

202 Traditionally associated with the Upādhyāya caste (ibid.). According to P.S. Jaini (personal communication), the last two, including the current Bhaṭṭāraka Cārukīrti II, who is a non-Shetty (Śreṣṭhi) Jain, were not of that caste. There is a trust comprising members of all three local castes (Shetty, non-Shetty, Upādhyāya) who selected the current *bhaṭṭāraka* (on suggestion of Bhaṭṭāraka Cārukīrti of Śravaṇabeḷagola).

203 The seat is associated with the Caturtha caste (ibid.), 'the only caste among the Jainas which follows agriculture as the main occupation' (Sangave 1980: 96), and is governed by Bhaṭṭāraka Jina Sena. The seat has three other *maṭhas* under its administration, in Kolhāpura, Tesdal and Belgāṁv – and in the past also in Dillī.

204 Associated with the Bogāra (and Kṣatriya and Vaiśya) caste and governed by Bhaṭṭāraka Lakṣmī Sena II of the Sena Gaṇa (Sangave 2001: 137).

205 The current seat was established in the tenth century and derives its descent from the Mūla Saṅgha Deśiya Gaṇa Pustaka Gaccha. It is associated with the Vaiśya caste (ibid.) and occupied by Bhaṭṭāraka Cārukīrti I.

206 A summary table of the relationship between specific castes and their principal *bhaṭṭāraka* seats can be found in Sangave 1980: 318. There were only nine *bhaṭṭāraka* seats left until the head of the Deśiya Gaṇa, Bhaṭṭāraka Cārukīrti of Śravaṇabeḷagola, created three more *bhaṭṭāraka* seats: in Karṇāṭaka Kambadahalli/Nagamaṅgala

(Bhaṭṭāraka Bhānukīrti), and Kanakagiri Maṭha in Maleyur (Bhaṭṭāraka Bhuvanakīrti), and in Tamil Nāḍu Tiruvannamalai (Bhaṭṭāraka Dhavalakīrti). Apart from the Hūmachā Maṭha, and the Svādī Maṭha in Sondā which is governed by Bhaṭṭāraka Bhaṭṭākalaṅka, all *bhaṭṭāraka* seats are presently under the authority of Lakṣmī Sena of Kolhāpura for the Sena Gaṇa, and of Cārukīrti of Śravaṇabeḷagola for the Deśiya Gaṇa.

207 Many castes of the Jains were founded by *ācāryas* and/or *bhaṭṭārakas*. The most important Śvetāmbara castes are the Osvāls and the Śrīmālīs. Of the Digambara Kāṣṭhā Saṅgha, the Nandītaṭ Gacch leader Rām Sena founded the Narasiṅhapura caste, his pupil Nemī Sena the Bhaṭṭāpurā caste, and the Ratnākar caste was apparently founded by Devendra Kīrti I. Of some Digambara castes the exogamous subgroups (*gotra*) or/and their *dasa* and *bīsa* subcategories are associated with different branches of the main *bhaṭṭāraka* traditions. The Baghervāla caste was partly founded by the Mūla Saṅgha *ācārya* Rām Sena (25 *gotras*) and partly by the Kāṣṭhā Saṅgha *ācārya* Loha (27 *gotras*). The Nāgaur branch of the Balātkāra Gaṇa commanded the following of several *gotras* of the Khaṇḍelvāla caste etc. (Joharāpurkara 1958: 13).

208 The *bhaṭṭārakas* of the Humaḍa, Narasiṅhapura and Khaṇḍelvāla castes until recently selected their own successor (? Kalol, Narasiṅhapura), while the *bhaṭṭāraka* of the Saitavāla, Caturtha, Pañcama, Upādhyāya, Bogāra, Vaiśya and Kṣatriya castes were chosen by the representatives (*pañca*) of these castes (Sangave 1980: 319f.). The only exception is the influential seat of Śravaṇabeḷagola, whose *bhaṭṭāraka* is since 1931 chosen by a committee of lay followers which is selected by the Government of Karṇāṭaka (ibid., Tuschen 1997: 33). Sangave 1980: 319–321 found that only the *bhaṭṭārakas* of the Humaḍa caste could be removed by their followers in the past. Although they preside over a particular caste, the *bhaṭṭārakas* do not need to be member of the caste and ideally represent all Jains. Lakṣmī Sena of Kolhāpura, for instance, was born in Tamil Nāḍu into the Saitavāla caste, but presides over the Pañcama caste.

209 In 1945, the Land Sealing Act of Karṇāṭaka led to the acquisition of most landholdings of the *bhaṭṭārakas* by the government in exchange for monetary compensation, whose ownership is in many cases still disputed in the courts between the Digambara laity and the *bhaṭṭārakas*.

210 According to Shāntā 1985: 134f., the *munis* apparently entirely disappeared in the seventeenth century.

211 Shāntā 1985: 134f. A modest revival of the institution of the *bhaṭṭāraka* was triggered recently because of the desire to spread Jainism across the borders of India and because of a renewed interest in community education. In response to modern demands, the *bhaṭṭārakas* made

themselves accessible to members of other castes than their own and created – without much success – a common institutional platform in 1969 and arranged the first *bhaṭṭāraka sammelan* (Sangave 2001: 143), which was followed by several others.

212 Carrithers 1989: 150. In 1926–7, Rāvjī Sakhārām Dośī, in G.P. Jauharī, in V. Śāstrī 1932: 7f., and G.P. Jauharī of the Akhil Bhāratvarṣīya Digambara Jain Mahāsabhā (ibid.: 56f.,) emphasised the need to re-introduce the *munis* to North India to propagate true religion ('*jain dharma kī yathārtha tathā utkṛṣṭa prabhāvanā*'), and unity amongst all Digambara societies in India (ibid.: 84–86).

213 Most Khaṇḍelvālas live in North India, where no *bhaṭṭāraka* seats exist anymore.

214 Some of the first disciples of Śānti Sāgar, such as Vir Sāgar and Candra Sāgar, were Khaṇḍelvāls. See D. Śāstrī 1985.

215 S.C. Jain 1940: 3f. In the twentieth century, after an earlier failure of transregional sect-caste associations, a number of Digambara Jain caste associations were established with the intention of reforming the Digambara community and creating transregional solidarities amongst geographically dispersed North Indian castes with a dominant Digambara Jain membership. The Jain Khaṇḍelvāla Mahāsabhā, for instance, which was founded in 1920, is today organised into 15 *prāntas*, or regions. Other examples are the Bagherväl Jain Mahāsabhā and the Jain Padmāvatī Porvāl Mahāsabhā. Similar organisations which strive to establish independent sect-castes are relatively rare among Śvetāmbara Jains, whose transregional organisations are usually founded exclusively on religious criteria (Kāsalīvāl 1992: 14f.). Cf. R.K. Jain 1999: 67.

216 The anti-printing movement called itself Śāstra-Mudraṇa Virodhī Āndolana: 'Murder threads were made against those involved in printing, and printing shops were blown up' (Sangave 1981/2001: 62).

217 At the time, Jain castes were generally divided in at least two ranked sections: the lower *dasa* and the higher *bīsa* sub-castes. The following social reforms were advocated by the Pariṣad: 1. child widow remarriage (*bāla-vidhvā vivāha*); 2. marriage across caste boundaries; 3. allowing members of *dasa* families to participate in the *pūjā pāṭha*, etc., within a society where mixed *dasa-bīsa* marriages were practised; 4. abolition of death feasts (*maraṇa bhojana*); 5. abolition of excessive feasts and gift-giving at *pratiṣṭhā* ceremonies (new *pratiṣṭhā pāṭha*: as a rule only old images should be consecrated); 6. raising the status of women through the foundation of womens' institutions (S.C. Jain 1940: 3f.).

218 Kāsalīvāl 1992: 11f. In 1902, the influential Bhāratvarṣīya Digambara Jain Tīrtha Kṣetra Kameṭī (BDJTKK) was founded by Maṇikcand

Hirācand Jauharī (1851–1913) in Bombay as a sub-committee of the Mahāsabhā. It became independent on 24 November 1930 and still has its office in the Hīrābāg Dharmaśālā compound in Mumbaī, owned by the Jauharī family trust. For administrative reasons, it divided India into six zones. Another national association, the Digambara Jain Mahāsamiti, was set up in 1974 by Sāhū Śānti Prasād in New Delhi for the promotion of Digambara unity during the year celebrating Mahāvīra's 2500th death day. In contrast to the Mahāsabhā, which is composed of individuals, it is organised in the form of a 'Jain *saṃsad*,' or parliament, that is, on the basis of regional representatives (Kāsalīvāl 1992: 12f.). However, after the death of its founder, the organisation failed to deliver and is now defunct. In 1983, the Kundakunda-Kahnā Tīrtha Rakṣā Trust was founded in order to promote the worship of Kānjī Svāmī (who declared himself to be a Digambara Terā Panthī) in his putative reincarnation as the *tīrthaṅkara* Sūrya Kīrti. This was in 1985 vigorously opposed both by the Mahāsabhā, whose patron saints were Muni Dharma Sāgar and Āryikā Jñān Mātā in Hastināpūr, and by the Mahāsamiti, whose patron saint was Muni Vidyānand in 1985. However, the main representatives of the Mahāsamiti, the Sāhū Jain family (Times of India) and Premcand Jain (Jayna Watch Co.) in Delhi, had once supported Kānjī Svāmī and failed to join the united front against the Kanjī Panth supporters at Soṅgaḍh (R.K. Jain 1999: 114–117). The Meerut Court decided on the 6 December 2000 that Kānjī Panthīs are not Digambara Jains (case no. 9/91, quoted by N.K. Jain, jain friends@yahoogroups.com, 21 June 2001). Both the Mahāsabhā and the Mahāsamiti are dominated by Khaṇḍelvāls. A rival organisation to the Tīrtha Kṣetra Kamaṭī, the Jaina Saṃrakṣaṇ Māñca, was recently set up in Jaypur, in order to protect old temples from partial demolition and reconstruction under instructions of modern *munis*.

219 V. Śāstrī 1932: 5 lists a number of '*nigrantha bhaṭṭārakas*' for the beginning of the nineteenth century. See Carrithers 1990: 148f. and Cort 2002: 71, n. 8 for further references on the so-called *nirvāṇ svāmīs*, who did not travel much and seemed to have dressed themselves in public.

220 K.P. Jain 1932: 158, n. 2: '*Mainapurī Digambara Jain Baḍā Mandir kā ek Guṭkā.*'

221 Ibid., citing Digambara Jain 9, 1: 18–23, ed. Mūlcand Kiśandās Kāpaḍiyā, Sūrat.

222 Eternal lights in the form of oil-lamps can be found at a variety of *samādhi mandiras* for Digambara *munis*; for instance at the Vimal Sāgar Samādhi Mandira in Madhuban.

223 ibid.: 159, citing Digambara Jain, Special Issue, 1916.

224 Carrithers 1990: 155.

225 K.P. Jain 1932: 159, citing Digambara Jain 14, 5–6: 7; cf. Mahias

forthcoming, p. 3.

226 Ibid. His name was Vardhamān Sāgar according to D. Śāstrī 1985: 54.

227 K.P. Jain 1932: 159. His name was Devappā Svāmī according to D. Śāstrī 1985: 55. Carrithers 1990: 155 identifies Devendra Kīrti as a *bhaṭṭāraka*.

228 K.P. Jain 1932: 159. Akkole 1987: 43 writes that the *kṣullaka dīkṣā* took place in 1916 and the *muni dīkṣā* in 1976 Phālguṇ Śuklā 14 (Śaka 1841). All initiations were given by Devendra Kīrti (Ibid.: 51–53, D. Śāstrī 1985: 56).

229 Cf. C.R. Jain 1931, Ghoshal 1932.

230 The original announcement of G.P. Jauharī was published in 1926 in the journal Jaina Bodhaka. It was reprinted by V. Śāstrī 1932: 46–48, whose book gives a detailed account of this momentous pilgrimage.

231 One should assume that the visit to Mount Śikhar would have helped the pending court cases between Digambara, Śvetāmbaras, and the Government concerning the control of the site.

232 K.P. Jain 1932: 161, Kāsalīvāl 1992: 35, Kāsalīvāl 1998, Kāsalīvāl 2001: 36ff., Śruta Saṃvarddhana Saṃsthān 2002: 3.

233 Ibid.

234 Ibid.: 3–5, Kāsalīvāl 2001: 26–29. Sūrya Sāgar's main disciples were Vijay Sāgar, Ānand Sāgar, Padma Sāgar and Kṣullaka Cidānand. Vimal Sāgar's main disciples were Nirmal Sāgar, Sumati Sāgar, Kunthu Sāgar and Kṣullaka Dharma Sāgar.

235 For one view of the resulting structure, see Kāsalīvāl 1998: n.p.

236 D. Śāstrī 1985, Rājkul Jain 2003: 213–221. Dates were converted with the computer program of M. Yano and M. Fushimi: http://ccnic15.kyoto-su.ac.jp/yanom/pancanga.

237 See Varṇī 1998 I: 334, Kāsalīvāl 1992: 30, 34. Personal communication Nīraj Jain, 12 June 2003, D.K. Jain 25 October 2003.

238 P. Śāstrī 1992: 212, cf. Varṇī 1998: 211–216. His childhood name Vidyādhar was derived from the famous 'miracle working' *samādhi* of Bhaṭṭāraka Vidyādhar in Karṇāṭaka (M. Jain 2001: 3). Both his father (Muni Malli Sāgar 1975) and his mother (Āryikā Samay Matī 1975) took *dīkṣā* from Ācārya Dharma Sāgar, and his three brothers (Muni Samay Sāgar 7 March 1980, Muni Yoga Sāgar, Muni Niyam Sāgar 15 April 1980) took *dīkṣā* from him (ibid.: 29–31). In 2003, his birthhouse has been converted into a temple.

239 *Āryikā* never receive foods in their hands nor in a standing posture, and apparently do not perform *keśa luñcana*.

240 The *ailaka*s, *kṣullaka*s and *kṣullikā*s are also called *tyāgī*s. See R.K. Jain 1999: 80. Similar debates on the status of women are known from early on (Jaini 1991). According to some early medieval

Digambara scriptures, at least some medieval Digambara or Yāpanīya traditions also formed a four-fold *saṅgha*, with nuns being recognised as mendicants rather than as laypeople (Schubring 2000: § 30, p. 61).

241 Personal communications by different Digambara *śrāvakas*.

242 This is emphasised in a proclamation by Ācārya Vimal Sāgar 23 October 1993, reprinted in Brahmacāriṇī Maināׂbāī Jain 1996: xv, which requests the laity to mediate the 'foolish' disputes between the two lineages with reference to the common Āgamas: '*samāj kā kartavya hai ki kisī kā vivād na karke donoṁ ācārya paramparā ko āgam sammat mānakar vātsalya se dharma prabhāvanā kareṁ.*' The writings of Ādi Sāgar were published by B.M. Jain 1996.

243 D. Śāstrī 1985: 344, 450–452.

244 His death memorial is in Madhuban at Sammet Śikhara.

245 The desire to became an *ācārya* and the abolishment of the once prevalent practice that an *ācārya* can be enthroned only after the death of his predecessor have contributed to the creation of many splits and independently roaming *ācāryas* (personal communication by Nīraj Jain, 12 June 2003).

246 According to Kāsalīvāl 2001: 35 he was a disciple of Mahāvīr Kīrti.

247 Kāsalīvāl 1992: 36–38.

248 D. Śāstrī 1985: 411–413. According to Ācārya Puṣpadanta, he was a disciple of Śānti Sāgar 'Dakṣiṇ' (personal communication, Mumbaī 24 October 2003). He was born in Kothalpur in Belgāṁv in Karṇāṭaka and died on the 22 May 1987.

249 Vir Sāgar 'Śolapur' is said to have been close to Kāñjī Svāmī's views, though his interpretation of the texts was slightly different.

250 This line is also claimed by the *bhaṭṭāraka* of Hūmachā today.

251 Copaḍe 1936.

252 On the dating of Kunda Kunda, see the divergent views of Upadhye 1935: 21 and Dhaky 1991: 193.

253 According to Dhaky (1991), this is because of 'the profound reverence and a very false notion as regards the antiquity of Kundakundācārya' (ibid.: 203, n. 30).

254 Personal correspondance, 25 September 2002.

255 This is also documented by M.U.K. Jain 1975: 126–128, Shāntā 1985: 489, and Carrithers 1989: 232.

256 Personal communication of Nīraj Jain, 16.6.2003.

257 Including, occasionally, demolishing old temples in order to replace them with new ones.

258 The Agravāla Digambaras, who are dominant in the Pañjāb and in

U.P., belong also to mixed Hindu-Jain caste.

259 Critics ask: 'Why only cows?'

260 '*vītarāg sādhu kā koī panth nahīṁ hotā*' (P. Śāstrī 1985b: 540).

261 Tuschen 1995: 50.

262 Saletore 1940: 124.

263 For information on the contemporary Digambara ascetics I wish to thank in particular Dr A. Jain, Dr N.L. Jain, Nīraj Jain and Manish Modi.

264 Jaini 1979: 246f., n. 8 reported the number of 175 ascetics in 1979 (65 *munis*, 60 *kṣullakas* and *ailakas* and 50 *āryikā* and *kṣullikās*) and 150–200 in 1991 (Jaini 1991: 24–26). Goonasekere 1986: 27 calculated the figure of 170 *munis* and altogether 400 mendicants (p. 116). Shāntā 1985: 489 mentioned 62 *āryikā* and 23 *kṣullikās*. Zydenbos 1999: 291 heard that there were only 120 *munis* in 1999 and emphasises their 'decline in numbers.' For 1990, Kāsalīvāl 1992: 35 quotes the figure of 32 *ācāryas*, 11 *upādhyāyas*, 130 *munis*, 154 *āryikā*, 22 *ailakas*, 80 *kṣullakas* and 45 *kṣullikās*. In 1992, Upādhyāya Kanak Nandi cited to me the figure of about 418 Digambara ascetics: 14–15 *ācāryas*, 2–3 *upādhyāyas*, 125 *munis*, 20–25 *ailakas*, 40–50 *kṣullakas* and about 200 *āryikā* and *kṣullikās*.

265 In 2002, only Ācārya Vidyā Sāgar provided complete data to B.U. Jain 2002: 324.

266 For 1996, B.U. Jain 1996: 326 gives the following sums, which differ from the detailed information on individual ascetic groups in his own text: 36 *ācāryas*, 143 *cāturmāsa* places, 352 *munis*, 305 *āryikā* and a total of 657 mendicants. For want of additional information, I was unable to check the extent of the inaccuracy of the figures. I met Muni Ānand Sāgar, who is now an *upādhyāya*, in 1981. He was then alone and apparently still is. In 1992, I observed that the group of Kunthu Sāgar had in all 34 ascetics, 18 *munis*, 3 *kṣullakas*, 2 *ailakas* and 11 *āryikā*, a figure which seems to corroborate B.U. Jain's numbers for 1987. The subsequent decrease in numbers can be explained by Ācārya Kanak Nandi's separation from Kunthu Sāgar in the early 1990s. My third example shows that the true number of ascetics must be much higher. Ācārya Rayaṇ Sāgar who is not included in the table, is listed by B.U. Jain as a single individual without mentioning the number of ascetics accompanying him. In 1999, his group had 8 members: 1 *ācārya*, 1 *upādhyāya*, 4 *munis*, 1 *ailaka* and 1 *kṣullaka*.

267 Roman alphabet.

268 The word *saṅgha* is used for groups of two and more ascetics.

269 On the definition of these categories as 'novices' see Carrithers 1990: 153, Flügel 2001: 76f.

270 There is no equivalent female category because *ailakas* (*elaka*) can

wear only one loin cloth, which is not considered to be proper for women.

271 The *ailācārya* corresponds to the *upādhyāya* amongst the Śvetāmbaras. The Digambara word *elācārya* is an ancient designation for 'a pontiff of the highest learning and for a qualified teacher of Jain doctrines, a position more or less equivalent of *vācaka, vācanācārya*, or *kṣamāsramaṇa* or *mahattara* in the ancient Northern Nirgrantha of which the Śvetāmbara Church is the off-shoot. Once a pontiff received the ecclesiastical title of *elācārya* his original monastic appelation apparently went into the background' (Dhaky 1991: 191).

272 The chosen successor, who is called *yuvācārya* among the Śvetāmbaras.

273 The titles have been given to only nine monks by the *ācārya*s Sanmati Sāgar (*ācāryakalpa* and *bālācārya*), Kunthu Sāgar (*ācāryakalpa* 2x, and *ailācārya*), Ajit Sāgar (*ācāryakalpa*), and Sumati Sāgar (*ailācārya*) (A. Jain 2001: 11).

274 For their names, see B.U. Jain's and A. Jain's publications.

275 This is evident in the mixed composition of the *ācāryas*' groups documented by A. Jain 2001: 1–11. See also Zydenbos 1999: 296f.; who cites questionable estimates that no more than 10–15 Digambara *saṅghas*, headed by an *ācārya*, exist.

276 The other bigger *saṅghas* are those of Ācārya Dharma Sāgar's successors Abhinandan Sāgar and Vardhamān Sāgar, Deś Bhūṣan's successors Bāhubalī Sāgar and Subal Sāgar, and Vimal Sāgar's successor Virāg Sāgar. Cf. A. Jain 2001: 1–11.

277 The accuracy of the data is confirmed by the identical names in A. Jain's lists. Through the comparison with the names listed by B.U. Jain (2002) the independently roaming groups of *muni*s and *āryikās* under the command of Vidyā Sāgar can be clearly identified. In 2001 the *saṅgha* had 188 members: 63 *muni*s, 10 *ailakas*, 113 *āryikā* and 2 *kṣullakas*. The changes between 2001 and 2002 are minimal: in 2002 the group had 3 more divisions of altogether 2 more independently roaming *muni*s, but 2 members less in the *ācārya*'s group, 4 *āryikā* less, and 2 *kṣullakas* less (A. Jain 2001). The *muni*s were divided into 17 divisions: the *ācārya*'s group, with 39 members (38 *muni*s including the *ācārya* and 1 *ailaka*), and 16 other groups of altogether 25 *muni*s. In addition, 1 unit of 2 *ailakas* roaming together, and 7 *ailakas* and 2 *kṣullakas* wandering alone. The 113 *āryikā* were divided in 17 divisions, which altogether represented 23.6% of all 72 divisions of Digambara nuns.

278 The word 'group' is not really applicable.

279 R.K. Jain 1999: 80 describes these '*tyāgīs*,' or renouncers, as regionally oriented 'priests' which can be compared to the *bhaṭṭārakas*, a

hypothesis which still needs to be tested.

280 According to B.U. Jain 1999: 372f., Vidyā Sāgar's order is the only mendicant group where the *āryikā* do not spend *cāturmāsa* at the same location as the *munis*.

281 Six groups of altogether forty seven *āryikā* spent *cāturmāsa* Kārañjā in Mahārāṣṭra (B.U. Jain 2002: 310).

282 According to M. Jain 2001: 494, cf. 539f., Vidyā Sāgar had initiated 195 disciples between 1972 and 2001: 62 *munis*, 114 *āryikā*, 10 *ailakas*, and 9 *kṣullakas*.

283 Shāntā 1985: 136.

284 Zydenbos 1999: 295. Svarṇa Matī (1), Viśuddha Matī (1), and Ananta Matī (1) are listed by D. Śāstrī 1985: 555, 567.

285 It happens that individuals, though initiated by other *munis*, are counted under the name of their new '*dīkṣā guru*' after changing to a new *saṅgha*. Personal communication by Nīraj Jain, June 2003.

286 D. Śāstrī 1985: 569.

287 A. Jain 2001: 23.

288 Cf. B.U. Jain 1999: 187, n. 107, cf. 320, 513f.

289 R.K. Jain 1999: 90.

290 Kāsalīvāl 1992: 38.

291 This is one of the biggest difference between Digambara *ācāryas* and *bhaṭṭārakas* as well as Śvetāmbara *ācāryas*.

292 See also Zydenbos 1999: 297.

293 This is the oldest method amongst the modern *muni saṅghas* according to Ācārya Puṣpadanta (personal communication Mumbaī 24 October 2003).

294 B.U. Jain 1996: 326, n. 4 notes an increase of about 100–125 mendicants between 1995 and 1996 and cites details of many new initiations.

295 An estimated figure of 10% was cited to me, which may be exaggerated.

296 The data are too unreliable to attach much significance to specific changes, such as the diminishing percentage of male mendicants.

297 See Fohr's article in this volume.

298 B.U. Jain 2002: 70 gives the summary figure of 12,469 Jain mendicants for the year 2002: Mūrtipūjaka 7,553, Sthānakavāsī 3,331, Terā Panth 691, Digambara 894. In 2005, the figure had risen to 13,307: Mūrtipūjaka 8,061, Sthānakavāsī 3,546, Terāpanthī 692, Digambara 1008 (B.U. Jain 2005: 25).

299 These percentages do not reflect a similar share of the Jain laity, for which no reliable data are available. Many Digambaras are affiliated

to reformist lay traditions without separate ascetic orders. The regional, caste and class background of the ascetics also varies. Most of the ascetics of the Śramaṇa Saṅgha and the independent Sthānakavāsī traditions stem from the Osvāl and Śrīmālī castes in Rājasthān, Madhya Pradeś, Mahārāṣṭra and the Pañjāb, but also from southern India (Shāntā 1985: 333). The Gujarātī Sthānakavāsī traditions and the Tapā Gaccha groups recruit their ascetics almost exclusively in Gujarāt and amongst the Gujarātī population in Mumbaī, the Kharatara Gaccha and the Śvetāmbara Terā Panth in Rājasthān, and the Digambara groups mainly in Karṇāṭaka and Madhya Pradeś, to name only the most important mendicant traditions. The average size of the itinerant groups in 1999 was 4–5 in all four traditions (Mūrtipūjaka 4.6, Sthānakavāsī 4.2, Terā Panth 5.69, Digambara 5.05).

300 The comparison is only meaningful because of the 'improvement in reporting of religion' in the censuses after 1971 (M.K. Jain 1986: 35). The doubling of the absolute number of Jains recorded in the censuses of 1951–1971 (which is not matched by the mendicant population) is generally interpreted as an effect of under-reporting during the colonial period. If this is true, then it must be concluded that – relative to the total population of India – the number of Jains is continually declining.

301 A variant of this approach is M. Spiro's theory of renunciation as a psychological defense-mechanism, which has been applied to the Jain case by Goonasekere 1986: 179f.

302 This figure more than doubles, if nuns and novices are included. See Bechert 1973: 580f.

303 The 2000 edition of the Vatican's Annuario Pontificio, gives for 1998 the figure of 57,813 monks and 814,779 nuns (ratio 1: 14). The monastic population as a whole represented 0.086% of all Roman Catholics. Overall numbers are declining, especially the population of nuns, which was 990,768 in 1978: http://www.sspxasia.com/Countires/World/NewsArchive.htm

304 For data confirming this for the Terāpanthīs see Flügel forthcoming.

305 'Socio-economically troubled families, especially those of the middle classes, often seek relief from their frustrations and insecurities by becoming religious' (Goonasekere 1986: 123).

306 Vallely 2002: 197 tried to solve the problem through re-definition: 'Within the order, desire to belong to the group, or attraction to a charismatic leader, is not treated as a "social" motivation, stemming from worldliness. Instead, it too is seen as evidence of a spiritual purity.'

307 Cf. Bloss 1987: 18, Kawanami 1990: 26.

308 'field investigations have revealed that this is more an accusation and a speculation than reality' (Goonasekere 1986: 179f.).

309 E.g. Bordiyā 1975: 265–80. Reasons which are rarely cited in the literature are (a) recruitment drives to satisfy the formal requirement of Mūrtipūjaka monks to have disciples in order to be able to advance in the monastic hierarchy, (b) family pressure informed by material considerations.

310 'In the decades since Independence, with the rise in the age of marriage and the increase in health standards, this [widows becoming *sādhvīs*, P.F.] has changed. Most Jain women are now married when they are in their early or mid 20s, and so even if they become widows they most likely have had children. Having to raise the children means that becoming a *sādhvī* is less of a realistic option for a widow. Changing social attitudes toward widows also makes it less likely that a Jain widow feels that she has little choice but to become a *sādhvī*. . . Today the vast majority of *sādhvīs* have never been married; becoming a *sādhvī* is now seen as an alternative vocation to that of a housewife' (Cort 1989: 111f.).

311 Most but not all *sādhvīs* come from Jain families, while an increasing number of *sādhus* are recruited from non-Jain tribal communities who seek material improvements through the association with the Jains. An unresolved difficulty for this interpretation is that, for reasons of tradition, educational opportunities are limited for Mūrtipūjaka *sādhvīs*.

312 In a personal conversation, the Tapā Gaccha *ācārya* Jay Sundar Sūri stated that men believe in 'heroism,' while women are 'more impressionable, more spiritual' (Mumbaī 23 October 2003). An investigation of the self-reported motives of Terāpanth mendicants showed, however, that 'religious' reasons were more prevalent amongst *sādhus* rather than *sādhvīs* (Flügel, forthcoming). Jay Sundar Sūri's disciples Prem Sundar Vijay and Harsad Vijay explained the increasing number of (male) mendicants with the increasing wealth of the Jain community, which now can afford to lose valuable workforce and to feed a growing community of materially dependent mendicants. Apparently, nowadays families of renouncers are more supportive than in the past (Mumbaī 1 November 2003).

313 By 1982, nine *ācāryas* alone had initiated some 300 ascetics (*munis, ailakas, kṣullakas, āryikās, kṣullikās*): Śānti Sāgar (20), Vir Sāgar (23), Śiv Sāgar (28), Dharma Sāgar (61), Vidyā Sāgar (18), Deś Bhūṣaṇ (33), Mahāvīr Kīrti (24), Sanmati Sāgar (26), Vimal Sāgar (65) (D. Śāstrī 1985).

314 At the moment, the increased mobility of the laity compensates only for the migration from rural to urban locations and abroad.

Bibliography

AISJC, Akhil Bhāratīya Sthānakavāsī Jain Kānfrens (ed.). *Akhil Bhāratvarṣīya Vardhamāṇ Sthānakavāsī Jain Śramaṇ Saṅghīya Samācārī.* Comp. Saubhāgyamuni 'Kumud.' Dillī: Akhil Bhāratīya Vardhamān Sthānakavāsī Jaina Kānfrens, 1987.

——. *Amṛt-Mahotsav Gaurav Granth.* Naī Dillī: Akhil Bhāratvarṣīya Śvetāmbara Sthānakavāsī Jain Kānfrens, 1988.

Akkole, Subhāścandra. *Śantśreṣṭha Parampūjya 108 Caritracakravartī Ācāryaśrī Śāntisāgar Caritra.* Śolāpūr: Jain Saṃskṛti Saṃrakṣak Saṅgh, 1987.

Appadurai, Arjun. 'Number in the colonial imagination.' *Orientalism and the Postcolonial Predicament.* Eds C.A. Breckenridge and P. van der Veer, 314–339. Philadelphia: University of Pennsylvania Press, 1993.

Baines, Jervoise Athelstane. *Census of India 1891— General Report.* London: Eyre & Spottiswoode, 1893.

Balbir, Nalini. 'Observations sur la secte jaina des Terāpanthī.' *Bulletin D'Études Indiennes* 1 (1983) 39–45.

——. 'Recent Developments in a Jaina Tīrtha: Hastināpur (U.P.) – A Preliminary Report.' *The History of the Sacred Places in India as Reflected in Traditional Literature.* Panels of the VIIth World Sanskrit Conference Vol. II. Ed. H. Bakker. General Editor: Johannes Bronkhorst, 177–191. Leiden: E. J. Brill, 1990.

——. 'La question de l'ordination des enfants en milieu jaina.' *Les Âges de la vie dans le monde Indien.* Ed. Christine Chojnacki, 153–182. Paris: Diffusion de Boccard, 2001.

——. 'The Añcalagaccha Viewed from Inside and from Outside.' *Jainism and Early Buddhism. Essays in Honor of Padmanabh S. Jaini.* Ed. Olle Qvarnström, 47–77. Fremont: Asian Humanities Press, 2003.

Banks, Marcus. 'Defining Division: An Historical Overview of Jain Social Organization.' *Modern Asian Studies* 20, 3 (1986) 447–460.

——. *Organizing Jainism in India and England.* Oxford: Clarendon Press, 1992.

Bechert, Heinz. *Buddhismus, Staat und Gesellschaft in den Ländern des Theravāda Buddhismus.* Bd. III. Bibliographie, Dokumente, Index. Wiesbaden: Otto Harrassowitz, 1973.

Bharill, Hukam Chand. *Kramabaddha Paryāya (Sequence Bound Modifications).* Tr. M. Jain. Jaipur: Pandit Todarmal Smarak Trust, 1980/1987.

Bloss, Lowell W. 'The Female Renunciants of Sri Lanka: The Dasasilmattawa.' *Journal of the International Association for Buddhist Studies* 10, 1 (1987) 7–31.

Böhtlingk, Otto and Rudolph Roth. *Sanskrit Wörterbuch. Dritter Theil.* St. Petersburg: Kaiserliche Akademie der Wissenschaften, 1861.

Brekke, Torkel. *Makers of Modern Indian Religion in the Late Nineteenth Century.* Oxford: Oxford University Press, 2002.

Budhmal, Muni. *Terāpanth kā Itihās. Pratham Khaṇḍ: Terāpanth ke Pratham Cār Ācārya.* 4th Revised Edition. Calcutta: Jain Śvetāmbar Terāpanth Mahāsabhā Prakāśan, 1964/1995.

Bühler, Georg. 'The Digambara Jainas.' *The Indian Antiquary* 7 (1878) 28f.

——. 'On the Authenticity of the Jaina Tradition.' *Vienna Oriental Journal* 1 (1887) 165–180.

——. 'Further Proofs of the Authenticity of the Jaina Tradition.' *Vienna Oriental Journal* 4 (1890) 313–331.

Carrithers, Michael. 'Naked Ascetics in Southern Digambar Jainism.' *Man (N.S.)* 24 (1989) 219–235.

——. 'Jainism and Buddhism as Enduring Historical Streams.' *Journal of the Anthropological Society of Oxford* 21, 2 (1990) 141–163.

——. 'On Polytropy: Or the Natural Condition of Spiritual Cosmopolitanism in India: The Digambar Jain Case.' *Modern Asian Studies* 34, 4 (2000) 831–861.

Clémentin-Ojha, Catherine. 'Ascetics' Rights in Early 19th Century Jaipur (Rājasthān).' *Asceticism and Power in South- and Southeast Asia.* Eds P. Flügel and G. Houtmann. London: Routledge, forthcoming.

Cohn, Bernard S. (ed.). 'The Census and Objectification in South Asia.' *An Anthropologist among the Historians and Other Essays*, 224–254. Delhi: Oxford University Press, 1987/1992.

Copaḍe, Tātyā Keśav. *Kīrtanopayogī Dharmadivākar Śrī 1008 Ācārya Śāntisāgar Caritra.* Bhoj: Rāygauḍā Devagaḍsā Pāṭīl, 1936.

Cort, John E. "Liberation and Wellbeing: A Study of the Mūrtipūjak Jains of North Gujarāt". PhD dissertation, Harvard University, 1989.

——. 'The Śvetāmbar Mūrtipūjak Jain Mendicant.' *Man (N.S.)* 26 (1991) 651–671.

——. 'Fistfights in the Monastery: Calendars, Conflict and Karma among the Jains.' *Approaches to Jain Studies: Philosophy, Logic, Rituals and Symbols.* Eds N.K. Wagle and O. Qvarnström, 36–59. University of Toronto: Center for South Asian Studies, 1999.

——. *Jains in the World: Religious Values and Ideology in India.* New York: Oxford University Press, 2001.

——. 'A Tale of Two Cities: On the Origins of Digambara Sectarianism in North India.' *Multiple Histories: Culture and Society in the Study of Rājasthān.* Eds L.A. Babb, V. Joshi and M. Meister, 39–83. Jaipur: Rawat Publications, 2002.

——. 'A Fifteenth Century Digambara Mystic and his Contemporary Followers: Tāraṇ Taraṇ Svāmī and the Tāraṇ Svāmī Panth.' (in this volume).

Darśanavijaya, Muni (comp.). *Paṭṭāvalī-Samuccaya.* Pratham Bhāg. Vīramgām (Gujarāt): Caritra-Smārak-Granthamālā, 1933.

Degenne, Alain and Michel Forsé. *Introducing Social Networks.* Tr. by A. Borges. London: Sage, 1994/1999.

Delamaine, Major James. 'On the Srawaks or Jains.' *Transactions of the Royal Asiatic Society of Great Britain and Ireland* 1 (1827) 413–438.

Deo, Shantaram Balchandra. *History of Jaina Monasticism from Inscriptions and Literature.* Poona: Deccan College, 1956.

Desāī, Ratilāl Dīpcand. *Seṭh Ānandjī Kalyāṇjī nī Peḍhī no Itihās.* Bhag 1–2. Amadāvād: Seṭh Ānandjī Kalyāṇjī, 1983–1986.

Devendramuni, Ācārya. 'Sant Sammelan: Ek Cintan (Śramaṇ Saṅgh).' *Jain Prakāś (Ānandṛṣi Janma Śatābdī Viśeṣāṅk)* 87, 73 (2000) 16–22.

Dhaky, Madhusudan A. 'The Date of Kundakundācārya.' *Paṇḍit Dalsukhbhāī Mālvaṇiyā Abhinandana Grantha I.* Sampādak: Madhusudan Ḍhākī & Sāgarmal Jain, 187–206 (English Section). Vārāṇasī: Pārśvanāth Vidyāśrama Śodha Saṃsthān, 1991.

Dullā, Pāsvīr Vīrjī 'Pārśva Śrī' (Prayojak). *Añcalgaccha Digdarśan.* Mulumḍ/Mumbaī: Mulumd Añcalagaccha Jain Samāj, 1968.

Dumont, Louis. *Homo Hierarchicus: The Caste System and its Implications.* Complete Revised English Edition. Chicago and London: The University of Chicago Press, 1966/1980.

Dundas, Paul. 'Somnolent Sūtras: Scriptural Commentary in Śvetāmbara Jainism.' *Journal of Indian Philosophy* 24 (1996) 73–101.

——. *The Jains.* Second Revised Edition. London: Routledge, 1992/2002.

——. 'Conversion to Jainism: Historical Perspectives.' *Religious Conversion in India: Modes, Motivations, and Meanings.* Eds. Rowena Robinson and Sathianathan Clarke, 125–148. Oxford: Oxford University Press, 2003.

Flügel, Peter. 'Jain Transactions: Food Restrictions as Interactive Matrices.' *DGV- Symposium Überbrücker von Unüberbrückbarem,* München, 17 October 1991.

——. *Askese und Devotion: Das rituelle System der Terāpanth Śvetāmbara Jains.* Doctoral dissertation, Johannes Gutenberg-Universität Mainz, 1994.

——. 'The Ritual Circle of the Terāpanth Śvetāmbara Jains.' *Bulletin D'Études Indiennes* 13 (1995–1996) 117–176.

——. 'Protestantische und Post-Protestantische Jaina-Reformbewegungen: Zur Geschichte und Organisation der Sthānakavāsī I.' *Berliner Indologische Studien* 13–14 (2000) 37–103.

——. 'R.K. Jain. 1999. The Universe as Audience: Metaphor and Community among the Jains of North India [review].' *Jinamañjari* 23, 1 (2001) 70–77.

——. "The Codes of Conduct of the Terāpanth Samaṇ Order." *South Asia Research* 23, 1 (2003a) 7–53.

——. 'Protestantische und Post-Protestantische Jaina-Reformbewegungen: Zur Geschichte und Organisation der Sthānakavāsī II.' *Berliner Indologische Studien* 15–17 (2003b) 149–240.

——. 'The Invention of Jainism: A Short History of Jaina Studies.' *Journal of Jaina Studies* (Kyoto) 11 (2005) 1–19 (also: *International Journal of Jain Studies* 1, 1 (2005) http://www.soas.ac.uk/ijjs).

——. 'The Unknown Loṅkā: Tradition and the Cultural Unconscious.' Eds C. Caillat and N. Balbir. *Proceedings of the Jaina Panel of the World Sanskrit Conference in Helsinki.* Delhi: Motilal Banārsīdāss (in press).

——. 'A Socio-Demographic Analysis of the Terāpanth Jain Monastic Order in Rājasthān.' *Paper delivered at the School of Social Sciences Research Seminar,* University of East London, 10 December 2003 (forthcoming).

Folkert, Kendall W. *Scripture and Community: Collected Essays on the Jains.* Ed. J.E. Cort. Atlanta: Scholars Press, 1993.

Ghoshal, Sarat Chandra. *The Digambara Saints of India.* Cooch/Behar: Digambar Jain Muni Raksha Committee, 1932.

Glasenapp, Helmuth von. *Der Jainismus: Eine indische Erlösungsreligion.* Berlin: Alf Häger Verlag, 1925 (English Translation: Delhi: Motilal Banarsidass, 1998).

Goonasekere, Ratna Sunilsantha Abhayawardana. 'Renunciation and Monasticism among the Jainas of India.' PhD dissertation. San Diego, CA: University of California, 1986.

Guérinot, A.A. *La Religion Djaina: histoire, doctrine, culte, coutumes, institutions.* Paris: Librairie Orientaliste P. Geuthner, 1926.

Hoernle, Rudolph A.F. 'Two Paṭṭāvalīs of the Sarasvatī Gachcha of the Digambara Jains.' *Indian Antiquary* 20 (1891) 341–361.

——. 'Three Further Paṭṭāvalīs of the Digambaras.' *Indian Antiquary* 21 (1892) 57–84.

Jacobi, Hermann. 'Kalpasūtra of Bhadrabāhu.' *Abhandlungen für die Kunde des Morgenlandes* 7, 1 (1879).

——. *Jaina Sūtras Part I.* Sacred Books of the East. Ed. M. Müller. Vol. 22. Oxford: Clarendon Press, 1884.

——. 'Jainismus.' *Zeitschrift für Religionswissenschaft* 18 (1915) 268–286.

Jain, Anupam (col.). *Sampark.* Hastināpur: Tīrthaṅkara Ṛṣabhdev Jain Vidvat Mahāsaṅgh, 2000a.

——. *Digambara Jaina Sādhu-Sādhvīyoṁ ke Varṣayoga – 2001 kī Sūcī.* Indaur: Akhil Bhāratīya Digambara Jaina Mahilā Saṅghaṭhan, 2000b.

—— (col.). *Digambara Jaina Sādhu-Sādhvīyoṁ ke Varṣayoga – 2001 kī Sūcī.* Indaur: Akhil Bhāratīya Digambara Jaina Mahilā Saṅghaṭhan, 2001.

Jain, Bābūlāl 'Ujjavala' (col.). *Samagra Jain Cāturmās Sūcī.* Bombay: Akhil Bhāratvarṣīya Samagra Jaina Cāturmās Sūcī Prakāśan Pariṣad, 1987.

—— (col.). *Samagra Jain Cāturmās Sūcī.* Bombay: Akhil Bhāratvarṣīya Samagra Jaina Cāturmāsi Sūcī Prakāśan Pariṣad, 1990.

—— (col.). *Samagra Jain Cāturmās Sūcī.* Mumbaī: Jaina Ektā Mahāmaṇḍal, 1996.

—— (col.). *Samagra Jain Cāturmās Sūcī.* Mumbaī: Ujjavala Prakāśan, 1999.

—— (col.). *Samagra Jain Cāturmās Sūcī.* Mumbaī: Ujjavala Prakāśan, 2002.

—— (col.). *Samagra Jain Cāturmās Sūcī.* Mumbaī: Ujjavala Prakāśan, 2005.

Jain, Brahmacāriṇī Mainā本bāī (comp.). *Ācārya Śrī Ādisāgar (Aṅkalīkar) kī Jhalak.* Dillī Ācārya Śrī Sanmati Sāgar jī Saṅgh, 1996.

Jain, Champat Rāy. *The Jain Law.* Madras, 1926.

——. *The Nudity of Jain Saints.* Delhi: The Jain Mitra Mandal, 1931.

Jaini, Jugmandir Lāl. *Jaina Law: 'Bhadrabāhu Saṃhitā.'* Text with Translation and Appendix Containing Full Text of an Important Judgement in a Jaini Case by the Original Side of the High Court of Judicature, Indore. The Library of Jaini Literature Vol. IV. Arrah: The Central Jaina Publishing House, 1916.

Jaini, Padmanabh S. 'Bhavyatva and Abhavyatva: A Jaina Doctrine of "Predestination".' *Mahāvīra and his Teachings.* Eds A.N. Upadhye, N. Tatia, D. Malvania, M. Mehta, N. Shastri and K. Shastri, 95–111. Bombay: Mahāvīra Nirvāṇa Mahotsava Samiti, 1977.

——. *The Jaina Path of Purification.* Berkeley: University of California Press, 1979.

——. *Gender & Salvation: Jaina Debates on the Spiritual Liberation of Women.* With a Foreword by Robert P. Goldman. Berkeley, CA: University of California Press, 1991.

Jain, Kailash C. *Jainism in Rājasthān.* Sholapur: Jaina Samskrti Samrakṣaka Saṅgha, 1963.

Jain, Kāmtā Prasād. *Digambaratva aur Digambar Muni.* Baraut: Digambar Jain Yuvā Samiti, 1932/1992.

Jain, K. Rājul. *Ācārya Jñānsāgar ke Hindī Sāhitya kā Samikṣātmak Adhyayan.* Sāṅganer: Bhagavān Ṛṣabhdev Granthamālā, 2003.

Jain, M.K. 'A Demographic Analysis on Jains in India.' *Jain Journal* 21, 2 (1986) 33–51.

Jain, Miśrīlāl. *Ātmaśilpī Ācārya Śrī Vidyāsāgar (Jīvan Darśan).* Amadāvād: Ahiṁsā-Ārmī Mānav Kalyāṇ Jīvdayā Ceriṭebal Ṭrasṭ 2001.

Jain, Muni Uttam Kamal. *Jaina Sects and Schools.* Delhi: Concept Publishing, 1975.

Jain, Rākeś (comp.). *Bīsvīṁ Sadī ke Divaṁgat Jaina Manīṣī.* Naī Dillī: Digambara Jaina Sāhitya-Saṃskṛti Saṃrakṣaṇ Samiti, 2002.

Jain, Ravindra K. *The Universe as Audience: Metaphor and Community among the Jains of North India.* Shimla: Indian Institute of Advanced Study, 1999.

Jain, Sureś Candra. *Jain Dharma-Bhūṣaṇ, Dharma-Divāraka Brahmacārī Śītalprasād jī (kī 61 vīṁ Jayantī ke Avsar Par Prakāśit).* Lakhnaū: Jaina Dharma Pravarddhanī Sabhā, 1940.

Jain Śvetāmbara Conference. *Jain Śvetāmbara Directory (Gujarāt).* Mumbaī: Jain Śvetāmbara Conference Office, Pāydhunī, 1909.

——. *Jain Śvetāmbara Directory.* Compiled by Ratancand Bhāstar and Dalsukhbhāī Vāḍīlāl. Mumbaī: Jain Association of India, 1915.

——. *Jain Śvetāmbara Directory.* Compiled by Ratancand Bhāstar and Dalsukhbhāī Vaḍilāl. Mumbaī: Jain Association of India, 1916.

Jauharī, Durlabhbhāī. *Sādhu-Sammelan kā Itihās.* Sampādak: Cimmanasiṅha Loḍhā. Samśodhak: Paṇḍit Śobhācandra Bhārill. Byāvar: Cimmanasiṅha Loḍhā (Mainejar, Śrī Mahāvīr Priṇṭiṅg Pres), 1946.

Jhaveri, Thakurdas Bhagavandas (comp.). *Shri Bharatvarshiya Digambara Jain Directory.* Bombay, 1914.

Jñān Matī, *āryikā. Digambara Muni.* 2nd edition. Hastināpur: Digambara Jaina Trilok Śodha Saṃsthān, 1980.

Joharāpurkara, V.P. *Bhaṭṭāraka Sampradāya.* Śolāpura: Jaina Saṃskṛti Saṃrakṣaka Saṃgha, 1958.

Joshi, A.P., M.D. Srinivas and J.K. Bajaj. *Religious Demography of India.* Chennai: Centre for Policy Studies, 2003.

Kanakanandi, Upādhyāya. *Śramaṇ Saṅgha Saṃhitā.* Jaypur: Dharmadarśan Vijñān Śodha Saṃsthān, 1994.

Kañcansāgarsūri, Sūryodaysāgar, Abhaysāgar (eds). 1977, 1983. *Āgama Jyotirdhara.* Vibhāg I-II. Āgamoddhārak Granthamālā Puṣpa 18–19. Kapaḍvañj (Kheḍā): Ramaṇlāl Jecandbhāī.

Kāsalīvāl, Kastūrcand. *Jaina Samāj kā Bṛhat Itihās.* Vol. 1. Jaypur: Jaina Itihās Prakāśan Sansthān, 1992.

—— (ed.) *Praśamamūrti Ācārya Śāntisāgar Chāṇī Smṛti Granth.* Meraṭh: Ācārya Śāntisāgar Chāṇī Granthamālā, 1998.

Kaṭariyā, Milāpbhand. 'Terā Panth aur Bīsa Panth.' *Jaina Nibandha Ratnāvalī.* Bhāg 1, 383–385. (xerox copy).

Kawanami, Hiroko. 'The Religious Standing of Burmese Nuns (*thila shin*): The Ten Precepts and Religious Respect Words.' *Journal of the International Association of Buddhist Studies* 13, 1 (1990)

17–39.

Keshory, Seth Kesree Chand. 'Account of the Terāpanthī Sect of Swetambar Jains.' *Census of India 1921*, Vol. I. India, Part I. Report. Ed. J.T. Marten. Appendix IV, xiii–xiv. Calcutta: Superintendent Government Printing, 1924.

Klatt, Johannes. 'The Samachari-Satakam of Samayasundara and Paṭṭāvalīs of the Anchala-Gachcha and other Gachchas (Revised with Additions by Ernst Leumann).' *Indian Antiquary* 23 (1894) 169–183.

Lath, Mukund. *Half a Tale: A Study in the Interrelationship between Autobiography and History. The Adhakathānaka. Translated, introduced and annotated.* Jaipur: Rājasthān Prakrit Bhāratī Sansthān, 1981.

Leumann, Ernst. *Die Āvaśyaka-Erzählungen.* (Abhandlungen für die Kunde des Morgenlandes herausgegeben von der Deutschen Morgenländischen Gesellschaft. X. Band, No. 2). Leipzig: F. A. Brockhaus, 1934.

——. *Übersicht über die Āvaśyaka Literatur.* Aus dem Nachlass herausgegeben von Walther Schubring Alt-und Neuindische Studien. Hamburg: De Gruyter, 1934.

Mahias, Marie-Claude. *Délivrance et convivialité: Le système culinaire des Jaina.* Paris: Éditions de la Maison des Sciences de l'Homme, 1985.

——. '*Āhāra dāna*, the Gift of Food to Digambara Ascetics (*muni*).' *Purushartha* (forthcoming).

Maṇilāl, Muni. *Śrī Jainadharmano Prācīn Saṅkṣipt Itihās ane Prabhu Vīr Paṭṭāvalī.* Amadāvād: Jīvaṇlāl Chaganlāl Saṅghvī, 1934.

Marriott, McKim (ed.). *Village India: Studies in the Little Community.* Chicago: University of Chicago Press, 1955.

Mehta, Rama. *Inside the Haveli.* London: Penguin, 1977/1996.

Mitchell, Clyde. 'The Concept and Use of Social Networks.' *Social Networks in Urban Situations: Analyses of Personal Relationships in Central African Towns.* Ed. J.C. Mitchell, 1–50. Manchester: Manchester University Press, 1969.

Nair, V.G. *Jainism and Terehpanthism.* Bangalore: Shri Ādināth Jain Śvetāmbar Temple, 1970.

Natarajan, B. *Indian Census through a Hundred Years.* Part I. Census Centenary Monograph No. 2. Census of India 1971. New Delhi: Office of the Registrar General. Ministry of Home Affairs, 1971.

Nathmal, Muni [now: Ācārya Mahāprajña]. *Acharya Bhiksu: The Man and his Philosophy.* Translation of *Bhikṣu Vicār Darśan* by N. Sahal. Cūrū: Ādarś Sāhitya Saṅgha Prakāśan, 1959/1968.

Navratnamal, Muni. *Śāsana Samudra.* Vol. 1–25. Published by Uttamcand Sethia. Calcutta: Śrī Jain Śvetāmbara Terāpanthī Mahāsabhā Prakāśan & Lāḍnūṁ, Jain Viśva Bhāratī, 1981ff.

——. *Terāpanth Pāvas Pravās.* Lāḍnūṁ: Śrī Jain Śvetāmbar Terāpanthī Sabhā, 1991.

Padmarāja, Paṇḍit. A Treatise on Jain Law and Usages. Bombay: Karnatak Press, 1886.

Plowden, W. Chichele. *Report on the Census of British India taken on the 17th February 1881.* Vol. I–III. London: Eyre & Spottiswoode, 1883.

Prakāśacandra, Muni. *Ā Che Aṇagāra Amārā.* Mumbaī: Śrī Naval Śāhitya Prakāśan Maṇḍal, 1989/1998.

Premī, Nāthūrām. "Bhaṭṭāraka." *Jaina Hitaiṣī* 7 (1912) 59–69, 9: 13–24, 10–11: 1–9; 8, 2 (1913) 57–70 [cited from a reprint of unspecified selections, no date].

——. (ed.). *Kavivar Banārsīdās viracit Ardha Kathānaka.* Bombay: Hindi Granth Ratnākar, 1957.

Ratna Prabhā Vijay, Muni. *Śramaṇa Bhagavān Mahāvīra.* Vol. 5.2. Ahmedabad: Śrī Jaina Siddhānta Society, 1948.

Reynell, Josephine. 'Honour, Nurture and Festivity: Aspects of Female Religiosity amongst Jain Women in Jaipur.' PhD dissertation, University of Cambridge, 1985.

Śāh, Mālti. *Nagarśeṭh Śāntidās Jhāverī.* Amadāvād: Gūrjar Grantharatna Kāryālay, 1987.

Saletore, R.N. 'Monastic Life in Śravaṇa Beḷagoḷa.' *Jaina Antiquary* 5, 4 (1940) 123–132.

Sandesara, Bhogilal, J. 'Kṣetrādeśapaṭṭaka issued by Ācārya Vijayadharaṇendrasūri of Tapā Gaccha.' *Journal of the Oriental Institute* 24 (1974) 228–233.

Sangave, Vilās A. *Jaina Community*. 2nd revised edition. Bombay: Popular Prakashan, 1959/ 1980.

——. *Facets of Jainology: Selected Research Papers on Jain Society, Religion and Culture.* Mumbai: Popular Prakashan, 2001.

——. 'Karavīravaibhav Śrī Lakṣmīsena Bhaṭṭārak Pīṭh: Paramparā va Kārya.' *Paṭṭācārya Bhaṭṭārak Ratna Svastiśrī Lakṣmīsena Mahāsvāmī Ṣaṣṭyabdipūrtī Gaurav Aṅk.* Sampādak: Prācārya Śrīdhar Heravāḍe, 1–4. Kolhāpura, 3 August 2003.

Śāstrī, Dharmacandra. *Digambara Jain Sādhu Paricay*. Sanghastha: Ācārya Dharmasāgara. Dillī: Lālā Śyāmlāl Ṭhekedār, 1985.

Śāstrī, Nāthūlāl. 'Bīs Panth Terah Panth Carcā.' *Jain Pracārak* (2002) 10f., 17.

Śāstrī, Phūlcand 'Siddhāntācārya' (ed.). *Khāniyā Tattva-Carcā.* 2 Vols. Jaypur: Ācāryakalpa Paṇḍit Ṭoḍarmal Granthamālā, 1967.

——. 'Songaḍh aur Jainatattvamīmāṃsā.' *Siddhāntācārya Paṇḍit Phūlcand Śāstrī Abhinandan-Granth.* Ed. Bābūlāl Jain Phāgull, 527–532. Vārāṇasī: Siddhāntācārya Paṇḍit Phūlcand Śāstrī Abhinandan Granth Prakāśan Samiti, 1985a.

——. 'Mūlasaṅgh Śuddhāmnāyakā Dūsrā Nām hī Terāpanth hai.' Ibid., 535–540, 1985b.

——. 'Śrī Jin Tāraṇataraṇa aur unkī Kṛtiyāṁ.' Ibid., 385–408, 1985c.

——. *Parvār Jain Samāj kā Itihās.* Jabalpur: Bhāratvarṣīya Digambar Jain Parvār Sabhā, 1992.

Śāstrī, Prakāś Hitaiṣī. 'Jaypur Khāniyā Tattva-Carcā: Ek Samikṣā.' *Siddhāntācārya Paṇḍit Phūlcand Śāstrī Abhinandan-Granth.* Ed. Bābūlāl Jain Phāgull, 643–661. Vārāṇasī: Siddhāntācārya Paṇḍit Phūlcand Śāstrī Abhinandan Granth Prakāśan Samiti, 1985.

Śāstrī, Vaṃśīdhar. *Ācārya Śrī Śāntisāgar Mahāmuni kā Caritra.* Solāpur: Rāvjī Sakhārām Dośī, 1932 (2nd edition, Mumbaī: Guṇamālāben Javherī, 1995).

Schubring, Walther. *Die Lehre der Jainas. Nach den alten Quellen dargestellt.* Berlin: Walter De Gruyter & Co., 1935.

——. *The Doctrine of the Jainas. Described after the Old Sources.* Tr. Wolfgang Beurlen. 2nd English edition. Delhi: Motilal Banarsidass, 1962/2000.

——. 'Jinismus.' *Die Religionen Indiens III.* Hg. v. A. Bareau, Walther Schubring, Christoph von Führer-Haimendorf, 217–242. Stuttgart: Kohlhammer, 1964.

Sen, Amulyachandra. *Schools and Sects in Jaina Literature.* Calcutta: Visva-Bhāratī Boos Shop, 1931.

Shāntā, N. *La Voie Jaina: Histoire, Spiritualité, Vie des ascètes pèlerines de l'Inde.* Paris: OEIL, 1985.

Sharma, Jagdish P. 'Jainas as a Minority in Indian Society and History.' *Jain Journal* 10, 4 (1976) 137–148.

——. 'The *Jinasattvas*: Class and Gender in the Social Origins of Jaina Heroes.' *Approaches to Jain Studies: Philosophy, Logic, Rituals and Symbols.* Eds N.K. Wagle and O. Qvarnström, 72–85. University of Toronto: Center for South Asian Studies, 1999.

Śīlcandra Vijay, Muni. *Śāsan Samrāṭ.* Ahmedabad: Tapāgacchīya Śeṭhśri Jinadās Dharmadās Dhārmik Trust, Kadambagiri Vāṭī, 1973.

Singh, Munshi Hardyal. *Report on the Census of 1891. Vol. II. The Castes of Marwar. Illustrated.* Jodhpur: Published by the Order of the Marwar Darbar, 1894.

Śivprasād. *Tapāgacch kā Itihās.* Bhāg 1, Khaṇḍ 1. Vārāṇasī: Pārśvanāth Vidyāpīṭh, 2000.

——. *Añcalgacch kā Itihās.* Vārāṇasī: Pārśvanāth Vidyāpīṭh, 2001.

SJCS, Samagra Jain Cāturmās Sūcī Prakāśan Pariṣad Bambaī. 'Pariṣad ke Baṛhte Kadam.' *Samagra Jain Cāturmāsi Sūcī.* Ed. B.U. Jain, 67f. Bombay: Akhil Bhāratīya Samagra Jaina Cāturmās Sūcī Prakāśan Pariṣad, 1987.

Śrut Saṃvarddhan Saṃsthān (Ed.). *Śrut Saṃvarddhan Saṃsthān dvārā Pravartit Pāñc Śrut Saṃvarddhan Vārṣik Puraskāroṁ evaṃ Sarāk Puraskār Varṣ – 2002: Paricay Pustikā.* Preraṇāstrot Upādhyāy Muni Jñānsāgar. Merath: Śrut Saṃvarddhan Saṃsthān, 2002.

Syādvādmatī, *āryikā* (comp.). *Vimal Bhakti Saṃgraha*. Vārāṇasī: Bhāratvarṣīya Anekānt Vidvat Pariṣad, 2000.

Tāraṇataraṇasvāmī. *Śrāvakācāra*. Anuvādak: Brahmacārī Sītalprasād. Surat: Śrī Tāraṇataraṇa Samāj ke Jain Caityālay – Sāgar Kī Or Se, Mathurāprasād Bajāj, Baṛā Bājār, 1933.

Ṭhāṇa = *Ṭhāṇa* (*Sthānāṅga Sūtra*). Vācanā Pramukha: Ācārya Tulsī. Sampādaka Vivecaka: Muni Nathamala. Lāḍnūṁ: Jaina Viśva Bhāratī, 1976.

Tomgia, V.G. 'Changing Patterns of the Status of Women in the Jain Community. Traditional and Modern Trends in their Status.' *Indian Journal of Social Research* 32 (1991) 283–288.

Ṭoṅgyā, Rameś, Amit Ṭoṅgyā and Atul Pāṭedī (comp.). *Ācārya Śrī 108 Vidyāsāgarjī* Mahārāj Sasaṅgh. Gommaṭagiri – Indaur Cāturmās 1999. *Saṅgh Paricay evaṃ Ahārdān Vidhi*. Indaur: Sugan Grāphiks & Ṭoṅkya Ṭelīkamyūnikeśans, 1999.

Tuschen, Stefanie. 'Das Bhaṭṭāraka-Amt bei den Digambara-Jainas in Karṇāṭaka.' Magisterarbeit, Philipps-Universität Marburg, 1997.

Upadhye, Adinath Nemīnath. 'Introduction.' *Śrī Kundakundācārya's Pravacanasara (Pavayanasara). A Pro-Canonical Text of the Jainas* (2nd edition), i-cxxvi. Bombay: Sheth Manilal Revashankar Jhaveri (Rāyacandra-Jaina-Śāstra-Mālā 9), (1930) 1935.

——. 'Yāpanīya Sangha: A Jaina Sect.' *Journal of the University of Bombay* 1, 4 (1933) 224–231.

——. 'A Paṭṭāvalī of the Senagaṇa.' *Jaina Antiquary* 13, 2 (1948) 1–9.

——. 'On the meaning of Yāpanīya.' *S. Srikantha Sastri Felicitation Volume*, 197–198. Mysore, 1973.

Upadhye, Adinath Nemīnath. 'More Light on the Yāpanīya Saṅgha.' *Annals of the Bhandarkar Oriental Research Institute* 55, 1–4 (1974) 9–22.

Vallée-Poussin, Charles Louis Joseph, de la. 'Religious Orders (Indian).' *Encyclopaedia of Religion and Ethics* Vol. 10. Ed. Hastings, 715–718. Edinburgh: T. & T. Clark, 1918.

Vallely, Anne. *Guardians of the Transcendent: An Ethnography of a Jain Ascetic Community*. Toronto: University of Toronto Press, 2002.

Varṇī, Kṣullaka Jinendra. *Jainendra Siddhānta Kośa*. Bhāg I-V. Chaṭhā Śaṃskaraṇ. Naī Dillī: Bhāratīya Jñānpīth, 1970/1998.

Vidvatratna, Sumerucandra Divākara. *Caritra Cakravartī. Śramaṇ Siromaṇa Suvargiya Ācārya Śāntīsāgar Mahārāja kā Puṇya-Caritra*. Vārāṇasī: Mahāvīra Press, 1972.

Vijayanunni, M. *Religion*. Census of India 1991. Series 1. India. Paper 1 of 1995. New Delhi.

Weber, Max. *Gesammelte Aufsätze zur Religionssoziologie*. Bd. II. Tübingen: J.C.B. Mohr (Paul Siebeck), 1920/1978.

——. *Wirtschaft und Gesellschaft: Grundriß der Verstehenden Soziologie*. Studienausgabe. Ed. Winckelmann. Tübingen: J.C.B. Mohr (Paul Siebeck), 1920/1978.

Williams, Robert H.B. *Jaina Yoga*. Delhi: Motilal Banarsidass, 1963/1983.

Zydenbos, Robert J. 'The Ritual Giving of Food to a Digambara Renunciant.' *Approaches to Jain Studies: Philosophy, Logic, Rituals and Symbols*. Eds N.K. Wagle and O. Qvarnström, 291–303. University of Toronto: Center for South Asian Studies, 1999.

2

Sthānakavāsī Jain Tradition

The origins of the Sthānakavāsī (lit. hall-dweller) Śvetāmbara Jain tradition can be traced to the Gujarātī Jain reformer Loṅkā Śāh, Luṅkā or Lumpaka (c. 1415-1489), who protested against the laxity of the contemporary Tapāgaccha Mūrtipūjāk Śvetāmbara Jain mendicants, because their conduct did not match the prescriptions of the oldest canonical texts. Loṅkā was the first layman who started a new religious movement within the Jain tradition. Because he copied manuscripts for Jain monks, he had unique access to the Jain scriptures and noticed that the oldest Śvetāmbara scriptures do not mention the practice of merit-making by giving money as religious gifts *(dāna)* for the construction of temples, nor the performance of image-worship *(mūrtipūjā)* or similar ostentatious rituals involving the breaking of flowers and other acts of violence. On the contrary, the scriptures prescribed possessionlessness and strict asceticism: nonviolence, self-restraint, and penance. Loṅkā, therefore, rejected both image-worship and the authority of fourteen (or fifteen) of the forty-five canonical texts that contain references to it. He also denounced the legitimacy of the existing image-worshipping monastic orders and started to live as an uninitiated ascetic, following the oldest textual prescriptions himself.

The surviving original sources for Loṅkā's biography and doctrine are not entirely reliable. But most texts agree that, in contrast to common practice, Loṅkā accepted alms from all castes but no money, that he did not possess a mouth-mask *(mukhavāstrikā)*, a stick *(daṇḍa)*, or a broom *(rajoharaṇa)*, and that he practiced neither image-worship nor the Jain rites of purification *(pratikramaṇa* and *posaḍha)*, which also involved elements of image-worship. Loṅkā quickly gained a large following among the Jains in Gujarat. Although he did not create a monastic order himself, he laid down instructions for his followers. The original texts were thought to be lost until 1964, when D.D. Malvaniya claimed to have rediscovered them in the L.D. Institute library in Ahmedabad in the form of anonymously written manuscripts: *Luṅkā Nā (Luṅkā Nī Huṇḍī) Aṭhāvan Bolo* and *Luṅkā Nī Huṇḍī*.

The Loṅkāgaccha mendicant tradition was formed by Loṅkā's first disciple, Bhāṇa, who apparently initiated himself and forty-five followers of Loṅkā's doctrine sometime between 1471 and 1476 by accepting the five great vows of the Jain ascetics *(mahāvrata)*. In the first decades of the sixteenth century the Loṅkāgaccha split into several more or less organized regional or revisionist Loṅkāgaccha groups, most of which comprised lay-ascetics, or *yatis*, who did not accept all of the five great vows or reverted to image worship. In the mid-sixteenth century, the Loṅkā tradition was split into more than thirteen independent branches, which further divided into separate subgroups. Until the demise of the Loṅkāgacch *yatis* in the nineteenth and twentieth centuries, only four branches survived: the Lāhaurī Loṅkāgaccha (founded c. 1504); the Nāgaurī Loṅkāgaccha (c. 1528); the Gujarātī Loṅkāgaccha Moṭā Pakṣ (Varsiṅha Pakṣ, or Keśav Pakṣ) (c. 1555); and the Gujarātī Loṅkāgaccha Nāṇa Pakṣ (Kuṃvar Pakṣ) (c. 1555).

In protest against the renaissance of image-worship and the renewed laxity of conduct of most Loṅkāgaccha (lay) ascetics, five reformers — the so-called *pañca muni* — split off from the Keśav Pakṣ, the Kuṃvar Pakṣ, and the Ekal Pātriyā Panth (a lay movement of unknown origin) in the early sixteenth century and founded the principal Sthānakavāsī mendicant traditions, which still exist today. The five traditions share three doctrinal characteristics: (1) rejection of image-worship,(2) strict ascetic conduct in accordance with the prescriptions in the thirty-two accepted Jain scriptures, and (3) compulsory use of a mouthmask to prevent the swallowing of living beings such as insects and dust. The square white mouthmask is now the principal external feature of all Sthānakavāsī mendicants (the Terāpanth Śvetāmbara mendicants use a rectangular blue mask). Sthānakavāsī laity generally reject material forms of worship *(dravya)* and practice only asceticism *(tapas)* and inner forms of worship *(bhāva)*, such as meditation *(dhyāna)* and study *(svādhyāya)*. Instead of images, they venerate the mendicants as living symbols of the Jain ideals.

They also practice *dayā dharma*, the religious work of compassionate help *(dāna)* for animals and human beings, in order to accumulate merit *(puṇya)* and thus to advance on the path of salvation. These three typical forms of ritual practice are known under the titles *guṇa pūjā, deva guru,* and *dāna-dayā.* In 1760, Muni Bhīkhaṇ, the founder of the TERĀPANTH ŚVETĀMBARA JAIN TRADITION, severed himself from the Dharmadāsa Sthānakavāsī tradition because he rejected merit-making as such, in favor of a purely salvation-oriented ascetic style of life.

The Sthānakavāsī Jain tradition is presently divided into twenty-six mendicant orders whose origins can be traced to one or more of the five principal reformers *(kriyā uddhāra)* of the aniconic Jain tradition, although the available sources are in consistent:(1) Jīvarāja has been made responsible for all crucial innovations of the Sthānakavāsī tradition, though some sources give priority to Lava. He lived sometime between 1524 and 1641 (probably having been born in Surat) and separated himself from the Kuṃvar Pakṣ in 1551, 1609, or 1629. Apparently it was he who selected the thirty-two Śvetāmbara scriptures that are now accepted by all Sthānakavāsīs (possibly by adding the *Vyavahārasūtra* or the *Āvaśyakasūtra* or both to Loṅkā's list, but there is no compelling evidence), and who introduced the mouthmask *(mūhapatti)*, the *rajoharaṇ*, and other paraphernalia used by present-day Sthānakavāsī mendicants.(2) Dharmasiṃha (1599-1671) severed himself from the Kuṃvar Pakṣ in 1628, 1635, or 1644 in Dariyāpurī in Ahmedabad and founded the Āṭh Koṭi (eight class) tradition. He was a scholar and wrote vernacular commentaries *(ṭabbo)* on the Prakrit Jain scriptures. He introduced a special pratikramaṇa rite for his lay followers and taught that there is no accidental death, because the lifespan of a living being is determined by its own karma. (3) Lava or Lavjī Ṛṣi (c. 1609-1659), the founder of the Ḍhuṇḍhiyā (seeker) tradition, also known under the name Ṛṣi Saṃpradāya, was born in Surat and split from the Keśav Pakṣ in 1637, 1648, 1653-1655, or 1657. (4) The founder of the Bāīsṭola (twenty-two schools) tradition, Dharmadāsa (1645-1703) from Ahmedabad, was originally a member of the Ekal Pātriyā Panth, but under the influence of Lava and Dharmasiṃha founded his own tradition in 1660 through self-initiation. (5) Hāra, the ancestor of the Sādhumārgī tradition (a branch of the extinct Kota Saṃpradāya), separated himself from the Kuṃvar Pakṣ in 1668 or 1728.

The name *Sthānakavāsī* (hall-dwellers), though in evidence in a text written in 1630, was not regularly used as a common designation for all five traditions until the unification movement of the early twentieth century. Doctrinally, only Dharmasiṃha's Āṭh Koṭi tradition in Gujarat differs significantly from the other four schools, which disagree only on minor points of philosophy and ritual. The Sthānakavāsī traditions as a whole nowadays are divided along regional lines between the Gujarātī and the non-Gujarātī (North Indian) traditions. The non-Gujarātī traditions are further subdivided into those who joined the reformist and centrally organized Śramaṇasaṅgha, which was founded in 1952 in Sadari in Rajasthan in a merely partially successful attempt to unite all Sthānakavāsī groups, and those who remained outside or left the Śramaṇasaṅgha. Both the Śramaṇasaṅgha and the independent traditions include mendicant orders that derive from four of the five main Sthānakavāsī traditions (the exception is the Āṭh Koṭi tradition), which were split into some thirty-three different organized groups at the beginning of the twentieth century. Although they are nominally under the command of one single *ācārya* whose consent is essential for all initiations and excommunications (at present, Ācārya Dr. Śivmuni), the original twenty-two founding traditions of the Śramanasaṅgha continue to operate within its framework more or less independently.

Some monastic orders never joined the Śramaṇasaṅgha, among them all Gujarātī Sthānakavāsī traditions, the Jñānagaccha of the Dharmadāsa Rāmratna tradition (founded by Jñānacandra, Ujjain 1732), and the Nānakgaccha of the Jīvarāja tradition (Nānakrām, eighteenth century). Because of perpetual discord between the founding traditions, many disappointed senior ascetics left the Śramaṇasaṅgha again and established their own independent groups: Muni Hagāmīlāl, and the modernist Arhat Saṅgha (Suśīl Kumār 1926-1994, New Jersey, 1974) of the Jīvarāja tradition; the Māyārām Saṃpradāya (Māyārām,1854-1912) of the northern Lava tradition; Ācārya Nānālāl of the Hara Sādhumārgī tradition (Hukmīcand, early nineteenth century); and four groups of the Dharmadāsa tradition: the Jamyamalagaccha (Jaymal, 1708-1796; Rajasthan,1748 or 1783); the Ratnavaṃś (Ratnacandra, Rajasthan,1796); the Dharmadāsa Saṃpradāya (Umeśmuni, late twentieth century) and Upādhyāy Amarmuni (1901-1992), the inspirational force behind the modern Vīrāyatan order, which was founded by Sādhvī Candanā in Ragriha,1974.

None of the Gujarātī groups joined the Śramaṇasaṅgha, which is essentially a Hindi-speaking order. With the exception of the Khambhāt Saṃpradāya (Lava, Ahmedabad, 1648) and the three

Āṭh Koṭi traditions — the Dariyāpurī Āṭh Koṭi Saṃpradāya (Dharmasiṃha, Ahmedabad, 1628); the Kacch Āṭh Koṭi Moṭā Pakṣ (Kṛṣṇa, originally Dharmadāsa Saṃpradāya, Kacch 1715-1782); and the Kacch Āṭh Koṭi Nāṇā Pakṣ (Jasraj, Kacch, 1786) — the majority of the independent Sthānakavāsī traditions in Gujarat descend from Mūlacandra (1651-1725), one of Dharmadāsa's twenty-two leading monks. Mūlacandra's main disciples formed separate local groups after a dispute at a mendicant assembly in 1788 in Limbḍī. Not all of the emerging Gujarātī Dharmadāsa traditions survived, and some of them split further into subgroups labeled great *(moṭā)* and small *(nānā)*. The seven principal orders of today are all named after the place of origin that is also their main seat: Limbaḍī Cha Koṭi Moṭā Pakṣ (founded by Ajrāmar, Limbaḍī, 1788); Limbaḍī Cha Koṭi Nānā Pakṣ (Hemcand and Gopāl, Limbaḍī, 1859); Goṇḍal Moṭā Pakṣ (Ḍuṅgarśī, Goṇḍal, 1788); Goṇḍal Saṅghaṇī (Gaṅga Svāmī, Goṇḍal, 1794); Barvāḷā (Moṭā Kahān, Barvāḷā, 1788); Boṭād (Jasā, Boṭād, c. 1850); and Sāyalā (Nāga, Sāyalā,1772-1812). They are not led by an elected administrator cum teacher *(ācārya)*, like the independent traditions outside Gujarat, but by the male ascetic with the highest monastic age, or *dīkṣā paryāya,* who may or may not be called *ācārya.* His main decisions have to agree with those of the often hereditary leader *(saṅghapati)* of the lay community.

The overall number of Sthānakavāsī mendicants is much higher than generally assumed. In 1999 there were 3,223 mendicants, 533 *sadhus,* and 2,690 *sādhvīs* — that is, 27.5 percent of all Jain mendicants, distributed in roughly equal proportions among the Śramaṇasaṅgha (1,096), twelve Independent traditions (967), and the thirteen Gujarātī traditions (1,160). The nationwide umbrella organization of the Sthānakavāsī laity, the All India Śvetāmbara Sthānakavāsī Jain Conference, the motivating force behind the movement toward unity, was founded in 1906 in Morvi in Gujarat, but it split in 1984 into two independent organizations because of the irreconcilable differences in ritual, culture, and language between Gujarātī and Hindi speaking Sthānakavāsī traditions.

Addresses:

Akhil Bharatvarsiya Śvetāmbara Sthānakavāsī
Jain Conference(Hindi)
Jain Bhavan
12 Sahid Bhagat Singh Marg
New Delhi 101001 (India)

Akhil Bhāratvarṣīya Śvetāmbara Sthānakavāsī Jain Conference (Gujarātī)
1 Vijay Vallabh Cauk
Paydhuni
Mumbai 400 002 (India)

Sources:

Flügel, Peter. "Protestantische und Post-Protestantische Jaina-Reformbewegungen: Zur Geschichte und Organisation der Sthānakavāsī I." *Berliner Indologische Studien* 13-14 (2000): 37-103.

——. "Protestantische und Post-Protestantische Jaina-Reformbewegungen: Zur Geschichte und Organisation der Sthānakavāsī II.' *Berliner Indologische Studien* 15-17 (2003):149-240.

Hastīmal, Ācārya. *Jain Dharma Kā Maulik Itihās.* Vol. 4. Jaypur: Jain Itihās Samiti, 1987, 1995.

Hastīmal, Ācārya, comp. *Paṭṭāvalī Prabandha Saṅgraha.* Edited by Narendra Bhanawat. Jaipur: Jain Itihās Nirmāṇ Samiti, 1968.

Jñānasundara, Muni *Śrīmad Lauṃkāśāh.* Phalodī. Śrī Jñāna Puṣpamālā,1936.

Mālvaṇiyā, D. "Lokāśāh Aur Unkī Vicār-Dhārā." In *Gurudev Śrī Ratna Muni Smṛti-Granth,* edited by Vijay Muni Śāstri and Harīśankar Śarmā, pp. 365-383. Āgrā: Gurudev Smṛti Granth Prakāśak Samiti, 1964.

Maṇilāl, Muni. *Śrī Jaindharmano Prācīn Saṅkṣipt Itihās Ane Prabhu Vīr Paṭṭāvalī.* Amadāvād: Jīvanlāl Chaganlāl Saṅghvī, 1934.

3

Historical Sources on the Loṅkāgaccha- and Sthānakavāsī-Traditions in Johannes Klatt's Jaina-Onomasticon[1]

In the absence of extensive archaeological evidence, monastic chronologies and hagiographies, inscriptions and the information in the colophons of handwritten or printed Jaina texts are almost the only sources available for the reconstruction of Jaina religious and social history. This fact was highlighted by Walther Schubring who, in his classical work on the Śvetāmbara doctrines of the Jainas, emphasised that '[a]ll history of literature, a building, as it were, has for its ground-floor the bio-bibliographical materials.'[2] Schubring lamented the early demise of Johannes Emil Klatt (1852-1908) who had dedicated his short life to the study of the historical records of the Jainas. Klatt left behind the nearly completed manuscript of his monumental *Jaina-Onomasticon*, a collection of proper names (Greek: *onoma*) of Jaina authors, legendary figures, texts and place names with explanatory historical notes, handwritten in English, which is still unpublished. 'Jain research would have enjoyed the great luck of having them [the Jaina bio-biographical materials] at its disposal, if Klatt's Onomasticon had been completed and printed,' Schubring wrote. 'Eight volumes from his own hand in alphabetical order contain what was within his reach to collect data concerning Jain authors and works. But he fell severely ill and never recovered. The work was estimated to fill some 1,100 pages in print, but no more than 55 pages have been printed as a specimen thanks to Weber and Leumen.'[3]

Few biographical details are known about Johannes Klatt. The only sources are brief notes in academic publications of his teacher and colleagues and in the autobiography of his son Fritz Klatt.[4] He was born on 31.1.1852 in Filehne, Posen, and died after a long illness in Bonn on 28.8.1908. He studied Indology under Albrecht Weber (1825-1901)in Berlin between 1868 and 1872 and in 1873 completed his doctorate at the University of Halle with a dissertation entitled *De trecentis Cāṇakyae poetae indici sententiis.*[5] Klatt worked at the Royal Library in Berlin, part time from 1872, as assistant from 1874, then as *Kustos* (custodian) from October 1880 and finally as *Bibliothecarius* (librarian) from April 1889.[6] He was married to Margarete *née* Patzig (1861-1928) with whom he had two sons, the pedagogue Fritz Klatt (1888-1945), who pioneered adult education in the Weimar Republic,[7] and the painter Albert Klatt (1892-1970). Klatt's published research focused on Jaina manuscripts and on the history of Jaina monasticism, based on the available chronologies and biographies. In his preface of 15 October 1892 to the fifty-five page revised edition of a sample of Klatt's *magnum opus*, Klatt's teacher Albrecht Weber (1892: iii) referred to the 'tragic catastrophe' that prematurely ended Klatt's efforts of ten years to complete his *Jaina-Onomasticon*, apparently because he had 'unduly exerted himself' for this 'grandiose' achievement, and in future would probably never be able to work again 'at the same speed.' At the time, Weber still expressed his hope that Klatt would recover, which he never did. Yet, already on 21 April 1892, because Klatt was no longer able to do so himself, Weber had presented to the Royal Prussian Academy of Sciences a specimen of Klatt's work, featuring information on important Śvetāmbara commentators such as Abhayadeva, Umāsvāti, Haribhadra, Jinabhadra and all other names beginning with Jina.[8]

A biographical note on Klatt was published during his lifetime by Klatt's '*gurubhāī*' and friend Ernst Leumann (1859-1931).[9] It took the form of a mock *paṭṭāvalī*, which turned out to be one of the main sources of our meagre knowledge of the great chronographer's own life:

> 'The chronology of his life, presented by way of one of the Paṭṭāvalīs so happily brought to light by his researches, is as follows: Johannes Klatt: born 1852 A.D. as the son of the postmaster of Filehne (in the Prussian province of Posen); dīkshā (matriculation) at the Berlin University 1868; after four years' study there, he took his Doctor's degree by presenting (see Boehtlingk's Indische Sprüche, 2nd ed., Part III, Preface) a paper on "Chāṇakya's Sentences" to the University of Halle; 1873 'Volunteer' at the Berlin Royal Library (still earning his living for a couple of years as official stenographist in the Prussian House of Commons), 1880 'Custos,' 1882-92 (nominally also 1893) "Librarian."'[10]

In his note, published as a footnote to Klatt's last published work, Leumann also mentioned that no further contribution of Klatt 'can come from his pen,' and noted the 'irreparable loss' caused by the sudden 'disappearance from literature' of 'the eminent Indianistic Chronicler and Bibliographist' 'as a year or two more of work would have allowed him to complete what has been slowly growing into shape in his study during the past ten years' (ibid.). Leumann was familiar with Klatt's work. Over many years, he supplied his friend with supplementary information for the *Jaina-Onomasticon*.[11] In addition to editing the last fifteen pages of the *Specimen*, which Klatt had prepared before his progressing illness rendered work impossible, Leumann also brought Klatt's last article to publication, and in 1893 took over the task of arranging the parts of the text that Klatt left behind. He had them 'bound into eight stately volumes' (ibid.), which his student Schubring later deposited in the library of the Seminar für Kultur und Geschichte Indiens, which is now integral to the library of the Asien-Afrika-Institut of the University of Hamburg.

Klatt's encyclopaedic compilation of literary-bibliographical information on Jaina authors, texts and biographies is still without parallel. Mehta and Chandra's (1970-72) work *Prakrit Proper Names* covers somewhat similar ground. But Mehta and Chandra focus exclusively on the Śvetāmbara *Āgamas* and their commentaries however, while Klatt concentrates on post-canonical sources from both Digambara and Śvetāmbara authors. Klatt based his work on the lists of Jaina manuscripts published by Weber (1853-1892), Bühler (1869-1880), Bhandarkar (1882-1897), Kielhorn (1869-1882), Peterson (1882-1899), Khatavate (1891-1901) and all other relevant textual, bibliographical and epigraphic sources at hand.[12] His search for information motivated family holidays, for instance in Italy, where he conducted research on the manuscript collections of Florence, Milan, and elsewhere.[13]

Even without updates, for the historian of Jainism Klatt's *Jaina-Onomasticon* is an invaluable resource. This was recognised by his contemporaries. Klatt's text was praised both by A. Weber, E. Leumann[14] and W. Schubring as one of the landmarks of modern scholarship in this field. They all agreed that the 4,132 pages long manuscript, starting with <Aïara> and ending with <Hlāsiyā>, was ready for publication, albeit with two or three years of editing work remaining. On 15 October 1892, A. Weber (1892: iii-iv) estimated the size of the printed *Onomasticon* at ca. 1120 pages, twenty times the size of the *Specimen*, if a system of abbreviations is used to save space, while conceding, because Jaina Studies was still in its infancy, that additions could have been made already half a year later, even to the published *Specimen.*[15] Schubring (1935 § 4: 8, n. 2) concurred with Weber's verdict that the manuscript was basically ready for publication (albeit in need of supplementation): 'At the time, the manuscript would presumably have been ready for the press, given a practicable technique of abbreviation and onesided type.' Yet, though the work deserves to be accessible to the wider world of scholarship, Johannes Klatt's *Jaina-Onomasticon* remains unpublished to this day. The task to prepare the manuscript for the press is still a *desideratum* for modern Jainology.

In 2010, the Centre of Jaina Studies at SOAS initiated the first steps towards the publication of Klatt's work. With the support of the Library of the Asien-Afrika-Institut in Hamburg, which kindly made the original manuscript available, the text is currently being transcribed and prepared for editing. An initial trial for its transcription has been funded through the Arts and Humanities Research Council (AHRC) Grant AH/I002405/1 and Leverhulme Trust Research Project Grant RPG-2012-620 has funded the production of a print edition of Klatt's text. It is hoped that the English text, once published both in print and in an expandable electronic format, will serve as a valuable research tool to future generations of scholarship.

'Luṅkā' and 'Ḍhuṇḍhaka'

The remainder of this article is devoted to a brief illustration, at the hand of two examples, the terms 'Luṅkā' and 'Ḍhuṇḍhaka' of the difficulties faced by the editors of this text, and an analysis of the implications of the sources available to Klatt on his text. To assess the feasibility of the project, selected texts from Klatt's Vol. III and IV have been transcribed by Christopher Gibbons and the present writer. Klatt's text and the references mentioned therein were checked (as far as possible) and, in parts, corrected and re-formatted; sometimes following suggestions by Klatt, who structured his text occasionally according to the historical sequence of *his* primary sources, that is, mainly catalogues and reports on manuscript collections. Nāgarī keywords were transliterated into Roman script. To make the text more accessible, indentations, italics and small caps were added. For Klatt's abbreviation 'S.' (Saṃvat), 'VS' (Vikram

Saṃvat) is used. Abbreviations such as 'Ḍh.' (Ḍhuṇḍhaka), 'a.' (anna), fr.b. (from bottom), 'l.' (line[s], or leave[s]), n. (catalogue number, or note), s. (see), and acronyms for references have been spelled out in this article to enhance readability. Others, like p. (page), Guj. (Gujarātī), and others such as rg. possibly referring to an officially 'registered' nineteenth century print publication, have been maintained. Missing diacritics, for instance in 'Lálaji' (Lālajī), have also occasionally been supplemented. The aim of consistency could however not be accomplished. Systematically imposing new editorial conventions to disambiguate Klatt's use of abbreviations and acronyms will obliterate much of the historical information preserved in the text. Klatt generally accepted the diverse methods of transcribing Indic words used in his sources and merely added analytical word-divisions. This makes his manuscript stylistically incoherent. At the same time, it offers valuable insights in the fluid state of knowledge amongst leading scholars of the period confronting a flood of entirely new information. 'Ḍhuṇḍhaka,' for instance, is rendered as 'Ḍhuṇḍhakar,' 'Dhundhiā' or 'Dhundiā,' though only the category 'Ḍhuṇḍhaka' is listed. Instead of the now preferred term 'Loṅkā,' 'Luṅkā' is used. However, another entry designating the same individual is 'Laukā.'

Only the proper name 'Luṅkā' and the sect-designations 'Lumpāka-matam' and 'Ḍhuṇḍhaka-matam' and some related names listed in the *Onomasticon* will be investigated here to probe into Klatt's methods and sources. Klatt's manuscript is of considerable value for identifying rare and yet unexplored sources, not least for the study of the aniconic or 'protestant' Jaina traditions, which have produced only few original texts in their more than five hundred year long history, since they put a premium on the sole authority of the *āgamas.* Many of their surviving scriptures continue to be suppressed by their opponents from the image-worshipping Jaina traditions. The aniconic traditions were launched in fifteenth century Gujarāt as a protest movement against the 'laxity' of contemporary mendicants by a Śvetāmbara layman known as 'Loṅkā' or 'Lumpaka,' the 'breaker' of images or 'violator' of tradition, who inspired the creation of the Loṅkāgaccha mendicant orders, from which a variety of new reform movements split in the seventeenth century which are now collectively known as 'Sthānakavāsī' or 'hall-dweller'[16] traditions. One of the original five of these schismatic aniconic monastic movements are the 'Ḍhuṇḍakas,' or 'searchers,' called 'Ḍhūṃḍhakas,' the ruin-dwellers[17] by their Jaina opponents. This particular 'Sthānakavāsī tradition was created by Lavajī Ṛṣi from Surat sometime between 1648 and 1656.[18] Most of the founders of the other four principal Sthānakavāsī movements, such as Dharmasiṅha,[19] the founder of the Āṭh Koṭi tradition, and Dharmadāsa,[20] the founder of the Bāīstola tradition, and a few of their successors, are also registered in the Jaina-Onomasticon, and some of their literature.

The full real name of 'Loṅkā' is unknown.[21] Ācārya Hastīmal[22] notes that Loṅkā is variously called *lumpaka* (which he interprets as *luṭerā*, thief) or *luṅgā* (which he interprets as *luccā*, scoundrel), etc., by his opponents. A. Weber[23] and D.D. Mālvaṇiyā[24] interpret *lumpaka* as the Sanskrit rendering of *luṃkā* (*lauṃkā*), the 'breaker' or 'destroyer' of (the worship of) images or of the tradition (from the Sanskrit "√lup, to break, violate; *lopaka*, violating). See Turner (1966/1973: 643,645) on *lupyatē*, and for the uncertain meaning of *luṅka*, which he hypothetically derives from *lukka* (Sub. *lupta*). At the time of Klatt, whatever was known about the aniconic Jaina traditions was based on reports from their Mūrtipūjaka critics, such as Dhamasāgara-gaṇin (d. 1596)[25] and Ācārya Vijayānandasūri (1836-1896), also known as Ātmārāma (his earlier Sthānakavāsī name) or Ātmānanda (his Mūrtipūjaka name), with whom many European Indologists communicated via letter and intermediaries.[26] Hence, the polemical term *Luṅkā* was used to describe the founder of the Lumpaka tradition and the *Ḍhūṃḍhakas* are listed under the name *Ḍhuṇḍhaka*.

Most of the references to primary sources on Loṅkā and the members and literatures of the Loṅkāgacchas collected by Klatt and others have not yet been systematically studied.[27] The following are the main entries he gives on Loṅkā and the Lumpākamatam:[28]

LUṄKĀ Lekhaka[29] founded VS 1508 the *Luṅkā-matam jinapratimotthāpana-param*, INDIAN ANTIQUARY XI 256[a] no. 52, WEBER II 1013 line 14-5,[30] AJÑĀNA-TIMIRABHĀSKARA, kh[aṇḍa]. 2, p. 43.

Ratnacanda of the Vṛihan-nāgorī-Luṅkā-gaccha VS 1942, WEBER II 788 line 9-10.[31]

Rājasiṅha and Raghunātha, VS 1857, of the Vṛihal-lauṅkā-gaccha, see PĀRÇVA-JINAVARA-MAHIMAḤ STOTRA, Kāçī 1880, p. 32.[32]

Jaina-tattvādarça, p. 583 following succession: ṛishi Bhāṇā (Bhānaka, Bhaṇḍārkar Report 1883/4 p. 154) VS 1533, Rūpajī 1568, Jīvājī-ṛishi 1578, Vṛiddha-vara-Siṅhajī 1649, isa Lumpaka-mata ke tīna nāma hūe, 1 Gujarātī, 2 Nāgorī, 3 Uttarādhī iti Lumpaka-matotpattiḥ.

Miles. Transactions of the Royal asiatic society III 346 mentions a Lunca Paṭṭāvalī.[33]

Origin VS 1527, Zeitschrift der Deutschen Morgenländischen Gesellschaft 38, [p.] 9,[34] in Aṇahalla-pattana in Gujara-deça by Luṅka of the Prāgvaṭa-kula, ib. p. 13. 40.[35]

Çrī-Loka-gacchīya-Çrāvakasya sārtha-pañca-pratikramaṇa-sūtra, Bombay, Jagadīçvar press 1883. 236 p. Rs. 1. Succession from Hīrākara-sūri VS 1640 till Amṛtacandra-sūri VS 1939, see... [?] Bhagavatī, Ben. [Benares] VS 1938, title.

Rāmacandra-gaṇi and his pupil Nānakacanda VS 1937, see Sthānāṅga ed. Ben. VS 1937. Tejasiṅgha VS 1766, Lokag[acchīya]-Pratikr[amaṇa-sūtra], Bomb[ay] 1887, p. 219-35.

Lonka-gacchīya-çrāvakasya sārtha-pañca-pratikramaṇa-sūtra, Bombay Jagadiçvar press 1882. 218 p. Re. 1. 4a (Catalogue Bombay 1882 IV 16-7).

VS 1572 Rūpacand Sorānā of his own accord put on the monks' garb and originated the Nāgorī Lumpaka sect, Ātmārāmjī's paṭṭa-vṛiksha (Hoernle).

Nāga-purīyāhvā Luṅkā-gaṇe at the end of Anuttaraupapātika, Calc[utta], Lokā-gacchīya çrāvakasya sārtha-pañca-pratikramaṇa-sūtra. 3. ed. Bombay, Jagadiçvār Press VS 1943, 6, 270 p. [...]

Lumpākamatam[36] Indian Antiquary XI 256ª n. 55, Weber II 1013 line 24, 30.[37] From it the Vīja-matam arose VS 1570.

ib. 1013f. line 25. Journal of the Bombay Branch of the Royal Asiatic Society I 98 n. 23.

Lumpāka-mukhya-kumata combatted by Vimalaharsha, Ms. Or. Fol. 673 n. 32.

Lumpākānāṃ pratimā-nishedhaḥ their principal heresy, Bhāṇḍārkar Report 1883/4 p.456 line 7 from bottom. Weber II 956 note [3].

Lumpaka-gaṇopāsaka Rāya [Bāhādur] Dhanapatisiṅha, see Samavāyāṅga, ed. Ben[ares] VS 1937.[38]

Lupaka-gacche çrī Amṛitacandra-sūri, see Aupapātika, ed. VS 1936.[39]

Lavajī, grandson of Borā Vīrajī of the Lumpaka sect originated VS 1709 the Ḍhuṇḍhaka sect. Likhārī of the Lumpaka sect originated VS 1734 a sect which rejects the Jina image and the holy scripture.[40]

LUMPĀKAMATAKUṬṬANA comp. by followers of the Kharatara-gaccha VS 1687, beg[ins] Natvā çruta-jñānam-ananta-bhedaṃ, 21 [leaves] BENDALL JOURN[EY] p. 47, 63.[41] [...]

LAUKĀ[42] lekhaka erected VS 1608 a statue in Ahamadāvāda,[43] there the Laukā-matam arose VS 1524, INDIAN ANTIQUARY XI 249^b n. 57, WEBER II 1050 line 7-8, INDIAN ANTIQUARY VIII 311.[44]

In contrast to 'Luṅkā' and 'Lumpākamatam,' 'Lumpākamata-kuṭṭana' and 'Laukā,' the main entry on 'Ḍhuṇḍhaka' includes references to primary literature of this monastic tradition, in particular a *paṭṭāvalī*. One text, however, the *Aṭṭhāvana bolo* was most likely composed by Loṅkā himself.[45] Textual references are presented by Klatt generally after the historical data related to an author or tradition. However, further additions were simply appended in the manuscript:[46]

ḌHUṆḌHAKA-matam originated VS 1709 under Vijayaprabha-sūri †VS 1749, JAINA TATTVĀDARŚA, p. 592.

The Ḍhuṇḍhakas separated VS 1724 from the Luṅkas, MILES TRANSACTIONS III, p. 365. They do not worship images, according to the Persian work MIRĀT I AHMADĪ, even 355.[47]

Controversies between the Dhondhiās and Tapās, see GAZETTEER OF THE BOMBAY PRESIDENCY, vol. 8, Kāthiāvār, p.148 note 2.

Jeṭhmaljī of the Dhundhiā sect composed before 75 years *Samakita-sār*, CATALOGUE BOMBAY 1888 II 70.[48]

Ātmārāmajī is said to have been a Ḍh[uṇḍhaka], ib.

Dhundhiāno rāsado, or a poem relating to a sect called Dhundiā. Guj., by Uttama Vijaya. Ahmedābād, Nāran Krishnarām 1869. 12 p. 4°, lith. 2 a[nna], see CATALOGUE BOMBAY 1869 III 6.

Siddhānta-sāranī Ḍhālo, or verses giving substance of the established truth, Guj., Ahmedabad 1887. 32 p. 2 a[nna] (condemns the worship of an image of any of the tīrthaṅkars, as well as pilgrimage to holy places),[49] see CATALOGUE BOMBAY 1888 I 24.

Bṛihad-āloyanā, or the great work on return from sin, Mārvādi. By Lālājī Sāheb Ranajita-siṅha-jī. Ahmedabad, Union Printing Press, published by Chaganlāl Behecardās 1888. 48 p. 3 a[nna] (A tract of the Dhundiyā sect), see CATALOGUE BOMBAY 1888 IV 42.[50]

Aṭṭhāvana bola,[51] Guj., KUNTE REPORT 1881 p. 48 n[umber] 225. Founded by Lābhājī from Surat, son of Bīro Birjī Srī Māl and Phulā Bāī, see MONIER-WILLIAMS, JOURNAL OF THE ROYAL ASIATIC SOCIETY N.S. 20 (1888) 286.[52] KUNTE REPORT 1880-1881, dated 24. January 1881 p. 3-4 (dated 6. June 1881 p. 4).[53]

In VS 1709, Lavajī, the adopted son of Phūlā Bāī, the daughter of the Borā Vīrajī, of the Lumpaka sect, together with Dharmadās, the cotton printer, originated the sect (panth) of the mouth-covering Ḍh[uṇḍhaka]. These divided into 22 sections,[54] COMMUNICATION OF ĀTMĀRĀMJĪ.

Opposite to the Ḍh[uṇḍakas] is *Vīra-stuti,* composed VS 1849, PRAKARAṆA-RATNĀKARA III p. 569-696.

Dhūdhūkā-gaccha, name of a gaccha in GACCHA-NĀMĀNUKRAMAṆIKĀ No. 60.

Ḍhuṇḍhakamatotpatti, see SAMAKITA-SALYODDHĀRA Bombay 1885 p. 1-8.

Ḍhuṇḍhakamata-paṭṭāvalī, ib. p. 8-11.

Ḍhūṇḍhaka-mata-nirākaraṇa, printed R[upee]s 3, CATALOGUE JYEṢṬHARAM MUKUNDJEE 1892, p. 13ª.

ḌHUṆḌHAKOTPATTI by Lakṣmīvijaya, 4 l[eaves]. PETERSON REPORT III Appendix [II] p. 213 n. 39.[55]

Concluding remarks

The brief review of the entries on Luṅkāmatam and Ḍhuṇḍhakamatam, etc., shows that a lot could have been learned about the aniconic traditions already more than a century ago had Johannes Klatt's yet unpublished *magnum opus* been utilized. Since this was not done, hardly any of the standard textbooks on Jainism offers even basic information on the aniconic traditions, with the exception of the well known work by Paul Dundas, which made a start. Even Klatt's information stemmed largely from the works of opponents of the protestant traditions. This was unavoidable at the time, since no other information was made available. The state of knowledge on the aniconic traditions reflected in the pages of the *Jaina-Onomasticon* is still embryonic and in itself unreliable, which probably is the reason why it was shunned by previous generations of indological scholarship.[56] However, it points to yet untapped sources the critical study of which will lead to more certain reconstructions of the history of a tradition which today comprises of about one third of all Jainas.

Sources Used By Klatt

Ātmārāma, Ācārya [Vijayānandasūri, also: Ātmānanda]. *Jainatattvādarśa.* Bhāg 1 & 2. Ed. Banārsīdās Jain. Pañcama Saṃskaraṇa. Bambaī: Ātmānanda Jaina Sabhā, 1881/1954.

—. *Samyaktva Śalyoddhāra.* Lahore: Ātmānanda Jaina Sabhā Pañjāb, [1885] 1884/1909. [Hindī translation of the original Gujarātī text]

—. *Ajñānatimirabhāskara.* Mumbai: Jainadharma Hitecchu Sabhā, 1888/1906 (2. Edition: Jaina Ātmānand Sabhā in Bhāvnagar).

—. *Paṭṭa-vṛiksha* (Hoernle).

—. Communication by Letter with J. Klatt.

Bayley, Edward Clive. *The History of India As Told by Its Own Historians: The Local Muhammadan Dynasties. Gujarāt.* London: W.H. Allen and Co., Publishers to the India Office, 1886 (Reprint: S. Chand & Co., 1970).

BENDALL JOURNEY. *See* Bendall 1886.

Bendall, Cecil. *A Journey of Literary and Archaeological Research in Nepal and Northern India, During the Winter of 1884–85.* Cambridge: University Press, 1886 (Appendix II: Rough List of MSS. In the Jain Mandir at Rāmghāt, Benares).[57]

Bhandarkar, Ramakrishna Gopal. *Report on the Search for Sanskrit Manuscripts in the Bombay Presidency During the Year 1883-1884.* Bombay: Government Central Press, 1887.

Bhandarkar, Shridhar Ramakrishna. *Report of a Second Tour in Search of Sanskrit Manuscripts made in Rajputana and Central India in 1904-05 and 1905-06.* Bombay: The Government Central Press, 1907.

Bhandarkar, Shridhar Ramakrishna (Comp.). *A Catalogue of the ... [Sanskrit] Manuscripts Deposited in the Deccan College [Poona].* With an Index. Bombay: Government Central Press, 1888.

CATALOGUE BOMBAY. *See* Sāthe.

Catalogue of Sanskrit Books for Sale at the Pandit Jyeshtharam Mukundjee's Book Depot. Bombay 1892 [Electronic Reproduction: Hathi Trust Digital Library, 2011].

Dharmasāgaragaṇi. *Gūrvāvalīsūtram* (Ms. Or. Fol. 997). In: Weber 1892: 997-1015.

GACCHA-NĀMĀNUKRAMAṆIKĀ.

Gazetteer of the Bombay Presidency. Vol. VIII. *Kāthiāwār.* Bombay: Government Central Press, 1889.

Hemacandrasūri, Ācārya. *Viśeṣāvaśyaka-vṛtti.* In: Weber (1888: 788).

Jacobi, Hermann. 'Ueber die Entstehung der Çvetāmbara und Digambara Sekten.' *Zeitschrift der Deutschen Morgenländischen Gesellschaft* 38 (1884) 1-42.

Journal of the Bombay Branch of the Royal Asiatic Society I.

Khān, Alī Muḥammad. *Mir 'āt-i Aḥmadī-i ṣūba-i Aḥmadābād Gugrāt. The Political and Statistical History of Gujarāt.* Translation of the Persian of Ali Mohammed Khān, the Revenue Minister of the Province; to which are Added, Copious Annotations, and an Historical Introduction by James Bird. London: Bentley, 1835 (Oriental Translation Fund 47).

—. 'Mirāt-i-Aḥmadī.' *See* Bayley 1886.

Kunte, Kāshi Nāth. *Report on Sanskrit Manuscripts for (1) Quarter July to September 1880, (2) Quarter Oct. to December 1880, (3) Year 1880-81, (4) Quarter April to June 1881.* Lahore, 1882. [BL: W 988]

Logan, William. 'The Six Tīrthaka.' *The Indian Antiquary* VIII (1879) 311-314.

Manāk, Bhīmasiṃha (ed.). *Prakaraṇa-ratnākara.* Vol. III (4 Vols). Bombay, 1876-78.

Miles, Lieut.-Colonel William. 'On the Jainas of Gujarat and Mārwār.' *Transactions of the Royal Asiatic Society of Great Britain and Ireland* 3 (1835) 335-371 (Communication of the Bombay Branch of the Royal Asiatic Society, Read 7th of January 1832).

Monier-Williams, William, Rang Lāl & (Colonel) William Davies. [32.1.1888: On the Jains.] In: Thomas Wade 'I. Reports of Meetings of the Royal Asiatic Society, Session 1887–88.' *Journal of the Royal Asiatic Society of Great Britain & Ireland N.S.* 20, 2 (1888) 277-288.

Paṭṭāvalīvācanā. Anonymous Text of the Kharataragaccha. In: A. Weber 1892: 1030-1056.

Peterson, Peter. *A Third Report of Operations in Search of Sanskrit Mss. in the Bombay Circle April 1884–March 1886.* Extra Number of the

Journal of the Bombay Branch of the Royal Asiatic Society. Bombay: Society's Library, Town Hall/London: Trübner & Co., 1887.

Ratnanandin, Ācārya. *Bhadrabāhucaritra* (15th-16th C.E.). *See* Jacobi (1884: 9).

Samavāyāṅga. Edited by Rāya Dhanapatisiṃha Bahādura. Benares, VS 1937 (1880).

Sāthe, G.M. (Registrar of Native Publications). *Catalogue of Books Printed in the Bombay Presidency*. During the Quarter Ending 31st March 1888 – 10th February 1891. Bombay: Government Central Press, 1888-1891.

Weber, Albrecht. *Verzeichniss der Sanskrit- und Prākṛit-Handschriften der Königlichen Bibliothek zu Berlin*. Zweiter Band. Erste Abtheilung. Die Handschriften-Verzeichnisse der Königlichen Bibliothek zu Berlin. Fünfter Band. Berlin: A.W. Schade, 1886.

—. *Verzeichniss der Sanskrit- und Prākṛit-Handschriften der Königlichen Bibliothek zu Berlin*. Zweiter Band, Zweite Abtheilung Die Handschriften-Verzeichnisse der Königlichen Bibliothek zu Berlin. Fünfter Band. Berlin: A. Asher & Co., 1888.

—. *Verzeichniss der Sanskrit- und Prākṛit-Handschriften der Königlichen Bibliothek zu Berlin*. Zweiter Band. Dritte Abtheilung. Die Handschriften-Verzeichnisse der Königlichen Bibliothek zu Berlin. Fünfter Band. Berlin: A. Asher & Co., 1892.

General Bibliography[58]

Bender, Ernest. 'An Early Nineteenth Century Study of the Jains.' *Journal of the American Oriental Society* 96, 1 (1976) 114-119.

Böhm, Winfried. 'Klatt, Fritz.' *Neue Deutsche Biographie* 11 (1977) 710-711.

Hartwig. O & K. Schultz (Hg.). *Centralblatt für Bibliothekswesen*. Leipzig: Otto Harrassowitz, 1884 ff.

Flügel, Peter. 'Protestantische und Post-Protestantische Jaina-Reformbewegungen: Zur Geschichte und Organisation der Sthānakavāsī I-IV.' *Berliner Indologische Studien* 13/14 (2000) 37-103, 15-17 (2003) 149-240, 18 (2007) 127-206, 20 (2012) 37-126.

—. 'The Unknown Loṅkā: Tradition and the Cultural Unconscious.' *Jaina Studies*. Papers of the 12th World Sanskrit Conference Vol. 9. Eds. Colette Caillat & Nalini Balbir, 181-278. Delhi: Motilal Banarsidas, 2008. (https://eprints.soas.ac.uk/3195/)

—. 'Changing Self-Perceptions: Reflections on the Social History of Modern Jainism.' *The Jaina and the British.* Universität Tübingen, 19.2.2010.

—. *Die Sthānakavāsī Śvetāmbara Jaina-Orden in Nordindien. Protestantische und Post-Protestantische Jaina-Reformbewegungen.* Wiesbaden: Harrasowitz Verlag (Forthcoming).

Hastīmal, Ācārya. *Jaina Dharma kā Maulik Itihās,* IV. Jaypur: Jaina Itihās Samiti, 1987/1995.

Jain, Sāgarmal & Vijay Kumār. *Sthānakavāsī Jain Paramparā kā Itihās.* Vārāṇasī: Pārśvanāth Vidyāpīṭh, 2003.

Klatt, Fritz. *Biographische Aufzeichnungen. Mit einer Vorbemerkung zu den Briefen von Gertrud Breysig und der Bibliographie seiner Schriften und Beiträge von Ursula Schulz.* Bremen: Bremer Volkshochschule, 1965 (Bremer Beiträge zur Freien Volksbildung, Heft 7).

Klatt, Johannes Emil. Klatt, Johannes. *De trecentis Cāṇakyae poetae Indici sententiis.* Dissertatio inauguralis philologica, quam consensu et auctoritate amplissimi philosophorum ordinis in Academia Fridericiana Halensi cum Vitebergensi consociata ad summos in philosophia honores capessendos d[ie] XV m[ensis]. Febr. a. MDCCCLXXIII hor[a]. XII una cum thesibus publice defendet scriptor Johannes Klatt Brombergensis : adversariorum partes susceperunt Konrad Zacher, cand. phil., Aemilius Gaessner, cand. phil. Academia Fridericiana, Halis Saxonum, 1873 (Berolini, Typis: A W. Schadii).

—. 'Dhanapāla's Ṛishabhapañcāçikā.' *Zeitschrift der Deutschen Morgenländischen Gesellschaft* 33 (1879a) 445-477.

—. 'Die Jaina-Handschriften der K. Bibliothek zu Berlin.' *Zeitschrift der Deutschen Morgenländischen Gesellschaft* 33 (1879b) 478-483.

—.'Vorderindien.' *Zeitschrift der Deutschen Morgenländischen Gesellschaft. Jahresbericht der Deutschen Morgenländischen Gesellschaft* 34 (1880) 13-43.

—.'Vorderindien.' *Zeitschrift der Deutschen Morgenländischen Gesellschaft. Jahresbericht der Deutschen Morgenländischen Gesellschaft* 35 (1881) 20-59.

—. 'Indien.' *Jahresbericht der Geschichtswissenschaft. Im Auftrage der Historischen Gesellschaft zu Berlin herausgegeben von F. Abraham, J.*

Hermann und E. Meyer. II. Jahrgang 1879. Berlin: Ernst Siegfried Mittler & Sohn, [1880] (1881) 1-26.

—. 'Islam.' Ibid. (1881) 237-249.

—. 'Indische Drucke.' *Zeitschrift der Deutschen Morgenländischen Gesellschaft* 35 (1881) 189-206.

—. 'Extracts from the Historical Records of the Jains.' *The Indian Antiquary* XI (1882) 245-256.

—. 'Christian Lassen.' *Allgemeine Deutsche Biographie* 17 (1883) 784-788.

—. *Literatur-Blatt für orientalische Philologie.* Band 1-4. Hg. Ernst Wilhelm Adalbert Kuhn. Unter Mitwirkung von Johannes Klatt. Leipzig: Schulze, 1883-1886 (Later: Orientalische Bibliographie).

—. 'Eine apokryphe Paṭṭāvalī der Jainas.' *Festgruss an Otto von Böhtlingk zum Doktor-Jubiläum 3. Februar 1888 von seinen Freunden,* 54-59. Stuttgart: W. Kohlhammer, 1888.

—. 'Friedrich August Rosen.' *Allgemeine Deutsche Biographie* 29 (1889) 192-195.

—. 'The Date of the Poet Māgha.' *Vienna Oriental Journal / Wiener Zeitschrift für die Kunde des Morgenlandes* 4 (1890) 61-71.

—. 'Die Handschriften-Verzeichnisse der Königlichen Bibliothek zu Berlin.' *Centralblatt für Bibliothekswesen* 7, 5 (1891) 177-196.

—. 'Specimen eines Jaina-Onomastikons (Vorgelegt von Hrn. Weber).' *Sitzungsberichte der Königlich Preussischen Akademie der Wissenschaften zu Berlin.* Jahrgang XXII 1892. Erster Halbband. Januar bis Mai. Gesamtsitzung 21 April, 349-362. Berlin: Verlag der Königlichen Akademie der Wissenschaften, in Commission bei Georg Reimer, 1892a. http://www.biodiversitylibrary.org/pdf3/005781000093352.pdf

—. *Specimen of a literary-bibliographical Jaina-Onomasticon.* [Fifteen of the Fifty-Five Pages Corrected by Ernst Leumann. With a Preface in German by Albrecht Weber.] Leipzig: O. Harassowitz, 1892b.

—. *Jaina Onomasticon.* Berlin 1893 (Manuscript Bound in Eight Volumes. Hamburg, Institut für Indologie und Tibetologie).

—. 'The Samachari-Satakam of Samayasundara and Pattavalis of the Anchala-Gachcha and other Gachchas (Revised with Additions by Ernst Leumann).' *The Indian Antiquary* XXIII (1894) 169-183.

Leumann, Ernst. '[Biographical Note on Klatt].' In: Klatt (1894) 169, n.2.

—. 'An Klatt geschickte Ergänzungen zum bibliographischen Index der Jaina-Literatur. 27 loose leaves.' In: Plutat (1998) 32.

Mālvaṇiyā, Dalsukh D. 'Śrī Loṅkāśāh nī ek Kṛti.' *Svādhyāya* 2, 1 (1963a) 50-82.

—. 'Śrī Lokāśāh ane temnā Mat.' *Svādhyāya* 2, 2 (1963b) 143-155.

—. 'Loṅkāśāh Mat kī Do Pothiyāṃ.' *Muni Śrī Hajārīmal Smṛti Granth*: Ed. Śobhācandra Bhārill, 184-188. Byāvar: Muni Śrī Hajārīmal Smṛti Granth Prakāśan Samiti, 1965.

Mehta, Mohan Lal & K. Rishabh Chandra. *Prakrit Proper Names.* Vol. I-II. Ahmedabad: L.D. Institute, 1970-1972.

Plutat, Birte (comp.). *Catalogue of the Papers of Ernst Leumann in the Institute for the Culture and History of India and Tibet.* University of Hamburg. Stuttgart: Franz Steiner Verlag, 1998.

Rau, Wilhelm (ed.). *Bilder 135 deutscher Indologen. Zweite erweiterte und verbesserte Auflage.* Wiesbaden: Steiner Verlag, 1965/1982 (Glasenapp-Stiftung Band 23).

Turner, Ralph Lilley. *A Comparative Dictionary of the Indo-Aryan Languages.* London: Oxford University Press, 1966. Reprint 1973.

Schubring, Walther. *Die Lehre der Jainas. Nach den alten Quellen dargestellt.* Berlin: Walter De Gruyter & Co., 1935.

—. *The Doctrine of the Jainas. Described after the Old Sources.* Translated from the Revised German Edition by Wolfgang Beurlen. 3rd English Edition. 1962. Reprint, with three Indices, enlarged and expanded by Willem Bollée and Jayandra Soni, Delhi: Motilal Banarsidass, 2000.

—. *Die Jaina-Handschriften der Preussischen Staatsbibliothek: Neuerwerbungen seit 1891.* Unter redaktioneller Mitarbeit von Günther Weibgen. Leipzig: O. Harrassowitz, 1944.

Walker, Alexander (Colonel). *Narratives of Mahrattah History and an Account of the Jeyn, or Shravaca Religion.* India Office Library Mss. Eur. D.582, ca. 1807-1830.

Weber, Albrecht F. 'Über den Kupakshakauçikāditya des Dharmasāgara. Streitschrift eines orthodoxen Jaina, vom Jahre 1573.' *Sitzungsberichte der Königlich Preussischen Akademie der Wissenschaften zu Berlin* 37 (1882) 793-814.

—. *Verzeichniss der Sanskrit- und Prākṛit-Handschriften der Königlichen Bibliothek zu Berlin. Die Handschriften-Verzeichnisse der Königlichen Bibliothek zu Berlin.* Band 5.2-3. Berlin: A. Asher & Co., 1888 & 1892.

—. 'Vorwort [15 October 1892].' In: Klatt (1892b) iii-iv.

Notes

1 The introductory part of this article was first published in *Jaina Studies – Newsletter of the Centre of Jaina Studies* no. 6 (2011: 58-61).

2 Schubring (1935 § 4; 1962/2000 § 7).

3 Ibid.

4 F. Klatt (1965: 189; cf. 1977: 710). I am indebted to Klaus Karttunen, University of Helsinki, for sharing his records on Johannes Klatt. They include the name of Klatt's son Fritz and pointed me to the photograph in Rau (1982). Rau's caption of the photo gives different biodata than F. Klatt: birth Filehne 31.10.1852, death Berlin 27.8.1903.

5 On Three Hundred Maxims of the Indian Poet Cāṇakya (Kauṭalya).

6 Hartwig & Schulz (1884: 25, 1889: 510, 1891: 31). See Klatt (1891) on the manuscript collections of the library.

7 For autobiographical notes, see F. Klatt (1965). Since Fritz was older, his brother Albert could not have been born in 1880 as suggested in the appendix of the book and by Böhm (1977: 710).

8 F. Klatt (1965: 11f.) characterizes his father, who was hospitalized in 1892, as 'an extremely quiet earnest man, with a pale face ... [who] lived entirely for his work and disliked going to social events ... [and] had to die so early, because he kept the dark manner in which he perceived life locked inside himself and did not find an expression for it. He felt so much within and took refuge in his studies, and frantic work.'

9 Later referred to as 'obituary' by Schubring (1962/2000 § 7: 10, n.2, cf. 1935 § 4: 8, n. 2).

10 Leumann (1894: 169, n. 2).

11. See Plutat (1998: 32).

12 See Weber (1892 II.3: xvii) on Klatt's contribution to his pioneering catalogue of Jaina Mss.: 'Klatt besonders durch eine grosse Zahl bibliographischer und literargeschichtlicher Daten aus seinen reichen Sammlungen der Art, in welchen er das einschlagende Material aus den trefflichen Reports von Bühler, Kielhorn, P. Peterson, R.G. Bhāṇḍārkar, Rājendra Lāla Mitra etc. vollständig eingetragen hat, für die ausserhalb des *siddhānta* stehende *Jaina*-Literatur, zu ganz besonderem Danke verbunden. Beide Gelehrte [Leumann & Klatt] haben damit diesem meinem Werke ihrerseits so wesentliche Dienste geleistet, dass ich ihnen dafür die wärmste Anerkennung schuldig bin.'

13 F. Klatt (1965: 9ff.).

14 Leumann also in Plutat (1998: 42).

15 See Schubring (1944: VII) on formal imperfections of the *Specimen* of Klatt's 'unique guide.'

16 In contrast to the 'temple-dwelling' *caityavāsins.*

17 The second term is also used as a self-designation. It refers to the original rejection by the members of these reformed mendicant orders of residencies that were specially constructed for them, with reference to the rules in the āgamas. Later, plain halls (sthānakas = upāśrayas) for mendicants were deemed acceptable. Hence, the members of the reformed mendicant traditions that severed from the Loṅkāgaccha orders were called 'sthānakavāsins', or 'hall-dwellers.' On 'dhūṇḍh-' and '*ḍhūṇḍh' see Turner (1973: 391). The term '*Sthānakavāsī*' was used as a self-designation only in the 20th century. See Flügel (2008:210).

18 The sources are inconsistent. Klatt (1893: 3388f.), referring to Ātmārāma and Hoernle, cites VS 1709 = 1653. On the history of the Sthānakavāsins, see Hastīmal (1995), Flügel (2000, 2003, 2007, 2008, 2012), and Jain and Kumār (2003).

19 Klatt (1893: 1749f.).

20 Klatt (1893: 1717).

21 Flügel (2008: 185 n. 8).

22 Hastīmal (1995: 769).

23 Weber (1882: 807f.).

24 Mālvaṇiyā (1965: 185).

25 See Weber's (1882) study.

26 Flügel (2010).

27 For pioneering preliminary work see Mālvaṇiyā (1963a, 1963b, 1965) and the sources mentioned in footnote 19.

28 Klatt (1893: 3417-3422).

29 See Kharataragaccha *Paṭṭāvalīvācanā* 57, No. 1989 in Weber (1892: 1050): 's. *1508 hamadāvāde Lauṃkākhyena lekhakena pratimā utthāpitā, tathā* s. *1524 Lau(ṃ)kābhidhaṃ mataṃ jātaṃ.*'

30 According to Dharmasāgaragaṇi's undated (Tapā-gaccha) *Gūrvāvalīsūtram* 54, at the time of the Tapā-gaccha Ācārya Ratnaśekharasūri (VS 1457-1517 = 1401-1460), the scribe Loṅkā founded the Luṃkā-mata in 1452, his follower Bhāṇa the Veṣadhara tradition in 1477: '*tadānīṃ Luṃkākhyāl lekhakāt saṃ 1508 varshe jinapratimotthāpanaparaṃ Luṃkāmataṃ pravṛittaṃ; tanmate veshadharās tu saṃ 1533 varshe jātāḥ tatra prathamo veshadhārī ṛi° Bhāṇākhyo 'bhūt*' (In: Weber II.3 1892: 1013). Section 57 of the text further mentions that the Kaṭuka-māta was founded in VS 1562 = 1506, in VS 1570 =

1514 the Vīja-māta, a 'Veṣadhara' splinter group of the Luṃkā-mata led by Vījā (Vīja), and in VS 1572 = 1516 the creation of the Nāgapurīya Tapāgaṇa (ib., 1013f.). Section 60 mentions the re-conversion of the Luṃpāka '*matādhipati*' Ācārya Megha to the Tapā-gaccha in Ahamadāvād at the time of the inauguration of Ācārya Hīravijayasūri (VS 1583-1652 = 1527-1596) in 1552: '*tathā Ahammadāvādanagara eva Lumpāka matādhipatiḥ ri° Meghajī svakīyasamudāyādhipatyaṃ durgratihetur iti matvā*' (In: ib., p. 1015; footnote reference to 'Methajī' in Bhāṇḍārkar 1883/4: 133).

Dharmasāgara's earlier *Kupākṣakauśikāditya* of VS 1629 (1477) uses almost identical words: '*Luṃpākamataṃ Vi° 1508 varshe Lumpaka - lekhakāt prarūpanāṃ adhikṛitya pravṛittaṃ, tatprarūpaṇā ca jina pratimānishedhamūlikā; tanmate veshadharāḥ punar Vi° sam° 1533 varshe Mārodī pratyāsannā'raghaṭṭaka vāstavya prāgvāṭajnātīya Bhānākhyād eva pravṛittā, etadutpattivistāras tu etannāmnā'shṭama viçrāme rakshyate, ayam ca pracavana(yacana!) bāhye bālagopālāṃganānām api pratītaḥ*' (In: Weber II.3 1892: 959; see also pp. 960, 967, 971f.).

31 A modern copy of Hemacandrasūri's *Viśeṣāvaśyaka-vṛtti*, a commentary on Jinabhadra's *Viśeṣāvaśyaka-bhāṣya* I (*sāmāyika*), mentioned in Weber's catalogue was prepared by Ratnacandra as indicated at two different places in the manuscript: "*saṃvat* 1942 (also: A.D. 1886) *rā vaiçasha suda 7 tithau ḥri / Ratnacaṃda nāgorī Luṃkā Jesalamera ma* 4" (fol. 144[b]) and "*Ratnacaṃda vṛihanāgarī luṃkāgachai*" (fol. 145[a]) (Weber 1888: 788).

32 As an example for further information on this order, that is not cross-referenced in the manuscript, see for instance the entry on the following Loṅkāgaccha monk in Klatt (1893: 1793):

'**Nagarāja** bhikshu, of the Vṛihan-nāgapurīya-Lauṅkā-gaccha, honored by the kings, see Bhagavatī ed. Benares VS 1938, f[olio] 1936b v[erse] 20.

N. of the Lauṅkā-gaccha, preceptor of Raghunātha, about VS 1890, see Prajñāpanā col[ophon].

N.'s pupil Rāmcandra, author of a padam, Pada-Ratnāvalī (Benares), p. 327 l. 1, reg. p. 31.'

33 Miles (1933: 346): 'Lūnca Patāvali.'

34 Jacobi (1884: 9), referring to the *Bhadrabāhucaritra* of Ratnanandin (15th-16th C.E.).

35 Jacobi (1884: 13, line 40), summarizing Ratnanandin: 'Im Jahre 1527 nach dem Tode Vikramas entsteht das Luṅkāmata (156). Ein Çvetāmbara Namens Luṅka aus dem Prāgvāṭakula stürzt die Jinabilder. Auch diese Sekte theilt sich wieder in mehrere (160).'

36 Klatt (1893: 3420-3422).

37 Dharmasāgara, in: Weber (1892: 1013).

38 See Bhūmika (entry on Dhanapatisiṃha on p. in Klatt 1893 III: 1662).

39 Because the title *sūri* is used exclusively by Mūrtipūjaka traditions, Amṛtacandra cannot have been a Lumpāka. The work was edited in Calcutta.

40 The unmentioned source must be Muni Ātmārāma, mentioned in Kunte (1882: 3).

41 Bendall (1886: 63) lists this text under 'Mss. Personally Collected.' The description on page 63 begins line 19 and the quotation starts line 24: '*Lumpāka-mata-kuṭṭana* is the subscription of a short work (of 21 leaves). Outside is written in a much later hand "Lokāyata-kuṭṭana." The Lumpāka mata was a school founded in Vikr. Saṃvat 1508 (A.D. 1461). See Dr Klatt *Ind. Antiq.* XI. 256 (September 1882). The treatise is in the main a compilation from the Siddhānta or canon of the Çvetāmbaras and begins:*Natvāçruta-jñānam-ananta-bhedaṃ / pāraṅgataṃ cetasi sannidhāya / siddhānta-vākyāni karomi samyak /* [citation printed in Nāgarī]. Its compilers belonged to the Kharatara-gaccha and wrote the work in Saṃvat 1687.'

42 Klatt (1893: 3443).

43 This is impossible because of the date and because of his rejection of image-worship.

44 The original text refers wrongly to: 'The Jain as who followed the Lokāyātas' (Logan 1879: 311). The mix up of 'Loṅkā' with 'Lokā' occurred frequently in 19th century reports. See footnote 26.

45 See Mālyaṇiyā (1963a: 80-82, 1965: 188). For a Hindī summary see Jain and Kumār (2003: 118-20). For a discussion and English translations, see Flügel (2008: 223ff.).

46 Klatt (1893: 1279-1283).

47 The reference could not be located in the English translations of the works by Bird (1835) and Bayley (1886). See Khān, Alī Muhammad.

48 Sāthe's (1888 II: 70f.) entry No. 373 refers to the 'second translation' of the *Samyaktva Śalyoddhāra* (of Ātmārāma 1994/1909) under the name of 'Bhāvnagar Jain Dharma Prasārak Sabhā, Translators': 'The work of Jethmalji, which has evoked the present refutation of it, is said to be 75 years old and was recently reprinted.'

49 Original text, Sāthe (1888 I: 25): 'Mentions the duties of a follower of Jainism and condemns the worship of an image of any of the Tirthankars or sanctified teachers of Jainism, as well as pilgrimage to certain holy places.'

50 No. 255 in Sāthe (1888 IV: 42f.).

51 Original Kunte (1880-81: 48f.): 'Atthāvan Bola' (Gujarātī), 'old and incorrect; prose. Gujarāthī. Very rare.' The text was attributed to Loṅkā by Mālvaṇiyā (1963a).

52 Original: Rang Lāl (Jain), in Monier-Williams, Lāl and Davies (1888: 286): 'I must finish now with one more remark, and it is about a sect of Jains called 'Dhundye,' but more commonly 'Munh-bandhe,' owing to their habit of keeping their mouth covered with a piece of cloth – something very much like a respirator in this country – because the first principle of Jainism is not to destroy*life*, however insignificant. As there are animalcule in the air, they say that when they breathe the hot breath kills them, so they use this cloth to keep away these animalcule. They have no temples, but simply a place of meeting, where they sit, meditate, say their prayers, and study religious books. A great number of those who belong to this sect are a sort of monks, who have given up the world, but there are very few laity.'

53 The original text of Kunte (1880-81: 4) is based on 'the conversation I had with a Jain mendicant, Ātmā Rām' in Gujarāṃvālā (ib., No. 28, p. 3, cf. No. 22, p. 3), that is, with the Ex-Sthānakavāsī Mūrtipūjaka Muni Ātmārāma (Vijayānandasūri): 'Dhūndhiyā is a sect said to have been founded by Lābhājī, a native of Sūrat. He was the son of Bīro Birji Srī Māl, by Phulā Bāī. The Dhūndhiyās are a branch of the Śvetāmabaris, but they discard the worship of the image of the Tīrthankaras. They are generally given to meditations or practices of the yoga, and attach great importance to the preservation of life, so much so that they do not light a lamp at night and generally tie a piece of cloth on their mouths to prevent the insects being killed by the heat or the air they expire. They seldom walk by night. They say that in worshipping idols people light a lamp, offer scent, and breathe freely, which is all in contravention of the doctrine of the preservation of life.'

54 Now it is clear that Lavajī and Dharmadāsa founded rival monastic order and that these 'Bāīs Ṭolā' derive from Dharmadāsa. See the literature mentioned in footnote 19.

55 'List of the more important Paper Mss. preserved in the Temple of Santinath, Cambay' (Peterson 1887 III: 191).

56 Klatt did by no means cover every piece of information available on the tradition of Loṅkā and the Ḍhūṃḍhiyās. A. Walker's (c. 1807-1830) very tentative unpublished report, for instance, seemed to have escaped his attention, or was left out because it did not throw any light on literary history. Since this is one of if not the earliest report on the Loṅkāgaccha in a European language, E. Bender's (1976: 117f.) excerpt deserves to be quoted at length:

'[T]he Lounka Gatcha, both Jutties and Shravacas, differ considerable from the other sects.

They are more careful of animal life. They worship the Supreme Being alone, and wholly reject the agency of Dewtas, and the Arhyuntas [arihantas]. They despise the worship of the Arhyantas in the Jaina Temples, and ask how an Image can grant a Petition?

The High Priest of the Shravacas and Jutties [*yatis*] is called Shree Pooj [*śrīpūjya*].

The Sripuja of the Lounka Gaccha, or tribe, is at Baroda; this is his principal Station, but their duty is to take a circuit among their dependents every year; the High Priests of the sects are elsewhere.

The Lounka Gatch had four stations (of which one no longer exists) at which Thiveras [*sthaviras*] were stationed; vizt. Delhi, Ajimere, Jalour. Three Thiveras are Deputies or Legates, who are entrusted with a general superintendance over the Morals of the Yati.

The Sripuja is chosen by adoption, generally from among the Wannias [baniyās] of the Veesavosavar [Veṣadahara] Caste, the most respectable; when the Sripuja is on the point of death, the child is placed on the gaudee [gādi]. His lock of hair plucked out, and the MUntra particularly appropriated for this station is whispered in his Ear, and the assembly of Yatis are desired to obey their future Chief.

About 100 years ago, this sect gave birth to a new description of Yatis, who carry mortifications to great extreme.

It happened that a Yati of the Lounka Gatcha disputed the Mandate of the Sripuja, ...and founded the Sect of the Dhoundia...

These [pūja] ceremonies are not performed by the Yatis, and they are wholly rejected both by Shravacas and Yatis of the Lounka Gatcha...

Altho' any of the above Castes may become Converts, yet they do not choose their disciples or Chila's [chelas] from the Military Class. This is at least the case with the Lounka Gatcha.'

57 Bendall (1886: 24f.) believed to be the first European to have visited the Śvetāmbara Mandir at the *ghāt*s in Benares. He attended a committee meeting of the Bāla Sarasvatībhavana library, started at suggestion of his guide Paṇḍit Ḍhunḍhirāja Dharmādhikārī.

58 Including a complete bibliography of Klatt's publications and manuscripts.

4

The Unknown Loṅkā

Tradition and the Cultural Unconscious

In the last two decades, the main focus of Jaina research has shifted from the effectively a-historical exploration of the language, content and form of the Śvetāmbara canon in particular, to the historical and anthropological investigation of "strategies of transmission" of tradition, including "canonisation" and "transformation" (Bruhn 1987: 107f.). The guiding question in this research is how to conceptualise the relationship between continuity and change within the "Jaina tradition" (Carrithers 1990: 142). The investigation of this question became imperative after the philological deconstruction of earlier notions of a Jaina "urcanon" and the "dogmatic immutability" of the Jaina doctrine (Bruhn 1987: 104, 107), as a consequence of which even the core principles of "true Jainism" (Dundas 1993: 253) and the term "Jaina" itself (Flügel 2005: 2-5) became problematic.

The Present in the Past

In current academic studies, the history of the Jaina tradition is predominately presented as an interactive process between texts and practices through time (Cort 1990: 59). The emphasis is on the continuity of canonical histories, monastic traditions, and religious properties,[1] which offer alternative points of connection for the formation of variable group identities. In this model, scripture,[2] lineal descent, and the direct link to a charismatic teacher function as alternative sources of authority and legitimation as Granoff (1991: 76f.; 1993: 315), Dundas (1993: 250), Qvarnström (1998: 33f., 46) and Balbir (2003a: 267-269) have shown in their studies of late medieval Jaina sectarian traditions. Practice is not seen anymore as a mere enactment of rules, but also as an impetus for re-interpre-tation of rules or for the creation of new rules. Examples of such processes are particularly visible in the context of sectarian rivalry "expressing the stiffening of group identity, rather than the perse-vering of an archaic tradition" (Balbir 2003a: 267). Neither textual traditions nor descent constructs are now seen as static, despite the fact that innovations are within the Jaina tradition commonly intro-duced as "views well-rooted in the scriptural tradition" (Balbir 2003a: 263).

Although earlier views of the unchanging nature of the principal features of Jainism are being replaced by this new approach, the dominant lines of influence still run from the past to the present, from text to practice. Yet, with growing historical and ethnographical information, it seems both possible and necessary to reverse the perspective. After all, in any situation, the choice is not whether to obey or to disobey transmitted rules, but which rule to obey, as the anthropologists M. Gluckman and E. Leach both noted.[3] In the Jaina context, this is a truism. The amorphous nature of the canonical scriptures alone, not to mention the commentaries and imports from non-Jain traditions, forces strategies of selection and reduction of complexity on everyone who refers to them, even disregarding instrumental interests. The question is not whether to obey or to disobey the scriptures, but which scripture to obey, and how to interpret it.

W.C. Smith's (1962/1991: 168) concept of "cumulative tradition" already highlighted that "a tradition" presents itself not as an entity but as "a growing congeries of items" of diverse nature, which is only "unified in the conceptual mind, by processes of conceptual abstraction." J. Assmann's (2000: 39f.) notion of "cultural memory" covers similar ground. Yet, it puts less emphasis on processes of conscious transmission and revitalisation of a tradition through the faith of individual participants, as Smith's notion does, or the selective instrumentalisation of the past through the "connective memory" of particular groups, as current reconstructions of Jaina sectarian histories do, but focuses on the latent function of the entire "archive" (Derrida) of the amorphous "cultural unconscious." In Assmann's view, the interesting aspects of "cultural memory" are the forgotten, ignored, obsolete, hidden, excluded, suppressed or disrespected elements of a tradition, which are still accessible but unutilised and therefore "freely at one's disposal."[4] The term "cultural memory" is wider than the term "tradition," which in its restricted sense refers to a consciously constructed instrumentalisation of the past in terms of present needs and interests. Though inspired by Freud's notions of repression and latency, the "cultural unconscious" in this sense must be distinguished both from inferred processes of "unconscious thought" and "deep motivations" (Goonasekere 1986: 7), and from spheres of value within the realm of ideology which are not systematically expressed (Laidlaw 1985: 51f.), and in this sense "unconscious" (Cort 1990: 60). It overlaps, however, with the sphere of preconscious habits, dispositions and practices (Bourdieu 1992: 52ff.) in a yet to be explored way.

In this article, I will utilise this perspective for the analysis of the modern historiography of Loṅkā and the Loṅkāgaccha, by focusing on processes of canonisation and repression of memory, and on techniques of selective citation and re-combination of transmitted elements of the Jain tradition[5] through which authority was claimed both by Loṅkā and his successors and by modern authors who tried to establish Loṅkā as an ancestral figure for competing factions of the aniconic Jaina tradition, which Loṅkā is said to have founded on the basis of the scriptures alone. I will first explore the ways in which the teachings of Loṅkā and the Loṅkāgaccha tradition have been depicted in modern literature, and how the scant information on Loṅkā was compiled and redacted by different interested parties, and then turn to some of the texts which have been attributed to Loṅkā himself to delimit the scope of his influence on the still existing but ignored Loṅkāgaccha tradition, which has lost all memory of its own past and on the Sthānakavāsī and Terāpanth traditions. I am not trying to solve the presently unanswerable question of the accuracy of the transmitted historical knowledge on Loṅkā's biography and beliefs but will focus primarily on the ana-lysis of the effective history (*Wirkungsgeschichte*) of his ideas.[6]

The Unknown Loṅkā

The true nature of the biography and teachings of Loṅkā is still di-sputed within the Jaina tradition, even now, more than five hundred years after his death.[7] It is commonly accepted that Luṅkā or Loṅkā[8] was a layman who lived in Gujarāt sometime between 1415-1489. Because of his access to the Śvetāmbara scriptures, he was able to articulate a powerful, text-based critique of the laxity, *śithilācāra,* of contemporary Jaina mendicants, and to reject the prevailing practice of image-worship as "uncanonical," since, in his view, it was predicated on violence and attachment to property.[9]

No consensus exists, however, on the nature of Loṅkā's influence on the formation of the aniconic mendicant traditions which emerged in the aftermath of his protest: the Loṅkāgaccha tradition,[10] which was founded by Bhāṇā in the 1470s, and the Sthānakavāsī traditions, which were established in the early 17th century by different groups of dissenting *sādhus* of the Loṅkāgaccha who objected to the re-emergence of image-worship within the tradition. Due to a lack of reliable sources,[11] nothing certain can be said at present about the biography of Loṅkā, and even less about the early leaders of the Loṅkāgaccha, although this may change in due course.[12]

The dearth of historical sources is a consequence both of the long-standing suppression of all but the most basic information concerning Loṅkā by his opponents,[13] and of the lack of interest in the creation and transmission of literature by the followers of Loṅkā, who evidently were more concerned with the preservation of his basic ideas (*Sinnpflege*) than of the texts (*Textpflege*).[14] Emptied of historical memory, the modern image of Loṅkā can be painted in almost any colour, like contours on a white canvas. By the beginning of the 20th century, Loṅkā was revered as an ancestral figure not only by the Loṅkāgaccha traditions, but also by the rival Sthānakavāsī and Terāpanth traditions; each claiming to manifest his teaching in its purest form. The premise of this contest, that religious authority is conveyed not only by proper conduct in ac-cordance with the prescriptions of the scriptures (*siddhānta*) but also by either lineal or direct spiritual descent (*paramparā*) from a prestigious ancestor,[15] was not entirely new in the aniconic tradi-tion.[16] In addition to Mahāvīra, Loṅkā is mentioned as a source of authority in almost all surviving old *paṭṭāvalī*s of the Loṅkāgaccha and Sthānakavāsī traditions. However, although they are amongst the earliest written documents of the tradition, the oldest Sthānakavāsī *paṭṭāvalī*s cannot be dated much earlier than the beginning of the 19th century.[17] Before the modern Jaina revival in the second half of the 19th century, the institutional structures of the aniconic traditions were very rudimentary and, within the five main lines of tradition, in a state of permanent flux. Instead of *paṭṭāvalī*s, which trace the succession of group leaders, the dominant descent constructs were *gurvāvalī*s, that is lists which trace the *guru-śiṣya* lineages, as documented in the colophons of the oldest surviving manuscripts which contain mostly biographical poems and songs.[18] It seems, the perceived need for group organisation and ideological integration through elaborate descent constructs emerged in the Sthānakavāsī tradition only when, facing extinction under conditions of colonial domination, Hindu nationalism and sectarian rivalry, the quest for organisation, reform and competitive re-appropriation of the past had gained a new momentum.[19]

At the time, the sectarian struggle over the definition of the cultural memory of Loṅkā was particularly intense between the Sthānakavāsīs and the reformed "Saṃvegī" Tapāgaccha Mūrtipūjakas. For the Mūrtipūjakas (and the Digambaras) Loṅkā continued to be the prototypical heretic and one of the greatest threats to the survival of their own tradition. In an intriguing role-reversal, the Sthānakavāsīs and the Mūrtipūjakas re-enacted the ideological struggle between Loṅkā (and the Loṅkāgaccha) and his Mūrtipūjaka opponents in the 15th century. Yet, the agenda had significantly changed. At stake was not only the justification of image-worship on the part of the Mūrtipūjakas, but also the quest for legitimacy of a wide variety of new monastic orders and sectarian traditions which, by now, derived their religious identity directly from the layman Loṅkā – either through descent constructs or through the acceptance of his interpretation of the scriptures. At the centre of the controversies were idiosyncratic points of the customary law, *sāmācārī* or *maryādā*, of the monastic traditions[20] which are at the heart of the aniconic sects.[21] Monastic customary law is multidimensional in both form and content. Usually it is transmitted in the form of hand-written lists of proclamations (*bol*) in ver-nacular prose, often only comprising quotes from the scriptures with or without commentary, but also in form of poems or ques-tion-and-answer texts (*praśnottara*). It regulates not only the con-duct, but also the doctrinal outlook, organisation and liturgy of a particular group of mendicants.[22] As such, it provides a crucial link between doctrine and practice, scripture and community, and is prone to processes of canonisation.[23] A crucial point of contention between the Sthānakavāsī and the Mūrtipūjaka traditions was whether Loṅkā himself formulated a list of instructions which led to the formation of the Loṅkāgaccha, what exactly these instruc-tions were, and how they related to the customs of the various con-temporary Sthānakavāsī traditions. Currently, no records are known on disputes about Loṅkā's teachings amongst Sthānakavāsīs and members of the Loṅkāgaccha.

The key question, to what extent the prescribed[24] customary practices of the different aniconic traditions (and those of the Mūrtipūjakas) actually coincided with canonical prescriptions, triggered a series of heated disputes, which peaked in the 1930s, at the height of the nationalist and religious revivalist movements in India. At the time, the Śvetāmbara revivalist movements competed vigorously with one another and with Hindu revivalist groups, such as the aniconic Ārya Samāj of Svāmī Dayānand Sarasvatī (1824-1883),[25] and with Christian missionaries for support amongst the adherents of the traditional Jaina communities. Particularly virulent were the written exchanges between Sthānakavāsī mendicants and ex-Sthānakavāsī Mūrtipūjaka monks from the Pañjāb and Rājasthān, such as the polemicists Muni Buddhivijay (Būṭerāy) (1807-1882),[26] Ācārya Ātmārām (Vijayānand Sūri) (1837-1897)[27] and his Gujarāt-born disciple Muni Vallabhvijay (1870-1953), who were amongst the driving forces of the revival of the upright (*saṃvegī*) tradition of the Mūrtipūjaka Tapāgaccha in Gujarāt, which had to re-establish itself almost from scratch.[28] One of the fiercest critics of the aniconic tradition in the 20th century, the (ex-Sthānakavāsī) Mūrtipūjaka Muni Jñānsundar (1936: 131ff.), born in 1880 in Rajasthan,[29] who attempted to revive the Upakeśagaccha, has argued that contemporary Sthānakavāsī intellectuals such as Ācārya Amolakṛṣi (1877-1936),[30] Vāḍilāl Moṭīlāl Śāh (1878-1931), Muni Maṇilāl (1849-1932?),[31] and Muni Saubhāgyacandra "Santabāḷa" (died 1981),[32] who invoked Loṅkā's critique of image-worship both in their innovative historiography of Loṅkā and in their polemics against the Mūrtipūjakas, had deliberately fabricated (*kalpita*) an artificial portrait of Loṅkā as their common spiritual ancestor to promote the unification of the multiple strands of their divided tradition.[33] According to Jñānsundar, who perceived a unified Sthānakavāsī Śramaṇasaṅgha as a threat to the revival of the Mūrtipūjaka tradition, there was not a shred of evidence for Loṅkā's instructions to his followers in the literature of Loṅkāgaccha, the Sthānakavāsīs and the Terāpanthīs, except for one unspecific reference to Loṅkā's *upadeśa* in a Loṅkāgaccha text which was composed thirty-eight or forty-six years after Loṅkā's death and could, in his view, therefore not be trusted.[34]

The critique of the "lack of evidence" in the Sthānakavāsi literature on Loṅkā is a modern *topos* of the Mūrtipūjaka *praśnottara* literature. It was already articulated by Ātmārām (1884/1903) and repeated again by Jñānsundar (1936: 97) and Śeṭh (1962: 342), to name but a few. Proof and evidence (*pramāṇa*) are long-established criteria in Jaina scholasticism. However, the increasing influence of European historicism and academic jargon on modern Jaina vernacular historiographies cannot be underestimated.[35] The Jainas encountered the power of "scientific truth" and of historical "facts and figures" first in the colonial courts of law in the 19th century.[36] Its rhetoric quickly filtered into their internal sectarian and communal disputes soon after the introduction of the printing press and of modern means of communication and transportation which transformed Indian intellectual culture. Almost all printed vernacular texts on Loṅkā profess to be interested in history and often use scientific jargon. This does not mean that the texts are products of a scientific attitude, in the sense of Max Weber's *Wissenschaft als Beruf*, with at least a notional commitment towards objectivity. Most vernacular historiographies to date are partisan and often polemical works which explicitly aim at influencing the present through one-sided re-constructions and re-interpretations of the past.[37] To its credit, the new Jaina historiography has unearthed numerous important historical documents. Its authors also reflect on the method of writing history itself, but often only to discredit the work of opponents as "unreliable."

As Jñānsundar (1936: 7) rightly observed, the interest of the Sthānakavāsīs in Loṅkā seems to be greatest during periods of expansion, crisis and change. Whenever "Sthānakavāsīs" feel the need to assert their common doctrinal heritage and the need for institutional integration, both Loṅkā and the common opposition against image-worship are brought into play. And whenever the "Mūrtipūjaka" tradition as a whole comes under attack, it usually retaliates in kind. In this way the antagonism generates a sense of self-identity in both traditions and contributes to their social integration. Underlying the antagonism between the previously socially insignificant denominational super-categories such as "Mūrtipūjaka" and "Sthānakavāsī," incorporating several "sub-"sects, is the struggle over the definition of the "essence" of "true Jainism" (understood in the manner of the new book oriented *Religionswissenschaft*) under the banner of "Jain" unity. At stake was the ideological self-definition and thus political positioning of the entire "Jain community" at a time of the emergence of Jain religious nationalism.[38]

Essence of Right Belief

The Loṅkāgaccha tradition still exists today in small pockets in Gujarāt.[39] Yet, the contemporary followers of the Loṅkāgaccha remember nothing of Loṅkā or his teachings anymore, and have only the vaguest idea of the recent history of their tradition. Not even Loṅkā's name is mentioned in their few idiosyncratic rituals. With two negligible exceptions,[40] most of the modern texts on Loṅkā have been produced by Sthānakavāsī, Terāpanthī and Mūrtipūjaka mendicants and lay intellectuals. It appears that the first Sthānakavāsī text which explicitly sought support in Loṅkā's teachings was Muni Jeṭhmal's celebrated anti-Mūrtipūjaka polemic *Samakitasāra*, essence of right belief. The original Gujarātī text was prepared by several unnamed Sthānakavāsī lay followers, sometime after the religious debate (*śāstrārtha*) in which Jeṭhmal reportedly used the published arguments,[41] and printed in 1882 in Rājkoṭ by Śeṭh Nemicand Hīrācand Koṭhārī from Goṇḍal in Saurāṣṭra.[42] Two further Gujarātī editions were published in the following decades, and one revised Hindī edition of two parts in 1930[43] (with the translation of the original text forming part one).[44] The way in which this work was created offers insights into the strategies through which the effective history of a tradition is created and re-created, and suggests that an investigation of parallels in the history of the transmission of knowledge in the Jaina tradition may yield materials for an understanding of processes of identity-formation through the work of canonisation outside the canon, which have not yet been investigated.[45] First of all, Jeṭhmal was not the author of the published work. At the time, it was generally not considered appropriate for Sthānakavāsī *munis* to publish books under their own name, because of the violence of the printing press and because of the implicit promotion of egotism. Instead, lay-followers published lecture notes of the *pravacanas* of their gurus. In its prefaces and introductions, the text is described as a synopsis of the arguments used by Jeṭhmal in a public debate with the Tapāgaccha *saṃvegī munis* Vīrvijay and Yaśovijay on doctrinal differences which divided their religious traditions.[46]

The debate took place in Ahmedabad, either in 1808/9 (Saṃvat 1865)[47] or 1821/2 (Saṃvat 1878).[48] It was triggered by a communal dispute. According to Śāh (1909: 78f.), Sthānakavāsī mendicants were proselytising at the time in the town. In response, the locally dominant Mūrtipūjaka laity threatened to excommunicate all Sthānakavāsīs from their castes (*jñātī*). In order to help his beleaguered co-religionists in this situation, Ācārya Prāg from the Sthānakavāsī Dariyāpurī Sampradāya travelled from his abode in the village of Visalapura outside Ahmedabad to the Tabīā Poḷ in the Sāraṅgapura district of the city centre. He stayed in Gulābcand Hīracand's house and also imparted religious instruction to the families of Gīrdhar Śaṅkar, Pānācand Jhavercand, Rāycand Jhavercand, Khīmcand Jhavercand, and others, who, in turn, helped him to spread his word. In order to end the ensuing quarrels between Sthānakavāsīs and Mūrtipūjakas, both parties went to court. To educate themselves about the Jaina religion, the judges invited *munis* from both sides as expert witnesses. For Prāg's side the learned Muni Jeṭhmal, apparently a *suśiṣya* of Muni Rūpcand of the Bhūdhar Dharmadāsa Sampradāya in Rājasthān,[49] was present, together with twenty-seven other *munis*;[50] and for the Mandirmārgīs Muni Vīrvijay together with Yaśovijay and several monks and scholars (*śāstrī*) came to the court. According to "someone's" notes (*yādī*) of the court-proceedings, the judgement of 1878 *pauṣ śukla* 13 (6.1.1822)[51] apparently favoured the arguments of Jeṭhmal's side – described as *cetanapūjakas*, worshippers of living consciousness, in contrast to the *mūrtipūjakas*, worshippers of images – although in their respective literatures both sides claimed victory.[52]

Although there is no conclusive evidence, the timing of the belated publication was almost certainly related to the publication of what is probably the first polemic against the Sthanakavāsīs in print[53] in Ātmārām's (1881/1954, II: 539f.) work *Jainatattvādarśa* which appeared in Bhāvnagar in Saṃvat 1937. After his separation from and excommunication by the Sthānakavāsī Ācārya Amarasiṅha (1805-1881) of the Pañjāb Lavjīṛṣi Sampradāya and his re-initiation into the Tapāgaccha in Saṃvat 1932 (1875/6) in Ahmedabad, the ex-Sthānakavāsī Muni Ātmārām (Vijayānanda Sūri) contributed much to the Mūrtipūjaka revival in Gujarāt and in the Pañjāb. To revive the "Sanātan Jaina Dharma"[54] by attracting more followers, Ātmārām started a vigorous pro-image-worship campaign, which he had already instigated in his later years as a Sthānakavāsī monk, during which he criticised many of the contemporary practices of the Sthānakavāsīs. One of the points of contention before he left was that Ācārya Amarasiṅha did not answer twenty-one "legitimate" questions which were put to him in Saṃvat 1925 (1868) by certain Sthānakavāsī *śrāvakas* from Dillī.[55] Amarasiṅha and his successor

Ācārya Sohanlāl (1846-1936) of the Lavjīṛṣi tradition were the dominant Sthānakavāsī monks in his native Pañjāb at the time, and the main targets of his critique. After Ātmārām's excommunication and the publication of his *Jaina-tattvādarśa*, Sohanlāl sent – on request of Amarasiṅha[56] – a *praśnottara* of one hundred questions[57] to Ātmārām in Saṃvat 1938 *caitra śukla* 5 (4.4.1881), to which Ātmārām instantly replied in Saṃvat 1938 *caitra śukla* 7 (6.4.1881), without receiving a response.[58] Shortly thereafter, it seems, in Saṃvat 1938 (1882)[59] the polemical *Samakitsār* appeared in print with its sustained attack on *mūrtipūjā* and a long list of questions to the Mandirmārgīs. Immediately after receiving a copy of this book from a Sthānakavāsī layman in Delhi, Ātmārām (1884/1903) composed an equally polemical point-for-point reply under the title *Samyaktva Śalyoddhāra*, removal of the thorns from right belief,[60] and the work *Ajñāna Timira Bhāskara* (1888/1906), radiant darkness of ignorance, in which both the Ārya Samāj and the Ḍhūṇḍhiyās are systematically criticised.[61] This triggered a long series of tit-for-tat exchanges between leading mendicants (and laity) of the two (three) traditions, which subsided somewhat only after Indian Independence in 1949, though the conflict is still smouldering and can re-erupt at any time.

Of particular interest for us is the role of "Loṅkā" in this debate. Ātmārām's sharp criticism of the "heresy" (*nihṇava*) of the "*Ḍhūṇḍhiyās*" was provoked by Jeṭhmal's (1930:1-9) construction of a contrast between "the path of compassion" (*dayā mārga*) and nonviolence of the tradition of Loṅkā (in its Sthānakavāsī manifestation),[62] and "the path of violence" (*hiṃsā mārga*) of the Mūrtipūjaka *saṃvegī* mendicants, which were addressed as "yellow-clad pseudo-ascetics" (*pītāmbar bheṣadhārī*). As a synonym of *dayā mārga*, Jeṭhmal used the term *mokṣa mārga*, and compared the path of salvation of the Sthānakavāsīs, which he derived directly from Loṅkā, with the dual concern of the Mūrtipūjakas (and Digambaras) with salvation and with material well-being (*kuśaliyā darśana*).[63] The Mūrtipūjakas are spreading lies, he argued, because they convey to their followers the illusion that salvation can be reached through *pūjā*, while preventing them from reading the truth in the scriptures.[64]

In his long list of rejoinders, of which only the *Samyaktva Śalyoddhāra* and the *Ajñāna Timira Bhāskara* seem to have been published during his lifetime, Ātmārām (1903; 1908)[65] highlighted

Jeṭhmal's "misspellings" and "misunderstandings" of the scriptures, and furnished descriptions of the lax conduct of contemporary Ḍhūṇḍhaka mendicants. In his view, the Sthānakavāsīs generally did not observe the canonical prescriptions, and thus truly formed a religion of violence: *ḍhūṇḍhiye hiṃsā dharmī haim.*[66] In his critique of Jeṭhmal's account, Ātmārām (1903: 7f.) categorically stated that everything that "Jūṭhmal" wrote about Loṅkā's beliefs as the source of the Sthānakavāsī doctrines was a "self-imagined fabricated lie." In accordance with the conventions of the *praśnottara* genre,[67] he backed his claim with selected citations from the canon and from the writings of the Sthānakavāsī tradition itself.[68] Information on the true historical origin (*kharī utpattī*) of the "Ḍhūṇḍhak Panth,"[69] he argued, can be found in two other Sthānakavāsī texts which he summarised in a few pages: Hīrakalaśmuni's *Kumati Vidhvaṃsana Caupāī*, quatrain on the destruction of stupidity, and the *Ḍhuṇḍhak Paṭṭāvalī* of Amolakcand of the Pañjāb Amarasiṅha Sampradāya.

Although the furnished information on the lines of succession is rudimentary,[70] Ātmārām's version of the "actual history" contrasts favourably with the account offered by Jeṭhmal[71] in the style of "localised" versions of Jaina "universal history," i.e. the history of great beings or *mahāpuruṣas*, and doctrinal "cosmological history."[72] In his first verse, Jeṭhmal (1930: 1) wrote, *śrī dayā dharma phailā aur bhasma graha utarā jiskā vistār*, effectively arguing — as Devṛṣi's commentary explains – that Loṅkā's revival of "true Jainism" in the year Saṃvat 1531, exactly two thousand years after Mahāvīra's death, was predicted already by the canonical *Jiṇacariya* 129-131, which says that after a two thousand year period during which

> there will not be paid much respect and honour to the śramaṇas, the Nirgrantha monks and nuns (...) when the great [Bhasma] Graha, &c., leaves that natal asterism [of Mahāvīra], there will be paid much respect and honour to the śramaṇas, the Nirgrantha monks and nuns for an era of two-thousand years (KS 130f.).

This somewhat optimistic version of Jaina cosmological history, which allows for progressive intervals within the generally predicted decline, contrasts however with other passages in the scriptures. In his rejoinder, Ātmārām (1903: 4) cited the famous section Viy 20.8.4 in which Mahāvīra predicted that his teaching will survive for at least 21,000 years after his death. The same argument had previously been used by the 16th-century founders of two Sthānakavāsī orders,

Lava and Dharmadāsa, against the followers of the Loṅkāgaccha and the Ekal Pātriyāpanth, who indeed seem to have favoured the *Jinacaritra* passage, to which Jeṭhmal had reverted without fear of sanction, because the Loṅkāgaccha was already in terminal decline, and no competition for the Sthānakavāsīs anymore.[73] Since there is no independent criterion for judging which of the two versions is more authentic (even historical precedence would not solve the issue) any choice between them is a matter of personal preference and of sectarian interests. However, due to his correspondence with European scholars such as Hoernle[74] and the presence of his representative V.R. Gāndhī at the first Parliament of World Religions in Chicago in 1893, Ātmārām's writings were widely read outside India, and significantly influenced the image of the Jaina community projected by the first generations of modern Indologists. Jeṭhmal's text, by contrast, circulated only within the literary elite of the Sthānakavāsīs and Mūrtipūjakas. Thus, only the Mūrtipūjaka depiction entered European textbooks on Jainism.

The second round of the dispute was fought on behalf of Sohanlāl and Ātmārām between the Sthānakavāsī *mahāsatī* "Jainācārya"[75] Pārvatī Devī (1854-1939) from the Amarasiṅha Sampradāya and Ātmārām's disciple and future *ācārya* Muni Vallabhvijay (1870-1954). Pārvatī Devī was a remarkable Jaina nun[76] who on the 28.12. 1872 (1929 *mārgaśīrṣa kṛṣṇa* 13) in Delhi changed from the Manoharadāsa Sampradāya of Ācārya Ratnacandra (died 1864)[77] to the Pañjāb Lavjī Ṛṣi tradition of Ācārya Amarsiṅha (1805-1881).[78] According to Sarlā (1991: 299), she chose a less restrictive group in order to be able to preach in public, to publish books, and to wander alone.[79] Her official biography by P.L. Jain (1913/1923: 30), however, informs us that she joined the Amarsiṅha Sampradāya because its mendicants followed the scriptures more closely. Pārvatī Devī's pamphlet *Jñāna Dīpikā* (Lāhaur 1889), a critique of the *Jainatattvādarśa*,[80] and Muni Vallabhvijay's (1891: 9-71) reply, *Gappa Dīpikā*,[81] re-ignited the debate in the Pañjāb which was again conducted in the form of *praśnottaras*, in which for instance the difference between the thirty-one Āgamas which were allegedly accepted by Loṅkā and the thirty-two Āgamas of the Sthānakavāsīs was questioned by Vallabhvijay (1891: 130f.), who dismissed Pārvatī's book as a "work of sin" which calls for an atonement (*prāyaścitta*) since, in accordance with the rules of the scriptures, no *sādhvī* before her had ever written a book nor spoken in the assembly of men.[82] Vallabhvijay was, in turn, repudiated by an anonymous [?] pamphlet called *Gappa Dīpikā Samīr kā Gappa* and Paṇḍit Jiyālāl Jain's (1893) *Carcā Candroday Bhāg Tisrā*. According to Vallabhvijay's (1909: 14-18) chronology of the exchanges between 1881-1909,[83] in response to Vallabhvijay, Ācārya Sohanlāl wrote *Draupadīpūjā Khaṇḍan* (Amṛtsar),[84] Muni Ṛṣirāj *Satyārtha Sāgara* (Pune), and an unnamed author *Saṃvegīmat Sāguphā*, (Ambālā); which was countered by an unnamed author's text *Jahālat Ḍhuṇḍhiyā* (Ambālā). Three further Sthānakavāsī pamphlets, *Kāgahans Nirṇay* (Ambālā), *Manta kī Bahsa Pūjeraṃ* of Kanīyālāl (Paṭayālā), and *Samyaktva athavā Dharma no Darvājo* by V.M. Śāh (Ahmedabad), were countered by Muni Amarvijay's *Dharma nā Darvājā Jovā nī Diśā*, which in turn was criticised by a text published in Ahmadabad, *Kamalprabhā*. The response to Mahāsatī Pārvatī's *Satyārtha-Candrodaya-Jain* (Lāhaur: Lālā Meharcand, 1904) on the "stupid" worship of "lifeless objects" (*jaṛ pūjā*)[85] and on the *nikṣepas*[86] was Muni Amarvijay's (1908) *Ḍhūṇḍhak-Hṛday-Netrāñjanaṃ athavā Satyārtha-Candrodayāṣṭakaṃ*; and in response to the Sthānakavāsī pamphlet *Iśatahār-Amarāvatī*, an unnamed Mūrtipūjaka author wrote *Ḍhuṇḍhakpol Amarāvatī*, which was countered by the texts *Khulāsāpol Saṃvegīyāṃ* (Amṛtsar), Muni Ratnacand's *Saṃvegīmat Mardan* (Amṛtsar), and *Śāstrārtha Nābhā* (Ambālā). The last Mūrtipūjaka text on Vallabhvijay's list is *Ḍhuṇḍhakmat Parājay* (Ātmānand Jain Sabhā Pañjāb 1909) which gives information on the judgement of Mahārāja Hīrāsiṃha Bahādur of Paṭayālā in favour of Vallabhvijay in a debate with Sohanlāl on the scriptural foundations of their respective views in 5.2.1904.[87] It was followed by seven Sthānakavāsī responses, some of which are reprinted and criticised in the collection edited by Muni Amarvijay (1908): *Pītāmbarī Parājay* (Amṛtsar), Muni Rāmcandra's *Amṛtsar Saṃgraha* (Mumbaī), the *stavan* of Muni Mādhav *Taraṅgiṇī Dvitīya Taraṅg* (Āgrā 1908), Muni Saubhāgmal's *Vividh Ratna Prakāś* (Pune), Muni Kundanmal's *Pragaṭ Jaina Pītāmbarī Mūrtipūjakoṃ kā Mithyātva* (1908),[88] and his *Ātmārām Saṃvegī kī Karttūt, Ātmārām kī Ādat kā Namūnā* (n.d.), and finally V.M. Śāh's (1909) *Sādhumārgī Jaina Dharmānuyāyīoe Jāṇvā Jog Keṭalīk Aitihāsik Noṃdh*, a key text for the modern Sthānakavāsī unification movement, which attracted much critical response from the Mūrtipūjakas, not least from Vallabhvijay (1909),[89] Ujamcand (1909), and Jñānsundar (1936: 247ff.), because it again referred to Loṅkā as the common forefather of all Sthānakavāsīs and thereby started a new round of debates.[90]

Historical Notes

V.M. Śāh (1878-1931) was the first layperson to make an important intellectual contribution to the study of Loṅkā's legacy for the Sthānakavāsīs,[91] and the first Sthānakavāsī to collect some of the available though "untrustworthy" *paṭṭāvalīs* in order to tentatively reconstruct, in the manner of Ātmārām, an accurate history of the entire Sthānakavāsī tradition.[92] He was also a prime mover, behind the creation of the *All India Sthānakavāsī Jaina Conference* (AISJC) of the Sthānakavāsī laity in February 1906 in Morvī,[93] and publicised in his 1909 book for the first time the idea of creating a unified order of all Sthānakavāsī mendicants. Although Loṅkā was a layman, it was he alone who could serve as a common ancestor, because the Sthānakavāsī tradition was founded not by one but by several different ex-Loṅkāgaccha mendicants, who initially shared little more than the rejection of image-worship and the criticism of "lax conduct" of the Loṅkāgaccha *yatis*. After their creation between c. 1628-1668, the original five Sthānakavāsī mendicant traditions quickly split into numerous sub-groups which developed different customs and began to struggle with one another, until the AISJC finally called for an end of all "internal" antagonism. Conflicts between mendicant orders were divisive for the Sthānakavāsī laity as well and obstructed aim of the AISJC leadership to assert the political influence of Sthānakavāsī representatives on a national platform. From 1906 onwards, the AISJC, like the competing Conferences of the Digambaras and Mūrtipūjakas which were established in 1893 and 1902 respectively, held regular meetings on an all-India basis to prepare the ground for the first *mahāsammelan*, or great assembly, of representatives of all Sthānakavāsī mendicant traditions, which was finally held in 1933 in Ajmer.

Before the assembly congregated, a fourth edition of the *Samakitsār*, which was also the first Hindī edition, was published in 1930 under the auspices of *the Akhil Bhāratīya Sthānakavāsī Jaina Conference* after years of careful preparation of the translation by Muni Devṛṣi (1872-1942), who in 1936 succeeded Ācārya Amolakṛṣi (1877-1936) – one of the most influential Sthānakavāsī monks at the time who was the first to publish a printed edition and Hindī translation of the Sthānakavāsī Āgamas – as the leader of the Mālvā Ṛṣi Sampradāy. The plan was to make the ideas of Loṅkā available to everyone, in the national language of India, and to create a sense of unity amongst the Sthānakavāsī mendicants in opposition to the Mūrtipūjakas in particular. In this context, the author of the *Samakit Śalyoddhāra* became again a useful target. One of the three anonymous introductions to the *Samakitsār*[94] accused the "stubborn mischief maker" Ātmārām in an *ad hominem* attack for not understanding the substance of *samakita* (*samyaktva*), right belief, nor practising it, as his violent use of language testified. As proof for Ātmārām's wrongdoing, the following passage of the *Dasaveyāliya* is cited:

> When he notices that [a monk] who has mastered the Āyāra and the [Viyāha-]Pannatti [and] who is studying the Diṭṭhivāya, makes a mistake in speaking, he should not mock him (DVS 8.49).[95]

In other words, Ātmārām was chided for not seriously criticising the principles of the Sthānakavāsīs, which are beyond reproach, but only the lax conduct of individual ascetics, and in so doing harmed himself due to the aggressive style of his attack. The impressive *Loṅkāśāh* [sic!] *Jaina Gurukul,* which was built by the AISJC in 1951 in Sāḍaṛī as a fitting venue for the 1952 *mahāsammelan,* at which the Śramaṇasaṅgha was formally founded, still stocks dozens of copies of this edition of the *Samakitsār,*[96] which demonstrates the key role the text played during the constituent phase of the Śramaṇasaṅgha, both as a symbol of the doctrinal unity of the Sthānakavāsīs and as a common reference source for arguments against the Mūrtipūjakas.

The Ajmer *sammelan* identified the problem of harmonising the different *maryādās* of the Sthānakavāsī *sampradāyas* as one of the prime obstacles for the planned formation of a unified Śramaṇasaṅgha. Another obstacle was the lack of a common origin and lineage. One year after this momentous meeting, the first important study of the history of the Sthānakavāsī tradition as a whole appeared in print: the *Śrī Jaina Dharm ano Prācīn Saṅkṣipt Itihās ane Prabhu Vīr Paṭṭāvalī* by Muni Maṇilāl (1934) of the Līmbḍī Nānī Pakṣa.[97] The text contains a long chapter on the "great reformer" Loṅkā Śāh,[98] in which Maṇilāl – with debatable success – attempted for the first time to resolve the contradictions between the transmitted biographies of Loṅkā in order to clearly establish the historical links between Loṅkā and the various Sthānakavāsī lineages, which are subsequently described in the book. Maṇilāl unearthed much new material,[99] particularly on the Gujarātī traditions, and produced the first comprehensive work on the aniconic traditions, as far as his (not clearly referenced) sources permitted.[100] His work was nevertheless criticised by the General Annual Meeting of the AISJC on the 10.5.1936 for its "incomplete" nature because it does not give a sufficient account of the Ajmer *sammelan*, and probably also because it does not provide much evidence on the Sthānakavāsī traditions in North India.[101] Jñānsundar (1936: 16), whose own publication *Śrīmad Lauṅkāśāh* responded critically to the renewed Sthānakavāsī interest in Loṅkā, did not fail to mention this.

After the Ajmer *sammelan*, the role of Loṅkā as a "founding father" was made more prominent within the Sthānakavāsī movement, and for the first time entire books were devoted to the depiction of his religious reforms. The most widely read account of Loṅkā at the time was the *Dharmaprāṇ-Loṅkāśāh (Krānti no Yugasṛṣṭā)*, by the social reformer Muni Saubhāgyacandra "Santabāḷa" (1939) of the Līmbḍī Moṭī Pakṣa. It was apparently written already in the 1920s and first published in the journal *Sthānakavāsī Jain*, founded in Ahmedabad Pañcabhāī nī Poḷ in 1932,[102] and between 10.11.1935–13.1.1936 re-published in Gujarātī in the form of a series of articles in the journal *Jaina Prakāśa*, the mouthpiece of the AISJC. The text contains few references, although Deśāī's work is mentioned. In the same year (1935), the Sthānakavāsīs celebrated "Loṅkāśāh's birthday"[103] with a national poetry festival in the Rājasthān town Sojat Road. The festival was organised by "Marudhar Keśarī" Mantrī Muni Miśrīmal (1891-1984) of the Raghunātha Sampradāya, a fervent advocate of reform (*kṣetra viśuddhi*) and of the unification of all Sthānakavāsī traditions (Editors, in Miśrīmal 1936: 1), whose speech at the regional *sammelan* of the Sthānakavāsī *sādhus* [sic!] on the 10.3.1932 in the town of Pālī, on the necessity to strengthen the influence of the Sthānakavāsīs "in the world," is now celebrated as one of the pivotal moments of the unification movement.[104] At the time, no "reliable" biography of Loṅkā was available in Hindī, apart from the 1925 translation of V.M. Śāh's (1909) pioneering work. In 1936, Miśrīmal therefore published in Hindī a book entitled *Dharmavīr Loṅkāśāh.* This work relies mostly on V.M. Śāh, Maṇilāl, and Saubhāgyacandra, but also uses two newly discovered sources: a "Prācīn Paṭṭāvalī"[105] which he found in the Jaitāraṇ Bhaṇḍār, and a "few leafs" from the Loṅkāgaccha Upāśray in Kuraḍāyā.[106] It was followed in 1941 by a versified biography called *Krāntikārī Vīr Loṅkāśāh* in 1941, and in 1946 by a short collection of *dohā*s and *ḍhāl*s, biographical poems, called *Vīr Loṅkāśāh.* Saubhāgyacandra's and Miśrīmal's works spread the new

Sthānakavāsī "standard portrait" of Loṅkā throughout the north Indian Jaina world. However, both books contain, if at all, only general references and no critical evaluation of the available sources. Their "scientific" value was therefore dismissed not only by Muni Jñānsundar (1936) in his evidence-based critique of the contemporary Sthānakavāsī historiography, but even by the Sthānakavāsī Muni Suśīlkumār (1959: g), who further disagreed with Saubhāgyacandra's "extreme" (*ativāda*) interest in social reform.

A doctrinal response to Mūrtipūjaka criticisms was formulated in the book *Loṅkāśāh Mat-Samarthan*, "Confirmation of Loṅkā's belief," whose revised version was published in 1939.[107] It is one of four works which were published by Ratanlāl Ḍośī of Sailānā (M.P.) in the 1930s and 1940s to defend key Sthānakavāsī doctrines and practices, such as the rejection of *mūrtipūjā* and the permanent use of the *mukhavastrikā* (which Loṅkā reportedly never wore). Ḍośī was a leading lay intellectual of the orthodox Jñānagaccha and a personal devotee of its *ācārya* Samarthamal (1898-1972), who was opposed to the unification of all Sthānakavāsī traditions. In the work *Loṅkāśāh Mat-Samarthan* he compiled textual evidence from the Śvetāmbara canon in support of the proposition that image worship is uncanonical, which he associated with the name of Loṅkā in a general way. Kesarīcand Bhaṇḍārī's (1938: 92) widely circulated *Sthānakavāsī Jaina Itihās* – one of the first books with the 20th-century self-description "Sthānakavāsī" in the title[108] – also refers to "Ḍośī's (1939) text for authoritative doctrinal arguments. However, this work does not contain any references to Loṅkā's writings, for which no direct evidence existed at the time. The conventional counter-arguments of the Mūrtipūjakas against the "lying *sampradāyavādī*s" – the aniconic traditions – who undermine the "unity" of the Jaina *dharma* were repeated several decades later in the works of the Mūrtipūjaka layman Nagīndās Girdharlāl Śeṭh, *Mūl Jaina Dharma ane Hāl nā Sampradāyo* (1962), *Sthānakavāsī Jaino nuṃ Dharma Kartavya* (1963), and *Loṅkaśāh ane Dharmacarcā* (1964). Whereas Ḍośī worked on the premise that the Sthānakavāsīs continue Loṅkā's doctrinal tradition, Śeṭh (1962: 342) reiterated Jñānsundar's (1936: 171ff.) verdict that the followers of the Loṅkāgaccha and the Sthānakavāsīs are historical enemies. To this purpose, he cites the depiction of Loṅkā in early Mūrtipūjaka and Loṅkāgaccha sources,[109] published by Jñānsundar (1936: 234-240) and Deśāī (1926-44, II-III: 1931-1944), which had been entirely ignored by the Sthānakavāsī commentary literature until the 1960s.

Sixty-Nine Statements

Before the publication of two old manuscripts of the Loṅkāgaccha tradition in 1936 by Jñānsundar (1936: 234-240), "Loṅkā's" beliefs were only indirectly known through the early polemics of his Mūrtipūjaka and Digambara opponents. The earliest known sources for the views of Loṅkā written by his own followers are the *Dayādharma Caupāī*, composed by the Loṅkāgaccha "*yati*" (monk or lay-ascetic) Bhānucandra in Saṃvat 1587 (1521/2),[110] and the *Loṅkāśāha Siloko*, written in Saṃvat 1600 (1543/4) by the Loṅkāgaccha *yati* Keśavarṣi.[111] However, they were not widely circulated and had no notable impact. The oldest dated texts on the Loṅkā-tradition were written by their Mūrtipūjaka opponents. The *Asūtra-nirākaraṇa Batrīśī* of Muni Bīkā was written in Saṃvat 1527 (1470/1),[112] the *Luṅkāmata Pratibodha Kulak* was written by an anonymous author in Saṃvat 1530 (1473/4),[113] the *Siddhānta Caupāī* of Muni Lāvaṇyasamay in Saṃvat 1543 (1486/7),[114] and the short *Siddhānta Sāroddhāra* [*Caupāī*] of Upādhyāya Kamalsaṃyam of the Kharataragaccha in Saṃvat 1544 (1487/8).[115] A text that has often been cited by Sthānakavāsīs is the *Ath Loṅkāśāh nuṃ Jīvan* (ALJ), composed in Pāṭaṇ in Saṃvat 1636 (1579/60) by the Tapāgaccha *muni* Kāntivijay.[116] Apart from a short passage in Ācārya Ratnanandī's *Bhadrabāhu Caritra* vv. 155-163 of Saṃvat 1625 (1568/9), the only presently known Digambara critiques of Loṅkā are the *Loṅkāmata Nirākaraṇa Caupāī* of Sumatikīrti-sūri which was written almost a century after Loṅkā's death, in Saṃvat 1627 (1570/1),[117] and the *Sata Prābhṛta Mokṣa Prābhṛta Ṭīkā* (pp. 305f.) of Bhaṭṭāraka Śrutasāgara.[118] Most of these and similar texts are still difficult to access and have therefore not been properly studied. The only early sources on Loṅkā which were widely accessible in the 19th and early 20th centuries were short passages in Dharmasāgara's *Pravacana Parīkṣā* of 1572 (Saṃvat 1629) and his *Tapāgaccha Paṭṭāvalī Sūtraṃ* of 1589/1590 (Saṃvat 1646).[119]

The first published text which was directly attributed to Loṅkā himself was the *Loṅkejī kī Huṇḍī* (A), or *Ath Huṇḍī Lūṅkārī Likhyate*, which contains sixty-nine doctrinal assertions (*bol*). The printed text is based on a manuscript that was reportedly found in the Sarūpacanda Rāmacanda Upāśraya in Jaitāraṇ, a town in southern Rājasthān which was a centre of the Loṅkāgaccha Nānī Pakṣa until the beginning of the 20th century. It was first published by K.S. Caudharī (1936?: 338-430) in a book called *Jin Jñān Ratnākar*, together with the original *sūtra* texts, which are summarised by "Loṅkā's *bols*," an interpretation of their meaning (*bhāvārtha*) in Hindī, and several versified Rājasthānī commentaries in the *ḍhāl*, *dohā* and *soraṭhā* meters which were composed in 1926 in Jaypur by Gulābcand (Luṇiyā?), a devotee of the Terāpanth Ācārya Kālūgaṇi (1877-1936), who may have discovered the original manuscript.[120] The *bols* were published in a slightly different form and without any commentary by Āñcaliyā (1937: 120-128). Although Kālūgaṇi's oral explanations clearly informed Gulābcand's work,[121] no written commentary on Loṅkā's ideas has ever been created by any Terāpanth Ācārya.[122] The present Terāpanth Ācārya Mahāprajña (2000: 6) always cites the *Loṅkejī kī Huṇḍī* as an authoritative source on Loṅkā's teachings.

Like the famous *ṭabos* (*ṭabbā*) of the Sthānakavāsī Ācārya Dharmasiṁha (1599-1671) and of other, anonymous, authors – vernacular texts which offer rudimentary word-for-word translations of the Prakrit Jaina Āgamas without regard to their syntax – "Loṅkā's *bols*" were, it seems, deliberately disseminated by the lay disciples of Ācārya Kālūgaṇi and his successor Ācārya Tulsī in order to establish an easy access to the "essential teachings" of the Āgamas in a language which everyone could understand.[123] This was important, since, with few exceptions, Sanskrit and Prakrit scholarship was all but lost in the Jaina mendicant traditions in the early 19th century, and did not exist at all within the aniconic traditions before the Jaina revival in the late 19th century.[124] Even in 1936, few Terāpanthī ascetics knew Sanskrit and Prakrit. Another reason for the publication of the text must have been the desire to legitimate the Terāpanth doctrine, which had been the target of critique from all other Jaina sects, with direct reference to Loṅkā, who was accepted as an authoritative reference point within the Sthānakavāsī movement.

It remains doubtful whether this text can really be attributed to Loṅkā. In contrast to other texts attributed to him (see *infra*), the cited passages from the primary literature contain not a single quote from the commentary literature, only citations from the Āgamas,[125] together with the explanations (*bol*) of "Loṅkā" in a quasi stenographic Rājasthānī-Hindī mix (which indicates that these are not

Loṅkā's own words), and of Gulābcand in both Rājasthānī and Hindī. The citations are so skilfully woven together that the resulting text does not assume the form of a casuistic list of unconnected points, but reads like a coherently constructed argument.[126] Moreover, the content of the text corresponds entirely with the views of the Terāpanthīs at the time.[127] It focuses almost exclusively on the principles of proper monastic conduct,[128] as taught by the *kevalins*,[129] the condemnation of non-believers, heresies (*niṇhava*),[130] pseudo-monks,[131] on the strict distinction between the standards for the Jaina householder and the mendicant,[132] and on the prescribed atonements for transgressions.[133] It seems that indirectly the credentials of the Sthānakavāsī *dayā-dāna* theory are also deliberately undermined through the condemnation of the accumulation of good karma through gift-giving and acts of compassion, etc.[134] Instead, the priority of knowledge over compassion is emphasised, and that giving "pure gifts" to a mendicant does not lead to accumulating good karma but to the destruction of karma.[135] In contrast to the available indirect evidence on Loṅkā's teachings, there is no discussion of image-worship at all. It therefore remains doubtful whether the text, which has apparently not been commented upon by any author, is the product of Loṅkā; despite the fact that it also contains some of the most well known of "Loṅkā's" quotations from the canon.[136] Thus, by publishing a hitherto unknown text confirming their own views, together with a Terāpanth commentary, the Terāpanthīs could implicitly claim Loṅkā as their own predecessor while challenging the assertion of the Sthānakavāsīs to be Loṅkā's only legitimate successors.[137]

Our History

The appropriation of Loṅkā by the Sthānakavāsīs was explicit and on quite a different scale. It culminated in the period after the creation of the unified Śramaṇasaṅgha under the rule of only one *ācārya*, which was accomplished after forty-six years of preparation at the *mahāsammelan* in 1952 at the *Loṅkāśāh Jaina Gurukul* in Sāḍaṛī. The Gujarātī Sthānakavāsī *sampradāyas* refused to join the new organisation, which was dominated by Hindī-speaking mendicants. This may have been one of the reasons why, in the decade after the constituent assembly of the Śramaṇasaṅgha, two official histories of the Sthānakavāsī tradition in Hindī were commissioned by the

Śramaṇasaṅgha *ācārya* Ānandṛṣi and the AISJC respectively to put the significance of the new organisation into a historical perspective.[138] The resulting publications are Muni Suśīlkumār's (1959) *Jainadharma kā Itihās* (*Pramukhataḥ Śrī Śvetāmbara Sthānakavāsī Jainadharma kā Itihās*) and Sādhvī Candanākumārī's (1964) *Hamārā Itihās: Sthānakavāsī Śramaṇ-Sāṃskṛtik Paramparā kā Paricāyak*. Both works built on earlier standard histories of the Sthānakavāsī tradition, but did not make use of the published old sources on Loṅkā.[139] Suśīlkumār (1959: g) mentions that his work was initially based on an unpublished manuscript of Saubhāgyacandra "Santabāḷa," which was handed to him by the AISJC. Since he saw no historical value in the manuscript, he wrote an entirely new text on the basis of information from leading mendicant scholars and of unspecified historical sources from Bīkāner, which were made available to him by Agarcand Nāhaṭā in 1957, two years after he started his work.[140] Candanākumārī's book is to a large extent based on Suśīlkumār's text and offers a crisp summary of the historical literature of the Sthānakavāsīs at the time, but without providing any references.[141] Both texts contain extensive sections on Loṅkā, on the Sthānakavāsī-dominated "Loṅkā-śāha Yuga" and on the "Saṅgha Yuga" which begins, according to Suśīlkumār (1959: 2), with the foundation of the Śramaṇasaṅgha in 1952.[142] And both emphasise the differences between the Loṅkā-gaccha "*yatis*," whose tradition is characterised as negligible "after the 15th century," and the Sthānakavāsī "*sādhus*." Candanākumārī (1964: 105) contends that (in the view of the leading mendicants of the Śramaṇasaṅgha) the Sthānakavāsī traditions are the true followers of Loṅkā's doctrine (*siddhānta*) – if not his direct lineal successors.[143] In support of this view, she points to the common lay practice of *dharmadhyāna* in the *sthānakas*, which she interprets as a replication of the ancient institution of the *poṣadhaśālā*; which, according to early Mūrtipūjaka sources, Loṅkā himself is said to have rejected.[144] Both authors employ various strategies to bypass the conventional Mūrtipūjaka emphasis on the importance of a continuous teacher lineage for the transmission of the "authentic" Jaina tradition.[145] Rather than attempting to construct lists of succession in the form of a single *paṭṭāvalī*, which is generally not acceptable within the Sthānakavāsī movement due to the continuing existence of competing lineages or sub-groups with independent histories, the texts present chronological lists of important historical personalities in the Sthānakavāsi tradition.[146] They begin their respective narratives with Ṛṣabha, not with Mahāvīra, whose ancestry is generally favoured: In the work of Bhaṇḍārī (1938: 85-87), who ignored the Loṅkāgaccha tradition entirely, though not Loṅkā himself, it is asserted that "only the Sthānakavāsī *sādhus* are Mahāvīra's true disciples."[147] The opening pages of Bhaṇḍārī's book suggest that the only reason for including the *tīrthaṅkaras* of the "Ādi Yuga" (Suśīlkumār) in a "historical" account is to prove the *ancienneté* of the Jaina tradition *vis à vis* the competing Hindu and Buddhist traditions.

Instead of lists of succession, the concept of a common Sthānakavāsī "culture" (*saṃskṛti*) is invoked – which figures in the title of Canadanākumārī's book – with an emphasis on common scriptures and doctrinal principles. The Śramaṇasaṅgha has also a common code of conduct (*sāmācārī*);[148] but no common rituals and liturgy, which remain different amongst the constituent *sampradāyas*.[149] The "Varddhamāna" Śramaṇasaṅgha has not been able to construct a single official *paṭṭāvalī*, because no consensus could be established amongst the leading monks as to which names should be selected. Instead, it produces *abhinandana granthas* for eminent mendicants within the tradition. These texts comprise *paṭṭāvalīs* of the respective sub-tradition of a particular monk or nun, but not of the united Śramaṇasaṅgha as a whole.

Accordingly, Suśīlkumār and Candanākumārī present the history of the Sthānakavāsī tradition as a chronology of great individuals and their disciples, not as the history of a single lineage of succession going back to Mahāvīra, Pārśva or even Ṛṣabha, as preferred by the constituent sub-groups. Although their contents cannot be described as "mythological," the narrative form of the texts – the chronology of the deeds of selected great beings – represents a spectrum of compromises between the chronological history of modern historiography and the *paṭṭāvalīs* and *gurvāvalīs* on the one hand, and of the cosmologically informed Sthānakavāsī universal histories *à la* Jeṭhmal on the other.[150] As such, the peculiar combinations of history (without source references) and legend reflect the particular problems of legitimation of the Śramaṇasaṅgha.

An extreme example of a new Sthānakavāsī universal history is Ācārya Ghāsīlāl's (1983)[151] Sanskrit [sic!] poem *Śrī Loṅkāśāha Caritam*, which associates Loṅkā and the Sthānakavāsīs, taken together, directly with Mahāvīrā and Gautama,[152] without mentioning any structures of mediation. His *mahākāvya*, he concedes, is based on hearsay or oral (*jabānī*) history for which, as the editor Muni Kanhaiyālāl notes in his introduction, no trustworthy evidence exists.[153] Kanhaiyālāl's remarks show that a century of debate on "factual history" has generated a critical awareness within the Jaina tradition that even the questionable attempts of attributing all common doctrinal features of the "Sthānakavāsī" tradition, such as the rejection of image-worship, the "ur-canon" of thirty-two texts, and the permanent wearing of a *mukhavastrikā*, to the legendary founding father Loṅkā, utilise the toolkits of legend, historiography and canonisation.[154] The age-old method of excluding and including, compiling and re-compiling, of picking-and-choosing – and inventing – authoritative references from the amorphous sediments of the preserved tradition to legitimise contemporary preferences, has, to a certain extent, become self-reflective.[155]

The Discovery of Loṅkā's Scriptures

Thus far, our cursory review of the development of the pivotal role of Loṅkā in the new Sthānakavāsī historiography has shown that received models of "chronological" and "cosmological" history both informed the modern portraits of Loṅkā. Features of the two models were creatively mixed during the modern period of revival of the Jaina tradition, which consciously distinguished itself from earlier epochs through an increasing concern with verifiable "facts" as a principal source of legitimation. In the context of renewed sectarian rivalry, the analysis of vernacular Jain sources – which Schubring (1944: vi) saw as the next important step in the history of Jaina research – has started in India earlier than elsewhere. Methodical research was nevertheless largely confined to the post-independence period, probably benefiting from a slight easing of the overt sectarian tensions within the Jaina tradition.[156]

After more than one hundred years of inquiry, historical sources on Loṅkā and the Loṅkāgaccha from within the aniconic tradition are still extremely rare.[157] The same can be said of critical scholarship of the tradition. The first manuscripts composed by early Loṅkāgaccha *yatis* were discovered and described by Deśāī (1931) in Part II of his ground-breaking study *Gūrjar Kavio.* Two further texts (see *infra*) were published by Jñānsundar (1936: 234-240), who was the first monk to emphatically emphasise that only the study of historical sources itself can provide a more reliable picture of Loṅkā's life and work. Detailed information on Loṅkāgaccha (and

Sthānakavāsī) *paṭṭāvalīs* – in addition to the unreferenced materials provided by Ātmārām (1884/1903) and Vallabhvijay (1891), Śāh (1909) and Maṇilāl (1934), and others – was published in Part III of Deśāī's (1944: 2205-2222) work. Further historical materials on the Loṅkā tradition, such as *gurvāvalīs*, *paṭṭāvalīs*, historical poems and lists of *bols*,[158] were unearthed by the next generation of Jaina scholars in the 1950s and 1960s, in particular by Bhanvarlāl Nāhaṭā (1957), Agarcand Nāhaṭā (1958; 1964; 1966, etc.), Dalsukhbhāī Mālvaṇiyā (1963a; 1963b; 1964; 1965), and Ācārya Hastīmal (1968), who revolutionised the historiography of the aniconic Jaina tradition (see *infra*). Most of these authors con-tributed to the *Muni Śrī Hajārīmal Smṛti Granth*, edited by Śobhā-candra Bhārill (1965), which contains further important articles on the literature of the Loṅkāgaccha tradition by Muni Kāntisāgar (1965) and Ālamśāh Khān (1965).[159] Particularly significant for fu-ture research was Ācārya Hastīmal's (1968) compilation *Paṭṭāvalī Prabandh Saṅgrah*, which made the oldest surviving *paṭṭāvalīs* of the Loṅkāgaccha traditions and the North Indian Sthānakavāsī traditions available for the first time. This fertile period of historical research, during which almost every Sthānakavāsī tradition in-vestigated its own history in order to construct its own *paṭṭāvalī*, culminated in Hastīmal's (1987/1995) synopsis of most of the available material on Loṅkā in the fourth volume of his monumental work *Jaina Dharma kā Maulik Itihās*, after which only the book by Duggar (1989) furnished new information on the extinct lineages of the Loṅkāgaccha in the Pañjāb.

While the outlines of the structure of differentiation of the mendicant lineages of the aniconic tradition became clearly visible by the end of the 1960s, the teachings of Loṅkā, and the doctrinal and organisational differences between Loṅkā and the Loṅkāgaccha traditions, and the Sthānakavāsī traditions remained almost unknown – and to a large extent still are. The answers to these questions hinge on the credibility of the sources on Loṅkā's teachings, in particular Loṅkā's own writings – which probably neither Jñānsundar (1936: 97) nor his adversaries had known – since no traces of the rules and regulations of the various Loṅkāgaccha traditions, whose practices differed from Loṅkā's own, had ever been discovered.

In a series of path-breaking articles, D.D. Mālvaṇiyā (1963a, 1963b, 1964, 1965) identified for the first time two manuscripts in the Puṇyavijaya collection at the L.D. Institute in Ahmedabad which, in his view, can clearly be attributed to Loṅkā himself. The publication of this discovery changed the entire discourse on Loṅkā. The authenticity of the texts is now accepted within the aniconic tradition itself. They are the only documents which were published by the followers of the Loṅkāgaccha itself (Vārīā's 1976 modern Gujarātī translation, in P.T. Śāh 2001), together with summaries of Hastīmal's (1968) collection of Loṅkāgaccha *paṭṭāvalīs*. But Mālvaṇiyā's claim has not remained unchallenged, especially by Mūrtipūjaka authors.

The manuscripts can be attributed to Loṅkā in terms of their contents,[160] which clearly relate to the beliefs of Loṅkā or the Loṅkā tradition, and because both of the two key texts mention "Luṅkā" or the "Luṅkāmatī" at the end;[161] though Loṅkā's name has been deliberately cut out at two places at the beginning and at the end of the Ms. *Luṅkā nā Saddahiyā ane Kariyā Aṭhāvan Bol*, as Mālvaṇiyā (1964: 381) has pointed out.[162] Mālvaṇiyā (1964: 366, 1965: 188) believed that Loṅkā was either the author of these texts, or that the texts have been written under his instruction, since his opponents would have used the Sanskrit term Luṃpaka for Luṅkā, although no final proof has been furnished yet. Śeṭh (1964: 54) disputed Mālvaṇiyā's argument and attributed both texts to the Sthānakavāsī Ācārya Dharmasiṅha. His views were comprehensively rejected by Hastīmal (1995: 759-789)[163] because of the "lack of proof," and with reference to Pārśvacandra Sūri's[164] text *Lūṅkāe Pechela 13 Praśna ane Tenā Uttarī*, which cites Loṅkā's questions concerning image-worship: why should *vandana* be performed to non-living entities, why are *sādhus* not allowed to perform *dravya pūjā*, etc.[165] This 16th-century text is now routinely referred to as a significant source for Loṅkā's views, which indirectly confirms the authenticity of the disputed texts.[166]

Loṅkā's Fifty-Eight Proclamations

The first manuscript attributed to "Loṅkā," No. 2989, has been dated by Mālvaṇiyā (1964: 381) to the 17th century CE. It contains three texts which, judging on the evidence of the handwriting and the format of the texts, must have been written by three different individuals. The main text, *Luṅkā nā Saddahiyā ane Luṅkā nā Kariyā Aṭhāvana Bolo* (L), "Loṅkā's beliefs and fifty-eight assertions created by Loṅkā,"[167] has Loṅkā's name in its title. It is clearly the oldest text of the three. The text is framed by an untitled index of the fifty-eight topics at the beginning of the Ms., and at the end by a list of fifty-four questions to unnamed opponents, which is generally referred to as *Keha nī Paramparā Chai* (K), "Whose tradition is this?," in the secondary literature. Both of these supplementary texts, the index and the *praśnottara* text, must have been added sometime after the completion of the core text, which is the only document of "Loṅkā" which contains not just questions to opponents, but also positive doctrinal statements.[168] The main text (L) consists largely of selected quotations (*uddharaṇa*) from the Śvetāmbara scriptures, on both ethical and abstract doctrinal issues concerning Jaina mendicants as well as laity, and renditions of their meaning in Old Gujarātī. At the beginning of the text the citations form a logical sequence on *samyaktva* which can be read as an entirely new text on the "essence" of the Jaina scriptures, although many subsequent statements take the form of questions and can be attributed to the *praśnottara* genre. The method of weaving selected citations together to form a new text is not fundamentally different from the method of compilation of the Āgamas themselves. Loṅkā's work can therefore be interpreted as a case of secondary canonisation, since many of his tenets are still reflected in the Sthānakavāsī literature, although their original handwritten sources are either lost or hidden away. There are, as Bruhn (1987: 106) has indicated, many examples of canonisation outside the canon in the Jain tradition; and generally the post-canonical literatures achieve a higher degree of closure than the canon itself; which Schubring (1910: 63) pointedly described as a "chaos of atoms." Considering its form, content and function, it would be misleading to classify Loṅkā's *siddhānta* as an instance of a mere literature of use (*Gebrauchsliteratur*),[169] that is as an *ad hoc* composition, since, *de facto*, Loṅkā's teachings established an entirely new doctrinal school within the Jaina tradition.

The text starts with *Āyāra* 1.4.1, the precursor of the later *ahiṃsā vrata*, which uses the term *dayāiṃ dharma*, or law of compassion, to describe the law of non-violence. *Āyāra* 1.4.2.3-6 is then cited in the second statement which comprises the rejection of the negation of this proposition: many Brāhmaṇas and Śramaṇas say that there is nothing wrong in injuring living beings, but this is not true because all living beings fear pain. The third *bol* cites *Āyāra* 1.4.2.1-2 which describes the necessity to discriminate between actions which cause the influx (*āsrava*) of karma and actions which destroy karma (*nirjarā*). The fourth and fifth *bols* establish the importance of the law of compassion (non-violence) as the sole path to liberation (*Sūyagaḍa* 17), by contrasting it to violence, which produces only suffering (*Sūyagaḍa* 18). *Bol* 6 and 7 use for the first time more than one citation within a sustained argument, and leave the monastic sphere behind in order to apply the basic, principles of *bol* 1-5 "with discrimination" to the case of image-worship.[170] Point 6 establishes that unavoidable violence committed in the course of the prescribed duties of a monk, such as crossing a river, must be counteracted through atonements (*prāyaścitta*), and asks why the same rule is not applied to the image worship of the laity. *Bol* 7 argues that "according to the scriptures (*siddhānta*)" the path of liberation (*mokṣa mārga*) cannot be entered through image worship, since it only produces worldly gratification (*phal*). Any other interpretation is "opposed to the scriptures" (*sūtra viruddha*). *Bol* 8 states that liberation can only be accomplished by observing the five *mahāvratas*, the *guptis* and *samitis* on the level of the mendicants, and the *bārah vrata*, and the *ṣaḍāvaśyaka* rituals, etc., on the level of the laity, but not through image-worship, which most of the remaining *bols* address.

Mālvaṇiyā (1964: 382) classified the contents of L into three broad categories: *samyaktva* and *mithyātva;*[171] the inauthenticity of the commentary literature; and the problems associated with *mūrti-pūjā,*[172] such as image-making and installation, *prasāda*, the *sthāpanā nikṣepa,* and the term *caitya* (Pkt. *ceiya*).[173] Other categories could be created, for instance concerning the prominent issues of *tīrtha yātrā,*[174] lay or mendicant practices (generally all points concerning image-worship imply lay conduct), or assertions addressing particular opponents, such as in L 30 (Āgamikagaccha's rejection of *pūjā* with flowers) or L 26, which questions the scriptural basis for the dispute between the view of the Añcalagaccha (and Kaḍuāgaccha) that only the laity can perform *pratiṣṭhās* and other Mūrtipūjaka sects which regard the performance of this ceremony as a prerogative of the mendicants.[175] Only one statement (No. 27) explicitly refers to the Digambaras, asking where in the scriptures the issue of the naked representation of *tīrthaṅkaras* is discussed, which is controversial between Digambaras and Śvetāmbaras.

The analysis of the contents and exegetical procedures employed by the author of this text requires a separate study. A cur-sory view shows that all selected texts belong to the canonical literature (of thirty-two scriptures), though no new classification of the Āgamas is offered. Mālvaṇiyā (1964: 378) argued that Loṅkā only rejected those passages in the commentaries which are not in agreement with the scriptures, which made the creation of a new canon unnecessary.[176] He suggested that the various canons of the aniconic traditions were products of the early Loṅkāgaccha and Sthānakavāsī traditions.[177] These are open questions. The commentary literature – which the author of L evidently knew – is explicitly rejected in L 41, with reference to additional insertions concerning image worship which cannot be found in the original text, and in L 57, which argues that the elaboration of exceptions (*apavāda*) of the prescriptions of the Āgamas in the commentary literature[178] opens the door to laxity. However, the claim that Loṅkā rejected the entire Śvetāmbara commentary literature in the name of a "fundamentalist scriptural literalism,"[179] seems too broad, since all aniconic traditions accept the "philological commentary," while rejecting the "canonical commentary," which while explaining the meaning of the scriptures also mediates creatively between the closed canon and the openness of the world.[180]

If L was really composed by Loṅkā, and there are more arguments in favour than against this assumption, then there can be no doubt that he propagated the necessity for the mendicants to observe the five *mahāvratas*, and for the laity to observe the twelve lay vows (which include the *poṣadha vrata*), the *āvaśyaka* rituals (*sāmāyika, caturviṃśatistava* etc.), and to support the ascetics with offerings of food, *upāśrayas*, etc., if they wish to reap the fruit of salvation (*mokṣa nāṃ phal*).[181] He rejected, however, all rituals which are predicated on violence (against flowers and fruits, water, fire, etc.). The claim by his early Mūrtipūjaka opponents,[182] which Jñānsundar (1936: 98ff.) and Śeṭh (1964) cited in support of their own views, that Loṅkā had rejected the standard Jaina *sāmāyika, pratikramaṇa, poṣadha, dāna* etc. rituals entirely,[183] is neither confirmed by the two published manuscripts of "Loṅkā," nor by his "thirteen questions."[184] The *Dayādharma Caupāī* vv. 15-19 of 1521/2 of the Loṅkāgaccha *yati* Bhānucandra[185] explicitly mentions the practice of two *sāmāyikas* (in the morning and evening), one-day *poṣadha, pratikramaṇa* (not without taking a vow), *pratyākhyāna, dāna* to restrained individuals, *bhāva pūjā* (but not *dravya pūjā*), and the belief in thirty-two Āgamas (v. 19) within his own group;[186] Jñānsundar (1936: 237, n. 1) explains this away as the result of a post-Loṅkā reform, and further argued that no such lay rites could have been practised before probably Bhāṇa introduced them, because the *śrāvaka pratikramaṇa* is not part of the *Āvaśyaka Sūtra* (*Niryukti*) amongst the thirty-two accepted Āgamas, and because it is known that both Loṅkā and Kaḍuā were householders who rejected the *sāmāyika* (Jñānsundar 1936: 105-107). Yet, the statement that Kaḍuā was "also" against the *sāmāyika* is obviously fabricated, since several points of Kaḍuā's *Niyamāvalī* demand its performance.[187] Without taking note of Jñānsundar's writings, Mālvaṇiyā (1964: 367f.) merely mentions that the difference of opinion between Loṅkā and the Mūrtipūjakas over these issues developed only when in Saṃvat 1544 Loṅkā met Lakhamsī, who became his first associate. But Hastīmal (1995: 786-788) points out that nowhere in Loṅkā's own writings is *sāmāyika, poṣadha, pratikramaṇa, pratyākhyāna* or *dāna* rejected in principle. What is rejected is the manner in which these rituals are performed or not performed, for instance the ostentatious giving of gold and money in the context of *pratiṣṭhā*, etc., rituals. He also notices that there is no mentioning of any opposition to *sāmāyika, pratikramaṇa, poṣadha*, etc. in the report on the meeting between Bhāṇā and Kaḍuā in Saṃvat 1539 in the *Kaḍuvāmat Paṭṭāvalī* (*Paṭṭāvalī Parāga Saṃgraha*, p. 483), which would have recorded a debate between the two if Bhāṇā had indeed not practiced these rituals which Kaḍuā himself observed.[188]

Another controversial issue is whether Loṅkāgaccha mendicants observed the *mahāvrata*s, or whether they were *yati*s in the modern sense of half-ascetics from the outset; as apparently the Kaḍuāgaccha ascetics were, though this remains doubtful (Klatt 1888: 58f.; Dundas 1999: 21, cf. 30, n. 11). Modern commentators such as V.M. Śāh (1909: 49f.), Jñānsundar (1936: 97ff.), and Mālvaṇiyā (1964: 367-369), who stressed the difference between Loṅkāgaccha "*yati*s" and Sthānakavāsī "*sādhus*," expressed the opinion (backed by the reports of the Mūrtipūjakas Dharmasāgara and Kamalsaṃyam) that the first leader of the Loṅkāgaccha, Bhāṇā, was known for not observing the *mahāvrata*s and for not wearing the dress of a *sādhu*.[189] He therefore must have been a *yati*, i.e. neither a householder nor a monk; which would turn the Sthānakavāsī mendicants into the first truly *pañca-mahāvratī* ascetics of the aniconic tradition. If this is indeed true, then already the practices of the earliest Loṅkāgaccha ascetics would not have corresponded with the principles of Loṅkā, as articulated in L.

L ends with the statement that *mokṣa* can only be reached through the practice of protecting life (*jīvadayā*),[190] even now [sic!] and in future by everyone, as stated in the *Sūyagaḍa*:

> O ye monks, the virtuous (Jinas) that have been and will be, the followers of the law of Kaśyapa, they all have commended these virtues. Do not kill living beings in the threefold way, being intent on your spiritual welfare and abstaining from sins. In this way numberless men have reached perfection [*siddhā*], and others, who live now, and who are to come, (will reach it) (Sūy 1.2.3.20-21, translated by Jacobi).

Loṅkā's main ("*ekānta*")[191] focus was the doctrine of *dayā dharma*, or the law of compassion.[192] His interpretation of *jīvadayā* is, however, restricted to practising abstinence from violence in general, and does not explicitly recommend an active intervention into the world for the saving of life, as advocated today by most Sthānakavāsī traditions. Since L presents such practices as an aspect of worldly conduct, but not of the *mokṣamārga*, this text could be cited in favour of Ācārya Bhikṣu's interpretation of the dividing line between *laukika* and *lokottara dharma*, though his controversial equation of *puṇya* and *pāpa*, from the *niścaya* point of view, is not discussed in the text.[193] Notably, the text does not reject religious property per se, but declares the gift of *upāśraya*s (= *sthānaka*s) to the mendicants (*sādhu*) as a religious act.

Loṅkā's Thirty-Four Proclamations

The second manuscript, No. 4121, contains only one text, *Luṅkā nī Huṇḍī 34 Bol* (=LH), Loṅkā's list of thirty-four assertions,[194] which gives thirty-three examples from the commentaries for significant deviations from the scriptures under the label of *apavāda*, or exception. The statements No. 1-25 criticise various points of the *Niśītha Cūrṇī*, which cannot be found in the *Nisīha*, No. 26 does the same for the *Uttarādhyayana Vṛtti*, No. 27 for the *Vyavahāra Vṛtti*, Nos. 28-33 for the *Āvaśyaka Niryukti*, and the last section for the *Prajñāpanā Vṛtti*. The underlying ordering principle of the diverse list of topics is the reference to the five *mahāvrata*s. More than one example is given for excuses for the exceptional use of violence in self-defence (Nos. 1, 22, 26); for the violation of the vow on non-possession (Nos. 3, 4); for the violation of the vow of not taking what is not given (Nos. 2, 18, 28, 29); for the violation of the vow of celibacy (Nos. 14, 15, 23);[195] and for using living objects such as water, fire, earth, food, plants, etc., in various contexts. Because the text focuses only on explicit discrepancies between canonical and post-canonical monastic law, and on the use of *prāyaścittas* for normalising transgressions (No. 23), image-worship is not mentioned at all, and neither are issues of contemporary practice. Interestingly, both the *Vavahāra* and the *Āvassaya Sutta* are implicitly referred to, which are often cited in the modern secondary literature as the two texts whose canonical status may have been disputed between the early Loṅkāgaccha and the Sthānakavāsī traditions.[196]

Loṅkā's Fifty-Four Questions to the Image-Worshippers

The fifty-four rhetorical questions *Whose tradition is that?* (*Te Keha nī Paramparā Chai?*),[197] which are appended to the *Aṭhāvan Bol* in the L.D. Institute Ms. 2989, effectively ask (like some of the *Aṭhāvan Bols*) whether any of the listed practices (not beliefs), which must have been prevalent amongst the image-worshipping Jaina traditions of the time, are backed up by the "root" scriptures.[198] Since the answer is assumed to be "no" in all cases, the main function of the questions is to provide summary criticism of the key shortcomings of the addressees of these questions, which in accordance with the etiquette of the *praśnottara* genre are not explicitly mentioned. Fifty-two almost identical questions which were attributed to Loṅkā were published in Hindī in the fourth edition of Muni Jeṭhmal's (1930: 14f.) polemical work *Samakitasāra*.[199] The content of this slightly shorter list overlaps to a large extent with K, but comprises some extra questions, which points to the existence of other recensions which are yet to be unearthed, or to later interpolations.[200] The original text (K) can be translated as follows:

> The tradition is written. Someone says, Śrī Vīra's tradition says this. Where is that?[201]

1. To cause images to be made and to be installed (*maṇḍāvai*) in the house, whose tradition is that?[202] To buy male and female disciples (*celā-celī*), whose tradition is that?[203]
2. To give initiation to small children, whose tradition is that?[204]
3. To change the name (to give a different name at the time of initiation), whose tradition is that?
4. To cause the ear to be extended (*vadhārai*), whose tradition is that?[205]
5. To venerate (*viharai*) the forgiving *guru* (in the presence of symbols), whose tradition is that?[206]

6. To amuse oneself (*viharai*)[207] sitting in the householder's house, whose tradition is that?
7. To go every day to the same house (for food), whose tradition is that?[208]
8. To ask (someone) to take a bath, whose tradition is that?[209]
9. To make use (*prajuṃjai*) of the secret of astrology, whose tradition is that?
10. To tell the future, whose tradition is that?[210]
11. To cause a reception to be held at the time of entering into a town, whose tradition is that?
12. To consecrate sweets, whose tradition is that?
13. To cause the worship of religious books, whose tradition is that?
14. To cause the performance of *saṅghapūjā*, whose tradition is that?[211]
15. To perform installation ceremonies (of idols), whose tradition is that?[212]
16. To give books during *paryuṣaṇa*, whose tradition is that?[213]
17. And to sell pilgrimages, whose tradition is that?[214]
18. And to give a certain amount,[215] whose tradition is that?
19. And to bind garlands made of vegetation to arched gateways, whose tradition is that?
20. To keep specially prepared food (*ādhākarma*) for the ascetics in the *poṣadhaśālā*,[216] whose tradition is that?[217]
21. To create the impression of the importance of the scriptures but not reading them, whose tradition is that?[218]
22. To cause decorative pavilions (for images) to be constructed, whose tradition is that?[219]
23. To cause the fast in the name of[220] "Gautama" to be performed, whose tradition is that?
24. To cause the "Saṃsāratāraṇa" (vow to be taken), whose tradition is that?[221]
25. To cause the "Candanabālā" fast to be performed, whose tradition is that?[222]
26. To cause the "ladder of gold and silver" (*sonā rūpā nī nīsaraṇī*) to be created, whose tradition is that?[223]
27. To cause the "Lākhā Paḍavi" to be performed, whose tradition is that?[224]
28. To cause gifts to be given (*ḍhovarāvai*) to celebrate the end of a fast (*ūṃjamaṇā*), whose tradition is that?[225]
29. To cause the *pūjā* to be recited,[226] whose tradition is that?

30. To cause the "Aśoka-tree" (*āso vṛkṣa*) to be supported (*bharavāi*),[227] whose tradition is that?[228]
31. To cause the eightfold bath (*aṭṭhottarī snātra*) to be performed, whose tradition is that?[229]
32. To cause fresh rice and fresh fruit to be offered in front of an image, whose tradition is that?[230]
33. To put sandalwood powder[231] on the head of laymen and laywomen, whose tradition is that?
34. To be involved[232] in the search for possessions, whose tradition is that?[233]
35. To cause the laity to offer a head tax (*pāīṃ mūṇḍaka*) before ascending a hill (pilgrimage site), whose tradition is that?[234]
36. To place garlands (on persons or idols), whose tradition is that?[235]
37. To permit laymen and laywomen to walk together (during pilgrimages) by foot, whose tradition is that?[236]
38. To cause the "Nāndi"[237] to be erected, whose tradition is that?
39. To cause foot-prints (shrines) (*padīka cāṃka*) to be built, whose tradition is that?
40. To put powder (*bhūko*) into the water, whose tradition is that?[238]
41. To cause worship (*vāndaṇā*) to be offered, whose tradition is that?[239]
42. To move the broom (*oghā*) (in front of the idols), whose tradition is that?[240]
43. To keep the *deva dravya*, whose tradition is that?[241]
44. To wear a long covering garment (*pacheṛī*) down to the feet, whose tradition is that?[242]
45. To accept the *sūrimantra*, whose tradition is that?[243]
46. To recite the *sūrimantra* every day, whose tradition is that?[244]
47. To shine in starched[245] (white clothes), whose bright tradition is that?
48. To cause the "Bairakanhai" fast to be performed during *paryuṣaṇa*, whose tradition is that?[246]
49. To cause a waterpot (*ghaḍūlā*) to be made, whose tradition is that?[247]
50. To cause the *āyambila olī* fast to be performed together with the *siddha-cakra* (*pūjā*), whose tradition is that?[248]
51. To hold a ceremony of mourning (*ūṭhamaṇuṃ*)[249] after the death of an ascetic, whose tradition is that?

52. To cause the swinging of the images (of the fourteen dreams of Mahāvīra's mother) to be performed, whose tradition is that?[250]
53. To create a decorated table (*ṭhavaṇī*) in front of the feet (of an ascetic or an image),[251] whose tradition is that?
54. To perform the *pratikramaṇa* on the fourth day (of the second lunar fortnight) of *paryuṣaṇa*, whose tradition is that?[252]

Notably, the questions are addressed to a Jaina mendicant, not to the laity, and imply a mendicant perspective. The basic question, whether any of the fifty-four listed beliefs and practices corresponds to the teachings of the root scriptures seems, at first sight, to reflect an attitude of a-temporal lay-inspired scriptural literalism which deliberately ignores the commentary traditions of the teachers of the mendicant lineages.[253] However, a closer view reveals that Loṅkā may not have rejected commentaries per se, especially not those (such as the later vernacular *ṭabo*s) which merely explain the meaning of the *sūtra*s themselves, but only commentaries or parts of commentaries whose contents do not correspond at all to the teachings of the root scriptures. Mālvaṇiyā 1964: 377f. argued that this interpretation is supported by the fact that the two Mss. which have been attributed to Loṅkā make use of all available Jaina scriptures and commentaries. Further evidence for a positive attitude toward the commentaries in the aniconic Jaina tradition can be found in the published Sthānakavāsī and Terāpanth Āgama editions which make explicit use of all commentaries in order to establish the literal meaning of the *sūtra*s themselves, though some modern monks, such as Upādhyāya Amarmuni, argue that because of their condensed nature the *sūtra*s are intrinsically polyvalent and can therefore only be interpreted symbolically.[254] In contrast to Mālvaṇīya's view that the canon of thirty-two was codified after the emergence of the Sthānakavāsī orders, there is evidence that Loṅkā himself advocated for a restricted canon of thirty-two scriptures in Bhānucandra's *Dayādharma Caupāī* v. 19 of 1521/2, though, if Mālvaṇīya's source Dharmasāgara's *Pravacanaparīkṣā* of 1572/3 can be believed, it had not been canonised one hundred years later. According to Kāpaḍiā (1941/2000: 38, 53), even the current Mūrtipūjaka classification of forty-five scriptures emerged sometime after the 14th century. The construction of alternative Āgama classifications in the late medieval period thus appears to be generally a product of sectarian politics, predicated on the emergence of a new style of text-oriented critique in "reformed" *gaccha*s and *gaṇa*s.

The fifty-four questions are *de facto* commentaries themselves, whose contents have in parts been canonised in the aniconic tradition. Their rhetoric may be literalist and fundamentalist, but they function as means of innovation and of canonisation, since they censure certain customary practices which back them up, while favouring others which are not explicitly mentioned. The fluidity of the usage of textual allusions is illustrated by Loṅkā's objection to child initiation (K2) which contradicts the canonical *Vavahāra* 10.16f.,[255] and by the fact that the equally rejected custom of changing names at the point of initiation (K3) is nowadays practiced by several Sthānakavāsī traditions,[256] and by the Terāpanthīs. Since much of the meaning of the fifty-four questions is contextual and implicit, their interpretation must remain tentative. However, the collection and analysis of similar lists from the same period, as studied by Dundas (1999) and Balbir (2003a; 2003b), may in future produce a clearer view of the sectarian faultlines in the 15th and 16th centuries.

Loṅkā's Teachings According to Modern Sthānakavāsī Sources[257]

With the publications of Mālvaṇiyā and Hastīmal, in particular, fruitful comparisons between the early beliefs and customs of different aniconic traditions are rendered possible for the first time. Of special interest is the reconstruction of the early development of the Loṅkāgaccha for which still hardly any evidence exists. For the present investigation of the effective history of Loṅkā the comparison between "Loṅkā's" writings and versions of his teachings transmitted within the Sthānakavāsī tradition is important, as are preliminary observations on the differences between the customary law (*maryādā*) of the early Sthānakavāsī traditions and "Loṅkā's" proclamations.

To my knowledge, in addition to the paraphrases in Jeṭhmal (1930), only two texts are currently available on Loṅkā's rules in the Sthānakavāsī secondary literature. One was published by Sādhvī Candanākumārī (1964: 102)[258] and the other by Gulābacanda Nānacanda Seṭh (1970: 703f.).[259] This is somewhat surprising, given the importance of Loṅkā as the founder of the aniconic Jaina traditions. However, a recent survey by the present writer has shown that most of the ancient sources of the comparatively sparse literary output of the aniconic traditions before the 20th century has either been lost or not been catalogued or used. Even the writings of the founders of the Sthānakavāsī traditions have not been preserved in their original form. It is therefore not surprising that no literary traces of the debates between the followers of the Loṅkā traditions and the Sthānakavāsī (and Terāpanth) traditions have been discovered to date.[260] Candanākumārī (1964: 102) writes that several manuscripts of the regulations (*niyama*) which Loṅkā himself composed for the Loṅkāgaccha mendicants (*sādhu-saṃsthā*) can be readily found in old Jaina libraries. She therefore decided to publish only a selection of eleven particularly "useful" rules in summary form in Hindī under the title *Loṅkāgaccha kī Sāmācārī* (LS).[261] Without acknowledgement of the source, her list was republished in Gujarātī by Muni Prakāścandra (1998: 31) of the Līmbḍī Moṭī Pakṣa.

The code of conduct of the Loṅkāgaccha[262] :

1. Only the Sanskrit commentaries (*ṭīkā*) which agree with the scriptures are acceptable as authoritative.
2. One should live a steadfast disciplined life in agreement with the scriptures.
3. From the point of view of religion "image-worship" is not in agreement with the scriptures.
4. Genuine, pure vegetarian food can be accepted from every family [caste].
5. It is not necessary for anyone to set up the symbols of the monastic order (*sthāpanācārya*) [for worship].[263]
6. During the vows of *upavāsa*,[264] etc., absolutely all types of lifeless (*prāsuka*) water can be accepted.
7. The one-day fast (*upavāsa*) can even be performed on days other than the lunar holy days (*parva-tithi*).[265]
8. There is no need for monks to practise the skills of *mantra-tantra* and *yantra*, etc.
9. Laymen can beg, but cannot receive religious gifts (*dāna*).
10. To give gifts (*dāna*) to the poor due to the feeling of compassion is not a sin (*pāpa*), but rather the cause of merit (*puṇya*).
11. There is no need to keep a staff (*daṇḍa*).[266]

If this list was indeed composed on the basis of primary literature, then the information must have been selected from all the texts that have been attributed to Loṅkā to date. The critique of the validity of the Jaina commentary literature in point one, for instance, is mainly discussed in the *Loṅkā nī Huṇḍī 34 Bol*, and the *locus classicus* of Loṅkā's critique of image worship is the text *Luṅkā nī Aṭhāvan Bol.* Candanākumārī's method of extraction and her utilitarian criterion of "contemporary relevance" offers a glimpse into the rational of the strategies of selection, exegesis and transmission of chosen elements of the doctrinal tradition and of the customary law within the aniconic Jaina mendicant traditions.

A second Sthānakavāsī source for the rules and regulations of Loṅkā was published by Gulābcand Nāncand Seṭh (1970: 703f.), a poet who was hired to write down the results of the extensive historical research of Muni Cauthmal (died 1951) on the life of Ācārya Jaymal, which was completed by the *munis* Cāndmal (1908-1968), Jītmal and Lālcand, who in 1964 split from the Śramaṇasaṅgha in protest against the controversial institutional reforms of Ācārya Ānandṛṣi, and founded the independent Dharmadāsa Jayamala Sampradāya.[267] The bulky text, entitled *Jaydhvaj*, was published with the aim of strengthening the sectarian identity of the newly established tradition. The publication was supported by the influential Ācārya Hastīmal, who in 1968 also separated himself from the Śramaṇasaṅgha to re-establish the Ratnavaṃśa as an independent order. Hastīmal (1968) had already published a collection of *paṭṭāvalīs* of the Loṅkāgaccha tradition and of the Sthānakavāsīs, and systematically researched the history of the aniconic Jaina tradition during the following two decades.[268] The following twenty points (LN) which Seṭh attributes to Loṅkā have been summarised by him in Hindī without any reference to the original source. The introductory sentence only mentions that Loṅkā prepared this *sāmācārī* in Saṃvat 1531 (1474/5 CE) in order to prevent the rise of *śithilācāra*, or laxity, amongst the *sādhus* of Bhāṇā's newly created Loṅkāgaccha:[269]

1. Even without having completed the *upadhāna* fast one can study the scripture.[270]
2. From the point of view of religion, worshipping the Jina image is not in the forty-five scriptures.
3. Apart from the root aphorism (*sūtra*), the scripture (*āgama*) and the root teaching (*śāstra*), joined together with the Sanskrit commentaries (*ṭīkā*), other scripture and Sanskrit commentary is not to be believed in any respect.
4. It is forbidden to practice magical skills (*vidyā*).

5. The fast day (*poṣadha*) [and the] ritual of repentance (*pratikramaṇa*) is performed according to individual custom.
6. Apart from *cāturmāsa*, one can also use a seat (*pāṭa*) [during the rest of the year].[271]
7. One should not keep a staff.
8. One can possess books.[272]
9. Paying attention to genuineness and purity, one can collect alms from every family.
10. A layperson (*śrāvaka*) can also perform the almsround (*gocarī*).
11. A layperson (*śrāvaka*) cannot accept a religious gift (*dāna*).
12. During fasting (*upavāsa pratyākhyāna*) one can take lifeless whey (*āch*) of buttermilk.[273]
13. *Poṣadha* can even be performed without practising a one-day fast.[274]
14. A one-day fast (*upavāsa*) can even be performed on days other than the lunar holy days (*tithi parva*).
15. One can take the vow of a one-day fast together (in a group).
16. One should not enumerate the auspicious days (*kalyāṇaka*) amongst the lunar days (*tithi*).[275]
17. The day on which one takes a milk product, on that day one should not use hard (*dvidala* grains).[276]
18. It is not necessary to set up a *sthāpanācārya*.
19. Within forty-eight minutes (*do ghaṛī*) life is generated in waste water (*dhovaṇa*).[277]
20. From a religious understanding, to give a gift (*dāna*) to an unworthy one (*apātra*) must be violence to give to a poor person out of compassion is not the cause of the fault of one-sidedness (*ekānta pāpa*)).[278]

The list overlaps to a great extent with Candanākumārī's, and may indeed have served as the immediate source for Candanākumārī's selection of useful points. In many cases the wording is almost identical. Another indication is that Seṭh's list is much more detailed, and must have been available to Candanākumārī, because it was apparently composed by Muni Cauthmal, who died in 1951, although it was published much later.[279] It is an intriguing but currently unanswerable question whether all of these rules go back to Loṅkā, or Bhāṇa, or whether at least some of these rules have been created by subsequent Loṅkāgaccha or Sthānakavāsī writers. Rule 2 states wrongly that worshipping images is not mentioned in the "forty-five" scriptures.

Loṅkā and Kaḍuā

As indicated in the footnotes, most, but not all, points of the two largely overlapping lists concur with topics of "Loṅkā's" texts L, LH and K, and can be said to be historically akin to Loṅkā's teachings. However, certain points, particularly on gift giving and *jīva-dayā* (see *infra*), seem to be later additions,[280] while many of the more intricate points in Loṅkā's texts have been left out altogether. Although the wording sometimes differs, the contents of Candanākumārī's list (LS) are entirely covered by Seṭh's list,[281] which confirms its derivative nature. The two lists have only few issues in common with the reported *maryādā*s of three of the founders of the Sthānakavāsī tradition, Dharmasiṅha, Lava, and Dharmadāsa.[282] But many points mirror Kaḍuā's rules, which were, as Jñānsundar (1936: 327, n. 4, etc.) suspected, probably formulated in contradistinction to Loṅkā's rules or vice versa. Though they differ in certain details, many of the transmitted rules of Loṅkā and Kaḍuā address similar issues. The main common topics are "ascetic"[283] rituals for the laity, such as the *pratikramaṇa*, *sāmāyika*, *upadhāna*, and *poṣadha*, which is often discussed in connection with the *upavāsa* fast. However, because both authors discuss many areas of monastic conduct as well, which do not overlap, it cannot be inferred from this that the followers of either Loṅkā and/or Kaḍuā were advanced householders, or *yati*s, and not mendicants. If the two Sthānakavāsī lists are considered together ("Loṅkā's" writings), the following picture emerges with regard to the lay rituals:

> Both Loṅkā and Kaḍuā advocated the performance of the *pratikramaṇa* ritual, according to individual (LN 5) and group custom, not scripture (there are no *pratikramaṇa* texts in the Āgamas). However, Loṅkā (K 58) determined that, in accordance with the scriptures, the *Saṃvatsarī pratikramaṇa* should be performed on the 5th *bhadrapāda*, not on the 4th *bhadrapāda* as Kaḍuā (following the Tapāgaccha custom) prescribed (KS 4). Contrary to the scriptures, Kaḍuā also fixed the *pākṣika pratikramaṇa* for the 14th of every lunar fortnight, not for the 15th (KS 3), and additionally adopted the *tristuti* formula (KS 11), which has been introduced by the Āgamikagaccha into the *pratikramaṇa*.[284]

Loṅkā (K 8) and Kaḍuā (KS 6) also agreed that the *sāmāyika* should be performed repeatedly. But only Kaḍuā asserted that the laity should use a *muhapattī* during the ritual (KS 5), and should recite the *īryāpathika ālocanā* after the first *sāmāyika* (KS 15).

The *poṣadha* is the topic of many points. It is usually discussed together with the topic of the one-day-fast (*upavāsa*).[285] Both Loṅkā (LS 7) and Kaḍuā (KS 7) determined that *poṣadha* can be performed repeatedly according to individual preference (LN 5), even outside the *parvan* days, on which it is obligatory.[286] However, Kaḍuā (KS 13) prohibited the consumption of all food or water during the fast (*upavāsa*), whereas Loṅkā permitted the use of all types of lifeless water, and of the whey (*āch*) of buttermilk, the use of which was/is prohibited in many Sthānakavāsī traditions.[287] Kaḍuā stressed particularly that women can also perform *poṣadha* (KS 11). Loṅkā emphasised that one *upavāsa* can be performed together in a group (LN 15).

The statements KS 11 and LN 15 may refer to the collective *upadhāna* fast as well. The *upadhāna* is an extended *poṣadha* (*cum* study) exercise, that was propagated by Loṅkā and Kaḍuā, who both however rejected the ceremonial garlanding of the *tapasvīns* with flowers at the end of the fast (K 36, KS 9), as performed by the Mūrtipūjakas. At the time, the *upadhāna* must have been performed either with or without studying, otherwise Loṅkā would not have highlighted that one can study the scripture "even without having completed the *upadhāna* fast" (LN 1); although his rule may also reflect customary prohibitions for studying certain texts without prior fasting.

The principal difference between Kaḍuā and Loṅkā, according to the lists published by Seṭh and Candanākumārī, was that Kaḍuā, who assumed an intermediary position between Loṅkā and the Mūrtipūjakas (especially the dominant Tapāgaccha), also propagated image-worship (KS 1, KS 20),[288] though rejecting the installation (*pratiṣṭhā*) of images by monks rather than laity (KS 2). Kaḍuā also advocated the veneration of the *sthāpanācārya* (KS 10), which Loṅkā rejected as a "worship of dead objects" (LS 5, LN 18). These differences can be explained in terms of fundamentally different attitudes to the scriptures, because Kaḍuā accepted the authority of the post-canonical calendar,[289] and maybe (though there is no evidence) defined the auspicious days (*kalyāṇaka*) as moon days (*tithi*) which Loṅkā explicitly criticised (since this would artificially reduce the number of fast days) (LN 16), and commentaries such as the *Āvaśyakacūrṇi* (KS 13, KS 15) or the *Bṛhatkalpabhāṣya* (KS 8) which Loṅkā had rejected (L 57, LS 1),[290] though both referred to the "seniors" of the canon as the main source for monastic conduct (KS 18).[291]

Conclusion: Remarks on Compassionate Giving

One of the most controversial issues in the aniconic Jaina tradition is the question of the origins of the so-called *dāna-dayā* theory, the doctrine of the religious value of the protection of life through charity and active compassionate help, not only to Jainas but to all living beings. Under Ācārya Bhikṣu, the Terāpanth tradition split from the Sthānakavāsī Dharmadāsa Raghunātha Sampradāya because it believed that such actions contributed only to the accumulation of *puṇya*, but nothing to the reduction of the overall karmic load. From the absolute point of view (*niścaya naya*), therefore, compassionate help is an impediment to ultimate salvation, and in this sense a sin (*pāpa*). The Terāpanthīs tend to claim that Loṅkā already rejected the *dāna-dayā* theories of the Mūrtipūjakas and Sthānakavāsīs, and that they are presently the only aniconic tradition which still pursues Loṅkā's neo-orthodox point of view. It seems that the text *Loṅkejī kī Huṇḍī* was published deliberately by the Terāpanth tradition in the mid-1930s, when the sectarian disputes within the Jaina community peaked, to prove this point. By contrast, many contemporary Sthānakavāsīs believe that Loṅkā was the originator of their own interpretation of the *dāna-dayā* theory, which promotes merit-making through *dāna* for financing *gośālā*s rather than temples, although Jñānsundar (1936: 210, n. 1) and other critics of the aniconic tradition argued, with reference to early Mūrtipūjaka polemics against Loṅkā, that it must have been one of the early leaders of the Loṅkāgaccha who introduced this doctrine, since Loṅkā rejected the religious merit of gift giving altogether (for purposes other than sustaining the subsistence of worthy mendicants), though L commends the sponsorship of *upāśraya*s.[292] At the same time, most modern commentators underline that Loṅkā himself was not an initiated monk, and that even the early Loṅkāgaccha ascetics may have been *yati*s, half-ascetics in the modern sense, rather than *sādhu*s and *sādhvī*s, and thus must have stood with one foot in the world.[293] This remains an open question, although Loṅkā's own writings suggest that Loṅkā himself was vigorously opposed to a semi-ascetic lifestyle (L8 and LH whose structure is informed by the *mahāvrata*s). The example of contemporary Digambara *bhaṭṭāraka*s[294] indicates that even *yati*s tend to be *pañca-mahāvrati*s, they simply do not observe the rules strictly, or interpret them slightly differently, not unlike the *aṇuvrata*s for the laity.

of particular interest in this context are the three statements concerning compassionate gift giving (*dāna-dayā*) in the two Sthānakavāsī summaries of "Loṅkā's" teachings, LS and LN. For these statements, no equivalent assertions can be found in "Loṅkā's" texts L, LH, and K, which use *dayā dharma* and *jīva dayā* merely as synonyms of *ahiṃsā dharma*.[295] The rules LS 4 = LN 9 describe in a straightforward way that a renouncer can collect food from all families, without regard to caste and class, if the food and the manner of giving correspond to the canonical rules.[296] This contrasts both with the rule No. 75 of *101 Bol* of the Kaḍuāgaccha which prohibits the renouncers to visit houses of followers of the Loṅkāgaccha,[297] and with the Mūrtipūjaka preference for *vaṇik* (*vāṇiyā*) households as expressed in rule No. 2 of the *Pāṭīs Bol* (PB) of 1526/7 of the Mūrtipūjaka reformer Ācārya Ānandvīmalsūri (1490-1539).[298] The texts ascribed to Loṅkā himself remain silent on this point.

Rules LS 9 = LN 10+LN 11 are more puzzling. They state that "a layperson" can perform *gocarī* in the manner of an ascetic, but cannot receive *dāna* in the manner of an ascetic. How can this be understood? The use of the term *gocarī* rules out non-religious contexts of begging which are addressed in LS 10. The most likely explanation points to the definition of the intermediary stages between householder and mendicant, since the religious status of Loṅkā and the Loṅkāgaccha ascetics was disputed from the beginning in the literature. In the eleventh *pratimā*, or stage of spiritual progress for the laity, a lay person should renounce all business of the world, has the head shaven, is clad in a mendicant's garment, carries a broom (*rajoharaṇa*), and a begging bowl (*pātra*), and performs the begging round, though technically not in the same manner as a monk (Williams 1983: 178-180). This means that although a layperson who took the vow of the eleventh *pratimā* performs the almsround in exactly the same way as a mendicant, technically s/he does not qualify for being a worthy receiver (*supātra*) for a religious gift (*dāna*) which generates a destruction of *karma* (and the accumulation of *puṇya karma*) on the part of the giver.

The rules concerning giving must have been created or selected from an unmentioned source by the Sthānakavāsīs to clearly demarcate the status of a properly initiated mendicant from an advanced householder or (Loṅkāgaccha) *yati*.[299] A material gift can, after all, also become a means of material enrichment. This explanation corresponds well to LN 20, which is addressed not to the receiver but to the giver. The first part states: "From a religious understanding, to give a gift (*dāna*) to an unworthy one (*apātra*) must be violence." This statement coincides with the conventional view presented in the Āgamas and in the Śrāvakācāra literature.[300] However, rather than representing the summary of a statement of "Loṅkā," the second part of the assertion (in brackets) seems to introduce a new argument, which lends support to the dominant Sthānakavāsī position in the debate with the Terāpanthīs on the nature of the pure gift (*śuddha dāna*), seen from the transcendent (*niścaya*) and conventional (*vyavahāra*) perspectives: "to give to a poor person out of compassion is not the cause of the fault of one-sidedness" (*ekānta pāpa*).[301] In contrast to the first part of LN 20, the equivalent formulation LS 10 in the list of Candanākumārī is not entirely consistent with the previous rules on giving, by eliminating the brackets and by using the unqualified term *dāna*[302] for the compassionate giving to the "poor" (*garīb*), while avoiding the doctrinal term *kupātra*: "To give gifts (*dāna*) to the poor due to the feeling of compassion is not a sin (*pāpa*), but rather the cause of merit (*puṇya*)." This interpretation contrasts both with the Terāpanth distinction between *lokottara dāna* and *laukika dāna* and with the conventional Sthānakavāsī interpretation of religious charity, which also stresses the suboptimal, if sometimes acceptable, character of giving to a *kupātra* or *apātra*. Given the subsequent life-course of the author Candanākumārī, the founder of the reformist Vīrāyatan group of nuns who engage in social work in the manner of Christian nuns,[303] it must be assumed that the word *dāna* was used intentionally in an unqualified form. It should be interesting to trace the origins of this belief in *anukampā dāna*, a concept which is mentioned already in the canonical texts *Ṭhāṇa* 10.475 and *Viyāhapannatti* 304b but re-projected and attributed to Loṅkā within the Sthānakavāsī traditions which now regard it as their own distinctive teaching. The contemporary Loṅkāgaccha tradition itself has lost all written sources and retains no cultural memory anymore on the doctrinal views of Loṅkā or the earlier Loṅkāgaccha *ācāryas*.

References

Primary Sources

A = *Loṅkejī kī Huṇḍī*, of Loṅkā. (Reportedly based on a Rājasthānī Ms. of Saṃvat 1830 in the Rūpacanda Rāmacanda Upāśraya, Jaitāraṇa.) With a *dohā*-style commentary of Gulābcand (Luṇiyā?), written in Jaypur in 1926. Published in Caudharī 1936?: 338-430. A corrupted version of the Rājasthānī root text has been published under the title *Ath Huṇḍī Lūṅkārī Likhyate* in Āñcaliyā 1937: 120-128.

AB = *Asūtranirākaraṇ Batrīśī*, of the Mūrtipūjaka Muni Bīkā. Ca. Saṃvat 1527 (1470/1). Published in Jñānsundar 1936, Appendix 1, pp. 230-233; Koṭhārī 2001: 500-503.

ALJ = *Ath Loṅkāśāh nuṃ Jīvan*, of the Tapāgaccha Muni Kāntivijaya. Written in Pāṭaṇ in Saṃvat 1636 (1579/60). Published in Maṇilāl 1934:161f.; Hastīmal 1995: 752-759.

DC = *Dayādharma Caupāī*, of the Lauṃkāgacchīya Yati Bhānucandra. Saṃvat 1587 (1521/22). Published in Jñānsundar 1936, Appendix 2, pp. 234-237.

DVS = *Dasaveyāliya* (*Daśavaikālika Sūtra*), of Ārya Sayyaṃbhava. Edited by Ernst Leumann. And translated, with introduction and notes, by Walther Schubring. Ahmedabad: The Managers of the Sheth Anandji Kalianji, 1932. (Reprinted in: *Kleine Schriften* (ed. Klaus Bruhn): 109-248. Wiesbaden: Franz Steiner, 1977.) – *Arya Sayyanbhava's Daśavaikālika Sūtra.* Translation and Notes by Kastur Chand Lalwani. Delhi: Motilal Banarsidass, 1973.

J = *Jinacariya.* Translated by Hermann Jacobi as *Lives of the Jinas.* In: Sacred Books of the East, 22 (1884): 217-285.

K = *Keha nī Paramparā Chaī?*, of Loṅkā. Ms. No. 2989, L.D. Institute, Ahmedabad. A Hindī variation is published in Jeṭhmal 1930: 14f. The original is published in: Mālvaṇiyā 1963a: 80-82; Vārīā 1976: 127-130 with a Gujarātī translation; Hastīmal 1995: 691-693; reprinted in Jain & Kumār 2003: 537-539, with a Hindī translation pp. 118-120.

KS = "*Kaḍuā-Mat kī Sāmācārī,*" on the basis of Śāh Kalyāṇavijaya's Kaṭukamat Paṭṭāvalī. Saṃvat 1684 (1628/9). Translated by Dundas 1999: 21f. A slightly different extract was published by Muni Jñānsundar (1936: 326-336) under the title *Kaḍuā-Mat Paṭṭāvalī kā Sār.*

L = *Luṅkā nā Aṭhāvana Bolo*, of Loṅkā. Ms. No. 2989, L.D. Institute, Ahmedabad. See also Mss. No. 19224 and 19225, Oriental Institute, Baroda; Ms. Rājagranthāsāra, Prācya Vidyāpīṭha, Śāhajāpura (photographic reproduction in:

Jain & Kumār 2003, Pariśiṣṭa). Ms. No. 2989, L.D. Institute, published by Mālvaṇiyā 1963a: 52-82; Vārīā 1976: 1-127, with a Gujarātī translation; Hastīmal 1995: 655-691; reprinted in Jain & Kumār 2003: 403-537 with a Hindī summary pp. 124-139.

LH = *Luṅkā nī Huṇḍī Cauṃtīs Bol*, of Loṅkā [?]. Ms. No. 4121, L.D. Institute, Ahmedabad. Extract (*Loṅkāśāh ke Cauṃtīs Bol*) in Hastīmal, 1995: 648-655; reprinted in Jain & Kumār 2003: 499-503, with a Hindī summary pp. 120-123.

LN = "*Loṅkā's Niyamāvali.*" In Gulābcand Nāncand Seṭh 1970: 703f.

LP = *Loṅkāgacchīya Paṭṭāvalī* (Bābu Puraṇcandjī Nahār no Bhaṇḍār). In Koṭhārī 2001: 405-407. (First published in the Jain Śvetāmbara Conference Herald, April-June 1918, 169-171).

LS = *Loṅkāgaccha kī Sāmācārī*. In Candanākumārī 1964: 102.

LTC = *Luṅkā nū 13 nī Carcā*, of Pārśvacandrasūri of the Pārśvacandragaccha. Ca. 16th century CE. Mss. No. 24466, 30565, L.D. Institute, Ahmedabad. Extract (*Luṅkāe Pūchela 13 Praśna ane tenā Uttaro*) in Hastīmal 1995: 694f.; reprinted in: Jain & Kumār 2003: 439-441, with a Hindī translation pp. 115-117.

PB = *Paiṃtīs Bol*, of the Mūrtipūjaka Ācārya Ānandvīmalsūri. Saṃvat 1583(1526/7). Published in Hastīmal 1995: 582-584.

PP = *Pravacanaparīkṣā*, of Upādhyāya Dharmasāgara, 1572/3. Surat: Ṛṣabhadeva Keśaramalajī Śvetāmbara Saṃstha, 1937.

SC = *Siddhānta Caupāī*, of the Mūrtipūjaka Muni Lāvaṇyasamaya. Saṃvat 1543 Kārtik śukla aṣṭamī (5.11.1486/7). Published in Jñānsundar 1936, Appendix 1, pp. 209-227; Koṭhārī 2001: 486-499.

SS = *Siddhānta Sāroddhāra* [*Caupāī*], of the Kharataragaccha Upādhyāy Śrī Kamalsaṃyam. Saṃvat 1544 [1487]. Published in Jñānsundar 1936, Appendix 1, pp. 228f; Koṭhārī 2001: 499-500.

Sūy = *Sūyagaḍa (Sūtrakṛtāṅga Sūtra)*. Translated by Hermann Jacobi. In: Sacred Books of the East, 45 (1895): 233-435.

TPS = *Tapāgaccha Paṭṭāvalī Sūtraṃ*, of Dharmasāgara. Saṃvat 1646 [1589/90]. Published in Darśanavijaya 1933: 41-119.

Viy = *Viyāhapannatti (Bhagavaī). The Fifth Anga of the Jaina Canon.* Introduction, Critical Analysis, Commentary & Indexes. Brugge: Rijksuniversiteit de Gent, 1970.

Ṭhāṇa = *Ṭhāṇa (Sthānāṅga).* Mūla Pāṭha, Saṃskṛta Chāyā, Hindī Anuvāda tathā Ṭippaṇa. Vācana Pramukha: Ācārya Tulsī. Sampādak-Vivecaka: Muni Nathmal. Lāḍnūn: Jaina Viśva Bhāratī, 1976.

YŚ = *Yogaśāstra of Hemacandra. A Twelfth Century Handbook on Śvetāmbara Jainism.* Translated by Olle Qvarnström. (Harvard Oriental Series, 61.) Cambridge, Mass.: Harvard University Press, 2002.

Secondary Sources

AISJC = Akhil Bhāratīya Sthānakavāsī Jaina Kānfrens (ed.), *Akhil Bhāratvarṣīya Vardhamān Sthānakavāsī Jaina Śramaṇ Saṅghīya Samācārī.* Compiled by Saubhāgyamuni "Kumud." Dillī: Akhil Bhāratīya Varddhamaṇ Sthānakavāsī Jaina Kānfrens, 1987.

Amarvijay, Muni (ed.) 1908. *"Ḍhūṇḍhak Hṛday Netrāñjanaṃ" athavā "Satyārtha Candrodayāṣṭakam."* Amadāvād: Śrī Satyavijay Priṇṭing Pres māṃ, Śā. Sāñkulcand Harīlāle Chāṣyuṃ.

Amolakṛṣi, Muni [Ācārya] 1908/1920. *Jaina Tattva Prakāś.* Duliya: Amola Jñānālaya. (Fourth edition, Ahmednagar 1920.)

---- 1920. *Śāstroddhara Mīmāṃsā.* Sākandarābād: Jaina Śāstroddhara Mudrālaya.

Āñcaliyā Dhansukhdās Hīrālāl (ed.) 1937. *Śiśu Hit Śikṣa.* Gaṅgāśahar: Dhansukhdās Hīrālāl Āñcaliyā.

Assmann, Jan 1987. Kanon und Zensur als kultursoziologische Kategorien. In: Aleida & Jan Assman (eds.), *Kanon und Zensur. Beiträge zur Archäologie der literarischen Kommunikation,* II: 100-112. München: Wilhelm Fink.

---- 2000. *Religion und kulturelles Gedächtnis.* München: C.H. Beck. (English version: *Cultural Memory. Ten Studies.* Transl. by R. Livingstone. Stanford: Stanford University Press, 2006.)

Ātmānand Jain Sabhā Pañjāb 1909. *"Ḍhūṇḍhakmat Parājay arthāt Phaislā Śāstrārthanāmā" tathā "Phaislā Samānā Ilākā Mahārājā Paṭiyālā."* Lahaur: Ātmānand Jain Sabhā Pañjāb kī Ājñā se Ātmānand Pustak Pracār Maṇḍal ke Janral Sakreṭarī Ajmer ke Seṭh Hīrācandjī Secetī ne Chapdhāyā. (Tṛtīyā Vṛtti. Lahaur: Jasvantrāy Jaini, 1906.)

Ātmārām, Ācārya (Vijayānanda Sūri) 1881/1954. *Jainatattvādarśa*. Bhāg 1 & 2. Ed. Banārsīdās Jain. Pañcam Saṃskaraṇ. Bambaī: Śrī Ātmānand Jaina Sabhā.

---- 1884/1903. *Śrī Samyaktva Śalyoddhāra*. Third edition. Hindustānī Translation of the Gujarātī original. Lahore: Śrī Ātmānand Jaina Sabhā Pañjāb.

---- 1884/1908. *Śrī Samyaktva Śalyoddhāra Dohā Ḍhūṇḍhak Mat ke Śalya ko Dūrakare Niradhāra Satya Nāmaim Grantha kā Samākita Śalyoddhāra*. Dillī: Ātmānand Jain Pustak Pracār Maṇḍal.

---- 1888/1906. *Ajñāna-timira-bhāskara*. Bhāvnagar: Jaina Dharma Hitecchu Sabhā. (With the Exception of the Prastāvanā to the 1st Edition, Cited after the 2nd Edition of the Jaina Ātmānand Sabhā in Bhāvnagar, 1906.)

Ātmārām, Ācārya [1888-90] 1916. *Praśnottara-saṃgraha (Śrīmad-Vijayānanda-Sūrīśvarāj (Ātmārāmjī) Mahārājajī Kalkattā Esīāṭīk Sosāiṭī nā Sekreṭarī Ḍaṃkṭar Hornla nā Praśno nā āpelā Uttaro)*. Bhāvnagar: Jaina Ātmānand Sabhā Taraph thī Bhāvsār Gāṇḍālāl Māncand.

---- 1893/1900a. *Jainamata Vṛkṣa*. Second Revised Edition. Ed. Muni Vallabhvijay. Amadāvād: Śrī Ātmārām Jaina Sabhā Pañjāb.

---- 1895/1902. *Tattvanirṇayaprāsāda: 36 Stambha*. Samśodhankarttā: Muni Vallabh Vijay. Prasiddhakarttā: Amarcand P. Parmār. Mumbaī: Induprakāś Jāīṭasṭāṃk Kaṃ. Lī. meṃ chāpkar prasiddha kiyā.

---- 1900b. *Īsāī Mat Samīkṣā*. Bambaī: Jaina Jñāna Prasārak Maṇḍal.

Ātmārām, Upādhyāy 1914. *Śrīmad Jainācārya Śrī 1008 Amarasiṅha kā Jīvan Caritra*. Lāhaur: Pañjāb Ekāntomīkal Yantrālay.

---- 1942. *Sthānakavāsī*. Ludhiyānā: Lālā Valāyatī Rām Kastūrī Lāl Jain.

Bagasarāvāḷā, Rāma Deva Maḍīā 1894. *Loṅkāgacchotpatti ane Mahārāja Śrīpūjya Bhaṭṭāraka Kalyāṇa Candrajī Surīśvarjī nuṃ Jīvana*

Caritra. Mumbaī Ghī Royal Prīṇṭiṅg Pres Bāhārakoṭa Bhājīpālā Len. (Reprinted with additions as *Loṅkāgacchotpatti ane Upāśraya nā Praṇetā Pūjya Ācārya Śrī Kalyāṇacandrajī Sūriśvarjī nuṃ Jīvana Caritra.* Mumbaī: Śrī Mumbaī Loṅkāgaccha Jaina Saṅgha. Upāśraya nā Śatābdi Mahotsava Prasaṅge Sabhāsado ne Bheṭa, 11.3.2001.)

Balbir, Nalini 1993. *Āvaśyaka-Studien,* I: *Introduction générale et traductions.* (Alt- und Neuindische Studien, 45.1.) Stuttgart: Franz Steiner Verlag.

---- 2001. La question de l'ordination des enfants en milieu jaina. In: Christine Chojnacki (ed.), *Les āges de la vie dans le monde Indien*: 153-182. Paris: Diffusion de Boccard.

---- 2002/2003a. Samayasundara's Sāmācārī-Śataka. In: Piotr Balcerowicz (ed.), *Caturaranayacakram. Essays in Jaina Philosophy and Religion*: 253-277. (First Indian Edition: Delhi: Motilal Banarsidass.)

---- 2003b. The Añcalagaccha viewed from inside and from outside. In: Olle Qvarnström (ed.), *Jainism and Early Buddhism. Essays in Honor of Padmanabh S. Jaini*: 47-77. Fremont: Asian Humanities Press.

Bhaṇḍārī, Kesarīcand 1938. *Sthānakavāsī Jaina Itihās.* Amadāvād: Śrī Sthānakavāsī Jaina Kāryālay.

Bhārill, Śobhācandra (ed.) 1965. *Muni Śrī Hajārīmal Smṛti Granth.* Byāvar: Muni Śrī Hajārīmal Smṛti Granth Prakāśan Samiti.

Bloch, Maurice. 1977/1989. The Past and the Present in the Present. In: *Ritual, History and Power. Selected Papers in Anthropology*: 1-18. London: The Athlone Press.

Bourdieu, Pierre 1980/1992. *The Logic of Practice.* Translated by Richard Nice. London: Polity Press.

Bruhn, Klaus 1981. Āvaśyaka-Studies I. In: Klaus Bruhn & Albrecht Wezler (eds.), *Studien zum Jainismus und Buddhismus* (Gedenkschrift für Ludwig Alsdorf): 11-49. Universität Hamburg: Steiner Verlag.

---- 1983. Repetition in Jain Narrative Literature. *Indologica Taurinensia* 11: 27-75.

---- 1987. Das Kanonproblem bei den Jainas. In: Aleida & Jan Assmann (eds.), *Kanon und Zensur. Beiträge zur Archäologie der literarischen Kommunikation*, II: 100-112. München: Wilhelm Fink.

Budhmal, Muni. *Terāpanth kā Itihās. Dvitīya Khaṇḍ.* Saṃpādak: Muni Sumeramal 'Sudarśan' & Muni Mohanlāl 'Śārdūl.' Calcutta: Jain Śvetāmbar Terāpanth Mahāsabhā Prakāśan, 2001.

Būṭerāy, Muni 1878. *Muhapattī Viṣe Cārcā.* Racnār Śuddha Mārg nā Rāgī Śrī Būṭerāyjī Mahārāj Temnā Carītra Sāthe. Amadāvād: Māṇekcok āgal Kāgadīol nā sāme Śā. Hīrābhāi Puñjāsānā Makān māṃ Amadāvād Ṭāims Pres māṃ Kālīdās Sāṅkalcand chāpī prasiddha karī.

Candanākumārī, Mahāsatī 1964. *Hamārā Itihās. Sthānakavāsī Śramaṇ-Sāṃskṛtik Paramparā kā Paricāyak.* Sampādak: Ācārya Śrī Amṛtkumār. Ahmadnagar: Śrī Tilok Ratna Sthānakavāsī Jaina Dhārmik Parīkṣā Borḍ.

Carrithers, Michael 1990. Jainism and Buddhism as Enduring Historical Streams. *Journal of the Anthropological Society of Oxford* 21.2: 141-163.

---- 2000, On Polytropy: Or the Natural Condition of Spiritual Cosmopolitanism in India: The Digambar Jain Case. *Modern Asian Studies* 34.4: 831-861.

Carrithers, Michael & Caroline Humphrey (eds.) 1991. *The Assembly of Listeners. Jains in Society.* Cambridge: Cambridge University Press.

Caudhārī, Kastūrcand Sūrajmal (ed.) 1936? *Jinjñān Ratnākar.* Kalkattā: Mahāland Bayed "Osvāl Pres."

Chopra, Chogmal 1937/1945. *A Short History of the Terapanthi Sect of the Swetambar Jains and its Tenets.* 4th Edition. Calcutta: Sri Jain Swetamber Terapanthi Sabha.

Cort, John E. 1989. Liberation and Wellbeing. "A Study of the Mūrtipūjak Jains of North Gujarat". Ph.D. dissertation, Harvard University.

---- 1990. Models of and for the Study of the Jains. *Method & Theory in the Study of Religion* 2.1: 42-71.

---- 1991. The Śvetāmbar Mūrtipūjak Jain Mendicant. *Man (N.S.)* 26: 651-671.

---- 1995. Genres of Jain History. *Journal of Indian Philosophy* 23: 469-506.

Cort, John E. 2001. *Jains in the World. Religious Values and Ideology in India.* New York: Oxford University Press.

Dalmia, Vasudha, Angelika MALINAR & Martin CHRISTOF (eds.) 2001/2003. *Charisma & Canon. Essays on the Religious History of the Indian Subcontinent*. Delhi: Oxford University Press.

Darśanavijaya, Muni (col.) 1933. *Paṭṭāvalī Samuccayaḥ*. Prathamo Bhāgaḥ. Vīramgām: Cāritra Smārak Granthamālā. (Reprinted by the Jinaśāsana Ārādhanā Ṭrusṭ in Mumbaī in 1996.)

Dayanand Sarasvati, Svami 1882/1908. *Satyartha Prakash*. Translated into English by Durga Prasad. Lahore: Virjanand Press.

Deśāī, Mohanlāl Dalīcand 1926-44. *Jaina Gūrjar Kavio*. Mumbaī: Jaina Śvetāmbara Conference Office. (Second edition: Sampādak: Jayant Koṭhārī. Bhāg 1-5. Mumbaī: Śrī Mahāvīra Jaina Vidyalaya, 1988.)

Ḍośī, Ratanlāl 1939. *Loṅkāśāh Mat-Samarthan*. Hindī Anuvād. Jodhpur: Jaina Ratna Pustakālay. (Hindī translation of Jīvaṇlāl Bhāī's Gujarātī translation of lost Hindī original revised by the author.) (Reprint Byāvar: Akhil Bhāratīya Sudharma Jaina Saṃskṛti Rakṣak Saṅgh, Jodhpur, 2002.)

Duggaṛ, Hīrālāl 1989. *Madhya Eśiyā aur Pañjāb meṃ Jainadharma*. Dillī: Jaina Prācīn Sāhitya Prakāśan Mandir.

Dundas, Paul 1993. The Marginal Monk and the True Tīrtha. In: Rudy Smet & Kenji Watanabe (eds.), *Jain Studies in Honour of Jozef Deleu*: 237-259. Tokyo: Hon-no-Tomosha.

---- 1996. Somnolent Sūtras: Scriptural Commentary in Śvetāmbara Jainism. *Journal of Indian Philosophy* 24: 73-101.

---- 1998. Becoming Gautama: Mantra and history in Śvetāmbara Jainism. In: John E. Cort (ed.), *Open Boundaries. Jain Communities and Culture in Indian History*: 31-52. Albany: SUNY.

---- 1999. Jainism without Monks? The Case of Kaḍuā Śāh. In: N.K. Wagle & O. Qvarnström (eds.), *Approaches to Jain Studies. Philosophy, Logic, Rituals and Symbols*: 19-35. Toronto: University of Toronto, Center for South Asian Studies.

---- 2001. History in Future Mode: A Nineteenth Century Digambara Jain Prophetic Text. In: Jayendra Soni (ed.), *Vasantagauravam. Essays in Jainism*: 51-72. Mumbai: Vakils, Feffer & Simons.

--- 2002. *The Jains*. Second Revised Edition. London: Routledge.

Farquhar, J.N. 1915. *Modern Religious Movements in India*. New York: Macmillan.

Flügel, Peter 1995-96. The Ritual Circle of the Terāpanth Śvetāmbara Jains. *Bulletin d'Études Indiennes* 13: 117-176.

Flügel, Peter 2000. Protestantische und Post-Protestantische Jaina-Reformbewegungen: Zur Geschichte und Organisa-tion der Sthānakavāsī I. *Berliner Indologische Studien* 13/14: 37-103.

---- 2003a. Protestantische und Post-Protestantische Jaina-Reformbewegungen: Zur Geschichte und Organisation der Sthānakavāsī II. *Berliner Indologische Studien* 15/16/17: 149-240.

---- 2003b. The Codes of Conduct of the Terāpanth Samaṇ Order. *South Asia Research* 23.1: 7-53.

---- 2005. The Invention of Jainism: A Short History of Jaina Studies. *Journal of Jaina Studies* (Kyoto) 11: 1-19. (Also: *International Journal of Jain Studies* 1, http://www.soas.ac.uk/ijjs).

---- Forthcoming (a) 2007. Protestantische und Post-Protestan-tische Jaina-Reformbewegungen: Zur Geschichte und Organisation der Sthānakavāsī III. *Berliner Indologische Studien* 18: 27-206.

---- Forthcoming (b) 2012. Protestantische und Post-Protestan-tische Jaina-Reformbewegungen: Zur Geschichte und Organisation der Sthānakavāsī IV: *Berliner Indologische Studien* 20:37-124.

---- Forthcoming (c). The Loṅkāgaccha revisited. Paper presented at the 12th World Sanskrit Conference in Helsinki, July 2003, and at the 6th Jaina Studies Workshop at SOAS, March 2004.

Gadamer, Hans-Georg 1960/1990. *Wahrheit und Methode. Grundzüge einer philosophischen Hermeneutik*. Tübingen: J.C.B. Mohr (Paul Siebeck).

Ghāsīlāl, Ācārya 1983. *Śrī Loṃkāśāha Caritam*. Niyojaka: Muni Kanhaiyālāl. Ahmadāvād: Akhila Bhāratīya Śvetāmbara Sthānakavāsī Jaina Śāstradvāra Samiti Pramukha Baladevabhāī Ḍosābhāī Paṭel.

Glasenapp, H. von. 1925. *Der Jainismus – Eine Indische Erlösungs-religion.* (Kultur und Weltanschauung, 1.) Berlin: A. Hager.

Gombrich, Richard 1988. *Theravāda Buddhism. A Social History from Ancient Benares to Modern Colombo.* London: Routledge & Kegan Paul.

Goonasekere, Ratna Sunilsantha Abhayavardana 1986. *Renunciation and Monasticism among the Jainas of India.* Ph.D. dissertation. San Diego: University of California.

Granoff, Phyllis 1991. The Politics of Religious Biography: The biography of Balibhadra the Usurper. *Bulletin d'Études Indiennes* 9: 75-91.

---- 1993. Going by the Book: The Role of Written Texts in Medieval Jain Sectarian Conflicts. In: R. Smet & K. Watanabe (eds.), *Jain Studies in Honour of Jozef Deleu*: 315-338. Tokyo: Hon-no-Tomosha.

Guṇsundar, Muni 1938. *Ādarś Jñān. Śrīmān Jñānsundarjī Mahārāj Sāhib kā Ādarś-Jīvan.* Bhāg 1-2. Jodhpur (?).

Hastīmal, Ācārya 1968. *Paṭṭāvalī Prabandh Saṅgrah.* Ed. Narendra Bhanawat. Jaypur: Jaina Itihāsa Nirmāṇ Samiti.

---- 1971. *Jaina Ācārya Caritāvalī (Jaina Ācārya Paramparā kā Kāvyabaddha Rūpa).* Ed. Gajasiṅha Rāṭhoṛ. Jaypur: Jaina Itihās Samiti.

---- 1987/1995. *Jaina Dharma kā Maulik Itihās*, IV. Jaypur: Jaina Itihās Samiti.

Jacobi, Hermann 1880. Das Kālakācārya-Kathānakam. *Zeitschrift der Deutschen Morgenländischen Gesellschaft* 34: 247-298.

Jain, Jiyālāl 1893. *Carcā Candroday Bhāg Tisrā.* Ahmadāvād: Yuniyan Priṇṭiṅg.

Jain, Jyotindra & Eberhard FISCHER 1978. *Jaina Iconography*, I-II. Leiden: E.J. Brill.

Jain, Kamleś Kumār 2003. *Jaina Uddharaṇa Kośa.* Bhāg I. Dillī: Bhogīlāl Leharcand Bhāratīya Saṃskṛti Saṃsthān.

Jain, Mohanlāl 1892. *Durvād Mukh-Capeṭikā.* Lāhaur: Eṅglo Saṃskṛt Yantrālay.

Jain, Pannālāl L. 1913/1923. *Jainācārya Śrī 1008 Śrīmatī Pārvatījī ke Jīvan Caritra.* Pratham Bhāg & Dvitīya Bhāg. Hindī Anuvād: Dayācandra Jain. Lāhaur: Candra Lakhanpāl. (1st Edition in Urdū.)

Jain, Sāgarmal & Vijay Kumār 2003. *Sthānakavāsī Jaina Paramparā kā Itihās*. Vārāṇasī: Pārśvanāth Vidyāpīṭh.

Jain, Śrīnāth Modī 1929. *Muni Śrī Jñānsundarjī*. Jodhpur: Rājasthān Sundar Sāhitya Sadan.

Jaydayāl, Lālā, n.d. *Ḍhuṇḍhak Mat Samīkṣā*. (Photocopy without bibliographic references.)

Jeṭhmal, Muni 1882/1930. *Samakit-Sār I-II*. Prabodhak: Tapasvīrāj Śrī Devjīṛṣi. Prakāśak: Śrīmān Sardārmal Pugaliā, Nāgpur, Śrīmān Ratanlāl Pīrcand Pārasevanī evam Barār Jaina Śrīmān. Caturtha Saṃskaraṇ. Hindī Anuvād: Rastabcand. Ratlām: Jainoday Pustak Prakāśak Samiti.

Jhauharī, Durlabh Trībhuvan. 1922/1923. *Śrīlāljī Mahārāj kā Sacitra Jīvan-caritra*. Morvī-Jaipur: Durlabh Trībhuvan Jhauharī.

Jñānsundar, Muni 1936. *Śrīmad Lauṃkāśāh*. Phalodī: Śrī Jñān Puṣpamālā.

Kāntisāgar, Muni 1965. Śrī Loṅkāśāh kī Paramparā aur uskā Ajñāt Sāhitya. In: Śobhācandra Bhārill (ed.), *Muni Śrī Hajārīmal Smṛti Granth*: 214-253. Byāvar: Muni Śrī Hajārīmal Smṛti Granth Prakāśan Samiti.

Kāpaḍiā, Hīrālāl Rasikdās. *A History of the Canonical Literature of the Jainas*. Surat: Hiralal Rasikdas Kapadia, 1941. (Reprint: Ahmedabad: Shree Shwetambar Murtipujak Jaina Boarding, 2000.)

Kelting, Mary Whitney 2001. *Singing to the Jinas. Jain Laywomen, Maṇḍal Singing, and the Negotiations of Jain Devotion*. Oxford: Oxford University Press.

Khān, Ālamśāh 1965. Loṅkāgaccha kī Sāhitya-Sevā. In: Śobhācandra Bhārill (ed.), *Muni Śrī Hajārīmal Smṛti Granth*: 203-213. Byāvar: Muni Śrī Hajārīmal Smṛti Granth Prakāśan Samiti.

Kiraṇyaśāstrī, Mahārāj 1999. *Śrī Vijayānandjī ke Vāḍam kā Vihaṅgāvalokaṇa*. Baṛaudā: Mahilā Jaina Upāśray.

Klatt, Johannes 1888. Eine apokryphe Paṭṭāvalī der Jainas. In: *Festgruss an Otto von Böhtlingk zum Doktor-Jubiläum 3. Februar 1888 von seinen Freunden*: 54-59. Stuttgart: W. Kohlhammer.

---- *Onomasticon*. Bound copy. 8 vols. Hamburg: Institut für Indologie und Tibetologie.

Koṭhārī, Jayant 2001. *Prācīn Madhyakālīn Sāhitya Samgraha* (Mohanlāl Dalīcand Desāī Sampādit Laghukṛti Saṃgraha). Ahmedabad: L.D. Institute of Indology. [See AB, LP, SC and SS under Primary sources.]

Kundanmal, Muni 1908. *Pragaṭ Jain Pītāmbarī Mūrtipūjakoṃ kā Mithyātva. Amarāvatī. Mūlcand Jugrāj.* (The short *stavan* is reprinted in Amarvijay 1908: 34-36.)

———, n.d. *Ātmārām Saṃvegī kī Karttūt, Ātmārām kī Ādāt kā Namūnā.* Ambālā: Paṇḍit Bhīmasena.

Laidlaw, James 1985. Profit, Salvation and Profitable Saints. *Cambridge Anthropology* 9.3: 50-70.

——— 1995. *Riches and Renunciation. Religion, Economy, and Society among the Jains.* Oxford: Clarendon Press.

Lālas, Padmaśrī Sītārām (ed.) 1986-87. *Rājasthānī-Hindī Saṅkṣipt Śabda Koś*, I-II. Rājasthān Purātan Granthamālā. Prabandh Sampādak: Padmadhar Pāṭhak. Jodhpur: Rājasthān Prācyavidyā Pratiṣṭhān.

Leslie, Julia 2003. *Authority and Meaning in Indian Religions. Hinduism and the Case of Vālmīki.* Hants: Ashgate.

Leumann, Ernst 1934. *Übersicht über die Āvaśyaka Literatur.* Aus dem Nachlass herausgegeben von Walther Schubring. (Alt- und Neuindische Studien, 4.) Hamburg: De Gruyter.

Mādhav, Muni 1908. *Taraṅgiṇī Dvitīyā Taraṅg.* Āgrā. (Reprinted in Amarvijay 1908: 31-34.)

Mahāprajña, Ācārya 2000. *Jainism and Its Philosophical Foundations.* New Delhi: Anmol Publications.

Malukcand, Anūpcand 1908. *"Praśnottara-ratna-cintāmaṇī" aur "Aṭhārah Dūṣaṇa-nivāraka."* Ahmadābād: Rāy Bahādur Bābu Buddhasiṅghjī.

Mālvaṇiyā, Dalsukhbhāī 1963a. Śrī Loṅkāśāh nī ek Kṛti. *Svādhyāya* 2.1: 50-82.

——— 1963b. Śrī Lokāśāh ane temnā Mat. *Svādhyāya* 2.2: 143-155.

——— 1964. Lokāśāh aur unkī Vicār-Dhārā. In: Vijay Muni Śāstri & Harīśankar Śarmā (eds.), *Gurudev Śrī Ratna Muni Smṛti-Granth*: 365-383. Āgrā: Gurudev Smṛti Granth Prakāśak Samiti.

——— 1965. Loṅkāśāh Mat kī Do Pothiyāṃ. In: Śobhācandra Bhārill (ed.), *Muni Śrī Hajārīmal Smṛti Granth*: 184-188. Byāvar: Muni Śrī Hajārīmal Smṛti Granth Prakāśan Samiti.

Maṇilāl, Muni 1934. *Śrī Jaina Dharma no Prācīn Saṅkṣipt Itihās ane Prabhu Vīr Paṭṭāvalī*. Amadāvād: Jīvaṇlāl Chaganlāl Saṅghvī.

Mette, Adelheid 1974. *Piṇḍ'esaṇā. Das Kapitel der Oha-Nijjutti über den Bettelgang übersetzt und kommentiert*. Wiesbaden: Franz Steiner.

Miśrīmal, Mantrī Muni "Marudhar Kesarī" 1936. *Dharmavīr Loṅkāśāh*. Ṭāṇṭoṭī/Ajmer: Jaina Śvetāmbara Sthānakavāsī Sakal Śrī Saṅgh Ṭāṇṭoṭī.

---- 1941. *Krāntikārī Vīr Loṅkāśāh*. Jodhpur Sṭeṭ: Jaina Buddhavīr Smārak Maṇḍal.

---- 1946. *Vīr Loṅkāśāh*. Prakāśak: Śāh Mukancand Nemīcand Bahorā Jain. Jodhpur: Jaina Buddhavīr Smārak Maṇḍal.

Nahar, Puran Chand. 1918/1983. *Jaina Inscriptions*. Delhi: Indian Book Gallery.

Nāhaṭā, Agarcand 1958. Kaḍuā Mat kī Mānyatāoṃ par Prakāś. *Jaina Bhāratī* 6.2: 19f.

---- 1951. Uttarārdha Gaccha. *Jaina Bhāratī* 12.6: 268-275.

---- 1966. Nāgorī Loṅkāgaccha ke Sthāpak Hīrāsāh aur Rūpcand. *Jinavāṇī* 15: 2-4.

---- 1968. Bhūmikā. In: Ācārya Hastīmal, *Paṭṭāvalī Prabandh Saṅgrah* (Ed. Narendra Bhanawat): 33-39. Jaypur: Jaina Itihāsa Nirmāṇ Samiti.

Nāhaṭā, Bhanvarlāl 1957. Luṅkāśāh aur unke Anuyāyī. In: Agarcand Nāhaṭā et al. (eds.), *Śrīmad Rājendrasūri Smārak Granth*: 470-477. Āhora tathā Bāgarā (Mārvāṛ): Śrī Saudharmabṛhattapāgacchīya Jaina Śvetāmbara Śrī Saṅgh.

Nāhaṭā, Kuṃvar Lālcandra "Taruṇ." 1968. Lauṃkāśāh: Vyaktitva aur Vicār. In: Śobhācandra Bhārill (ed.), *Marudhar Kesarī Muni Miśrīmaljī Mahārāj Abhinandan Granth*: 159-168. Jodhpur: Marudhar Kesarī Abhinandan Granth Prakāśan Samiti.

Nair, V.G. 1970. *Jainism and Terehpanthism*. Bangalore: Shri Adinath Jain Svetambar Temple, 1970.

Pārvatī, Mahāsatī 1905a. *"Satyārtha-Candroday Jaina" arthāt "Mithyātva Timir-Nāśak." Jis ko Sanātan Satya Jaina*

Dharmopadeśikā Bāl Brahmacāriṇī Jainārыyājī Śrī Mahāsatī Pārvatījī ne banāyā. Lāhaur: Lālā Meharcandra Lakṣmīdās Śrāvak.

---- 1905b. *"Samyaktva Sūryoday Jaina" arthāt "Mithyātva Timir Nāśak." Jis ko Jainācāryya Pañjābī Śrī 1008 Śrī Parampūjya Amarasiṅhajī kī Sampradāya meṃ Sanātan Satya Jaina Dharmopadeśikā Bāl Brahmacāriṇī Jainācāryyājī Śrīmat Śrī 1008 Satījī Śrī Pārvatījī ne banāyā.* Hośiārpur: Lālā Kṛpārām Koṭūmal Śrāvak. (Second Edition: Rohtak: Jyotrām Seṭh kī Dharmapatnī Lā. Śerasiṅha.)

Prakāścandra, Muni 1998. *Ā Che Aṇagār Amārā.* Mumbaī: Śrī Naval Sāhitya Prakāśan Maṇḍal.

Puṣkarmuni, Upādhyāy 1977. *Jain Dharma meṃ Dān. Ek Samīkṣātmak Adhyayan.* Sampādak: Devendramuni & Śrīcand Surānā 'Sarat'. Agra: Śrī Tārakguru Jaina Granthālay.

Qvarnström, Olle 1998. Stability and Adaptability: A Jain Strategy for Survival and Growth. *Indo-Iranian Journal* 41: 33-55.

Śāh, Praviṇcand Tulsīdās 2001. *Dharma Priya Krāntivīr Lokāśāh nuṃ Jīvan Caritra (Saṅkṣep).* Mumbaī: Śrī Mumbaī Loṅkāgaccha Jaina Saṅgha.

Śāh, Vāḍīlāl Motīlāl 1909. *Śrī Sādhumārgī Jaina Dharmānuyāyīoe Jāṇvā Jog Keṭalīk Aitihāsik Noṃdh.* Amadāvād: "Jaina Samācār."

---- 1925. *Śrī Sādhumārgī Jaina Dharmānuyāyioe Jāṇavā Joga Keṭalīka Aitihāsik Noṃdh.* Hindī Anuvād, Mulatānmal Hīrācand Dhārīvāl. Ratan Rāypur C.P.: Jaina Pāṭhśālā ke Sahāya Tīrth.

Sarlā, Sādhvī 1991. *Sthānakvāsī Pañjāb Sampradāy kī Pramukha Sādhviyāṃ.* [Extract of: Sādhanā Path kī Amar Sāhikā.] In: Hīrābāī Boradiyā, *Jainadharma kī Pramukh Sādhviyāṃ evaṃ Mahilāeṃ*: 298-304. Sampādak: Sāgarmal Jain. Vārāṇasī: Pārśvanāth Vidyāśram Śodha Saṃsthān.

Śāstrī, Hansrāj 1915. *Svāmī Dayānand aur Jainadharma.* Gopipura/ Surat: Paṇḍit Hansrāj Śāstrī.

Saubhāgyacandra, Muni "Santabāḷa" 1939. *Dharmaprāṇ-Loṅkāśāh (Krānti no Yugasṛṣṭā).* Amadāvād: Sthānakavāsī Jaina Kāryālay. (First published in *Jaina Prakāś* 1935.)

Schubring, Walther 1935/2000. *Die Lehre der Jainas. Nach der alten Quellen dargestellt.* (Grundriss der Indo-Arischen Philologie und Altertumskunde, 3.7.) Berlin: Walter De Gruyter & Co. [Cited after the English translation: *The Doctrine of the Jainas. Described after the Old Sources.* Transl. Wolfgang Beurlen. 3rd English edition. Delhi: Motilal Banarsidass.]

---- 1944. *Die Jaina-Handschriften der Preussischen Staatsbibliothek.* Leipzig: Otto Harrassowitz.

Schubring, Walther 1957. Kundakunda echt und unecht. *Zeitschrift der Deutschen Morgenländischen Gesellschaft* 107: 537-574.

Seṭh, Gulābcand Nāncand 1970. *Jaydhvaj. Pūjya Ācārya Jaymaljī Mahārāj kā Jīvan Caritra.* Madrās: Jaydhvaj Prakāśan Samiti.

Seṭh, Nagīndās Girdharlāl 1962. *Mūḷ Jaina Dharma ane Hāl nā Sampradāyo.* Mumbaī: Jaina Siddhānta Sabhā.

---- (ed.) 1963. *Sthānakavāsī Jaino nuṃ Dharma Kartavya.* Satya Dharma Samāj vā Icchanāra ne Māṭe Ja. Jaina Siddhānta Granthamāḷā Aṅko 49 Mo. Mumbaī: Jaina Siddhānta Sabhā (Rajīsṭarḍ) nī Vatī Seṭh Nagīndās Girdharlāl. [Includes chapters 7-13 and 22-26 of Seṭh's Mūḷ Jaina Dharma ane Hāl nā Sampradāyo: E Pustak māṃ nā Ahīṃ Umerelā Mūrti ne Lagtā Prakaraṇo.]

---- 1964. *Loṅkāśāh ane Dharmacarcā.*

Shah, Umakant Premanand 1955a. *Studies in Jaina Art.* Varanasi: Pārśvanātha Vidyāpīṭha.

---- 1955b. A Forgotten Chapter in the History of the Svetambara Jaina church, or, a Documentary Epigraph from Mount Satrunjaya. *Journal of the Asiatic Society of Bombay* 30: 100-113.

Shāntā, N. 1985/1997. *La voie Jaina. histoire, spiritualité, vie des ascétes pèlerines de l'Inde.* Paris: O.E.I.L. (English version: *The Unknown Pilgrims. The Voice of the Sādhvīs: The History, Spirituality and Life of the Jaina Women Ascetics.* Transl. by M. Rogers. (Sri Garib Dass Oriental Series, 219.) Delhi: Shri Satguru Publications, 1997.)

Smith, Wilfred Cantwell. 1962/1991. *The Meaning and End of Religion.* Minneapolis: Fortress Press.

Surānā, Śrīcand "Saras" 1976. *Mahāprajña Pravartak Śrī Pannālālji*

Mahārāj. Jīvan, Vyaktitva aur Kṛtitva. Vijaynagar/Rājasthān: Śrī Prajña Jaina Smārak Samiti.

Suśīlkumār, Ācārya 1959. *Jainadharma kā Itihās (Pramukhtaṛ Śrī Śvetāmbara Sthānakavāsī Jainadharma kā Itihās)*. Kalkattā: Samyag Jñān-Mandir.

Ujamcand, Rikhabcand (Mumbaī) 1909. *Sthānakavāsī Sādhumārgī Satyatā Ūpar Kuhāḍo. Urphe. Bhī. Vāḍīlāl-kṛt Aitihāsik Khoṭī Noṃdh Upar Ṭīkā.* Bhāg 1. Amadāvād: Eṅglo Varnākyular Priṇṭiṅg.

Vallabhvijay, Muni (ed.) 1891. *Ḍhuṇḍṛak-hita-śikṣā Apanām Gappa-dīpikāsamīr.* Amadāvād: Śrī Jainadharma Prasārak Sanā. Nāvnagar.

---- 1902. Tapāgaccha Ācārya Śrīmad Vijayānandasūriśvarjī Prasiddha nām Ātmārāmjī Mahārājjī Jainī Sādhu kā Janmacaritra. In: Ācārya Ātmārām (Vijayānanda Sūri), *Tattvanirṇayaprāsāda: 36 Stambha*: 33-83. Samśodhan-karttā: Muni Vallabh Vijay. Prasiddhakarttā: Amarcand P. Parmār. Mumbaī: Induprakāś Jāīṭasṭāṃk Kaṃ. Lī. meṃ Chāpkar Prasiddha kiyā.

---- 1909. *Javābdāvā. Jain Samācār Ḍhūṇḍhak Patrādhipati kī Pūkār kā Javāb.* Written in Pālaṇpur, Gujarāt. Lāhaur: Jasvantrāy Jaini.

---- 1996. *Navyug Nirmātā (Nyāyāmbhonidhi Ācārya Śrīmad Vijayānand Sūri (Ātmārāmjī) Mahārāj kī Jīvan Gāthā).* Dvitīya Saṃskaraṇ. Pāvāgaḍh Tīrtha: Vijayānand Sūri Sāhitya Prakāśan Phāuṇḍeśan.

Varddhamāna Sthānakavāsi Jaina Śrāvaka Saṅgha, Jaypur (ed.) 1964. *Ajmer Śikhar Sammelan meṃ Saṃśodhit evaṃ Pārit – Varddhamān Sthānakavāsī Jaina Śramaṇ Saṅgh ke Prastāv, Vidhān evaṃ Sāmācārī.* Jaypur: Mantrī, Varddhamāna Sthānakavāsī Jaina Śrāvaka Saṅgha.

Vārīā, Ratanśī 1976. *Dharma Prāṇ Śrī Loṅkāśāh nā Aṭṭhāvan Bol.* Jāmnagar: Lālbāg (Ratanśī Vārīā).

Weber, Albrecht 1882. Über den Kupakshakauçikāditya des Dharmasāgara. Streitschrift eines orthodoxen Jaina, vom Jahre 1573. In: *Sitzungsberichte der Königlich Preussischen*

Akademie der Wissenschaften zu Berlin 37: 793-814.

Williams, Ronald. 1963/1983: *Jaina Yoga. A Survey of the Medieval Śrāvakācāras.* London: Oxford University Press.

Wujastyk, Dominik 1984. The Spikes in the Ears of an Ascetic: An Illustrated Tale in Brahmanism and Jainism. *Oriental Art (N.S.)* 30: 189-194.

Appendix I:

Keha nī Paramparā Chai – Text in Old Gujarātī[304]

paramparā likhīiṃ chaiṃ, ketalā eka ima kahai chai śrī vīra nī paramparā ima kahai chai, te kihāṃ chai.[305]

1. gharim pratimā ghaḍāvī maṇḍāvai chai, te keha nī paramparā chai?[306] – celā celī vecānā leī teha keha nī paramparā chai?[307]
2. nānhā chokarā nai[308] dīkṣā dii chai, te keha nī paramparā chai?
3. nāma[309] pheravai chai, te keha nī paramparā chai?
4. kāṃna vadhārai chai, te keha nī paramparā chai?
5. khamāsamāsaṇa[310] viharai chai, te keha nī paramparā chai?
6. gṛhastha (nī) gharaiṃ baisī[311] viharai, te keha nī paramparā chai?
7. dīhāḍī dīhāḍī[312] 2 teṇai[313] ghariṃ viharai, te keha nī paramparā chai?
8. aṅghola[314]kahai[315] kare,[316] te keha nī paramparā chai?
9. jyotiṣa nai marma prajuṃjai chai, te keha nī paramparā chai?
10. kalavāṇī karī āpai chai, te keha nī paramparā chai?
11. nagara māhiṃ paisatā paiṃ sāru sāhamuṃ karāvai chai, te keha nī paramparā chai?
12. lāḍūā pratiṣṭai[317] chai, te keha nī paramparā chai?
13. pothī pūjāvai chai, te keha nī paramparā chai?
14. saṅghapūjā karavai chai, te keha nī paramparā chai?
15. pratiṣṭā karai chai, te keha nī paramparā chai?

16. pajūsaṇaiṃ pothī āpai chai, te keha nī paramparā chai?
17. tathā yātrā vecai chai, te keha nī paramparā chai?
18. tathā mātra āpai chai, te keha nī paramparā chai?
19. tathā ghāṭaḍī donuṃ toraṇa[318] bāṃghai chai, te keha nī paramparā chai?
20. ādhākarma posāliṃ rahai chai, te keha nī paramparā chai?
21. siddhānta prabhāvanā pākhai na vāṃcai, te keha nī paramparā chai?
22. māṇḍavī karāvai chai, te keha nī paramparā chai?
23. gautama paḍagho[319] karāvai chai, te keha nī paramparā chai?
24. saṃsāra-tāraṇa karāvai chai, te keha nī paramparā chai?
25. candanabālā nu tapa karāvai chai, te keha nī paramparā chai?
26. sonā rūpā nī nīsaraṇī karāvai chai, te keha nī paramparā chai?
27. lākhāpaḍavi karāvai chai, te keha nī paramparā chai?
28. ūjamaṇā[320] ḍhovarāvai chai, te keha nī paramparā chai?
29. pūja pūḍhāiṃ chai, te keha nī paramparā chai?
30. āsovṛkṣa bharāvi[321] chai, te keha nī paramparā chai?
31. aṭṭhottarī sanātra karāvi chai, te keha nī paramparā chai?
32. navā ghāna navā phala pratimā āgali ḍhoi chai, te keha nī paramparā chai?
33. śrāvaka-śrāvikā nai māthai vāsa ghālai chai, te keha nī paramparā chai?
34. parigraha ḍhūṇḍha māṃ bāṃdhai chai, te keha nī paramparā chai?
35. śrāvaka pāīṃ mūṇḍakuṃ apāvī ḍuṅgara caḍhāvī[322] chai, te keha nī paramparā chai?
36. mālāropaṇa karai chai, te keha nī paramparā chai?
37. padīka śrāvaka śrāvikā suṃ bhelī jāiṃ chai, te keha nī paramparā chai?

38. nāndi maṇḍāvai chai, te keha nī paramparā chai?
39. padīka cāṅka bāṃdhai chai, te keha nī paramparā chai?
40. pāṇi māhiṃ bhūko[323] muṃkai chai, te keha nī paramparā chai?
41. vāndaṇā divarāvai[324] chai, te keha nī paramparā chai?
42. oghā pheravai chai, te keha nī paramparā chai?
43. devadravya rākhai chai, te keha nī paramparā chai?
44. pagai lāgai nīcī pacheḍī oḍhai chai, te keha nī paramparā chai?
45. sūrimantra leiīṃ iṃ chai,[325] te keha nī paramparā chai?
46. dīhāḍī sūrimantra gaṇai chai, te keha nī paramparā chai?
47. kalapaḍā ṭhaṭai[326] chaiṃ, te keha nī paramparā chai ūjalā?
48. pajūsaṇa māhiṃ bairakanhai tap karāvai chai, te keha nī paramparā chai?
49. ghaḍūlā karāvai chai, te keha nī paramparā chai?
50. āṃbila nī olī siddhacakra nī karāvai chai, te keha nī paramparā chai?
51. mahātamā nāla[327] karā pachī te ūṭhamaṇuṃ karai chai, te keha nī paramparā chai?
52. pratimā jhūlaṇuṃ[328] karāvai chai, te keha nī paramparā chai?
53. padīka āgali ṭhavaṇī[329]māṇḍai chai, te keha nī paramparā chai?
54. pajūsaṇa parva nai cauthaiṃ[330] paḍikamai chai, te keha nī paramparā chai?

Appendix II:

Loṅkā's assertions according to Candanākumārī 1964 in Hindī

1. āgam-sammat ṭīkāoṃ ko hī prāmāṇik mānā jāy.
2. āgam ke anusār dṛṛhatāpūrvak samaya meṃ jīvan vyatīt kiyā jāy.
3. dharmadṛṣṭi se 'pratimā-pūjan' śāstra-sammat nahīṃ hai.
4. śuddha sāttvik śākāhārī pratyek kul kā āhār liyā jā saktā hai.

5. sthāpanācārya kī sthāpanā kī koī āvaśyaktā nahīṃ hai.
6. upavās ādi vratoṃ meṃ sabhī prakār kā prāsuk jal liyā jā saktā hai.
7. parv-tithi ke binā bhī upavās kiyā jā saktā hai.
8. sādhuoṃ ko mantra-tantra tathā yantra ādi vidyāoṃ kā prayog nahīṃ karnā cāhie.
9. śrāvak bhikṣā kar saktā hai, par dān nahīṃ le saktā.
10. dayā bhāv se garīboṃ ko dān denā pāp nahīṃ hai, apitu puṇya kā kāraṇ hai.
11. daṇḍ nahīṃ rakhā jānā cāhie.

Appendix III:

Loṅkā's Sāmācārī according to Seṭh 1970 in Hindī

1. upadhān tap kiye binā bhī śāstra-abhyās karāyā jā saktā hai.
2. jin pratimā kī dharmadṛṣṭi se pūjā karmā 45 āgamoṃ meṃ nahīṃ hai.
3. mūl sūtra, āgam aur mūl śāstra, samasta ṭīkāoṃ ke sivāy anya āgam evaṃ ṭīkā sarvathā amānya hai.
4. vidyā kā prayog niṣiddha hai.
5. pauṣadh pratikramaṇ svatantra rīti se karmā.
6. cāturmās ke sivāy bhī pāṭ kā vyavahār jā saktā hai.
7. daṇḍ nahīṃ rakhā jānā cāhiye.
8. pustakeṃ rakhī jā saktī haiṃ.
9. sātvikta aur śuddhi kā dhyān rakhte hue pratyek kul meṃ gocarī kī jā saktī hai.
10. śrāvak bhī gocarī kar saktā hai.
11. śrāvak dān nahīṃ le saktā.
12. upavās pratyākhyān meṃ chāch-pānī kī āch prāsuk le sakte haiṃ.
13. binā upavās ke bhī pauṣadh kiyā jā saktā hai.
14. tithi-parv ke binā bhī upavās kiyā jā saktā hai.
15. ek sāth upavās paccakkhe jā sakte haiṃ.
16. kalyāṇakoṃ ko tithi meṃ nahīṃ ginnā cāhiye.
17. jis din goras liyā jāy us din kaṭhor (dvidal dhānya) kā prayog

nahīṃ honā cāhiye.

18. sthāpanācārya kī sthāpanā anāvaśyak hai.
19. dhovan pānī meṃ do ghaṛī ke anantar jīvotpatti sambhav hai.
20. apātra ko dharma buddhi se dān dene se hiṃsā hotī hai (*anukampā* se garīb ko denā ekānta pāp kā kāraṇ nahīṃ hai).

Picture:

Loṅkā nā Aṭhāvana Bolo, Ms. No. 2989,

L.D. Institute, Ahmedabad, p. 14b

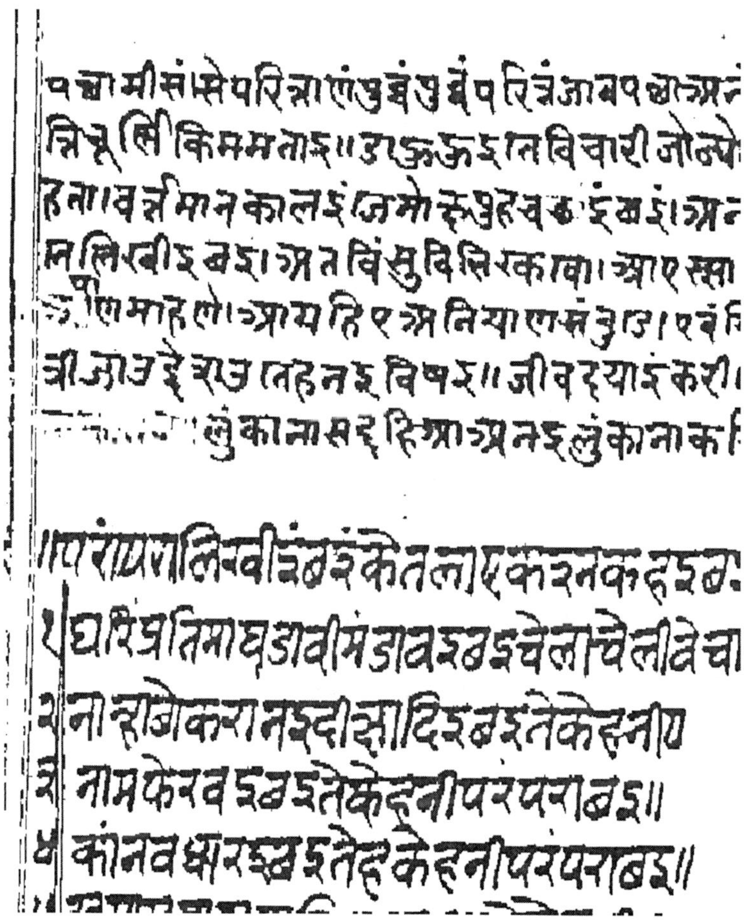

Notes

1 See the empirical studies on Jain laity in Carrithers & Humphrey 1991.

2 Used in a wider sense, including commentary, and ritual literature.

3 See Bloch 1989: 5; Bourdieu 1992: 53. See also Carrithers' (2000: 834) investigation of eclecticism or "polytropy" in the Jain tradition.

4 Assmann 2000: 34. His definition contrasts "cultural memory," based primarily on the medium of writing, with "communicative memory," the social aspect of individual memory, and with "collective" and "connective memory," which is primarily ritually constituted: "Das kulturelle Gedächtnis umfasst im Gegensatz zum kommunikativen Gedächtnis das Uralte, Abgelegte, Ausgelagerte und im Gegensatz zum kollektiven und Bindungsgedächtnis das Nichtinstrumentalisierbare, Häretische, Subversive, Abgespaltene" (p. 41). He uses the term "unconscious transmission" (p. 40).

5 "Source quotations play an essential part in the demonstration" (Balbir 2003a: 263). Important in this context is J. Leslie's distinction between authority and meaning (Leslie 2003: 74f.). Pioneering works on the use of quotations (*uddharaṇa*) in the Jaina scriptures itself are the *Berliner Konkordanz* of K. Bruhn and C.B. Tripathi, and the recent publication of K.K. Jain (2003). The re-combination of elements always involves aspects of creative invention.

6 See Gadamer 1990: 305ff.; also Bruhn 1981: 18; 1987: 111; Gombrich 1988: 21. For an analysis of the institutional conditions of this history see also Flügel 2000; 2003a; forthcoming (c).

7 On the history of research of the aniconic Śvetāmbara traditions see Flügel 2000: 40-46; Jain & Kumār 2003: 109-115.

8 Hastīmal (1995: 765) criticises that he is variously called *Luṃpaka* (from *luṭerā*, thief) or *luṅgā* (from *luccā*, scoundrel), etc., by his opponents, rather than by his real name. Weber (1882: 807f.) and Mālvaṇiyā (1965: 185) interpret *luṃpaka* as the Sanskrit translation of *luṃkā (lauṃkā)*, the "breaker" or "destroyer" of (the worship of) images, the creator of ruins. The real name of "Loṅkā" remains unknown. The first text which mentions "Śāh" as the family name seems to be the *Loṅkāśāha Siloko*, written in Saṃvat 1600 (1543/4) by the Loṅkāgaccha *yati* Keśavarṣi.

9 Mūrtipūjaka scholars such as Devagupta Sūri (1016 CE) of the Upakeśagaccha defined injury to living beings committed during the construction of temples and in the preparation of *pūjā* with flowers, fruits and water as a form of unavoidable or occupational violence (*ārambhajā hiṃsā*) (Williams 1983: 66). Digambaras additionally use the term *udyogī hiṃsā*, violence that is connected with a purposeful (religious) action.

10 Originally: "Jinamata."

11 Apart from Deśāī's ground-breaking survey of Gujarātī literature (1926-44), only two studies of an exploratory character are available to date on the meagre surviving textual material of the Loṅkāgaccha *yatis*: Ālamśāh Khān 1965, and particularly Muni Kāntisāgara 1965. Judging on the basis of these sources, it appears that most texts of the Loṅkāgaccha traditions are poems or songs of a hagiographic or biographical nature. Given their chronological precedence, it seems that the surviving Loṅkāgaccha *paṭṭāvalīs*, published by Hastīmal (1968), were composed on the basis of such earlier sources. See Flügel 2003a: 180f. Jñānsundar (1936: 27) rightly complained that the "unreliable" (*apramāṇika*) *paṭṭāvalīs* of the Loṅkāgacchas do not contain any information on the doctrine of Loṅkā or the Loṅkāgacchas nor on their forms of organisation.

12 The surviving biographical sources on the Loṅkāgaccha ascetics have not yet been studied.

13 The early Loṅkāgaccha tradition were opposed by local Mūrtipūjaka and Sthānakavāsī rivals, and to a lesser extent by Digambaras. References to Loṅkā were, literally, erased from the few surviving manuscripts which could have been attributed to him (see picture on p. 278). Even today, Mūrtipūjaka libraries are often instructed by the *ācāryas* of their tradition not to permit access to materials relating to Loṅkā.

14 See Assmann 1987 for the terms *Sinnpflege* and *Textpflege*.

15 As Dundas (1993: 253) pointed out, the Terāpanth did initially not refer to any predecessors and has still not published an official *paṭṭāvalī* which constructs a direct line of succession back to Mahāvīra or another Tīrthaṅkara. In this respect, the Terāpanthīs present themselves as direct disciples of Mahāvīra, like the Śramaṇasaṅgha. See Bhaṇḍārī 1937: 96; Flügel 2003a: 194ff.

16 See Balbir 2003a: 268f.

17 Cf. Hastīmal 1968. The fact that the chronologies are relatively young may be seen as confirmation for the general view that the Sthānakavāsī *muni* Jeṭhmal was the first to invoke Loṅkā as the *dharmaguru* of his tradition in 1808. See *infra*.

18 On the form and function of *paṭṭāvalīs* and *gurvāvalīs* see Flügel 2003a: 177-196.

19 Purification of the *saṅgha* was already an established motive for institution building in the Śvetāmbara tradition.

20 According to Dundas (1993: 248), one of the principal critics of the Loṅkā tradition, the Mūrtipūjaka monk Dharmasāgara, rejected in his *Pravacana-parīkṣā* the arbitrary basis of customary law with the remark that if custom were an acceptable criterion then even the views of the Loṅkāgaccha would be acceptable. Jñānsundar (1936: 182) also distinguishes between the Jaina *ājñā* and Loṅkā's *maryādā* in order to devalue the latter. On the Jain *maryādā* literature see Flügel 2003b.

21 The foci for processes of identity formation of the image-worshipping sects are both mendicant orders and temples.

22 Balbir (2003a: 259; 2003b: 53) stresses the difference between "ethics" and "abstract ideas and concepts."

23 On the problem of canonisation in the Jaina context see Bruhn 1987: 106.

24 Observed behaviour of individual monks was generally not the key point of criticism.

25 See for instance Dayānand's polemic against the Jains (1882/1908: 439ff.), which Śāstrī (1915) has also written about, the responses scattered throughout Ātmārām's work (1882/1906: 1-162, etc.), and a text of the Sthānakavāsī *sādhvī* Pārvatī (1905b), who attacked Dayānand's notions of god (*īśvara*) and *karma* based on the belief in liberation through transmigration. A vivid description of the exchanges from 1874 onwards can be found in P.L. Jain 1913/1923: 38ff. & II, 102-111. Farquhar (1915: 104) surmised that Dayānand's inexplicable rejection of image-worship was influenced by the Sthānakavāsī example in his native Morvī state in Gujarāt.

26 See Būṭerāy 1878. He was in 1831 initiated into the Sthānakavāsī Jīvarāja Malūkacandra Sampradāya in the Pañjāb. See Upādhyāya Ātmārām 1914: 57, n.; Duggar 1989: 338; Flügel 2000: 80, n. 78.

27 He was born in the Kṣatriya family of the soldier Gaṇeścandra Kapūr in the village Laharā in the Zīrā Tahasīl near Phīrozpur in the Pañjāb. After coming in close contact with Osvāl Sthānakavāsī Jains, he was initiated on 5.12.1853 (1910 *mṛgasār śukla* 5) by the Sthānakavāsī *muni* Jīvaṇrām (Jīvaṇmal), who probably belonged to the Jīvarāja Gaṅgarāma tradition. In 1874, he was re-initiated by the Mūrtipūjaka *ācārya* Buddhivijay (the ex-Sthānakavāsī monk Būṭerāy) in Gujarāt, and was given the name "Vijayānanda" when he became a *sūri* on 1.12.1886 (1943 *mṛgasār śukla* 5). See Ātmārām 1900a: 72f.; Vallabhvijay 1902: 33-85; 1996: 4ff.; Flügel 2000: 60 (n. 42), 79. Further details on his group affiliations before leaving the Sthānakavāsīs, which are not entirely clear in his official biographies, have been highlighted in Mohanlāl Jain's polemic *Durvādī Mukha-Capeṭikā* (1892), which was summarised by P. L. Jain 1913/1923: 246-249. Accordingly, Ātmārām left his guru Jīvaṇmal already in 1863 to study in Āgrā with Muni Ratnacandra of the Manoharadāsa Sampradāya. Thereafter, he returned to the Pañjāb and joined the Pañjāb Lavjīṛṣi Sampradāya of Ācārya Amarsiṅha. In Vallabhvijay's biography (1902: 52) it appears that despite his physical separation, Ātmārām did not formally cut his link with Jīvaṇmal.

28 See Cort 2001: 46.

29 See the biographies by S.M. Jain (1929) and Guṇsundar (1938).

30 See his monumental work *Jaina Tattva Prakāś* which was composed in 1903. The title of this not openly polemical text alludes to Ātmārām's *Jaina Tattva Ādarśa*. See also *Grantha Karttā kā Saṅkṣipt Jīvan Vṛttānta by* Kalyāṇmal Corādiyā in Amolakṛṣi 1908/1920: 3.

31 His dates 1849-1932, cited in sources of the Līmbḍī Nānī Pakṣ, are probably wrong, since he was still a young man in a photo published by Amarvijay 1908: 77f. Maṇilāl's 1934 work was criticised by the Annual General Meeting of the AISJC in Ahmedabad in 19.5.1936 as "insufficient," because of its incompleteness and lack of proof. See *Jaina Prakāśa* 17.5.1936, p. 342, in Jñānsundar 1936: 16, n.

32 Saubhāgyacandra "Santabāḷa" had publicised his views already in 1935 in the journal *Jaina Prakāśa*, the mouthpiece of the All India Sthānakavāsī Conference, and probably earlier in a book called *Viśvavaṃdya Prabhu Mahāvīr* (Ed. Ghīrajlāl Ṭokarśī Śāh), which is listed in Maṇilāl's bibliography (1934).

33 For details see Flügel 2000; 2003a.

34 *Dayādharma Caupāī* 11. The word *upadeśa* can also refer to Loṅkā's famous conversion of Lakhamsī which took place before the creation of the Loṅkā order. It is true that no details or references are offered by V.M. Śāh (1909: 49ff.) or Saubhāgyacandra (1939: 77ff.). Jñānsundar (1936: 136) writes that there is also no evidence in Jeṭhmal's (1930) work *Samakitsār*: *un meṃ in bātoṃ kā iśārā tak bhī nahīṃ kiyā hai*. However, on page 14f. of this text a *praśnottara* of fifty-two questions which are attributed to Loṅkā is published in Hindī, though no references to the original Ms. are given. The questions correspond to a list of fifty-four questions in a 17th-century text (K) attributed to Loṅkā which was published by Mālvaṇiyā (1963a: 80-82; 1964: 381).

35 See Cort 1995: 471, 491-494.

36 See for instance the report of Śāh (1909: 79) on the use of the courts to settle doctrinal disputes in 1822.

37 *Lokāśāh ke yug se lekar āj tak kisī bhī vidvān Sthānakavāsī muni ne athvā gṛhastha ne viśuddha itihās ke dṛṣṭikoṇ se kuch likhā ho, vah mere dekhne meṃ nahīṃ āyā. ... praśasti tathā guṇānuvād hī adhik hai – itihās us meṃ nahīṃ hai* (Mālvaṇiyā 1964: 365). The same is true for histories of Loṅkā by followers of other sectarian traditions.

38 Flügel 2005; forthcoming (b).

39 Flügel, forthcoming (c). The term *gaccha* can mean school, monastic order or sect.

40 I have found only two histories of Loṅkā in the Loṅkāgaccha *upāśrayas*, Bagasarāvāḷā 1894, and P.T. Śāh 2001. Both texts are derivative and do not add anything new on Loṅkā. The second text relies largely on Vāriā 1976.

41 *Usī carcā kā sārāṃś, anekoṃ jijñāsu sadgṛhastha ke āgraha se, pustakākār ke rūp meṃ ḍhāl diyā gayā* (Pratham Bhāg kī Bhūmikā, in Jeṭhmal 1930: 4).

42 Ātmārām 1903: 289; Vallabhvijay 1909: 14; *Bhūmikā* in Jeṭhmal 1930: 10.

43 Without access to the first three editions it is impossible to clearly identify different layers of commentary which may have been added to the original text in the published version of 1930.

44 V.M. Śāh (1909: 79) mentions a documentation of the counter-arguments of the Mūrtipūjakas, *Ḍhuṇḍhakmat Khaṇḍan Rās* by Muni Uttamvijay which was unavailable to me. Johannes Klatt's *Jaina Onomastikon*, III, p. 1281, mentions another polemical text of this author: *Dhundhiā no Rāsado* (Ahmadābād: Nāran Kṛṣṇarām, 1869).

45 On strategies of canonisation in the Jaina context see Bruhn 1987: 107, etc. To my knowledge, the term "secondary canonisation" was first used by Glasenapp (1925). The term "work of canonisation" was introduced by Assmann (1987: 19). For further studies on processes of canonisation in South Asia see Dalmia, Malinar & Christof 2003.

46 Jñānsundar 1936: 15 suggests that Jeṭhmal developed his arguments on the basis of a text called *Vivāha Cūliyā Sūtra*, which was unavailable to me.

47 Jñānsundar (1936: 15, 293) argued that the debate itself took place in Saṃvat 1865, because Jeṭhmal was already dead in Saṃvat 1878 (he does not give any information as to which Jeṭhmal he identified).

48 V.M. Śāh 1909: 78f.

49 Preface, in Jeṭhmal 1930: 4. Seṭh (1970: 1112, n. 1) writes that Jeṭhmal temporarily belonged to the orders of Ācārya Jaymal and of the Terāpanth *ācārya* Bhikṣu respectively. Other sources say that he worked under the directive of Ācārya Amarasiṅha (Flügel 2003a: 237).

50 Reportedly, twenty-five monks from Rājasthān were present, plus two monks from Prāg's group, and apparently Muni Mul (Mūḷ?) from the Sāyalā Sampradāya in Gujarāt who is said to have supported Muni Jeṭhmal from the Palanpur Sampradāya (Maṇilāl 1934: 227f.). This points to a concerted effort on the side of the Sthānakavāsīs, which may have required them to take recourse to Loṅkā to find a common platform.

51 Some sources say: 1878 *phālgun śukla* 1 (22.2.1822). The case is mentioned in V.M. Śāh 1909: 78f.; Maṇilāl 1934: 192f., 198f., 228; Jñānsundar 1936: 7, 15, 293; Candanākumārī 1964: 150, 192; Hastīmal 1971: 138f. See Flügel 2000: 68, n. 54 and 79, n. 77; 2003a: 237.

52 Only the *mūrtipūjak ono parājay thayo – cetanapūjak ono jay thayo*; and *jeṭho rīkh āvyore, kāgaḷ vāṃcī rarī; pustak bahu lāvyore, gāḍuṃ ek bharī* (in V.M. Śāh 1909: 79). Jñānsundar 1936: 15 simply states Jeṭhmal's defeat (*hār*).

53 *yah lok to sarva jainmat se viparīt calanevāle hai* (Ātmārām 1954, II: 540).

54 Ātmārām 1900a: 72.

55 Vallabhvijay 1891: 131f. The first question asked for the *paṭṭāvalī* of all *ācāryas* beginning with Mahāvīra, which apparently did not exist in this Sthānakavāsī tradition at the time: 1. *śrī mahāvīr svāmī se lekar āj tak pāṭānupāṭ kaun se ācārya hue unoṃ ke nām likhne* (p. 131).

56 In Vallabhvijay 1891: 72-82.

57 On the *śataka* format see Balbir 2003a; 2003b.

58 Published by Vallabhvijay 1891: 83-125.

59 Generally, the South Indian calendar applies in Gujarāt, therefore Saṃvat 1938 must be 1882, not 1881.

60 *Ḍhūṃḍhīye hī hiṃsādharmī haiṃ aur dayā kā yathārtha svarūp nahīṃ samajhte haiṃ* (Ātmārām 1903: 289). There are many texts in the Jaina *bhaṇḍāras* with titles such as *Samakit Sār Praśnottar Pacchīsī Sajjhāy* (L.D. Institute Ms. No. 4734 etc.) which may contain information on earlier exchanges between exponents of the two traditions.

61 The title alluded to Dayānand's book *Timir Bhāskar Jvālāprasād* (cf. P. L. Jain 1913/1923: 41). The work addressed the view of the two main rivals of Ātmārām in the Pañjāb. It was composed in two parts between 1882-85 in Ambālā, and first published in Bhāvnagar in 1888. Ātmārām's deliberation on the beliefs of the Christians, *Īsāī Mat Samīkṣā*, was published posthumously in the year 1900. See Kiraṇyaśāstrī 1999, Pariśiṣṭ I.

62 Jeṭhmal 1930: 9f. does not use the word "Sthānakavāsī," but refers directly to Loṅkā and his "true mendicant path": *lokā gaccha-sādhu mārga hī saccā hai* (p. 3).

63 Two realms of value in the Mūrtipūjaka tradition are also identified by Cort 2001.

64 In contrast to other Mūrtipūjaka *ācāryas*, Ātmārām opposed the publication of the scriptures. He permitted both *sādhus* and laity to read the *sūtras* only in the presence of a guru who could explain the meaning of the text, and prevented access to certain texts to women. See for instance Malukcand 1908: 182f.

65 See also his answers to Sohanlāl in Vallabhvijay 1891: 83-125.

66 Ātmārām 1903: 289. It is not entirely clear whether Ātmārām attacks both observed behaviour and customary law in this section. Since he does not address any particular order, though he may have had the Lavjīṛṣi Amarasiṅha Sampradāya in mind, his criticism is too vague to be considered in detail.

67 In her discussion of the Kharataragaccha monk Samayasundara's (1553-1645) *Sāmācārī śataka* of 1616, whose second section (and probably other points as well) is devoted entirely to the critique of "the Sthānakavāsīs" (probably the Loṅkāgaccha traditions, but since the canon of "thirty-two" is criticised in points 38 and 47 the Sthānakavāsī Jīvarāja may have been addressed), Balbir (2003a: 255, 257; 2003b: 56f.) argues that it was the conflict between Loṅkā and the Mūrtipūjakas which lead to the development of the *praśnottara* genre which reflects the formal features of oral debates. In her view it is the "tendency to stress divergencies" and the lack of "any global organising principle" which distinguishes the genre from the merely "literary" question-answer formats used in the canon, though the method of citing "authentic" written texts in the debates between the late medieval sectarian traditions (see Granoff 1993) seems to be the

principal difference: "such works are meant to discuss specific points that gave birth to different opinions within different Jain circles by referring to scriptures, with the idea to settle them according to the view in force within the order to which the author belongs" (Balbir 2003a: 256).

68 *Jeṭhmal meṃ jo lumpakmat kī utpatti likhī hai bilkul jhūṭhī aur svakapol kalpit hai* (Ātmārām 1903: 11).

69 Ātmārām 1954, II: 537 derives the term *Ḍhūṇḍhiya* or *Ḍhūṇḍhaka*, polemically from *Ḍhūṇḍha*, or ruin. The Sthānakavāsī themselves derive *Ḍhūṇḍhiya* from *Ḍhūṇṛhiya* or *Ḍhūṇṛhaka*, or seeker. See for instance Hastīmal 1995: 769.

70 Cf. Flügel 2000; 2003a; Jain & Kumār 2003.

71 Jñānsundar 1936: 29 used the same method of critique backed with more evidence of this kind in his rejoinder to the later Sthānakavāsī *itihāsa* literature.

72 Bruhn 1983: 37 defines Jaina universal history in terms of "a definite mythological subject, the history of the sixty-three great men." Cort 1995: 473 coined the loosely defined term "localised history" to describe similar narrative structures, focusing on great personalities, etc., within particular sectarian traditions. For the present purpose – the analysis of "historical narratives of great beings" – both definitions are too specific, and do not account for the cosmological themes in Jaina historical narratives. I would suggest to see "universal history," as defined by Bruhn, as a term which mediates between "chronological" and "cosmological history."

73 Flügel 2000: 72f.

74 Ātmārām 1916.

75 Book cover Pārvatī 1905b. "*Ācārya*" is here used as a honorific title.

76 According to Vallabhvijay's often polemical remarks on her biography (1891: 6-11), she was born in an Agravāl *baniyā* family of the village Luhāra near Āgrā, took *dīkṣā* from her teachers Muni Kuṃvarsena and Sādhvī Hīrāṃ of Ratnacandra's Sthānakavāsī Manoharadāsa Sampradāya on the 6.4.1867 (1924 *caitra śukla* 2). Kuṃvarsena did not follow Ratnacandra's command (*ājñā*) and separated himself later together with his disciples. Pārvatī's official biographer P.L. Jain (1913/1923) confirms her basic biodata. He relates the interesting detail that her father's brother followed the Digambara tradition, and her father the Sthānakavāsī tradition of Ratnacand's disciple Kuṃvarsena (p. 5).

77 Vallabhvijay 1902: 46.

78 Vallabhvijay 1891: 8 notes that the disputes between Pārvatī and Ātmārām, who left the Sthānakavāsīs in 1874, caused great discordance between the Jaina traditions in the Pañjāb: *pañjāb meṃ ākar bahut Jaina dharma kī nindā karāvegā.*

79 Her texts are published in the *praśnottara* format, and are probably based on protocols of oral conversations with her lay followers.

80 The contents can be inferred from Vallabhvijay's response (1891: 9-71). I have not been able to locate a copy of this or any other text mentioned in the following which is not listed in the bibliography. Further books of Pārvatī, which were inaccessible to me, are *Jaina Dharma ke Dās Niyam* (1889), *Go Rakṣā kā Upadeś* (1900), *Kuvyasan Niṣedh* (1915), *Mukti Nirṇay Prakāś* (1916), *Śrīmad Bhagavān Nemināth Rājīmatījī kā Jīvan Caritra* (1918), *Brahmacarya Vidhi* (1919), and *Vairāgya Prakāś* (1930). Further criticisms of Ātmārām, whom she met personally for the first time in 1863 in Āgrā, are summarised in P.L. Jain 1913/1923: 32-37, 249f., 278-283, II: 47-50, 71f. They concern issues such as the initiation of five year old children, or the habit of Ātmārām's mendicants of taking baths, which are defended in the *Jainatattvādarśa*, and in particular the "misrepresentation" of the Sthānakavāsī tradition in the last section of this book.

81 The title of Vallabhvijay's *Ḍhuṇḍhak-hita-śikṣā Apanām Gappa-dīpikā-samīr* (1891) alludes also to V.M. Śāh's *Hita-śikṣā*. Vallabhvijay quotes extensively from Ātmārām. His authorship of the work, as well as the attribution of the authorship of "Vijayrājendra Sūri's" *Caturtha Stuti Kuyukti Nirṇay Chedan Kuṭhār* to Vallabhvijay's disciple Dhanvijay, has been disputed by J. Jain (1893: 6f.), in response to the polemical attribution of Pārvatī's book to an anonymous Brāhmaṇ.

82 Vallabhvijay 1909: 1f.

83 With details supplemented from other sources.

84 The critique of image worship in the manner of Draupadī, who apparently only at her wedding under special circumstances venerated images, is a *topos* of the aniconic Jaina literature. See for instance L 7; Jeṭhmal 1930: 84-112. Compare: "The Story of Draupadi" in: Nagendra K. Singh (ed.), *Encyclopaedia of Jainism*, Vol. 22, pp. 5931-5945. New Delhi: Anmol Publications, 2001.

85 Like most topics of the sectarian debate, the issue was already addressed by Loṅkā, and discussed for instance in Samayasundara's *Sāmācārī śataka* 40 (Balbir 2003a: 260). However, like Ātmārām (Vijayānandsūri), Pārvatī (1905b) was also engaged in an ideological battle against the "Āryyās," i.e. the Ārya Samāj.

86 See Jeṭhmal's (1930) critique of the interpretation of the *nikṣepa* doctrine by the *hiṃsādharmī*, i.e. the image-worshippers. The Mūrtipūjaka tradition treats the four principal analytical standpoints, or *nikṣepa* (*nāma*, *dravya*, *sthāpana*, *bhāva*), as equivalent, whereas the Sthānakavāsī or *dayādharmī* tradition gives priority to the *bhāva nikṣepa*: *anuyogadvāra sūtra meṃ 4 nikṣepa kahe haiṃ yah to satya hai par cāroṃ hī nikṣepa vandanīk nahīṃ kahe. ek bhāv nikṣepa vandanīk kahā hai* (Jeṭhmal 1930: 54). The principal reply was formulated by Muni Ātmārām (1884/1908), who in turn was criticised by Mahāsatī Pārvatī

(1905a) in her work *Satyārtha Candrodaya Jaina*, which was rejected in Muni Amarvijay's *Ḍhūṇḍhak Hṛday Netrāñjanaṃ athavā Satyārtha Candrodayāṣṭakaṃ* (1908). An early Digambara critique of this view can be found in the *Sūryaprakāśa* of the year 1825. See Dundas 2001: 67, n. 44. For short summaries of Pārvatī's debates with Digambara laity see P.L. Jain 1913/1923.

87 Note that many pamphlets of the Mūrtipūjaka monks have been published under Ātmārām's name even after his death. See footnote 81.

88 Kundanmal belonged to the Raghunātha Sampradāya.

89 He described it as a "work of deceit." See V.M. Śāh's reply (1925: 3f.).

90 Muni [Ācārya] Amolakṛṣi's *Śāstroddhār Mīmāṃsā* (1920), an addendum to his Āgama edition is also a key text for the Sthānakavāsī revival. It contains a few pages on Loṅkā (pp. 57-60) and sustained a criticism of the Mūrtipūjakas and Digambaras. I only recently gained access to this book.

91 The Mūrtipūjaka layman Lālā Jayadayāl's *Ḍhūṇḍhak Mat Samīkṣā* (n.d.) must have been published in the Pañjāb sometime before 1908.

92 Śāh 1909: 5 singles out the *paṭṭāvalī*s of the Darīyāpurī Sampradāya, the Pañjāb (Lavjīṛṣi) Sampradāya and of the Mūrtipūjaka "Vijaya" and "Sāgara" Śākhā (which treated the Sādhumārgī and Loṅkagacchī as "*sammūrcchima*") for their untrustworthiness, but exempts the Cha Koṭī Saṅgha (Līmbḍī Nānī Pakṣa) *paṭṭāvalī*.

93 On the significance of V.M. Śāh and the text *Aitihāsik Noṃdh* see Flügel 2000; 2003a.

94 Written either by Devṛṣi or, more likely, by one of the editors of the book in Jeṭhmal 1930: 11-19.

95 Schubring's translation. Original cited in Jeṭhmal 1930: 18.

96 The Hindī edition of the *Śrīlāljī Mahārāj kā Sacitra Jīvancaritra* which was composed by Durlabh T. Jhauharī (1922/23), one of the principal leaders of the Sthānakavāsī laity at the time, is the only other text which is available in huge quantities.

97 Reprinted photos of Maṇilāl and Pārvatī Devī are mocked as "suitable evidence" for the "aniconic" credentials of the Sthānakavāsīs in Amarvijay 1908: 77f.

98 Maṇilāl 1934: 157-178. See also the chapter on the Loṅkāgaccha, pp. 179-186. There is no evidence in the oldest sources that Loṅkā's family name was Śāh, though this is commonly assumed in modern literature.

99 For instance, the Tapāgaccha *muni* Kāntivijay's *Ath Loṅkāśāh nuṃ Jīvan*, which he published in its entirety at the beginning of the chapter on Loṅkā (Maṇilāl 1934: 161f.). For a critique of this text and its influence on Maṇilāl see Jñānsundar 1936: 9ff.

100 Deśāī 1926-44, III: 2204 mentions that Maṇilāl edited the *paṭṭāvalīs* on which the published work is based in Saṃvat 1941. Śeṭh 1962: 342 quotes an additional book of Maṇilāl, *Prabhuvīr Paṭṭāvalī māṃ Loṅkāśāh nuṃ Jīvancaritra*. I was unable to trace these works; nor Jīvaṇlāl Kālīdās Vorā's (ed.) *Jaindharma Darpaṇ* of Saṃvat 1942 which, according to Deśāī, also contains *paṭṭāvalīs* of the aniconic traditions.

101 My earlier statement that Maṇilāl's work was declared as the official history of the AISJC has to be corrected. See Flügel 2000: 41. The Līmbḍī Nānī Pakṣa, to which Maṇilāl belonged, never joined the Śramaṇasaṅgha.

102 I have not been able to trace early editions of this journal.

103 The historical date is disputed, but the Sthānakavāsīs declared *kārtik śukla* 15 to be Loṅkā's birthday.

104 Miśrīmal, in Surānā 1976: 217f.

105 This may be the same text that was published in the collection of Hastīmal 1968.

106 Miśrīmal 1936: 64.

107 The published text has a complex history of translation from Hindī to Gujarātī (first edition) and back again.

108 In isolated form, the word "*sthānakavāsī*" occurs reportedly much earlier (Suśīlkumār 1959: 427), but even Upādhyāya Ātmārām (1942: 12, cf. 16), who devoted an entire article on the history of the word *sthānakavāsī* to prove that the principal Sthānakavāsīs are the *mokṣa*-seeking *bhāva sthānakavāsīs* not the *dravya sthānakavāsīs* (*sthānake bhāvasaṃyamādirūpe samyakcāritre vasati tacchīla iti sthānakavāsī*), did not cite earlier examples of its modern use as a self-description. John E. Cort mentioned to me that the word is used in a polemical Mūrtipūjaka text of the late 18th century.

109 Śeṭh 1962: 344-383.

110 Published by Jñānsundar (1936: 234-237) who located the Ms. in the Lābhasundarajī Jñāna Bhaṇḍāra.

111 Published in a Bombay paper on the 18.7.1936, and republished by Jñān-sundar (1936: 238-240). For bibliographic references of early Loṅkāgaccha sources see Deśāī 1926-44; Flügel 2003a: 219-222.

112 A manuscript of the Gokulbhāī Nānī Saṃgraha in Rājkoṭ was published by Desāī in *Jaina Yuga* (Bhādrapad 1985 – Kārtak 1986): 99-100 (reprint in Koṭhārī 2001: 501-503) and reprinted by Jñānsundar 1936: 230-233. For further bibliographic information on the following texts see Flügel 2003a: 230-233.

113 Ms. No. 5837, L.D. Institute, Ahmedabad, published with a Hindī translation in Hastīmal 1995: 642-646.

114 A manuscript of the Jñānbhaṇḍār in Pāṭaṇ was published by Desāī (reprint in Koṭhārī 2001: 486-499) and reprinted by Jñānsundar 1936: 209-227.

115 A manuscript of the Jñānbhaṇḍār in Pāṭaṇ was published by Desāī in *Jaina Yuga* 1.2 (Vaiśākh-Jeṭh 1986): 339-349 (reprint in Koṭhārī 2001: 499-500) and reprinted by Jñānsundar 1936: 228f.

116 Published in Maṇilāl 1934: 161f.; Hastīmal 1995: 752-759, Hindī summary by Jñānsundar 1936: 9f. A copy of one original Ms., which was with Yati Sundar of the Kacch Nānī Pakṣa, has been given to Ācārya Hastīmal 1995: 751.

117 Ms. Bīkāner Bṛhata Jñānabhaṇḍāra, Dānasāgara Saṃgraha No. 72. Padmanabh S. Jaini is currently publishing a book on the anonymous Digambara text *Cauryāṃsī Bol* which contains extensive criticism of the "Loṅkā" tradition.

118 The text is mentioned in Mahāprajña 2000: 7. The followers of Loṅkā are apparently accused by the author to be materialists and atheists, because they rejected the veneration of (protector) gods. It must be identical with the author's commentary to "Kundakunda's" Pāhuḍas in the *Ṣaṭprābhṛtādisaṃgraha*, which according to Schubring 1957: 559, describes the followers of Launka as "Pseudo-Śvetāmbaras" (*śvetāmbarābhāsa*) and as "sinful wrong believers" (*pāpiṣṭhā mithyādṛṣṭayaḥ*) because they reject images.

119 Published in Darśanavijaya 1933: 41-119.

120 No further information is available on the original Ms.

121 *huṇḍī jahe Loṅkā taṇī, acche purātan teha,*
tiṇmeṃ āgam sākṣi thī, bol unhattar jeha. (1)
sakal suguṇ śir sehrā, śrī kālū gaṇi rāy,
tāsu pasāye gulāb kahe, dohā rūp banāya. (3)
(Gulābcand, in Caudharī 1936?: 338, cf. 428f.).

122 Information from Muni Navratnamala, 12.8.2004, who also stated that according to Terāpanth sources, Loṅkā's original *Huṇḍī* (or rather the Ms.?) was written in Saṃvat 1583.

123 See Dundas 1996: 74 on Jayācārya's Rājasthānī translation of Abhayadeva Sūri's 11th-century Sanskrit commentary on the *Viyāhapannatti*, and Budhmal 2001: 419 on the introduction of the study of the Sanskrit commentaries into the monastic curriculum of the Terāpanth by Kālūgaṇi.

124 A standard critique of Ācārya Bhikṣu, even from the Sthānakavāsīs who were subject to the same criticism, was that he "had no knowledge of Sanskrit and Prakrit" (Muni Rajyash, in Nair 1970: iii). See already the complaints of Jñānsundar 1936: 97, and Mālvaṇiyā 1964: 378 cited in Dundas 2002: 247 and 250, on the lack of learning of the followers of the aniconic tradition in general, which prevented them from understanding the Ardhamāgadhī canon itself and the Sanskrit commentary; though Mālvaṇiyā excluded Loṅkā himself from this verdict, in view of his extensive citations from the canon. Jñānsundar (1936: 63-5, 109) and most Mūrtipūjakas credit Pārśvacandra Sūri of the Pārśvacandragaccha for the "translation" of

the Aṅgas into Gujarātī, whereas the Sthānakavāsī tradition refers to Dharmasiṁha as the author of the first *ṭabos*. See Flügel 2000: 62; 2003a: 195.

125 1. Sūy(agaḍa) 1.12.16, 2. Uvav(āiya) 2.19, 3. Viy(āhapannatti) 7.2 (294b), 4. DVS (Dasaveyāliya) 4.12, 5. Utt(arajjhāyā) 28.29, 6. DVS 4.10, 7. Viy 8.6, 8. Sūy 1.1.2.4, 9. DVS 7.48, 10. Pannavaṇā 22, 11. DVS 5.1.92, 12. Āyāra 1.8.4.13, 13. Sūy 1.1.2.14, 14. Uvav 2.20, 15. Utt 28.31, 16. Utt 36.260, 17. Uvav 2.20, 18. Āyāra 1.2.6.5, 19. Aṇuogaddārāīṃ 7 [?], 20. Sūy 1.6.7, 21. Sūy 1.9.1, 22. Sūy 1.1.4.10, 23. Sūy 1.10.3, 24. Utt 4.8, 25. DVS 1.1, 26. Nis(īha) 11.81, 27. Nis 11.91, 28. Nis 15.74f., 29. Nis 16.13f., 30. Nis 17.223, 31. Nis 11.11, 32. Nis 17.224, 33. Nis 8.12, 34. Nis 8.13, 35. Sūy 1.11.20, 36. Utt 20.44, 37. Pannavaṇā 11, 38. Dasāsuyakkhandha 9.9, 39. Sūy 1.10.15, 40. DVS 7.1, 41. Sūy 1.12.5, 42. Āyāra 1.6.4.1, 43. Āyāra 1.2.2, 44. Āyāra 1.5.6.1, 45. Uvav 2.19, 46. Utt 31.3, 47. Sūy 1.3.4.6-7, 48. Nis 12.1-2, 49. Ayāra 1.4.4.1f., 50. Utt 14.12, 51. Uvav 2.21, 52. DVS 6.19 [not: "6.21"], 53. DVS 4.[10], 54. Nis 4.22, 55. Utt 10.15, 56. Utt 21.24, 57. Nis 13.42-45, 58. Nis 12.17, 59. Ṭhāṇa 2.3.6, 60. Ṭhāṇa 2.1.25, 61. Ṭhāṇa 2.1.25, 62. Utt 28.36, 63. Utt 23.63, 64. Āyāra 1.4.2.1, 65. DVS 9.4.4, 66. Āyāra 1.1.7 [not: "1.2.4"], 67. Uvav 2.34, 68. Uvav (*samava-saraṇa adhikār meṃ*, four types of meditation), 69. DVS 7.47.

126 In this respect, it contrasts with many *maryādā* lists. See Mette 1974: 4f.; Flügel 2003a: 17.

127 That is, before the reforms of Ācārya Tulsī (1914-1997) after 1949.

128 Nos. 5-6, 10, 15, 22-25, 55, 62, 64-66, 68.

129 Nos. 1, 11-14, 17-18, 20-21.

130 Nos. 2, 8, 16, 41, 45, 50, 63.

131 Nos. 3, 9-13.

132 Nos. 39, 58-61, 67.

133 Thirteen points are concerned with *prāyaścittas* as outlined in the *Nisīha*, whereas not one of the *bols* of L, LH, and LTC deal with atonements. This, and the absence of any discussion of image-worship, indicates that the sixty-nine *bols* are probably the creation of a (Terāpanth) monk rather than a layman such as Loṅkā.

134 Nos. 6, 7, 36, 46-49, 55. An exception is No. 35: *je ya dāṇaṃ pasaṃsanti, vaham icchanti pāṇiṇaṃ; je ya ṇaṃ paḍisehanti, vitticcheyaṃ karanti te* – "Those who praise the gift, are accessory to the killing of beings; those who forbid it, deprive (others) of the means of subsistence" (Sūy 1.11.20, Jacobi's translation). This passage has been associated with the Sthānakavāsī *muni* Jaymal's defence against Bhīkhaṇ's famous critique of the value of gift giving for the purpose of accumulating *puṇya* (Seṭh 1970: 1004). It does not come as a surprise, then, that different interpretations of the Prakrit original are offered: "Loṅkā's *bol*" explains the verse as follows: *sāvadya dāna kī praśansā kare tiṇa ne prāṇī jīvāṃ ko badha bañchaṇhāro kahyo* (in Caudharī 1936?: 376).

Gulābcand's *dohā* says:
do sāṃsārika dāna rī, kare praśansā koya;
badha bañche kāya nūṃ, sūyagaḍāṅge joya (128).
adhyayana igyārahvāṃ ne viṣai, bīsmī gāthā māṃhi;
niṣedhiyāṃ varttamān meṃ, vṛtti cheda kahāhi (129)
(Caudharī 1936?: 376f.).
The *sorṭhā* finally objects to "Loṅkā's" insertion of the word *sāvadya*, blameful, in front of the word *dāna*, because it is not in the original text: *sāvadya śabda nahīṃ pāṭha meṃ, samuccai dān kaheha re* (p. 377). In order to explain the meaning, two types of gifts are distinguished: *supātra dāna* and *kupātra dāna*, and Viy 8.6.1 (No. 7. in the list of *bols*) is invoked which states that a gift of pure food to a worthy recipient (a pure monk) is a pure gift (*śuddha dāna*) "which brings about the annihilation of *karman*," rather than the influx of *puṇya* (which is *pāpa* from the "absolute" point of view that is favoured by the Terāpanth).

135 Nos. 6-7, 8, 55.

136 Nos. 5, 22-25. See *infra*.

137 The method of legitimising a particular sectarian interpretation of the canon by constructing a selective list of "authoritative" citations is not unusual (Balbir 2003a: 272). Today, it can be found for instance in the unpublished *Sāmācārī* of the Sthānakavāsī Kacch Āṭh Koṭī Nānī Pakṣa (personal communication by Ācārya Rāghav).

138 See Flügel 2000; 2003a.

139 See also Jain & Kumār's (2003: 109) critique.

140 Suśīlkumār (1959: N) received advice from Ācārya Ānandṛṣi, Upādhyāy Hastīmal, Upādhyāy Amarmuni, Muni Pyārcand, and "Marudhar Keśarī" Miśrīmal, i.e. from the Śramaṇasaṅgha *munis* who had the greatest interest and expertise in the study of history.

141 She received advice from Ācārya Ānandṛṣi, Upādhyāy Hastīmal, Upādhyāy Amarmuni, Pravartak Pannālāl, "Marudhar Keśarī" Miśrīmal, Muni Ambālāl, Muni Puṣkarmuni, and Muni Padmacandra (Prakāśakīya, in Candanākumārī 1964: 9).

142 Suśīlkumār 1959: 2 distinguishes five eras: 1. Ādi Yuga (pre 500 before V.S.), 2. Mahāvīra Yuga (500 before V.S. – 2nd century before V.S.), 3. Bhadrabāhu Yuga (2nd century before V.S. – 16th century V.S.). 4. Luṅkāśāha Yuga (16th century V.S. – 2007 V.S.), 5. Saṅgha Yuga (2007 V.S. – today). See Flügel 2000: 43, n. 11 for other emic periodisations of the Jaina history.

143 *vartamān meṃ pracalit śvetāmbar sthānakavāsī jain-samāj Loṅkāgacch kī vartamānkālīn kaṛī hai. isī samāj meṃ hameṃ āj sahī rūp meṃ śrī Loṅkāśāh-siddhānta ke darśan hote haiṃ* (Candanākumārī 1964: 105).

144 See the sources published by Jñānsundar 1936.

145 Cf. Dundas 1996: 79.

146 The idea for this procedure evidently stems from Ācārya Javāharlāl (1875-1943) whose arguments were rejected at the Ajmer *sammelan* in 1933. See Flügel 2003a: 195. On the incompatibility of many Sthānakavāsī *paṭṭāvalīs* see Ātmārām 1884/1908: 8-11; Vallabhvijay 1891: 67-70; V.M. Śāh 1909: 96ff., 103f.; Jñānsundar 1936: 296-300.

147 *phakat sthānakavāsī sādhuja mahāvīr nā sācā śiṣya che* (Bhaṇḍārī 1938:96).

148 AISJC 1987: 71ff. See Flügel 2003a: 195f.; forthcoming (a).

149 Cf. Cort's definition of *gacchas* = *sampradāyas* as "units, defining the boundaries within one can ritually interact" (Cort 1991: 662).

150 The texts are not stifled by formalism, whose significance for other genres of the Jaina literature was highlighted by Bruhn 1981: 36. Only the information on the "great beings" after Loṅkā can claim some historical credibility.

151 Ghāsīlāl (1884-1973) originally belonged to the Sādhumārgī tradition, which left the Śramaṇasaṅgha in the 1950s. He was apparently made an *ācārya* by Ācārya Javāharlāl in 1933, but left when Gaṇeśīlāl became leader, and founded his own splinter group, which does not exist today. See his disciple Kanhaiyālāl's *Bhūmikā*, in Ghāsīlāl 1983: 5f.; personal communication of Umeśmuni 13.10.2002.

152 Ghāsīlāl 1983: 2f.

153 Kanhaiyālāl's *Bhūmikā*, in Ghāsīlāl 1983: 12.

154 See Bruhn 1987: 107, 111f., also for the term "canon of research."

155 Although history writing as such was not always an issue, the "delicate balance between objectivity and in-depth analysis ... and aggressivity" is nothing, new in Jaina religious discourse as Balbir 2003a: 259, 268 has shown with regard to the 16th-century Kharataragaccha monk Samayasundara. Both "canonisation" and "creeping change" and the "reconstruction of history from the point of view of the present" are founded in one-sided interests, strategies of exclusion and inclusion, and in polemics. The contrast between "canonical interest" and "historical interest" proposed by Assmann (1987: 15) is therefore not as sharp in practice as the conceptual distinction suggests.

156 Several factors are responsible for this. Some explicit agreements were made between leading *ācāryas* to discourage the production and distribution of violently polemical pamphlets which can harm the public image of Jainism as a whole. Overt attacks and *ad hominem* denunciations are therefore nowadays largely confined to intra sectarian politics. Another factor was the accomplishment of the unification of most Sthānakavāsī traditions, and the end of the main period of institutional reform.

157 There are also hardly any sources concerning the founders of the Sthānakavāsī traditions.

158 See Nahar 1918: 38, etc. for short inscriptions of the Loṅkāgaccha.

159 Another widely read article on Loṅkā was written by K.L. Nāhaṭā (1968).

160 *ukt donoṃ pratiyoṃ kā sīdhā sambandh lokāśāh se avaśya hai. kyoṃki lokāśāh ke mat ko, unkī vicārdhārā ko usmeṃ spaṣṭ rūp meṃ prastut kiyā gayā hai* (Mālvaṇiyā 1964: 366).

161 *e sarva Luṅkāmatī nī yukti chai* (*Luṅkā nī Huṇḍī 34 Bol*) (L.D. Institute Ms. No. 4121). The early sources always use the term *mata*, doctrine or sect, and never *gaccha*, order, sect or school, as a designation of the Loṅkā tradition.

162 *iti ... Luṅkā nā saddahiyā anaī Luṅkā nā kariyā aṭhāvana bola anaī tehanuṃ vicāra likhauṃ chai. śubhaṃ bhavatu sramaṇasaṅghāya, śrī* (L.D. Institute Ms. No. 2989). Mālvaṇiyā's view is still vigorously opposed by orthodox followers of the Mūrtipūjaka tradition, who point out that the manuscript had been tampered with. Even today, many Mūrtipūjaka libraries, such as the Kailāśasāgarasūri Jñān Mandir of the Śrī Mahāvīr Jaina Ārādhana Kendra in Kobā, restrict access to texts of the aniconic tradition which criticise Mūrtipūjaka practices.

163 Hastīmal (1995: 759ff.) disproved Śeṭh's (1964: 43) "sectarian" view that Loṅkā had only a few followers with citations from the Tapāgaccha *paṭṭāvalīs*, and that his views were *adharmik* (Śeṭh 1964: 46) and that he had no knowledge of Ardhamāgadhī (p. 25) with Āgama citations from Loṅkā's *Aṭṭhāvan Bol*.

164 The founder of the Pārśvacandragaccha.

165 The thirteen questions, a selection of the longer text (L.D. Institute Mss. No. 24466, 30565), were published by Hastīmal (1995: 694f.) and re-published by Jain and Kumār (2003: 539-541), who also rendered the text into Hindī (Jain & Kumār 2003: 115-117).

166 Jain & Kumār 2003: 115-117. Hastīmal 1995: 762 also refers to Pārśvacandrasūri's *Sthāpanā Pañcāśikā*, which was not accessible to me.

167 The original text was published for the first time by Mālvaṇiyā (1963a), then together with a modern Gujarātī translation by Vāriā (1976), and again by Hastīmal (1995: 655-693). A Gujarātī summary of this text has been published by P.T. Śāh (2001), and a Hindī rendition by Jain and Kumār (2003: 124-139), who also re-published the version by Hastīmal and a copy of an unspecified hand-written manuscript of the text in an appendix (Jain & Kumār 2003: 503-537).

168 Only a future comparison of different manuscripts can establish whether K is always presented in conjunction with L.

169 Cf. Bruhn 1981: 18. In her *4th Annual Lecture on Jainism* at the London School of Oriental and African Studies on the 17.3.2004, "Thoughts on the meaning and the role of the Śvetāmbara canon in the history of Jainism," Nalini Balbir introduced the term "canon of use" which can be usefully applied in this case; though the difference between a primary and secondary canon is merely a matter of degree.

170 Most *praśnottara* texts address issues in the religious life "of the mendicant as well as of the layman" (Balbir 2003a: 259), which reflects the prevalence of "fourfold," etc., sectarian forms of organisation.

171 L 1-9, 17, 20-21, 40-52, 54-55, 58.

172 L 7-16, 18-19, 22-32, 34-39, 42, 53, 56.

173 L 57.

174 L 53 points to the inner journey advocated by Viy 18.10.4 for instance.

175 Balbir 2003b: 57 refers to "some inscriptions" as evidence for the view that A(ñ)calgaccha mendicants "take help from *ācārya*s belonging to other groups" for *pratiṣṭhā*.

176 Mālvaṇiyā 1964: 377 cites the key passage of Loṅkā's texts, and asks what harm there is to accept the commentaries which are in agreement with the *sūtras*: *'niryukti, bhāṣya, cūrṇī, vṛtti aur ṭīkāoṃ meṃ jo sūtra viruddha bāteṃ haiṃ, unheṃ pramāṇ kaise mānā jā saktā hai?' lekin jinkā siddhānta sūtroṃ ke sāth meṃ mel baiṭh jātā hai, unheṃ pramāṇ mānne meṃ kyā hāni hai*? He suggests that, judging on the basis of the two Mss., Loṅkā himself must have been of this view (Mālvaṇiyā 1964: 378).

177 According to Dharmasāgara's *Pravacanaparīkṣā*, in Mālvaṇiyā 1964: 378, some of Loṅkā's followers accepted twenty-seven scriptures, and others twenty-nine. Earlier Loṅkāgaccha sources, such as Bhānucandra's *Dayādharma Caupāī*, already mention the Loṅkāgaccha canon of thirty-two scriptures, though the canon of thirty-two may have originated with the Sthānakavāsī *ācārya* Jīvarāja. The modern association of a canon of thirty-one with Loṅkā seems to go back to Ātmārām 1881/1954, II: 519; 1888/1906: 204; in Vallabhvijay 1891: 131. Ātmārām wrote that the *Vavahāra* was added by the Sthānakavāsīs, whereas Jñānsundar (1936: 106) argued that it was the "*Āvaśyaka Sūtra*." Suśīlkumār (1959: 395, 431f.) tells us that the Sthanakavāsī *ācārya* Jīvarāja (died ca. 1641) created the present canon of thirty-two scriptures. Mālvaṇiyā (1964: 378f.) also believes that it was created after the emergence of the Sthānakavāsīs, because in all cases only thirty-two are mentioned in the later literature. See Flügel 2000: 49, n. 18 and 59, n. 38.

178 For instance, in the *Āvassaya Nijjutti* or the *Bṛhatkalpabhāṣya*.

179 Dharmasāgara, in Dundas 1996: 74; 2002: 62. See also Mālvaṇiyā's (1964: 376) critique of the "hard" (*dṛṛh*) dogmatism of the Sthānakavāsīs, who in his view do not tolerate differences of opinion.

180 The terms are from Assmann 1987: 13f.

181 ... *tathā śrāvaka naiṃ bāra vrata pālyā nāṃ phal śrī uvavāī upāṅga tathā sāmāiya cauvīsatthao ityādi āvaśyaka nāṃ phal ānuyogadvāra madhye, tathā śrāvaka naiṃ ju sādhu cāritrīā vandanīka chaiṃ tu sādh unai vāṃdyā nāṃ phal, tathā sādhu nī paryupāsti kīdhā nāṃ phal tathā annā pāṇī dīdhā nāṃ phal tathā upāśraya dīdhā nāṃ phal, tathā vastra pātra dīdhā nāṃ phal ityādi* (L 8).

182 See the *Asūtranirākaraṇa Batrīśī* of Muni Bīkā of 1470/1, the *Siddhānta Caupāī* of Muni Lāvaṇyasamay of 1486/7, and the *Siddhānta Sāroddhāra* of Upādhyāya Kamalsaṃyam of the Kharataragaccha in 1487/8. The *Loṅkāśāha Siloko* vv. 13-15 of 1543/4 by the Loṅkāgaccha *yati* Keśavṛṣi also contains similar statements, which is difficult to explain.

183 Jñānsundar 1936: 29, 97, App. 3; Mālvaṇiyā 1964: 367f.; Dundas 2002: 248.

184 *kintu Loṅkāśāh ke 58 boloṃ evaṃ 13 praśnoṃ ādi meṃ kahīṃ koī ek bhī aisā śabda nahīṃ. ... Loṅkāśāh ke virodha meṃ likhane vāle vidvānoṃ ke dvārā kiye gaye ullekhoṃ meṃ sthān-sthān par is prakār ke tathyoṃ kī andekhī dṛṣṭigocar hotī hai* (Hastīmal 1995: 751, cf. 759-789).

185 *sāmāika ṭālaiṃ be bāra, parva pare posaha parihār,*
paḍikkamaṇuṃ bina vrata na karaiṃ, paccakhāṇai kima āgāra dharaiṃ (17).
ṭālai asaṃyati naiṃ dāna, bhāva pūjā thī rūḍau jñāna,
dravya pūjā navi kahī jinarāja, dharma nāmaiṃ hiṃsāi akāja (18).
sūtra batīsa sācā saddahyā, samatā bhāve sādhu kahyā,
siri Luṅkā no sācco dharma, bhrame paṛiyā na lahai marma (19)
(Bhānucandra, in Jñānsundar 1936: 236).

186 This is evidently the first reference to the thirty-two Āgamas in the Jaina literature, which points to a pre-Sthānakavāsī origin of this classification.

187 Dundas 1999: 22. Jñānsundar 1936: 327 also cites Kaḍuā's list, but comments on the relevant point 4 (point 6 in Dundas' list) that Kaḍuā may have included it in the list to distinguish himself on paper from Loṅkā: *śāyad lauṃkā-śāh ne sāmāyik ko bhī asvīkār kiyā thā, isī lie kaḍuāśāh ko yah niyam banānā karā ho* (p. 327, n. 4).

188 Hastīmal 1995: 750 also points to the absence of any polemic along these lines in critique of Loṅkā in the Digambara *muni* Ratnanandī's *Bhadrabāhu Caritra* 158-163 of Saṃvat 1625.

189 A different picture is painted in the much younger *Vinaycandrajī-kṛt Paṭṭāvalī*, published by Hastīmal (1968: 141).

190 *jīvadayāiṃ karī mokṣa puhatā* (L 58).

191 L 46. See Mālvaṇiyā's (1964: 373-375) critique of the "one-sidedness" of Loṅkā's *niścaya-naya* approach, which does not take into account practical considerations of religious instruction for beginners: *dharma kī jo sādhana 13veṃ guṇasthāna se 14veṃ guṇasthāna meṃ jāne ke lie hotī hai, vahī sādhanā pratham guṇasthāna vāle ke lie bhī āvaśyak hai – is prakār kā āgrah karne se sāmānya vyakti ko dharma ke mārga par kaise lāyā jā saktā hai? sādhanā ke mārga par is prakār ekānta āgrah se kām nahīṃ caltā. kyoṃki sabhī sādhakoṃ kī yogyatā samān nahīṃ ho saktī.* This critique echoes the standard criticisms of the views of the Terāpanth *ācārya* Bhikṣu. The additional criticism, directed at the Sthānakavāsīs, that their emphasis on *dayā* unduly neglects the

importance of knowledge is, partly, polemical: *sthānakavāsī paramparā jñān-śūnya ban gaī* (Mālvaṇiyā 1964: 376).

192 See L 17 for a lengthy list of citations from the Āgamas using the term *dayā* in defence of his choice of catchphrase.

193 Cf. Mālvaṇiyā 1964: 373f., and Jain and Kumār's (2003: 140) summary of the text, which would also support this interpretation.

194 Mālvaṇiyā 1964: 382 cites the text as *Luṅkā nī Huṇḍī 33 Bol.* It was however published with an explanation in Hindī under the title *Cauṃtīs Bol* (34 assertions) by Hastīmal (1995: 648-655), and re-published under the same title by Jain and Kumār (2003: 499-503), who also give a summary in Hindī (Jain & Kumār 2003: 120-124). The numerical difference can be explained by the fact that Mālvaṇiyā did not count *bol* No. 34, because it contains only the general statement that only on the basis of the scriptures progress can be achieved.

195 See U.P. Shah 1955b for an inscription documenting historical cases.

196 See Flügel 2000: 18.

197 The text was first published by Mālvaṇiyā (1963a: 80-82), and reprinted in Hastīmal 1995: 691-693, and from Hastīmal's publication (without an indication of the original source) in Jain & Kumār 2003: 537-539. A Hindī summary can also be found in Jain & Kumār 2003: 118-120.

198 See Samayasundara's question "What are the textual references for such and such a rite, usage, etc.?" in his *Sāmācārī Śataka* cited by Balbir 2003a: 267.

199 Fourth edition with Hindī translation by Muni Devṛṣi (1872-1929), who became the *ācārya* of the Sthānakavāsī Mālvā Ṛṣi Sampradāya after Amolakṛṣi's death, and was the predecessor of Ānandṛṣi (1901-1963), the second *ācārya* of the Śramaṇasaṅgha in which the Mālvā Ṛṣi Sampradāya was incorporated in 1952. See Flügel 2000: 70, n. 62.

200 Jeṭhmal 1930: 14 has as question No. 6: *ghoṛā, rath, bail, ḍolī meṃ baiṭhte ho.* – To sit on a horse, chariot, bullock (-cart) or litter carried by porters; No. 8: *ghar jākar kalpa sūtra paṛhte ho.* – To read the *Kalpa Sūtra* after going to a house; No. 12: *rassī ḍore dete ho.* – To give strings of rope (as blessings); No. 13: *mantra, jantra, jhāṛ phūk karte ho.* – To perform *mantra, yantra,* exorcism; 14. *pustak, pātare becte ho.* – To sell leafs of a book (to sell knowledge); 15. *māl uṛāte ho.* – To indulge in property; 25. *ṭīp likhā rupaye lete ho.* – To take money for writing documents; 29. *tapasyā karākar paise lete ho.* – To accept money after performing a fast; 45. *mor piñch ke ḍaṇḍāsaṇ rakhte ho.* – To keep a peacock feather staff (Digambara style); 46. *strī kā saṅghaṭṭā karte ho.* – To keep the company of women; 49. *kapṛe dhulāte ho.* – To cause clothes to be washed. These are standard complaints against "domesticated" Jain mendicants.

201 On the uses of written texts in earlier medieval Jaina debates see Granoff 1993, and also Dundas 1996. On the role of written texts for the "protestant" Jaina reform movements see Flügel 2000: 38, 46.

202 Jain and Kumār (2003: 118) have *ghar meṃ pratimā banavāne yā citrit karavāne.* This sentence appears in Jeṭhmal 1930: 14 as No. 24: *māṇḍvī karāte ho.*

203 This sentence has only been published in Hindī in Jeṭhmal 1930: 14. It is not related to the first sentence of point 1, and should have been listed separately. The laxities of (some) medieval Mūrtipūjaka mendicants are well documented in an inscription published by U. P. Shah 1955b.

204 On *bāl dīkṣā* see Balbir 2001.

205 Or "split." On ascetics piercing their ears see Wujastyk 1984.

206 The word *khamāsamāsaṇu* refers to the *vandanā* ritual to the *kṣamāśramaṇa*, which begins with the words *icchāmi khamā-samaṇo vandiuṃ* – "I desire to venerate you forgiving monk," which Mūrtipūjaka ascetics (and laity) also perform in front of symbolic objects representing the *guru*, such as the *sthāpanācārya*, and in front of statues (*caitya vandanā*). See Leumann 1934: 7-10; Williams 1983: 199-203; Cort 2001: 65. The sentence is interpreted by Jain and Kumār (2003: 118) as: "*khamāsaṇā guru ko diyā jātā haim, dev ko nahīṃ.*" The issue is also addressed in Samayasundara's *Sāmācārī Śataka* 1 etc. (Balbir 2003a: 261).

207 Also: to spend time.

208 A common mistake, known in the scriptures as *nitya-piṇḍa* or *nitiya-piṇḍa*.

209 Jain and Kumār (2003: 118) have: *snān karne kā kahanā aur snān karnā.* – To ask (someone) to take a bath and to take a bath. LH 19 criticises that the *Niśītha Cūrṇī* permits taking a bath under certain circumstances, although the scriptures prohibit it unequivocally for mendicants. The question may also address the obligatory practice of image-worshipping lay Jainas to take a bath before entering the temple in order to "purify" themselves outwardly. See Williams 1983: 221, and Laidlaw 1995: 273 on the "incongruence between purity in *puja* and purity in asceticism."

210 In Rājasthānī (R.) *kalavāṃṇī*, means "dirty water" (Lālas 1986-87: 208). The question may thus alternatively refer to *sacitta* water that is left over from the ablutions of the ascetics and/or images, and distributed as a sacred object, or to "raw" water used at certain ritual consecrations. Cf. Williams 1983: 224. Jain and Kumār (2003: 118) have *kalavānī karke dete haiṃ.*

211 There are two uses of the term: (1) The prime recipients of the *saṅghapūjā*, which Williams 1983: 166 described as a "later development," are the mendicants, who during an annual ceremony (at the end of *paryuṣaṇa*) receive at once "blankets, cloth, needles, thread, staves, almsbowls, *rajoharaṇa*s, and other objects useful to an ascetic." Jeṭhmal 1930: 14 (question No. 18) uses the expression "to

extract" (*nikalnā*) the *saṅghapūjā*. (2) The "worship of the congregation" may also involve "giving every participant at some public religious function a small amount of money (usually a one-rupee coin) and a red forehead mark as a token of respect" (Cort 2001: 150). *Saṅghapūjā* is, for instance, performed in connection with the visit of prominent ascetics to the residence of a householder. The host invites his family and friends to participate in this event and prepares *kunkum* for auspicious *tilaka*s on the fronts of their heads and distributes money to each visitor after the monk or nun has left – a kind of *prasāda* (personal communication K. Śeṭh).

212 This question reflects L 26. The A(ñ)calagaccha did/does not allow this for its own mendicants. See Balbir 2003b: 57.

213 Jeṭhmal 1930: 14 understands this as: *paryuṣaṇ meṃ pothī, de rātra jāgaraṇ karāte*. – To cause night watches to be done to books given out during *paryuṣaṇ*. Loṅkā thus may have rejected the veneration of books as objects. Often, manuscripts are copied or books printed in honour of deceased parents, whose names are mentioned in the introductory sections of a text, and then offered to the mendicants during *paryuṣaṇa*. The objection may also have been directed against the payments for something that has been produced especially for the mendicants, or, more likely, against motivating the laity to auction the privilege of taking the *Kalpa Sūtra* home for one night.

214 For allocating the honour of leading specific rituals, auctions (*bolī*) are routinely held in many Jaina traditions. In the question, the practice of bidding for the privilege of leading the *saṅgha yātrā* as a *caitya paripāṭī* is addressed. Williams 1983: 234 indirectly confirms Loṅkā's suspicion. He writes: "The *tīrtha-yātrā* seems to be a later development."

215 The contextual meaning of *mātra* is unclear here. It could mean measure, a certain amount of money, etc. Jain and Kumār (2003: 118) interpret the half-sentence as: *mātrā (prasravaṇ) dene, prasravaṇa* meaning flow, outflow.

216 *posāliṃ*; see R. *posāla*, S. *pāṭhaśālā*. The *poṣadhaśālā* is a special room that is used for the collective performance of a one-day fast, or *poṣadha*, during which the practising laity imitates the lifestyle of the ascetics. A variety of fasts can be performed. Because not all of them require the complete renunciation of all nourishment, food and drink may be brought to the *poṣadhaśālā* from home (Yaśovijay, in Williams 1983: 145). Since *poṣadha* does not involve performing an almsround, only specially prepared food can be eaten. Therefore, Loṅkā must have disagreed with eating food at all during *poṣadha*, apparently in agreement with the Añcalagaccha and the Kaḍuāgaccha, but in contrast with the Tapāgaccha and Kharataragaccha (Samayasundara) at the time (cf. Balbir 2003b: 60).

217 *Ādhākarma* is discussed in L 21 as well.

218 Loṅkā advocated open access to the scriptures.

219 The word *māṇḍavī* (H. *maṇḍapa*) can also signify a temple, or the entrance hall of a temple.

220 Literally, the sound or echo (*paṛagho*, G. *paḍaghī*). Jeṭhmal 1930: 46-52 lists fifteen practices opposed to the scriptures (*sūtra*) which the *hiṃsā dharmī*, i.e. the image-worshippers, associate with the name of Gautama. Vārīā 1976: 129 explains the question as: *gautam paḍaghā nuṃ tap karāve che.* Jain and Kumār (2003: 119) read the word *paṛagho* as *pratipadā* (*paṛvā*) – the first day of the lunar fortnight. Though Jeṭhmal does not mention this, the question may also refer to the *sūrimantra* (cf. Dundas 1998) which is addressed explicitly in questions 45 and 46, or, more likely, to Gautama's invocation during the annual *pūjā* of the account books at Dīpāvalī (cf. Cort 2001: 168-70).

221 *Saṃsāra-tāraṇa* means literally "to cross the ocean of existence." John Cort informed me that this practice is listed as a fast in the Tapāgaccha monk Jinendravijaygaṇi's *Taporatna Mahodadhi* (Lākhāvāḷa-Śāntipuri: Harṣapuṣpāmṛta Jaina Granthamālā 101, 1982) which is based on the Kharataragaccha *ācārya* Vardhamāna's 15th-century *Ācāradinakara.* Jeṭhmal 1930: 14 speaks of the *Saṃsāra-tāraṇa* "*telā*," i.e. a continuous three-day fast. Most, if not all, of the practices mentioned in questions Nos. 24-27 are likely to be special fasts, which involve auctions of the meritorious act of giving the first drink and food to a *tapasvin(ī)* to conclude, or "break," the fast (*pāraṇa*).

222 This fast takes four days: three one-day fasts (*upavāsa*), followed by one day eating only one meal (*ekāsana*) with or without practising *āyambila* (to eat only one unsalted cereal). Both the privilege of the first feeding of the *tapasvī/n(ī)* on day four, and of the first feeding at the time of the breaking of the fast on day five are auctioned (Kelting 2001: 46). For the story of Candanā see Shāntā 1997: 122-128.

223 This is probably another fast involving public auctions. Alternatively, the question may or may not refer to one of the following practices: (a) a ladder of gold is often given by grandsons to grandfathers; (b) ladders are often used to reach a large statue for *pūjā* (personal communication K. Śeṭh).

224 John Cort suggested to me, this may refer to the *lakṣa pratipada* fast (G. *lākhī paḍavo*), which is listed in modern Gujarātī Jaina compilations of fasts.

225 G. *ujamaṇuṃ*, R. *ujamaṇau, ujavaṇau*, a celebration at the end of a fast, involving donations of money to the fasting person(s). Jain and Kumār (2003:119) translate *ūṃjamaṇā* as "*udyāpana*," which signifies the concluding ceremony or the dedication of a temple on completion. The meaning of the word *ḍhovarāvai* (? S. *ḍhauk*, P. *ḍhovaṇa*, to offer, to give gifts) is not entirely clear. It may generally refer to celebrations. Jeṭhmal 1930: 15 has "*ḍhurāna*."

226 Or to be sung (*pāḍhāī*).

227 The Hindī verb *bharvāī* or *bharvāna*, to have something filled, makes less sense here than the Rājasthānī verb *bharvāī*, to carry, nurture, maintain, or pay for.

228 Mahāvīra renounced the world under an Aśoka-tree; which is also one of the twelve symbols of the *arihantas*. The tree is associated with the worship of portable Jina images, and is believed to have wish-fulfilling powers. Models of it are often installed on the roofs of temples (Jain & Fischer 1978, II: 3, 7f., 24, Plate XIIb). The *aśoka vṛkṣa* is also listed as a fast in Jinendravijaygaṇi's *Taporatna Mahodadhi*, the breaking of which was possibly auctioned off in various ritual contexts (personal communication of John Cort). The word *bharavāi* could refer to an auction as well. Kanubhāī Śeṭh (personal communication 7.7.2003) informs me that the expression may also point to a decorative curtain with a tree motif (though it seems unlikely). These curtains are made with gold and silver inlays to adorn the wall behind the seat of a monk. Today, they are called *choḍa*, a small tree or shrub. They contain the name of the donor, his family members, and the name of the inspiring monk or nun. After being used as an adornment, they are later venerated in the house of the donor. Sometimes sixteen or eighteen curtains of this type are requested to be made, to be presented to women who have performed a long fast.

229 This question refers back to L 35, which questions the canonical basis of the "upper eight" (Skt. *aṣṭottarī*, Pkt. *aṭṭhottarī*) ritual of installation of images, which includes the use of fire in *āratī*, the rite of throwing "living" salt into the fire, etc.

230 This was also rejected by the A(ñ)calagaccha. See Balbir 2003b: 60. Since image-worship is rejected *per se*, this point is redundant, and may have been imported simply to add more venom to the attack.

231 S. *vāsakṣepa*, colloquial *vāskṣep* or *vāskep*, to sprinkle with scented powder. Mūrtipūjaka ascetics charge sandalwood powder with *mantras* and sprinkle it on the heads of their devotees to transfer their blessings-*cum*-spiritual energy to them.

232 *bāṃdhai*, H. *baṃdhnā*.

233 An alternative reading would be: "To set a limit (for individual laymen) in their search for possessions." Jain and Kumār (2003: 119) interpret the meaning of the passage as *upadhi ādi poṭaliyoṃ meṃ bāṃdhte haiṃ* – to tie up/bring together property etc. in small parcels.

234 The religious legitimacy of the pilgrimage sites of Śatruñjaya, Girnār, Ābū, etc., and *tīrthas* other than the *caturvidhasaṅgha* is questioned for instance in L 36, L 38, L 39, L 41, L 44.

235 The privilege of giving garlands, for instance for the successful performers of the *upadhāna tapa*, is also auctioned off amongst Mūrtipūjakas.

236 Samayasundara, in Balbir 2003a: 260, similarly questioned the co-wandering of monks and nuns, which is still practised within the Tapāgaccha.

237 The questioned issue is not clear. Maybe the word *nāndi* refers to the *nandīśvara-paṭa* which is venerated in the context of the *nandīśvara* fast (U.P. Shah 1955a: 121; Williams 1983: 232; Jain & Fischer 1978, II: 19). It could also (though unlikely) refer to the bull *Nandin*, who is associated with Śiva, or to an inauguration involving praise of the gods (*nāndī*).

238 G. *bhūko* or *bhūkā*, powder, is related to R. *bhūkau* (Lālas 1986-87: 296). The question addresses a common form of water sterilisation amongst the Jainas through "killing" *sacitta* water by adding a different living substance such as lime powder (*cūnā*). Hastīmal 1995: 693 transcribes the original *bhūko* as *bhūṃkā*. Jain and Kumār (2003: 119) interpret *bhūṃkā* as G. *thūṃka* or H. *thūka*, saliva, spittle. The issue of *cūrṇa*, or powder, is also addressed in Samayasundara's *Sāmācārī Śataka* 37 etc. (Balbir 2003a: 261).

239 The sentence apparently means: "to cause veneration to be given (to an ascetic or image)," since R. *vāndaṇau* (*bāndaṇau*) is equivalent to S. *vandana*, to worship. Jain and Kumār (2003: 119) translate *vāndaṇā dirāvai* as *bāṃdhanā dilānā* – to cause someone to give an oath (to bind him/herself). They derive *vāndaṇā* from S. *bandhana*, to bind, R. *bāṃdhaṇau*. Cf. Lālas 1986-87: 194f.

240 Jain and Kumār (2003: 119) render the words *oghā phervai chai* as *āśīrvād svarūp kisī par oghā phernā*. Loṅkā apparently did not use an *oghā* at all (Mālvaṇiyā 1964: 369).

241 The donations given "to the gods" should only be used for the maintenance of the temples, etc. Jeṭhmal 1930: 15 has as question No. 44: *gāṃṭh meṃ paisā rakhte ho*. – To keep money in the pocket.

242 To wear a long *pacchevaṛī* (P. *pacchāga*) is considered wasteful. It seems, Loṅkā himself used one almsbowl (*pātra*), one loincloth (*colapaṭṭāka*) and one short *pacchevaṛī* (*cādar*) (L.D. Institute Ms. No. 2328, in Mālvaṇiyā 1964: 369). He rejected the *oghā*, *muhapattī*, *kambala*, and *daṇḍa*. See Mālvaṇiyā 1964: 369; he cites Ghelārṣi, a contemporary of Loṅkā, who reportedly (L.D. Institute Ms. No. 7588, question 86) asked him in which *sūtra* it is written to wear a *colapaṭṭa*, or loincloth: *āp jaisā colpaṭṭak pahante haiṃ, vaisā kis sūtra meṃ likhā hai?*. From this, it can be deduced that the ascetics at the time did not wear a *colapaṭṭa*; though *colapaṭṭa*s are mentioned in the canon (Viy 8.6.2 (374), etc.). Jñānsundar (1936: 173f.) writes that in the 20th century (?) Loṅkāgaccha ascetics wore *colapaṭṭaka*s and *caddar*s (*cādar*), but in a slightly different form than the Sthānakavāsīs. In contrast to the Sthānakavāsīs, they did not wear a *muhapattī* permanently, but carried an *oghā*, *kambal*, and *daṇḍa*, etc. I have never seen any evidence of a Loṅkāgaccha *yati* carrying a *daṇḍa* though of *oghā* and *kambal*.

243 For the tantric cult of the *sūrimantra* in the Mūrtipūjaka tradition see Dundas 1998: 36-46. He points out that it is not used by the Sthānakavāsīs because they claim "during the fifth century C.E. there occurred a major interruption of the teacher lineage through which the formula was transmitted" (Dundas 1998: 36).

244 The *mantra* was recited to acquire mystical powers, and in order to strengthen the commitment to the particular lineage.

245 Jain and Kumār (2003: 119) translate the expression *kalapaṛā* with the Hindī word *kalaf*, starch.

246 Jain and Kumār (2003: 120) identify this fast as the *vajra-kṛṣṇa* (*vaira-kannai*), or black thunderbolt-fast. No further information is given.

247 G. *ghaḍūlo*, small pitcher, water pot. Pots and bowls should be produced by the ascetics themselves. K. Śeṭh informs me that the question may point to welcoming celebrations for ascetics (*nāgara praveśa*) performed by women with auspicious water pots on their heads, for which see the photo on the dustjacket of Cort 2001. The Hindī rendition of Jain & Kumār 2003: 120 reads: *jhaḍūle karvānā* (*bāl utarvānā*), i.e. to cause the hair to be shaved (R. *jhaḍūlau* signifies the hair of a newly born child). Jaina ascetics should pluck their hair or have it plucked by another ascetic.

248 For a description of this ritual, which comprises the use of flowers and fruit and the veneration of images and gods, see Jain & Fischer 1978, II: 2-4; Cort 2001: 162f. Jain and Kumār (2003: 120) have: *siddhacakra ke āyambīl kī bolī karvānā*, to cause the auction of the *siddhacakra āyambila* fast to be done, which must have been one of the main objections implied by the question.

249 In Rājasthānī, *uṭhāvaṇau* denotes collective mourning. In the case of ascetics, this is the *guṇānuvāda sabhā*, the auspicious praise of the deceased ascetic. A special carpet is used in this context.

250 This ritual is performed by the Mūrtipūjaka Jaina laity on the fifth day of *paryuṣaṇa*, which is called Mahāvīra Jayanti, though the actual birthday of Mahāvīra falls on an earlier date in the year. For details of this ritual, which is performed for well-being and involves extensive bidding for ritual acts, see Cort 2001: 154-7, who also cites earlier literature.

251 Jain and Kumār (2003: 120) use the word *gavalī* (*uṃbaṇī*) for *ṭhavaṇī*.

252 This refers to the practices of the Tapāgaccha and the Kharataragaccha to perform the final *saṃvatsarī pratikramaṇa* not, like most Jaina traditions, on *bhādrapad śukla* 5 but already on *bhādrapad śukla* 4, apparently following the advice of Kālakācārya (cf. Jacobi 1880). In contrast to Loṅkā, Kaḍuā seems to have accepted "the general practice established by Kālakācārya" (in Dundas 1999: 22), but not the A(ñ)calagaccha (Balbir 2003b: 59).

253 Dundas 1996: 74, 89f.

254 See Flügel 2003a: 162, n. 49; 195, n. 140; 196, n. 145. Dundas (1996: 80, 83, 86) has discussed similar remarks of Abhayadeva, Prabhācandra and Dharmasāgara.

255 Schubring 1935/2000: 250; Balbir 2001: 154. Amongst the Śvetāmbara sects, only the Śramaṇasaṅgha rejects child initiation.

256 Amongst the Sādhumārgīs only women change their names. The empirical situation is complex.

257 Original source not cited in Candanākumārī 1964: 102; Prakāścandra 1998: 31.

258 It is possible that Candanākumārī extracted the rules from the book by Suśīlkumār (1959), which was one of the main sources for her work. I cannot disconfirm this, since several pages of the chapter on Loṅkā are missing in my own xerox-copy of Suśīlkumār's text.

259 The texts were also published in Flügel 2000: 52; 2003a: 233.

260 Flügel 2000; 2003a; forthcoming (c).

261 *prācīn śāstra-bhaṇḍāroṃ meṃ in niyamoṃ ke anek patra prāpta hote haiṃ. un sabhī niyamoṃ kā likhnā yahāṃ āvaśyak nahīṃ hai. un meṃ se kuch upayogī niyam jānkārī ke lie yahāṃ diye jā rahe haiṃ* (Candanākumārī 1964: 102).

262 Translated by the author.

263 The A(ñ)calagaccha allowed its use only for mendicants, not for the laity as most Mūrtipūjaka traditions. See Balbir 2003b: 59f.

264 The word *upavāsa* signifies either fasting in general, or a specific thirty-six-hour fast (Pkt. *cauttha bhatta*, Skt. *caturtha-bhakta*) without any food, but with or without drink. I have preferred the more specific meaning in all translations, since the *upavāsa* performed in the context of *poṣadha* is addressed, though often fasting in general may have been the intended meaning in a particular case.

265 This rule is identical with one of the stipulations of Kaḍuā (KS 7); though Jñānsundar 1936: 327, n. 5 expressed the opposite view. The point was rejected by the A(ñ)calagaccha and the Kharataragaccha (Samayasundara), but accepted by the Tapāgaccha (Balbir 2003b: 59). Dundas 1999: 22 understands the meaning of rule KS 7 slightly differently – that "the *poṣadha* fast can be celebrated when it does not fall on an observance day (*parvan*)."

266 The prototype must be LH 22, which criticises the *Niśītha Cūrṇi*'s permission for using an *acitta* staff for purposes of self-defence, which contradicts the *Niśītha* 5 itself.

267 Varddhamāna Sthānakavāsī Jaina Śrāvaka Saṅgha Jaypur 1964; Flügel 2003a: 164-168; forthcoming (a).

268 See Hastīmal 1968; 1971; 1987/1995, and his collection of Mss. in the Lāl Bhavan Sthānak in Jaypur.

269 Translation by the author.

270 The *upadhāna tapa* is a special, extended (usually thirty-five or forty-seven day long) collective *poṣadha*, a collective fast-*cum*-study exercise which, according to Cort 2001: 137, has been first described in the 7th-century *Mahā-nisīha* 3.3.15-3.36.1. At the end of the programme, which demands image-worship three times a day, "each lay faster takes a garland of flowers used in temple worship and puts it over the head of the mendicant leader." Dundas 1999: 22 cites the stipulation of Loṅkā's younger contemporary, Kaḍuā, that "One should not perform garlanding (*mālāropaṇa*) at the end of *Upadhāna*

Tapas," which he interprets as the ceremony of the "lay votary being garlanded by the presiding monk" (Dundas 1999: 30, n. 21). The objection expressed in the text that is attributed to Loṅkā addresses another aspect of *upadhāna*, i.e. that one is not allowed to study without a prior fast.

271 The meaning of this statement is not entirely clear, though there is a certain resonance with point 6 in Dharmadāsa's critique of Lava (in Seṭh 1970: 368, n.) on the use of seats, which are unnecessary luxuries, even outside of *cāturmāsa*. The printed text has the word *pāṭakā*, which may be a corruption of S. *pāṭaka*, part of a village, which would make even less sense.

272 The issue of the possession of books is touched upon in a different context in K 16 on the distribution of books during *paryuṣaṇa*. It was also a point of contention between the "bookish" Dharmasiṅha and Lava, who rejected the possession of books. See *Prācīn Paṭṭāvālī* in Hastīmal 1968: 186-192.

273 Cf. Dharmadāsa's critique of Dharmasiṅha, who apparently upheld Loṅkā's rule, in Seṭh 1970: 369, n.: *upavās meṃ chāch kī āch pīnī nahīṃ*. – One should not drink the whey of buttermilk during a fast. The Sthānakavāsī traditions of Raghunāth (Dharmadāsa Sampradāya), Amarsiṅha, Dīpcand, Malūkcand (Jīvarāja Sampradāya), Khetsī and Khemsī (Hara Sampradāya) also touched on this issue in a common decree of 1753 whose wording is, however, not entirely intelligible: 2. *tapasyā meṃ telā uparānt dhovaṇ tathā āch aur chāch kī āch pīnī nahīṃ. pī lī jāye to ādhe tap kā prāyaścit* (Seṭh 1970: 919f.; cf. Flügel 2003a: 237f.). The Terāpanth mendicants, which emerged from the Dharmadāsa traditions as well, however, use *āch* during fasts: "When they undertake long fasts they take, if available, the greenish water floating on boiled whey, after the thicker portion of the boiled whey has settled down, otherwise they take boiled water only" (Chopra 1945: 27, n.).

274 Even in the *Śrāvakācāra*s of the image worshippers, *poṣadha* is not identical with *poṣadhopavāsa*. See Williams 1983: 142f. on the four spheres of application of the *poṣadha* vow. The issue is also addressed in Samayasundara's *Sāmācārī Śataka* 25, 29 which accepts this practice (Balbir 2003a: 260), as did the Tapāgaccha, but not the A(ñ)calagaccha (Balbir 2003b: 60).

275 Cf. L 22. For another debate concerning the *kalyāṇaka*s, in Samayasundara, see Balbir 2003a: 263ff.

276 Soft food made of milk, such as yoghurt, and hard food made of grains that are (under their skin) split into two parts (S. *dvidala*) should not be eaten on the same day. The rule is identical with one of the stipulations of Kaḍuā (KS 8 citing the *Bṛhatkalpabhāṣya*); though Jñānsundar (1936: 327, n. 6) expressed the view that Loṅkā permitted the use of *dvidala*. It is also mentioned in the lists of forbidden food (*abhakṣya*) in the medieval *Śrāvakācāra* texts under the name *ghola-*

vaṭāka, buttermilk in tiny lumps (Williams 1983: 110f.). Here, *dvidala* are described as "pulses which when ground yield no oil." They should not be consumed because they contain many micro-organisms; in particular not in combination with milk products "for in this latter instance it is the combination of sour food and milk-product which curdles the milk product and thus results in the generation of innumerable organisms" (Cort 1989: 271). The issue is also addressed in Samayasundara's *Sāmācārī Śataka* 7 (Balbir 2003a: 261).

277 It is believed that new micro-organisms develop in lifeless water after forty-eight minutes. *Dhovana* (P. *dhovaṇa*) water has been used by Jaina ascetics from the outset (see AS 2.1.7.7-9, DVS 5.1.75-79, 5.1.47-55), although some Jaina traditions insist nowadays that only boiled water is acceptable (see Sūy 1.2.2.18, 1.2.2.20, DVS 5.2.22). Often *dhovana* water is filtered and thus kept much longer than forty-eight minutes.

278 This rule is oriented towards a layperson. It resonates with the debate on the nature of the pure gift (*dāna*) between the Sthānakavāsīs Raghunāth and Jaymal on the one hand and the founder of the Terāpanth, Bhīkhan (Bhikṣu), on the other. The Terāpanthīs argued that for the seeker of salvation, the imperative to get rid of all *karma* is authoritative. Giving for reasons of compassion is counterproductive, and thus a form of violence against the self, because it contributes to the accumulation of more *karma*, i.e. *puṇya*. The Sthānakavāsīs argued that compassionate giving, even to a nonascetic or to a bad ascetic, is nevertheless a religious act, since both the relative point of view (*vyavahāra naya*) of conventional morality and the absolute point of view (*niścaya naya*) of the *karma* theory are part of religion. See Flügel 1995-95: 123f.; 2000: 96, n. 107. The statement in the "Loṅkā's" *sāmācārī* supports both Bhikṣu's view, which is based exclusively on the *niścaya naya*, and Raghunāth's belief that the more fundamental Jaina principle of non-onesidedness (*anekāntavāda*) supports the ethics of compassionate help, because it is predicated on the irreducible complementarity of the absolute and the conventional point of view.

279 I asked Candanākumārī personally which sources she used for this list, but she said she could not remember anymore.

280 LN 6 (using a seat) and LN 8 (possession of books) touch on issues which were controversial between Dharmasiṅha, Lava and Dharmadāsa. See Flügel 2000; forthcoming (b).

281 LS 8 (*mantra-tantra*) and LN 4 (*vidyā*) cover similar ground, as does future telling and astrology which "Loṅkā" criticised for instance in K 9, K 10.

282 Seṭh 1970: 368, n. & 369, n. See Flügel, forthcoming (b).

283 "Ascetic" rather than "symbolic" or reflective rituals such as *pūjā*.

284 See Dundas 1999: 30, n. 23.

285 In the *Śrāvakācāra* literature of the image-worshipping traditions, which Williams (1983: 142) studied, *poṣadha* usually means "the fast on the *parvan* day." The term *poṣadhopavāsa* therefore appears to be "etymologically tautological," though other interpretations of *poṣadha* can be found as well, such as "that which strengthens or fattens the religious life" (YŚ 3.85) or "the supreme mendicant" (Cāritrasundar).

286 Jñānsundar 1936: 327, n. 5 deliberately misunderstands the respective rules.

287 See footnote 273.

288 Image-worship is also a traditional ingredient of the *upadhāna*.

289 See Jñānsundar 1936: 328, n. 2; Dundas 1999: 31, n. 31.

290 Dundas 1999: 31, n. 31.

291 Dundas 1999: 31, n. 30.

292 See L 23 and DC 18 for the distinction between worthy (*yogya*) and unworthy mendicants.

293 See for instance V.M. Śāh 1909: 54, 65; Jñānsundar 1936: 105; Suśīlkumār 1959: 426; Mālvaṇiyā 1964: 368.

294 Joharāpurkar in Shāntā 1985: 186, n. 99; Flügel 2006: 382, n. 190.

295 See for instance L 17, which lists several passages from the canon where the word *dayā* occurs.

296 The same conviction is expressed by the contemporary Loṅkāgaccha laity, though no universally recognised *yatis* exist anymore.

297 In Jñānsundar 1936: 333.

298 *keval vaṇik jāti ke viraktoṃ ko hī śramaṇ-śramaṇī dharma meṃ dīkṣā karnā, anya jāti ke logoṃ ko nahīṃ* (PB 2, in Hastīmal 1995: 582).

299 As in the case of Digambara *bhaṭṭārakas*, only few *yatis* existed in the Loṅkāgaccha traditions between the 17th and 21th centuries, often only single individuals without disciples who were in charge of the property and religious ceremonies of a particular *gaccha*.

300 See Williams 1983: 152 for the difference between a *kupātra*, a poor person of a more or less righteous lifestyle but wrong belief, and an *apātra*, a person devoid of all good qualities. Both are normally not considered worthy recipients of religious gifts in the *Śrāvakācāra* literature, nor are adherents of non-Jain traditions. See Viy 8.6.

301 The reasons for interpreting *anukampā dāna* to a *kupātra* or *apātra* as an acceptable and even meritorious act are discussed by Puṣkarmuni (1977: 504).

302 Ṭhāṇa 10.97 distinguishes between ten forms of *dāna* only one of which is called *dharmadāna*.

303 See Flügel, forthcoming (b).

304 Text based on L.D. Institute Ms. 2989, pp. 14b-15a.

305 The meaning (*vivaraṇa*) of this sentence has been given by Vārīā (1976:127) as follows: *have paramparā lakhīie chīe. keṭalāk ema kahe che ke vīra prabhue ā rīte paramparā kahī che.śrī loṅkāśāha praśna kare che ke ā paramparā kayāṃ śāstro māṃ kahīi che te batāvo.* The text was reproduced *verbatim* by Hastīmal (1995) (and Jain & Kumār 2003), which shows that the subsequently published versions are all based on Vārīā's transcription.

306 Vārīā's (1976: 127) reproduction of the text uses the past tense here and in the following question: "*te keha nī paramparā thai.*" Since the L.D. Institute Ms. No. 2989 uses the present tense, I have amended the printing mistakes in the published version in these two cases.

307 This sentence has been left out in all published versions of L.D. Institute Ms. No. 2989, probably because it is regarded as too controversial.

308 Hastīmal 1995: 691: *chokaranaiṃ.*

309 Hastīmal 1995: 691 added in brackets: (*dīkṣa kāle*).

310 Hastīmal 1995: 691: *khamāsamāsaṇu.*

311 Hastīmal 1995: 692: *baisi.*

312 Hastīmal 1995: 692: *dīhāṛī* and added in brackets: (*pratidin*).

313 Hastīmal 1995: 692 added in brackets: (*usī ek*).

314 Hastīmal 1995: 692 added in brackets: (*snān*).

315 Hastīmal 1995: 692 added in brackets: (*koī*).

316 Hastīmal 1995: 692: *karai.*

317 Hastīmal 1995: 692: *pratiṣṭhaī.*

318 Hastīmal 1995: 692: *ghāṭaṛī* and added in brackets: (*vanaspati ke toraṇ*).

319 Hastīmal 1995: 692: *paṛagho.*

320 Hastīmal 1995: 692: *ūṃjamaṇā.*

321 Vāriā 1976: 129: *bharrvaī.*

322 Hastīmal 1995: 693: *dūṅgara caḍhāvaī.*

323 Vāriā 1976: 129: *bhūṃko muṃkai*; Hastīmal 1995: 693: *bhūṃko mukai.*

324 Hastīmal 1995: 693: *dirāvai.*

325 Vāriā 1976: 130: *sūrimantra leīṃ chaī.*

326 Vāriā 1995: 693 *thaṭai.*

327 Vāriā 1976: 130: *kāla.*

328 Vāriā 1976: 130: *jhūlaṇaṃ.*

329 Vāriā 1976: 130: *Uaṃbaṇī.*

330 Hastīmal 1995: 693: *cauthanaiṃ paḍikamai chaiṃ.*

5

A Jaina Mendicant Council

Proceedings of the 8th Sthānakavāsī Jaina Bṛhad Śramaṇa Saṅghīya Sādhu-Sādhvī Sammelana, Indore 20-29 March 2015

Śvetāmbara Jaina mendicants peregrinate in small groups from village to village without much contact with other members of their own order.[1] Gatherings for special purposes or general assemblies are held only sporadically, when matters of common concern are to be resolved. An exception is the Terāpanth, whose fourfold community assembles annually near the *ācārya* for a legislative meeting, called *maryādā-mahotsava* or "great festival of restraint." Qua rule, established by Ācārya Jītamala in 1864, the final day of the event is always *māgha śukla saptamī*. Members of other Jaina mendicant orders meet at irregular intervals only. Large gatherings of the representatives of several different orders are extraordinary occasions. Because of their rarity, monastic councils of the latter variety are often events of great significance. The most famous council, literally "recitation" (*vācana*), in the history of Jainism was held in 466 C.E. at Valabhī (Gujarat) by Śvetāmbara monks under the leadership of Devarddhigaṇi Kṣamāśramaṇa. Reportedly, at this occasion the Śvetāmbara canon was redacted and for the first time written down.[2]

After the legendary council of Valabhī, the "fourth" and "last" of Śvetāmbara historiography, local meetings of monks of one or other group are documented, but rarely a council, were members of more than one mendicant tradition, not to speak of all (Śvetāmbara) Jaina mendicants, came together. The currently largest monastic order of the Sthānakavāsī tradition, the Śramaṇasaṅgha, which comprises more than 1,000 monks and nuns wandering in regions as far apart as Kashmir and Tamil Nadu, hails the first common assembly of representatives of all Sthānakavāsī mendicant orders in Ajmer in 1933 as an event on par with the council of Valabhī. At this occasion, leading monks of 32 regional Sthānakavāsī traditions resolved to abandon their differences and to integrate into a new nationwide organisation with a common

Depiction of the council of Valabhī in the memorial temple Valabhīpura Tīrtha, 2010. Photo: Peter Flügel

purpose and set of rules under the new leadership of just one *ācārya*. It took another 19 years and two further "great assemblies of the ascetics" (*bṛhad śramaṇa sammelana*) until the dream was finally realised at the Great Council of Sāḍarī in 1952, where the leaders of 22 of the original 32 signatory traditions renounced their positions and submitted to the authority of the newly selected first *ācārya* of the Śramaṇasaṅgha, Ācārya Ātmārāma "Panjābī" (1882-1962). A provisional set of rules was agreed, but many issues were yet to be settled. After much deliberation, in a series of three councils, a compromise was agreed upon at the seventh "great assembly" in Pune in 1987, and published under the editorship of Muni Saubhāgyamal "Kamala" (AISJC 1987). For 28 years no general assembly was held until the eighth great council in Indore, from 20-29 March 2015, which was attended by 175 monks, 400 nuns, and up to 100,000 laity.[3] The barefoot journey of the mendicants to Indore took several months in most cases, and involved great physical hardships.[4]

At the *sammelana* in Pune nuns were for the first time permitted to listen to the deliberations of the monks, which would affect their own lives, but not allowed to speak.[5] Thus it was a major innovation of the organisers of the meeting in Indore (the *ācārya* and his advisors) to grant the nuns the right to fully participate in the discussions. The council, which was previous known as *Sthānakavāsī Paramparā Bṛhat Śramaṇa Sammelana,* "Great Assembly of the Ascetics of the Sthānakavāsī Tradition," or *Akhila Bhāratīya Muni Sammelana,* "All India Assembly of Monks," was renamed accordingly, as *Sthānakavāsī Jaina Śramaṇasaṅgha Bṛhad Sādhu-Sādhvī Sammelana,* "Great Assembly of the Monks and Nuns of the *Sthānakavāsī Jaina Śramaṇasaṅgha.*"[6] This new development reflects the enhanced role of the nuns, in contemporary Jainism, who are increasingly educated and articulated.

The general assembly in Indore was long overdue, not least because of the advancing age of the present fourth *ācārya* of the Śramaṇasaṅgha, Dr. Śivamuni (born 1942), and the undecided question of succession.[7] The meeting had already been postponed several times, due to minor differences of opinion between leading monks. Two issues were at stake at the *sammelana*: (a) selection of the predestined successor to the head of the order, (b) constitutional reform. The most interesting aspects of the Great Assembly in Indore, for a participant observer, were the unscripted rules of procedure. The proceedings were held behind closed doors, every morning from 9.45-12.00 (after voluntary "Arhaṃ" meditation[8] between 6.40-7.40) and in the afternoon from 14.00-16.00. They were only accessible to two committee members of the lay community, assisting the *ācārya,* who were not allowed to speak in the assembly. Nonetheless, interviews with participants together with material published before,[9] during[10] and after[11] the *sammelana* established the effective procedures for decision taking, which this report briefly summarises.

(a) The Sthānakavāsī Śramaṇasaṅgha is the only Jaina monastic order, besides the Terāpanth, which, by rule, is headed by a single *ācārya,* who also acts as spiritual leader of the fourfold community (*caturvidha saṅgha*) of monks, nuns, male and female laity. But in contrast to the Terāpanth *ācārya*, his position is weak. In the constitution (*saṃvidhāna*) of the Śramaṇasaṅgha the *ācārya* is defined as the head (*pradhāna*) of an all-male monastic working committee (*kārya samiti*), the *saṃcālaka maṇḍala*, also comprising the deputy leader (*upācārya*), the leader-in-waiting (*yuvācarya*), up to seven members from the circle of tutors (*upādhyāya maṇḍala*) and the circle of regional heads (*pravartaka maṇḍala*), and a maximum of nine members of the monastic advisory council (*parāmarśa samiti*), with a single chief counsellor (*mahā-mantrī*)[12] mediating between the circle of tutors and the circle of regional heads.[13] The advisory council is chaired by the *ācārya*. It was introduced by Ācārya Ātmārāma in 1956, to strengthen his authority, after fending off the proposal to establish the exclusive right of the working committee to take decisions, discussed at the Great Council of Bikaner on the 4-6.4.1956, which would have reduced the *ācārya* to a mere figurehead.[14] The ideal of consensual decision making remains enshrined in the published current constitution of the Śramaṇasaṅgha, the *Samācārī*, agreed at the Council of Pune in 1987. At the same time the *ācārya* is granted special authority as leader of the order and guide to the fourfold community. This arrangement reflects the continuing indirect influence of the founding traditions.

The published rules of the Śramaṇasaṅgha concerning the procedures for the appointment of a successor (*yuvācārya pada niyukti*) state that when the head of the order, the *ācārya*, the one who knows, teaches and implements the monastic rules of proper conduct (*ācāra*), is getting old, or is ill, then a successor, either an *upācārya* or a *yuvācārya*, should be appointed. Usually, the *yuvācārya* is the deputy-leader and dedicated successor of the *ācārya*. If both roles are filled, then the *upācārya* is superior and will automatically succeed after the demise of the *ācārya*. In the history of the Śramaṇasaṅgha, this happened only once, at Pune in 1987, where the new position of *upācārya* was created to amicably resolve a succession dispute.

The appointment of a *yuvācārya* is a delicate matter, especially in a weakly centralised organisation as diverse and geographically widely spread as the Śramaṇasaṅgha, whose members roam in almost all regions of India (with the notable exception of Gujarat, a state which is dominated by independent Sthānakavāsī orders that in

1952 decided not join the Śramaṇasaṅgha after all). The rules of the Samācārī state that the appointment should be made by the *ācārya* in consultation with senior advisors:[15]

> "The authority for making the appointment of deputy-leader (*upācārya*) and/or leader-in-waiting (*yuvācārya*) is chiefly that of the eminent leader (*ācārya*), the tutor, the circle of regional heads and the members of the advisory committee."

A supplementary rule states:

> "The announcement of the deputy-leader and/or leader-in-waiting will be made by the *ācārya*."[16]

The general rules delineating the powers (*adhikāra*) of the *ācārya* specify that he should take all important decision together with the chief monks after prior consultation with (leading) members of the fourfold community (i.e., the nuns and the laity):

> "His choice will be made together with (if there is no *yuvācārya* then) the circle of regional heads and the advisory circle (Consultation of the fourfold community is necessary)."[17]

The assembly of Indore was regarded as a success, because a decision on the successor was actually taken, and not postponed any further, as at previous attempts. On 27 March 2015, two days before the end of the *sammelana,* to the surprise of everyone, the *ācārya* announced to the morning assembly of the fourfold community, that was held daily between 8.30-9.30, that Mantrī Muni Mahendra Ṛṣi has been selected as *yuvācārya* and will be publicly consecrated at the final gathering of the fourfold community one day after the *sammelana* in the centre of Indore. The unexpected manner of the announcement can be seen as a response to the increasing rumours, nervousness and palpable tension amongst the thousands of lay followers that had made the journey to Indore to be part of this momentous event. Although, by rule, the selection of the successor is an internal matter of the order, and no-one should know about the selection before its public announcement, many lay activists treated it like an election campaign and lobbied intensely for one or other perceived potential candidate. It transpired that the selection issue was not discussed at the *sammelana.* Apparently the decision was taken some 12 days before the council, soon after the arrival of 450 monks and nuns led by Ācārya Śivamuni in Indore on 8 March 2015, by the *ācārya* himself together with some of the main office holders and senior monks, notably the influential Pravartaka Rūpacandra, who was involved in the selection of the last two *ācārya*s, but could not attend due to illness.

The two main candidates, according to rumour, were both members of the Mahārāṣṭra based Ṛṣi Saṃpradāya, a southern branch of the Lavajī Ṛṣi Saṃpradāya, both initiated by the second *ācārya* of the Śramaṇasaṅgha, Ānanda Ṛṣi (1900-1992), and both Osavālas and well educated. Upādhyāya Pravīṇa Ṛṣi (born 1957 into a Desaraḍā Osavāla family, in a village near Ahmadnagar, *dīkṣā* 1974) was not only senior in physical—and initiation age (*dīkṣā-paryāya*), but also the personal educator (*śikṣā-guru*) of Mantrī Muni Mahendra Ṛṣi (born 1967 in a Bhaṭevarā Osvāl family in a village near Puṇe, *dīkṣā* 1982). Pravīṇa Ṛṣi was very popular, because he appeared often on TV, had a "personal touch," and a social vision, focussing on the alleviation of the personal suffering of the "common man" through a new form of meditation, and inspired the creation of many religious, social and educational institutions. His visualisation based method of meditation was intent on strengthening personal vision ("make dreams come true") to increase happiness and success in the world (*puruṣākāra parākrama dhyāna sādhanā*). The younger Mahendra Ṛṣi was more extroverted and also a good speaker. The perceived "contest" was not personal. At least two other monks were considered serious contenders. In the end, the *ācārya* was the key factor in the imprecisely regulated and informal decision making process.

(b) The principal business of the nine day-long *sammelana* was the discussion and ratification of rule changes. Updating the monastic regulations had become an urgent task in the light of changes of the social circumstances and mendicant practices since the last *sammelana* in 1987. The procedures were as follows. At the beginning of the *sammelana* Sumana Muni (Sumana Kumāra) (born 1936, *dīkṣā* 1950), *pravartaka* for the region of North India, the most experienced monk who witnessed all previous general assemblies of the Śramaṇasaṅgha, was assigned the role of chairperson (*adhyakṣa*) or peace keeper (*śānti rakṣaka*). Reportedly, Sumana Muni dominated the proceedings with his sharp intellect. Whatever he said effectively closed the discussion. Seated on the podium behind him, also in front of microphones, were the main (male) decision makers, facing a large group of nuns on their left and a smaller contingent of monks on their right: the *ācārya*, Dr. Śiva Muni (b. 1942, d. 1972), flanked by the *mahā-mantrī*, Saubhāgya Muni "Kamala" (b. 1937, d. 1950), and by the oldest *upādhyāya* present in Indore, Muni Mūlacandra (Mūl Muni). Behind them was the *mantrī*, Śirīṣa Muni (born 1964, *dīkṣā* 1990). Other prominent monks were placed at the edges of the dais, but no nuns.

Not everyone was allowed to speak. Only the main attending office holders (*padādhikārī*): 4 *upādhyāyas* (of 7), 4 *pravartakas* (of 8), 4 (*mahā-*) *mantrīs* (of 5), and 3 *pravartinīs* (of 3) (the leaders of the nuns in Madhya Pradeśa, Mahārāṣṭra, and Rājasthān; in the Pañjāb only *upa-pravartinīs* existed at the time). All other monks and nuns could only indirectly make their voice heard by passing questions to their regional heads, the *pravartakas* or *pravartinīs*, who would articulate them. But some group-leaders (*siṃghāṛapati*) were also allowed to speak. Up to three points per day were discussed. The main role of Upādhyāya Mūlacanda and Mahāmantrī Saubhāgyamuni was to translate salient passages from the Āgamas. All decisions had to be based on the scriptures. The main reference work used in addition was Vijaya Rājendra Sūri's *Abhidhānarājendrakośa.* Forms of conduct that are not regulated by the 32 Āgamas were decided by a fresh assessment of the current situation. Two monks took minutes, which were then typed by office staff and passed on to Ācārya Śiva Muni and Pravartaka Sumana Muni, who edited the drafts and the final record. Decisions were taken after deliberation of pre-circulated proposals. Most issues were resolved. Very few questions were left open. All interviewees agreed: the atmosphere was very amicable. No voices were raised. Decisions were not opposed or controversially discussed. This was due to the fact that most issues were settled already before the assembly. The agenda was set two months prior to the *sammelana*, during the foot-journey of the mendicants to Indore. Apparently more than 50,000 letters (e-mails) were exchanged between the *ācārya* and leading monks and nuns, who shared all letters between them. Expert advice was taken. The office bearers of the national lay organisation of the Śramaṇasaṅgha, the All India Sthānakavāsī Jaina Conference, who finance the infrastructure of the order, and organised the *sammelana* (at the cost of Rs. 30 crore), were also consulted.[18] Since the mendicants themselves are not permitted to write personal letters or to use electronic means of communication, all communications had to be conducted through lay followers. To accomplish his administrative tasks, the *ācārya* and Mantrī Śirīṣa Muni, who always accompanies him, were supported by a team of office staff, who follow his itinerant group with a van filled with books, computers, and communication equipment.

The published "agreement to be observed" (*samācaraṇīya nirdhāraṇa*) includes some significant new points, such as the permission to initiate gifted 9-12 year old children (*bāla-dīkṣā*), which the Samācārī did not allow (AISJC 1987: 52). Though agenda of the *sammelana* was infused by the challenges of modernisation, its response was generally conservative. The main problem was that, over the years, new practices, such as the use of flush toilets, electric light, mobile phones, sandals made of cotton during long itineraries, transportation of books by cars, etc., became prevalent in the order which were, strictly speaking, not in line with the Samācārī, and could be justified at best as exceptions (*apavāda*). The main thrust of the *sammelana* was pragmatic: to ratify new practices, if they do not (like flush toilets) contradict scripture, or to regulate them. Hence it was decided that electric light can be used, but only if it is switched on by householders, without asking; mobile phones are prohibited, but messages can be conveyed via householders, etc. It was also decided to support the creation of a "third tier" of lay ascetics, called *sādhaka* (f. *sādhikā*), comparable to institutional innovations of the Terāpanth. Some practices were highlighted as not being in line with the lifestyle demanded of a Sthānakavāsī mendicant, inevitably incurring punishment, for instance: using cars, fund raising, engaging in political associations, hand reading, magic, carrying out image worship, using washing machines, etc. A orthodox nun, who disagreed with rule-relaxation (regarding the use of microphones, etc.), said that it made no difference in practice for her if some rules were relaxed, because no-one could force her to give up her old austere lifestyle: "everyone can decide."

This brief overview of the main proceedings of the council of Indore shows that the *ācārya* of the Śramaṇasaṅgha does not take decisions alone, but in consultation and agreement with senior monks and nuns, in view of the scriptural and the social acceptability of rule-changes both within the order itself and the fourfold community. It also confirms that the proceedings are not intended to be conducted in a democratic way. Votes are not taken. Consensual decision making is the ideal. Procedural rules have not been scripted in detail to retain the flexibility of the decision making process. Not all Śramaṇasaṅgha mendicants present in Indore took part in the *sammelana*. As at all congresses, the often most interesting and enjoyable encounters emerged at the fringes of the official procedures of the council, which enabled hundreds of monks and nuns from different parts of India to share their thoughts and information, and thousands of devotees to come in direct contact with their revered spiritual guides.

Notes

1 Fieldwork on invitation of Ācārya Dr. Śivamuni. See Anonymous (2015).

2 See Wiles 2006.

3 The dates of the seven great mendicant assemblies of the Sthānakavāsīs are: 1. Ajmer (5.4.-19.4.1933), 2. Madrās (24.-26.12.1948), 3. Sāḍarī (27.4.-6.5.1952) 4. Sojat (17.1.-30.1.1953), 5. Bhīnāsar-Bīkāner (16.2.-6.4.1956), 6. Ajmer-Sikhar (16.3.1964), 7. Puṇe (2.5.- 13.5.1987), 8. Indore (20. 29.3.2015). On the history of the Sthānakavāsī tradition, see Flügel 2000-2012 (and forthcoming).

4 The assembly was held in a half-completed Dharmaśālā adjacent to the Pārśvanātha Jaina Śvetāmbara Mandira and Dādābāṛī, at Mahāvīr Bāg, Erodram Road, which was rented from the local Kharataragaccha Trust.

5 AISJC (1987: 6).

6 The official title displayed in the assembly room itself added: "Ascetic assembly with a vision of the (true) self" (*ātmadṛṣti santa samāgama*), which refers to Mahāvīra.

7 The four *ācāryas* of the Śramaṇāsaṅgha were selected from three different older traditions: Ātmārāma "Punjābī" (r. 1952-62): Pañjāb Lavajī Ṛṣi Saṃpradāya; Ācārya Ānanda Ṛṣi (1962-92): Ṛṣi Saṃpradāya (Mahārāṣṭra); Ācārya Devendramuni (r. 1992-99): Jīvarāja Saṃpradāya (Mevār); Ācārya Dr. Śivamuni (r.1999-): Pañjāb Lavajī Ṛṣi Saṃpradāya.

8 A new meditation method developed by Ācārya Dr. Śivamuni.

9 Bāṇṭhiyā (2015), *Ahimsa Times* 176 & 177 (2015).

10 Local press, leaflets.

11 Saubhāgya (2015), Jain (2015).

12 Canonical precedents do not exist for many current monastic positions, such as *upācārya* and *mantrin*, not only in the Śramaṇasaṅgha.

13 AISJC (1987: 73).

14 Flügel (2003: 63, 88).

15 "*upācārya, yuvācārya kī niyukti kā adhikāra mukhyatayā ācārya pravara, upādhyāya, pravartaka maṇḍala aura parāmarśadātā samiti ke sadasyoṃ ko hai*" (AISJC 1987: 77).

16. "*upācārya, yuvācārya kī ghoṣaṇā ācārya śrī kareṅge*" (AISJC 1987: 77).
17. "*unakā cunāva (yadi yuvācarya na ho to) pravartaka maṇḍala evaṃ parāmarśaka maṇḍala milakara kareṅge / (caturvidha saṅgha kā parāmarśaka āvaśyaka hai)*" (AISJC 1987: 73).
18. Followers of other Sthānakavāsī orders also tried to influence the process, e.g., Bāṇṭhiyā (2015).

References

Ahimsa Times. "Sthanakwasi Sadhu Sadhvi Conclave 2015." Vols. 176 March 2015: http://www.jainsamaj.org/magazines/ahimsatimes.php

AISJC = Akhila Bhāratīya Sthānakavāsī Jaina Kānfrens. *Akhila Bhāratvarṣīya Vardhamāṇa Sthānakavāsī Jaina Śramaṇa Saṅghīya Samācārī*. Sampādaka: Muni Saubhāgya "Kumuda." Dillī: Akhila Bhāratīya Vardhamāṇa Sthānakavāsī Jaina Kānfrens, 1987.

Anonymous. "Jarmanī Se Śodha Karane Sammelana Meṃ Pahuñce Pīṭar." *Rāj Express* 28.3.2015.

Bāṇṭhiyā, Nemīcand. "Indaur Sammelana Hetu - Samācaraṇīya Sujjhāva." *Samyag-Darśana* 3 2 March (2015) 11-14.

Flügel, Peter. "Protestantische und Post-Protestantische Jaina-Reformbewegungen: Zur Geschichte und Organisation der Sthānakavāsī I-IV." *Berliner Indologische Studien* 13-14 (2000) 37-103, 15-17 (2003) 149-240, 18 (2007) 127-206, 20 (2012) 37-124.

Jain, Dharmacand. "Jayatu Indaura-Sammelanam." *Jinavāṇī* 10 April (2015) 7-11.

Jauharī, Durlabha Trībhuvan (Prayojaka). *Sādhu-Sammelan kā Itihāsa*. Sampādaka: Cimmanasiṅha Loḍhā. Saṃśodhaka: Paṇḍita Śobhācandra Bhārilla. Byāvar: Cimmanasiṅha Loḍhā (Mainejar, Śrī Mahāvīr Priṇṭiṅg Pres), 1946.

Saubhāgya, Muni "Kumuda." "Bṛhad Sādhu Sammelan Indaur Svīkṛta Prastāva (Samācaraṇīya Nirdhāraṇa)." *Jaina Prakāśa* 109, 1 April (2015) 9-21.

Wiles, Royce. "The Dating of the Jaina Councils: Do Scholarly Presentations Reflect the Traditional Sources?" *Studies in Jaina History and Culture: Disputes and Dialogues*. Ed. P. Flügel, 61-85. London: Routledge, 2006.

6

Terāpanth Śvetāmbara Jain Tradition

The Terāpanth Śvetāmbara Jain Tradition was founded by Muni Bhīkhaṇ (1726-1803), who was later called Ācārya Bhikṣu. Bhīkhaṇ was born in India in the village of Kantaliya near Jodhpur. His parents were Bīsa Osvāls of the Saṅklecā *gotra* (clan) and followed the Mūrtipūjak Jain tradition. After the death of his wife, Bhīkhaṇ renounced the world and became initiated into the itinerant mendicant order of Ācārya Raghunāth (1706 or 1708-1790) of the Dhannā Dharmadāsa Sthānakavāsī tradition in 1751. However, on June 28, 1760, he split from the "lax" Sthānakavāsīs with four other monks and founded his own mendicant order in Kelva near Rajsamand. In the beginning, his group had only thirteen male members, and his opponents scorned it as the path of the thirteen, or *terāh panth*. Bhikṣu later paraphrased *terah panth* as *terā panth*, or your path, and interpreted the number thirteen in terms of the principal rules of conduct for Jain ascetics, the five great vows, or *mahāvratas*; the three restraints, or *guptis*; and the five comportments, or *samitis*—which he attempted to follow by the letter.

The cause of the schism was a disagreement over a technical point of Jain karma theory. The Jain canonical scriptures teach that the soul can be liberated from its *kārmic* letters only through the renunciation of all violence—that is, all action. The Dharmadāsa Sthānakavāsīs, like most extant Jain traditions, also propagate compassion, or *anukampā*, as a religious value and emphasize the positive *kārmic* consequences of charity *(dāna-dayā)* and the protection of life *(jīva dayā)*. In contrast, Bhikṣu argued that because ultimately both bad *karma (pāpa)* and good *karma (puṇya)* obstructs the liberation of the soul, a salvation seeker must avoid both. Because he privileged this perspective, he even regarded acts of compassion performed for the purpose of accumulating *puṇya* as sinful (*pāpa*). The most concise discussion of this issue from the Terāpanth point of view can be found in Bhikṣu's treatise *Anukampā Rī Caupāī*, written in 1787 in the local Marvari language. Bhikṣu distinguishes there (and elsewhere) between relative or worldly compassion *(laukika dayā)* and absolute or religious compassion *(lokottara-* or *dharma dayā)*—that is, absolute nonviolence. He argues that although material acts of charity are positive from the social point of view *(vyavahāra naya)*, they are negative from the religious point of view *(niścaya naya)*. In his conception, *puṇya* can be gained only as a side-effect of acts of renunciation, not independently through acts of material help or other "mixed" actions. His criticism of the laxity of the Sthānakavāsī mendicants and other Jain traditions is directed against their nonrecognition of the difference between religion and worldly morality.

The terminology of Ācārya Bhikṣu's teaching of absolute renunciation is influenced not only by the writings of the Digambara Ācārya Kundakunda (c. second to third centuries C.E.) and the Digambara commentaries of Umāsvāti's *Tattvārtha-sūtra* (c. third to fifth centuries C.E.) but also by the *ṭabbas* (vernacular commentaries) of the Ācārya Dharmasiṁha (1599-1671), the founder of the Dariyāpurī Sthānakavāsī tradition. Dharmasiṁha also taught the futility of compassionate help and nonintervention on the grounds that from the absolute point of view the moment of death of every living being is pre-determined by its life-span *(āyuṣya) karma*, even if the causes of death appear to be accidental, and therefore preventable, from a conventional point of view. For other Sthānakavāsīs the name Terāpanth indicates that Ācārya Bhikṣu's views are akin to those of the proponents of the image-worshipping lay movement of the Digambara Terāpantha (which should otherwise not be confused with the aniconic Śvetāmbara Terāpanth order), whose adherents also claim to practice Jainism from an absolute perspectiveor *niścaya naya*. The denial of the necessity of the practical point for a nonomniscient living being is, for them, a form of *ekānta-vāda* (theoretical absolutism) that contradicts the Jain theory of *anekānta-vāda* (non absolutism).

Although the principal outlook of the Terāpanth has not changed during its 240-year history, its forms of application and its institutions have changed. To prevent schisms and laxity, Ācārya Bhikṣu made the rule that there should be only one *ācārya* (teacher-cum-group leader) and that he should be chosen by his predecessor. On that basis, the fourth *ācārya*, Jītmal (*Jayācārya*; 1803-1881), created an elaborate institutional framework for the growing monastic order from 1852 onward. The ninth *ācārya,* Tulsī (1914-1997), ruled the order from 1936. He modernized the Terāpanth and turned it from a world-negating mendicant order into a world-transforming religious movement by emphasizing the significance of education, worldly morality, and social reform. In 1949 he created the "nonreligious" *aṇuvrata* (small-vow), movement for the implementation of nonviolence and morality in social life. In 1952 he abolished the dogma of non accidental death and later promoted "worldly" charity for his educational projects. The communal good-will movement in 1954 was followed in 1960 by the *nayā moḍ* (new turn) initiative that sought to eradicate "outdated" social customs among the Terāpanth laity, such as rituals, casteism, and female *purdha.* In 1970 the Jain Viśva Bhāratī was opened and gained the status of a "Deemed to be University" in 1991. It is located in Ladnun, the birthplace of Ācārya Tulsī, and it functions today as the physical center of the Terāpanth, though all important decisions are taken by the permanently itinerant *ācārya.* In 1980, Ācārya Tulsī introduced a new category of novices, the *samaṇ(ī)s,* who are permitted to use public transport and to travel abroad on missionary tours. For many Jains living outside India, the *samaṇs* and *samaṇīs* are the only Jain mendicants they can meet. The present leader of the Terāpanth is Ācārya Mahāprajña (b. 1920). After his death in 2010, Ācārya Mahāśramaṇa became leader, who was inaugurated in 1994. Mahāprajña contributed greatly to the Terāpanth edition of the canonical scriptures, or *āgama* (1974ff.), and the publication of the Terāpanth literature in Rajasthani. Under the impression of the success of Goenkas *vipassanā* (meditation) classes in Rajasthan, he introduced a Jain version of insight meditation, *prekṣa dhyāna,* in 1975. And in 1980 he introduced the science of living program, *jīvana vijñāna,* a step-by-step guide for a nonviolent way of life for children and adults, intended for schools and universities in particular. The chosen successor of Mahāprajña is Yuvācārya Mahasraman (b.1962).

At present, the Terāpanth has about 250,000 followers all over India (including non-Jain members of the *aṇuvrata* movement); several thousand in Nepal, the UK, and the United States; and a few families in many commercial centers around the world. Most Terāpanth lay followers belong to the traditional business families of the Osvāl castes. Because of the influence of the missionary tours of the *samaṇs* and *samaṇīs*, the influence of the Terāpanth is currently spreading worldwide, though primarily among expatriate Jains. The principal religious practices of the Terāpanthīs are fasting, meditation, and study. Because image worship is rejected, lay people venerate the mendicants of the Terāpanth order as symbols of Jain ideals.

Address:
Jain Vishva Bharati
Ladnun 341 306
Rajasthan India

Sources:

Budhmal, Muni. *Terāpanth Kā Itihās. Pratham Khaṇḍ: Terāpanth Ke Pratham Car Ācārya.* 4th rev. ed. Calcutta: Jain Śvetāmbara Terāpanth Mahāsabhā Prakāśan, 1964, 1995.

Flügel, Peter. "The Ritual Circle of the Terāpanth Śvetāmbara Jains." *Bulletin D'Etudes Indiennes* 13 (1995-1996): 117-176.

Mahāprajña, Yuvācārya. *Preksha Dhyana: Theory and Practice.* 2d rev. ed., edited by Muni Mahendra Kumar. Lāḍṇuṃ: Tulsī Adhyatmā Nidam, 1992.

Nathmal, Muni [Ācārya Mahāprajña]. *Acharya Bhiksu: The Man and His Philosophy. Translation of Bhikṣu Vicār Darṣan* by N. Sahal. Cūrū: Adarś Sāhity Saṅgh Prakāśan, 1959, 1968.

Tulsī, Ācārya. *Anuvrat: A Shield against Immorality.* Ladnun: Jain Vishva Bharati, 1989.

——. ed. *Bhikṣu-Granth Ratnākar Khaṇḍ 1-2.* Saṅghrāhakartā: Muni Cauthmal. Prabhandh Sampādak: Śrīcand Rāmpuriyā. Calcutta: Jain Śvetāmbara Terāpanth Mahāsabhā, 1960-1961.

Tulsī, Ācārya, and Yuvācārya Mahāprajña, comps. *Terāpanth: Maryādā Aur Vyavasthā.* Sampādak: Muni Madhukar. Jayācāryā Series Vol. 9. Lāḍṇuṃ: Jain Viśva Bhāratī, 1983.

7

The Ritual Circle of the Terāpanth Śvetāmbara Jains[1]

The empirical investigation of the changing role of pilgrimage and religious networks as forms of socio-political integration is one of the most fertile areas of South Asia research to date. Yet the related theoretical debate which broadly opposes Durkheimian[2] and Weberian[3] approaches suffers from the fact that the proponents of both camps share the Neo-Kantian view of history as a manifestation of cultural ideals. The former argue that religious rituals resolve conflicts and promote social integration, whereas the latter emphasise the dual functions of rituals for the reproduction of both social solidarity and the legitimation of power. It is now widely accepted that both theories are fundamentally a-historical and mainly rewarding for those who regard the values of socially dominant elites as paradigmatic for society as a whole. A slightly different, although still culturalist, approach was developed by Parsons and later applied to South Asia by Dumont (1980):

> "From this point of view, the systems of ultimate values are of two types: in the first, all spheres of life come immediately and formally under the same values; in the second, certain spheres have their own values, special but, by definition absolute within their sphere. Moreover, the first type corresponds to group religion; in the second religion is attached to the individual person" (p.316).

Dumont argued that although the hierarchical aggregation of the first and the second model accurately represents the ideology of the majority of the people of rural 'traditional India', the second model alone is increasingly relevant for an understanding of the processes of modernisation in the Indian cities (p. 217-31). In other words, even for him religion in India has already lost part of its function to represent and to mediate the social process as a whole, although this is apparently not yet reflected in the structure of the dominant *brāhmaṇic* ideology.

In contrast to Dumont who operates with an artificially monolithic notion of Hinduism (p. 296), and dogmatically assumes that even today "the politico-economic domain is encompassed in an overall religious setting" (p. 228). I don't think it is merely "the relation between the ideological and the empirical aspects which is at stake" here (p. 45), but a fundamental theoretical problem: From a Neo-Kantian perspective social change cannot be thought of in terms of the internal structural limitations of a given historical situation, but only as "a momentary compromise between the functional imperatives of the situation and the dominant value-orientation patterns of the society" (Parsons 1951:203). I therefore follow Habermas' (1981:338-51) suggestion to investigate culture (symbolic systems), society (norms), and personality (aims) not anymore in terms of free-floating transcendental meanings, but as the three principal empirical components promoting social integration in concrete lifeworld situations (notwithstanding their normative content). I also drop the culturalistic identification of lifeworld and society and analyse society from two complementary perspectives: as a "system of action which is both socially [via the three components of the lifeworld] and systemically [through the unintentional consequences of the ongoing struggle for existence] integrated" (p. 228). The dualism between the imperatives of culture and survival does not vanish in his model, which circumvents the radically functionalist position of Luhmann who focus esexclusively on the complexity of a social system disregarding the self-perceptions of the participants, but it takes a more realistic form by giving primacy not to cultural values but to the lifeworld itself. Habermas' approach allows us to understand the integration of a society as the perpetually contested renewal of a compromise between two series of imperatives: the internal conditions of the social integration of the lifeworld, and the exernal conditions of its functional integration vis-à-vis an only partially controllable environment. If values and functions don't match, then a compromise holds only as a long as the actual functions of social orientations remain latent. In the following I want to show that this shift of theoretical perspective has consequences for our understanding of the systemic and the social, personal and cultural role of contemporary Jain pilgrimage.

Although important studies of contemporary Buddhist, Vaiṣṇava, Śivaite and Liṅgāyat sects, and of the link between pilgrimage and religious nationalism have emerged in the last two decades, there is a lack of monographs on pilgrimage and the various sectarian movements within modern Jainism, even though the Jains are widely consi-dered to be the Indian pilgrims *par excellence.*[4] From a Jain point of view, pilgrimage is the paradigmatic form of renunciation, and one of the keys to the understanding of Jainism itself. According to modern Jain cosmology the wandering of souls in the world is brought about by their being charged with *kārmic* matter as a consequence of their desire for external objects, and this, too, is the primary cause of the world structure *(saṃsār)* itself. The manifold forms of existence are seen as the results of differential forms of interpenetrations of essentially pure individual souls (*jīv,* lit. life-force) on the one hand and unanimated matter *(ajīv)* on the other. Every form of life thus appears to embody a dual orientation both towards the external world of desirable objects, and to the essentially unlimited potentialities of the inner life-force itself, which can be realised through renunciation *(tyāg)*. If the liberation of the soul from embodiment can be achieved through acts of restraint, then, conversely, it is the power of human desire *(rāg)* that attracts matter and generates material life and rebirth. The dual perspectives are not mutually exclusive but hierarchically complementary within the continuum of the total cosmic field, which is considered phenomenologically homologous with the field of consciousness. This is why acts of self-limitation may appear as forms of potentialisation.[5]

From an observer's point of view, the main ideological function of Jainism is to sever the ritual links of the dominant socio-cosmic hierarchy and to reduce it to a collection of individuals. In contrast to the brāhmaṇical social system *(varṇa),* Jains, like Buddhists, traditionally use the term *saṅgh* (assembly) to delineate discrete social unit.[6] From this perspective society appears "as a mere aggregate of men," surrounding a spiritually superior individual, whose ideal autonomy also implies a claim to status-superiority in hierarchical societies (Dumont 1980:300). According to Jain doctrine, assemblies spontaneously emerge at the place of the sermon *(pravacan)* of the wandering ascetics. Within the context of the assembly social differences and conflicts are temporarily suspended. Everyone is a pupil *(śiṣya)* and equal in submission to the supreme authority of the teacher *(guru),* who should be the exemplary embodiment of the Jain soteriological values of non-violence *(ahiṃsā)* and world-renunciation *(tyāg),* regardless of social differences in rank, status, caste or class outside the context of the assembly.

However, in practice the situation is not as fluid as the ideal suggests. As in Buddhism and Hinduism, time enduring structures have emerged amongst Jains through the development of permanent links between ascetic groups and certain lay elites, who support religious networks and pilgrimages not only for religious purposes but also as means of both status acquisition and political and economic integration. The main stabilising element of these emerging power-structures is religious property. In South Asia monastic groups without property tend to divide and subdivide and split along the lines of geography, charisma, demography, and lay patronage.[7] Yet, with the crystallisation of an infrastructure of religious institutions the question of control arises. Until recently most Jain temples and rituals were administered by a category of sedentary political monks, called *bhaṭṭāraks* among the Bīsapanthī Digambars and *yatis* or *śrīpūjyas* among the Mūrtipūjak Śvetāmbars, who exercised control over both religious property and their lay followers. Modern Jain sects have widely abolished the institutions of monastic landlordism, because the centralisation of political power and the collapse of feudal tributary systems have made them superfluous. Instead they revived the role of the propertiless wandering *sādhu,* while delegating the administration of religious property to the laity and conceding political control to the modern state.

There is however a wide variety of responses to the changing social environment within present-day Jainism. In this article I will show how one particular Jain subsect–the Śvetāmbar Terāpanth–organises the ritual interaction between ascetics and laity on a supraregional basis, and in which way it is strategically orientated within the overall field of South Asian religion and politics today. Jain doctrine and ritual is taken as an intermediary level, generative of both universally meaningful religious experiences and social harmony, but simulaneously serving as a vehicle for the mobilisation and legitimation of particularistic political interests. In the first part I describe the history and the internal functioning of the ascetic community *(dharmasaṅgh)* of the Terāpanth, as well as the religious organisation of their ritualised annual itinerary *(vihār)*. In the second part I focus on the role of the main lay association, the *Terāpanth Mahāsabhā,* for the maintenance of this ritual and, indirectly, for the welfare of the members of the lay community *(samāj),* before concluding, in part three, with a few comparative observations on the changing politial role of Terāpanth pilgrimage in the context of the modern Indian state.

I. The Terāpanth Śvetāmbar Jain Dharmasaṅgh

The Terāpanth ascetics belong to the non-image-worshipping section of the Śvetāmbar Jain mendicants, for which there is no Digmbar equivalent. This tradition emerged in 1451 as an anti-*yati* movement amongst the Mūrtipūjak-laity in Muslim-ruled Ahmedabad, led by the Rajasthani-Osvāl court-jeweller, and copyist of Jain manuscripts, Loṅkā Śāh (ca. 1415-1489). Loṅkā noticed a widening discrepancy between precept and practice among contemporary ascetics because he did not find any references to idol-worship nor to sedentary monasticism in the oldest textual tradition. With the help of the Jain minister L.B. Bhansali from Patan he then started a revivalist ascetic tradition on his own in 1471 under circumvention of monastic rules of linear succession. Although Loṅkā never initiated himself, it was he who drafted a set of organisational principles for the new Loṅkā Gacch in form of 69 maxims *(Loṅkā Śāh Kī Huṇḍī).* These rules played a paradigmatic role for all subsequent iconoclastic Śvetāmbar movements. They explicitly rejected idolatry and sedentary monasticism, and stressed the ultimate authority of 31 of the ca. 45 scriptures of the Śvetāmbar 'canon' *(āgam),* and the importance of ascetic wandering *(vihār)* for the maintenance of a propertiless *(aparigrah)* monastic order into which 'only *baniās* [merchants] should be initiated.[8]

The last point is particularly interesting, because it illustrates that often religious reform and socio-economical interests go hand in hand in Jainism. As a rule, the impetus for Jain religious reform arises first within the ascetic community itself, as long as it maintains its monopoly of religious knowledge and stays aloof of the laity. However, the modified or non-image-worshipping traditions that later emerged in North India under Mughal-rule, like the Śvetāmbar Kaḍuā Gacch, founded by Kaḍuā Śāh (1438-1507), and Tāraṇsvāmī's (1448-1515) Digambar Tāraṇpanth and its successor movements which are today associated with the Digambar Terāpanthīs,[9] were all initiated by religiously educated lay people which were eager to gain socio-religious autonomy vis-à-vis the tutelage of the *śrīpūjyas* and *bhaṭṭāraks.* Most of them rejected the ritualistic basis of the ascetics' claim to the monopoly of socio-religious leadership in the name of textual knowledge *(jñān)* and true inner religious experience *(samyag darśan).* Yet the problem of such anti-authoritarian ('protestant') lay movements, which can be found all over Asia, is their inability to continuously produce exemplary religious leaders. The presumed compatibility of religious leadership and householder status[10] has therefore often been criticised as a mere expression of greed and uncharitability.[11] This might have been one of the reasons for Loṅkā's decision to steer between the extremes in emphasising the importance of 'real', i.e. propertiless and rule-abiding, ascetics. However, some years later, after Loṅkā was apparently murdered by the followers of a rival sect, the Loṅkā Gacch split into factions and the cycle of reform and routinisation started again. In protest against the renewed lax behaviour *(śithilācār)* of the ascetics and the re-emergence of temple-worship the *munis* Jīvrāj, Lavjī und Dharmsiṅhjī split off the Gujarātī Loṅkāgacch between 1628-1657 in Surat and Dariyāpur/ Ahmedabad founded the Ḍhūṇḍhiyā (seekers) and Dariyāpurī Sampradāy sects, Manohardās and Dharmadāsa in 1660 whose group then divided itself into 22 schools *(bāīsṭolā)* and later became known as the Sthānakvāsī (hall dwellers) tradition. For similar reasons *muni* Bhikṣu (1726-1803) and four *sādhus* broke away from the Bāīsṭolā *ācārya* Rughanāth (Raghunāth) in 1760 in Bagṛī (Mārvāṛ) and founded the Terāpanth *gaṇ* four months later in Kelvā through a collective rite of self-initiation *(bhāv dīkṣā)*.[12]

In the beginning the Terāpanth was mainly an ascetic reform movement that was remarkable for its radical doctrinal and institutional innovations, some of which have since been imitated by other Jain sects.[13] The most significant doctrinal innovation was Bhikṣū's attempt to eradicate the legitimacy of religious property once and for all by strictly distinguishing religious *(dhārmik)* acts of penance *(tap or pāramārthik dān)* from social *(laukik)* acts of charity *(vyāvahārik dān)*, arguing that "if the act of giving is considered an act of religion then it is the rich people who would monopolise religion and a place in heaven" (L.P. Sharma 1991:100). Popular *pūjā*-rituals and material gifts were thus deprived of religious value, with the notable exception of the offering of food, drink etc. to the (Terāpanth) ascetics themselves *(saṃyati dān)*. Instead Bhikṣu emphasised the importance of a renunciatory disposition *(tyāg)* and of the 'gift' of knowledge *(jñān dān)* and of non-violent conduct as such *(abhayadān)* AK I:56, Tulsī 1985:173), and recommended rigorous asceticism *(tap)* as well as internalised forms of religious practice, like meditation *(dhyān)* or religious study *(svādhyāya)*, even for the laity: "*Tyāga* is possible even without offering anything to anybody" (p. 158).

On a doctrinal level the strict separation between religion and society, propagated by the Terāpanth, dissolves the characteristic ambiguity of key concepts of 'popular Jainism'[14] by differentiating between pure and impure forms (e.g. religious merit *(lokottar puṇya)* and social merit *(laukik puṇya))*.[15] The consequence of this doubling of traditional Jain concepts is that the social ritualism that pervades the life of every Indian family is considered to be 'non-Jain' or 'Hindu.'[16] Yet, the overall emphasis on the internal rather than the external aspects of religion does not suggest egalitarian ('protestant') forms of lay-dominated religious individualism, as one might assume. On the contrary, the additional importance given to outward ascetic conduct assures the reaffirmation of the authority of the *ācārya* and the ascetic order and its constitutive principle of 'hierarchical' individualism.[17] The difference between Bhikṣu's Terāpanth and many traditional ('hinduised') image-worshipping sects, which ambiguously combine considerations of ascetic purity and social power or auspiciousness within hierarchical cosmological systems, pivoting around a notion of moral kingship *(dharmarāj)*, is that in the Terāpanth system the 'world-transcending' *ācārya* alone can be the ideal king *(mahārāj)*.[18]

The refusal to recognise the religious merit of *pūjā* rituals and charitable giving, which are essential for the traditional ritual legitimation of power and the development of popular forms of religion, has let the idol-worshipping Mūrtipūjaks and Bīsapanthīs to question the religious value of the absolutist *(ekānta)* doctrinal literalism of the new sect as a form of islamisation (Jaini 1979:314, n.63); —an allegation which was countered by the Terāpanthī's claim for greater religious purity: "Some people say that by dividing religion into worldly and spiritual segments Ācārya Bhikṣu has really cut down life itself into various sections. We do not deny the charge but must also admit at the same time that we cannot help such fragmentation of life. Lord Mahāvīra has divided religion into secular and religious parts in 'Nikṣepa Vyavasthā'" (Nathmal 1968:15). Digambar Terāpanthīs, on the other hand, rejected automatic claims to spiritual superiority that are based on the outward characteristics of monkhood alone.[19] However, the strongest opposition to Bhikṣu's ideas came from Sthānakvāsī ascetics, like the ex-Śramaṇ Saṅgh *muni* Suśīl (1926-1994) who advocated social reform and services to mankind. They objected in particular to the 'selfishness' and the 'a-humanism' of Bhikṣu's radical pursuit of world-renunciation, which showed no concern for the alleviation of suffering in the world.[20] Like Kundakunda Bhikṣu was indeed convinced that the protection of life could only count as an act of social compassion *(laukik dayā)* but not as a religious act of liberation *(lokottar dayā)*. In the eyes of many Sthānakvāsīs, this doctrine was predicated on "the economic perspective of the 'survival of the fittest' in a society of famines and droughts, poverty, starvation and death" and therefore merely "the natural product of the miserable social conditions prevalent in Rajasthan in the days of Bhikṣu" (Nair 1969:39): "Bikhanji's message of deliverance [through self-help] was a great boon to the economically weak, the miserly, the ungenerous and the selfish people. The money saved from giving charity could be accumulated to one's own benefit" (p. 378).

Obviously, the question of the social implications of such a radical separation of religion and society is a point of intense dispute within the Jain tradition itself. From a Durkheimian point of view the doctrinal distinction between 'pure' and 'impure' forms of giving must be seen as an ideological expression of the experience of increasing social differentiation and the growing importance of 'organic solidarity' for the adherents of Jainism (cf. Dumont 1980:227). Parry (1986), for instance, suggested "that an elaborated ideology of the 'pure' gift is most likely to develop in state societies with an advanced division of labour and a significant commercial sector" (p. 467). This argument is widely accepted, although its precise implications are obscure. Certrainly, Bhikṣu's emphasis on the internal, renunciatory aspects of giving, in opposition to the external, material aspects, cannot be explained in terms of the calculatory 'long-term' function of disinterested giving, as Parry suggests, because this would involve precisely the reduction of the gift to exchange which the Terāpanthīs criticise.[21] They interpret 'the gift' not transactionally but primarily ontologically, as a non-violent form of existence. Life itself, they argue, should be a perennial sacrifice, ideally embodied in the exemplary renunciatory conduct of the *ācārya* who, as a symbol of the corporate purity of the *saṇgha* as a whole, regenerates the bifurcation of the spheres of religion and society as the precondition of the ritual circle of ascetic wandering and its implied social exchanges. While acknowledging the possibility of cheating by performing 'objectified rituals' with dual purposes in mind, which has been stressed by Laidlaw (1995:230) and Johnson (1995:310), Terāpanthīs have always insisted that the difference between religious *(saṃyam pravṛtti)* and worldly orientations *(laukik pravṛtti)* is not only subjectively felt but also visibly manifest in the overall conduct of an individual.[22] From their point of view, ascetic power invariably encompasses transactional rationality.

In spite of these conceptual refinements the new doctrine of Bhikṣu has effectively not been able to overcome the fundamental problem of routinisation as described by Weber (1985:142-8). It merely generated a new set of practical paradoxes. Generally, the increased degree of differentiation of religion and society produced both a greater immediacy and a greater indirectness of the links between the *dharmasaṅgh* and the laity. But the role of religious property has effectively not changed. As I will show in greater detail in the second part, a popular Terāpanth Jainism exists today, and there are Terāpanthī rituals of charitable giving, contrary to the official doctrine, although they are less visible and deprived of immediate religious value. Compared to Bhikṣu's vision of a purely ascetic Jainism, the Terāpanth of today has considerably changed, particularly through a series of controversial innovations that were introduced by *ācārya* Tulsī in the first decades after Indian Independence (1949-1981). In order to secure the growing influence of the Terāpanth under the changed social conditions, Tulsī gradually reverted back to a traditional Jain system by forming closer bonds with the laity and promoting programs of religious and moral education for the society as a whole. He showed great ingenuity in the construction of an all-inclusive corporative sectarian organisation by creating a new network of 'socio-religious' institutions for the laity, to carry the *Aṇuvrat* (small vow, 1949), *Prekṣa Dhyān* (insight meditation, 1975) and *Jīvan Vijñān* (science of living, 1980) movements, without directly violating Bhikṣu's principles.[23] Officially the lay-movements of the Terāpanth were simply defined as purely social activities. The only problem was that, in order to attract sufficient funds for the massive publishing and building projects involved, Tulsī had to amend Bhikṣu's theory of the gift. His modified version of 1970 is known as the doctrine of *visarjan* (lit. dispersion, abandonment, parting from possessions), and asks the laity to practice acquisition together with renunciation *(visarjan)* of ownership. It concedes that under certain conditions monetary donations may count as religious acts of renunciation *(tyāg)*[24] and promises an influx of meritorious *karmas (puṇya)* depending on the intention of the giver. It is said that giving for a good cause *(dān)* both contributes to the destruction of *karma (nirjarā)* and liberātion of the self from attachments *(aparigrah, anāsakti)* and generātes good karma *(śubh karma)* for the giver. But giving in order to increase one's social prestige *(mān)* diminishes the chances of liberation and generates bad karma *(pāp, aśubh karma)*. Critics say that giving for the purification of the soul *ātmaśuddhi)* has only been invented in order to raise money for the 'good purpose' of Tulsī's construction programs, and point to the fact that, by publicly asking for donations and promising merit, today's ascetics merely create opportunities for 'big men' to put their name plaques on the new Terāpanth buildings. The ideology that donations are only meritorious if they are not given to anybody specific but 'just being left for the use of society' (Mahāprajña 1987:16) — that is the religious trusts of the Terāpanth (AK II:154) — has not only provoked cynical comments but also motivated several discontented Terāpanth ascetics to split off.[25] Tulsī's reply that all the funds he had collected had been for the benefit of humanity, and that it is necessary to move with the times, has, on the other hand, been well received by the Sthānakvāsīs and the more traditional image-worshipping Jain sects (Muni Rājyaś, in: Nair 1969:xxxxi).

The principles of the *aṇuvrat, prekṣa dhyān* and *jīvan vijñān* initiatives clearly cover the same ground as the traditional *śrāvakācāra* regulations (cf. Williams 1983). But there are still important differences. Although having inserted a new ambiguous socio-religious sphere between the domains of religion and society, Tulsī has not entirely reverted a Hinduised version of popular Jainism. The compilations of recommended rules and regulations for the Terāpanth laity are different from the *śrāvakācāras* of the image-worshipping sects. Charitability, for instance, is merely presented as a value of social morality and Hemacandra's classification of seven fields of giving *(kṣetradān)* (p. 165) is not accepted. However the Terāpanth lay community of today reproduces itself increasingly with the help of a standardised body of text-oriented rituals and of organisational rules, some of which were codified only recently (AK). These are scaled down versions of the religious practices and the idiosyncratic institutional rules of the Terāpanth ascetics, which were Bhikṣu's second important innovation.

Bhikṣu tried to contain the segmentary tendencies of Jain ascetic groups not by exploiting the stabilising effect of religious property but through discipline and a more detailed regulation of interascetic conduct. For this reason he introduced, from 1775 onwards, a new set of organisational rules *(maryādā)*, which he subsequently amended in a series of additional writings *(likhats)*. Rules like these have not yet been investigated, although they can be found in less elaborated form amongst all Jain sects (Schubring & Caillat 1966:87). Together with the older and more widely accepted *Ācārāṅga*, the *Cheda Sūtras*, and the *Mūla Sūtras* they form the Jain equivalent of the Buddhist *Vīnaya* code and its extensions. They are important for the monastic jurisprudence, but of diminished religious value: "Non-violence and mere organisational rules are two things" (Nathmal 1968:114). Today, one of the distinctive organisational features of the Terāpanth ascetic order is its constitution *(maryādā patr)*, written down by Bhikṣu in 1802 *(māgh śuklā saptamī)* shortly before his death. It determines that there can be only one *ācārya* within the sect, and that it is he alone who initiates novices, excommunicates, and determines his successor *(yuvācārya)*, as well as the overall policy of the sect.[26] The *ācārya* fulfils both spiritual and administrative, legislative and judicative functions within the order. By means of such a constitutionally fixed, centralised organisation, and a rigorous policy of excommunication, permanent schisms have been preventable so far.[27]

The Monastic Organisation

The Terāpanthī subsect *(gaṇ)* is today (1991) one of the largest organised ascetic groups among the Jains, with 149 *sādhus* (male ascetics), 554 *sādhvīs* (female ascetics)[28] and about 80 novices of different categories *(samaṇ, mumukṣu, upāsak)*.[29] The *sādhus* and *sādhvīs* are at the moment divided into 126 *siṅghāṛas* (Skt. *saṃghāṭa*-gathering), which are small itinerant groups of 3-5 ascetics, each led by a senior called a *siṅghāṛpati* or *agraṇī* (chief). In order to prevent schismatic tendencies, due to personal or regional attachments, their individual members are rotated every year by the *ācārya* (*'mahārāj'*) whose own group, called the *rāj* or *gurukul*, comprises of 34 *sādhus* and 54 *sādhvīs* (see Table I). Like a royal court, the *rāj* (lit. stretching oneself out) embodies the principle of unity of the 'divine kingdom' of the *dharmasaṅgh* as a whole, because it is the only monastic group that encompasses subunits of both male and female ascetics, which is a necessary condition for the capacity to generate a complete *caturvidh saṅgh*, and thus to establish an independent subsect in the Jain tradition.[30] The structure of the monastic hierarchy can be summarised diagramatically.[31]

Ācārya Śrī Pūjyaji Mahārāj	
Yuvācārya	
Mahāśramaṇ	Sādhvī Pramukhā (Mahāśramaṇī)
Agraṇī (Siṅghāṛpati)	Agraṇī (Siṅghāṛpati)
Sādhu	Sādhvī
Niyojak	Niyojikā
Samaṇ	Samaṇī
Sanyojak	Sanyojikā
Yojak	Yojikā
Mumukṣu Bhāī	Mumukṣu Bahan
Upāsak	Upāsikā

The various ascetic groups spend 7-8 months of the year on their *vihār* with or away from the *ācārya (bahir vihār)* and the four months of the rainy season *(cāturmās)* in residence in one particular place. Because temple worship is rejected, the *vihār* of the ascetics is the major form of ritual integration of the Terāpanth sect, and carefully planned. The way in which this is done today deserves close attention, not only because it involves the pivotal political processes within the sect, but especially because it comprises a new set of religious institutions, formerly unknown to Jainism, which combine ancient ascetic rituals with modern principles of organisation. They have been introduced in 1853-1864 by *ācārya* Jītmal (1803-1881) to prevent the fragmentation of the expanding ascetic order. Jītmal (Jayācārya) was the major consolidator and legislator of the sect. Not only did he re-introduce sanskritic literacy into monastic education, and invented an innovative system of monastic division of labour *(gāthā praṇālī)*, but he also compiled, condensed and codified Bhikṣu's *likhats* in various ways for their recitation in ceremonial contexts. In order to guarantee the continuous implementation of these rules, he set up a system of three interconnected rituals: the *likhat,* the *hājarī,* and the *maryādā mahotsav,* each being based on the compulsory performance of an oath of acceptance of certain rules peculiar to the Terāpanth monastic organisation. The *lekh patr* or *likhat* (formular) contains the thirteen essential rules of the order and has to be individually recited and signed first thing every morning.[32] The *hājarī* (presence) is a ceremony of group purification cum teaching *(gaṇaviśuddhī-karaṇ)*. It was first organised by Jayācārya in 1853 as a fortnightly assembly of all the ascetics of the *rāj* (and each *siṅghāṛ)* for the recitation, explanation and acceptance of the *likhat* and other rules, as well as for public examinations of novices. Nowadays the *hājarī* is only performed at special occasions, and the *maryādā patr* – a new compilation of Bhikṣu's and Jayācārya's rules made by Tulsī – is read out in the presence of a large audience. In this way the general public is made familiar with the *maryādās* and can monitor the conduct of the ascetics independently. Afterwards the *sādhus* and *sādhvīs,* all standing in a row according to the seniority of initiation *(dīkṣā paryāya),* recite the *lekh patr* and accept it one after the other. The *hājarī* differs from the Buddhist *pātimokkha* because penances and confessions do not take place before or during the *hājarī* (Tulsī & Mahāprajña 1983:186-198). However, the most important ceremony of the Terāpanth is the annual *maryādā mahotsav* (=MM) (festival of restraint). Like the *hājarī,* it was originally (1864) a ritual for the ascetics only, but has developed into a meeting of the whole fourfold assembly, which takes place for three or more days in January/February, and often attracts up to 50,000 pilgrims. The festival celebrates the date of the recording of Bhikṣu's last *likhat,* the constitution of the sect, through the recitation of the original text *(samūhik maryādā)* and the performance of an oath of allegiance to the '*dharma, gaṇ, ācārya,* and the *maryādā*' by the ascetics (p. 467–70).[33]

This annual meeting of all ascetics and important leaders of the sect is unique among Jain sects (although vaguely resembling the Buddhist *uposatha).* In its bureaucratic form it resembles a tributary royal ritual, and is the only festival of the year where – if possible – all the ascetics are assembled around the *ācārya,* together with representatives of the various Terāpanth lay communities from all over India. The effective community of the Terāpanth sect as a whole is manifest only on this occasion, where all the organisational, political and religious affairs of the Terāpanthīs are decided. Today not only the ascetics, who are obliged to participate, but also the laity are encouraged to vow allegiance to the *ācārya,* and to resolve their disputes, redistribute the fruits *(phal)* of their past year's socio-religious work *(kārya),* discuss new projects and receive new directives for the coming year. The importance of the collective oath of loyalty *(viśvasanīyatā kī śapath)* is underlined by the fact that it is considered as a form of self-sacrifice, generating the organisational unity and thus the potency *(śakti)* for all the religious activities of the year to come. In this way the annual cycle of ascetic wandering synthesises traditional religious and modern organisational rituals into a unitary process. The overall pattern of the Terāpanth religious year takes the shape of a polarised process of fragmentation and reintegration of both the *saṅghapuruṣ* – the corporate unity of the *saṅgh,* embodied in the *ācārya* as the moving centre of the sect – and the local *cāturmās* assemblies of the laity at the poles of the annual *vihār.* Interwoven with the agricultural cycle and related seasonal festivals *(utsav),* there is an inbuilt alternation between traditional ascetic Jainism, which is prominent during *cāturmās,* and modern festive Jainism after the rains (the traditional season of marriages, wars, and business ventures), when the fruits of asceticism are harvested and redistributed, particularly at the MM.

In accordance with this overall cosmological design, the main organisational tasks of the MM are the rotating of the ascetics amongst the *siṅghāṛas,* and decisions about the next *cāturmās* residencies as well as the *vihār* route for each of the *siṅghāṛas.*[34] It is an important rule that the choices of *cāturmās* localities for all the groups are determined by the *ācārya* alone. However, the local lay communities are competing for visits from the ascetics, because there are more lay communities than *siṅghāṛas.* This is done publicly in a series of religious assemblies prior to the MM, where lay representatives praise the merits of their local communities (e.g. moral restraint, charity), and through invitation letters *(vijñapti patr)* repeatedly ask the *ācārya* to send ascetics. Competitive invitations are the only Terāpanth equivalent to the customary auctioning *(bolī)* of ritual acts among idol-worshipping Jains, and therefore particularly elaborated. The Terāpanth laity have a strong desire to be close to their saints, because the opportunity to worship the ascetics directly is crucial for non-image-worshipping Jains, not only for religious reasons, but also in terms of the implicated prestige *(man)* and the auspiciousness *(maṅgal),* that in their eyes is generated particularly by a visit of the *ācārya* himself. Often the *ācārya 'mahārāj* is treated like an idol, and venerated for his 'life-giving' and miraculously 'wish-fulfilling' *(camatkārik)* powers through the practice of secretly taking vows during *darśan: 'If you help me to become prosperous, I will donate ... % of my earnings to your religious projects.'*

Such popular Jain practices are considered to be inconsistent with the main teachings of the religion (Schubring 1978:316-7), but they are often "so thoroughly assimilated with them now that they are no longer perceived as alien" (Jaini 1991:187). At the end of the MM, when all decisions are taken, the assembly disperses, and the small groups of ascetics set out for their new *cāturmās* destinations, which might be a considerable distance and, after *cāturmās,* on to the place where the *ācārya* will hold the next MM. In this way, the fundamental ritual structure for the interaction between ascetics and laity is organised one year in advance.

Territorial Organisation

The Terāpanthīs use a formal system of geographical categories to allocate circumscribed regions *(vihār kṣetr)* for each *siṅghāṛ.* It takes the territorial boundaries of the contemporary Indian states *(prānt:* province) as its basis, but gives a special priority to Rajasthan, the place of origin and the major focus of activity for the sect. Rajasthan has been further sub-divided into five regions *(sambhāg),* which do not correspond to the administrative districts of modern Rajasthan, but to the former territories of the principle *rājput* kingdoms. The elementary administrative units are the local region or circle of villages/lay communities *(grām maṇḍal),* the village *(gāṃv)* and the household *(ghar).* Unlike Mūrtipūjak or Sthānakvāsī ascetics, who reside in community buildings *(upāśrays)* or meditation halls *(sthānaks),* Terāpanthī ascetics originally could not stay in purpose-built residences but relied on the homes of their lay followers for accomodation (which requires greater restraint and gives the laity more influence).[35] To avoid disputes, each ascetic group receives a written list *(parcī)* of villages to be visited. These areas which are demarcated by a mental boundary *(sīmā)* are called *cokhlā* (Buddhamall 1995:417, Nathmal 1968:137, 147-8).[36] The free acceptance of such limitations of movement *(dig)* is considered as a form of religious self-denial in Jainism (BKB 1.51-2). In any region which has more than one *siṅghāṛ* allocated to it, the most senior of the *siṅghāṛpatis* fulfills supervisional functions for all the other *siṅghāṛs* and organises the further distribution of villages and houses among them with the help of local lay-supporters. Important decisions, however, are always taken by the *ācārya* himself, who keeps in contact with all *siṅghāṛpatis* through written messages which are

TABLE I: Territorial Distribution of Terāpanth Ascetics' Cāturmās 1991

	Groups			Ascetics'		
	Śramaṇ	*Śramaṇī*	*Sum*	*Śramaṇ*	*Śramaṇī*	*Sum*
1. Rajasthan Prānta						
a. Jodhpur Sambhāg						
Tulī's group	x	x	1	34	54	88
other	4	16	20	11	76	87
b. Bikaner Sambhāg	9	18	27	39	139	178
c. Udaipur Sambhāg	6	19	25	19	88	107
d. Jaipur Sambhāg	2	3	5	7	15	22
e. Ajmer Sambhāg		2	2	-	8	8
sum	21	58	79	110	380	490
2. Madhyapradesh Prānt	1	2	3	3	9	12
3. Maharashtra Prānt		5	5		25	25
4. Gujarat Prānt	2	5	7	9	24	33
5. Andhrapradesh Prānt		1	1		5	5
6. Karnataka Prānt	1	2	3	3	11	14
7. Tamil Nadu Prānt	2	1	3	6	5	11
8. Orissa Prānt		1	1		5	5
9. Bengal Prānt	1		1	4		4
10. Bihar Prānt		2	2		10	10
11. Assam Prānt	1	1	2	2	5	7
12. Haryana Prānt	2	9	11	6	42	48
13. Punjab Prānt	1	5	6	3	23	26
14. Delhi	1	1	2	3	5	8
15. Nepal		1	1		5	5
sum	12	36	48	39	174	213
Sum	33	94	127	149	554	703

(*Source:* Navratanmal 1991)

personally delivered by the laity who act as channels of communication as Jain ascetics are traditionally not allowed to use modern means of communication or transport.

The mode of distributing ascetics around the geographical zones and the routes of their *vihārs* changes every year. It reflects the general politico-religious aims of the *ācārya* who selects certain centres as loci for sectarian activity, and determines the basic structure of the *vihār* with regard to changing social circumstances. The *prānt* system itself, for instance, was only adopted after 1949, when *ācārya* Tulsī finally recognised the demands of the lay diaspora and decided to 'modernise' his sect and to extend the permitted range of the *vihār* of his ascetics in order to spiritually incorporate the whole territory of the new Indian state (and Nepal) (cf. map in Mahāprajña 1987:61). He initiated this process by symbolically turning his back on his former allies, the once all-powerful Gaṅga Siṅgh (1880-1943) and his son Sadul Siṅgh (1902-1950) – the *rājās* of Bikaner – by selecting first the new state capital of Jaipur and then the national capital, Delhi, for his *cāturmās* in 1949-1950 — an illustration of 'how power and religion go hand in hand' (L.P. Sharma 1991:252; cf. Mahāprajña 1994:64-70). Today, as a rule, half of the ascetics (especially the older and weaker ones who cannot walk long distances) remain in Rajasthan or close to the *ācārya.* The other half are distributed in such a way that the sect can be said to have covered the whole of India (including Nepal). This new nationwide orientation distinguishes the Terāpanth gaṇ from the Mūrtipūjak *gacchas* who, due to a lack of centralised organisation, do not form effective groups beyond the level of *śākhās* (branches) and operate only regionally, although there are national organisations for the laity. However, at present even Terāpanth transregionalism appears merely as an example of a 'masked expansion' of a particular regional religious movement (Balbir 1983:44). Table I shows that the centres of Terāpanth activity in 1991 were Bikaner and Jodhpur, the traditional heartland of the Terāpanth sect.

Fields of Influence

Formal territorial divisions like *prānt* and *sambhāg* have to be distinguished from functional regions, that is the places effectively visited by ascetics. Traditionally they are called *kṣetras* (fields of influence), and are characterised not in objective territorial terms, but by recurrent personal contact and mutual support between ascetics and lay followers. *Kṣetr* is a relational category, signifying a selective religious evaluation of people-cum-territory. From the ascetic point of view, *kṣetr* is a 'place worthy of residence' (Schubring & Caillat 1966:71), whereas from the lay point of view *kṣetr* is a "recipient worthy to be given alms" (Williams 1983:165). The *Terāpanth Kṣetr Pad* for instance is an annually published list of addresses of those privileged lay families or local associations *(sabhas)* who will be visited by ascetics during *cāturmās* (Navratanmal 1991). The *guru kṣetr* is the total field of influence of the *ācārya* himself which encompasses the networks of personal allegiances of all the ascetics. Its fluctuating size is dependent on the scale and success of the annual *vihār,* which ritually regenerates the effective unity of the *saṅgh.*

The process as a whole resembles the continually shifting and unstable segmentary state system *(maṇḍal)* of ancient India, where a king was merely *a primus inter pares* who had to prove his authority perennially through an "ever-renewed sacrificial contest as the mediating and organising institution" (Heesterman *1985*:150). Jain *ācāryas,* like ideal kings, are considered as the 'life force' of their *kṣetras,* which they have to contest every year after *cāturmās* in a process perceived as one of self-sacrifice and sociocosmic regeneration (UtS IX, XVIII). Like ancient Indian kings, Jain ascetics are sometimes regarded as the quintessence of the people, and their ritual wandering and entering of houses is symbolically associated with processes of symbolic incorporation of their followers, which is ontologically perceived as a process of the expansion of the soul, that is as an act of transcendence of differences and attachments. The soul of an ascetic is believed to be capable of entering the body of another person through a process of epansion: "The soul has a shape which is not like that of a material body. It is like a field of energy, which is not identical with shape [and which] .. pervades the body in the sense that it can feel any sensation in any part of the body [and] .. in any part of the cosmos by developing the relevant power. .. In all kinds of expansion, the points of the soul project themselves outside the body, and thereby the shedding off the relevant *kārmic* matter is effected in large measure. In the expansion related to the omniscient, the soul pervades the whole cosmic space" (Tulsī 1985:151-3).

Terāpanth ascetics perceive themselves as spiritual warriors and their *vihār* as a *karma*-shedding form of self-denial and spiritual (self-) conquest. Always accompanied by lay-followers they roam barefoot throughout India, from one village or town to the next *(padyātrā)*, collecting alms *(gocarī)*, giving sermons *(pravacan)*, and trying to attract converts by persuading them to make binding vows of allegiance in form of public or written statements of intent *(saṅkalp patr)*. With the permission of the *ācārya*, individual ascetics and *siṅghāṛs* compete in terms of *padyātrā*-miles, charisma *(tej)* generating austerities *(tap)*, religious programs, and the number of (lay-) conversions *(prabodhit)*.[37] The *agraṇīs* keep diaries *(kul yātrā vivaraṇ)* in which they write the names of the villages they visited, how many days they stayed, how much cloth *(vastr)* and medicine *(auṣadhi)* they received, and from whom, special achievements of each ascetic *(tapasyā, svādhyāyā)*, religious programs *(prekṣa dhyān)*, pacifications of quarrels *(vigrah śaman)*, the number and type of vows administered, and the services given and received from other ascetic groups *(bhakti)*. These diaries have to be scrutinised every year during MM by the *ācārya*, who then evaluates the conduct of each ascetic *(sāraṇa vāraṇa)*, and distributes rewards (so called *kalyāṇak* points) and punishments *(prāyaścitt)* accordingly.[38]

Particularly fierce is the rivalry between ascetics of different organised Jain subsects roaming in the same region. They compete as groups for status in terms of the idiom of behavioural purity and non-violence. These rivalries are fought with the help of the laity and sometimes take the form of open conflict for sectarian superiority in certain regions. The present dominance of the Terāpanth *gaṇ* in Bidasar and Ladnun (Bikaner), for instance, was gained through a focused campaign by *ācārya* Jayācārya from 1872-1877 against his Sthānakvāsī rival *ācārya* Javāharlāl. The Terāpanthīs maintained their commanding position in the region ever since, although in 1922 and 1926 Sthānakvāsīs and Mūrtipūjaks together tried to end their dominance by systematically disrupting the Bikaner *cāturmās*, including an alleged attempt to assassinate the *ācārya*. The defamation campaign was averted, however, through the intervention of Gaṅga Siṅgh, the ruler of Bikaner, who finally expelled some Sthānakvāsī mendicants and laity (L.P. Sharma 1991:177, 229-34). Negative campaigning was later (1954) ruled out by Tulsī, who – in the interest of the renewed proselytization of Jainism – advocated for a more positive approach towards public relations: "Views of others should be tolerated. Hatred or disrespect towards other sects and their monks should not be preached" (in Nagaraj 1959:28).

Religion and Politics

The structure of the Terāpanth *vihār* as a whole appears at first sight as an ideal manifestation of an ancient peripatetic asceticism. A closer view, however, reveals not only how a centralised bureaucratic organisation has been added to the pristine segmentary system of personal *guru-śiṣya* relationships, but also how the laity were gradually incorporated into an overarching framework, which nowadays combines traditional forms of moral sovereignty *(dharmarāj)* over a population-cum-territory *(janpad)* with modern 'democratic' ways of political-territorial organisation (cf. Dumont 1980:229, 332).[39] Most of these changes were introduced only recently under *ācārya* Tulsī in an attempt both to preserve the traditional way of life of the monastic community and to maintain its social influence under changed social conditions (territorial unification, spatial mobility, emancipation of economics, globalisation). Tulsī employed basically four strategies after 1949:[40] (1) the expansion and systematisation of ascetic wandering, (2) the use of modern media of mass-communication, (3) the regulation of popular religion and (4) the differentiation of monastic institutions. In order to create an integral religious system that is capable to address a nationwide mass audience, without violating the Terāpanth principles of centralisation and of direct interaction between ascetics and the laity, Tulsī first tried to stretch the ascetics' capability for barefoot walking to its physical limits (having covered more than 70,000 miles himself). In order to compensate for the self-created centrifugal tendencies he then had to improve the communication between the now even more widely scattered groups and to organise lay support in remote areas. He therefore decided (a) to draft a moral code of conduct for the laity (AK) (while remaining silent about their actual convictions)[41] and (b) to reform the monastic organisation; by modernising certain rules of conduct (use of microphones, flush toilets etc.), introducing a new system of administration *(nikāya),* and institutionalising and expanding the novice status. The reform program was finally completed with the introduction of the *samaṇ* order, that is a third category midway between the ascetic and the householder for the proselytization of Jainism abroad, in 1980. The media could now be legitimately used by the *dharmasaṅgh* without conceding control entirely to the laity, or blurring the distinction between religion and society. Bechert's

(1970) remarks on recent changes in Sinhala Buddhism also apply to the Terāpanth today:

> "Practically, a dual structure had come into existence in the historical development of the Theravāda *saṅgha:* it was organized along more modern organizational lines, but it had to keep the old structures as prescribed by the *vinaya.* The new structures were necessary, no doubt, for the survival of the *saṅgha* — but the old one had to be preserved in order to make the proceedings of the *saṅgha* lawful" (p. 773).

How are the spheres of religion and society related in practice? The crucial point is that, even though Bhikṣu renounced traditional notions of group religion and thereby ratified the relative autonomy of social life, from a devotee's point of view, religious values should still encompass all social pursuits. But in contrast to the former *śripūjyas* and *bhaṭṭāraks* the Terāpanth *ācāryas* (indeed most modern *ācāryas)* cannot directly control (religious) property or the social life of their lay followers anymore. Processes of control therefore operate indirectly, through 'secular' institutions, and through the individual religious *persona* of their followers, which may become progressively fixed (ethicised) through a competitive ritual system of self-imposed behavioural commitments *(vrats)* that are associated with specified religious status categories which imply the moral right to expect respect and religious services from the lower ranks. It is important to note that abstract Jain religious principles, like *ahiṃsā,* in practice always carry pragmatic – even legal – implications and presuppose systems of religious sanctions and customary behavioural specifications which are less visible. The actual observance of vows can, if at all, only be enforced informally via public opinion and sanctioned through a system of freely acceptable penances which is administered through various forms of religious book-keeping. Such a religious system of control through *Seelsorge* (Weber 1985:283) differs from modern state-bureaucracy because it does not operate in a disembodied way, but is predicated on the personal interaction of *guru* and *śiṣya* and on the exemplary conduct of the *ācārya,* who is the final authority of religious knowledge and sectarian religious law. However it shows features of the old patrimonial bureaucracy (loyalty, personal authority, and favor) (p. 127-131, 692ff.) which prevailed in the former princely states (Rudolph & Rudolph 1983:194). But although the monastic community itself is governed like a little kingdom on the basis of organisational rules *(maryādā)* and central offices *(pad),* its jurisdiction does not formally extend towards the laity. Religious sanctions *(prāyaścitt)* can only be imposed on their own demand.

There is no space here to provide a detailed analysis of the multiple layers of Jain (socio-) religious regulations and the history of their emergence. It is sufficient to re-state the general principle of self-referentiality:[42] Internal processes of rule-selection and specification always reflect wider processes of social differentiation and historical change. They combine at each stage the past and the present, universal religious principles and specific institutional rules, as is manifest in our sketch of the historical elaboration of Terāpanthī monastic law through the extension of the traditional method of imposing religious vows. Involution is evident in the existence of at least two different layers of rituals and rules, generated by the doctrinal distinction between predominantly religious and social orientations: (1) Jain 'canonical' rituals (e.g. *āvaśyak, pakkhī, paryuṣaṇ)* and (2) Terāpanthī 'organisational' rituals (e.g. *likhat, hājarī, maryādā mahotsav);*[43] plus analogous structures among the laity, who additionally participate in 'Hindu' group religion.

This result leads us to the question of the relevance of the (post-) colonial setting for the emergence of new doctrinal interpretations and the development of bureaucratic and communal structures among the Terāpanth. In his celebrated paper *Nationalism and Communalism* Dumont (1980) argued that communalism as "the affirmation of the religious community as a political group" (p. 315) is a hybrid phenomenon, a janus-faced transitional state — intermediary between traditional group religions and modern religions of the individual. He further argued that communalism is the ideological manifestation of an emerging class-culture, which developed mainly through the impact of colonial rule and the christian missionary model[44] Particularly the middle-class elites were enabled to free themselves from traditional forms of religious and political hegemony, and to transform themselves into dominant social groups. In the context of overall social change, many of these elites drifted increasingly towards the newly emerging forms of lay religiosity, based on doctrines of 'this-worldly asceticism' on the one hand and corporate lay associations on the other.[45]

As we have seen, the same combination of modernised religious doctrines and bureaucratic organisation can be found among the

Terāpanth as well. But a lay revolution has not taken place, and the continuous dominance of the ascetic orthodoxy and caste prevented attempts to combine old and new features into a new communalist form of Jainism. Moreover, the fundamental principles of the Jain 'lay-revolution' go back to the 15th C., and Śvetāmbar reformers never rejected monasticism as such, while Digambar lay movements retained most features of traditional Jain group religion (image-worship etc). The emergence of these principles cannot be attributed to the historical influence of colonialism or christian protestantism. In contrast to Theravāda Buddhism, Jain codes of 'this-worldly asceticism' *(śrāvakācāra)* have 'canonical' roots and can hardly be interpreted as a modern phenomenon. Thus, everything speaks for a more cautious theory of Jain religious reform. Ācārya Tulsī himself, who has worried for national integration and Jain unity throughout his life, "is not in favour of the amalgamation of different sects into one" (Mahāprajña 1994:188) and has always opposed communalism in the name of 'pure' religion and freedom of thought. In Dumontian terms, the Terāpanth presently employs a 'mixed' strategy of modernisation, by striving to hierarchically encompass an increasingly modern social system within a traditional religious system. In accordance with the overall pattern, the legislation of the modern state had a greater impact on the formation of contemporary Terāpanthī lay-associations, which mediate between secular and religious law, than on the monastic order itself. Within the monastic order adaptation to changed social circumstances occurred mainly through hierarchical differentiation, that is the development of intermediary institutions between the ascetics proper and the laity. But on secondary levels the tenuous co-existence of religious and social orientations is intensely felt by the laity. As it becomes more functionally differentiated, modern Indian society corresponds less and less to the ancient system of hierarchically differentiated classes *(varṇa)* and, for the middle classes at least, the relevance of the religious principle of hierarchy is progressively reduced to guaranteeing the psychological compatibility of an increasingly compartmentalized way of life with the ideal of an integral personality. In the words of Mahāprajña (1994) "The individual today represents the capitalist aspect of vested interests. By presenting him with the principle of renunciation, Acharya Sri has given extension to the individual and added a new dimension to his social character" (p. 187).

The real situation of the Jains in India today corresponds less to a Hocartian than to a Dumontian (1980:299-301) scenario, where the ideas of moral kingship, which inform ritual exchanges of 'protection' and prestations, appear as rationalisations of actual social practice. I wish to argue, that the (inevitably paradoxical) attempt of a strict separation between religion and society, that is the simultaneity of religious reform and secularist tendencies (Bechert 1970:767) which is gaining organisational force among the Terāpanth and other contemporary Jain sects, allows only for a weak form communalism, by confining religious practice to the individual while strengthening the importance of dominant social practices, in contrast to traditional attempts to incorporate conflicting views within a cosmic hierarchy dominated by a Jain king and to the modern desire of image-worshipping lay reformers to "eradicate every non-Jaina element from the Jaina community" (Sangave 1980:410).[46]

But how are the Terāpanth laity organised? In the next section I focus on the political and economic implications of the *vihār*. Many studies have noted the ways in which modern South Asian elites instrumentalise religion for political ends. The most important strategy being the formation and control of sectarian lay-organisations which act on behalf of the religious community within the modern political and legal system. Jain organisations like these typically have an universalistic agenda although they are controlled by influential potentates and serve exclusively for the material benefit of their own, caste and class-based, membership.[47] Thus, two complementary developments can be observed: On the one hand, the tendency to create a unified religious community and to overcome internal doctrinal differences by focusing on few general religious principles, and, on the other hand, the tendency to harden internal boundaries with regard to social issues, like the control of religious property (p. 397). The paradoxes and ideological effects generated by these simultaneous tendencies towards external religious universalism and internal social separation cannot be solved once and for all. This is evident among the Terāpanth, who strictly distinguish religious and social issues on the level of doctrine, but whose laity is effectively integrated into a plural nationwide framework of exclusive lay-associations paralleling the monastic organisation, like in any other contemporary Jain sect.

II. The Terāpanth Laity and Their Organisations

There are today about 500,000 [Griswold 1934:148 cites the number of 200,000, some Terāpanthīs say: 1 million] followers of the Terāpanth ascetics. They are organised and tightly integrated with the ascetic community in a variety of ways. Most of them were born into the sect, however, for converts it is mandatory to have an interview with the *ācārya,* and to undergo the formal lay initiation into the right belief *(samyaktva dīkṣā).* This ritual, which transforms individuals into second-order ascetics, or 'real' *brāhmaṇs* (Schubring 1978:285), is usually publicly performed under the guidance of the *ācārya,* who only under special circumstances also excommunicates *śrāvaks.* Ideally the candidates take a vow to accept the Jain doctrine and practice in general *(aṇuvrat),* and another vow to accept the *maryādā* of *ācārya* Bhikṣu, to support the Terāpanth ascetics, to monitor their behaviour, and to maintain exclusive loyalty to the *ācārya* throughout their life *(śrāvak niṣṭh patr)* (AK I:360-376).[48] A candidate, therefore, accepts not only the universal moral principles of Jainism, but also the specific institutional regulations of the sect as a corporate group. The commitment to these vows is nominally strengthened through their collective recitation in public assemblies *(hājarī)* and by a system of religious sanctions, which the ascetics apply to adjudicate confessed transgressions. Most effective, however, are informal social sanctions attached to prevailing notions of honour and face, which need not be enforced by the *sabhāpatis* (the leaders of the local lay-communities) who only intervene in the case of crime. In this way a strong moral and indeed legal bond is established between the *ācārya* and his laity, who are expected to adhere strictly to his political guidance and regulations (cf. Sangave 1980:379). Although the *ācārya* cannot exercise any political authority over his laity, his directives have great persuasive power and become rule for all practical purposes, simply by the fact of his constitutive role both for the reproduction of Jain religion and of the Terāpanth community. In practice, there is a certain overlap between various forms of jurisdiction (religious, social, legal). This is manifest both in the occasional mediating role of the *ācārya* in social disputes between members, and of his mirror-image, the Terāpanth lawyer, who acts in the courts on behalf of the sect. In sum, the Terāpanth, like other Indian sects, combines religious universalism with social exclusivism, and thus constitutes a well-organised and therefore powerful pressure-group that mediates between state, caste and family.

The great majority of the Terāpanth laity (and ascetics) are Rajasthani Bīsa Osvāl *baniās*. The fact that the Terāpanth, like most Jain subsects (Sangave 1980, Banks 1992:121-2), is closely associated with a particular caste *(jāti)* is also the historical consequence of an explicit rule which prescribed that only Bīsa Osvāl *baniās* should be initiated and accepted as lay followers. It was abandoned only in the 1950s, under the impact of the anti-caste politics of the Indian government.[49] The Rajasthani Osvāls are seen as a subcategory of the Mārvāṛīs, who are today a very mobile and wealthy segment of the Indian population (G.D. Sharma 1984:200).[50] Over the last 300 years many of them migrated from Rajasthan, which at times offered few economic prospects, to the major cities of India, where they now form small, semi-permanent trading communities (Timberg 1978:93). Traditionally they operate through kinship links and maintain well organised joint-family firms with communal assets which are controlled by the head of the family. Like the Terāpanth *ācārya*, the head of the Mārvāṛī family firms exercises civil jurisdiction over his sons and employees and rotates his personnel (mainly relatives and long-term associates of the family from Rajasthan) in order to prevent their attachment to a particular local branch and thus tendencies towards the premature division of the family business (p. 131,135). He also decides on the locations for a network of branches *(śākhā, koṭhī)* in promising trading locations where he sends his younger sons, often "by a process of uncles calling nephews, and fathers-in-law sons-in-law" (Timberg 1971:76). Even today diaspora Terāpanthīs maintain an attachment to the houses *(havelīs)* of their ancestors *(pitṛ)* in Rajasthan, where the cooperating members of the family lineage *(kuṭumb)* periodically assemble for marriages and funerals (i.e. feasts which involve the pooling and transfer of resources), as well as to Osiyān, the legendary place of origin of the Osvāl *jāti* near Jodhpur, where the lineage goddess *(kuldevī)* Saciyā (Durgā) is worshipped (cf. Babb 1996:137-160).[51] According to Timberg (1978:38) this combination of a network of branches and a centralised control with the family-firm explains the 'organisational superiority' of the Mārvāṛīs, which he regards as the key to their success. Between families of the same sub-caste *(jāti)* exist only weak status differences. Hindus and Jains still intermarry freely among Bīsa Osvāls and no ranking of exogamous group *(gotra)*, lineages *(kul)*, cooperating family lineages *(kuṭumb)*, and families *(parivār)* can be observed. In certain contexts, of course, differences of political influence and economic power become rele-vant, and the principles of solidarity and seniority also operate between families, and between members of religious communities, which are nominally equal.[52]

In the following I will concentrate on the implications of the *vihār* for the Terāpanth (Osvāl) laity, in demonstrating the important political and economic functions of their lay-associations. Timberg (1978) argued that Mārvāṛi commercial expansion "had little to do with the community" (p. 82). He denies the importance of cultural factors for economic development per se (p. 3-6), although he mentions the strong symbolic identification of the 'Mārvāṛīs' with Rajasthan and its culture, and the important indirect economic role of religious and family networks (p. 195). Bayly (1983), on the other hand, suggests that "the corporate identities of the later commercial middle classes were, at base, formed around conceptions of religion and credit" (p. 8) and that there is a direct relationship between mercantile credit and common sectarian attachment (p. 389). In focusing not only on the institutions of the family, but also on those of the religious community and caste, which Timberg neglects, I wish to combine religious and socio-economic perspectives. Although I do not share Bayly's (p. 383-5) appreciation of Jain stories as evidence for the presumed direct economic efficacy of proper religious conduct, I wish to emphasise the constitutive duality of the Terāpanth ritual circle, which plays both a religious and a social role, both conditioning and being conditioned by a dispersed community of lay supporters. The indirect function of the Terāpanth community as a socio-economic 'resource network' is less visible than in other Jain sects, because religion is officially divorced from the world of property. But its role as a political 'pressure group' is manifest.[53] Yet no formal organisation of Terāpanth lay followers existed until the founding of the Terāpanth *Sabhā* (assembly) in Calcutta in 1913. Local communities assembled informally in the houses of leading *śrāvaks* to meet visiting ascetics or for other religious events. Only after independence were a whole variety of community associations founded and nationally to materially support the new educational programmes of *ācārya* Tulsī, most notably the *Aṇuvrat* movement in Delhi 1949, and the *Pāramārthik Śikṣaṇ Sansthā* (= PSS), a religious school for young women *(upāsikā)* and novices *(mumukṣu)* in Ladnun in 1949, and the *Jain Viśva Bhāratī* (=JVB) in Ladnun in 1970 (Mahāprajña 1987:11-12, 43-44). These organisations operate independently under the spiritual guidance of the *ācārya* and are financed by the *Aṇuvrat Trust* (1949) and the *Tulsī Foundation* (1980) respectively.[54] However, the most important organisation, the Terāpanth *Mahāsabhā* (=MS), which now funds the PSS, nowadays forms a national council of lay representatives, and provides a centralised organisational framework for the Terāpanth laity, parallel to the religious organisation of the ascetics.

The Jain Śvetāmbar Terāpanth Mahāsabhā

The Terāpanth Mahāsabhā was founded in 1913 in Calcutta by a number of Terāpanth Mārvāṛī businessmen and lawyers to foster the interests of the local Terāpanthī community. The Terāpanthī Mārvāṛīs of Calcutta belonged to the second wave of migrating businessmen, who came mainly from the Bikaner, Jodhpur and Shekhavati regions of Rajasthan and arrived in Calcutta in greater numbers from 1880 onwards. Timberg (1971) especially mentions the Koṭhārī family-clan from Bikaner, and other families such as the Baiṅgāṇīs and Baids from Ladnun and the Dugaṛs, Rāmpuriās, Nāhaṭās and Gadhaiyās from Sardārśahar and Ratangarh in Churu district. One might add the Corariyās, Dāgās, Seṭhiyās, and Surāṇās, "On the border of Bikaner and Jodhpur states, four towns in particular (Ladnun, Chapar, Sujangarh, and Bidasar) sent a large number of Osvāls into the jute trade, especially in East Bengal" (p. 77). These families have produced the most prominent lay followers of the Terāpanthī ascetics and many of the office bearers of the *Terāpanthī* MS in Calcutta. It is therefore safe to say that not only did most of the Terāpanthī Osvāl Mārvāṛīs come from Bikaner district, but also that most of the leading Bikaneri Mārvāṛīs in Calcutta were Terāpanthī Osvāls (cf. Timberg 1978:195). How close the relationship between Bikaner and the Calcutta Mārvāṛīs was (and is) illustrates the remark of Mahārāja Surat Siṅgh from Bikaner in 1883: "Calcutta and Bikaner is one" (G.D. Sharma 1984:200). Most of the Mārvāṛīs traded in cloth and jute, and slowly established themselves in the business world of Calcutta by gaining more and more *baniāships* (guaranteed commission agencies) from British merchant companies. During the First World War they achieved an economic breakthrough and established the institutional and financial basis for their present position as one of the most influential business communities in post-independence India.

The history of the Mārvāṛīs is well known and it is sufficient to stress that, although there was a cultural bond which united the Rajasthani *baniās* in Bengal, a great diversity of social circles existed within the general regional category of 'Mārvāṛīs.' Not only because initially their families had to remain in Rajasthan,[55] Terāpanthī Mārvāṛīs kept mainly to themselves, maintaining closer links to their ancestral homes, and to other Bīsa Osvāl families all over India, rather than with their neighbours (Jain 1988). They participated of course in the activities of the main Mārvāṛī organisations *(Mārvāṛī Chamber of Commerce, Jute Association, Mārvāṛī Samāj Calcutta* (1898), *All India Mārvāṛī Federation, Mārvāṛī Relief Society)* and other cross-cutting economic interest groups, as well as the main Jain organisations *(Jain Sabhā, Jain Śvetāmbar Pañcāyatī Mandir)* (Sukhalāl 1991:47). The emergence of these two separate types of special interest groups illustrates the increasing compartmentalization of economic and socio-cultural spheres among Indian business people (Singer 1968:438). However, the focus of the socio-religious activities of the Terāpanthīs became the Terāpanth *Sabhā,* which was modelled on similar self-regulating institutions among other sects.[56] The establishment of the *Sabhā* as a formally registered religious association occurred only in 1913, in response to the *Navalik Cela Registration Bill* of 15.9.1913, which threatened to classify young Jain mendicants with 'professional beggars', and to imprison them if caught begging on the streets. L.S. Siṅgh proposed a four-point resolution to the legislative council of the government of the United Provinces, "to prevent minor boys and girls from being turned into beggars, mendicants or sādhus during the period of their minority either by the parents who make them over to the so-called sādhus or by sādhus who make them such by force or false representations" (Siṅgh 1914:518). All Jains were alarmed by the plans of legislative council, which, if passed as a bill, would have made the traditional itinerant life of the Jain mendicants (who distance themselves vehemently from 'brāhmaṇical beggars') impossible. The Terāpanthīs in Calcutta joined with the Mūrtipūjaks to protest against the resolution (which never became law: the beggars act of 1948 distinguishes *sādhus* from 'beggars') and R.B.G. Mukim from Bikaner, the trustee of the *Jain Śvetāmbar Pañcāyat Mandir* in Calcutta, was invited to coordinate Jain protest. But very soon problems in working together emerged, apparently regarding the accountability of the trustee, who was forced to declare that the

Mūrtipūjaks 'did not take any money' for running the temple for all the local Jains (Sukhalāl 1991:46-7). K.C. Koṭhārī then decided that the Terāpanth tradition *(sampradāy)* would establish its own independent organisation. A *Sabhā* meeting under the presidency of Talu Rām was called, and Dhadeva was elected president and K.C. Koṭhārī secretary of the new Terāpanthī *Sabhā*. The *Sabhā* thus came into being as a formal organisation not only to resist the *Navalik Cela Registration Bill,* and to please the colonial government with social reforms, but also to protect the shares of the Terāpanthīs in the religious property of the Jain community in Calcutta.

Although it fulfilled secondary social, political and economic functions, the *Sabhā* was primarily a vehicle for the defence of community interests in the courts. One of the main activists and the second president of the Terāpanth *Sabhā* was Chogmal Copṛā (1883-1976). He was an Osvāl, born in Derajsar (Bikaner), where his mother stayed in the family house *(havelī),* while his father Pūsrāj Copṛā worked in Rangapur (Bengal) as an accountant *(munīm)* of I.C. Nāhaṭā, an important jute merchant. I.C. Nāhaṭā was the first Jain Osvāl who broke the religious rule against travelling overseas and went to the UK in 1887. He was therefore declared an outcaste by the Bīsa Osvāl *pañcāyat* for the rest of his life, and even Chogmal's father suffered from his close contacts with Nāhaṭā. C. Copṛā differed from the rest of the Terāpanth business community through his higher education. In 1908 he gained a law degree in Calcutta, the first of the Mārvāṛī families from Bikaner to do so, and worked as a specialist in insurance law until he was 60. He was famed for the free legal advice he gave to 'people in need' – mostly prominent Terāpanth Mārvāṛīs (who today control the majority of the great law firms in Calcutta) – and developed into one of the most active social workers *(kāryakarta)* of the Terāpanth community (p. 39, 46). The fact that not a businessman, but a lawyer, a man of education, became the most influential community leader is not untypical for Jain communities. Jain businessmen do usually not dispose of the necessary 'cultural capital' to be able to construct a sufficient ideological platform on which to build a lay community. This is why they need intellectuals to do this on their behalf. The intellectuals, on the other hand, often do not possess 'economic capital.' The characteristic relationship of hierarchical complementarity between ascetics and laity is thus replicated within the laity itself, whose leading members are intellectuals on the one hand and businessmen on the other.

Most of the decisive *Sabhā* members of the time belonged to the conservative wing of the Terāpanth *śrāvaks* and were supporters of the National Congress. They reacted to state-legislation but did not press for reforms within the Terāpanth sect itself. They were opposed by the young radicals of the now defunct Terāpanth *Taruṇ Saṅgh* (youth assembly), headed by Bhanvarmal Siṅghī, who even challenged the monastic orthodoxy itself. The changes they demanded were not only related to social customs (women, untouchability etc.) and business interests, which were best served by maintaining good working-relationships with the British,[57] but also concerned with the abolition of child initiation *(bāldīkṣā),* old fashioned excretionary practices of ascetics in towns, ritualistic inhibitions against industry, foreign travel, and the movement of wives, children and ascetics outside Rajasthan (cf. Timberg 1978:69). Most, but not all (viz. *bāldīkṣā*) of those demands were ratified by *ācārya* Tulsī forty years later in the course of the general social changes after Indian Independence and are now part of the official socio-religious policy of the Terāpanth (Mahāprajña 1987:10-13).

In the early decades of its existence, the *Sabhā* was an organisation designed purely for the interests of the Calcutta Terāpanthīs. The organisation was closed to Terāpanthīs from other regions of India. Only later, under the influence of *ācārya* Tulsī (1946-1960), was the membership of the *Sabhā* widened, and the organisation transformed itself into the first nation-wide institution of the Terāpanthī laity by recognising similar local Terāpanth communities all over India as affiliate members. From then on, the Calcutta *Sabhā* was named *Akhil Bhāratīya Terāpanth Mahāsabhā,* the great all Indian assembly of the Terāpanth laity. Today almost all of the Terāpanth lay associations are *sabhās.* Only a very few, mostly small, local communities in remote are, still assemble aroundas prominent family, as is indicated by the names given in the annual lists of *cāturmās* locations of the asceties (Navratanmal 1991). In due course the MS acted as the central coordinating organisation of the Terāpanthī laity for all India, under direct instruction of the *ācārya.* The main outward sign of systematic co-operation between the independent local communities became the centralised planning of the material infrastructure of the ritual *vihār* from the two central offices *(śākhā)* of the MS in Calcutta and Ladnun, and the sharing of expenses for the four months of *cāturmās* of the *ācārya* and his group, which are about Rs. 2,000,000 (Goonasekere 1986:207) which are usually paid by the local *sabhāpati*. Also in recent years major investments have been made in order to create a permanent infrastructure for the new community institutions, i.e. the Terāpanthī-centre in Ladnun and assembly houses *(sabhābhavans)* with libraries for the laity in major cities.

Formal Organisation

How is a Jain lay-association, like the MS, organised? And how does it handle property? The prime official aim of the MS is to represent the interests of the Terāpanth community vis-à-vis the institutions of the modern Indian state, that is "to consider, (and) promote or oppose any legislation or other measures and enactments affecting Jainism, its tenets, culture or order of Jain Sādhus, Sādhvīs, Shrawaks and Shrawikas" (JSTM 1987:5). The MS is also particularly concerned with maintaining legal control over its charitable funds as with similar charitable associations of the Jains (cf. Banks 1992:104-6). However, until *ācārya* Kālūrām's recognition of the MS, the concept of community welfare was rejected by the Terāpanth on doctrinal grounds. Instead, the family, and caste were favoured as the elementary social units (there are still no community meals among the Terāpanth laity). As non-image-worshippers, the Terāpanthīs could not promote the construction of temples and also rejected the Sthānakvāsī notion of charitable 'social work' as religiously illegitimate, arguing that the propagation of social charity as a religious value would only serve the rich (Tulsī 1985:163ff., Oldfield 1982:71). In accordance with Tulsī's reforms the MS therefore chose as its main aim the promotion of 'educational work' (i.e. the propagation of Terāpanthī Jainism), stressing particularly the importance of meditation and the preservation and publication of books, which is a traditional concern of Jains (JSTM 1987:1-6).[58] Members of the association can be "any Shrawaka or Shrawika who has attained the age of 18 years irrespective of caste, colour, race and nationality" (p. 3). It thus appears as if membership of the MS is open to all Jains. But this is not the case, on the contrary, the general Jain terms *śrāvaka* and *śrāvikā* (male and female laity, lit. 'listeners' of the sermons of the Jinas) have been given a narrow, sectarian interpretation, reserving them for lay members of the Terāpanth sect alone: "'Shrawak' or 'Shrawika' means a person who has implicit faith in the Acharya of the Jain Swetambar Terāpanthī Sect, and his religious views, and in his rules of conduct and limitations, and in the Sādhu who follows his order, and also in the religious principles of the Jain Swetambar Terāpanthī Sect" (p.3). Membership of the MS is thus predicated on discipleship to the *ācārya*. This partly explains the *ācārya's* power, because no excommunicated individual can remain in the MS.[59]

The organisational framework of the MS is designed to guarantee a centralised nationwide coordination of socio-religious activities of the Terāpanth laity. Its formal structure is modern and democratic, and combines features of bureaucratic centralisation and territorial segmentation, parallel to the *dharmasaṅgh*. The highest representative body of the MS is the *General Meeting* of all members. But more important with regard to the running of the day-to-day affairs of the organisation is the biannual *Annual General Meeting* of at least 51 members, who assemble at the site of the *maryādā mahotsav*. Its main function is the election of a president, who acts as the *sabhāpati* (leader of the lay community) and is the formal equivalent to the *ācārya* within the overall hierarchical structure of dual leadership, which is typical for modern Jain sects. The *sabhāpati* fulfils mainly representative and general supervisional functions. He should ensure that the rules and regulations of the *ācārya* and the MS are correctly observed, and has the right to criticise the behavioural 'laxity' of its members. During his presidency he is nominally forced to neglect his own business because he is preoccupied with visiting and supervising meetings and functions of the local *sabhās* throughout India. Like the *ācārya* or the head of a traditional Mārvāṛī 'great firm' he is constantly on the move. However, effectively, the MS is managed and supervised by a *Working Committee* of 100 members (incl. the president) who are directly nominated by the president (and with the consent of the *ācārya*) for a two years term. The *Working Committee* transacts all necessary business of the MS. It meets four times a year and is mainly responsible for the framing of regulations, the creation of new departments or committees, and the setting up and management of charities and funds. It appoints the general secretary, the treasurer, and the heads *(sanyojak)* of state-committees, and prescribes their duties (p. 15-8). The key person in the actual running of the organisation is not the president but the general secretary. He acts as the public spokesman of the MS and operates its office in Calcutta, where the accounts and the voters list etc. are kept. His main responsibilities are to keep proper accounts, to undertake any legal actions, and to sign all necessary papers in the name of the MS (p. 26-30). The two other key persons are the treasurer and the chief trustee. A system of mutual controls between them and the general secretary is to prevent the misuse of office (p. 30-31).

Status and Power

One of the main incentives for being a candidate for any of the key positions is to gain control over the management of the assets of the MS trusts. The community properties of the Terāpanth sect are, like those of other contemporary Jain sub-sects, held in the name of the sect *(saṅgh),* but managed by the elected, usually male leaders of the lay communities *(samāj),* thus establishing a system of balances that are crucially dependent on the maintenance of a strict separation between ascetics and laity. Decisions about investments in new socio-religious projects are usually taken by leading members of the Terāpanth community which assemble 'at the feet' of the *ācārya* to discuss the issue informally *(āntarik goṣṭhī).* The *ācārya* does not legally own any property, but he is informed of all new developments and always asked for his advice on where to donate surplus money for charitable (educational) purposes and how to spend the funds of the Terāpanth foundations. He will give his blessings only if he agrees with a project, and nobody will act against his recommendations. This arrangement is the norm among contemporary Jains, with the exception of the Digambar Terāpanth movements.[60]

It is necessary to distinguish between the charitable institutions, on the one hand, and the trusts and landed property owned by them and their members, on the other. Whether a particular fund is treated as 'secular' or as 'socio-religious' property depends entirely on the context. The statute that "any proprietary concern whose proprietor is an associate of (the) Mahāsabhā" (JSTM 1987:4) can also be a member, facilitates the temporary transformation of any business controlled by Terāpanthīs into a charitable institution. Charitable funds are sometimes used as communal sources of credit and fulfil major economic functions within Jain communities. In fact, the crux of disputes over pilgrimage sites and the internal political dynamic of Jain associations is often the battle for the control of community assets which have been accumulated over decades or even centuries.[61] These funds have to be invested in the best interests of the community. Therefore the most prosperous and capable individuals are usually elected to the posts of chief trustee, treasurer and general secretary, who take all economic decisions for the MS trusts and manage the funds of the association as if it were a business (Mahāprajña 1987:11).[62] This *potlatch*-like system favours the rich and supplies them with access to community assets and prestige, in the expectation that the community itself can profit from their prosperity, because it is expected that those in control, in turn, donate generously to the various fund of the organisation and pay all the expenses occurring during their two years in office. As a rule, only renowned 'social workers' *(prabhāvaka, kāryakarta),* who donate regularly to the socio-religious projects of their sect, will be elected.[63] Among the Terāpanth all this was rendered possible only through Tulsī's doctrine of *visarjan,* which turned charitable donations into an attractive proposition even for businessmen. However, the continuing doctrinal devaluation of charitable giving generated two paradoxical effects: Firstly, the property held in the name of the sect is regarded as 'social' from the religious point of view and as 'religious' from the social (legal) point of view. Secondly, the prestigious process of giving money is hidden from public view, although the names of the donors and the donated sums are published by community magazines. The consequence of the fact that several candidates are involved in secret competitive giving *(maunsevā),* particularly during the process of issuing invitations for *cāturmās,* is that the total assets continue to grow, thus, reinforcing the incentive to give even more.

How do Terāpanthīs, then, conceive of the relationship between status and power? No doubt, lay people often venerate ascetics only because of their presumed magico-religious powers *(ojas, tejas, śakti)* which, they think, can be transmitted through direct contact with their toes, hands, and eyes. Charitable transactions, on the other hand, are considered to be merely of socio-religious value. As a rule, asceticism generates respect and attracts religious support. Similarly, charitableness attracts social support. In theory, therefore, two parallel status-systems operate within the community, a religious one, culminating in the *ācārya,* and a socio-religious one, culminating in the *sabhāpati* (who is not necessarily the individual with the greatest economic power). Purely socio-economic status criteria, like wealth *(dhan)* or power *(śakti)*, are regarded as non-religious, as are *brāhmaṇic* notions of purity.[64] In practice, however, religion and power are often two sides of the same coin. As Dumont (1980:187, 215), Bechert (1970:766) and Tambiah (1984:49) have shown, traditionally both Buddhists and Jains recognise a hierarchical continuum between power and renunciation, and operate with ambiguous status-categories which mediate between *dharma* and *artha*. The fundamental notion, informing socio-religious life, being the concept of the spiritually superior person *(mahāpuruṣ)*, i.e. the socially encompassing moral hero, who through exemplary acts of renunciation converts raw power into status, and who rules primarily through personal moral authority. The Terāpanth system is nominally different but operates in exactly the same way, except that only the *ācārya* has the power to invest a person formally with socio-religious status: Terāpanth community leaders are considered to be the protectors of the religion in the social sphere, thus embodying both morality *(dharma)* and power *(artha)*, like ideal Jain or Buddhist kings *(dharmarājā)*. They present themselves in public therefore as individuals of religious education and of flawless moral character. Politico-economic power is presupposed, but hidden away and not explicitly emphasised in socio-religious contexts.

There are only few legitimate avenues for charitable donations. Most lay-projects concern religious publishing and Tulsī-inspired building projects. The MS, for example, promotes the construction of *dharmśālās* and of memorials *(smāraks)* in the villages of Rajasthan to honour those who have 'served the cause of Jainism' (JSTM 1987:3, 6). The most famous of these are the *Bīkhāṇjī kā janm sthān* in Kanṭāliyā, the *Jaitasiṃhajī kī chatrī* in Bagṛī, and the *Bhikṣu smārak* in Siriyārī, which mark the important events *(kalyāṇak)* in Bhikṣu's life, and which became second order places of pilgrimage along with Tulsī's birthplace and the JVB in Ladnun and the site of his cremation in Gaṅgāśahar, which both will be marked with new memorials.[65] In order to qualify as a form of socio-religious service *(sevā)*, community work has to be validated through public appraisal by the *ācārya*, who alone holds the right to confer socio-religious titles. Tulsī bestowed no less than 49 different types of honorific titles *(sambodhan)* during his reign, on both ascetics and laity; and the Terāpanth foundations give cash awards *(puraskār)* of up to 1 *lakh* rupees to acknowledged lay individuals who did 'good work for community and religion', including members from other sects (cf. Mahāprajña 1987:12). The motivating effect of public honours on community workers can be explained by a combination of rational and empirical factors: For Terāpanthīs honorific titles are desirable not only because they guarantee public recognition but also because they substantiate claims to real assets. For outstanding contributions ascetics receive *kalyāṇak* bonus points from the *ācārya*, which may be cashed in as compensation for penances received for negligent conduct, and lay people receive cash awards. In order to motivate service to the community the Terāpanthīs also employ a great variety of social status categories, which they reinterpret in terms of the Jain concept of the spiritually superior person. The ascetics, for instance, often allude to the Mārvāṛī ethos of moral respectability *(ābrū)* and family honour *(izzat)*, or they refer to the pride *(mān)* associated with access to high office and proximity to the holders of politico-religious power, even though, from a strictly doctrinal point of view, this can only be considered as a form of *kārmic* delusion *(māyā)*. Public honouring *(sammān)* and dishonouring *(apmān)*, both in religious and social contexts, are a common means of generating status differentials among the nominally egalitarian Māvāṛīs, which affects their social credibility and stirs competitive instincts.[66] Laidlaw's (1995:354) theory – derived from Bayly's (1983) study of North Indian society 1770-1870 – that among Jains socio-religious status translates 'directly' into economic credit seems however implausible (this presupposes monopoly markets), particularly in the light of growing complaints about vanishing community spirit and growing egotism. Today, even among Jains, and despite the moral recommendations of the ascetics, business is one thing, and religion another. But, it is crucial for the individual to get the balance right.[67]

In sum, through the mediation of the value-ideas of *karma*, status, and honour, which focus on the social *persona* of an individual, Jain charitable institutions ideally transform the relative competitive advantage of wealthy families into a form of well-being and security for the whole community. They grant them access to the charitable funds but expect adequate returns in the form of religious donations flowing back into the institution. The system aims at synthesizing individual self-interest and community well-being to help the successful members legitimate their wealth and to become even more successful, if they are prepared to limit themselves and to share some of that wealth with the community. The social pressures and competitive constraints of this system, which in the case of the Terāpanth is restricted to the funding of the annual pilgrimage and Tulsī's moral-educational projects and practically excludes the wider society, explains the political importance of the selection processes preceding the *vihār.*

Regional and Local Assemblies

The selection of members of the *Working Committee* by the president is carefully regulated: 20% of the committee members are selected from representatives proposed by the various affiliated Terāpanth institutions, and 80% are nominated directly from the 'state assem-

TABLE II: Territorial Distribtion for the selection of working committee members.

1. Rajasthan		7. Assam	2
(a) Jodhpur Sambhāg	5	8. Orissa	1
(b) Ajmer Sambhāg	1		
(c) Udaipur Sambhāg	5	9. Tamilnadu	2
(d) Jaipur Sambhāg	2	10. Karnataka	2
(e) Bikaner Sambhāg	6	11. Andhra Pradesh	1
2. Haryana	3	12. Maharashtra	3
3. Punjab	3	13. Gujarat	2
4. Delhi	2	14. Madhya Pradesh	2
5. Bihar	2	15. Uttar Pradesh	1
6. Bengal			
(a) excluding Calcutta	2	16. Nepal &	
(b) Calcutta	31	other foreign countries	2

(*Source:* JSTM 1987:11-12)

blies' of the Terāpanthī sect, according to the following territorial quotas:

The table shows the highly disproportionate number of reserved seats for the members from Calcutta, who still control the *All India Jain Śvetāmbar Terāpanthī Mahāsabhā.* It also shows that the territorial divisions of the modern Indian state have been incorporated not only within the 'religious' but also within the complementary 'secular' organisational structure of the Terāpanth. However, these territorial divisions are merely formal structures, and important only with regard to electoral matters and for the allocation of *vihār* regions. The limits of effective communities are, in fact, impossible to determine in terms of clearly demarcated geographical areas (Weber 1985:217). Jain communities, like others, are not substantive, territorially bound entities, but situationally shifting segmentary structures, perceived by the participants in terms of widening circles of personal allegiances and overlapping commitments to a whole variety of informal and formal institutions, which are often intentionally constructed for specific purposes. Although the Jain laity are organised and tend to live together in urban neighbourhoods of families of common regional, sectarian, caste, or class background, they do not form monolithic 'corporative entities' which 'press their interests upon their members', as Carrithers & Humphrey (1991a:6-7 *pace* p. 8-9) assume, but multiple overlapping networks of social, economic and religious relationships. As a rule these are focused on the male householders, who compete not only economically but also in terms of socio-religious status. In spite of the coordinating activity of the MS, and the efforts of Ācārya Tulsī to transform the entire fourfold *saṅgh* into a corporative religious organisation, actual community among the Terāpanthīs is always a situational, temporary affair, and manifests itself in the assemblies of the members of those dormant lay institutions, which are temporarily activated by visiting ascetics, whose translocal *vihār* serially links several local Terāpanth associations in a spatio-historical chain of revived community institutions.

Within the framework of the MS the segmentary dynamic manifests itself through the process of committee formation. The system of constituting (sub-)committees, which are given the powers to raise funds independently, is one of the crucial mechanisms for the articulation of the competition for control within the MS. Committees are temporary organisations which are formally established by the *Working Committee* for a specific socio-religious purpose, and therefore the equivalent of the *siṅghāṛas* of the ascetics and the branches of Mārvāṛī firms.[68] Examples are legal committees or committees for the promotion of educational or charitable causes (libraries, scholarships, meditation camps *(śibir)*, free medical help etc.). The paradigmatic case for committee formation occurs during the *vihār* of the ascetics, whose infrastructure is organised as communal effort by a whole series of state and local committees, and during *cāturmās*, when the ascetics are maximally dispersed among the lay communities. Their presence requires 'local action' for organising a whole variety of religious and social functions, and special-purpose committees are elected by local *sabhās*. Terāpanthīs tend to stress the organisational 'unity' of their lay associations in order to limit the 'artificial' competition between the local *sabhās*, which are substantively independent and not under direct control of the MS. Throughout the year the Terāpanthī institutions are formally united and form a single body of members. The rivalry between local *sabhās* surfaces only before the *maryādā mahotsav*, when temporary local committees are set up under the auspices of the MS to compete for the visits of ascetics during *cāturmās*.

The crucial point about committee selection is the role of the charitable trusts. The local *Sabhās* maintain religious trusts administered by elected committees. Various members compete for the control of these funds allocated to a specific sub-committee to finance a particular religious event, which they may treat as a form of credit. However, the main incentive is the prospect of gaining temporary access to the wider national pool of all community funds combined. This is possible, because it is the duty of MS "to assist, promote, aid or subscribe to the establishment and maintenance of any institution, association, fund, trust or charity for the benefit of Jains and the cause of Jainism" (JSTM 1987:6). Leaders of any local *sabhā* can approach the *Working Committee* and ask for help in organising specific religious events, once they have gained the blessings of the *ācārya* for their religious or educational project. The moral principle underlying this selection process is that all Terāpanth associations, families, individuals have to support the selected family or committee for the time being, materially and socially. Even a relatively poor committee or family can momentarily become the focus of the Terāpanth lay activities, and draw onto resources from the whole India-wide network of the Terāpanth Mārvāṛīs for the support of the *ācārya* and his projects. In this limited way, the lay community acts also as a socio-economic resource group. Similar principles concerning the pooling of resources also apply between Jain subsects, once agreement has been reached between their *ācāryas* to support certain religious events.

Community is thus functionally defined with reference to specific socio-religious projects, like organising provisions for the *vihār*. Despite the obvious tendencies towards corporatism and bureaucratisation, the *vihār* is a volatile and contested process which not only integrates but also systematically dissolves the unity of the elements which have been temporarily assembled. A *total* communal integration and reification of a Terāpanth community is systematically prevented because of the principally unpredictable and arbitrary way in which the *ācārya* distributes his favours. His actions continually break open a social space which vested interests, like the local *sabhās* or powerful families, try to control and monopolise. In this sense the autocratic religious regime of the Terāpanth *ācārya* is indeed the precise opposite of a dictatorial political organisation, as the Terāpanthīs maintain (Nathmal 1968:123). Although he has no immediate control over community property or the social life of his followers, he is not only the source of spiritual power, but also the effective organisational focus of the sect. The potential for community formation – and consequently the ability to mobilise the resources of the community – is literally embodied in his 'life-giving' personality, as the tangible manifestation of Jain values. His social strength derives not only from his religious position, but also from his functional contribution to the maintenance of a balance between the latent competitive tensions between independent business families which are nevertheless loosely interdependent and tied by marriage links and therefore interested to submit to a common social framework vis-à-vis competing social groups and the state.[69] There is a residue of the ancient role of the moral king in the institution of the *sabhāpati,* who mediates between the *dharmasaṅgh,* the laity, and the modern state. His relative weakness, compared to the *ācārya,* may be peculiar to the Terāpanthīs. However, it can be explained through the dynamic structure of competitive interdependence among the laity, which is both reinforced and regulated through the strategic choices of the *ācārya,* who, paradoxically, through his autocracy, prevents the emergence of monopoly structures among the members of his sect (whatever their powers outside his sphere of influence).

Non-Violence and Dispute Resolution

> "A non-violent being participating in community life does accept the restraint of a social system but his orientation is more towards freedom from systems" (Nathmal 1980:119).

For Jains it is essential to maintain a public image of non-violence and purity, because this determines their social status, both individually and as organised group.[70] In practice, however, the value of non-violence inevitably encompasses its contrary. It is the eternal dilemma of Jainism that "the lay estate cannot exist without activity and there can be no activity without the taking of life" (Williams 1983:121). In order to reconcile this contradiction Jains employ a multitude of strategies:[71] One strategy was Bhikṣu's attempt to differentiate clearly religious and social orientations on a doctrinal level. Another was chosen by the MS, who ruled that no information about internal conflicts should become public knowledge, on pain of social stigmatisation or excommunication: "No member shall indulge in any activity prejudicial or derogatory to the interest of Mahāsabhā or of the Jain Swetamber Terapanthi Sect or its tenets" (JSTM 1987:10). Similar regulations apply within the ascetic community (Tulsī & Mahāprajña 1981:93, Nathmal 1968:145). The existence of such rules is often hidden from the public gaze, although they were already elevated to religious principles in the medieval *śrāvakācāras:* "faults committed by co-religionists should, as far as lies within one's power, be concealed" (Williams 1983:44). This shows that the principle of self-regulation *(samiti)* of conflicts, the control of information about them, and the monitoring of corporate purity is one of the constitutive ideals of Jain organisations, in contrast to the state-controlled and therefore relatively open monastic communities in the countries of Theravāda Buddhism, where disputes are generally adjudicated by government-sponsored ecclesiastical courts.[72]

As we have seen, disputes among Jains often concern property. In one way or another all the major scandals within Jain communities revolve around community assets, and sometimes the struggle for the control of pilgrimage sites and religious trusts even degenerates into violence[73] or is fought out in the public courts.[74] In order to avoid such outbursts of public self-humiliation the Terāpanth prefer a centralised regime of dispute management not only for the ascetics but also for the laity. Osvāls settle their disputes traditionally through the mediation of their local *pañcāyats* under the leadership of an elder whose advice is widely respected. He is called the *kartā* (doer), and informally chosen among prominent local caste members. Many disputes concerning matters that are regulated by customary law are still settled this way; and even though the *kartā* has lost his legal powers, his judgements are enforceable through the District Magistrate Courts. A modern equivalent of this institution is the

Terāpanth MS board of arbitrators. Disputes among the members of the MS have to be mediated by an elected *Board of Arbitrators*. This is to prevent recourse to judicial courts regarding internal affairs of the members of the sect (JSTM 1987:35): "No member shall file any suit or take any legal action in any court of law with regard to any matter relating to or concerning the Mahāsabhā before referring such matter to the Board of Arbitrators" (p. 10).[75] The process of arbitration takes place in secret and involves only the parties directly concerned and the arbitrators, who keep records of the proceedings and who also have summary powers (p. 36). However, if conflicts between community members cannot be resolved, the *ācārya* himself is asked for advice and often settles the disputes. "Ācārya is he who pacifies the raging conflict between thou and me" (Nathmal 1968:134). Religious and social adjudication was one of the traditional duties of the *śrīpūjyas* and *bhaṭṭāraks,* who fulfilled royal functions among Mūrtipūjaks and Bīsapanthīs (Sangave 1980:101, 319). The Terāpanth *ācārya,* however, like the *kartā,* has no political and legal authority over the laity anymore, and the acceptance of his suggestions are based entirely on respect for his superior judgement and the implicit threat of excommunication (cf. Mahāprajña 1994:77).

From a Neo-Kantian perspective it may seem that the most important means for resolving disputes and promoting social cohesion is the outward orientation towards Jain ascetic values themselves. After all, religious forms of conflict management are visibly manifest at the time of the obligatory ethical rituals of repentance *(pratikramaṇ)* and of mutual forgiveness *(kṣamā yācan)* on the evening of *saṃvatsarī,* the most sacred holiday of the Jains. The localaity assemble for this occasion and beg each other for forgiveness for the injuries inflicted upon each other during the past year: *'micchā mi dukkaḍaṃ'*, 'may the evil of it be in vain'. Marcel Mauss argued that the reason for such communal rites of repentance must be sought in the desire to neutralize feelings of envy which may threaten social co-operation within segmentary societies with weak authority structures.[76] Weber (1985:201-7, 277ff.) similarly indicated not only the link between asceticism and individualism, but also how ascetic soteriological cults facilitate the constitution of exclusive and often elitist 'exemplary communities' which cut across family ties and political boundaries, and often intersect with economic interests. Certainly, among North Indian merchants "the devotion to a *guru* or a set of precepts which attracted a group of devotees from seve-ral different castes fulfilled the requirement that involuted social relations had to subsist with wider business contacts" (Bayly 1983:389). However, religious and economic interests are not isomorphous, and the resolution of social conflicts between group-members is, if at all, rarely achieved through the participation in communal rituals, which is strictly voluntary, and can be avoided if necessary.[77] Among the Terāpanth neither common discipleship nor membership in a religious (or caste) association implies the right to expect material help in times of distress. This is symbolically manifest in the absence of communal meals after *saṃvatsarī*.[78] As in most public 'therapeutic' rituals, the performative effect of the *kṣamāpaṇā* is largely confined to transitory experiences of communal feelings which often amounts to nothing more than a formal exercise of communal self-affirmation (cf. Kapferer 1983:82, 87, 104). Effectively, periodical celebrations of religious communality happily coexist with economic antagonism, social competition and friction in other contexts, even though the ideology of communality may help preventing openly violent conflicts between members.

Jain sects have to be situated in a wider historical context and analysed as integral social sub-systems, encompassing both ascetics and laity and their relationships to the rest of society, if one wants to understand the actual social functions of Jainism. To avoid reductionist interpretations a variation of both religious and social perspectives is required.[79] An example of the problems associated with a monistic approach is Marriott's (1976:123-8) analysis of the 'inborn *varṇa* strategies of castes' which focuses exclusively on religious transactions. The onesidedness of his depiction of 'the' Jains (indeed all *vaiśyas*) as 'minimal transactors' is revealed once both religious and religious non transactions are taken into consideration.[80] It then becomes clear that effectively Jain traders combine the role of minimal transactors in the religious sphere and of maximal transactors in the social sphere, as Bayly (1983:386-9) demonstrated for 19th cent. North Indian merchants, in general. In Marriott's (1976) own terms this type of behaviour corresponds not to the 'minimal strategy' but to the 'optimal strategy', which he unfortunately reserved for the *brāhmaṇs* alone:

> "The Brahmans earn, through refusal or controlled acceptance, the minimal transactor's gain of nonmixture and integrity for their

> own substance-code. They also earn, through their wide distributions, the maximal transactor's gain of universal domination. Their tactic thus may be considered as an asymmetrical compromise made up of the more rewarding parts of those two opposite symmetrical tactics" (p. 129).

Marriott presumes that the 'Western common sensical assumption' of a 'separability of action from actor, of code *(dharma)* from substance *(śarīra)*' is generally absent in India (p. 110).[81] I wish to argue, on the contrary, that the main social function of the dualist Jain doctrine was to contribute to a relative de-substantialisation of popular preconceptions. If this interpretation is correct, it seems that in orientating themselves towards a 'minimal transactional' Jain ascetic code of conduct, and thereby de-coupling themselves from the substantivistic underpinnings of the *brāhmaṇ* social system, Jain laity were enabled to become competitors of the *brāhmaṇ* priests in the social transactional sphere and also to engage legitimately in the maximisation of profit.[82]

However, my main point is different: A historical-comparative perspective shows that it is unrealistic to assume that religion generates social integration per se but not conflict. Yet, from a Neo-Kantian perspective one has no other option than to assume that disputes and conflicts are deviations from the Jain ideal of religious harmony, or that its values are contradictory.[83] I argue, differently, that the principal effect of using the 'ready-made' value-ideas of Jainism, i.e. schematised ritual procedures or decontextualised symbolic codes, is not the avoidance of conflict per se but its formalisation. If Jainism is seen from the perspective of the functioning of a code, it paradoxically contributes not to the repression but to the proliferation of chances of conflict.[84] Habermas (1981:92ff.) suggested that abstract interpretative schemes, like ethics and law, backed up by institutions, effectively function as protective mechanisms for society, or second order rituals, because they anticipate conflicts and thereby transform them into manageable affairs which do not threaten the collapse of the social order per se but are internal to the social fabric.[85] By framing expectations, classifying types of proper and improper conduct as well as religious rewards and penances, ethics and law provide not only sophisticated languages for conflict analysis but also procedures for negotiating antagonistic interests without having to resort to physical violence. Similarly, doctrinal Jainism can be analysed as a set of interpretative and procedural schemata that are constructed through a series of binary oppositions: the principal Jain categories can for instance be generated with the help of the asymmetrical code violence / non-violence combined with secondary codes like soul / body, prohibited / permitted, etc. Because of the specific semantic content of the fundamental opposition of non-violence / violence, which cuts across the *brāhmaṇic* distinction between pure / impure discussed by Dumont (1980:42-7, 191), and its predominant application to the actions of individual living beings,[86] Jainism is uniquely disposed to the minute classification of types of actions and corresponding states of being. With the help of the Jain conceptual system the individual devotee is enabled to anticipate, discriminate and to pre-judge types of events, and may acquire a sharpened awareness of the moral *(kārmic)* implications of alternative modes of conduct, and eventually develop a generalised social competence which can be of use in both religious and social pursuits. In other words, Jainism can be seen as a cultural-specific action-theory which motivates strategic reasoning, and by means of which conflicts become calculable:[87] In the words of the Ācārāṅgasūtra "He who knows the violence done for the sake of special objects, knows what is free from violence; he who knows what is free from violence, knows the violence done for special objects" (AS 1.3.1.4). Jainism can thus be interpreted as a protective divice, a historically adaptive 'immune-system', which compensates for the vulnerabilities that are structurally inbuilt in a given pattern of social differentiation.

One can add a historical dimension to this type of analysis in correlating the changes in the Jain doctrinal and ritual system with changes in the relative predominance of the principal forms of social differentiation, that is segmentary, hierarchical, and functional differentiation (economically constituted class-societies).[88] Studies of the social division of labour have shown that under conditions of functional differentiation, paradoxically, both individual independence and mutual dependency increase, and that processes of individuation and social integration generated through competitive interdependence are complementary both in a socio-economic and a moral sense. If indeed "what happens within one actor is by nature not much different from what happens between actors" (Dumont 1980:xxxvi)[89] then it follows, first, that a social ethos changes in accordance with the type of social differentiation, and, second, that moral education via generalised ethical rules and regulations will only be effective if these reflect some genuine sentiments in the world — and if their actual social functions remain latent. Because the complementarity of socialisation and individuation explains the prominent role of personality-structures for social integration, and therefore the social implications of asceticism, a general theory of asceticism may be predicated on the fact that, within society, a sense of freedom from external constraints can only be achieved by way of internalised modes of self-control, even though their precise form varies indirectly in accordance with social pre-conceptions and the type of constraints experienced.[90]

III. A Comparative Perspective

In this article I have focused almost exclusively on the intracommunal processes and structures of the Terāpanth, although I have indicated the way in which processes of internal differentiation reflect changes in the social environment. I have concentrated on the description of the catalytic function of the ritual circle as a key mechanism for the maintenance of a self-regulating social system whose contextual functions are predicated on the dynamic interdependence of conflicting interests, and are ultimately unplanned. Now I want to add a few final observations about the wider social implications.

The historical development of the Terāpanth, from an introverted and conservative ascetic splinter to a proselytising modern religious organisation with a self-proclaimed mass appeal, can only be understood before the background of the initial religious marginalisation of the ascetics and the relative poverty of the laity, who did not belong to the class of influential court officials, like other Bīsa Osvāl Jains, but to a group of highly specialised overland traders, who operated in the arid western districts of Rajasthan.[91] The diminishing importance of the caravan routes through the *Thār* desert and the scarcity of local resources generated increased competitive pressures which forced most of them into a semi-permanent diaspora, which in turn contributed to the strengthening of various forms of social and religious co-operation. Within the wider category of the Mārvāṛīs, religious sectarianism combined with local, caste and class differences and contributed to the emergence of socially self-conscious groups, which were able to defend common interests vis-à-vis the institutions of the modern state and the traditional caste society. The internally valued egalitarianism of their family-centred segmentary system, which principally only acknowledges differences of individual status, was thus combined with an outward emphasis on hierarchy and the claim to superior corporative status relative to the rest of society. Group status was not primarily determined by birthright but functionally, in terms of economic success and the collective behavioural purity. In this way classificatory principles gradually encompassed those of caste and genea-logy. It is yet another irony of history that the once liberating iconoclastic anti-ritualism of a subaltern elite, like the Terāpanth, who regard "possession in all its forms as the root of sin" (Mahāprājña 1987:16), has turned into a system of legitimation for a now economically dominant group, whose members combine politico-economic secularism with a form of religious individualism which does not demand expensive social charity (beyond the contributions to the communal *potlatch),* but propagates a cult of self-development and national character building via asceticism and moral education. The critique of charity thus allowed the Terāpanthī to sever their substantive ritual links with the rest of the society, while maintaining an universalist façade through the propagation of abstract ethical values for the private religion of the individual.[92] In the words of Nair (1969:40) "the outcome of Bhikṣu's crusade against traditional religion was freedom to a small section of society from the conventions of collective responsibility for promoting social welfare."

In response to such criticism and to the changed social circumstances *ācārya* Tulsī launched his reform programme. He made it clear from the beginning that the *Aṇuvrat* movement in particular was not intended as a religious programme but as a social initiative for the improvement of the moral standards of society.[93] In his analysis the fundamental problems of post-independence India are caused by the transformation of the feudal caste society into a modern class society: "Today's society is tortured by class consciousness. Both the haves and the haves-not seem intent upon denying each other's existence" (Mahāprajña 1994:187); "the accumulation of wealth in one pole gives rise to the attempts towards aggression and destruction from the other pole and neither philanthropy nor violent class struggle will resolve this conflict" (Tulsī in Guseva 1971:102). For him the only practical solution of this problem is a combination of (Jain) moral education and state socialism, involving three elements: (a) the reduction of the 'grabbing instincts' through attitudinal change and behavioural modification, (b) the reduction of the number of beggars through the limitation of charity ("the more is given to the poor, the more will be the number of the poor in this world" (p. 101),[94] and (c) the reduction of the social violence through the just redistribution of the means of production by the state, and the organisation of co-operative efforts of all members of society.[95] However, such lip-service to state-socialism combined with a critique of private charitability effectively deepens the rifts in society, because it releases the rich from their traditional social obligations, while notionally delegating all social responsibilities to an impoverised and increasingly corrupt state apparatus. Guseva comments:

> "In the opinion of Acharya Shri Tulsī, in a socialist state like India it is the government which must direct social life, realise just distribution of riches and adjust a just mutual relationship between various groups in the society. This programme is a reflection characteristic of many bourgeois scholars and a part of Indian bourgeoisie, looking upon state as a public organ above class" (p. 102).

More importantly, the Indian state is conceived as a public organ above religion. Indian rules were always forced to support several religions at the same time in order to transcend religious differences to a certain extent. The option for the control of the socially disruptive side-effects of capitalism through an all-encompassing religious nationalism is blocked in this situation. Not surprisingly, social elites have therefore traditionally chosen the alternative individual-centred option, that is the ideology of the integral personality, which remains indifferent and self-controlled even in situations of conflict and tension. Today the moral potency of Jain asceticism is used in multiple ways by spatially dispersed social elites in order to promote the ideological hegemony of non-violent pluralism within the context of the Indian state in competition with similar icons of religious nationalism,[96] like Gandhi, who was initially criticised by the Terāpanthīs for instrumentalising asceticism for political ends (Chopra 1945:35), or the BJP hero *Rām,* whose violent depiction in Hindu mythology is also rejected (Mahāprajña 1994:215-243). In contrast to many of its competitors the Terāpanth openly admits the political character of its new *Aṇuvrat* and *Vijñān* initiatives, which correspond to Gandhi's *Sarvodaya* (universal welfare) movement, but for one difference. Aṇuvrat propagates primarily self-control for 'the masses', instead of a charitable redistribution of wealth: "It does not call for people to gift away what they have in excess but simply exhorts them to leave it for use by society" (Mahāprajña 1987:16). Not surprisingly this recommendation appealed only to few members of the dominant strata, and is at present not a serious option for the country as a whole. In practice no distribution of riches has taken place, and as with Gandhi's *Sarvodaya* movement, nothing but the defence of particularistic interests and the vain attempt of disciplining the rich remained. Effectively the Terāpanth legitimised the regime of the Congress Party after Independence, but faces difficulties in the changed political climate of today, where Hindu-Nationalism seems the only ideological intrument left for the traditional elites to contain the growing tensions between the classes (cf. Van der Veer 1994:94-8).

The only real impact the Terāpanth reform programme could have is in the field of moral education, i.e. in the field of socialisation from above, but only if the attempts to move the Government to include *prekṣa dhyān* and *jivan vijñan* into the national curriculum take fruition. Critics perceive this endeavour primarily as a sectarian initiative, although the Terāpanthīs themselves "criticised the Acharya by declaring that he no longer insists on the people becoming Jainas" (L.P. Sharma 1991:287). In their stress on meditation and innerworldly asceticism these initiatives resemble Anagārika Dharmapāla's reforms in Śri Laṅkā, which have been characterised in the literature as a form of 'Buddhist modernism' or 'protestant Buddhism', in extension of the Weber thesis.[97] Weber (1978 II:203, 212, 217) himself broadly contrasted 'protestant' and 'hinduistic and buddhistic' religions, only excepting Jainism to a certain extent from his broad opposition of western 'innerworldly asceticism' and South Asian 'otherwordly asceticism.' His analysis of 'Jain protestantism' as a still ritualistic and therefore 'internally contradictory' intermediary doctrine, which associates Jainism as a whole with aristocratic and middle class consciousness, informs much of the recent sociological writing on the Jains. However, as critics like Elias (1978 II:312), Luhmann (1984) and Habermas (1981:421) have argued, Weber's individualist bias led him to exaggerate the role of rational thinking and of soteriological ideologies for processes of modernisation. Instead they stress the unplanned character of historical processes, and investigate the dynamics of social differentiation through competition, generating both greater independence and interdependence. The inbuilt structural tensions of such processes which enforce both the individualisation and the compartmentalization of roles, they argue, may compel the individual (and society) to develop far-sightedness, self-control and other features of rationality. The various forms of Jainism and other religions, I argue, are rationalisations of the social-psychological processes involved. In fact, Durkheim's[98] theory of 'competitive modernisation' and of the emergence of 'religions of the individual', can be modified, and it may be argued, that the transition from predominantly segmentary and hierarchical forms of social differentiation to modern forms of functional differentiation, is necessarily accompanied by different types of individualism: (1) the heroic individual of segmentary society, (2) the hierarchical individual of feudal society, and (3) the atomised individual of modern society. A strict separation between religion and society is only possible in the latter case, where it necessarily takes the form of anti-ritualistic subjectivism. Modern Jainism, this is the argument of this paper, reveals various intermediary solutions within the global trend towards modern cults of the individual.[99]

Dumont (1980) distinguished three general types of interaction between traditional and modern features in India: "rejection, mixture, in which traditional and modern features exist happily side by side, and combination, which unites them intimately in new forms of a hybrid nature and ambiguous orientation [here: communalism, religious totalitarianism]" (p. 229). Similar adaptive strate-gies can be found in any context of modernisation. The Terāpanth attempt to encompass modern socio-economic secularism within a traditional religious framework signifies in Dumont's terms a shift from a radical rejectionist strategy to a mixed strategy. In contrast to Bhikṣu's original 'ascetic Jainism' today's Terāpanthīs promote most of the features of reformism (focus on scripture, meditation, anti-ritualism, scientific outlook, modern lay-associations, innerworldly asceticism, etc.) but contain them within an orthodox ideological and institutional framework, with the *ācārya* as the social focus. This approach differs markedly both from the 'traditional Jainism' of the Mūrtipūjaks and Bispanthis and the 'lay Jainism' of the Digambar Terāpanthīs, because by strictly separating society and religion the Terāpanth still restricts the sphere of Jain group religion to a bare minimum.[100] Although from a 'traditional' Jain perspective it may still appear as an exclusivist ascetic movement, after Independence the Terāpanth was the first Jain tradition to symbolically incorporate the new structures of the modern Indian state, and to reject Jain communalism in favour of a Gandhiesque policy of religious tolerance; whereas the principal image-worshipping traditions, because of their different doctrinal and organisational structure, continued to combine sectarianism on a regional level with a lay dominated Jain communalism on a national level. In other words, from different starting-points both 'traditional' and 'protestant' movements drift towards a 'combined' strategy, although at present only the Digambar lay movements have the potential to develop egalitarian forms of religious communalism. The radically changed social circumstances after Independence thus turned traditional inclusivists into exclusivists, and exclusivists into inclusivists. Because of their great internal diversity the Sthānakvāsīs must be treated as a special case. Many Sthānakvāsī traditions are very orthodox even though their biggest sub-sect, the Śramaṇ Saṅgh, adopted a centralised organisation structure and modest reforms similar to the Terāpanth. Other Sthānakvāsī groups, like Amar Muni's Vīrāyatan, are engaged in social work, thus blurring the distinction between ascetics and laity. In one respect the Bīsapanth traditions resemble the Terāpanth more closely than any other Jain sect, because they too responded to adaptive pressures through organisational involution, that is by recognising two different types of ascetics. Yet the administrative focus of their sects are the

Traditional Jainism

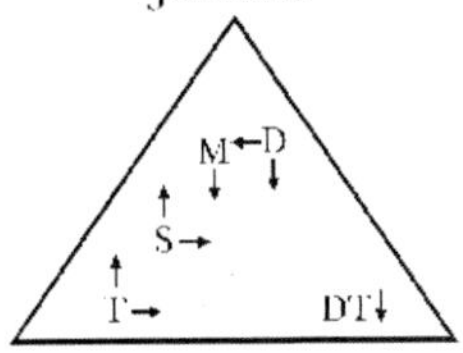

REJECTION — Ascetic Jainism — Lay Jainism — COMBINATION

bhaṭṭāraks and not the *ācāryas*. The relative strategic position of the main contemporary Jain sects can be summarized in diagrammatical form:[101]

MIXTURE

To conclude, the Terāpanthī reforms between 1760-1980 are

unique because they effectively replaced the traditional system of medieval Jainism, where ideally all spheres of life are formally encompassed by religion, with a mixed traditional and modern ideological system where 'certain spheres have their own values, special but, by definition absolute within their sphere' (p. 316).

References

AK = Jinprabhā, Sādhvi & Sādhvi Swarnrekha. *Amṛt Kalaś.* 2 Volumes. 7. Edition. Lāḍnūn: Ādarś Sāhity Saṅgh, 1990.

AS = *Ācārāṅga Sūtra.* Tr. H. Jacobi, *Sacred Books of the East* Vol. 22 (1884) 1-213.

Babb, Lawrence A. *Absent Lord: Ascetics and Kings in a Jain Ritual Culture.* Berkeley: University of California Press, 1996.

Balbir, Nalini. "Observations sur la secte jaina des Terāpanthī." *BEI* 1 (1983) 39-45.

----. "Recent Developments in a Jaina Tirtha: Hastinapur (U.P.) – A preliminary Report." In *The History of the Sacred Places in India as Reflected in Traditional Literature.* 177-91. Leiden: E.J. Brill, 1990.

Banks, Marcus. *Organising Jainism in India and England.* Oxford: Clarendon Press, 1992.

Bayly, C.A. *Rulers, Townsmen and Bazaars: North Indian Society in the Age of Expansion.* Cambridge: University Press, 1983.

Bechert, Heinz. "*Theravada Buddhist Saṅgha*: Some General Observations on Historical and Political Factors in its Development." *JAS* 29 III-IV (1970) 761-778.

BKS = *Bṛhat Kalpa Sūtra.* Tr. W. Schubring "The Kalpa-Sūtra. An Old Collection of Disciplinary Rules for Jaina Monks." *The Indian Antiquary* 39 (1910) 257-267.

Buddhamall, Muni. *Terāpanth kā itihās. Pratham khaṇḍ: Terāpanth ke pratham cār ācārya.* 4th Revised Edition. Calcutta: Jain Śvetāmbar Terāpanth Mahāsabhā Prakāśan, (1964) 1995.

Caillat, Colette. *Atonements in the Ancient Ritual of the Jaina Monks.* L.D. Series 49. Ahmedabad: L.D. Institute of Indology, 1975.

Carrithers, Michael. "Passions of Nation and Community in the Bahubali Affair." *Modern Asian Studies* 28 (1988) 281-310.

----. "Naked Ascetics in Southern Digambar Jainism." *Man* N.S. 24 (1989) 219-235.

Chopra, Chogmal. *A Short History of the Terāpanthī Sect of the Swetambar Jains and its Tenets.* 4th Edition. Calcutta: Sri Jain Swetamber Terāpanthī Sabhā, (1937) 1945.

Cort, John E. *Liberation and Wellbeing: A Study of the Mūrtipūjak Jains of North Gujarat.* Ph.D. dissertation, Harvard University, 1989.

----. "The Śvetāmbar Mūrtipūjak Jain Layman." *Journal of Indian Philosophy* 19 (1991a) 391-420.

----. "The Śvetāmbar Mūrtipūjak Jain Mendicant." *Man* (N.S.) 26 (1991b) 651-671.

----. *Defining Jainism: Reform in the Jain Tradition.* The 1994 Roop Lal Jain Lecture. University of Toronto: Center for South Asian Studies, 1995.

Dumont, Louis. *Homo Hierarchicus: The Caste System and its Implications.* Complete Revised English Edition. Chicago: The University of Chicago Press, 1980.

Elias, Norbert. *Über den Prozess der Zivilisation I-II.* Frankfurt am Main: Suhrkamp, (1939) 1978.

Flügel, Peter. *Askese und Devotion: Das rituelle System der Terāpanth Svetambara Jains.* Doctoral Dissertation, Johannes Gutenberg-Universität Mainz, 1994.

Gombrich, Richard & Gananath Obeyesekere. *Buddhism Transformed: Religious Change in Sri Lanka.* Princeton University Press, 1988.

Goonasekere, S.A. *Renunciation and Monasticism among the Jains of India.* Ph.D. thesis, University of California, 1986.

Guseva, N.R. *Jainism.* Bombay: Sindhu Publications, 1971.

Habermas, Jürgen. *Theorie des kommunikativen Handelns.* 2 Bände. Frankfurt am Main: Suhrkamp, 1980-1981.

Heesterman, Jan C. *The Inner Conflict of Tradition: Essays in Indian Ritual, Kingship and Society.* Chicago: The University of Chicago Press, 1985.

Holmstrom, Savitri. *Towards a Politics of Renunciation: Jain Women and Asceticism in Rajasthan.* M.A. thesis, University of Edinburgh, 1988.

Humphrey, Caroline & James Laidlaw. *The Archetypal Actions of Ritual: A Theory of Ritual Illustrated by the Jain Rite of Worship.* Oxford: Clarendon Press, 1994.

Jain, Ranu. "'Jain-Osvāl' of Calcutta as an 'Ethnic Group.' A Socio-historical Perspective." *Man in India* 67,4 (1987) 383-403.

Jaini, J.L. "Parricidal Desecration of Sri Kesaria Parsvanath." *The Jaina Gazette* XXIII,5 No. 263 (1927) 146-149.

Jaini, Padmanabh S. *The Jaina Path of Purification.* Berkeley: University of California Press, 1979.

----. "Is there a Popular Jainism?" In *The Assembly of Listeners.* Ed. M. Carrithers & C. Humphrey, 187-99. Cambridge: Cambridge University Press, 1991.

Johnson, W.J. *Harmless Souls. Karmic Bondage and Religious Change in Early Jainism with Special Reference to Umāsvāti and Kundakunda.* Delhi: Motilal Banarsidass, 1995.

JSTM = *Memorandum of Association & Articles of Association.* Calcutta: Jain Swetamber Terāpanthī Mahāsabhā, 1987.

Kapferer, Bruce. *A Celebration of Demons.* Bloomington: Indiana University Press, 1983.

Laidlaw, James. *The Religion of the Śvetāmbar Jain Merchants in Jaipur.* Ph.D thesis, Cambridge University, 1990.

----. *Riches and Renunciation: Religion, Economy, and Society among the Jains.* Oxford: Clarendon Press, 1995.

Luhmann, Niklas. *Funktion der Religion.* Frankfurt am Main: Suhrkamp, (1977) 1982.

----. *Soziale Systeme.* Frankfurt am Main: Suhrkamp, 1984.

Mahāprajña, Yuvācārya. *Steering the Wheel of Dharma (A Biography of Acharya Tulsī).* Ladnun, Jain Vishva Bharati, (1986) 1994.

----. *Ācārya Tulsī: A Peacemaker Par Excellence.* Rajsamṇḍ: Aṇuvrat Viśva Bhārati, 1987.

Mahias, M.C. *Délivrance et convivialité: Le système culinaire des Jaina.* Paris: Éditions de la Maison des Sciences de l'Homme, 1985.

Marriott, McKim. "Hindu Transactions: Diversity without Dualism." In *Transaction and Meaning: Directions in the Anthropology of Exchange and Symbolic Behavior.* Ed. B. Kapferer, 109-142. Philadelphia: Institute for the Study of Human Issues, 1976.

Mehta, M. *The Ahmedabad Cotton Textile Industry: Genesis and Growth.* Ahmedabad: New Order Book Company, 1982.

Nagaraj, Muni. *Glimpses of Terāpanth,* Calcutta: The Jain Swetamber Terāpanth Mahāsabhā, 1959.

Nair, V.G. *Jainism and Terehpanthism.* Bangalore: Shri Adinath Jain Svetambar Temple, 1969.

Navratanmal, Muni. *Śāsan Samudra* Vol. 1-18. Published by Uttamcand Sethia. Calcutta: Śrī Jain Svetāmbar Terāpanthī Mahāsabhā, 1981.

––––. *Terāpanth Pāvas-Pravās.* Lāḍnūn: Śrī Jain Śvetāmbar Terāpanthī Sabhā, 1991.

Nathmal, Muni [today Ācārya Mahāprajña]. *Acharya Bhikṣu. The Man and His Philosophy.* English Version of 'Bhikṣu Vicār Darśan.' Tr. N. Sahal. Delhi: Adarsh Sahitya Saṅgh Prakashan, 1968.

––––. *Shraman Mahavir.* Tr. D.C. Sharma. New Delhi: Today & Tomorrow's Printers and Publishers, 1980.

Oldfield, Kenneth. *Jainism Today: A Study of the Jain Community in a Rajasthani Village in 1982.* M.A. thesis, University of Lancaster, 1982.

Parry, J. "*The Gift,* The Indian Gift and the 'Indian Gift.'" *Man* (N.S.) 21 (1986) 453-473.

Parsons, Talcott & Edward A. Shils (eds.) *Towards a General Theory of Action.* New York: Free Press, 1951.

Renou, Louis & Marie-Simone Renou. "Une secte religieuse dans L'Inde contemporaine." *Études* t. 268, Janvier-Mars (1951) 343-351. Reprinted in L. Renou, *Choix d'Études Indiennes.* Réunies par Nalini Balbir et Georges-Jean Pinault. Paris: EFEO, 1997 (Réimpression n° 9), Vol. 2, 919-927.

Reynell, Josephine. *Honour, Nurture and Festivity: Aspects of Female Religiosity amongst Jain Women in Jaipur.* Ph.D. Dissertation, University of Cambridge, 1985.

Rudolph, Lloyd & Susanne Hoeber Rudolph. "Oligopolistic Competition among State Elites in Princely India." In *Elites. Ethnographic Approaches.* Ed. G.E. Marcus, 193-220. Albuquerque: University of New Mexico Press, 1983.

Sangave, Vilas. *Jaina Community.* 2nd ed. Bombay: Popular Prakashan, 1980.

Schubring, Walther. *The Doctrine of the Jainas.* Delhi: Motilal Banarsidass, 1978.

Schubring, Walther & Colette Caillat. *Drei Chedasūtras*. Alt- und Neuindische Studien 11. Hamburg: De Gruyter, 1966.

Shāntā, N. *La Voie Jaina: Histoire, Spiritualité, Vie des ascètes pèlerines de l'Inde*. Paris: OEIL, 1985.

Sharma, G.D. "The Mārvāṛīs: Economic Foundations of an Indian Capitalist Class." In *Business Communities in India*. Ed. by D. Tripathi, 9-25. Ahmedabad: Manohar, 1984.

Sharma, L.P. *Advent and Growth of the Terāpanth Jain Sect: A Comprehensive Historical Study*. Unpublished Ph.D. Dissertation, Jodhpur University, 1991.

Sheth, N.R. "Theoretical Framework for the Study of Indian Business Communities." In *Business Communities in India*. Ed. by D. Tripathi, 185-207. Ahmedabad: Manohar, 1984.

Singer, Milton. "The Indian Joint Family in Modern Industry." In *Structure and Change in Modern Indian Society*. Ed. M. Singer & B.S. Cohn, 423-452. Chicago: Aldine, 1968.

----. "Max Weber and the Modernization of India." In *Max Weber in Asian Studies*. Ed. A. Buss, 28-45. Leiden: E.J. Brill, 1985.

Singh, Lala Sukhbir et. al. "Resolution." In *Abstract of the Proceedings of the Council of his Honour the Lieutenant-Gobernor, United Provinces of Agra and Oudh, Assembled for the purpose of Making Laws and Regulations. 1913*, 518-32, Allahabad: Office of the Superintendent, Government Press, United Provinces, 1914.

Sukhalāl, Muni (Ed.). *Purūṣārtha kī Gathā*. Calcutta: Jain Śvetāmbar Terāpanthī Mahāsabhā Prakāśan, 1991.

Sumeramal, Muni (Ed.). *Jay Tithi Patrak*. Lāḍnūn: Jain Viśva Bhārati, 1992.

Tambiah, S.J. *The Buddhist Saints of the Forest and the Cult of Amulets*. Cambridge: Cambridge University Press, 1984.

Timberg, Thomas A. "A Note on the Arrival of Calcutta's Marwaris." *Bengal: Past and Present* 90 (1971) 75-84.

----. *The Marwaris: From Traders to Industrialists*. New Delhi: Vikas, 1978.

Todarmalji, Pandit Acharyakalp. *Moksha Marg Prakashak (The Illuminator of the Path of Liberation)*. Bombay: Shri Kund-Kund Kahan Digambar Jain Tirtha Suraksha Trust, Shri Todarmal Smarak Bhawan, 1992.

Tulsī, Ācārya. *Illumination of Jaina Tenets (Jaina Siddhānta Dipikā).* Tr. S. Mookerjee. Ladnun: Jain Vishva Bharati, 1985.

Tulsī, Ācārya & Yuvācārya Mahāprajña (eds.). *Victory of Discipline.* Jayācārya Series Vol. 1. Ladnun: Jain Vishva Bharati, 1981.

----. *Terāpanth: Maryādā Aur Vyavasthā (Jayācārya).* Ladnun: Jain Vishva Bharati, 1983.

UtS = *Uttarādhyayana Sūtra.* Tr. H. Jacobi, *Sacred Books of the East* Vol. 45 (1895) 1-232.

Van der Veer, Peter. *Religious Nationalism: Hindus and Muslims in India.* Berkeley: University of California, 1994.

Weber, Max. *Gesammelte Aufsätze zur Religionssoziologie II.* Tübingen: J.C.B. Mohr (Paul Siebeck), 1978.

----. *Wirtschaft und Gesellschaft.* Tübingen: J.C.B. Mohr (Paul Siebeck), 1985.

Williams, R. *Jaina Yoga.* London, 1963, reprint Delhi: Motilal Banarsidass, 1983.

Résumé

Le présent article montre comment une secte jaïne spécifique – les Śvetāmbara Terāpanthī – organisent l'interaction rituelle entre les ascètes et les laïcs sur une base suprarégionale, et comment elle s'agence de manière stratégique au sein de l'ensemble du contexte politique et religieux dans le sous-continent d'aujourd'hui. La doctrine et le rituel jaïns apparaissent comme un niveau intermédiaire, générateur d'expériences religieuses significatives et d'harmonie sociale; mais, en même temps, ils font office de moyens destinés à mobiliser et à légitimer des intérêts politiques particularistes.

La première partie décrit l'histoire et le fonctionnement interne de la communauté monastique *(dharmasaṅgh)* des Terāpanthī, ainsi que l'organisation religieuse de leurs pérégrinations annuelles *(vihār).*

La seconde partie souligne le rôle de la principale organisation laïque, la *Terāpanth Mahāsabhā,* pour le maintien du rituel de pérégrination et, indirectement, pour la prospéité de la communauté des laïcs *(samāj),* tandis que la troisième partie se termine par des observations comparatives sur les orientations de l'évolution des principales sectes jaïnes dans le contexte de la société indienne moderne.

Notes

1. The ethnographic present of this paper is the year 1991-1992, although fieldwork in India has been conducted in stages between 1988 and 1993. The leader of the Śvetāmbar Terāpanth during this period was Ācārya Tulsī (1914-1997). He renounced his position (which he held for 58 years) on health grounds in March 1994 at the *maryādā mahotsav* in Sardārśahar in favour of his successor Mahāprajña (1921-2010) but retained the title of *gaṇādhipati* (leader of the sect) until his death in Gaṅgāśahar June 23 1997. Without his generous support my research on the Terāpanth would not have been possible. Earlier drafts of this paper have been presented to the 12th European Conference on Modern South Asian Studies, Berlin, September 1992, Panel 7, and to the Seminar of the Department of Anthropology, University College, London, February 1994. I am indebted to the participants, and to Maṅgilal Baid, Bahram Mirzai, and Roger Smedley for their helpful comments. I wish to thank Bruce Kapferer in particular, who inspired me with his enthusiasm and critical insight.
2. E.g. Mauss, Marcel & Beuchat, H. "Essai sur les variations saisonnières des sociétés Eskimo." In *Sociologie et Anthropologie*. Paris: Presses Universitaires de France, (1904/1905) 1968; Turner, Victor W. "The Center out there: Pilgrim's Goal." *History of Religions* 12 (1973), 191-230; Eck, D.G., "India's *Tīrthas* 'Crossings' in Sacred Geography." *History of Religions* 20 (1981), 322-344; Gold, Ann G. *Fruitful Journeys: The Ways of Rajasthan Pilgrims*. Berkeley: University of California Press, 1990; Chojnacki, Ch., "Lieux saints jaina dans le *Vividhatīrthakalpa* (XIVe s.): représentation, fonction, panthéon." *BEI* 9 (1991), 37-59; Granoff, Phyllis. "Worship as Commemoration: Pilgrimage, Death and Dying in Medieval Jainism." *BEI* 10 (1992), 181-202.
3. E.g. Redfield, Robert & Milton Singer. "The Cultural Role of Cities." *Economic Development and Cultural Change* 3 (1954) 53-73; Cohn, Bernhard S. & McKim Marriott. "Networks and Centres in the Integration of Indian Civilization." *Journal of Social Research* 1,1 (1958), 1-10; Marriott, McKim. "Changing Channels of Cultural Transmission in Indian Civilization." *Journal of Social Research* 4 (1961), 1-13; Sopher, David E. "Pilgrim Circulation in Gujarat." *The Geographical Review* (1968) 392-425; Stein, Burton. "Circulation and the Historical Geography of Tamil Country." *Journal of Asian Studies* 37,1 (1977) 7-26; Burghart, Richard. "Regional Circles and the Central Overseer of the Vaishnavite Sects in the Kingdom of Nepal." In *Changing South Asia: Religion and Society*. Ed. K. Ballhatchet & D. Taylor, 165-179. Hong Kong: Asian Research Service, 1984; Van der Veer, Peter. "Structure and Anti-Structure in Hindu Pilgrimage to Ayodhya." In *Changing South Asia: Religion and Society*. Ed. K. Ballhatchet & D. Taylor, 59-67. Hong Kong: Asian Research Service, 1984.
4. No study has yet been devoted to the investigation of the complex

regional and supraregional networks of both laity and ascetics, nor of the translocal forms of ritual integration of Jain subsects as a whole. As a consequence, Jainism still appears as an elusive phenomenon. Recent empirical studies of the Jains have concentrated either on the description of local lay congregations (Oldfield 1982, Mahias 1985, Cort 1989, Laidlaw 1991, Carrithers 1988, 1991, Reynell 1991, Banks 1992, Babb 1996) or of Jain ascetics in general, without clearly distinguishing between individual organised Jain sub-sects, and neglecting the pivotal role of the renouncers in the ritual constitution of lay congregations (Shāntā 1985, Goonasekere 1986, Holmstrom 1988, Carrithers 1989, Cort 1991b).

5. According to H. Jacobi *"Jainism."* ERE (1914), 472 the *karma*-theory is an integral part of Jainism, and its constitutive soul-body dualism not an import from Brahmanism but based on "Being as given in common experience" (p. 468). E. Husserl *Cartesianische Meditationen.* Hamburg: Meiner, (1929) 1987 similarly argued that, by both living in the world and being conscious of the world, humans are constituted by a dual orientation towards the material world and towards the encompassing sphere of the transcendental consciousness. Because of this parallelism, phenomenological interpretations of intentionality could be more fruitful for the analysis of Jain ontological concepts than, for instance, approaches based on Weber's notion of subjective purpose or Peirce's objectivist concept of the indexical symbol. All-encompassing phenomenological approaches à la Dumont (1980:34) should, however, be complemented by a recognition of the tenuous co-existence of totalising ideologies and/or subjective experiences and the objective compartmentalisation of social life (cf. p. 316).

6. The word *saṅgh* refers to the ideal fourfold assembly *(caturvidh saṅgh)* of all Jains including the male and female laity *(śrāvaks, śrāvikās)*. In Buddhism the word *saṅgh* is reserved for the ascetic community alone, although the notion of the fourfold assembly *(cattāro parisā)* or community *(cātuddisa saṅgha)* is similarly used. Different from the terms *gaṇ, gacch, śākhā panth* or *dharmasaṅgh,* which refer exclusively to ascetic communities within particular sectarian traditions *(sampradāy, parampara),* the word *saṅgh* is also used to describe any category or group of Jains. Even lay organisations are called *saṅgh.*

7. Cf. Miller, David M. & Dorothy C. Wertz. *Hindu Monastic Life: The Monks and Monasteries of Bhubaneswar.* Montreal & London: Mc-Gill-Queen's University Press, 1976:130, Goonasekere 1986:201-4, Cort 1989:104, n. 20.

8. Loṅkā's rules are only known through Dharmasagara's 1572 polemic *Pravacanaparikṣā* (L.P. Sharma 1991:31-4). Similar rules were subsequently composed, for instance by Kaḍuā Śhāh (see Paul Dundas, "Jainism without monks?: The Case of Kaḍuā Śhāh." In *Approaches to Jainism: Philosophy, Logic, Ritual and Symbols.* Ed. O.

Qvarnström & M.K. Wagle, 181-195. University of Toronto: Center of South Asian Studies, forthcoming). On the scriptures of the Loṅkā Gacch and the Sthānakvāsīs (who additionally accepted the *Vyavahāra Sūtra)* see Jaini 1979:49 n. 12.

9. The Śvetāmbar Terāpanthīs should not be mixed up with the equally reformist, but older and temple-worshipping tradition of the Digambar Terāpanthīs which are the dominant tradition among the Digambar today. Their present organisation in Jaipur was apparently started by Pandit Amar Cand Badarya from Sanganer in 1626. Other sources quote the name Amar Siṅgh, although the Terāpanthīs were clearly influenced by the earlier Adhyātma (Vāraṇasīya) movement (1635+669) of Rājā Todarmal (-1589) and Banārsidās (1586-1644), which they later incorporated. When the name Terāpanth became current, the *bhattāraks* called their system Bisapanth "since the number 20 exceeds 13 by 7" (Nathmal 1968:7). Closely associated with the Terāpanthīs in Jaipur, Agra, and Varanasi are today the Digambar Totāpanthīs in Nagpur and the followers of Śrīmad Rājcandra (1867-1901) and Kānji Svāmi (1889-1980) in Gujarat. All of these institutionally independent movements are spiritually guided by competing *Pandits* who derive their inspiration from Kundakunda's mystical work *Samayasāra,* which denies the necessity of ritualised ascetic practice. On the monastic context of Kundakunda's original teaching, and his foreshadowing of the Śvetāmbar Terāpanthīs' doctrinal view of the futility of purely internalised forms of religion unaccompanied by external ascetic practice, see Johnson 1995:183 n. 132, 309-10.

10. Cf. Todarmal 1992:23. "He should not be of low caste" (p. 21).

11. Cf. Vijayaratnasūri, in Lath, M. *Half a Tale: A study in the interrelationship between autobiography and history.* The Ardhakathanaka. Translated, introduced and annotated by M. Lath. Jaipur: Rajasthan Prakrit Bharati Sansthan, 1981:219-22.

12. Bhikṣu criticised the Sthānakvāsīs in his *Ācār Rī Caupāī* (reproduced in Buddhamall 1995:22-5) which has been summarised by Nathmal (1968:5): "1. Monks of today stay in the houses built for them. 2. They make people purchase books, papers and habitation. 3. They are absorbed in vilifying others. 4. They make householders promise that they would be initiated by them alone and not by anyone else. 5. They purchase disciples. 6. They do not transcribe books. 7. They send messages with householders. 8. They keep more cloth than prescribed or permitted. 9. They take delicious diet in violation of the rules. 10. They go to public feasts for alms. 11. They are eager to have disciples – both male and female. They are concerned not with the life of a monk but only with the continuance of their sect. 12. They try by hook or by crook to prevent people from going to other monks. They sow the seeds of friction in their families. 13. Today asceticism is on the

decline. What is prospering is simulation." The pattern of this critique is conventional. It follows closely the example of Haribhadra's condemnation of the *caityavāsins* in the 6th century. The name Terāpanth combines *terah* (thirteen) and *terā"* (your) and either means the 'path of the thirteen' (at one stage it comprised only 13 *sādhus)* or 'your path' (Buddhamall 1995:69-76). It also refers to the presumed thirteen basic rules of Mahāvīr (5 *mahāvrats,* 5 *samitis,* 3 *guptis)* (cf. Nathmal 1980:148-9).

13. For example by the Sthānakvāsī Ścamaṇ Saṅgh, whose centralised organisation was introduced in 1952 in Sādari/Rajasthan by an assembly *(sammelan)* of 32 *ācāryas* who chose *ācārya* Ātmārām as their leader (cf. Sangave 1980:377, 1991).

14. Cf. Williams (1983:xix), Carrithers (1991:266-7285), Cort (1989:449-70), Johnson (1995:310), Laidlaw (1995:354), and Babb (1996:98-101) on the ambiguous use of the terms *guṇa, samāj, lābh, maṅgal, udhar, sakh* etc. among image-worshipping Jains. Interestingly, only few of these concepts, like *pūja* or *kriyā,* were incorporated into the *śrāvakācāra* systems of collective lay-rituals. Jains are careful to distinguish semantic ambiguity from philosophical perspectivism *(anekāntavād, syādvād, nikṣepa),* which is seen as an analytic instrument for disambiguation: "Whereas in the fallacy of *chhal* (fraud), one word has two meanings, no word in this argument (of *syādvād*) is of such nature.... To declare the existence of an object from one point of view and to declare its non-existence from another point of view, is not to indulge in *a pun,* and thus to be guilty of this fallacy" (L. Kannoomal. *The Saptabhangi Naya or The Pluralist Aspects of the Jaina Dialectics.* Agra: Atmanand Jain Pustak Pracharak Maṇḍal, 1917, p. 16. cf. C.R. Jain. *Faith, Knowledge and Conduct.* Allahabad: The Indian Press, 1929, p. 8, 16-18). See my paper "Power and Insight in Jain Discourse." In *Doctrines and Dialogues.* Ed. A. Henn & H. v. Skyhawk, Delhi: Manohar (forthcoming).

15. Cf. Tulsī (1985:68-71) on the Terāpanth notion of pure merit *(śubhkarma puṇya)* as a side-effect of penance. On the ambiguous case of the two-fold causal function of *puṇya*-generating penance, i.e. the destruction as well as bondage of *karma,* see the concept of *kṣayopaśama* (destruction-cum-subsidence of *karmas)* (p. 44, 63, 70, 80).

16. Cf. Dumont 1980:275.

17. The present Terāpanth *ācārya* Mahāprajña quotes UtS 5.19-20 in order to demonstrate that Mahāvīr himself conceded the possibility of householders reaching enlightenment if they are both knowledgeable and restrained. For him, preparation for enlightenment within a monastic setting is entirely conventional (Nathmal 1980:157-163). Cf. Johnson (1995:306-7) on the difference between the personal (intentionalist) and the social (rule-oriented) view of renunciation, and his theory of the strategic role of the Jain

doctrine of the manifold aspects *(anekāntavād* and *syādvād)* for holding together these contradictory perspectives (p. 232), evading confrontation with other schools (p. 253), and bridging the gap between ascetics and laity (p. 79-90). With regard to Jain lay practices, Laidlaw (1995) similarly argues that "the conflicts between these different ways of being Jain are resolved, in so far as they are, in a wider domain of sociality" (p. 20-1). For a different interpretation see K.W. Folkert, *Scripture and Community:* Collected Essays on the Jains. Ed. J.E. Cort. Atlanta : Scholars Press, 1993: 215-27.

18. On cosmic kingship and the hybrid nature of 'traditional' popular religion cf. Dumont (1980:229, 300-34), Heesterman (1985), Tambiah (1984), Kapferer (1983), and Gombrich & Obeyesekere (1988:15-29). Cort (1989) has recently observed that, although "kingly notions of power have almost totally disappeared from the contemporary Jain ideological universe," "the two dominant realms of value within the Jain context are *mokṣa-mārga* and well-being" (p. 15). He notices that there is a "different situation among the Jains of Marwar," who still "tend to imitate Rajputs in many social [sic!] customs" (p. 80, n. 80). But strictly speaking, there can be nothing 'Jain' about ideologies of political or economical power *(artha),* whatever their historical efficacy. Precisely this is one of the main agendas of present day revivalism, which, as we have seen, is particularly strong in Marwar. Terāpanthīs clearly do not recognise a separate realm of worldly 'Jain' values. Instead they are trying to implant ascetic principles of conduct into social life. Accordingly, the 21 qualities of the ideal Terāpanth layman *(śrāvak guṇ),* which were codified only recently by Tulsī (AK 11:317), differ from Hemacandra's list of 35 qualities, which is popular among the Mūrtipūjaks (YS I.47-56, Williams 1983:260-269, Cort 1991a), by being unequivocally otherworldly. Moreover, popular social functions in connection with the completion of fasts etc. were ruled out by Tulsī again in 1960 (Mahāprajña 1987:34). The fact that Terāpanthīs confer royal attributes exclusively to the *ācārya 'mahārāj,* is not unusual for Jain ascetics (cf. Carrithers 1988:830-1, 1989:228-9). Already the medieval Jain commentaries emphasised the equivalence of the administrative virtues demanded from both religious superiors and kings (Caillat 1975:55). According to Jainism, the ideal king is a renouncer, not a worldly ruler, and moral authority the ultimate form of power. Indeed, the predominant foci of 'group religion' – even among most modern Śvetāmbar and Bīsapanthī Jain sects – are today not quasi sacred kings, like the medieval *bhaṭṭāraks* and *śrīpūjyas* or today's *saṅghpatis,* but the *ācāryas* themselves, who fulfil certain 'royal' functions with respect to religion amongst their followers, while leaving the surrounding society standing as it is.

19. For a critique of the uneasy coexistence of renunciatory ritual behaviour and injurious everyday behaviour among 'Dhoondhakar' laity see Todarmal 1992:225-226.

20. Cf. Dumont (1980:274-5). In his eagerness to demonstrate the futility

of intervening into worldly affairs, both for one's own and other's spiritual progress, Bhikṣu gave many controversial examples why ascetics should not help saving lifes, even if they could (Tulsī 1985:162-76, Nair 1969:App.1). From his purely monastic and liberation-oriented point of view *'ahiṃsa* lies solely in the spirit of non-cooperation', a perspective which renders the world empty of religious meaning in which charity is not only irreligious but also tends to perpetrate social inequality: "The undue emphasis on charity indirectly accepts the practice of exploitation. Terāpanth teaches the principle of non-exploitation and non-accumulation" (Nagaraj 1959:12).

21. J. Derrida *Given Time: I. Counterfeit Money*. Chicago: The University of Chicago Press, 1991:76 makes this point and shows in turn how the general paradoxes of 'donating consciousness' may be better understood in terms of Heidegger's theory of *Dasein* as the constitutive ontological ground for subject-object distinctions *per se,* which are presupposed by 'the figure of the circle of exchange' (p. 24). I cannot enter into the epistemology/ontology-debate here.

22. Cf. Kundakunda (Johnson 1995:230) and Todarmal (1992:16-7). Both Laidlaw and Johnson associate Jain doctrines with a limited set of social functions (social mobility, status maintenance, social integration, community survival). However, it seems that Jainism, like most religious doctrines, is compatible with a wide range of social contexts and not an ideological expression of limited class interests per se.

23. Numerous codes of conduct were set up both for Terāpanthīs and the general population alike. The *aṇuvrat* movement basically tried to overcome the unpopularity of the small vows among the Terāpanth laity in particular, in order to raise its standards of morality (AK 1:27). There is a great deal of overlap between the various initiatives. The principal directives of Jain life-style *(jīvan vijñān),* for instance, are: "1. Equality: Not to behave hostile to someone on the basis of caste, not to consider anybody untouchable. 2. Peacefulness: To practice peaceful cohabitation. To avoid family quarrels. Not to be merciless in matters of dowry etc. 3. Labour: To develop self-sufficiency. Not to exploit labour. 4. Non-violence: To develop fearlessness. Not to commit suicide, murder, and abortion. To avoid unnecessary violence. To avoid substances produced through acts of violence and cruelty. 5. Moderation of desire: Not to acquire wealth by means of mixing food products, smuggling, trade in eggs and meat etc. To practice acquisition together with renunciation *(visarjan)* of ownership. To limit the enjoyment of an object. 6. Pure food and release from addiction: To keep to the pure manner of eating and drinking — To give up eggs, fish, meat etc. To live a life free of addiction — To avoid alcohol, intoxicating substances, gambling etc. 7. *Anekant:* Not to be contumacious and, as far as possible, attempting to settle controversial matters harmoniously. 8. Worship of resemblance: Studying the

scriptures, equanimity etc. To do the prescribed *jap* of 5 *Navkār Mantras* three times every day — at dawn after getting up, before meals, and before sleeping. 9. Affection for the co-religionist: To behave fraternally to one of the same faith or religion (one who faithfully repeats the *Navkār Mantr)"* (tr. Tulsī, in: Māṇakcand Paṭāvarī (ed.). *Upāsanā.* Mitra Pariṣad Ātma Sādhanā Kendra: Calcutta, 1991:27-8).

24. AK 11:153-5. According to Mahāprajña "there is a difference between donation and renunciation" (1994:109). Theoretically "acquisition can be seen as (1) its psychological counterpart (non-discrimination) and (2) the overt cause — (the object)" (Nathmal 1980:186). One of the four possible combinations of these two aspects being present or absent is the *visarjan dān,* which should be based on the ideal "to possess only the bare necessities" (p. 187). Surrendering possessions merely in order to gain self-awareness and social control is a form of acquisition (p. 188). *Visarjan* thus acts as an ambiguous intermediary category between 'worldly transactions' and the three 'religious gifts' of fearlessness *(abhay),* knowledge *(jñān),* and self-castigation *(saṃyati)* — not unlike the Khartar Gacch practices described by Laidlaw (1995:294-301) and Babb (1996:190). The only difference is that, even if the intention is religious, materially mone-tary donations are still considered social or socio-religious. *Visarjan* is thus the result of an extension of the cognitive principle *(śubh upayoga)* underlying the restrained gift *(samyati)* to money, which, in contrast to food, cannot be handled by ascetics.

25. Ācārya Tulsī has been accused by the renegade *muni* Candanmal, whose orthodox Nav Terāpanth movement split off in 1981 after the introduction of the *samaṇ śreṇi,* of being too much involved in secular politics and in the administration of charitable trusts (cf. Muni Candanmal. *Ādhunik praśnoṃ ke sandarbh meṃ.* Calcutta: Viśva Cetanā, 1979 [published anonymously]; id. *Ācārya Sri Tulsī ko bhejā gayā Muni Śrī Candanmalji kā mukti patra.* Jaipur: Milāp Bhavan, 29.10.1981; id. *Kyā āp jānanā cāheṅge?* Ratangaṛh, Rajaldesar, Parhihara: Jain Saṅgam, May 1985; *Dān dayā: ek viśleṣaṇ.* Bikāner: Akhil Bhāratiya Jain Saṅgam, N.N.). Tulsī, in turn, points at the fact that the Nav Terāpanthīs themselves (1993 only Candanmal and nine *sādhvīs* remained, most male ascetics started their own initiatives) have given up wandering and begun setting up social institutions like the Arham Āśram in Gaṅgāpur (cf. Muni Candanmal. *Arham Āśram.* Dronañcal, Gopalpura (Ḍūṅgar): Arham Āśram, 29.1.1990). Sthānakvāsīs applaude Tulsī's turn towards "social service" and humanitarian deeds as a major improvement upon Bhikṣu's 'misguided' doctrines (Muni Rājyaś, in Nair 1969:viii,xxxi). However, other Terāpanth *sādhus* left monkhood altogether, because for them Tulsī's U-turn was not radical enough and because they disliked his 'authoritarian' style of leadership (S. Kumar. *No Destination.* Bideford: Green Books, (1978) 1992, 35-6). The two forms of internal protest are characteristic for orthodox

asceticism and lay Jainism respectively. See Mahāprajña's (1994:204-215) description of recent internal conflicts.

26. The *sādhvīs* initially operated relatively independent. The central position of the chief female ascetic *(sādhvī pramukhā),* who is also appointed by the *ācārya,* has only evolved under *ācārya* Jītmal between 1853-1869 (Buddhamall 1995:403-6). Similar organisational rules are known from other Rajasthani sects, like the Vaiṣṇav Rāmasanehī sect of Rāmcaraṇ, a friend of Bhikṣu (p. 46-7). More recent *gacch* constitutions are mentioned by Sangave 1980:377-8. An important Jain rule concerns the irreversibility of renunciation, and the social stigmatisation of excommunicated ascetics. See Bechert (1970:768f.) on the ('uncanonical' nature of pupillary succession rules in Theravāda Buddhism.
27. Jain *ācāryas* have always fulfilled administrative functions with regard to the ascetic order. In the past *yatis* and *bhaṭṭārakas* exercised also a form of theocratic control over the laity (Sangave 1980:93-101, 317-22, L.P. Sharma 1991:131, 212). However, the Terāpanth *ācārya* has 'swallowed the institution of the *yati'* (Cort 1991b:667) only to the extent that he controls his laity. The Jain situation was always different from the overall pattern in Theravāda Buddhism, where – as a rule – the king (or the government) determines the *saṅgharāj* and manages monastic disputes.
28. Cf. Weber (1985:297) on the sociology of the religious emancipation of women.
29. The introduction of the *samaṇ* category in 1980 is another notable innovation of the Terāpanth. *Samaṇs* can be compared to *yatis* and *bhaṭṭāraks.* They are initiated ascetics whose vows have been relaxed to allow them the use of modern means of transport and communication — but not to own property. They are utilised for overcoming the communication problems associated with the geographical expansion of the *vihār kṣetr* under Tulsī. One can be a *samaṇ or samaṇī* either temporary *(sāvadhik)* or lifelong *(yāvatjīvan).* A similar ambiguity underlies the categories of *upāsak* and *mumukṣu* — which are comparable to the Digambar *brahmacārin, ailak* and *kṣullak* — which either signify lay practitioners of the *pratimās* (doctrinal stages of lay religiosity) in general *(śrāvak upāsak* or *mumukṣu)* or members of two new categories of lay novices that were introduced by Tulsī. The possibility to become a temporary ascetic is new in Jainism and contributes to a further integration of the laity. At least among Digambars and Śvetāmbar Terāpanthīs, *pratimas* are not 'fossilized relics' as claimed by Cort 1991a:396.
30. A capacity already given to the ascetic families *(parivār)* – the equivalent of the *siṅghāṛs* – among the image-worshipping Jain ascetics (cf. Shāntā 1985, Carrithers 1989:233, n. 4, Cort 1989:154, n. 7). There are 7-8 subunits within the Terāpanth *raj,* which correspond to the *siṅghāṛs*

outside: 5 groups of *sādhus,* called *sājh* (partners), and 2-3 groups of *sādhvīs* under the rule *(niśrā)* of the *sādhvī pramukhā,* called *cittasamādhi* (lit. calm mind), because their members support each other by right. On the history of the *sājh* see Buddhamall 1995:392.

31. Double lines indicate key initiatory stages. The *niyojak* and *sanyojak* and their female equivalents are the leaders of all the *samaṇs* and all the *mumukṣus* and *upāsaks* respectively, but the *yojaks* lead only one group of *mumukṣu* novices. They can be compared to the *agraṇīs* among the *sādhus* and *sādhvīs.*

32. Vows *(vrats)* are accepted either by real or mental signature among the Terāpanth. The thirteen rules of the *lekh patr* are: "1. I shall not disobey you. 2. I shall follow your commands in every activity I undertake to do. 3. I shall always proceed on ascetic ramblings, rainy retreat etc. as ordered by you. 4. I shall have no disciples of my own. 5. I shall never indulge in forming factions. 6. I shall not meddle with your affairs. 7. I shall not use undesirable language in the least against you or any of the monks and nuns. 8. If any fault is found or comes to my notice in any monk or nun, wanting in conduct, I shall apprise him or the Ācārya-Śrī rather than propagating it elsewhere. 9. In any controversial dispute pertaining to principles, rules and regulations or traditions, I shall abide by your verdict with all reverence. 10. I shall have no connection whatsoever with anybody either excommunicated or resigned from the order. 11. I shall claim no ownership over the books, manuscripts and documents of the order. 12. I shall not become a candidate for any post. 13. I shall unhesitatingly abide by the orders of your successor" (tr. Tulsī & Mahāprajña 1983:480).

33. Cf. Buddhamall 1995:401-17, Renou & Renou 1951, Nagaraj 1959:4-6, Nathmal 1968:147-9, L.P. Sharma 1991:169-70. Terāpanthī scriptures mention three sect-specific festivals introduced by Jītmal: Jayācārya's succession-day *(paṭṭotsav),* Bhikṣu's last day *(caramotsav),* and the MM. The succession and *nirvāṇa* days of all *ācāryas* are holidays today. Historically the separate veneration of the organisational rules in addition to the succession-days developed through the generalisation and thereby depersonalisation of the *paṭṭotsav* celebrations. The MM, it is said, represents the *paṭṭotsavs* of all Terāpanth *ācāryas.* Originally it was celebrated together with the Jayācārya paṭṭosav *(māghśuklā pūrnimā)* which later was split into two different festivals (Buddhamall 1995:408-17, AK 1:43). Ācārya Tulsī introduced additionally the separation-day *(abhiniṣkramaṇa)* and founding-day celebrations *(Terāpanth sthāpanā divas).*

34. Bīsapanth and Mūrtipūjak subsects do not rotate the ascetics of their subgroups. Shāntā (1985:330-1), Cort (1989:105,n.21), Carrithers (1989:229) and Banks (1992:29) report a similar 'scriptedness' for their *vihār,* but do not mention any particular sub-sect organisation.

35. Cf. Buddhamall (1995:71-2). Exceptions are the *sevā kendras* (service centres) for elderly ascetics in Rajasthan, and the *sabhābhavans* (assembly houses) of local Terāpanthī lay communities, which are sometimes used by visiting ascetics in big cities. In Rajasthan the ascetics use the mostly empty ancestral houses of their followers.

36. In parts of Rajasthan the word *cokhlā* is still used to signify regional marriage circles, i.e. "an unit of caste (sub-caste) spread over a number of contiguous villages, binding the members of the caste to certain codes and regulations considered to be falling within the traditional jurisdiction of the caste (sub-caste) organization in that area, and subjecting the members to some effective controls through collective action" (Brij Raj Chauhan. *A Rajasthan Village.* New Delhi: Associated Publishing House, 1967:119).

37. That is vows given. Practices of self-sacrifice *(tyāg)* are seen to generate respect *(vandanā)* and to attract support *(dān)*.

38. The present rules of the Terāpanth ask *sādhus* not to stay more than one month in one village *(sādhvīs:* two months), not to carry more than 69 hands *(hāth)* of cloth (which should not be accepted during *cāturmās)*, to perform 30 days of fast each year, to avoid medical treatment etc. If an ascetic cannot comply with these basic rules, he/she has to atone for each mistake at the end of the *vihār.* The ascetic rules of conduct underwent numerous changes during the centuries, and no present Jain sect can legitimately claim to be orthodox anymore (cf. Nair 1969:50). Tulsī's main innovations are described in Mahāprajña 1994:170-1. The paradigmatic *yātrā vivaraṇ* is Sādhvīpramukhā Kanakaprabhā's account of Tulsī's religious conquest of southern India 1967-1971 *(Ācārya Tulsī: Dakṣin Ke Añcal Meṃ.* Chūrū: Ādarś Sāhity Saṅgh, 1977: 885-990).

39. The monastic organisation has been described by ācārya Mahāprajña himself as a feudal "mixture of despotism and democracy," because it combines the ideal principle of segmentation with an element of functional differentiation and centralised bureaucratic rule (Nathmal 1968:123, Balbir 1983:43). Democracy, because rules are not imposed, but are freely accepted; despotism, because one of the main functions of the *ācārya* is the 'royal' privilege to settle disputes and to impose sanctions on transgressors of monastic rules.

40. Cf. Singer's (1968:438ff., 1985:35) rather negative notion of 'adaptive' strategies.

41. A typical 'church' strategy to account for the *hiatus* between dogma and practice which Luhmann (1982:305-7) contrasts with the three strategies of popular religion: 1. unreflective orthodoxy, 2. interruption of interdependence, 3. reflective doubt. A version of the second strategy, where 'belief is not believed as a system but as it

were topological: point for point' (p. 307), has recently been described by Humphrey & Laidlaw (1994:123-4).

42. See Parsons' argument that the increasing external differentiation of a sub-system has to be compensated both by a higher level of internal differentiation and the generalisation of its principle of differentiation; and Goonasekere's (1986:39) and Cort's (1991b) observation that within the 'Śvetāmbar mendicant orders "one finds a replication of many elements of the social order" (p. 652) — and *vice versa* (Banks 1992:122-3). The Terāpanth case of an ascetic order that combines both the principles of segmentary differentiation and bureaucratic organisation shows the non-generalisability of the thesis of Caillat (1975:27), Reynell (1985:1), Goonasekere (1986:39), Cort (1991b:661-2) and Babb (1996:54), that Jain ascetic groups are modelled on the organisational principles of kinship and caste.

43. In practice the distinction between personal and social aspects of Jain practices proposed by Johnson (1995:307) and Laidlaw (1995) etc. dissolves. Although 'canonical' rituals nominally address the individual, both types of rites are obligatory and are performed collectively under supervision, and the details of universal 'Jain' rites differ from sect to sect. Even voluntary religious practices *(tap, dhyān* etc.) have to be permitted by the group leader and are highly ritualised exercises among Jains and Buddhists alike (cf. Tambiah 1984:324).

44. Dumont's (1980: 229, 315) view that social change in contemporary India should not be understood as a mere colonial imposition but either as a 'mixture' or a 'combination' of the old and the new (p. 229, 315) has been echoed even by his critics (cf. van der Veer 1994:76).

45. The details of this general trend vary. They include devotional forms of worship *(bhakti)* of personal guardian deities *(iṣṭa devatā),* spirit possession *(bhūt-pret),* socialist or Gandhiist movements, or religious totalitarianism (cf. Dumont 1980:220-234, Bechert 1970, Gombrich & Obeyesekere 1988, van der Veer 1994).

46. Cf. Sangave 1980 on the failures of the latter. Interestingly, both forms of Jain 'communalism' – traditional-hierarchical and modern-segregational – are associated with image-worshipping sects.

47. Cf. Mehta 1982:100-4, Nair 1969:148, Sangave 1980:313, 321, 329, 350-1.

48. "1. I dedicate myself to the *maryādā* of Ācārya Bhikṣu, the disciples of the Terāpanth *dharn,* and the head of the order. 2. I shall perpetually remain vigilant regarding the indivisibility of the order. 3. I shall not give refuge to anyone who has been excommunicated by the order. 4. I shall not concur with any attitudes which are not in concord with the orders of the *ācārya*. 5. If I find any faults in any *sādhu* or *sādhvī* of the order, I will inform them directly or the *ācārya*. I shall not publicise it. 6. I shall maintain the purity of my food and drink. 7. I shall devote

every day one *sāmāyik* [48 minutes] or at least twenty minutes to religious observances" (tr. AK 1991 I:376). Although the ascetics propagate this, born Terāpanthīs rarely accept the *samyaktva dīkṣā* or the *aṇuvrats* because these are very general and demand a lifelong commitment. More popular are the ten types of more specific ritualistic vows *(das pratyākhyān)* which are principally taken as part of the sixth *āvaśyak* (obligatory rite), either for a limited period or lifelong *(ĀvS* 6.1-10 in AK I:29, cf. Cort 1989:260, Laidlaw 1995:174). The *Aṇuvrat* movement has only gained 40.000 adherents in nearly 50 years and is seen by many Terāpanthīs more as a media show and an unnecessary formalism. The *śrāvak niṣṭh patra* has been introduced in 1982 by Tulsī on demand of the former education minister of Rajasthan, Candanma Baid, who considered it a good idea to have sect-specific *maryādās* for the laity as well. It remains to be seen how effective this attempt of expanding monastic organisational rules to the laity will be.

49. This rule goes back to Loṅkā. Similarly, Terāpanth accepted "only those with whom they can eat together" (Siṅgh, Munshi H. *The Castes of Marwar.* Being a Census Report of 1891. Jodhpur: Books Treasure, 1991:110). Historically, it is rules like these and the political interests behind them, which are primarily responsible for the present close link between Jainism and commerce, in addition to the quasi 'protestant ethos' embodied in the Śvetāmbar *Śrāvakācāra* literature itself (cf. Weber 1978:207, Williams 1983:xxii).

50. The Gujarati Osvāls migrated earlier, mainly during the period of the Chalukya rule (974-1238 A.D.), from Rajasthan to Gujarat. Today they speak Gujarati and are predominately followers of the local Mūrtipūjak ascetics. They do not intermarry or interdine with Rajasthani Osvāls, which they consider as a lower status group (because they 'still eat onions'). Rajasthani Osvāls are internally divided in up to four status classes *(Heta, Pañca, Dasa, Bīsa)*. The Bīsa Osvāls (Mv. *Baṛā Sājan)* are considered status-higher than the Dasa Osvāls (Mv. *Choṭā Sājan)*. Cf. Babb (1996:137-73) on Osvāl origin myths, and Sopher (1968:424) on the lasting influence of the Chalukya empire on current patterns of Mūrtipūjak pilgrimage circulation.

8

The Codes of Conduct of the Terāpanth Samaṇ Order[1]

ABSTRACT The article investigates the relationship between canonical rules *(dharma)* and customary rules *(maryādā)* in contemporary Jain mendicant life. It focuses on an analysis of the Terāpanth Śvetāmbara Jain mendicant order and presents translations and analyses of the rules and regulations and initiations rituals for a new category of Jain novices, the *samaṇ* order, which was introduced by the Terāpanth in 1981. It is argued that variations and cumulative changes in post-canonical monastic law can be understood in terms of rule specification and secondary canonization and not only in terms of exceptions to the rule. The article contributes both to the anthropology of South Asian asceticism and monasticism and to the exploration of the *maryādā* and *āvaśyaka* literatures of the Jains.

KEYWORDS: *asceticism, āvaśyaka literature, canonization, initiation, Jainism, Jain religious practice, monastic law, modernisation, renunciation, rites of atonement, vinaya literature*

Introduction

Surprisingly few details are known about the history and organization of contemporary Jain mendicant orders. Although the canonical Jain *vinaya* literature has been studied extensively during the last hundred and twenty years of academic scholarship,[2] the codes of conduct of current Jain mendicant orders[3] remained largely unexplored, mainly because they are not easily accessible and written in vernacular languages rather than in Prakrit or Sanskrit. In this article, I will present a commented translation of the current *Niyamāvalī*, or list of rules, of the Terāpanth Śvetāmbara *samaṇ*[4] order. The *samaṇ* order is a new category of Terāpanth ascetics,[5] intermediate between mendicants[6] and laity, and therefore of particular interest.[7] It was created in 1980 by the modernist leader of the Terāpanth, the late Ācārya Tulsī (1914–97), for the dual purpose of spreading the Jain doctrine all over the world and to teach the new socio-religious programmes of the Terāpanth for the 'moral transformation of humankind'[8]; for example the practice of small vows *(aṇuvrata)*,[9] a Terāpanth Jain version of insight meditation *(prekṣā dhyāna)* and the so-called science of living *(jīvan vijñān)*.[10] Technically, the *samaṇs* are novices with relaxed rules which enable them to travel abroad and to use money ('safety dollars'), means of transport, means of communication, shoes, flush toilets, to leave their abode at night, to live permanently at one place, and to accept food that was especially prepared for them, all of which is traditionally prohibited for fully initiated Jain mendicants. In this respect they resemble the *yatis* and *bhaṭṭārakas*, or half-mendicants, who accept only four of the five canonical *mahāvratas*, and who played a dominant role in the Jain community during the Mughal period and under British rule. However, in contrast to the *yatis*, who do not observe the vow of non-possession *(aparigraha)*, the permanent possession of private property beyond the minimal requirements of a Jain mendicant is strictly prohibited for the *samaṇs*, who accept all five vows, though they do not have to observe them as strictly as the *sādhus* and *sādhvīs*. Most of them leave the householder life forever, and their rules and regulations are similar to the code of conduct of the Terāpanth mendicants. The *samaṇs* can therefore speak with the authority of established saints, in contrast to the missionaries *(pracāraka)* and social reformers of other Jain traditions, who are either lay followers or mendicants of low prestige who step outside the canonical rules.

Monastic Reforms

The Terāpanth is the most centralized of all Jain mendicant orders. By rule, it is the *ācārya* alone who takes all important decisions. He initiates all mendicants and novices, determines his successor and rotates the personnel of the itinerant groups. He is also the principal legislator and reformer of *saṅgha*. The present modernist agenda of the Terāpanth was also instigated by the presiding *ācārya*. Between 1947–80, institutional frameworks for new categories of novices were developed step-by-step by Ācārya Tulsī. In order to raise the standards of education of the Terāpanth nuns he founded in 1949 the *Paramārthik Śikṣaṇ Saṃsthān* (PSS) at his birthplace Lāḍnūṁ in Rājasthān. The PSS is an institution for the religious education of young girls and prospective female candidates for initiation, called *vairāgiṇīs*, that is those who are free from desire. Previously, individual candidates for initiation received instruction during the *cāturmās* period or simply followed the group *(siṅghāṛa)* of the *sādhu* or *sādhvī* of their choice on its itinerary *(vihāra)* for a period of probation which lasted from four months up to three years. The only condition for receiving pre-monastic education from the mendicants was the formal acceptance of the small vows *(aṇuvrata)* of the Jain laity. In 1962, in Udaypur, the idea of a third order between mendicants and laity crystallized in Tulsī's mind, and in November 1980 two different categories of novices, the *mumukṣus* and the *samaṇīs*, were created, and the first initiations performed (the first *samaṇs* were initiated in 1985). In 1971, the *Śikṣā Kendra*, a separate study centre for Terāpanth mendicants, was opened in Lāḍnūṁ and in 1977 integrated into the *Jaina Viśva Bhāratī* (JVB), the new physical centre of the Terāpanth in Lāḍnūṁ which was also founded in 1971. In 1991, the JVB Institute gained the status of a 'deemed to be university' and nowadays provides for the academic education of the members of the Terāpanth *samaṇ* order in particular, although it is open for non-Terāpanthīs and non-Jains as well.

As the consequence of the institutional reforms of 1980, there are now two categories of Terāpanth mendicants: the ascetics proper, or *śramaṇs*, and the *samaṇs*, and there are three categories of novices: the *samaṇs*, the *mumukṣus*, or seekers of salvation, and the *upāsakas*.[11] The *mumukṣus* are a pre-monastic category of celibate laywomen and laymen who practice temporary renunciation in an institutional setting. This category was introduced as a replacement for the category of the *vairāgiṇī* in order to allow young girls, in particular, to live for an extended period like mendicants and to study Jainism systematically without undergoing a full initiation. During this time of sustained study and religious practice they can test their resolve and after completing their course either advance further on the path of salvation or return to the householder life.

The full course of education of the *mumukṣus* takes seven years and most candidates for initiation remain *mumukṣus* for five to ten years before they move on to be initiated into the *samaṇ* category. During the first year in the PSS, a candidate initially enters the category of a celibate layman *(upāsaka)* or laywoman *(upāsikā)* with the acceptance of limited formal vows (in the scriptures '*upāsaka*' is a generic term for 'laity'). In contrast to the *brahmacārīs* and *brahmacāriṇīs*, that is the Jain laity who practice the vows of celibacy while continuing their normal life at home, the Terāpanth *upāsakas* (lit. servants) live together with the *mumukṣus* in the PSS, dress in white cotton and practice the life of a religious student. One of their main duties is to serve the *mumukṣus* and to cook for them, because the *mumukṣus*, like Jain mendicants and the *samaṇs*, are not allowed to use fire, although, unlike the *samaṇs*, they are not permitted to perform the alms round. During their year as *upāsakas*, the candidates receive a basic education while their aptitude for entering the *mumukṣu śreṇī* is tested.

At the point of initiation the candidates have to vow to follow the code of conduct of the *mumukṣus*,[12] not to make marriage arrangements during their life as a *mumukṣu*, to see their relatives only for one month a year, not to leave the training centre without permission, to fast for two days per month and to perform the obligatory rites of atonement *(pratikramaṇa)* once every fortnight on the full moon and new moon days. A great number of *mumukṣus*, who are technically still householders, move on to become properly initiated mendicants, first *samaṇīs* and then *sādhvīs*.

The religious status of the *mumukṣus* can be compared with the one of the *kṣullakas* (fem. *kṣullikā*) and the *ailakas* (fem. *ailikā*), the four categories of neophytes of the Digambaras which correspond to the 10th and 11th or last stage of the *pratimā* scheme of spiritual progress of an ideal Jain layperson which is more popular amongst the Digambaras (cf. Williams, 1963: 172–81), whereas the *upāsakas* are located somewhere between the stage of the *brahmacāriṇ* (no. 6) and the stage of abandoning the activity of a householder (no. 8). By contrast, the *samaṇs* and *samaṇīs* are partially initiated mendicants, and therefore of a higher status, somewhat similar to the Digambara 'nuns,' or *āryikā*. To mark their difference in status, *upāsikās* and *mumukṣus*, *samaṇīs*, and *sādhvīs* live in three separate buildings in Lāḍnūṁ.

Monastic Hierarchy

The hierarchy of the Terāpanth order currently comprises 23 categories: (1) *gaṇādhipati*, the retired leader of the order; (2) *ācārya*, teacher and head of the order; (3) *yuvācārya*, designated successor; (4) *mahāśramaṇa*, administrative assistant to the *ācārya* and *yuvācārya*; (5) *sādhvī pramukhā (mahāśramaṇī)*, head nun; (6) *agraṇī (siṅghāṛapati)*, leader of a group of male ascetics; (7) *agraṇī (siṅghāṛapati)*, leader of a group of female ascetics; (8) *sādhu*, monk; (9) *sādhvī*, nun; (10) *niyojaka*, head of the *samaṇs*; (11) *niyojikā*, head of the *samaṇīs*; (12) *nirdeśaka*, leader of a group of *samaṇs*; (13) *nirdeśikā*, leader of a group of *samaṇīs*; (14) *samaṇa*, male novice; (15) *samaṇī*, female novice; (16) *sanyojaka*, head of the *mumukṣu* brothers; (17) *sanyojikā*, head of the *mumukṣu* sisters; (18) *yojaka*, leader of a group of *mumukṣu* brothers; (19) *yojikā*, leader of a group of *mumukṣu* sisters; (20) *mumukṣu bhāī*, male neophyte; (21) *mumukṣu bahen*, female neophyte; (22) *upāsaka*, celibate layman; (23) *upāsikā*, celibate laywoman. Outside these categories of renouncers are the *srāvakas*, or common laypeople. The structure of the hierarchy is summarized in the following chart:

Table 1: **The structure of the Terāpanth hierarchy**

<table>
<tr><td colspan="2">gaṇādhipati</td></tr>
<tr><td colspan="2">ācārya</td></tr>
<tr><td colspan="2">yuvācārya</td></tr>
<tr><td>mahāśramaṇa</td><td>sādhvī pramukhā</td></tr>
<tr><td>agraṇī (siṅghāṛapati)</td><td>agraṇī (siṅghāṛapati)</td></tr>
<tr><td>sādhu</td><td>sādhvī</td></tr>
<tr><td>niyojaka</td><td>niyojikā</td></tr>
<tr><td>nirdeśaka</td><td>nirdeśikā</td></tr>
<tr><td>samaṇa</td><td>samaṇī</td></tr>
<tr><td>sanyojaka</td><td>sanyojikā</td></tr>
<tr><td>yojaka</td><td>yojikā</td></tr>
<tr><td>mumukṣu bhāī</td><td>mumukṣu bahen</td></tr>
<tr><td>upāsaka</td><td>upāsikā</td></tr>
</table>

Some of the categories are, at times, purely theoretical.[13] After the death of Gaṇādhipati Tulsī in 1997, Mahāśramaṇ Muditkumār was promoted to be *yuvācārya*, but no new *mahāśramaṇa* was selected. There are four *mumukṣu* brothers at the moment, who travel with the *ācārya*. Apart from them and the four *samaṇs*, the entire system of novice categories is currently of practical relevance only for female candidates. The roles of the *nirdeśaka* and the *nirdeśikā* became only in recent years more prominent. The *mumukṣu* sisters, too, did not always have a formal leader, since a *samaṇī* is the administrative head of the PSS in Lāḍnūṁ. The fact that a great number of organiza-tional changes occurred even within the last decade shows how dynamic the structures of Jain mendicant orders are and how flexible organizational rules and regulations are handled in practice.[14]

Initiation

Formal initiation rituals have been established by Ācārya Tulsī for all categories of novices and mendicants of the Terāpanth.[15] The principal stages of initiation are marked by different sets of vows. They are the *upāsaka dīkṣā*, the *mumukṣu dīkṣā*, the *samaṇa dīkṣā* and *śramaṇa dīkṣā*.[16] These initiations do not have to be taken in sequence. In fact, with permission of the *ācārya* it is even possible to gain initiation into the mendicant order straight away – an option that is often granted to male candidates who are more difficult to attract to monastic life. However, the *ācārya* will give his permission only on condition of certain educational qualifications of the initiants. These are still rare amongst female candidates. For young girls in particular it is therefore recommended to study Jainism first and to live a celibate life like a mendicant for a fixed period before taking on any further ascetic commitments. As a rule, no one without prior training in the PSS and/or a basic degree in Jainism from the Jain Viśva Bhāratī Institute in Lāḍnūṁ will nowadays be initiated into the mendicant order.[17]

From an early period, probably from the time of Mahāvīra himself, initiation and ordination have been treated as separate rituals both in Jainism and in Buddhism. Mahāvīra apparently introduced the ordination ritual in order to distinguish his own strictly ascetic regime from the somewhat less stern followers of Pārśva, who demanded only the initiation. According to the canon (*KS* 6.14), the Śvetāmbara monastic life is divided into six initiatory stages (cf. Schubring, 1935: § 136). However, only the first two, the initiation and ordination are still practised. The initiation ritual, or *sāmāyika dīkṣā*, is a lengthy and elaborate public event and performed with great pomp. The principal rites are the change of dress (*veśa parivartana*), the plucking of the hair (*keśa luñcana*), and the acceptance of the *sāmāyika vrata*, the vow of renouncing all violence for the rest of one's life. The ordination ritual, or *chedopasthāpanīya dīkṣā*, by contrast, is not a special public event but a rather short internal monastic procedure during which the five great vows (*mahāvrata*) and the codes of conduct of (Terāpanth) Jain mendicants are formally accepted by reciting the text *Cāritradharma* of the *Chajjīvaṇiyā* section in the *Dasaveyāliya Sutta* (*DVS* 4.11–17). After the *sāmāyika dīkṣā* an initiant has gained the status of a *śramaṇa*, a Jain mendicant. He or she is accepted as a fully initiated member of the monastic community only after the ordination (cf. Prasad, 1972: 13f.). The ordination ceremony is usually performed between two weeks and four months after the initiation. During the intervening period, the newly initiated monk or nun is introduced into the monastic code of conduct and the routines of mendicant life, and learns by heart the *Dasaveyāliya Sutta* and the *Śramaṇa Pratikramaṇa* which contain the essential canonical rules of conduct and the formulae of the principal rite of purification. Before the ordination, a *sādhu* or *sādhvī* participates fully in the mendicant life, but does not share food with the other mendicants, which indicates his or her liminal status.

The Terāpanth *samaṇs* are a different category. The *samaṇ* status is defined through the specific vows which are accepted during the initiation ritual of the *samaṇs*, the *samaṇ dīkṣā*. There are two types of *samaṇ dīkṣās*: (1) temporary (*sāvadhik samaṇ dīkṣā*), and (2) lifelong (*yāvajjīvan samaṇ dīkṣā*). Almost anyone–even short term visitors–can be temporarily initiated as a *samaṇ* or a *samaṇī* and thus easily acquire some status of sanctity, which is quite unique in Jainism.[18] Accordingly, the *sāvadhik samaṇ dīkṣā* ceremony is a simple, informal procedure. It merely involves the change of dress, the recitation of the *Samaṇa Sāmāiya Sutta* (Skt. *Samaṇa Sāmāyika Sūtra*), that is the vow of abstaining from all violence for a temporary period, and the acceptance of the code of conduct of the *samaṇs*. The *yāvajjīvan samaṇ dīkṣā*, on the other hand, is a big public event, like the *śramaṇ dīkṣā*. It requires the formal permission of the relatives of the initiant and involves four key elements: (1) the change of dress, (2) the shaving of the hair, (3) the acceptance of the lifelong *samaṇ sāmāyika* vow, and (4) the explanation of the rules and regulations for the *samaṇs* or *samaṇīs*.

1. Like the *upāsikās* and the *mumukṣus*, who have their own dress code, the *samaṇīs* (and *samaṇs*) are given special clothes, called *kavac*, and a white handkerchief (*mukhavastra*), which clearly marks them off from the *sāmaṇeras*. In contrast to the *sāmaṇeras*, the *samaṇs* are not equipped with a broom (*rajoharaṇa*) and a mouthmask (*mukhavastrikā*) at their initiation, the two outward status symbols of an ascetic of the aniconic Jain mendicant tradition. However, they do receive a new name. The names of the *samaṇīs* usually end in the suffix *-prajñā*, in contrast to the *sādhvīs*, whose new names usually end in *-prabhā*, *-śrī*, *-latā* or *-vibhā* (Sanmatiprajñā, 1996: 14–16).

2. The rite of plucking a small tuft of hair which is deliberately kept after the shaving of the head, symbolizes the transition from householder to renouncer. The fact that it is not performed during the *samaṇ dīkṣā* indicates that the lifelong *samaṇ* is not a fully initiated mendicant. In contrast to *sādhus* and *sādhvīs*, *yāvajjīvan samaṇs* are also not obliged to pluck their hair twice a year after their initiation.

3. The text of the newly composed *Samaṇa Sāmāiya Sutta* (Skt. *Samaṇa Sāmāyika Sūtra*) was written in Prakrit especially for the new lifelong *samaṇ* order by Ācārya Tulsī and Yuvācārya Mahāprajña. It contains an innovative preamble with the repeated use of Prakrit words such as *uvasaṃpajjāmi*, 'I accept,' and *vajjayāmi*, 'I renounce,' and a variation of the traditional *Sāmāiya Sutta* at the end of the text. The severity of the limitations implied by the five vows (*pañcavrata*) in the text is ranked by Sanmatiprajñā (1996: 24f.) somewhere between the *aṇuvratas* for the laity and the *mahāvratas* for the mendicants:

> *Samaṇa Sāmāiya Sutta*[19]
>
> I engage, your reverence, in the *sāmāiya* and renounce harmful activity.
>
> I accept the fourfold religion of the ascetic –
> forbearance, gentleness, straightforwardness, humility.[20]
>
> I give up the four faults born in the mind – anger, pride, deceit, greed.
>
> I accept the five ascetic abstentions –
> abstention from injury to living beings, abstention from lying, abstention from theft, abstention from sex, abstention from possession.[21]
>
> I accept the three ascetic disciplines –
> mental discipline, verbal discipline, physical discipline.[22]

I accept the ascetic virtue – peacefully living together.

I give up the four sinful activities –
quarrel, false accusation, backbiting, censuring others.

I accept the five ascetic circumspections –
circumspection in walking, circumspection in speaking, circumspection in using food, circumspection in using utensils, circumspection in excretion.[23]

I accept the four ascetic means (of salvation) –
study, meditation, reflection, ascetic exercise.

I accept the observance of doctrine –
Right conduct concerning the knowledge is of eight types, with regard to time, discipline, respect, attentive repetition, non-denial (non-concealment), word, meaning, and the connection of both (word and meaning).[24]

I accept the observance of right insight –
(The excellence of faith depends on) eight points: that one has no doubts (about the truth of the tenets), that one has no preference (for heterodox tenets), that one does not doubt its saving qualities, that one is not shaken in the right belief (because heretical sects are more prosperous), that one praises (the pious), that one encourages (weak brethren), that one supports or loves the confessors of the law, that one endeavours to exalt it (with good works for the propagation of the Jain religion).[25]

In the presence of the *guru* and in the presence of my soul I accept all this *for all my life*. I will not violate it or cause it to be violated (by others) or approve of others violating it. I repent such wrongdoing, your reverence, and I reprehend and censure and abandon myself (if I have done so in the past).[26]

4. The explanation of the rules and regulations of the *samaṇs*, the so-called *pāṭī-* or *baṛī-samaṇa dīkṣā*, is very short during the public ceremony and usually involves merely a general explanation of the degree of observance of the five vows that is expected of *śrāvaks*, *samaṇs* and *sādhus*. Within one week after the initiation ceremony, the *samaṇs* are acquainted with three types of rules: (a) the 700 verses of the *Dasaveyāliya Sutta*, which ideally have to be learned by heart within one month after initiation, (b) the general rules of the *samaṇ* order, that are codified in a short text called *Saṅkalpa Patra*, and (c) the specific rules and regulations which are laid down in the *Niyamāvalī*, which is translated in this article. The *Niyamāvalī* is a lengthy document which contains the specific rules and regulations of the customary law of the *samaṇ* order, both for *samaṇs* and *samaṇīs*, which have to be learned after initiation. The *Saṅkalpa*

Patra, by contrast, is a short list of the general rules of the *samaṇ* order and has the form of a legal contract. Each lifelong *samaṇ* and *samaṇī* should sign the *Saṅkalpa Patra* first thing every morning – at least in their mind – to confirm their commitment to the constitution of their order.[27]

Resolution letter[28]

I express my reverence, faith and inclination in Śrāman Lord Mahāvīr and his ascetic teachings and resolve humbly and with folded hands that the code of conduct as set by the proceeding pontiffs such as Bhikṣu, Bhārīmāl, and others as well as by the present pontiff his holiness Ācārya Tulsī is acceptable to me.

Gurudev! You are the very life of the order and the leader of the *śrāmaṇ* tradition. I have complete faith in you.

1. I shall not transgress the discipline enjoined upon us by you.
2. I shall not ignore the injunctions of the *niyojak/niyoyikā* appointed by you.
3. I shall follow the code of conduct of the *samaṇ* order conscientiously.
4. I shall be completely devoted and humble towards the monk (ascetic) order.
5. I shall observe equanimity in dealing with all the *samaṇs/samaṇīs* initiated in the *samaṇ* order. I will not attempt to make anyone my own (disciple).
6. I shall be humble towards my elders and magnanimous towards the juniors.
7. I shall practice the rainy retreat and the ascetic itinerary in accordance with your views.
8. I shall not include anybody else in the *samaṇ* order of my own accord.
9. I shall not speak insultingly against any of my co-religionists.
10. If I happen to detect any fault in anybody, I shall apprise him of it or the authorities concerned directly. I shall never mention it elsewhere.
11. In any controversial matter I shall gladly obey the orders of you or the authority appointed by you.

I have accepted the clauses contained in this pledge reverentially and not with hesitation, fit of emotion or influence.

Signature ______________________________ (as a mark of acceptance)

Date

Samaṇ/ī ______________________________

The two basic categories of novices in the Terāpanth are the *mumukṣus* and *samaṇs*. They are again subdivided into temporary and (semi-) permanent categories (*upāsakas* and *mumukṣus*, *sāvadhik samaṇs* and *yāvajjīvan samaṇs*) and according to gender. The system as a whole thus comprises altogether eight fundamental categories which have to be distinguished from the fully ordained male and female *śramaṇas*. However, there are only two significant initiatory stages in the reformed path from novicehood to mendicancy: the *yāvajjīvan samaṇ dīkṣā* and the *śramaṇ dīkṣā*. The transition from the status of a lifelong *samaṇ/ī* to a *sādhu/sādhvī*, the *śramaṇ dīkṣā*, is marked merely by a small ceremony, which is performed in conjunction with the initiation of new *samaṇ/īs*. For an initiated lifelong *samaṇ/ī*, no second public celebrations are held before entering the mendicant order, because the transition from householder to renouncer has already been accomplished. The candidates simply accept first the *śramaṇ sāmāyik* vow and later the *mahāvratas*.

Canonical and Customary Codes of Conduct

The significance of the two principal initiation rituals is reflected by the fact that only for the *yāvajjīvan samaṇs* and the *śramaṇs* have elaborated sect-specific codes of conduct been produced by the Terāpanth. The contents and functions of such non-canonical rules amongst Jain mendicant orders is not well understood. In the last fifty years, the Terāpanth became the focus of a number of historical[29] and ethnographic[30] studies, not least by the Terāpanth mendicants themselves, due to the efforts of Ācārya Tulsī (1914–97) and his successor Ācārya Mahāprajña (born 1920) to promote research in the (Terāpanth) Jain tradition. Today, it is the most intensely studied contemporary Jain mendicant order.[31] However, even on the basis of the vernacular historiographic literature of the Terāpanth itself it is difficult to get a clear picture of the procedures and the complex layers of formal and informal rules and regulations currently governing monastic life. The reason for this is that there are different types of written rules amongst Jain mendicant orders, canonical and customary rules. As a matter of principle, only the first are publicized, often in print, while the latter circulate only in handwritten form within the order. Already the canonical *Vavahāra* 10.9 mentions the existence of specific non-canonical organisational rules, called *saṃṭhii* (*maryādā*) in the *Vavahārabhāsa*, which are created from time to time by the *ācāryas* of individual monastic orders (*gaṇa*) in addition to the general canonical rules for Śvetāmbara Jain mendicants, their *dharma* (Schubring and

Caillat, 1966: 87). Whereas the canonical rules are fixed, the customary law of the *maryādās* is constantly revised by the monastic authorities and adapted to changing historical contexts.[32] The fact that the customary law (Pkt. *jīyakappa*, Skt. *jītakalpa*) of a particular mendicant order is somewhat discontinuous, flexible and more or less arbitrarily determined by the monastic authorities is not considered to be improper if the canonical rules (Pkt. *suyakappa*, Skt. *śrutakalpa*) are not directly violated. According to the scriptures, there is a hierarchy of procedures: '[All] proceedings (*vavahāra*) . . . are determined by superior knowledge (*āgama*), tradition (*suya*), an order (*āṇā*), a rule (*dhāranā*) or an accepted practice (*jīya*), the following criterion always coming into force in default of the proceeding one' (*Viy* 383a).[33] As a consequence, it is possible to transgress the law of the order but not the *dharma* (*Vav.* 10.9).

On the basis of canonical rules alone it is, therefore, impossible to understand the internal procedures and function of a specific Jain mendicant order. In the commentary literature, both scholastic and academic, this problem is generally treated in terms of 'exceptions' (*apavāda*) and 'pragmatic choices' under contextual pressures.[34] However, in the case of the Terāpanth the *maryādā* literature itself underwent a process of canonization. The general rules and regulations, which the founder of the Terāpanth, Ācārya Bhikṣu (1726–1803), laid down on 30 January 1803 (shortly before his death) in a document called *Sāmūhik Maryādā*, are now accepted as the constitution (*saṃvidhān*) of the order. This document establishes the fundamental principle that there can only be one *ācārya*, who determines his own successor and takes all important decisions concerning the ascetic order (Bhikṣu, in Tulsī and Mahāprajña, 1983: 467–70). Apart from general rules such as this, all specific rules can be changed or abolished by the ruling *ācārya*. During the history of the Terāpanth, important innovations have been introduced in particular by Ācārya Jītmal (1803–81) in his four works *Baṛī Maryādā* and *Choṭī Maryādā* (Jaypur, 30 September 1852), *Paramparā nāṃ Bol* (Indore, 2 February 1855), and *Paramparā rī Joṛ* I–VII (Lāḍnuṁ 1857–60). Some of his new organizational rules have also de facto been canonized by the editors of his texts, Ācārya Tulsī and Yuvācārya Mahāprajña (1983), who published a selection of his legal treatises under the title *Terāpanth Maryādā aur Vyavasthā*. As a consequence of this process of secondary canonization,

Terāpanth mendicants currently observe three basic types of written rules: (1) canonical, (2) constitutional, and (3) customary rules. However, only the canonical and the constitutional rules are accessible in print, although much of the day-to-day life of the ascetics is regulated by custom and not by canon. In addition, a large body of unwritten customary rules such as the oral explanations of the *pañca vratas* by the *ācārya*, is in evidence, some of which may be codified in future. Hence, the existing corpus of rules and regulations is cumulative and multi-dimensional. Rule selection and authentication depends in the last instance on the *ācārya*.

The current lists of customary rules have all been created by Ācārya Tulsī. During his long reign from 1936–94 he has introduced significant legal changes and devised several lists of new customary rules and penances for the mendicants, such as the *Maryādāvalī* (1960) and the *Prāyaścitta Vidhi* (1962) which were both revised in 1989, and the *Niyamāvalī* for the *samaṇs*. None of these lists has been published. The current customary law of the Terāpanth is therefore only known to the mendicants themselves. As a matter of principle, the lists of current rules and regulations, called *samācārī*, *maryādāvalī* or *niyamāvalī* exist only in form of handwritten documents amongst Śvetāmbara ascetics. The lists are nowadays copied by hand by each mendicant into his or her diary. Since the details of these rules are often revised and old diaries rarely kept, it is difficult to find a complete historical record of all changes of rules and regulations. Only few of the presumably numerous *maryādāvalīs* of the medieval and early modern periods have survived. The Terāpanth seems to be the only order which recently began to collect the old lists of rules and regulations of its *ācāryas*. Some of these historical lists have been published (Tulsī and Mahāprajñā, 1983). However, in the past, even obsolete *maryādā* lists were never publicized (like the canonical literature itself) or passed on to members of other Jain orders, because they enable potential critics to compare the actual behaviour of the ascetics with their current set of rules.[35] Since these lists are concerned with minute aspects of behaviour, they are sometimes at variance with individual canonical rules and picked upon by rival mendicants for petty criticism.[36] They also contain lists of routine atonements (*prāyaścitta*) whose publication might harm the public image of the order, since they imply the recurrence of specific transgressions.[37]

Because the sect-specific rules and regulations embody the identity-defining criteria of a specific mendicant order, they are also bestowed with a certain aura of sanctity, although the rules themselves are rather pragmatic and unremarkable. With notable exceptions, the majority of the rules are vernacular renditions or running commentaries of selected canonical prescriptions.

The Niyamāvalī *of the Samaṇ/īs*[38]

At the outset, no specific rules existed for the lifelong *samaṇs* and *samaṇīs*, only the *Saṅkalpa Patra*. Additional rules were formulated orally by the *ācārya* when certain problems were encountered and noted down by the *samaṇs* and *samaṇīs* in their diaries. The necessity for a systematic code of conduct for the regulation of both individual conduct and communal life was only felt when the number of *samaṇīs* started to grow. The following list of rules for the *samaṇs* and *samaṇīs* was devised by Ācārya Tulsī on 28 January 1991. Individual rules have been added by Ācārya Mahāprajña later on in response to recurrent problems. Special rules (*viśeṣ niyam*) are regularly changed and updated by the *ācārya* at the annual assembly of the mendicants, the *maryādā mahotsava*. At this occasion, all rule changes are noted down by the mendicants in their diaries. The handwritten form emphasizes both the somewhat provisional and changeable character of the rules, which are devised in response to specific events and experiences, and their non-public character. *Maryādā* lists tend to be published – if at all – only when they are obsolete. Lay people generally do not know the specific internal norms of the mendicant orders, and (as I was told) 'do not need to know' (though in principle they should be able to monitor the conduct of the mendicants on the basis of their rules).[39]

The *Niyamāvalī* has a casuistic character.[40] The current text is formally divided into 14 sections:[41] (1) code of conduct (*ācāra saṃhitā*), (2) daily work (*dina-caryā*), (3) rules of organization (*vyavasthā sūtra*), (4) cloth (*vastra*), (5) bowls (*pātra*), (6) begging (*bhikṣā*), (7) medicine (*auṣadha*), (8) rules of education (*śikṣā sūtra*), (9) rites of atonement (*prāyaścitta*), (10) annual report (*vārṣika vivaraṇa*), (11) cleaning of clothes (*vastra prakṣālana*), (12) food (*āhāra*), (13) service (*bhakti*), (14) method of atonement for the laity (*śrāvaka kī prāyaścitta vidhi*).[42] The model of the special rules (*viśeṣ niyam*) of the *samaṇ/īs* are the special rules of the

Terāpanth *sādhus* and *sādhvīs*. Therefore, many rules and regulations are shared, for example those for begging alms and medicine, which generally correspond to canonical prototypes. Other prescriptions, such as the *Ācār Saṃhitā*, *Vyavasthā Sūtra* and *Dinacaryā* rules were especially designed for the *samaṇ/īs*, while the *Śikṣā Sūtra* contains a mixture of shared and special rules. A comparison with the 17 sections of the *Maryādāvalī* of the mendicants (Tulsī, 1989a) shows that the wording of sections 6, 7, 10 and 14 is almost identical with corresponding sections in the *Maryādāvalī*, though slightly shorter, and that the topics of sections 4, 5, 9, 13 and of individual rules considerably overlap (both texts contain a list of atonements, though the mendicants possess a separate and more extended *Prāyaścitta Vidhi* text).[43] However, sections 1–3 and 8, which contain the general rules for the *samaṇ/īs*, are almost entirely distinct. The *samaṇ/īs* observe slightly different rules in India and abroad. In India the rules are stricter. For example, money ('safety dollars') should not be kept and electrical appliances should not be used: doorbells should not be rung, light should not be switched on and off, lifts should not be used (except in cases of illness and only if the destination is higher up than the third floor), and so on. The main reason is that in most locations in India tasks such as switching on electrical appliances can be performed for the *samaṇ/īs* by the well organized Terāpanth laity. There are a number of distinct rules for comportment abroad beyond those published and written down. These are special allowances (*ājñā*) and directives (*sandeś*) of the *ācārya*, whose word overrules all written and unwritten customary rules. Although all *Niyamāvalī* rules have to be copied into the personal diaries, their actual wording is not well known to most *samaṇ/īs*, since proper conduct is mainly learned through imitation and not by the book. The rules are, however, consulted if specific problems occur and serve as a general orientation. Although I found that the actual conduct of the *samaṇs* and *samaṇīs* corresponds very closely to the rules and regulations, which they have vowed to observe, there are systematic discrepancies with regard to certain regulations (concerning for instance photography) which seem to be intended from the outset to function as regulative ideals rather than as factual limitations.

For aesthetic reasons, I have put the commentary on individual rules into the notes rather than in the main text.

List of Rules[44]

Code of conduct[45]

1. The *samaṇs* and *samaṇīs* of the *samaṇ* order will remain under the spiritual discipline of the *ācārya.*
2. *Samaṇīs* will practise religion under the custody of the *sādhvīs* and the *samaṇs* under the *sādhus.*
3. Without informing her *niyojikā* or *nirdeśikā* a *samaṇī* will not go outside the place of residence.
4. In their own group, any *samaṇ* and *samaṇī* may be exchanged and appointed as *niyojaka* or *niyojikā.*
5. *Samaṇīs* will not be able to go anywhere alone.
6. A single *samaṇ* cannot have a conversation with a single sister/woman or *samaṇī*, nor a single *samaṇī* with a single *samaṇ* or brother/man. If it is necessary for a conversation to take place, then some third person should be present within a distance of seven 'hands.'[46] The third should not be blind, deaf, dumb or less than nine years of age.
7. When a transgression of the essential code of conduct or discipline occurs, then the *samaṇs* and *samaṇīs* will do their penance near the *ācārya* or a person pointed out by the *ācārya.*
8. If even after having been initiated in the *samaṇ* order some *samaṇ* or *samaṇī* proved to be unsuitable from the point of view of right conduct and discipline, then s/he can be separated from the *samaṇ* order.
9. One should not keep the hair growing. Normally, one should cause the hair to be cut or plucked out twice a year (in August/September and February/March).[47]
10. A meal must take place in accordance with the proper begging procedure. Begging can be done both invited and uninvited.[48]
11. Normally, one should do the work of sewing clothes, dyeing bowls, cleaning the place of residence oneself.[49]
12. One should not correspond by letter.[50]
13. Normally, one should not use a telephone.[51]
14. Normally, one should have only one meal,[52] renounce rich foods or perform a one-day fast[53] on the eighth and fourteenth (pure thirteenth)[54] [of every fortnight].

15. Normally, one should not go to the place of the *sādhus* [*sādhvīs*] at night.
16. If one goes outside the place of residence, one should use [the expression] '*āvassahī*' at the time of departure and '*nissahī*' at the time of return.[55]
17. One should inspect (*pratilekhanā*) the various paraphernalia, books, clothes, etc. every two weeks and monthly.[56]

Daily work

1. One should practise getting up at approximately four o'clock in the last part of the night.
2. One should not sleep before nine or ten o'clock in the night.
3. After a meal half an hour's rest can be taken.[57]
4. One should spend at least three hours [per day] with the rites of repentance, meditation, etc.
5. Generally, the practice of yogic posture is compulsory.
6. One should perform the rites of repentance, *arhat vandanā*, etc. collectively.
7. A group meeting should be held once in a fortnight. In this one should reflect on mutual interactions or other problems.
8. One should maintain the practice of daily mutual ceremonial greeting and fortnightly begging of forgiveness.[58]
9. Generally, one should perform three meditations (*kāyotsarga pratimā*)[59] of 45 minutes length on the eighth, fourteenth and fifteenth [of every fortnight]. (Away from home or in proximity of the *ācārya śrī* [only two meditations of] one and a half hours).[60]

Rules of organization

1. One should take the permission of the *niyojikā* for every activity, such as washing clothes, alms, water, conversation with monks [nuns], etc.
2. At night, the sleeping order should normally be arranged according to monastic seniority or sometimes in the reverse order.[61]
3. In the acceptance of a ceremonial greeting one should use the word '*arham*' with both hands folded.

4. One should submit an annual diary in written form [to the *ācārya*] at the occasion of the festival of rules (*maryādā mahotsava*) (medicine, tea, coffee, clothes, fasting etc.).[62]
5. A mutual exchange of things borrowed from householders should generally not take place between *sādhvīs* and *samaṇīs*[63] (one should not take a tub, bucket, notebook, diary, pencil, etc. in a case of special need without making it known [to the group leader]).
6. The sequence of shifts for the newly initiated should be determined after one month.[64]
7. If at the time of the sermon facilities are not available for all, then the *nirdeśikā* or the one who gives the sermon is able to use the high seat for just that time.
8. In the presence of several *sanyojikās*, generally the eldest in the order of seniority will maintain responsibility for the organization. Special circumstances are a different matter.
9. Generally, one should not use a lift for up to three storeys.[65]
10. Thirty one-day fasts are done per year.[66]
11. If *samaṇs* and *samaṇīs* rely only on water during a fast, then taking food from the whole group after breaking the fast is done in the following sequence of days:[67] for each day beyond breaking one three-day fast, half the days of the fast days;[68] for four days *āyambil* one day, for eight days two days, and so on for every four days one day more.[69]
12. After performing a fast, one is permitted to sleep as long as full energy has not returned.
13. After seven days of a threefold fast and after four days of a fourfold fast[70] (in the case of buttermilk and buttermilk-water fasts, after 15 days) one should not continue to do the collective work and the almsround, and after breaking the fast, for half of the number of days on which one receives food from the group, one should abstain from doing the almsround and the collective work. If one lives off the work of the collective for odd numbers of days, then 'half a day' should be understood as 'one day.'[71] Thus, if after ten days of fast one remains for five days in the collective, then one will also not have to endure the collective work in it for up to three days.

Cloth

1. Whenever one asks for[72] cloth, one should accept it from the hands of the householder. One may bring a cloth to be borrowed by one's own hand, but if one asks for it too, then one should accept it from the hands of the householder.[73]
2. One can keep more cloth than permitted by rule (uniform,[74] woollen blanket or mat, undercloth, shawl) continuously for up to one and a half months. In winter one can keep one and a half metre additional cloth.
3. The cloth that is kept for *khaṇḍiya* one should not wear and not wrap around onself.[75] One should not keep more than one metre's length [of *khaṇḍiya* cloth].
4. If one accepted a woollen shawl (*alvān*), etc., expensive cloth, glasses, a spongy blanket or a head scarf made of prefabricated threads on an outside itinerary, then one should inform the *niyojikā*.
5. One should not keep more than the prescribed limit of bedding and covering cloths. The prescribed limit is of the following type: 5 overclothes, 2 underclothes, 3 bodices (with long arms), 2 uniforms, 1 shawl, 1 woollen shawl, 2 blankets, 1 wrapping cloth, 3 small bodices (with short arms), 2 handkerchiefs (to hold in front of the mouth), 2 mouthmasks, 1 towel, 2 glasses, 2 ball-point pens, 2 pens, 2 toothbrushes.

Observing the prescribed limit of cloth is obligatory even in a state of bad health, etc.[76]

Bowls

1. One should not keep more than three bowls. One should not eat from bowls made of metal. A bowl must be of plastic, wood or clay.[77]
2. If the water in which a bag, a cloth for cleaning pots, etc. is washed is continuously poured in a bucket etc., then it should only be discarded when all the work is completed.[78]
3. Borrowed utensils should be handed back after being washed well with powder, etc.
4. If two *samaṇīs* go on a journey, then they can keep five bowls and one jug. Additionally, a bucket[79] and an earthen water pot can be kept. Dishes which were accepted for one's own use from a householder cannot be returned.[80]

5. One should not use more than four tubs and two buckets for washing the clothes of up to the number of five [*samaṇīs*].[81] If necessary, additional tubs and buckets can be asked for. But they must be returned to the householder on the same day.

Begging[82]

1. Green chilli, raw mango, lemon etc. which have been cut and pickled with salt and pepper, such pickle one should not accept for up to three days [after it was made].[83] If an onion has not been cut into separate pieces, then one should also not accept its pickle after three days.[84] But if a pickle of it has been made by putting it into clarified butter or oil, etc., then it can be accepted after three days.[85]
2. One should not accept roasted *mothī* seeds,[86] *dhuṁgārī* foods,[87] millet bread,[88] seed-pods of the *phalī* beans,[89] unripe beans of the *khejaṛī* tree,[90] (dry) black capers,[91] *phogalā*[92] and green chilli which contain seeds.[93]
3. One should not take seed-corns of pomegranate and mashed raw mango if salt and pepper have been added.[94]
4. One should not accept rice with unboiled spiced curd[95] and onion *caṭnī*.
5. One should not accept juice of plants inhabited by infinite living beings[96] (onion, green ginger, carrot, etc). which is not mixed with a sufficient quantity of other things.[97]
6. Normally, where vegetation is one should not go for alms. But if there is enough of a path to support a thumb, then it is possible.
7. One should not accept more than half a kilo of milk, and half a measure (approximately 25 grams) of clarified butter or butter per day.
8. One should refuse to accept custard-apple[98] and (entire) corn-cobs.[99]

Medicine

As medicine one can take things [such as] dry ginger or cloves by one's own hand,[100] otherwise not.[101] For the purpose of anointing, one can take oil etc. by one's own hand. Even as medicine, sugar candy, sugar cake, raw sugar, un-crystallized coarse sugar, clarified butter, milk, yoghurt, etc. should not be taken by one's own hand (for special information read *Paramparā kī Joṛ Dhāl* 7).[102] One should not take jam (fruit of the tree *emblic myrobalan*, etc.)[103] and dry fruit (almond etc.) by hand; even as medicine, taking much should not be considered. If medicine is brought to someone who stays in a certain locality, then it should usually be returned to the house from which it was fetched.[104] If this medicine is from a store or doctor, then it can also be handed over to some other householder.

Rules of education

1. Without special order, a *samaṇ* should not individually teach the sisters and a *samaṇī* not the brothers.
2. Apart from the community works, a *samaṇ* should not teach the sisters individually at night and a *samaṇī* not the brothers, nor perform service. Without taking the permission of the leader of the accompanying *samaṇ/īs*, service should also not be performed during the day.
3. At night time, a *samaṇ* should normally sit at a distance of at least three 'hands' from women and a *samaṇī* from men.
4. A householder's shoulders etc. should not be touched.
5. Cloth should be washed unaccompanied, and water should be used with restraint during this work.[105]
6. If one has borrowed utensils etc. during a long stay at one place or a long journey away from home, then one should only leave at the time of departure after having returned them oneself to the place from which they were received.
7. One should not explain *mantras* of gods and goddesses and also the repetition (*jap*) of some *mantras* for material success to householders.
8. One should not explain horoscopes and the good and bad consequences of the lines on the palm of the hand to householders.[106]
9. One should not have a sacred thread, *yantra, mantra* etc. made, nor order it from another place. If it is required, then one should accept a penance in writing.[107]
10. One should not give incitement to any householder or photographer for taking a photo. And one should not keep personal photos with oneself. One should also forbid [photography] for a personal album, video etc.[108]

11. One should not watch TV. If some householder shows a community programme merely for information, this is another matter.
12. If some householder wishes to fill a cassette with devotional songs etc., then this should not be done without the knowledge of the *niyojikā* or *nirdeśikā*.[109]
13. One should not keep books, clothes, etc. in a closed box for a long time.
14. The *kāyotsarga pratimā* should be practised collectively every day, in so doing repetition (*jap*), meditation, etc. should be performed.[110]
15. If one uses indecent words and sheds tears in front of householders, having been overcome by an excess of emotion, then one should avoid six rich foods for one day and produce a written report.
16. Normally, without a reason one should not possess coloured glasses (which change their colour in the sun) and also sunglasses.
17. One should not ask for a [spectacle] frame made only of metal rods.[111]
18. One should not use more than one plastic bag during the work of begging.[112]
19. If a [plastic] bag has lost its fold, one should not fetch it with the hand [supporting the] outside of the bag.
20. One should not accept boiled onion, betel leaf and rolled betel leaf (fresh or dry).[113]
21. Without boiling, fresh water-chestnuts are alive, therefore one should not accept them.
22. Seedless grapes with a small branch one should also not accept.
23. Packaged salt that has not become lifeless one should also not accept.[114]
24. Normally, other than during illness, one should not ask for tea, hot water, etc. to be prepared.[115]
25. One should normally not use things brought for an ill person for another purpose.
26. In their personal life *samaṇs* and *samaṇīs* should practise to remain self-dependant and self-reliant at the most.

27. 'Stay completely alone in the group.' If one keeps this moral stipulation of Ācārya Bhikṣu in front [of one's mind], then one will not attempt to make anyone else one's own even if one enjoys the communal life of *samaṇs* and *samaṇīs*.[116]
28. One should not give one's own written diary [to anyone].[117]
29. One should not ask for a personal watch etc.[118]
30. One should not have one's personal work (writing diary etc.) done by some *mumukṣu* or *upāsikā* or householder permanently resident away from home (in Lāḍnūṁ).[119]
31. The use of vehicles for begging alms remains prohibited. Bottles of water should not be kept open, and if they are open, then one should keep them in sight.[120]
32. If the *samaṇ/īs* pay a visit to someone to give *darśan*, then they should not sit down in that place, except for special circumstances such as long fasts, death fasts.

Rites of atonement

The means of purification for knowingly or unknowingly commiting an error in the observation of the vows is — atonement.

The atonements are of several types, such as *kāyotsarga*, *svādhyāya*, *dhyāna*, *ekāsana*, *upavāsa*, *tapa*, etc.[121] The atonement of a special transgression should, if possible, only be received from the *ācārya*. There are several types of common atonements:

1. For accepting living things [during the almsround] – 1 *ekāsana*.
2. For eating living things – 1 *upavāsa*.
3. For keeping edible substances over night, or washing powder, toothpaste etc.[122] – half an hour standing meditation (*dhyāna*) or recitation (*svādhyāya*).[123]
4. For losing a pen, pencil or needle – 100 *śvāsocchvāsa kāyotsargas*.
5. For losing expensive things such as a watch, etc. and for breaking a thermos, thermometer, bowl, etc. – 1 *āyambila*.
6. For confessions relating to the deeds of day and the deeds of the night – 25 *śvāsocchvāsa kāyotsargas*.[124]
7. For confronting each other or arguing with one another, for an outburst of an excess of emotion – 100 *śvāsocchvāsa kāyotsargas*.
8. For transgressing the code of conduct – 25 *śvāsocchvāsa kāyotsargas*.

9. For not speaking the truth – 25 *śvāsocchvāsa kāyotsargas*.
10. For talking while moving around – 25 *śvāsocchvāsa kāyotsargas*.[125]
11. For transgressing the permitted limit of sleep during the day – 100 *śvāsocchvāsa kāyotsargas*.[126]
12. For transgressing the directives of the *niyojikā* – 100 *śvāsocchvāsa kāyotsargas*.
13. For not keeping confessions confidential – standing recitation (*svādhyāya*) of 100 verses.[127]
14. For shedding tears – 25 *śvāsocchvāsa kāyotsargas*.
15. For harming the five immobile bodies – 100 *śvāsocchvāsa kāyotsargas*.[128]
16. For harming two-to-four-sensed creatures – recitation (*svādhyāya*) of 200 verses (*gāthā*).[129]
17. For accepting what is not properly given – 1 *belā*.[130] For harming five-sensed beings – 1 *upavāsa* or 1 *belā*.
18. For keeping more than the fixed limit of utensils – 1 *belā*.[131] For eating at night – 1 *upavāsa*.
19. For entering the open space at night – 6 *śvāsocchvāsa kāyotsargas*.
20. For a transgression at the time of the *pratikramaṇa* – 25 *śvāsocchvās kāyotsargas*.
21. For leaving some objects in the open space – 12, 25 *śvāsocchvāsa kāyotsargas*.[132]
22. For keeping cutting instruments etc. during the night – 25 *śvāsocchvāsa kāyotsargas*.[133]
23. For not doing the *pratikramaṇa* – 1 *ekāsana*.
24. For leaving the collection bowl for more than 48 minutes – 4 *logassas* in meditation.[134]
25. For quarrel, defamation, etc. – 100 *śvāsocchvāsa kāyotsargas*.
26. For dreams connected with the five causes of karmic influx (*āsrava*)[135] – 100 *śvāsocchvāsa kāyotsargas*.
27. For violent, untruthful dreams – 100 *śvāsocchvāsa kāyotsargas*.
28. If vomiting occurs at night, then for one or two times – 25 *śvāsocchvāsa kāyotsargas*.
29. If wet clothes are wrung out during the rainy season, then 2 *logassas*.[136]

30. If by mistake food and drink was accepted and enjoyed before sunrise – 1 *upavāsa.*

Annual report[137]

1. Before each four-monthly rite of repentance (*caumāsī pakkhī pratikramaṇa*), the prepared 'list of customary rules' should be read out once by the entire group.
2. The 'rite of atonement' (*prāyaścitta vidhi*) should be read out by the entire group without fail once every year.
3. A record should be kept of the village in which cloth was received, from whom, how much and of which type. Of small cloths, such as bags, cloths for wrapping books, cleaning cloths, etc. only the amount should be written.
4. A record should be kept from which village and from whom one received anything special (āyurvedic medicine (*dhātu*), etc.). The name and number of injections and allopathic pills should be written down.
5. A record should be kept of fasting, renunciation of rich foods and special religious practice.
6. A record should be kept of where one stayed, how many days, and how many regions the group visited.
7. A record should be kept of special help [offered] to calm conflicts, of the support of new individuals to the *guru*,[138] and of the works effecting discipline.[139]
8. A record should be kept of who incites memorization, recitation, study and teaching, and who creates literature.
9. It should be written down if by mistake borrowed objects (book, seat, high seat, medicine, mortar, knife, scissors, etc.) were not given back to the owner.
10. It should be written down if glasses were accepted during the work of water procurement (lit. 'thermos bottle work').[140]

Cleaning of clothes

1. Normally clothes should be washed once every week. In the hot season, in April–July, it can be done after five days.
2. If one travels one night or day by train or bus, then one dress can be washed, and if the journey is continuous, then one dress can be washed after two days.

3. Washing clothes can be done one day earlier, if required, but next time it should be done in the previous order.
4. After arrival at a certain place, if one wishes, either one undercloth may be washed or one dress, [but] one should count it on the washing day.
5. During journeys by foot the interval of washing clothes will remain weekly.

Food

1. During meals, one should share by distributing portions.
2. To a new initiate a share of [leftover] food[141] should not be given for up to four months.
3. Until one has not reached a condition to share food with others, due to fever or typhoid, nothing will be given.
4. If during the abstention from wholesome food, or the renunciation of some edible thing, or [during a partial fast] some use [of food] continues, then one will continue to get an equal share (the only exception is the practice of giving up salt).[142]
5. If one completely refuses to take food, one will not be given a share; but if one becomes a sharer of even one thing, an equal share will be given out.[143]
6. If seasonal [fruits], pomegranate,[144] orange, grape or the juice collected from them was accepted and if at midday or evening coffee or tea was taken, then five rich foods should be avoided.
7. If juice of a watermelon,[145] syrup of wood-apples, [or] juice collected from tomatoes was accepted, then one should avoid three rich foods.[146]

'Service'[147]

1. If one has to go by early morning train, then one should take one's proper turn [of service] the previous day. If one is going by evening train, then (after the meal of the second quarter of the day) [one should still do] evening service.
2. If one arrives at a certain place before twelve o'clock in the night, then one shall carry out the proper sequence of turns, and will do service once [during the next day].[148]

3. If two groups arrive in one town, then the group which arrives first should perform service to the second group.
4. During an ongoing journey, service should be performed once [to an arriving party], and if one stays somewhere permanently, then one full day service should be performed for an arriving group.
5. If someone arrives in Lāḍnūṁ (or a place of collective residence away from home) after two and a half months, then one day service should be performed.[149]
6. Within three days of coming back, you will take your turn in the sequence of turns.

Method of atonement for the laity

1. If thorns are extracted during the *sāmāyika* – 25 *navkāra mantras*.
2. If raindrops fall [on a householder during the *sāmāyika*] – 1 *navkārsī*.
3. If the *sāmāyika* was too short or someone kept sitting [for too long] – 2 or 3 *navkārsīs*.
4. If the *sāmāyika* is broken – 1 *sāmāyika*.
5. If a 12-hour *pauṣadha* is broken – 3 *sāmāyikas*.
6. If an 18-hour *pauṣadha* is broken – 4 *sāmāyikas*.
7. If a 24-hour *pauṣadha* is broken – 5 *sāmāyikas*.
8. If water was drunk during *pauṣadha* – 1 *belā*.
9. If during a fast food, etc. is taken at night – 1-day fast or 1 month giving up sweets.

The Text – Niyamāvalī

arham

ācāra-saṃhitā:

1. samaṇ śreṇī ke samaṇ samaṇī par adhyātmik anuśāsan ācārya kā rahegā. 2. samaṇ sādhuoṁ ke aur samaṇī sādhviyoṁ ke saṃrakṣaṇ meṁ sādhanā karegī. 3. samaṇī apnī niyojikā athvā nirdeśikā ko sūcit kiye binā nivās sthān se bāhar nahīṁ jāyegī. 4. samaṇ aur samaṇī ke apne apne varga meṁ koī ek parivartit rūp se niyojak yā niyojikā niyukt hotī rahegī/ rahegā. 5. samaṇī kahīṁ bhī akelī nahīṁ ja sakegī. 6. akelā samaṇ bahin se akelī samaṇī se aur akelī samaṇī akele samaṇ yā bhāī se bātcīt na kareṁ.

bātcīt karnā āvaśyaka ho to sāt hāth tak koī tīsrā vyakti rahnā cāhie. tīnoṁ meṁ koī acakṣu, bahrā, mūk aur nau varṣ se kam avasthā kā na ho. 7. maulik ācār yā anuśāsan kā atikramaṇ hone par samaṇ aur samaṇī ācārya yā ācārya dvārā nirdiṣṭa vyakti ke pās uskā prāyaścitt kareṅgī/ kareṅgā. 8. samaṇ śreṇī meṁ dikṣit hone ke bād bhī koī samaṇ yā samaṇī ācār aur anuśāsan kī dṛṣṭi se ayogya pramāṇit ke jāe to use samaṇ śreṇī se pṛthak kiyā jā sakegā. 9. keś bādhā kar nahīṁ rakhnā. sāmānyataḥ varṣ meṁ do bār (bhādrav pad phālgun meṁ keśāpanayan yā keś loc karānā. 10. bhojan bhikṣā vidhi se hogā. bhikṣā āmaṇtrit aur anāmaṇtrit donoṁ kī jā saktī hai. 11. sāmānyataḥ vastroṁ kī silāī, pātroṁ kī raṅgāī, sthān kī saphāī ādi kārya svayaṃ karnā. 12. patra vyavahār nahīṁ karnā. 13. sāmānyataḥ ṭelīphon nahīṁ karnā. 14. sāmānyataḥ aṣṭamī, caturdaśī (śuklā trayodaśī) ko ekāsan, vigay-varjan yā upavās karnā. 15. sāmānyataḥ rātrī meṁ sādhuoṁ ke sthān par nahīṁ jānā. 16. nivās sthān se bāhar nikalte samay 'āvassahī' lautne samay 'nissahī' kā prayog karnā. 17. pustakeṁ vastra ādi vividh upakaraṇoṁ kā pākṣik athvā māsik pratilekhan karnā.

dina-caryā:

1. paścim rātrī meṁ lagbhag cār baje uṭhne kā abhyās karnā. 2. rātrī meṁ 9 yā 10 baje se pahle nahīṁ sonā. 3. bhojan ke bād ādhā ghaṇṭā viśrām kiyā jā saktā hai. 4. pratikramaṇ dhyān ādi meṁ kam se kam tīn ghaṇṭe kā samay lagānā. 5. sāmānyataḥ anivārya rūp se yogāsan kā abhyās karnā. 6. pratikramaṇ arhat vandanā ādi sāmuhik rūp se karnā. 7. paks meṁ ek din sāmuhik goṣṭhī rakhnā. jis meṁ pāraspārik vyavahār athvā anya samasyā ke bare meṁ cintan karnā. 8. paraspar pratidin abhivādan aur pākṣik kṣamā yācanā kā kram banāe rakhnā. 9. sāmānyataḥ aṣṭamī caturdaśī va pakkhī ko 45 minuṭ kī tīn kāyotsarg pratimā karnā (bāhar athvā ācārya śrī ke sānidhya meṁ 1.5 ghaṇṭā karnā).

vyavasthā-sūtra:

1. pratyek kārya meṁ niyojikā kī svīkṛti lenā. jaise vastra-prakṣālan, bhikṣā pānī sādhuoṁ se bātcīt ādi. 2. rātrī meṁ sone kā kram sāmānyataḥ dīkṣā paryāy se kiyā jāe yā kabhī paścānupūrvī kram se kiyā jāe. 3. abhivādan svīkṛti meṁ donoṁ hāth joṛ kar 'arham' śabda kā prayog karnā. 4. vārṣik vivaraṇ likhit rūp meṁ maryādā mahotsav ke avsar par prastut karnā (auṣadhī, cāy, kāfī, vastra, tapasya ādi. 5. sādhviyoṁ samaṇiyoṁ meṁ paraspar pāḍihāriya vastuoṁ kā vinimay prāyah na rahe (ṭab, bālṭī, kāṁpī, ḍāyrī, pensil ādi viśeṣ apekṣā meṁ jñāt kie binā na leṁ. 6. navdikṣit kī bārī kā kram ek mahīne ke bād niścit rahe. 7. vyākhyān ke samay sab ke lie suvidhā na ho to nirdeśikā yā jo vyākhyān de vah utne samay tak patt kā upayoga kar saktī hai. 8. anek sanyojikāoṁ kī upasthiti meṁ sāmānyataḥ dīkṣā paryāy meṁ jeṣṭhā sanyojikā vyavasthā kā dāyitva sambhālegī. viśeṣ sthiti kī bāt alag hai. 9. sāmānyataḥ lifṭ kā prayog 3 maṃzil tak na kareṁ. 10. varṣ meṁ 30 upavās karnā hai. 11. samaṇ samaṇī keval jal ke sahāre tapasyā kare to pārṇe ke bād samuccay āhār lene ke dinoṁ kā kram is prakār hai. tele ke pārṇe meṁ ek din āge jitne dinoṁ kī tapasyā hogī, us se ādhe din. āyambil meṁ 5 din kī tapasyā meṁ 1 din 8 din meṁ 2 din āge pratyek cār din meṁ 1 din bādhāe. 12. tapasyā karne ke bād pūrṇ śakti na āe ṭab tak sone kī ājñā hai. 13. tivihār tapasyā meṁ 7 din bād aur cauvihār tapasyā meṁ cār din bād (āch tathā chāch ke agār se tapasyā 15 din bād) samuccay ke kārya va bhikṣā na karāī jāe aur pārṇā karne par jitne din samuccay kā āhār le unse ādhe din tak samuccay ke kārya aur bhikṣā na karāī jāe. kārya meṁ samuccay rahne ke dinoṁ kī saṁkhyā viṣam ho to ādhe din kā ek din samajhā jāe. jaise 10-10 din kī tapasyā meṁ pāṁc din samuccay meṁ rahtā hai to tīn din tak us meṁ samuccay kā kārya bhī nahīṁ rahegā.

vastra:

1. kapṛā jāṁce ṭab gṛhastha ke hāth se leṁ. pāḍihāriya vastra apne hāth se lāe, use bhī jāṁce ṭab gṛhastha ke hāth se leṁ. 2. ḍeṛh mās tak kalpa se adhik vastra (kavac, luṅkār, antarīya, śāl) rakhe jā sakte hai. 1.5 mītār kapṛā sardī meṁ atirikt rakh sakte haiṁ. 3. khaṇḍie ke lie jo kapṛā rakheṁ use na pahne na oṛhe. ek mītar se adhik lambāī meṁ na rakheṁ. 4. bahir vihār meṁ unī śāl (alvān) ādi kīmatī vastra, caśmā, spañj kambal yā kṛtrim dhāgoṁ vālā maphalar jāṁce to niyojikā ko mālum kareṁ. 5. oṛhne bichāne ke vastroṁ ko nirdhārit sīmā se adhik nahīṁ rakhnā. nirdhārit sīmā is prakār hai: uttariya 5, antarīya 2, colak 3, kavac 2, śāl 1, alvān 1, kambal 2, kholī 1, choṭā colak 3, mukhvastra 2, mukhvastrikā 2, proñchan paṭṭ 1, caśme 2, pain 2, doṭ 2, braś 2. asvasthā ādi kī sthiti meṁ bhī vastra kī nirdhārit sīmā kā pālan anivārya hai.

pātra:

1. pātra tīn se adhik na rakheṁ. dhātu ke pātroṁ meṁ bhojan nahīṁ karnā. pātra plāsṭik kāṭh yā miṭṭī ke ho. 2. jholī, pallā ādi kā dhoyā huā pānī bālṭī ādi meṁ dālā jāe to kārya pūrṇ hote hī paraṭṭha diyā jāeṁ. 3. pāḍihāriya bartanoṁ ko pāuḍar ādi se acchī tarah dhokar vāpas saumpeṁ. 4. yadi do samaṇī jī yātrā par jāeṁ to pāṁc pātra va ek jag rakh sakte haiṁ. bālṭī va ghaḍā atirikt rakh sakte hai. gṛhastha ke pātra apne kām meṁ lekar nahīṁ lauṭā sakte. 5. pāṁc kī saṅkhyā tak vastra prakṣālan ke lie cār ṭab aur do bālṭī se adhik prayog nahīṁ karnā. yadi āvaśyaktā ho to atirikt ṭab bālṭī jāṁc sakte hai, kintu ve usī din gṛhastha ko lauṭānī hogī.

vārṣik vivaraṇ:

1. prastut 'maryādāvalī' pratyek caumāsī pakkhī se pahle ek bār sab milkar paṛheṁ. 2. 'prāyaścitt vidhi' varṣa meṁ ek bār [sab milkar] avaśya paṛhe. 3. vastra jis gāṁv meṁ jis se, jitnā aur jis prakār kā jāṁceṁ uskī tālikā rakheṁ. jholī, pallā, luhaniyā ādi choṭe vastroṁ kā keval parimān likheṁ. 4. jis gāṁv se jisse jo viśiṣṭa (dhātu ādi kā) lī uskī tālikā rakheṁ. iñjekśan tathā elopathik goliyoṁ ke nām tathā saṅkhyā likheṁ. 5. tapasyā, vigay-varjan tathā viśeṣ sādhanā kī tālikā rakheṁ. 6. kahāṁ kitne din raheṁ aur kul kitne kṣetroṁ kī yātrā huī, tālikā rakheṁ. 7. viśeṣ upakār vigraha śamaṇ, naye vyaktiyoṁ ko guru dhāranā tathā śāsan prabhāvanā ke kāryoṁ kī tālikā rakheṁ. 8. prerak saṁsmaraṇ, svādhyāy, adhyayan, adhyāpan aur sāhitya racnā kī tālikā rakheṁ. 9. paḍihāriya (pustak, pāt, bājoṭ, auṣadh, kharal, cākū, kaiñcī, ādi vastu bhūl svāmī ko na dī gaī ho to likh kar rakheṁ. 10. tharmas kām meṁ le, caśmā jāṁce to likh kar rakheṁ.

vastra prakṣālan:

1. sāmānyataḥ saptāh meṁ ek din vastra prakṣālan kareṁ. garmī meṁ vaiśākh, jeṭh, āsāṛh meṁ pāṁc din ke bād kar sakte haiṁ. 2. ek rāt yā din kī ṭren yā bas kī yātrā kareṁ to ek ḍres dho sakte haiṁ aur yadi yātrā nirantar ho, to do din bād ek ḍres dho sakte hai. 3. vastra prakṣālan apekṣā ho to ek din pahle kiyā jā saktā hai kintu aglī bār pūrv kram se kareṁ. 4. niścit sthān par pahuṁcne ke bād cāhe ek utarīya dhoe yā ek ḍres dhoe, prakṣālan kā din usī ko ginā jāe. 5. pad yātrā meṁ vastra prakṣālan kā kram sāptāhik hī rahegā.

āhāra:

1. āhār meṁ pānti kā vibhājan saṃvibhāg pūrvak kareṁ. 2. nav dīkṣit ko āhār kī pānti cār mahīne tak na dī jāe. 3. bukhār va ṭāifāiḍ meṁ jab tak sāmānya āhār kī sthiti meṁ na aeā ṭab tak nahīṁ dī jāegī. 4. pathya-paṛhez meṁ yā kisī khādhya vastu ke tyāg ho yā koī prayog cal rahā ho to pānti barābar kī jāegī (sirf namak parihār ke prayog meṁ apavād hai). 5. āhār kā sarvathā niṣedh karne par use pānti nahīṁ dī jāegī kintu ek bhī dravya meṁ – bhāgidār hone par samān pānti kī jāegī. 6. mausambī, nāraṅgī, anār, aṅgūr yā inkā ras samuccay se le tathā madhyāhna, sāyaṃ meṁ kāfī, cāy le to pāṁc vigay ṭāleṁ. 7. matīre kā pānī, bel kā śarbat, ṭamāṭar kā ras samuccay se le to tīn vigay ṭāleṁ.

'bhakti':

1. prātaḥ kālīn ṭren se yadi jāeṁ to pahle din apnī bārī yathāvat calāeṁ. yadi śām kī ṭren se jānā ho to (dūsrī prahar ke āhār ke bād) śām kī bhakti. 2. rātri ke bārah baje se pahle yadi niścit sthān par pahuṁc jāe to bārī kā kram yathāvat calegā, ek samay kī bhakti kī jāegī. 3. ek śahar meṁ yadi do grup pahumcte haiṁ to pahle pahuṁcne vālā grup dūsre varga kī bhakti kareṁ. 4. cal yātrā meṁ ek samay kī bhakti kareṁ aur yadi sthāyī rūp se kahīṁ par raheṁ to āne vāle varga kī ek din kī bhakti kareṁ. 5. Lāḍnūṁ meṁ (athavā jahāṁ sāmūhik pravās ho) vadhyam [aṛhāī] mahīne bād yadi koī pahuṁce to ek din kī bhakti kareṁ. 6. tīn din ke bhītar vāpas ā jāe to bārī ke kram meṁ bārī calegī.

śrāvaka kī prāyaścitta vidhi:

1. sāmāyik meṁ kāṇṭā nikāle – 25 navkār. 2. varṣā kī būnde lag jāe – 1 navkārsī. 3. sāmāyik kam pār le yā baithā raheṁ – 2 yā 3 navkārsī. 4. sāmāyik bhaṅg ho jāe – 1 sāmāyik. 5. pauṣadh cau-prahārī bhaṅg ho jāe – 3 sāmāyik. 6. pauṣadh chav-prahārī bhaṅg ho jāe – 4 sāmāyik. 7. pauṣadh aṣṭa-prahārī bhaṅg ho jāe – 5 sāmāyik. 8. pauṣadh meṁ pānī pī leṁ – 1 belā. 9. tyāg meṁ rātrī bhojan ādi kar leṁ – 1 upavās yā 1 mās miṭhāī choṛnā.

Appendix

Kāyotsarga Pratimā

The *kāyotsarga pratimā* is a new obligatory form of insight meditation (*prekṣā dhyāna*), which was introduced by Ācārya Mahāprajña for the *samaṇ/īs*[150] in order to help them to 'pacify their emotions (*kaṣāya*)' through regular exercises of relaxation and meditation. *Sādhus* and *sādhvīs* are not obliged to practise this form of meditation, since they should have conquered their emotions already. Of the three meditation exercises per day which should be performed regularly by the *samaṇ/īs* on the eighth, fourteenth and fifteenth of every fortnight of the lunar calendar, one should be performed collectively by the members of a group. The times for meditation are not prescribed, but the collective *kāyotsarga pratimā* is usually performed early in the morning, before or after the *pratikramaṇa*, and the individual meditations at noon and before or after the evening *pratikramaṇa*. The *kāyotsarga pratimā* is commonly performed in the sitting or standing posture. Lying down, the third of the traditional *kāyotsarga* positions, is for obvious reasons prohibited (cf. Schubring, 1935: § 161). After the initial *kāyotsarga* resolution (cf. *ĀvS* 5.3), the group meditation is performed in three parts. Generally, but not necessarily, the group leader announces the beginning of each section by reciting its Prakrit opening verse: (1) *aiyaṃ paḍikkamāmi*, 'I repent my past mistakes'; (2) *paḍipunnaṃ saṃvareṃi*, 'I restrain myself at present'; (3) *aṇāgayaṃ paccakkhāmi*, 'I renounce my future mistakes'. After reciting the section title of the first part, the group leader (or another ascetic) announces for instance, 'We reflect now on anger committed during the last __ days.' Every *samaṇ/ī* then meditates silently for two to three minutes on this subject. During the thematically focused meditation, which may or may not involve the repetition (*jap*) of the following verses composed by Ācārya Mahāprajña, concrete instances of anger may be recalled and repented. The second part of the *kāyotsarga pratimā* focuses, in the same way, on the curtailment of anger, etc. in the present, and the third part on its renunciation in future, etc. Each of the three parts lasts about 12–26 minutes. The exercise ends with the meditative recitation of verses suggesting the progressive self-realization of the soul. In essence, the ritual replicates key features of the *pratikramaṇa*. In contrast to the *pratikramaṇa*, however, the compulsory *kāyotsarga* meditation is not merely a formulaic ritual, although the text of the ritual is fixed, but repents concrete mistakes.

Kāyotsarga Pratimā

Keep the body unmoving, relaxed and free from tension. Keep the spinal cord and neck straight. Give up your unrestrained desire. Keep your mind centred on the throat and create in the entire body a feeling of relaxation.

The aphorism of intention:

'Making an additional effort, performing penance, performing purification, extracting evil from myself, I stand in the *kāyotsarga* in order to make an end to sinful acts.'[151]

State of discrimination:

Discriminate the heterogeneous and the essential qualities in order to understand your own nature. Practice reflection –

I am not anger. Anger is not my nature.

I am not pride. Pride is not my nature.

I am not deceit. Deceit is not my nature.

I am not greed. Greed is not my nature.

I am not fear. Fear is not my nature.

I am not grief. Grief is not my nature.

I am not hatred. Hatred is not my nature.

I am not desire. Desire is not my nature.

I am not falsehood. Falsehood is not my nature.

Practise controlled breathing after each experience. Reflect upon it yourself, with full alertness and concentration.

State of abandoning the body:

'I repent the past'

I repent for the things I have done in the past.

If I have been angry, then may all the evil of mind, speech and action have been done in vain.

If I have been proud, then may all the evil of mind, speech and action have been done in vain.

If I have been deceitful, then may all the evil of mind, speech and action have been done in vain.

If I have been greedy, then may all the evil of mind, speech and action have been done in vain.

If I have been fearful, then may all the evil of mind, speech and action have been done in vain.

If I have been aggrieved, then may all the evil of mind, speech and action have been done in vain.

If I have been hateful, then may all the evil of mind, speech and action have been done in vain.

If I have been desirous, then may all the evil of mind, speech and action have been done in vain.

If I have been dishonest, then may all the evil of mind, speech and action have been done in vain.

'I stop the present.'

I stop the flux of Karma at present.

The feeling of forgiveness is developing.
The feeling of softness is developing.
The feeling of honesty is developing.
The feeling of patience is developing.
The feeling of fearlessness is developing.
The feeling of bliss is developing.
The feeling of friendship is developing.
The feeling of forgiveness is developing.
The feeling of chastity is developing.

'I renounce the future.'
I renounce sinful acts in the future.
I will not get angry.
I will not get proud.
I will not get deceitful.
I will not get greedy.
I will not get fearful.
I will not get aggrieved.
I will not get hateful.
I will not get desirous.
I will not get dishonest.
Controlled breathing.
The experience of one's true nature:
I am full of consciousness. I feel that my understanding is waking up.
I am full of bliss – my mental health is developing.
I am full of energy and power – my tolerance is growing.

The Text – Kāyotsarga Pratimā

śarīr ko sthir, śithil va tanāvamukta kare. pṛṣṭharajju aur gardan ko sīdhā rakheṁ. maṃśapeśiyoṁ ko dhīlā choṛ de. citt ko kaṇṭh par kendrit kareṁ aur pūre śarīr meṁ śithiltā kā anubhav kare.

saṅkalpa-sūtra

'tassa uttarī-karaṇeṇaṃ pāyacchitta-karaṇeṇaṃ visohī-karaṇeṇaṃ visallī-karaṇeṇaṃ pāvāṇaṃ kammāṇaṃ nigghāyaṇ-aṭṭhāe ṭhāmi kāusaggaṃ.'

viveka pratimā

apne svarūp ko jānne ke lie vijātīya tattvoṁ kā vivek kare. cintan kare – maiṁ krodh nahīṁ hūṁ. krodh mera svabhāv nahīṁ hai.

maiṁ mān nahīṁ hūṁ. mān mera svabhāv nahī haiṁ.

maiṁ māyā nahīṁ hūṁ. māyā mera svabhāv nahīṁ hai.

maiṁ lobh nahīṁ hūṁ. lobh mera svabhāv nahīṁ hai.

maiṁ bhay nahīṁ hūṁ. bhay mera svabhāv nahīṁ hai.

maiṁ śok nahīṁ hūṁ. śok mera svabhāv nahīṁ hai.

maiṁ ghṛṇā nahīṁ hūṁ. ghṛṇā mera svabhāv nahīṁ hai.

maiṁ kām nahīṁ hūṁ. kām mera svabhāv nahīṁ hai.

maiṁ mithyātva nahīṁ hūṁ. mithyātva mera svabhāv nahīṁ hai.

pratyek anubhav ke paścāt svās saṃyam kā prayog kareṁ. svayaṃ ko bhāvit kareṁ. pūrī jāgarūktā ke sāth, ekāgratā ke sāth.

kāyotsarga pratimā

'aīyaṃ paḍikkamāmi' maiṁ atīt kā pratikramaṇa kartī hūṁ.

maiṁ ne krodh kiyā ho to manasā, vācā, karmaṇā tassa micchāmi dukkaḍaṃ.

maiṁ ne mān kiyā ho to manasā, vācā, karmaṇā tassa micchāmi dukkaḍaṃ.

maiṁ ne māyā kiyā ho to manasā, vācā, karmaṇā tassa micchāmi dukkaḍaṃ.

maiṁ ne lobh kiyā ho to manasā, vācā, karmaṇā tassa micchāmi dukkaḍaṃ.

maiṁ ne bhay kiyā ho to manasā, vācā, karmaṇā tassa micchāmi dukkaḍaṃ.

maiṁ ne śok kiyā ho to manasā, vācā, karmaṇā tassa micchāmi dukkaḍaṃ.

maiṁ ne ghṛṇā kiyā ho to manasā, vācā, karmaṇā tassa micchāmi dukkaḍaṃ.

maiṁ ne kām kiyā ho to manasā, vācā, karmaṇā tassa micchāmi dukkaḍaṃ.

maiṁ ne mithyātva kiyā ho to manasā, vācā, karmaṇā tassa micchāmi dukkaḍaṃ.

'paḍipuṇṇaṃ saṃvaremi' maiṁ vartamāna kā saṃvara kartī hūṁ.

anubhav kare kṣamā kā vikās ho rahā hai.

anubhav kare mṛdutā kā vikās ho rahā hai.

anubhav kare ṛjutā kā vikās ho rahā hai.
anubhav kare santoṣ kā vikās ho rahā hai.
anubhav kare abhay kā vikās ho rahā hai.
anubhav kare ananda kā vikās ho rahā hai.
anubhav kare maitrī kā vikās ho rahā hai.
anubhav kare brahmacarya kā vikās ho rahā hai.

'aṇāgayaṃ paccakkhāmi' maiṁ bhaviṣya kā pratyākhyāna kartī hūṁ.
maiṁ krodh nahīṁ karūṅgī.
maiṁ mān nahīṁ karūṅgī.
maiṁ māyā nahīṁ karūṅgī.
maiṁ lobh nahīṁ karūṅgī.
maiṁ bhay nahīṁ karūṅgī.
maiṁ śok nahīṁ karūṅgī.
maiṁ ghṛṇā nahīṁ karūṅgī.
maiṁ kām nahīṁ karūṅgī.
maiṁ mithyātva nahīṁ karūṅgī.
svās saṃyam.

svarūpa kā anubhava –
maiṁ caitanyamay hūṁ. anubhav kareṁ merī prajñā jāg rahī hai.
maiṁ anandamayā hūṁ – merī mānsik svāsthya vikasit ho rahā hai.
maiṁ śakti sampann hūṁ – merī sahiṣṇutā baṛh rahī hai.

Notes

1 I wish to thank Samaṇī Pratibhāprajñā, Samaṇī Ṛjuprajñā, Mumukṣu Anita and Samaṇī Caritraprajñā, who explained to me the *Niyamāvalī* of the *samaṇ/īs* in August–October 2001. I am also indebted to Adelheid Mette and Lalita Du Perron for their valuable comments on earlier drafts of this article, and to Samaṇ Sthitiprajñā, who introduced me to Ācārya Tulsī in 1992.

2 The pioneers in this field were A. Weber, Jacobi, Leumann and Schubring. For further references see the text editions and translations cited in this article.

3 Today, there are eight to ten schools (depending on definitional criteria) and some 57 independently organized mendicant orders

in the Śvetāmbara tradition. The Digambara ascetics are currently not organized into tightly regulated mendicant orders (see Flügel, in press b).

4 With the exception of certain technical terms at their first occurrence, I have not transliterated the inherent Sanskrit vowel 'a' in roman script, in accordance with the conventions established by McGregor, 1993: xi.

5 For a general analysis of the structure and the function of rules in the Terāpanth mendicant order see Flügel, 1994: 107–45.

6 A translation of the *Maryādāvalī* of the monks is currently in preparation by the author.

7 For the history, doctrine and organization of the Terāpanth see Sharma 1991, Flügel, 1994, 1995–96, 2000. The Terāpanth split from the aniconic Dhannā Dharmadāsa Sthānakavāsī tradition in Rājasthān in 1760 under the leadership of Muni Bhīkhan (1726–1803). Bhīkhan disagreed with the Sthānakavāsī *ācārya* Raghunāth (1710–90) over the issue of the religious value of charity and compassionate help and advocated strict ascetic practice as the only path to salvation. In the late 19th century Ācārya Jayācārya (1803–81) established the present stronghold of the Terāpanth in the kingdom of Bīkāner where it remains the dominant aniconic Jain tradition to date. Until the reign of Ācārya Tulsī, the influence of the Terāpanth was largely confined to Rājasthān. Tulsī was a modernizer who, under the impact of the Indian independence in 1947, changed the inward-looking orientation of the order and promoted (Terāpanth) Jain moral values for the transformation of the world. He initiated social and monastic reforms and widened the geographical sphere of influence of the Terāpanth to India as a whole and Nepal. In 1980, he created a new category of Terāpanth Jain mendicants for the purpose of the Terāpanth mission in the subcontinent and abroad.

8 'The aim of establishing this new category of ascetics was not merely to help and facilitate the spread of Jainism abroad but it was also felt that it would open up new avenues of work since the Samaṇs and Samaṇis would not have to observe the vow of travelling on foot. Their mobility would result in the rapid expansion of constructive projects' (Mahāprajña, 1987: 37).

9 Ācārya Tulsī's *aṇuvrata*s are newly composed 'non-religious' small vows for specific spheres of application which supplement the rather general traditional Jain *aṇuvratas* which are formally identical with the *mahāvrata*s and rarely practised by Jain laity.

10 The Terāpanth distinguishes between religious (*dharmik*) values of world renunciation and moral (*naitik*) values of world transformation. For details on its programmes for the moral upliftment of mankind see the relevant publications of Ācārya Mahāprajña.

11 The meaning of the word *samaṇ* has been explained by Tulsī (1990: 8): 'There is a word *Samaṇa* in the Prakrit language. Its Sanskrit form *Śramaṇa* has three meanings: 1. One who exerts himself or has diligence (*Śrama*). 2. One who is calm and maintains equanimity *(Śama)*. 3. One who treats every one equally *(Sama)*. The *Śramaṇa* culture is grounded in these three main principles namely, exertion, equanimity and equality.' In this article I will call the *samaṇ*s 'novices' and the *mumukṣus* 'neophytes.'

12 The code of conduct of the *mumukṣus* is more severe than the *aṇuvratas* for laity and does not include any reference to the religious duties of a Jain householder, such as gift-giving: 'The aims of the *mumukṣus* are: 1. Pure mind or release from passions. 2. Introduction into religious practice by the *samaṇ*s or *muni*s. 3. To balance education with religious practice. PSS legislation: Entry qualifications: 1. Emotionally felt desire for the attainment of salvation. 2. Letter of consent of the relatives. Code of conduct of the *mumukṣus*: 1. To develop non-violence mentally and ideologically. 2. Not to tell lies. 3. Not to take things not given. 4. To observe celibacy. 5. To develop selfless sentiments. 6. To develop genuineness and fearfulness of sin. There are some vows worth knowing not only for external discipline but also for the development of self-discipline: 1. Not to be angry, to develop tolerance. 2. Not to have pride, deceptiveness, and licentiousness. 3. Not to waste time with futile amusements. 4. Not to squander time with gossip and sleep. 5. Joyfully to admit mistakes. For the development of religious devotion it is mandatory to practice every day *sāmāyik, navkārsī, arhat vandanā, dhyān-yogāsan,* to study three hundred religious verses, to write a diary, and also to practice self-contemplation.' In the Hindī

original: *mumukṣu ke dhyey haiṁ: 1. cit śuddhi yā kaṣāya mukti. 2. samaṇ yā muni bhūmikā kī sādhanā. 3. śikṣā aur sādhanā kā santulan. – paramārthik śīkṣaṇ saṃsthā kā vidhān: praveś yogyatā: 1. mumukṣā bhāv. 2. abhibhāvakoṁ kī svīkṛti patra. – mumukṣu ācār-saṃhitā: 1. mānasik evaṃ vaicārik ahiṁsā kā vikās. 2. asatya sambhāṣaṇ nahīṁ karnā. 3. adatt vastu grahaṇ nahīṁ karnā. 4. brahmācārya kā pālan karnā. 5. nirmamatva bhāvanā kā vikās karnā. 6. pāpabhīrutā tathā prāmāṇiktā kā vikās. –yahāṁ keval bāhyānuśāsan hī nahīṁ atmānuśāsan ke vikās hetu bhī kuch ek habandu jñātavya haiṁ: 1. krodh nahīṁ karnā, sahiṣṇutā kā vikās karnā. 2. abhimān, chal, ucchṛṅkhalatā nahīṁ karnā. 3. hāsya-kutūhal meṁ vyartha samay nahīṁ gaṁvāṇā. 4. atinidrā va dantakathā meṁ samay kā apavyay nahīṁ karnā. 5. apnī truṭi saharṣ svīkār kar lenā. sādhanā-vikās hetu pratidin, sāmāyik, navkārsī, arhat vandanā, dhyān-yogāsan, tin sau gāthāoṁ kā svādhyāy karnā, ḍāyrī likhnā evaṃ atmacintana karnā anivārya hai* (Mahāśramaṇ Muditkumār, via letter from J.C. Jain, 20 April 1996).

13 In 2001, the Terāpanth had 144 *sādhus*, 534 *sādhvīs*, 4 *samaṇs* and 83 *samaṇīs*. In 1992 it had 60 *mumukṣu* sisters, 10 *upāsikās* and the occasional *upāsaka* (I have no later figures for these categories).

14 Compare the situation represented by the diagram in Flügel, 1995–96: 131.

15 Even a – rarely performed – initiation ritual for Terāpanth laity (*śrāvaka dīkṣā*) has been designed. The status of a 'Jain layperson' is either acquired by birth or/and by a informally performed vow of allegiance to the *ācārya* in his presence. Since the laity do not form an exclusively organized group, there are in practice no formal membership criteria (though vegetarianism is taken for granted).

16 The first two involve little more than signing the respective rules and regulations. The principal initiatory stages are indicated by double lines in the chart.

17 This applies to unmarried girls, not to widows and older women.

18 Generally, Jain mendicants must renounce the world for life. There is no turning back, since the lay community will not accept them again. In practice, only men have made use of the possibility of temporary renunciation so far. Young women find it

embarrassing to return to their families with short hair after their period of temporary renunciation (the shaving of the head is required at the initiation).

19 *samaṇa sāmāiya-suttam:*

karemi bhaṃte! sāmāiyaṃ sāvajjaṃ jogaṃ paccakkhāmi –
uvasaṃpajjāmi ṇaṃ cauvvihaṃ samaṇa-dhammaṃ –
khaṃtiṃ, maddavaṃ, ajjavaṃ, lāghavaṃ.
vajjayāmi ṇaṃ cauvvihaṃ ajjhattha-dosaṃ –
kohaṃ, māṇaṃ, māyaṃ, lohaṃ.
uvasaṃpajjāmi ṇaṃ paṃcavihaṃ samaṇa-veramaṇaṃ. –
pāṇāivāyāo veramaṇaṃ, musāvāyāo veramaṇaṃ, adinnādāṇāo veramaṇaṃ, mehunāo veramaṇaṃ, pariggahāo veramaṇaṃ.
uvasaṃpajjāmi ṇaṃ tivihaṃ samaṇa-aṇusāsaṇaṃ –
mana-aṇusāsaṇaṃ, vaya-aṇusāsaṇaṃ, kāya-aṇusāsaṇaṃ.
uvasaṃpajjāmi ṇaṃ samaṇa-sīlaṃ –
santaṃ sahavāsaṃ.
vajjayāmi ṇaṃ cauvvihaṃ pāvaṃ –
kalahaṃ, abbhakkhāṇaṃ, pesuṇṇaṃ, paraparivādaṃ.
uvasaṃpajjāmi ṇaṃ paṃcavihaṃ samaṇa-vivegaṃ –
gamaṇa-vivegaṃ, bhāsā-vivegaṃ, bhoyaṇa-vivegaṃ, uvagaraṇa-vivegaṃ, ussagga-vivegaṃ.
uvasaṃpajjāmi ṇaṃ cauvvihaṃ samaṇa-sāhaṇaṃ –
sajjhāyaṃ, jhāṇaṃ, aṇuppehaṃ, ṭhāṇaṃ.
uvasaṃpajjāmi ṇaṃ suya-sāmāiyaṃ –
kāle, vinae, bahu-māṇe, uvahāṇe, tahā a-ṇiṇhavaṇe, vaṃjana-, attha-, tad-ubhae, attha-viho ṇāṇa-m-āyāro.
uvasaṃpajjāmi ṇaṃ daṃsaṇa-sāmāiyaṃ –
nissaṃkiya-, nikkaṃkhiya-, nivvitigicchā, a-mūdhada-diṭṭhī ya, uvavūha-, thirī-karaṇe-, vacchalla-, pabhāvaṇe aṭṭha.
jāvajjīvaṃ eyaṃ savvaṃ uvasaṃpajjāmi appasakkhiyaṃ gurusakkhiyaṃ. aikkamaṇaṃ na karemi, na kāravemi, karaṃtaṃ pi aṇṇaṃ na. samaṇujāṇāmi. tassa bhaṃte! paḍikkamāmi niṃdāmi garihāmi appāṇaṃ vosirāmi

(Sanmatiprajñā, 1996: 49f.).

20 These ethical principles are the counterparts to the four passions (*kasāya*) anger, pride, deceit, greed. For their canonical origins see Schubring, 1935: § 174.

21 See *DVS* 4.11–15. The *samaṇ/īs* accept the *mahāvratas* in name, but not the specifications that are detailed in the DVS.

22 For these, so-called, three *guptis* see *Utt* 24.19–26 and *TS* 9.4.

23 The five *samitis* are treated in *Utt* 24.1–18.

24 This quotation corresponds to verse 184 (edition Bollée) of the *Dasaveyāliya Nijjutti* with parallels in other texts, in particular the *Niśītha Bhāṣya* 8. I am indebted to Kornelius Krümpelmann and Adelheid Mette for this information. See Leumann, 1892b: 651, and Bollée, 1995: 49, fn. 335 who also cites another parallel. Adelheid Mette has provided me with a translation of this verse in German.

25 The translation is an adaptation of Jacobi's rendering of *Utt* 28.31 (= *DVN* 182 = *Niśītha Bhāṣya* 23) to which this texts corresponds. For further parallels see Bollée (1995: 49, Fn. 335). Adelheid Mette pointed out to me that the *Niśītha Bhāṣya* may be the source of both *DVN* quotations in the *Samaṇa Sāmāiya Sutta*, because the verses are cited in the same sequence, not in accordance with the sequence in the *DVN*. See also Williams (1963: 43f.) on the *aṅgas* of *samyaktva*.

26 The *cha koṭi/nau koṭi* issue, so important for the differentiation of the *sāmāyik* ritual of Jain mendicants and lay-people (Flügel, 2000: 63–5), is sidestepped in this formula by not mentioning 'in mind, speech and body, *maṇasā, vayasā, kāyasā*' at all. Cf. Leumann, 1934: 6, 42; Williams, 1963: 132; Bruhn, 1981, 1997–98; Balbir, 1993. See also Shāntā (1985: 244–246, 354, 536–537, 543, n. 15) and the version of the Terāpanth laity in *AK* I: 272.

27 For similar practices amongst the Terāpanth *śramaṇs* see Flügel, 1995–96: 132.

28 *saṅkalpa patra: maiṁ śramaṇ bhagavān mahāvīr tathā uske nigranth pravacan meṁ śraddhā pratīti aur ruci-vyakta kartā/kartī hūm. tathā savinay śraddhāñjali yah saṅkalpa svīkār kartā/kartī hūṁ ki śrī bhikṣu, bhārīmāl ādi pūrvaj ācārya tathā vartamān ācārya śrī tulsī gaṇi dvārāā pradatta anuśāsan mujhe mānya haiṁ.*
gurudev ! āp saṅgh ke prāṇ haiṁ śramaṇ paramparā ke adhinetā haiṁ. āp par mujhe pūrṇa śraddhā hai.

1. *maiṁ āp ke anuśāsan kā atikramaṇ nahīṁ karūṁgā/karūṁgī.*
2. *maiṁ apne/apnī niyojak/niyoyikā ke anuśāsan kā atikramaṇ nahīṁ karūṁgā/ karūṁgī.*
3. *maiṁ samaṇ śrenī ke sāmāyik kā ātma-sākṣī se anuśīlan karūṁgā/karūṁgī.*
4. *maiṁ muni saṅgh ke prati pūrṇ niṣṭhāvān tathā vinamra rahūṁgā/rahūṁgī.*

5. *maiṁ samaṇ-śreṇī meṁ dīkṣit sabhī samaṇ-samaṇiyoṁ ke prati sam vartāv karūṁgā/karūṁgī. kisī ko apnā banāne kā prayatna nahīṁ karūṁgā/karūṁgī.*
6. *maiṁ apne se baṛoṁ ke prati vinamra rahūṁgā/rahūṁgī tathā choṭoṁ ke prati udār rahūmgī/rahūṁgī.*
7. *maiṁ pravās aur yātrā meṁ āp kī dṛṣṭi kā aṇusaran karūṁgā/ karūṁgī.*
8. *maiṁ apnī icchā se kisī ko samaṇ śreṇī meṁ sammilit nahīṁ karūṁgā/karūṁgī.*
9. *maiṁ kisī bhī sādharmik kī utartī bāt nahīṁ karūṁgā/ karūṁgī.*
10. *maiṁ kisī meṁ dos jān paṛegā to use yā usse sambaddha adhikārī ko batāūṁgā/ batāūmgī. anyatra uskī carcā nahiṁ karūṁgā/karūṁgī.*
11. *maiṁ kisī bhī vivādāspad viṣay meṁ āp yā āp dvārā nirdiṣṭ vyakti ke nirṇay ko sahajtā se svīkār karūṁgā/karūṁgī. yah saṅkalpa patra maiṁ ne śraddhāpūrvak svīkār kiyā hai, saṅkoc, āveś yā prabhāvvaś nahīṁ.*
svīkarttā/svīkarttrī samaṇ/samaṇī

(Sanmatiprajñā, 1996: 45f.).

29 The majority of the historical studies have been produced by the Terāpanth mendicants themselves who from 1946 onwards published original documents and general historiographic accounts covering the period from the schism of the Terāpanth from the Sthānakavāsīs in 1760 up to the eighth Ācārya Kālugaṇī (1877–1936). These works are based almost entirely on Terāpanth sources. They comprise mainly doctrinal, biographical and legal materials written in Rājasthānī by the founder of the Terāpanth, Ācārya Bhikṣu (1726–1803), and by its chief organizer, Ācārya Jītmal (1803–81). They contain only few details on subsequent developments. See Tulsī 1960–61; Tulsī and Mahāprajña, 1981, 1983; Navratanmal 1981–2001; Sharma, 1991; Budhmal, 1995, 2001.

30 The presently available ethnographic studies focus mainly on the overt aspects of ascetic conduct, the rituals and ceremonies of contemporary Terāpanth mendicants, and their widely publicised socio-religious projects. See Balbir, 1983; Shāntā, 1985; Goonasekere, 1986; Holmstrom, 1988; Flügel, 1994, 1995 –96; Vallely, 2002.

31 To date, the only study of other Jain mendicant orders is Flügel, 2000, 2003.

32 Nowadays, the term *samācārī* (*sāmācārī*) is often used for the current non-canonical vernacular lists of *maryādā*s. However, the word can refer both to canonical and non-canonical or customary rules. Mette (1974: 6f.) has suggested that the meaning of the Prakrit term *samāyārī* (*sāmāyārī*) was extended already in the early medieval period from the old lists of 10 monastic duties (*Utt* 26.1–7, etc.) to a whole range of disciplinary canonical texts, such as the *PK* and the *ON*, which she interprets as a running commentary ('fortschreitender Kommentar') of the *DVS* 5.

33 *Viy* 383a (8.8.2) = *Vav.* 10.2 = *Ṭhāṇa* 317b (5.124), tr. Deleu, 1970: 152. The Terāpanth Ācārya Jayācārya [Jītmal] (in Tulsī and Mahāprajña, 1983: 341), for instance, legitimated his innovations explicitly with reference to the *jīyakappa* rule.

34 See for instance Caillat, 1965 [1975]: 113, 213 who investigated rule changes in the canonical *vinaya* literature. Rayanade (1982) writes: 'The emphasis is not so much on the rules so much as on personal choice' (p. 14). Following Amarmuni, he deduces from the fact that rules cannot be followed literally that the terms of the canonical *vinaya* literature have to be interpreted 'symbolically' (p. 5) – an interpretation that is favoured by 'modern' Jain mendicants.

35 The only printed currently-used list is, to my knowledge, the *Samācārī* of the Sthānakavāsī Śramaṇsaṅgh (AISJC, 1987).

36 The canon is not of one piece and some of its rules and statements are mutually contradictory.

37 In addition, special handwritten lists of atonements are drafted which overlap with those in the *maryādāvalī* texts. The ancient penitential literature is only consulted in difficult cases (see Flügel, in press b).

38 Access to the specific rules and regulations of Jain mendicant orders is still frequently prevented in order to protect the order from outside interference. The fact that the Terāpanth mendicants made their current rules and regulations freely available to me reflects the outward-looking attitude of their present leadership.

39 See also Rayande (1982: 15).

40 That is, it is structured according to lists of points (*pada vibhāga*). See *ĀvN* 665 and *Mūlācāra* 124 in Mette, 1974: 4f.

41 Nowadays, most of the themes are conventionalized across sectarian divisions.

42 The *prāyaścittas* for laity are a recent innovation of the Terāpanth (see Flügel, in press a, b).

43 Tulsī 1989b.

44 Translation of Tulsī 1991.

45 For a different and rather general list of nine 'essential' *ācār saṃhitās* see Sanmati-prajñā, 1996: 18f.

46 One hand (*hāth*) is the measure of the length of a forearm.

47 In *bhādrapad* and *phālgun*.

48 In contrast to the *sādhus* and *sādhvīs*, *samaṇs* and *samaṇīs* can accept food that is especially prepared for them. However, they have to observe the proper procedures of begging and usually do not eat in the presence of lay people.

49 Laypeople should not work for mendicants.

50 Cf. *Nisīha* 6.13, in Schubring and Caillat, 1966: 97.

51 This is routinely done, however.

52 The *ekāsan* fast requires not to eat more than once a day. Terāpanthīs commonly practise the following fasts (I follow the spelling in their ritual literature): *navkārsī* – fasting for 1 *muhūrta* after sunrise; *porsī* – fasting for 1 *prahar* (*pahar*) after sunrise (1/4 of the bright half of the day: *ca.* 3 hours); *ḍeṛh porsī* – fasting for 1.5 *prahar* after sunrise; *do prahar* (*purimaḍḍha*) – fasting for 2 *prahar* after sunrise; *apārdha* – fasting for 3 *prahar* after sunrise; *ekāsan* (*ekāśan*) – only 1 meal a day; *beāsan* – only 2 meals a day; *nīvī* (*nīvī, nirvigay, nirvikrti*) – not to eat *vigay* food, such as milk, yoghurt, butter, etc. for 1 day (salt permitted); *ekal ṭhānā* (*ek sthān*) – to eat only once a day, within one hour, silently, in only one position; *āyambil* (*āmbil*) – to eat only once a day one unsalted cereal; *upavās* – 1 day fasting (to drop three meals); *cauttha* – 1.5 days fasting (to drop three meals); *belā* – 2 days continuously fasting; *caṭṭha* – 2.5 days fasting (to drop five meals); *telā* – 3 days continuously fasting; *aṭṭham* – 3.5 days fasting (to drop seven meals); *colā* – 4 days continuously fasting; *pañcolā* – 5 days continuously fasting; *che* (*chah*) – 6 days continuously fasting; *sāt*

– 7 days continuously fasting; *aṭhāī* – 8 days continuously fasting (*aththaī*); *nau* – 9 days continuously fasting; *das* – 10 days continuously fasting; *pakkhvard* (*pakṣman*) – 15 days continuously fasting; *māskhamaṇ* – 1 month continuously fasting [or: *gāthā svādhyāya, paraṭhaṇā, purimaḍḍha, nīvī, āyambil, ekāśan* etc.]; *chomāsi* – 4 months continuously fasting; *chemāsi* – 6 months continuously fasting; *ekāntarā* – alternating 1 day fasting and 1 day eating; *belā telā* – alternating 2 days continuously fasting and 1 day eating; *telā telā* – alternating 3 days continuously fasting and 1 day eating; *colā telā* – alternating 4 days continuously fasting and 1 day eating; *soliyā* – 16 days alternating one day fasting and one day eating (often practised by freshly wedded couples); *varṣī* – 13.5 months alternating one day fasting and one day eating only once; *oḷī* (lit. line) – variable combination of different fasts (*āyambil, upavās,* etc.); *naupad oḷī* – practising 9 days continuously *nivi* or *āyambil,* in April and September for 4 years; *anaśan* – to renounce food forever: beginning of the death fast (*santhārā*). Compare the conventional *Āvassaya Sutta* list of ten renunciations (Pkt. *paccakkhāṇa,* Skt. *pratyākhyāna*): 1. *namukkāra sahiya* (Skt. *namaskāra sahitya,* Hd. *navkārsī*) – not to eat during the first *muhūrta* (*ca.* 48 minutes) after sunrise, 2. *porisī* (Skt. *pauruṣī,* Hd. *prahar*). – not to eat in the first quarter of the bright half of the day after sunrise (*ca.* 3 hours), 3. *purimaḍḍha* (Skt. *purimārddha, dina pūrvārddha*) – not to eat until midday, 4. *egāsana* (Skt. *ekāśana,* Hd. *ekāsan*) – not to eat more than once a day [Schubring 1935: § 156, 2000: 'if one half of the day [first or second] remains without a meal being taken' (p. 275)], 5. *egaṭṭhāṇa* (Skt. *eka-sthāna,* Hd. *ek sthān*) – to eat only once a day, within one hour, silently, in only one position, 6. *āyambila* (Skt. *ācāmla*) – to eat only once a day one unsalted cereal, 7. *abhattaṭṭha* (Skt. *abhaktartha,* cf. Pkt. *cāuttha bhatta*) – to fast for 24 hours, or to drink only water (*anupavāsa*), 8. *divasa carima* (*carama*) – not to eat or drink one hour before sunset, 9. *abhiggaho* (Skt. *abhigraha*) – not to accept food without prior fulfillment of special conditions (e.g. only from a woman), 10. *nivvīgaiya* (Skt. *vikṛti niṣedha, nirvikrti,* Hd. *nirvigay*) – not to eat *vikṛti* (*vigaya*) food, i.e. products such as milk, yoghurt, butter, molasses etc. that have changed their taste by having undergone a transformation through cooking or bacteria (*ĀvS* 6.1–10, cf. *AK* I: 31f., Williams, 1963: 207–13, Schubring, 1905: 14, n. 1).

53 The *nirvigaya* fast demands the avoidance of the conventional ten forms of 'transformed' food (*vigaya*, Pkt. *vigaiya*, Skt. *vikṛti*), i.e. (rare) items which changed their taste (*ras calit*) due to cooking or bacteria. The ten are milk (*dūdh*), yoghurt (*dahī*), clarified butter (*ghī, ghṛt*), oil (*tail*), molasses (*guṛ*), butter (*navnīt*), a dish made of rice cooked in oil (*avagāhim*) as well as three items which have to be always avoided: alcohol (*madya*), honey (*madhu*), meat (*māṃsa*). The standard lists vary slightly (cf. *Ṭhāṇa* 204b, 450b, in Schubring, 1935 § 156; *Yogaśāstra* 3.130, in Williams, 1963: 39f.). The Terāpanthīs usually list the first five and sweets (*miṭhāī*) in contrast to Khartargacch Jains who apparently regard salt as the sixth *vigay* (Laidlaw, 1995: 182). They also assume that, due to the transformation process, *vigay* food is lifeless, which is not accepted by other mendicant orders.

54 This rule is commonly found in the Dharmadāsa Sthānakavāsī traditions in Rājasthān, for instance in the Jñāngacch. The conventional five fast-days (*pāṁcū tithi*) of the Terāpanth are the second, fifth, eighth, fourteenth and fifteenth. The eleventh, called silence eleven (*maun ekādaśī*), which is popular in Gujarāt, is not observed.

55 Cf. Jayācārya, 1981: 82. Jain mendicants should not leave the abode of their *guru*, unless it is necessary, and only with permission. They return back (from the world) without elaborate formula of politeness. The formulae *āvassahī* (Pkt. *āvassiyā*), conventionally used at the point of departure from the abode, and *nissahī* (Pkt. *nisihiyā*), used at the point of return to the abode, are two of the ten canonical deportments of Jain mendicants (*Utt* 26.1–7, etc.). Leumann (1934: 9f.) followed the commentators Śāntyācārya and Lakṣmīvallabh, *ĀvN* 7.29–36 and *Mūlācāra* 4.5f., in translating *āvassiyā* as 'obligatory, duty' ('Pflicht-Nöthigung') and *nisihiyā* as 'departure/turning away' ('Abkehr'). The terms were later incorporated into lay Jain rites of image worship, where *nissahī* is uttered when the temple is entered and *āvassahī* when it is left. Notably, the points of reference are reversed.

56 The obligatory inspection (Pkt. *paḍilehaṇā*, Skt. *pratilekhanā*) has to be performed at least twice a day and consists of scrutinizing all possessions and gently removing insects from cloths, books, brushes, etc.

57 This relaxation of the traditional prohibition of sleeping during the day has been introduced by Ācārya Mahāprajña for both *śramaṇs* and *samaṇs.*

58 After the evening *pratikramaṇa* the junior *samaṇ/īs* ceremonially greet all senior *samaṇ/ īs* by performing the *vandanā* rite. With hands folded, they individually approach the group leader first and ask: *vandāmi namaṃsāmi, samaṇ/ī jī āpke sukhsātā hai* – 'I bow to you and greet you *samaṇ/ī jī,* are you happy (do you need anything)?' Usually, the answer is no, and the group-leader responds with a short informal blessing, such as touching the head of the junior *samaṇ/ī* with her/his hand and saying '*arham*' – 'worthy of worship.' The word *arham* is said to be indicative of non-attachment and is also used as a *mantra* and for the practice of *jap* (cf. Sanmatiprajñā, 1996: 16). If the answer is yes, then the junior *samaṇ/ī* will inquire whether s/he can do anything to ease the problem at hand. *Vandanā* is performed once a day to every senior *samaṇ/ī* and twice a day to the respective group leader, i.e. the *niyojak/niyojikā* or the *nirdeśak/nirdeśikā,* who is greeted not only in the evening but after both daily collective *pratikramaṇa* (Pkt. *paḍikkamaṇa*) rituals. Senior ascetics never perform *vandanā* to junior ascetics. Every two weeks, after the *pakkhī pratikramaṇa,* which atones the sins of a fortnight, and the *vandanā,* the rite of mutual forgiveness, *kṣamā yācanā* is performed. The following formula is used: *vandāmi namaṃsāmi, pakkhī sambandhī koī avinay āśātanā huī ho to bārambār khamāijyo* – 'I bow to you and greet you, if during the past fortnight discourtesy [or] improper behaviour towards you occurred, then I beg you repeatedly for forgiveness' (the scriptures (*DVS* 3, etc.) distinguish 33 forms of improper behaviour towards a senior (Pkt. *asāyaṇā,* Skt. *āśātanā*; see Schubring, 1935: § 158, Williams, 1963: 225–9). A different *vandanā* formula is used by the *samaṇ/ īs* vis-à-vis the *sādhus* and *sādhvīs* (*matthaena vandāmi* – 'I venerate you with the head [bowing down]'). This formula has been characterized by Leumann (1934: 9) as a simplified version of the original *laghu guru vandanā* formula to be used by the Jain laity. The innovative formula *vandāmi namaṃsāmi* which was created for ceremonial greetings amongst the *samaṇ/īs* is an alternative simplification of the ritual performed by the mendicants.

59 See Appendix.

60 The expression *bāhar*, away from home or abroad, implicitly refers to the Terāpanth centre Lādnūṁ where the *samaṇs* and *samaṇī/īs* are trained, though technically Terāpanth *samaṇ/īs* are 'homeless.' Especially when the *samaṇ/īs* go abroad or visit the *ācārya*, time is short and particularly valuable. The *kāyotsarga pratimā* is therefore only performed twice on each of the three *tithis*. In recent years, compulsory meditation has been generally reduced from three times to two times on the eighth, fourteenth and fifteenth of every lunar fortnight, because of the 'lack of time' of the *samaṇ/īs*, who are in great demand.

61 In the summer heat, everyone wants to sleep close to the window and in winter away from it. In order to avoid quarrel, the rule has been made that the distance to the window is determined by seniority (order of initiation). However, sometimes the sequence can be reversed to give the juniors also a chance of a good night's sleep. Sleeping outside the abode is prohibited. See *Bṛhat Kalpa Bhāṣya* 1574f., in Tatia and Kumar, 1981: 52. The problem is acute at the occasion of the annual assembly of the mendicants, when many *samaṇīs* have to sleep in one room.

62 See the specific rules against the use of addiction-inducing intoxicants and on writing reports below. If ratified by the *ācārya*, the achievements listed in the reports are nowadays published by Muni Sumeramal (1997ff.).

63 The technical Prakrit term *pāḍihāriya* (Skt. *prātihārika*) refers to items that are borrowed from householders. There are two types of objects: those which are potentially harmful (*śāstra*), such as scissors, needles, etc. and those which are not. Objects of the first type have to be returned before dusk, whereas other items, books, pencils, etc. can be kept indefinitely, but have to be returned personally to their original owner.

64 Freshly initiated mendicants enjoy a period free of duty to allow them to acclimatize. All other mendicants have to perform their equal share of daily routine work, such as cleaning the floor (*sāphā-pānī*), filling up the water pitcher (*ghaṛā, matkā, maṭkī*), washing (*dhonā*), etc. The *samaṇīs* take turns. In small groups, one *samaṇī* performs all routine work for the entire group for one day, or the tasks are divided up.

65 This rule relates to the peculiarities of the modern way of life. Exceptions are granted in cases of illness, weakness due to

excessive fasting, etc. Monks and nuns are not allowed to use modern technology at all.

66 The 30 obligatory fasts comprise 24 hour fasts (*upavāsa*) on the 24 *pakkhī* days, three two-day fasts (*belā*) on the three *cāturmāsik pakkhī* days which overlap with three one-day fasts of the 24 *pakkhī* days, and one three-day fast (*telā*) on the annual *saṃvatsarī* day: (24x1) + ((3x2) – (3x1)) + (1x3). If for some reason a *samaṇī* cannot perform the fasts according to this ideal pattern, an equivalent number of lighter fasts (e.g. two *ekāsanas* instead of one *upavāsa*, etc.) can be performed or other religious performances, with special permission of the *ācārya*.

67 Rare and costly types of food, such as fruit juice, dry fruits, etc., which may be important for curing illness, etc. are considered to be the property of the entire group of ascetics at one particular place. In contrast to ordinary food, such as bread, which can be eaten by the members of each itinerant group, the availability of these types of food has to be reported to all groups in a particular location in order to be allocated to the needy by the most senior mendicant (see *ON* 503, 525–6).

68 Breaking a fast means completing it. E.g. for two days after a four-day fast, three days after a six-day fast, five days after a ten-day fast, etc. any type of food can be taken from the whole group. This unwritten rule reflects the need for specific types of food, which are sometimes unavailable in one group, for nurturing an individual back to full strength after a long fast.

69 The *āyambila* (*ācāmāmla*), or 'sour' fast, of the Terāpanthīs requires the eating, only once a day, of one unsalted cereal 'cooked only in water with a sour flavouring' (*āmla-rasa*)' (Williams, 1963: 40, cf. 209). For the meaning of the word *āyambila* see Schubring, 1935: § 156.

70 The threefold (*tivihār*) fast permits drinking water, whereas the fourfold (*cauvihār*) fast requires complete abstinence. See Williams, 1963: 39.

71 That is, a one and a half day release from compulsory collective work is rounded up to two days, two and a half days to three days, etc.

72 The polite expression *jāṁcnā* (Pkt. *jāyaṇā*, Skt. *yācanā*), to investigate, here means to ask for, to receive or accept, begging, soliciting.

73 Terāpanth mendicants may touch objects belonging to a householder but cannot borrow them without asking and receiving them formally from the hand of the owner.

74 The uniform of the *samaṇ/īs* and *samaṇīs*, called *kavac* (lit. armour), is a specially designed white cotton frock with the word '*arham*' stitched in red colour onto the chest.

75 *Khaṇḍiya* are small pieces of fabric that are torn off a larger piece of cloth to be used for cleansing the body orifices and the paraphernalia of the mendicants.

76 This list of possessions is not exhaustive (*khaṇḍiya* clothes for instance are not mentioned). In addition, the *samaṇ/īs* borrow most essentials for their daily use, such as soap, toothpaste, etc. from the householders.

77 *Samaṇ/īs* cannot accept vessels made of metal. Today, the buckets used both by *samaṇ/īs* and *sādhu-sādhvīs* are usually made of plastic, and should only comprise insignificant pieces of metal, such as a handle. Metal is avoided, because it is regarded as a valuable possession, and because it is produced in a process involving violence. Orthodox Jain mendicants also do not accept plastic vessels or vessels containing small pieces of metal.

78 The technical term for discarding, which should take place not later than 48 minutes, is *paraṭhaṇā* (Pkt. *pariṭṭhavaṇa*, Skt. *pariṣṭhāpana*). See *ON* 303; Mette, 1974: 138f., 143; Mette (in press); Flügel (forthcoming).

79 Or a pitcher, both made of plastic.

80 In contrast to other objects borrowed from householders, bowls and plates used for eating should not be returned. That is, the *samaṇ/īs* should only eat from their own bowls.

81 The use of both water and utensils should be minimised.

82 Cf. *AS* 2.1.8, etc. The term *gocarī* should not be used for the begging round of the *samaṇ/īs*, to distinguish them clearly from the *śramaṇas*.

83 Pieces of raw fruit may contain life even after being pickled. They are only considered dead after a transformation of taste induced by the admixture of different substances. The acceptability of various types of pickles is a contentious issue in the Jain tradition. For the Sthānakavāsī *sacitt-acitt* debate see

Flügel, 2000: 83, Fn. 83, 2002. For a critique of such 'non-canonical' practices from a Mūrtipūjak standpoint see Atmārām, 1903: 291.

84 A peeled raw onion which has not been cut into pieces and remains whole on the outside should not be eaten, even if it is pickled. Cf. *Viy* 21.1–21.2–10 (800a–801b); *Viy* 23 (804a); Deleu, 1970: 19f., 260–262; *Utt* 36.97–100, tr. Jacobi 1895: 216, fn. 11.

85 The implication is that all life in a peeled but uncut onion is killed after three days through the contact with heated substances such as clarified butter and oil. This rule is significant because, in contrast to most other Jain ascetics and lay people, Terāpanth (and some north Indian Sthānakavāsī) mendicants and laity do eat onions, potatoes and even garlic and carrots if they have been boiled or transformed into something else without having being boiled (e.g. carrots used in the sweet dish *gājar halvā*, potato chips, dried ginger). This practice divides, for instance, the members of the Terāpanth and Mūrtipūjak Osvāl castes, in Rājasthān and Gujarāt respectively, and has been criticised by Mūrtipūjak *ācāryas* such as Atmārām (1903: 292). To avoid conflict, Ācārya Mahāprajña abolished this rule during his itinery to Gujarāt in 2003. The argument in support of eating onions and potatoes has been explained by him in his own *Bhagavatī Sūtra Bhāṣya* (*BSB*) (p. 352f., and *Viy* 7.3.66). He writes that the scriptures distinguish only two types of plants: *praktyakṣa* and *ananta-kāya*, and that it is not explicitly mentioned in the Āgamas that one should not eat roots. There are, he writes, three different opinions in the scriptures: (1) The *Utt* 36.96–99 says, it is forbidden to eat root vegetables such as onions and garlic because they are *ananta-kāya*. (2) The *Jīvājīvābhigama* 1.73 and *Viy* 23.1–2 do not mention this. (3) *Pannavaṇā* 1.48.43 (cf. 1.32, 1.48.1–7) says that there is only one soul in one body. The *āluya* mentioned in *Viy* 23.3 is the sweet potato (the words potato and chilli are of South American origin). Though potatoes, like peanuts, grow underground, they are not root vegetables. Potatoes are stem tubers not root tubers (BSB, p. 353). Other arguments are discussed for instance in *AS* 2.1.8 and 2.7.2, where the distinction between raw and cooked substances is applied. Uncooked raw garlic that has partly been eaten by animals is described as eatable. The same argument could of course be applied to meat, though both partly eaten garlic and unboiled

meat contain of course microorganisms. The argument against eating potatoes, for instance, is that it contains many souls, since it can reproduce even after being cut into pieces.

86 The *mothī*, 'a kind of sweet, yellow, leguminous seed' (McGregor, 1993: 836), was once a speciality of the town of Chāpar in Rājasthān, but is even there not anymore available. This old rule is therefore obsolete for all practical purposes.

87 The *dhuṁgāra* (smoking) method uses the taste of burning charcoal for the seasoning of food, usually without using much oil. There are two techniques: (1) a plate of vegetables, etc. is placed on top of the burning charcoal, and (2) vegetables are cut in a bowl and heated by inserting one piece of burnt charcoal on which some clarified butter is poured which starts to burn. Its flames are contained with a lid. The consumption of *dhuṁgārī* food is prohibited for the mendicants because one cannot be certain that the food is thoroughly cooked. A reason given in *M* 3.44.134 is that alms should not be (de-) selected for their good (or bad) tastes.

88 Mārvāṛī: *sogarau*, a thick bread of the Jodhpur area, made of millet, salt, water and sometimes green vegetables and traditionally baked in hot ash.

89 Hindī: *phalī, cyamopsis psoralioides,* here: seed-pod.

90 Mārvāṛī: *sāṅgarī,* of the desert tree *prosopis cineraria.*

91 Mārvāṛī: *kair,* Hindī: *karīr, capparis aphylla.*

92 A dried vegetable product of a desert bush.

93 These substances share the quality of uncertainty that they will be entirely lifeless, i.e. thoroughly cooked and/or without any living seeds.

94 Unboiled or unheated salt and pepper are considered substances which are alive.

95 *rāytā,* curd with vegetables or fruits; Mārvāṛī: *chamkau,* Hindī: *chauṁk,* seasoning.

96 Root vegetables also belong to these *ananta kāya* plants (see Kohl, 1953: 91–95 and Williams, 1963: 113–16). 'Those plants which are classified as *ananta-kāya*s seem to be chosen because of certain morphological peculiarities such as the possession of bulbs or rhizomes or the habit of periodically shedding their leaves; and in general they are characterised by possibilities of vegetative reproduction' (p. 114).

97 The doctrinal argument is that living substances of one kind are killed through the process of mixing with living substances of another kind (see *AS* 1). Thus, if juices made of root vegetables are mixed at the ratio of at least 50 per cent with acceptable substances, such as tomato juice or mango juice, they are regarded acceptable. Some mendicants also believe that it is just the indulgence in these highly desirable foods which is objectionable. Fruit juice is not acceptable at all in other Jain mendicant traditions. For this reason, presumably, this rule was abolished by Ācārya Mahāprajña in 2003.

98 *sītāphal*: custard-apple, *anona squamosa*; sweet pumpkin or musk melon, *cucurbita moschata* (McGregor, 1993: 1020).

99 Corn can only be eaten if the seeds are removed from the cob and boiled.

100 Alms are usually accepted from the hand of a householder. The expression *hāth se* here refers to exceptional cases, such as medicine and borrowed items, which mendicants can pick up 'with their own hands' after prior permission of their host. The subject is discussed extensively in Jayācārya's *Paramparā nīṁ Joṛ* 7, as mentioned later in this section (Jayācārya, 1983: 377–80). In the opening verse, Jayācārya clearly stated that the rules of taking/not taking with one's own hand fall under the *jīta-kalpa* rules, which can be added by the *ācārya*s to the existing rules of the tradition: *kuṇ-kuṇ vastu hāth sūṃ, leve mahā munirāy, ṛhāl sātmī ne viṣai, jīta paramparā māṃya* (p. 377).

101 *Paramparā nīṁ Joṛ* 7.10 states that foods with medicinal qualities can be taken by one's own hand if they are not alive, i.e. cut, boiled, etc. but only as medicine. Verses 7.18 and 7.21–22 also emphasize that, normally, root vegetables such as ginger cannot be taken at all, except as medicine, but then even by one's own hand (Jayācārya, 1983: 377f.).

102 See *Paramparā nīṁ Joṛ* 7.23–25 (Jayācārya, 1983: 378). The reason is to prevent the temptation to eat too much of these most attractive foods.

103 *phyllanthus emblica* (McGregor, 1993: 77).

104 Unused medicine must be returned.

105 The clothes of the *samaṇ/īs* should not be washed by the laity.

106 Many *samaṇs* and *samaṇīs* are, nevertheless, trained in hand-reading and other 'occult' sciences and apply this knowledge systematically during their travels.

107 Except for *mantras*, etc. received from the *ācārya*, to perform magic is considered to be a serious offence which can only be atoned by a private confession to the *ācārya*. The form of a penance qua private letter has been prescribed to avoid spreading detailed information on such practices.

108 The rule is intended to prevent egotism. Officially, only passport photographs are allowed. Photos and videos of the *samaṇ/īs* are, nevertheless, regularly taken – even on request.

109 The *sanyojikā* is the overall leader of the *mumukṣu* sisters, that is the 'seekers for salvation,' a category of lay-ascetics *cum* novices, which sometimes accompany the *samaṇīs*.

110 See appendix.

111 Other traditions, such as the Jñāngacch, do not even accept frames containing merely parts made of metal.

112 Orthodox mendicants reject the use of utensils made of plastic and metal altogether. One reason for the restriction of plastic bags to only one during the almsround is that it 'does not look good,' and also that it is not necessary to prevent, for instance, the *pāpar* bread from crumbling by transporting it in a separate bag. It is one of the oldest rule of the Dharmadāsa Sthānakavāsī tradition that bags should not be carried with two hands (see Flügel, 2003).

113 As part of a meal, boiled onions are acceptable to the Terāpanth ascetics, though most Jain mendicants and laity reject this. This rule was abolished in 2003.

114 Salt is killed by frying it in a pan on a small flame.

115 Specially prepared food or drink is under no circumstances acceptable to fully initiated Jain mendicants. Because they are intoxicants and can lead to addiction, tea and coffee are usually taboo. However, many monks and nuns drink tea in the morning and accept minor penances for this. In the year 2000 Ācārya Mahāprajña decided that morning teas are free of blemish. However, afternoon teas continue to be banned. The penance for taking both morning and afternoon teas are five days without evening tea. Three days without evening tea or afternoon tea but no food are the penance for drinking afternoon tea.

116 In this sense, the term monasticism, from the Greek word *monos*, 'alone,' 'solitary,' is indeed applicable to Jain mendicants.

117 The personal diary contains information on the current rules and regulations, personal transgressions, etc. which should not be passed on without permission of the *ācārya*.

118 Ācārya Tulsī introduced the principle of time-keeping some 15–20 years ago and decided that each group of mendicants should be given a watch or clock owned by the order as a whole.

119 This is allowed in other places, where few other *samaṇ/īs* reside.

120 (Thermos-) bottles which have been opened for cooling boiled water should not be covered with a pot, etc. but kept in sight. This rule was originally listed together with the next point but is clearly unconnected and has therefore been translated independently. Many of the rules of this section, especially from point 20 onwards, seem to be later additions. Additional rules are probably always listed under the category *śikṣā-sūtra*.

121 In contrast to the principal ten atonements practised by fully initiated mendicants, the atonements of *samaṇs* and *samaṇīs* comprise only controlled breathing (*śvāsa-ucchvāsa*) in one of the three 'motionless' *kāyotsarga*-postures, recitation of verses (*svādhyāya*), white colour meditation (*dhyāna*), and different varieties of light fasting *cum* reduction of food-intake (*tapas*). In the canon, *svādhyāya* and *dhyāna* are recognized as forms of asceticism, but rarely as atonements. See *Viy* 920A (25.7e) = *Ṭhāṇa* 484a; *Uvavāiya* 30.1, etc.; *ĀvN* 19 in Leumann, 1892a: 1195f; Schubring, 1935: § 161f.; Flügel, in press b.

122 All items which are borrowed from householders have to be returned before darkness.

123 *Svādhyāya*, or study, here means reciting verses without controlled breathing.

124 Before the obligatory rites of atonement, called *āvaśyaka* or *pratikramaṇa*, to be performed twice a day at dawn and dusk, Jain mendicants ask their preceptors to grant them confession (*alocanā*). The penance of 25 controlled breaths is routinely given for the unavoidable acts of violence committed during

routine activities of day and night. Additional infringements should also be confessed before the *pratikramaṇa* and are rewarded with special penances.

125 Jain mendicants should take great care not to crush any greenery, insects or other living beings while walking. They should therefore remain silent during the almsround (*gocarī*) and the itinerary (*vihāra*) from one village to the next.

126 *Samaṇ/īs* can rest for up to half an hour in the afternoon. While sleeping during the day was traditionally not allowed for Jain mendicants, new rules introduced by Ācārya Mahāprajña in 1998 allow Terāpanth *sādhvīs* and *sādhus* to sleep up to 45 minutes in the afternoon.

127 One verse, or *gāthā*, here means any kind of writing using 32 syllables (1 *anuṣṭubh śloka*). Many such recitations implicitly refer to specific religious texts with the required number of verses. The *DVS*, for instance, the basic code of conduct for Jain mendicants, contains seven hundred *gāthās*.

128 In addition to the mobile living beings, or *trasa*, Jain scriptures distinguish the five types of immobile living beings, or *sthāvara*: fire, water, earth, wind, plants (*DVS* 4).

129 Jain biology classifies types of living beings according to the number of senses they appear to have. The two types of single-sensed beings (*ekendriya jīva*), the sub-microscopic *nigodas* and the elements of earth, water, fire, wind and certain types of vegetation have only the sense of touch (*sparśa*). The two-sensed beings (*dvindriya*) such as worms or leeches also possess the sense of taste. Ants, bugs and similar three-sensed creatures (*trindriya*) possess in addition the sense of smell (it is known today that some species of ants have eyes too). Bees, flies, mosquitoes and similar four-sensed creatures (*caturindriya*) additionally possess the sense of sight. Human beings belong to the class of five-sensed creatures (*pañcendriya*) who possess the additional sense of hearing (*Utt* 36). Two-to-four-sensed creatures are classified together as *vikalendriya-trikam*, three types of beings with incomplete senses, as they show no difference with regard to the *karma* doctrine (See Ṭhāṇa 2.155–60, 2.158, Glasenapp, 1915: 65ff., Williams, 1963: 110–16). In addition to these biological classifications, certain supernatural capabilities are distinguished, which are only possessed by gods, pure ascetics and liberated souls.

130 *Adatta* here means that which is given without the permission of the mendicants.

131 *Samaṇīs* should keep not more than the possessions listed above. If a *samaṇī* keeps deliberately more than permitted, out of attachment for a particular object, then this relatively harsh penance is applied.

132 If an object was left outside for one to two hours, only 12 breaths are given, if longer than 25, etc. On the various reasons informing the prohibition to enter the open space (*achāyāṃ*) at night and to leave objects outside see Flügel, forthcoming.

133 Scissors, needles, etc. (*śāstra*) are regularly borrowed from laypeople. They have to be returned before dusk.

134 The *samādhi pātra* (Pkt. *samāhi mattaya*), literally collection bowl (*KS* 1.16f., Schubring, 1910: 260, n. 15, 1935: § 144; cf. Mette, 1974: 59ff., 148 on *mallaya*), is a vessel used for collecting waste, urine, faeces, etc. Unlike other Jain mendicant orders, Terāpanth ascetics collect their excreta at night and discard them within the prescribed period altogether. This is done to minimize violence, since only one person has to leave the abode for emptying the chamber pots. Excreta are said to be dead for one *muhūrta* (*ca.* 48 minutes), but afterwards bacteria, etc. start growing, insects are attracted, etc. Discarding the excreta after 48 minutes therefore involves harming life. Performing the *logassa* requires a recitation of four *caturviṁśiti-stavas* in meditation.

135 The five principal causes of karmic influx (*āsrava*) and bondage (*bandhā*) are: 1. wrong belief (*mithyātva*), 2. non-observance of the vows (*avirata*), 3. carelessness (*pramāda*), 4. passion (*kasāya*), 5. activity (*yoga*) (*TS* 8.1). The rule refers to persevering violations of the *mahāvratas* in dreams (for instance dreams about violence or sex).

136 Wringing out clothes causes the killing of the water elements.

137 On the role of the personal diaries and the written annual reports of the group (*siṅghāṛapati*) to the *ācārya* for awarding punishments and rewards see Flügel, 1995–96: 138, in press.

138 *Guru dhāraṇā*, the act of support or acceptance of *dharma, deva, guru* (*ācārya*) is a formal promise of a layperson by way of repeating a few sentences recited by a mendicant. Sometimes,

but rarely a public initiation ritual is performed for laity (*samyaktva dīkṣā*). See *AK* I: 365–78; Williams, 1963: 41–50, Jaini, 1979: 164–6, Shāntā, 1985: 538, 544, fn. 30.

139 That is, insight meditation (*prekṣā dhyāna*) camps, events related to the small vow (*aṇuvrata*) movement, etc.

140 The rules for water procurement are not further specified in the *Niyamāvalī*. By rule, the water collected in the first *prahar* (a quarter of bright/dark half of the day) cannot be stored until sunset by *sādhus* and *sādhvīs*. Only water collected in the second *prahar* can be kept until dusk, but not longer. The remaining water has to be consumed or disposed of in an appropriate way. However, the relaxed rules of the *samaṇ/īs* allow them to keep even the water collected during the first *prahar* for the rest of the day. The rationale of being allowed to keep water from 9.00–17.00 but not from 6.00–17.00 is inconsistent with the general presumption that food and water becomes re-populated by micro-organisms already after 48 minutes. These rules are based on tradition. However, nowadays, it is even permitted for Terāpanth *sādhus* and *sādhvīs* to consume food and water collected early in the morning (first *prahar*) at late afternoon (fourth *prahar*). See also the regulations of the Sthānakavāsī Sādhumārgī mendicants, which have seasonal rules for water consumption: In the cold season between November/December and February/March (*mārgaśīrṣ-phālgun*) water is said to remain lifeless (*acitta*) for three *prahar*; in the hot season between March/April and June/July (*caitra-āsāṛh*) for five *prahar*; and between July/August and October/ November (*śrāvaṇ-kārtik*) for four *prahar* (Gaṇeśmāl, 2000). For a critique of similar rules of North Indian Sthānakavāsī groups who apparently accepted raw water during *vihār*, see Ātmārām, 1903: 290.

141 A new mendicant (*nayā*) is given special treatment.

142 Salted and unsalted foods cannot easily be separated.

143 Jain mendicants should not leave any leftovers. If by mistake too much food was collected and one mendicant is fasting, then all the remaining food has to be eaten by the other mendicants of the group. In order to help them consume the food, the fasting mendicant may break his/her fast, but then

must eat an equal share, not just picking selected items. For the contrast between the rules of this so-called *pāristhāpanika-bhoktr* practice and the older *AS* 2.1.9.6, see *ON* 586–95 in Mette, 1974: 139–42.

144 *anār* = *dāṛim*, pomegranate.

145 Mv. *matīrau.*

146 Raw fruits with many seeds are not permitted for Jain ascetics. The rule is listed because sometimes juices are required for health reasons. Juice, dry fruits and certain expensive and rare foods are considered to be the property of the entire *samaṇ* or *samaṇī* order (currently *ca.* 40 groups of 2–4 *samaṇ/ī*s which generally operate as self-contained units) and have to be shared if several groups stay at one place.

147 In this section, the conventions of mutual hospitality (offering food etc.) between members of the Terāpanth (*samaṇ-*) order are laid out, as well as exceptions to the rule that every mendicant has to take his/her turn of daily community work, such as begging alms, washing clothes, etc. (see Flügel, in press a). Begging alms is done by rotation, by special order, and under exceptional rules. Members of other Jain monastic orders are generally not served.

148 The first turn early in the morning will be spared for a *samaṇ/ī* who arrives in the night before midnight. If s/he arrives after midnight, s/he remains a guest for an entire day, made up of three turns between a maximum of four group members.

149 Only one day service will be provided for a *samaṇ/ī* who arrives within a period of thirty days away from home, i.e. Lāḍnūṁ or other Terāpanth centres, where a group of *samaṇ/ī*s lives.

150 It should not be confused with the *kāyotsarga pratimā*, the so-called 'stage of continence by day,' which is one of the 11 scripted stages of the spiritual path for the ideal Jain lay-person. See Schubring (1935: § 157, § 163) and Williams (1963:172–81) on the 12 *pratimā*s (Pkt. *paḍimā*) for the mendicants and the 11 *pratimā*s for the laity.

151 First sentence of the *Kāyotsarga Sūtra* (*ĀvS* 5.3, cf. *ĀvN* 779a), translated by Williams, 1963: 213.

References

Primary Sources

AS *Āyāraṃga Sutta* (*Ācārāṅga Sūtra*). Translated by Hermann Jacobi. *Sacred Books of the East* Vol. 22. *Jaina Sūtras* Part I: 1–213. Oxford: Clarendon Press, 1884.

ĀvN *Āvassaya Nijjutti* (*Āvaśyaka Niryukti*). With Haribhadra's Ṭīkā. Bombay: Agamodaya Samiti, 1916–1917.

ĀvS *Āvassayaṃ* (*Āvaśyaka Sūtra*). In: *Navasuttāṇi* 5. Vācanā Pramukhah: Gaṇādhipati Tulsī. Saṃpādak: Ācārya Mahāprajña, 3–23. Lādnūṁ: Jaina Viśva Bhāratī, 1985.

DVN *Dasaveyāliya Nijjutti* (*Daśavaikālika Niryukti*). Edited by Willem B. Bollée, 1995, pp. 31–73.

DVS *Dasaveyāliya Sutta* (*Daśavaikālika Sūtra*). Edited by Ernst Leumann. And Translated, with Introduction and Notes, by Walther Schubring. Ahmedabad: The Managers of the Sheth Anandji Kalianji, 1932 (reprinted in: W. Schubring.*Kleine Schriften.* Hg. K. Bruhn, 109–248. Wiesbaden: Franz Steiner Verlag). Also translated by Kustur Chand Lalwani. *Arya Sayyanbhava's Daśavaikālika Sūtra.* Translation and Notes. Delhi: Motilal Banarsidas, 1973.

KS *Kappa Sutta* (*Kalpa Sūtra*). Translated by Walther Schubring, 1905, 1910.

M *Mahānisīha* (*Mahāniśītha*). Chapters 1–5 translated by Jozef Deleu and Walther Schubring, *Studien zum Mahānisīha.* Kapitel 1–5. Herausgegeben und übersetzt. Alt- und Neu-Indische Studien 10. Hamburg: De Gruyter, 1963.

NIS *Niśītha Sūtram,* with *Bhāṣya* and *Cūrṇi* by Ācārya Jinadāsa Mahaṭṭar. Part I: *Pithikā.* Edited by Upādhyāy Amarmuni and Muni Kanhaiyālāl 'Kamal.' Second Revised ed. Delhi: Bharatiya Vidya Prakashan, (1960) 1982.

ON *Oha Nijjutti* (*Ogha Niryukti*). Verses 331–595 (*Piṇḍ'esaṇā*) translated by Adelheid Mette, 1974.

PK *Pajjosavaṇā Kappa* (*Sāmāyārī*). Translated by Hermann Jacobi. *Sacred Books of the East* Vol. 22. *Jaina Sūtras* Part I: 296–311. Oxford: Clarendon Press, 1884.

Utt *Uttarajjhāyā Sutta* (*Uttarādhyayana Sūtra*). Translated by Hermann Jacobi. *Sacred Books of the East* Vol. 45. *Jaina Sūtras* Part II: 1–232. Oxford: Clarendon Press, 1895.

TS *Tattvārtha Sūtra*, of Umāsvāti/Umāsvāmī. Translated by Nathmal Tatia. San Francisco: Harper Collins, 1994.

Ṭhāṇa *Ṭhāṇa Sutta (Sthānāṅga Sūtra)*. Vācanā Pramukha: Ācārya Tulsī. Sampādaka Vivecaka: Muni Nathamala. Lādnūṁ: Jaina Viśva Bhāratī, 1976.

Vav *Vavahāra Sutta* (*Vyavahāra Sūtra*). Translated by Walther Schubring and Colette Caillat. *Drei Chedasūtras des Jaina Kanons. Āyārodasāo, Vavahāra, Nisīha.* Alt- und Neuindische Studien 11, 48–91. Hamburg: De Gruyter, 1966.

Viy *Viyāhapannatti Sutta* (*Bhagavatī Sūtra*). Translation of Śataka 1–11 by K.C. Lalwani. *Sudharma Svāmī's Bhagavatī Sūtra.* Vol. I–IV. Prakrit Text with English Translation and Notes based on the Commentary of Abhayadeva Sūri. Calcutta: Jain Bhawan, 1973–1985. Analysis by J. Deleu, 1970.

Modern Works

AISJC = Akhil Bhāratīya Sthānakavāsī Jaina Kānfrens, ed. (1987) *Akhil Bhāratvarsīya* Vardhamaṇ *Sthānakavāsī Jaina Śramaṇ Saṅghīya Samācārī.* Dillī: Akhil Bhāratīya Vardhāman Sthānakavāsī Jaina Kānfrens.

AK = Jinprabhā, Sādhvī and Sādhvī Svarnrekha, eds (1990) *Amṛt Kalaś.* 2 Volumes. 7th edn. Lādnūṁ: Adarś Sāhitya Saṅgh.

Ātmārām, Ācārya (Vijayānand Sūri) (1888/1903) *Śrī Samyaktva Śalyoddhār* (Hindī Translation of *Samyaktva Sulodhār*). Lahore: Śrī Atmānand Jaina Sabhā Pañjāb.

Balbir, Nalini (1983) 'Observations sur la Secte Jaina des Terāpanthī,' *Bulletin D'Etudes Indiennes* 1 (1983) 39–45.

Balbir, Nalini (1993) *Āvaśyaka-Studien. Introduction Générale et Traductions,* Alt- und Neuindische Studien 45, (1). Stuttgart: Steiner Verlag.

BSB = Ācārya Tulsī (Vācanā Pramukha) and Ācārya Mahāprajña (Bhāsyakāra) (2000) *Bhagavaī (Viāhapaṇṇattī)* Khaṇḍ 2, Śatak 3–7. Mūlpāṭh, Saṃskṛt Chāyā, Hindī Anuvād, Bhāṣya tathā Abhayadevasūri-krt Vṛtti evaṃ Pariśiṣṭ-Sabdānukram ādi sahit. Lādnūṁ: Jain Viśva Bhāratī.

Bollée, Willem B. (1995) *The Nijjuttis on the Seniors of the Śvetāmbara Siddhānta: Āyāranga, Dasaveyāliya, Uttarajjhāyā and Sūyagaḍa, Text and Selective Glossary*. Stuttgart: Franz Steiner Verlag.

Bruhn, K. (1981) *Āvaśyaka Studies I, Studien zum Jainismus und Buddhismus* (Gedenkschrift für Ludwig Alsdorf). Hg. K. Bruhn and A. Wezler, 11–49. Hamburg: Franz Steiner Verlag.

Bruhn, K. (1997–2001) 'Five Vows and Six Avashyakas: The Fundamentals of Jaina Ethics.' Ed. C. Geerdes. http://here-now4u.de/eng/spr/religion/Bruhn.html

Budhmal, Muni (1964/1995) *Terāpanth kā Itihās. Pratham Khaṇḍ: Terāpanth ke Pratham Cār Ācārya*. 4th revised edn. Calcutta: Jain Śvetāmbar Terāpanth Mahāsabhā Prakāśan.

Budhmal, Muni (2001) *Terāpanth kā Itihās. Dvitīya Khaṇḍ*. Sampādak: Muni Sumeramal 'Sudarśan' and Muni Mohanlāl 'Sārdūl.' Calcutta: Jain Śvetāmbar Terāpanth Mahāsabhā Prakāśan.

Caillat, Colette (1965/1975) *Atonements in the Ancient Ritual of the Jaina Monks*. Ahmedabad: L.D. Institute of Indology. (Translated from the original French: *Les Expiations dans le Rituel Ancien des Religieux Jaina*. Paris: E. de Boccard.)

Deleu, Jozef (1970) *Viyāhapannatti (Bhagavaī). The Fifth Anga of the Jaina Canon. Introduction, Critical Analysis, Commentary and Indexes*. Brugge: Rijksuniversiteit de Gent.

Flügel, Peter (1994) *Askese und Devotion: Das rituelle System der Terapanth Śvetambara Jains*. Doctoral dissertation, Johannes Gutenberg-Universität Mainz.

Flügel, Peter (1995–6) 'The Ritual Circle of the Terāpanth Śvetāmbara Jains,' *Bulletin D'Etudes Indiennes* 13: 117–176.

Flügel, Peter (2000) 'Zum Ursprung der Terāpanth Śvetāmbara Jaina Tradition.' http://www.here-now4u.de/zum_ursprung_der_terapanth_sve.htm

Flügel, Peter (2000) 'Protestantische und Post-Protestantische Jaina-Reformbewegungen: Zur Geschichte und Organisation der Sthānakavāsī I,' *Berliner Indologische Studien* 13–14: 37–103.

Flügel, Peter (2003) 'Protestantische und Post-Protestantische Jaina-Reformbewegungen: Zur Geschichte und Organisation der Sthānakavāsī II,' *Berliner Indologische Studien* 15–16.

Flügel, Peter (in press a=2003) 'Spiritual Accounting: The Role of the *kalyānaka patra* in the Religious Economy of the Terāpanth

Jain ascetics,' in O. Qvarnström (ed.) *Jainism and Early Buddhism in the Indian Cultural Context, Festschrift in Honour of P. S. Jaini.* Freemont: Asian Humanities Press.

Flügel, Peter (in press 2006b) 'Demographic Trends in Jain Monasticism,' J.R. Bhaṭṭacharyya (ed.) *Professor Satya Ranjan Banerjee Felicitation Volume.* Delhi: Motilal Banarsidass.

Flügel, Peter (forthcoming) 'Atonements in the Rituals of the Terāpanth Śvetāmbara Jains.' Paper presented at the conference *Aspects of Jainism,* University of Warsaw, 7–8 September 2000.

Gaṇeśmāl, Ācārya (2000) *Nirgrantha Saṅgha Samācārī.* Handwritten copy.

Glasenapp, Helmuth von (1915) *Die Lehre vom Karma in der Philosophie der Jainas.* Leipzig: Otto Harrassowitz.

Goonasekere, Ratna Sunilsantha Abhayawardana (1986) *Renunciation and Monasticism among the Jainas of India.* Ph.D. dissertation. San Diego: University of California.

Holmstrom, Savitri (1988) *Towards a Politics of Renunciation: Jain women and asceticism in Rajasthan.* M.A. Thesis, University of Edinburgh.

Jacobi, Hermann (1879) 'Kalpasūtra of Bhadrabāhu,' *Abhandlungen für die Kunde des Morgenlandes* 7, 1.

Jaini, Padmanabh S. (1979) *The Jaina Path of Purification.* Berkeley: University of California Press.

Jayācārya, Ācārya [Jītmal] (1852) *Baṛī Maryāda.* Jaypur: Gaṇ Vidhān Saṅgrah Gadhya. (Ms.)

Jayācārya, Ācārya (1852) *Choṭī Maryādā.* Jaypur Gaṇ Vidhān Saṅgrah Gadhya (Ms.).

Jayācārya, Ācārya (1855) *Paramparā nāṁ Bol: Sayātar.* Gocarī Sambandhī. (Ms.).

Jayācārya, Ācārya (1857–60/1983) 'Paramparā nīṁ Joṛ.' *Terāpanth: Maryādā aur Vyavasthā.* Compiled by Ācārya Tulsī and Yuvācārya Mahāprajña. Sampādak: Muni Madhukar. Jayācārya Series Vol. 9, 339–80. Lādnūṁ: Jain Viśva Bhāratī.

Jayācārya, Ācārya (1981) *Victory of Discipline. Jay Anuśāsan.* Sampādak: Muni Mahendrakumar. Comp. Ācārya Tulsī and Yuvācārya Mahāprajña. Tr. S.K.L. Goswami. Jayācārya Series Vol. 1. Lādnūṁ: Jain Viśva Bhāratī.

Kohl, J. F. (1953) 'Pflanzen mit gemeinsamem Körper nach der Lehre der Jainas,' *Zeitschrift für Ethnologie* 78: 91–95.

Laidlaw, James (1995) *Riches and Renunciation: Religion, Economy, and Society among the Jains.* Oxford: Clarendon Press.

Leumann, Ernst (1892a) 'Jinabhadra's Jītakalpa, mit Auszügen aus Siddhasena's Cūrṇi,' *Sitzungsbericht der Preussischen Akademie der Wissenschaften* 55: 1195–1210.

Leumann, Ernst (1892b) 'Daśavaikālika-Sūtra and -Niryukti nach dem Erzählungsgehalt Untersucht und Herausgegeben von E. Leumann,' *Zeitschrift der Deutschen Morgenlän-dischen Gesellschaft* 46: 581–663 [Reprinted in E. Leumann. *Kleine Schriften.* Ed. N. Balbir, 207–59. Stuttgart: Steiner, 1998].

Leumann, Ernst (1934) *Übersicht über die Āvaśyaka Literatur.* Aus dem Nachlass herausgegeben von Walther Schubring. Alt- und Neuindische Studien 4. Hamburg: De Gruyter.

Mahāprajña, Yuvācārya (1987) *Acharya Tulsi: A Peacemaker par Excellence.* Ed. and tr. S.L. Gandhi. Rajsamand: Aṇuvrat Vishva Bharati.

McGregor, R.S. ed. (1993) *The Oxford Hindi-English Dictionary.* Oxford: Oxford University Press.

Mette, Adelheid (1974) *Piṇḍ'esaṇā. Das Kapitel der Oha-nijjutti über den Bettelgang.* Wiesbaden: Franz Steiner.

Mette, Adelheid (in press 2003) 'Waste Disposal (*pariṭṭhavaṇa-vihi*) in Ancient India. Some Regulations for Protection of Life from the Rules of the Order of Jain Monks,' in P. Balcerowicz and M. Mejor eds. *Essays in Jaina Philosophy and Religion.* Delhi: Motilal Banarsidass.

Navratanmal, Muni (1981–2001) *Sāsana Samudra.* Vols. 1–26. Published by Uttamcand Jain Sethia. Calcutta: Śrī Jain Śvetāmbar Terāpanthī Mahāsabhā Prakāśan and Lādnūṁ: Viśva Bhāratī.

Prasad, Nand Kishore (1972) *Studies in Buddhist and Jaina Monachism.* Vaishali: Research Institute of Prakrit, Jainology and Ahimsa.

Ratnacandra, Ācārya (comp.) (1923/1988) *An Illustrated Ardha-Magadhi Dictionary.* Re-print. Delhi: Motilal Banarsidass.

Rayanade, B.B. (1982) 'Jaina Literature,' in *Niśītha Sutram,* with *Bhāṣya* and *Cūrṇi* by Ācārya Jinadāsa Mahaṭṭara. Part I: Pīthīka. Edited by Upādhyāy Amarmuni and Muni Kanhaiyālāl 'Kamal.' Delhi: Bharatiya Vidya Prakashan.

Sanmatiprajñā, Samaṇī (1996) *Samaṇ Dīkṣā: Ek Paricay*. Lādnūṁ: Jain Viśva Bhāratī.

Schubring, Walther (1905) *Das Kalpa-Sūtra*. Die alte Sammlung jinistischer Mönchsvorschriften. Einleitung, Text, Analysen, Übersetzung, Glossar. Indica 2. Hg. E. Leumann. Leipzig: Otto Harrassowitz.

Schubring, Walther (1910) 'The Kalpa-Sūtra. An Old Collection of Disciplinary Rules for Jaina Monks' [Revised by the Author and Translated into English by J. A. S. Burgess], *Indian Antiquary* 39: 257–67.

Schubring, Walther (1935) *Die Lehre der Jainas. Nach den alten Quellen dargestellt*. Berlin: Walter De Gruyter & Co. (Translated into English by Wolfgang Beurlen (1962/2000) as *The Doctrine of the Jainas*. Delhi: Motilal Banarasidass.)

Schubring, Walther and Colette Caillat (1966) *Drei Chedasūtras des Jaina Kanons. Ayārodasāo, Vavahāra, Nisīha*. Alt- und Neuindische Studien 11. Hamburg: De Gruyter.

Shāntā, N. (1985) *La Voie Jaina: Histoire, Spiritualité, Vie des ascétes pélerines de l'Inde*. Paris: O.E.I.L.

Sharma, L.P. (1991) *Advent and Growth of the Terapanth Jain Sect: A Comprehensive Historical Study*, Ph.D. Dissertation, Jodhpur University, 1991.

Sumeramal, Muni, ed. (1997) *Terāpanth Digdarśan 1995–96*. Kalkattā: Jain Śvetāmbar Terāpanth Mahāsabhā.

Tatia, Nathmal and Muni Mahendra, Kumar (1981). *Aspects of Jaina Monasticism*. Ladnun: Jain Vishva Bharati.

Tulsī, Ācārya. (comp.) (1960–61) *Bhikṣu-Granth Ratnākar*. Khaṇḍ 1–2. Saṅgrahkartā: Muni Cauthmal. Prabandh Sampādak: Śrīcand Rāmpuriyā. Kalkattā: Jain Śvetāmbar Terāpanth Mahāsabhā.

Tulsī, Ācārya (1989a) *Maryādāvalī*. 2nd Revised Version. 20 September 1989 (2046 bhādrapad kṛṣṇa 5) (Typescript) (Lādnūṁ: 1960).

Tulsī, Ācārya (1989b) *Prāyaścitta Vidhi*. 2nd Revised Version. Yuga Pradhān Śrī Tulsī Dvārā Nirdhārit. 20 September 1989 (2046 bhādrapad kṛṣṇa 5) (Ms.) (Lādnūṁ: Jain Viśva Bhāratī, 31 March 1962).

Tulsī, Ācārya (1990) *Arhat Vandana.* Cūrū: Ādarś Sāhitya Saṅgha.

Tulsī, Ācārya. (1991) *Niyamāvalī.* Lādnūṁ 28 January 1991 (Handwritten copy).

Tulsī, Ācārya and Yuvācārya Mahāprajña (eds), (1981) *Terāpanth ke Tīn Ācārya.* Jayācārya Series, Vol. 6. Lādnūṁ: Jain Viśva Bhāratī.

Tulsī, Ācārya and Yuvācārya Mahāprajña (comp.) (1983) *Terāpanth: Maryādā aur Vyavasthā.* Sampādak: Muni Madhukar. Jayācārya Series Vol. 9. Lādnūṁ: Jain Viśva Bhāratī.

Vallely, Anne (2002) *Guardians of the Transcendent. An Ethnography of a Jain Ascetic Community.* Toronto: University of Toronto Press.

Weber, Albrecht (1883–85) 'Über die heiligen Schriften der Jaina,' *Indische Studien* 16–17: 211–479, 1–90. (Translated into English by H.W. Smyth (1882–92) in *The Indian Antiquary* 17–21).

Williams, Ronald W. (1963) *Jaina Yoga: A Survey of the Medieval Śrāvakācāras.* London: Oxford University Press.

9

Spiritual Accounting

The Role of the *Kalyāṇaka Patra* in the Religious Economy of the Terāpanth Śvetāmbara Jain Ascetics[1]

In his seminal article *The Pure and the Auspicious in the Jaina Tradition,* Padmanabh Jaini has argued that the equation of ascetic purity *(śuddha)* and auspiciousness *(maṅgala)* was a historical innovation of Buddhists and Joins, who "attempted to assimilate the ascetic ideal into *maṅgala,* not by degrading the *śuddha,* but instead by raising *maṅgala* to a new status which incorporated both the worldly *śubha* and the supramundane *śuddha.* In this new scheme, anything which was not *śuddha* was considered to be *aśuddha:* activities which were not productive of salvation. However, this *aśuddha* was subsequently subdivided into the mundane pure *(śubha)* and the mundane impure *(aśubha)*".[2] As a consequence, *maṅgala* was not only reserved for worldly, meritorious activities *(puṇya),* but came to refer "both to the transcendental *(śuddha),* as well as to that portion of the mundane sphere which was pure *(śubha)*" by virtue of "an association with the "truly" holy *(maṅgala)*".[3]

Today, most practising Jains agree that, ultimately, only acts of renunciation are truly auspicious. But whether or not material acts of worship *(pūjā)* and religious gift giving *(dāna)* can also be classified as forms of renunciation *(tyāga)* is a conundrum that divides the Jain community.[4] The classical account of the second interpretation of purity and auspiciousness, mentioned by Jaini, is found in Umāsvāti's *Tattvārtha Sūtra,* which endorses auspicious acts of charity *(dāna)* and compassionate help for all living beings as a means of advancing on the path of salvation *(mokṣa mārga).*[5] Auspicious acts *(śubha),* it states, produce good *karma,* or merit *(puṇya),* and inauspicious acts *(aśubha)* produce bad *karma,* or demerit *(pāpa)*[6]. The sequential transformation *(saṃkrama)* of *puṇya* and *pāpa* of the same basic type is automatically generated by the karmic mechanism.[7] Because the highly influential *Tattvārtha Sūtra* presents both purity and material wellbeing as products of good *karma,*[8] many Jain lay people, as John Cort observed, seem to act and live on the "assumption that one can have it both ways: following practices of the *mokṣa-mārg* brings one wellbeing and pursuit of wellbeing (within certain boundaries) advances one at least a small way along the *mokṣa-mārg*".[9] This conception is popular in the Bīsapanth, Mūrtipūjak, and Sthānakavāsī Jain traditions. However, Śvetāmbara Terāpanthīs do not recognise the practice of accumulating merit through charity as a religious value and, accordingly, strictly distinguish between religious *(dhārmik)* acts of asceticism *(tapas)*, and social *(vyavahārik)* acts of charity *(dāna)*,[10] as taught by the founder of their tradition, Ācārya Bhikṣu (1726-1803).[11] The distinction is not only applied to the sphere of lay religiosity, but is in similar form replicated within the monastic community itself, although its codes of conduct are regarded as *dhārmik* by definition.

Asceticism and service

Max Weber has argued that there is a universal tendency for an originally strictly anti-economic monastic asceticism, practised as a means for individual salvation, to become transformed into an asceticism which motivates mendicants to work in the service of the hierocratic authority.[12] He also noticed that, in contrast to other Indian ascetics, the Jains (Nirgranthas) were "from the beginning" organised orders of "professional monks".[13] Walther Schubring and Colette Caillat have similarly shown how the growth of the Jain monastic orders after Mahāvīra led to the development of hierarchical institutions, based on the principles of inequality and group discipline and headed by *ācāryas*. These changes are reflected both in new organisational rules and in the formulation of a monastic jurisprudence in the *Cheda Sūtras*,[14] as well as in the emerging difference between a eremitical *(jinakalpa)* and a cenobitical *(therakalpa)* mendicant culture.[15] On the basis of their investigations of this second layer of disciplinary canonical texts, both Schubring and Caillat concluded that, "theoretically, the Jaina monks live in complete subordination to one another,"[16] and that the "extremely hierarchical structure of the Jaina community favoured exchanges of service and the progress of everyone".[17] They found that the *Cheda Sūtras* differentiate between superior acts of self-purification *(tapas)* and inferior acts of monastic service *(vaiyāvṛttya)*, but treat asceticism and service as hierarchically complementary tasks,[18] somewhat analoguous to the above mentioned hierarchical relationship between other-wordly purity and this-wordly auspiciousness (second interpretation). From a strictly soteriological point of view, service, like *dāna,* is a anomaly.[19] It does not conform to early canonical ideals of world-renunciation, because it is predicated on the value of the wellbeing of the monastic community and involves not only compulsory work for *tapasvīs* and the sick but also for all seniors and the *ācārya.*[20] However, theoretically, a Jain monastic order is a purely voluntary *(icchākāra)* organisation. Jain ascetics should be "absolutely independent and self-supporting" and have no right "for getting service from any other monk".[21] Presumably in an attempt to reconcile the contradiction between asceticism and service, service was in late-canonical texts somewhat euphemistically defined as a form of 'voluntary' internal asceticism.[22]

The benefits of devoted service have been described in early Jain *vinaya* texts as being both spiritual and material, though the exact nature of the material rewards is not entirely clear.[23] Three types of benefits have been distinguished: karmic benefits, honours, and material benefits.[24] However, although during a penance a monk had to do some service, such as disposing of excretions (KS 4.26), service was not recognised as a standard form of penance.[25] It was therefore excluded from the mathematical calculation of karmic purity, which was introduced by the Jains, but originally restricted to the rites of atonement *(prāyaścitta).* Individual merit accounts were not used by early Jain mendicants.[26] Scholars of Jainism have therefore generally assumed that the aim of merit-making was limited to the sphere of the laity, the more so since all actions conducted in accordance with monastic law were defined as producing either only *nirjarā* or both *puṇya* and *nirjarā.*[27] However, nowadays the monastic economy of the Terāpanth is mediated by a form of money of accounts based on personalised merit-books, or *kalyāṇaka patras,* which allow the calculation of the value of each mendicant's contributions to the common good, and an indirect trade-off between services and penances. By tracing its history and analysing the current function of the *kalyāṇaka patra,* this article attempts to show that, for Jain monastic jurisprudence, group service poses doctrinal problems similar to *dāna* in the sphere of the laity, since it involves not only self-restraint but also material benefits.

The Verse System

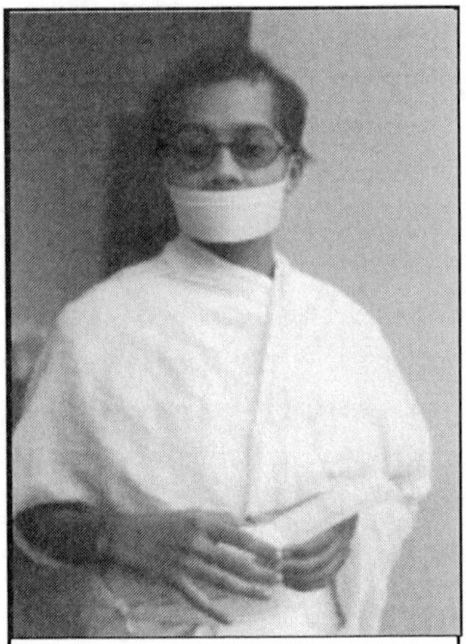

Muni Kumārśramaṇ with his *kalyāṇaka patra* in 1999.

Ācārya Bhikṣu's constitution *(saṃvidhāna)* for the Terāpanth monastic order was written shortly before his death, on the 30.8.1803 (Bhādrapad Śukla 13, 1860). It is still in force today, but has been supplemented by a number of additions and re-interpretations, most notably by Ācārya Jitmal (1803-1881) and Ācārya Tulsī (1914-1997). Jītmal, the fourth Terāpanth *ācārya,* is known under his epithet Jayācārya. He ruled the *saṅgha* from 1852 for thirty years, and introduced a number of institutional innovations between 1852 and 1865, which laid the foundations for the organisation *(vyavasthā)* of today's Terāpanth *śramaṇa saṅgha.* In 1852 the Terāpanth was in a desolate state. It was formally under the rule of a single *ācārya,* but effectively divided into smaller peripatetic groups *(siṅghāṛa),* lead by senior male and female ascetics *(agraṇī),* who acted virtually independently. With the permission of the *ācārya,* the *agraṇīs* recruited their own disciples and also privately owned religious manuscripts. Both personal disciples and certain material objects are regarded as inalienable 'possessions' by Jain mendicants. Jayācārya skillfully exploited this shared characteristic by shifting attention away from his prime objective of re-establishing central control over all members of the *saṅgha* to the issue of common access to monastic property. Access to the scriptural tradition was difficult at the time, not only because none of the *sādhus* knew Sanskrit and few *sādhvīs* could read at all, but also because the Terāpanth mendicants were initially not permitted to own any property beyond the canonically prescribed limits and relied on the libraries *(bhaṇḍāra)* of their lay followers and of other Jain sects.[28] The few texts owned by the male *agraṇīs* had to be carried by the junior monks, which set a natural limit to their possessions. At the time of Jayācārya's succession, the differential ownership *(svāmitva)* of disciples and books created friction and threatened to fragment the ascetic community. The order came also under demographic pressure, due to the increasing influx of female recruits, who were only insufficiently incorporated into the still rudimentary organisational structure and not under the direct control of the *ācārya*.[29]

According to Jayācārya, the main problem of the order was the private property held by the *agraṇīs,* which impeded both equal access to the sacred scriptures and the re-integration of the *śramaṇa saṅgha* under the central command of the *ācārya,* who alone could enforce the purification of individual conduct in accordance with Ācārya Bhikṣu's austere vision of disciplined ascetic behaviour. Immediately after his inauguration in Bīdāsar on the 5.2.1852 (Māgh Śukla 15, 1908), he succeeded in persuading the ascetics of the advantages of establishing communal ownership of manuscripts under the overall control of the *ācārya,* but only after ruling that junior ascetics could not be asked to carry privately owned manuscripts, only texts belonging to the *saṅgha.* From the 22.4.1852 (Vaiśākh Śukla 3, 1909), at their first meeting in Lāḍnūn, the *agraṇīs* began to hand their books over to Jayācārya for redistribution.[30] His next aim was to increase the total number of available scriptures, in preparation for an improvement of the generally low standard of education of the ascetics. For this purpose, Jayācārya ordered the systematic copying of manuscripts from the *bhaṇḍāras* of other sects. The writing had to be done in microscript *(laghu patra)* to make transportation easier. To maintain the motivation for the copying work *(prati-lekhana)* and for writing well, he decided at first to allow the ascetics to keep the works which they had copied themselves in their own possession, even though they belonged to the *saṅgha.* But when the output began to decrease, he decided, in the same year, to provide spiritual and material incentives for the production of manuscripts, since he had no means of forcing the ascetics to engage in this task. The idea was that for every *śloka* (32 syllables) written, whether copying or producing one's own, a monk would be remunerated with one bonus point, called *gāthā* or verse,[31] which could be cashed in for certain goods and services within the monastic community. This innovative arrangement was called the verse system *(gāthā praṇālī)* and regarded as an economic system *(artha praṇālī)* for the *sādhus* and *sādhvīs.*

The spiritual rewards for producing verses were obvious. Writing was, by then, recognised as a legitimate Jain religious practice *(sādhanā)* for the enhancement of mental concentration *(dhyāna),* asceticism *(tapas)* and religious knowledge *(jñāna)*. But why should anyone collect *gāthās,* given the fact that the Terāpanth doctrine does not even accept the accumulation of *paṇya* as a legitimate aim?[32] To solve this problem once and for all, Jayācārya simply imposed a 'tax' *(kara)* of writing 25 *gāthās,* that is 800 syllables, per day on the *agraṇīs* for the duration of their leadership.[33] He decided that the female equivalent of the *gāthā* tax would be the production of one broom *(rajoharaṇa)* and one hand-brush *(pramārjanī)* per year by the female *agraṇīs,* and of one string *(ḍorī)* by every *sādhvī.* The value of a set of brooms — the ultimate status-symbol for the Śvetāmbara ascetic — was therefore rated at 25 x 365, that is 5125 *gāthās.*[34] Although violating early canonical prescriptions in so doing,[35] after a while, Terāpanth ascetics produced themselves most of the utensils they needed in their daily life, such as begging-bowls *(pātra),* mouthmasks *(mukhavastrikā)* and garments *(kapṛa).* They received the raw materials from the laity as *bhikṣā.*[36] The division of labour between the *sādhus,* who performed the intellectual labour, and the *sādhvīs,* who performed the manual labour, replicated the division of labour that was operating within the average Jain family. The products of their obligatory work, that is manuscripts on the one hand, and brooms, begging-bowls, mouthmasks and needlework on the other, were annually offered to the *ācārya* and then either re-distributed by the *ācārya* or stored away for future use in the *servā kendra* in Lāḍnūn, which was the only permanent abode of the Terāpanth in the late 19th century.[37]

The daily routine work, which is "not strictly speaking spiritual or intellectual, but practical or artistic,"[38] such as emptying the chamber pots, cleaning the abode, washing up, doing the laundry, apportioning food, etc., had to be organised as well. In the time of Ācārya Bhikṣu, the number of ascetics was small and not much routine work had to be undertaken. The monastic economy was traditionally governed by the "principle of inequality,"[39] and the rights and duties were determined by the order of seniority *(dīkṣā paryāya).* The rule was that junior ascetics would perform service for the seniors *(sevā vyavasthā).* With the increasing ambitions and numbers of the Terāpanth ascetics, the tasks became more complex and had to be centrally organised, at least in the *ācārya's* own group, called the *rāj,* which usually comprises 30-70 *sādhus* and *sādhvīs.* Jayācārya felt that without supervision and a fixed institutional framework, community duties would not be performed to everyone's satisfaction. He therefore introduced, on the 30.9.1852 (Kārtik Kṛṣṇa 2, 1909) in Jaypur, compulsory community work based on the principles of equality and mutual help *(upakāra)*, division of labour and job rotation.[40] The hierarchical order of seniority was thereby stripped of its traditional economic implications and encompassed by a strictly centralised and in this sense 'egalitarian' system, with only one principal *guru-śiṣya* relationship and a functional differentiation of tasks which cut accross group boundaries.[41] The new monastic division of labour *(śrama vibhāga)* was predicated on the distinction between necessary *(āvaśyaka)* work for the community and unnecessary *(anāvaśyaka)* work for the individual, which corresponds to the canonical distinction of two types of monastic property, communal *(samuccaya)* and personal *(vyaktigata)*.[42] The community work was compulsory and of three types: work for the whole community *(samuccay kā kārya)*,[43] work for the *ācārya (bājoṭ kā kārya)*,[44] and work for the *sājh (sājh kā kārya)*, that is for a commensal group *(saṃbhoga)* within the *rāj*.[45]

In 1857, the first *sevā kendra*, or service centre, a nursery home for elderly nuns, was opened in Lāḍnūn and periodic service to the old and sick nuns was made compulsory *(sevā anivāryatā)* for all *sādhvīs*. Subsequently, Jayācārya incorporated community service into the *gāthā* system, and determined that the value of one day of *sevā* was also worth 25 *gāthās*. Slowly, more and more routine work was made compulsory for all *sādhvīs* and *sādhus* and rewarded with *gāthās*, for instance, carrying the baggage of the group, sewing clothes,[46] dyeing and varnishing the almsbowls, etc. The respective *gātha* values of all essential works were fixed by decree *(nirṇay)*. However, the system was flexible. Individual tasks could be avoided through the simple payment of a certain amount of *gāthās* to other monks or nuns who would perform the work instead. But it was decided to apportion the overall compulsory workload of each mendicant into 25% writing and studying *(svādhyāya)* and 75% service *(sevā)* and work *(śrama)*.[47] Because *sevā* was now recognised to be proportionally more important than writing, it was also determined that no *sādhu* or *sādhvī* could refuse serving an elderly or sick monk or nun, no matter how many *gāthās* they had accumulated. But they would always receive the appropriate amount of bonus points for their work.

With time, the *gāthās* acquired the role of a medium of exchange *(vastu-vinimay kā mādhyam)* and effectively functioned as a kind of money *(dhana)*, because almost all obligatory works and services were evaluated in terms of *gāthās*. Muni Budhmal noticed that under Jayācārya 'voluntary' service that was once undertaken for the reduction of one's karmic burden *(nirjarārthitā)* slowly became replaced by compulsory service *(sevā kārya)* undertaken in exchange for *gāthā* bonus points.[48] With the express permission of the *ācārya,* for a certain amount of *gāthās,* services and other requisites, even manuscripts, could be acquired for personal possession or consumption. The rate of exchange *(bhāva)* fluctuated, but the value of certain essential works, such as sewing and dyeing, was fixed by decree of the *ācārya*. During their lifetime, the ascetics could dispose of their *gāthā* capital *(pūñjī)* as they wished. With permission of the *ācārya,* they could spend it on works and services done for them, or give it away *(pradāna)* as presents. However, on the point of death their *gāthā* accounts were closed. In this way, no inheritance or capital accumulation could take place. Moreover, the traffic of goods and services was not straightforward. Ācārya Bhikṣu had stressed that ascetics should not exchange their personal possessions.[49] Transactions between individual ascetics could therefore not take place directly, but only through the mediation of the *ācārya* who — like a patrimonial king — redistributed the gifts (and tributes) which he received according to individual need.[50] All exchanges were (and still are) clad in the form of gifts *(bhemṭ)* or presents *(upahāra)* which were given without any expectation of return in kind.[51] The words *bhakti* and *dāna* are still used to stress the anti-economic form of these transactions. Conversely, everything that was given by the *ācārya,* who bestowed, as it were, 'exchange value' on the objects and services he received, was acceptable. Because direct exchange, or barter, was not permitted within the monastic community, all gifts and services, particularly those between *sādhus* and *sādhvīs,* whose chances for interaction are limited,[52] had to be noted down to be (retrospectively) authorised by the *ācārya,* who monitored all monastic transactions with the help of an elaborate system of book-keeping.

The accounting of the *gāthās* was first done whenever there was free time, but later always at the *maryādā mahotsava,* the annual assembly of all Terāpanth ascetics in January-February, which was first held in Balotara in 3.2.1865 (Māgh Śukla 7, 1921) for the principal purpose of rotating the mendicants amongst the *agraṇī*-lead itinerant groups and checking their individual contributions to the common good of the order.[53] At these occasions, a few ascetics *(lekhākartā)* were appointed to undertake the calculations for each *sādhu* and *sādhvī* in descending order of seniority. Any ascetic could get his or her *gāthās* recorded and then accepted by the *ācārya.* Before the accounts, the ascetics had to show their *gāthā* record *(lekhā patra)* and their work to the *ācārya* and had to confirm their dedication to the *saṅgha* in his presence. Then they received a stamp *(mudrāṅkan)* and went to the accountants, where they left their records, the copied manuscripts and other work. The accountants counted the number of syllables of the first four or five lines of each piece of writing and on this basis estimated the average number of syllables per line. The total number of *gāthās* of a given text was then calculated by counting the lines of one page multiplied by the number of pages, times the average number of syllables per line. Finally, the entire account of incomes and expenditures *(āy-vyay)* was established for each individual and recorded on the *lekhā patra,* a copy of which was given to the individual concerned. The completed account recorded the types of activities (services or writing) and their value.[54] If a *sādhu* copied a manuscript for himself, he was not entitled to receive any *gāthās* nor the seal of approval. The text was not considered to be the communal property of the *saṅgha* until his death, after which the *ācārya* could redistribute the book, since Bhikṣu ruled in 1803 that everything that was "made or accepted while staying in the *saṅgha*" was communal property.[55] Copies which were unacceptable to the *ācārya,* because they were badly written or unnecessary, could be kept both for personal use or to be given away. To distinguish between the books which were personal possessions and those which were the communal property of the *śramaṇa saṅgha,* the latter were marked with a special stamp from 15.5.1857 (Jyeṣṭh Kṛṣṇa 7, 1914).[56] Personal possessions are still labelled by writing one's name on the object concerned.

Individual and Corporate Purification

It is not known why Jayācārya imposed the exact figure of 25 *gāthās* as a 'tax' on his ascetics. But it must be assumed that it was not chosen arbitrarily, since it also plays a role in the obligatory rites of repentance *(āvaśyaka* or *pratikramaṇa),* which are the most important daily ritual practices of the Terāpanth ascetics.[57] The most significant part of these rites is the fifth or *kāyotsarga āvaśyaka.* It involves asking for forgiveness for one's transgressions *(Prāyaścitta*

Sūtra), assuming a posture of motionlessness in body and mind *(Kāyotsarga Sūtra)* and reciting the inspirational hymn to the 24 Tīrthaṅkaras *(Caturviṃśatistava* or *Logassa)* four times in meditation and once aloud, in order to cast off the body and to 'realise' the true self.[58] The repetitive and motionless recitation of the *Logassa* is performed with the sole aim of destroying *(nirjarā)* the short-term or *īryāpatha karmas*, which were accumulated in a specified time-period. If no acts of unavoidable violence or small transgressions of monastic rules were committed, the *kāyotsarga* is believed to contribute to the further reduction of the karmic burden.[59]

The 7 verses of the *Caturviṃśatistava* comprise 257 syllables, or 8 *ślokas*. Although there is no hard and fast rule, it is often said that the *Logassa* should be recited in meditation in no more than 25 controlled breaths *(śvāsa ucchvāsa)*. Inhalation and exhalation are counted as a single breath.[60] These are sometimes also called *gāthās*, which offers a clue to the symbolism underlying Jayācārya's *gāthā* system.[61] During the daily *rātrik* and *daivāsik pratikramaṇas*, which expiate the sins of twelve hours, the mendicants recite the *Caturviṃśatistava* 4 times in meditation, which conventionally requires a maximum of 4 x 25 = 100 breaths.[62] The ascetic aspect of the performance is enhanced on the days of the fortnightly *pakkhī pratikramaṇas* (12 recitations in 300 breaths), the quarterly *cāturmāsik pratikramaṇas* (20 recitations in 500 breaths), and on *saṃvatsarī*, the day of the annual *paryuṣaṇa pratikramaṇa*, which expiates the minor wrongdoings of one year (40 recitations in 1000 breaths).[63] The mendicants control their breathing during the course of the recitations as an exercise of atonement (which may be one of the reasons why the recitation is performed in meditation). In the words of the present Terāpanth Ācārya Mahāprajña:

"*Kāyotsarga* is simulation of death. Two conditions are essential — (i) total cessation of voluntary movements, that is relaxed condition... of all skeletal muscles, and (ii) extremely slow rate of respiration as if the system has stopped working. Total relaxation is when there is an acute perception of this state which is neither imagination nor auto-suggestion but a real experience. The body is forgotten and cast away. It is further characterised by an actual experience of floating outside one's body and this is 'death' while living.... The essence of this exercise is the actual awareness of the truth that the conscious element is not identical with the inert body".[64]

Outwardly, the *kāyotsarga* appears purely as an act of non-action. Yet, the achievement of absolute motionlessness and the "attempt to stop all activities of body and mind, including even breathing"[65] is not regarded as an aim in itself, but merely as preparatory for achieving the ultimate goal of all forms of Jain meditation, that is discriminating insight or the direct experience of the soul, which is traditionally conceived as a life-force that is intrinsically active *(vīrya),* all-knowing *(sarvajñāna)* and fundamentally distinct from the body it animates. For Jains, as for Hindus, breath *(prāṇa)* is the bridge between the body and the vital energy *(prāṇa śakti)* of the soul.[66] Only under this premise can the control of breathing *(prāṇāyāma)* be conceived as a conduit for releasing life-energy (both from *niścaya-* and *vyavahāra naya).*[67] Although the control of breathing during the *kāyotsarga āvaśyaka* is primarily practised for achieving self-purification through the annihilation of obstructive *karma,*[68] it is simultaneously believed to be a means of psychophysical empowerment. Moreover, amongst the Terāpanth mendicants, the two functions, purification and empowerment, are automatically transposed from the individual to the corporate level by virtue of the fact that the mendicants perform the *pratikramaṇa* collectively.[69] Individual and corporate purification are fused qua aggregation through subtle forms of social coercion.

Why was service as such not recognised as a form of atonement? The standard canonical list of ten atonements *(prāyaścitta)* can be broadly divided into the atonements which are directly or indirectly related to the *āvaśyaka* rituals (1-5) and those which are not (6-10).[70] The *āvaśyaka* rituals are unique because they combine different atonements, and are obligatory, routinely performed collective rituals. They are also the only expiatory rites which atone exclusively for the unavoidable violence committed during routine actions within the order.[71] Atonements for specific transgressions are received individually from the *ācārya,* either on request, after prior confession, or imposed as a punishment.[72] Traditionally, the "atonement par excellence" was penance no. 6, *tapas,* or fasting, which replaced the older *parihāra,* or isolation from the group, "at a fairly early date".[73] However, the atonements 6–10 were, at least in theory, treated as mutually interchangeable, if only for the purpose of calculating the appropriate intensity of the penance which, as Colette Caillat has shown, had to be "exactly proportional to monastic status".[74] Service *(vaiyāvṛttya)* was not included in the standard list of atonements. However, it was accepted as one of the six forms of internal asceticism *(abhyantara tapas),* along with study *(svādhyāya),* meditation *(dhyāna),* and, paradoxically, the atonements *(prāyaścitta)* themselves.[75] Caillat's evidence suggests that, according to the *Cheda Sūtras,* service could not be substituted for any of the *prāyaścittas,* because it was not acknowledged as a form of atonement-cum-punishment for a particular sin,[76] but merely as a voluntary form of asceticism for the elimination of *karma* in general.[77]

Under Jayācārya, the somewhat fictitious distinction beween "compulsory" atonements and "voluntary" asceticism was abandoned, and specific services and works categorised as *pariṣṭhāpana* (Mv. *paraṭhaṇā*), discarding, became the preferred means of atonement of transgressions of the basic organisational rules of the Terāpanth. However, they were not measured in terms of *gāthās.*[78] Nowadays, service and routine wrork is regularly bestowed as a penance for specific rule transgressions within the Terāpanth. This new development was rendered possible through the introduction of an element of compulsion into monastic service; a decision which – like the imposition of the *partikramaṇa* ritual by Mahāvīra – begged the question of legitimacy, since in principle, "no coercion or compulsion is desirable in monastic deportment".[79] It seems, the unit of '25 *gāthās*' was contrived to answer to the problem o[legitimacy. Conceivably, Jayācārya tried to transform mandatory work into a intrinsically meaningful religious endeavour by associating community service with established forms of monastic morality, particularly the compulsory disciplinary rites of repentance. But an acceptable asso-ciation between community service and the rituals of corporate puritication, i.e. compulsory work and compulsory atonements, could only be constructed artificially, through the formal analogy between the '25 *gāthās*' of daily obligatory monastic labour and the '25 breaths' that are recommended for the recitation of the *Caturviṃśatistava* during the *kāyotsarga āvaśyaka* rites.[80]

Official merit

With the recognition of *vaiyāvṛttyas* a form of internalised asceticism in late-canonical texts such as the *Uttarādhyayana Sūtra,* self-purification and 'voluntary' service became theoretically fused, and in principle, the door was open for a transformation of the self-imposed "rule of religion" into a command economy. Apparently,

Jayācārya was the first Jain *ācārya* to take this step, by shifting the emphasis from 'voluntary' service to obligatory work *(kārya)* and group discipline *(anuśāsana)*. He also abandoned the traditional penitential system, in which the severity of the atonements is proportional to monastic status, in favour of an egalitarian system, predicated on the rule that everyone receives the same penance for a certain type of transgression.[81] The contradiction between the ideal of self-purification and the artificial constraints of organised collective life was thus, in principle, no longer bridged by the institutions of monastic seniority and office, but by a system of mediation based on the symbolic medium of the *gāthās* and a central 'bank of accounts.'[82] In other words, the old system of ascribed hierarchical status was encompassed by a new 'egalitarian' system based on achievement and merit, as judged by the *ācārya*, who not only bestowed public honours in return for meritorious acts, but also supervised the fair and just allocation of goods and services. The *gāthā* value of a recognised 'act of merit', i.e. official merit[83] as opposed to putative karmic merit,[84] existed only in the flexible judge-ment of the *ācārya*. In this sense, the *ācārya* acted as the universal equivalent for the services and products exchanged, somewhat similar to money in a market economy.[85] However, although a 'meritorious deed' gained social currency only through his official acknowledgement, the *ācārya* was not regarded as the source of merit himself but only as its witness.[86]

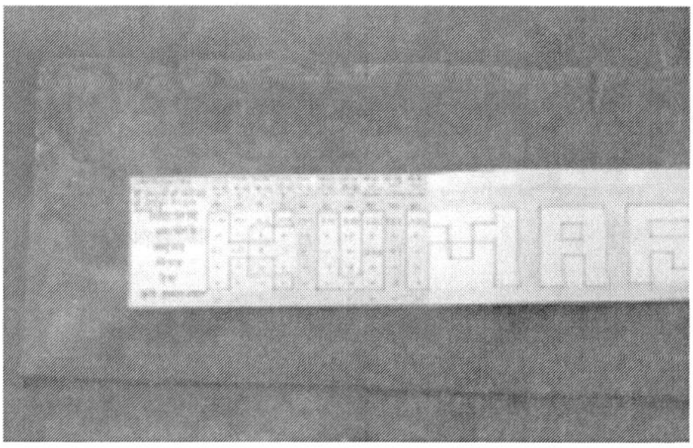

Detail of the *kalyāṇaka patra* of Muni Kumārśramaṇ in 1999.

To some ascetics, such as Chog and Caturbhuj, who severed themselves from Jayācārya, whose reforms they rejected, the emerging discourse of monastic merit-making was an embarrassment, because of Ācārya Bhikṣu's vehement rejection of the late- and post-canonical morality of good deeds *(puṇya)*. However, although it was employed as an attribute of 'good deeds', i.e. positive contributions to the material wellbeing of the order, technically, the concept of merit underlying the *gāthā* system referred to individual 'acts of asceticism' *(tapas)*.[87] 'Good deeds', ordained by the *ācārya*, were rewarded on the grounds that, by definition, all rule abiding actions of a mendicant contribute to the shedding of *karma*,[88] and that the main characteristic of an act of asceticism is the inner attitude of self-restraint.[89] A more fundamental problem, which could not be deflected so easily, was the principal incompatibility of the ontology of *karma* and the symbolic medium of the *gāthās*. Compulsory' work performed for *gāthā* bonus points could not be integrated with the rites of atonement, predicated on the doctrine of individual *karma*, withtout producing a contradiction. Collecting *gāthā* bonus points was thus simply defined as a pragmatic, socio-religious endeavour without ultimate religious significance.[90]

The main point is that after Jayācārya's reforms, the rites of purification and the regulation of the monastic economy through the *gāthā* currency were only theoretically integrated into a single coherent symbolic system revolving around the 'life-giving' personality of the *ācārya*. In practice the *ācārya* acted as the exemplary embodiment of the value of discipline, which alone bridged the contradiction between individual asceticism and group organisation.[91] Max Weber highlighted the universal significance of 'rational discipline' for the 'rationalisation of charisma', noting that it "eradicates not only personal charisma but also stratification by status groups, or at least transforms them into a rationalizing direction".[92] In his analysis, 'rational discipline' consists in nothing but the "methodically prepared and exact execution of the received order, in which all personal criticism is unconditionally suspended".[93] However, he also stressed that instrumental rationality, metaphysical rationality, and ethical rationality rarely coincide. Effectively, the fundamental contradiction between karmic merit and official merit – between the rites of atonement and the *gāthā* economy – remained unreconciled within the Terāpanth, because Jayācārya did not permit the reckoning of services performed for *gāthā* bonus points and services performed as atonements. An extensive trade-off between religious work and penances was not possible until the reforms of the late Ācārya Tulsī, who attempted to integrate the two spheres by proclaiming work performed as a penance to be also equivalent to a certain amount of *gāthās*. With this, a sufficient degree of rationalisation of the realm of "innerwordly asceticism" within the Terāpanth order was finally achieved, without recognising merit-making as a value in itself. After Jayācārya, monastic economy of the Terāpanth was threatened with the prospect of the development of an internal market within which the *gāthā* currency was sought after as a value in itself, and thus with an ensuing collapse of its ideal monastic communism.[94] The prevention of such a development along with the reduction of the role of compulsion in monastic life must have been important considerations, informing Ācārya Tulsī's decision to abolish the *gāthā* system "for the time being" in 1970. However, the main reason was the fact that the increasing use of the printing press made the compulsory copying of scriptures by hand superfluous.[95]

The record of achievement

Once established, the practice of reckoning works and services was difficult to stop. On the 4.11.1960 (Kārtik Pūrṇimā 2017), Ācārya Tulsī therefore promoted the *pariṣṭhāpana* system as a replacement for the *gāthā* system, and decided that 20 *gāthā* points could be converted into one *pariṣṭhāpana* (Mv. *paraṭhaṇā*) bonus point.[96] The word *pariṣṭhāpana* denotes the carefully regulated practices of discarding (fifth *samiti*), such as throwing away what is inedible or emptying the chamberpots at night, which is usually done in rotation and often imposed as a *prāyaścitta*. The *pariṣṭhāpana* was one of the Terāpanth-specific collective works-cum-atonements, which Jayācārya imposed for transgressions of basic organisational rules.[97] Its precursor was a *prāyaścitta* called *maṇḍaliyā*. The *maṇḍaliyā* was a piece of cloth that was spread on the floor, upon which the food was divided among the monks.[98] The washing of a certain number of floor cloths was either given as a *prāyaścitta* or recorded as a meritorious deed which could compensate for a future *prāyaścitta* of the same kind. This innovative idea of balancing the account of negative and positive deeds lies at the heart of Ācārya Tulsī's *pariṣṭhāpana* system, although the *maṇḍaliyā* penance itself was discountinued in 1949 due to the abolition of the system of central distribution of food within the *rāj*. In 1978, at the *maryādā mahotsava* in Rājaldesar, Ācārya Tulsī replaced the somewhat negative word *paraṭhaṇā*, discarding, with the word *kalyāṇaka,* or auspicious action, and introduced the individual record of achievement, or *kalyāṇaka patra,* for the recording of the merits and de-merits which the *ācārya* ascribes to the reported deeds of each mendicant.[99]

The *kalyāṇaka patra* comprises five categories: *amar nidhi,* fixed deposit; *cal nidhi,* withdrawal; *anugrah,* credit; *nigrah,* debit; and *dey,* debit balance. At the time of initiation, each initiate is granted a fixed deposit of 101 *kalyāṇaka* points by the *ācārya* to open his or her *kalyāṇaka* account.[100] The first performance of *keśa luñcana,* the obligatory plucking of the hair and beard, is rewarded with 150-200 *kalyāṇakas.* Further credits are either awarded for specific individual achievements, such as exemplary service to the order, the production of works of art, oratory, writing, singing and study, or indiscriminately for all monks and nuns on auspicious occasions, such as the installation ceremony *(paṭṭotsava)* of a new *ācārya,* or at special anniversaries. *Kalyāṇakas* are usually not granted for exemplary performances of voluntary fasting, but regularly for short term fasts *(vigaya varjana).* There are thus two occasions for bestowing *kalyāṇakas: Kalyāṇakas* are given in recognition of the religious work of an individual, and in acknowledgement of the collective achievement of the whole community. An exception is the gift *(bakhśiś)* of a temporary or lifelong exemption from service, which is occasionally granted to an individual as a reward for consistently outstanding contributions.[101]

Kalyāṇaka points can only be added or deduced by the *ācārya.* They cannot directly be claimed as payment for services from another monk. The bestowal of *kalyāṇaka* points is always an act of grace of the *ācārya.* But there are two exceptions. With permission of the *ācārya, agraṇīs* may bestow a maximum of 3x9 *kalyāṇakas* per annum to a maximum of three ascetics under their supervision for special services.[102] The *sādhvī pramukhā* may also impart a limited amount of *kalyāṇakas.* Additionally, she can perform deductions on the *sādhvīs'* accounts without asking the *ācārya* for permission. The *ācārya,* the *yuvācārya* and the *sādhvī pramukhā* are the only mendicants who do not possess *kalyāṇaka* accounts themselves, because this would interfere with their administrative status. The *ācārya* himself does not need *kalyāṇakas,* because, qua office, he is merit personified. In principle, there is no limit to the amount of *kalyāṇakas* he may bestow, since he acts not as an individual, but as the trustee of the purity and well-being of the community as a whole. *Kalyāṇakas* are not awarded through a transfer of personal merit *(puṇya),* which is impossible according to Jain doctrine, but as the quas-material correlate of the official recognition or honouring *(sammān)* of a mendicant's work.[103] This procedure presupposes a conceptual separation of inward and outward aspects of 'good deeds', that is putative karmic merit *(nirjarā)* and official merit *(kalyāṇaka).*[104] Honours and *kalyāṇakas* share with knowledge the characteristic that they can be handed out without substantial loss to the giver. However, once created, the *kalyāṇaka* bonus points can be used as currency for the transfer of merit from one mendicant to another under the premise that one ascetic's gain is another's loss, which is accepted practice amongst contemporary Terāpanth ascetics.[105] Although their methods of measurement may appear crude and arbitrary, there can be no doubt that the stout pragmatism of the Terāpanthīs assures that only real efforts demanding great restraint are rewarded.

Kalyāṇaka bonus points function in two ways: as rewards and punishments. If the *ācārya* is pleased with the work of an ascetic, he may credit his or her account with a gift *(upahāra)* of as many *kalyāṇaka* points as he sees fit. Conversely, when a *sādhu* or a *sādhvī* does something wrong, a certain amount, corresponding to the gravity of the offence, is debited to his or her account. All minor transgressions of the *mahāvratas,* the *guptis,* the *samitis* or the *maryādās,* or any other oversight *(prāmādya)* or fault *(doṣt)* committed during the course of duty can be sanctioned with a deduction of *kalyāṇakas. Kalyāṇaka* points are debited, for instance, when a ascetic leaves his abode at night to go out for excretory or other puposes. During the night, a mendicant is not permitted to enter the *acchāya,* the unprotected terrain under the open sky, because of the danger of inadvertently stepping on small insects, etc. As a rule, one should not go out in the dark unless it is absolutely necessary, for instance for purposes of study. Even then, one has to cover one's head to protect it from the moisture of the dew and should later ask for the appropriate penance. A similar unwritten rule is that nothing belonging to the *saṅgha* should be left outside overnight. All minor transgressions of this sort usually have to be atoned for as soon as possible.[106] Deductions are also imposed if food and water are kept overnight, if medication is taken after dark, or if the possessions of the ascetics have not been properly inspected. If a *sādhvī* did not perform the *pratilekhanā,* the inspection of her clothes and other utensils, she has to report this to the *sādhvī pramukhā* and receives from her a deduction of 2-5 *kalyāṇakas.* If a *sādhu* or a *sādhvī* collected untreated living *(sacitta)* water from a well or from a pipe outside a house, he or she receives a *nigrah* of 2-3 points. The following list indicates typical transgressions sanctioned by *kalyāṇakas* and the values accorded to them. Actual punishments vary, because individual circumstances are taken into account:[107]

individual circumstances are taken into account:[107]

Transgressions	*Deductions*
1. If small things, like a thread, were left under the open sky during the night.	1
2. If medium-size things were left under the open sky during the night.	3
3. If large things, like a loin-cloth, were left under the open sky during the night.	5
4. If things became wet.	9
5. If the inspection has not been done for small things, like a hand brush.	1
6. If the inspection has not been done for the curtain, and the high stool.	3
7. If a needle was broken, or kept overnight.	1
8. If a needle was lost, or if a knife or scissors were kept overnight.	2
9. If a pen has been broken, or lost.	5
10. If a mortar or large medicine bottle has been broken.	9
11. If the inspection has not been done for the broom, or the loin-cloth, etc.	2
12. If one forgot to remind the next monk to take his turn doing the collective work.	1
13. If one forgot to do the collective work.	5
14. If one had walked more than thirty feet without a broom.	1-2
15. If the doors of the nuns' abode were left open during the night.	5
16. If one forgot one's belongings, and if a householder had to return them.	5-9
17. If anything belonging to a monk or nun fell from a multi-storied building.	1 per floor
18. If water has been spilled from a drain.	5
19. If water has been spilled at the place of a sermon, or on a householder.	9
20. If a manuscript that was tried with a thread was dropped on the floor.	13
21. If the wooden cover of a manuscript was broken.	9

Initiates are instructed never to get into deficit, which is recorded in the *kalyāṇaka patra* under the rubric of debit balance *(dey)*, and, if ever this should be the case, to atone for any debit as soon as possible. There are two principal ways of squaring one's debt, both of which are considered as forms of atonement: work for others and work for oneself, i.e. community service, on the one hand, and canonical forms of atonement such as fasting, on the other. The most common method to gain *kalyāṇaka* points is to undertake extra work for the community under the overall supervision of the *ācārya*. For instance, stitching clothes, varnishing *pātras* or emptying the chamberpots for the old or sick monks or nuns, which is not necessarily an obligatory daily duty, but may earn 5 *kalyāṇakas*. Alternatively, one may fulfil more than one's quota of compulsory work, such as inspecting the abode and the *acchāya* and collecting all items that are left *(cokīkarnā)* (25-50 points for 10 days), preparing the list of required food items (until 1949), washing the cotton wrappings *(pallā)*, which are used to cover the hand-written manuscripts, or to inspect the *cilmlī*, the large white curtain which protects the ascetics from public view while they are eating. Renouncing one or more of the 10 processed foods *(vigaya)* for a defined period or performing other fasts is also accepted as a method of scoring *kalyāṇaka* points, though it is rarely practised for this pupose, and tables of equivalencies of fasts and services have been drafted in 1989.[108] However, if one has gathered a debit of more than 20 points and does not compensate for it, the *ācārya* may impose special penances such as reciting a certain number of *gāthās*, or performing compulsory *paraṭhaṇās* or one of the ten types of fast *(pratyākhyāna)*. All atonements can only be performed with permission of the *ācārya* or the *sādhvī pramukhā*.

Withdrawals *(cal nidhi)* are recorded separately from deductions *(nigrah)*, as fluctuations can occur in two different ways. The *ācārya* may punish an offender with a deduction, and *sādhus* and *sādhvīs* can withdraw *kalyāṇaka* points from their account to "trade" them for services, in the same way as *gāthā* bonus points in the earlier system. For instance, if a *sādhu* with a positive account needs help with the stitching of his clothes, he may be helped by a *sādhvī* for a certain amount of *kalyāṇaka* points.[109] However, *kalyāṇakas* are not a currency in the market economic sense, though they function as a means of payment, money of accounts (book credit), and capital within the centrally regulated monastic economy.[110] It is only with the express permission of the *ācārya* that one may "barter" the *kalyāṇaka* points which were earned through his grace. The mendicants are never indebted to each other, only to themselves, or rather to the *ācārya,* to whom they 'owe' good behaviour, because he ensures that the ascetics reduce their karmic burden and contribute to the well-being of the community. Although a deduction of *kalyāṇaka* points can buy services and compensate for minor transgressions, the quantity of the individual *kalyāṇaka* capital has no immediate bearing on the overall religious status of a monk or nun, whether conceived in terms of monastic seniority, administrative position, or putative karmic purity. The official recognition of meritorious deeds through the bestowal of *kalyāṇaka* points has only an effect on the compulsory workload and what may be called the socio-religious capital of a mendicant.[111] At stake is not a system of transactional ranking, but a centrally regulated system of justice.[112] What counts is merit acquired through recognised acts of exertion, that is religious work done both for one's own karmic benefit and for the community. After all, the most significant innovation of Jayācārya and Tulsī was not the introduction of a gift economy into the monastic order, but the recognition of community work as a form of atonement. Their main intention was to infuse monastic life with an element of economic rationality and to complement the traditional system of religious sanctions with a system of tangible rewards as opposed to putative karmic effects in order to create a positive motivation for religious work.

The internal safeguards of the supervised system of accounting methodically prevents individual profiteering by not only recording positive deeds on their own, which is common for instance in Buddhist lay merit accounts, but negative deeds as well. In contrast to the earlier disjunction of *prāyaścittas* and *gāthās,* the record of achievement computes both atonements for specific transgressions and positive efforts to reduce one's karmic burden through religious work on a single scale and thus allows a trade-off between debits and credits. Through the mediation of the *kalyāṇaka patra,* services and minor fasts can be treated as functional equivalents. Minor atonements, such as optional fasts, study or meditation, can therefore be avoided by a simple deduction of *kalyāṇaka* points.[113] This decidedly modern procedure can either be interpreted as a further decline in ascetic standards[114] or as a more flexible form of proportional justice, which not only punishes transgressions, like the canonical rules and regulations, but also rewards positive contributions to the welfare of the community.

Modern atonements

Fast and services are still not entirely congruent. But service is today one of the five types of atonement recommended for Terāpanth mendicants. Most of them are derived from the standard list of six types of internal asceticism: 1. *kāyotsarga,* 2. *svādhyāya,* 3. *dhyāna,* 4. *tapas,* and 5. *kalyāṇaka.*[115] Each of these atonements expiates different types of transgressions, though no systematic tabulation exists.[116] In practice, there is considerable overlap and flexibility in the implementation of these categories. *Kāyotsarga* is commonly performed for the expiation of acts of unintentional violence against (microscopic) living beings committed during the almsround (1 *Logassa)* or at night outside the abode.[117] It is practised by assuming a motionless posture while breathing in a controlled way *(śvāsocchvāsa).* Sometimes, additionally either the *Namaskāra Sūtra* or the *Logassa* is recited in meditation (5 *Namaskāra Sūtra* = 1 *Logassa).* For the expiation of specific transgressions, alternatively the recitation of verses *(vācana),* study *(svādhyāya),* meditation *(dhyāna)* or fasts *(pratyākhyāna)*[118] can be performed. The equivalents of one day fasting *(upavāsa),* for instance, are either the faultless recitation of 2000 *gāthās,* the study of 1200 *gāthās,* or the meditation and reflection upon the meaning of 8 *gāthās* selected from the *Āgamas.*[119] Evidently, the abbreviation *'gāthā'* has multiple contextual meanings. From 1989, meditation is also practised in the form of insight meditation *(prekṣā dhyāna),* i.e. without concentrating on a text.[120] Small fasts, such as renouncing one or more of the processed foods *(vigaya,* Skt. *vikṛti),*[121] or omitting soup, vegetables or other foodstuffs for one or more meals, are traditionally performed for minor transgressions of the basic ascetic rules, unconnected to collective work. The *nirvikṛti* fast is, for instance, given for sleeping during the day, crying in public, overeating, or asking for specific items during the almsround, etc.[122] From this, it emerges that between 1960 and 1989, fasts became slowly replaced by study and meditation as the preferred atonement. The main official reason for this is that mendicants who fast are too weak to work. In other words, the old ascetic morality is progressively substituted by a modern work ethic. However, compulsory fasts are still imposed for violations of the basic ascetic rules, i.e. the *mūla guṇas* and the *uttara guṇas,* while the deduction of *kalyāṇakas* is applied to transgressions of the organisational rules *(vyavasthā guṇa)* and offences related to compulsory service.[123] The *ācārya* invariably imposes severe punishments *(daṇḍa),* notably monthly, four-monthly and six-monthly fasts, etc., for transgressions of the *mahāvratas,* such as killing five-sensed beings, sexual misconduct, stealing, or repeated transgressions, which are considered too serious to be compensated with a deduction of *kalyāṇaka* points.

Spiritual accounting

Most Terāpanth ascetics live in small groups *(siṅghāṛa)* of three to seven mendicants who roam independently from the central group of the *ācārya* and therefore cannot receive instant assessment of their deeds. In such cases, all infringements are written down and later reported to the *ācārya.* However, to prevent a fresh influx of *karmas* adhering permanently to the soul, a transgressor should perform penances immediately and not wait for the *ācārya's* verdict. The official judgement is still received only once a year during the annual congregation of the Terāpanth ascetics in January/February, culminating in the *maryādā mahotsava,* festival of restraint, on Māgh Śukla 7. Not unlike Indian merchants, who settled their accounts before the beginning of the traditional business year on *dīvālī,* Terāpanth ascetics settle their spiritual accounts before the *maryādā mahotsava,* which marks the beginning of the Terāpanth religious year.[124] The following example of the merit account of Muni Ṛṣabhkumār, who was in his mid-twenties in 1995 and served the then *mahāśramaṇa*[125] Muni Muditkumār within the *rāj,* shows that both of his two major credits for the years 1989-1995 were given a few days before the *maryādā mahotsava,* on Māgh Śukla 3/4 and Māgh Śukla 5. The eighteen deductions were made irregularly, although six were made in the week before *cāturmāsa,* and three before *pakkhī* days.[126] It is not known to me why exactly they were imposed, but most likely as a result of routine confessions and purifications before the onset of *cāturmāsa* or *pakkhī.*[127] Interestingly, none of the alterations took place on the auspicious days *(kalyāṇaka divas)* of the Jain Tīrthaṅkaras, as one might expect,[128] but on significant dates of the Terāpanth ritual calendar, which revolves around the periodal ceremonies for the corporate self-purification of the *saṅgha* – the *pañca pratikramaṇas* and the *maryādā mahotsava* – and the auspicious events *(puṇya tithi)* in the lives of the Terāpanth *ācāryas* and in the history of the order.[129]

At the annual *maryādā mahotsava,* the merits and demerits of the conduct of each ascetic are evaluated by the *ācārya* on the basis of the annual report *(vihāra vivaraṇa),* written by the group leader, and personal interviews, a process called *sāraṇā vāraṇā,* or purging and restraining. At the moment of his/her arrival, the *agraṇī* is obliged to go immediately to the *ācārya* to hand over his/her disciples, their books and reports and the products of their past year's labour for redistribution and assessment.[130] After reading the report of the group leader, the *ācārya* makes inquiries on the observance of the rules, the atonements, the mutual relations between the ascetics, and on the individual ascetic's progress in study, teaching and writing. Finally, he rewards each ascetic with *kalyāṇaka* bonus points for accomplishments, and imposes deductions or additional atonements for transgressions.[131] Until the process of appraisal is complete, all members of the *sriṅghāṛa* must fast.

The amendment of a *kalyāṇaka* account does not necessarily take place in the presence of the *ācārya.* Like the earlier and much more complex *gāthā* accounts, the records of achievement are monitored and updated by specially appointed ascetics. Of late, this work was done by the *mahāśramaṇa* Muni Muditkumār, the present Yuvācārya Mahāśramaṇa (born 1962), who is responsible for much of the administrative work within the *śramaṇa saṅgha.* Once the value of the accomplishments of an ascetic, minus the transgressions, has been determined by the *ācārya,* an entry is made in the individual account. First, the submission under the *niśrā,* or authority, of the *ācārya* is confirmed in writing, using the shortened *mā.* for *mānatā* or *ācārya śrī tulsī ko maiṃ tīrthaṅkara devatulya mānatā hūṃ* – "I believe in Ācārya Śrī Tulsī as the equal of the Tīrthaṅkara God".[132] Then the account is settled and the ascetic concerned confirms the correctness of the calculations by ticking off the respective date on the account sheet. Finally, the *kalyāṇaka patra* is returned to the ascetic. Its contents are usually not disclosed to the general public, but they are not secret. According to Ācārya Mahāprajña, the *kalyāṇaka patra* "is nothing but a record of appreciation by the *ācārya* of the distinctive works of the disciples".[133]

Conclusion

The interpretation of *sevā,* devoted service, as 'social work' is one of the hallmarks of religious modernism in South Asia.[134] This article has shown how, through a series of reforms from 1851, the Terāpanth *ācāryas* Jayācārya (1803-1881) and Tulsī (1914-1997) transformed originally 'voluntary' monastic service into a compulsory system of religious work for the welfare of the Terāpanth order. They motivated their disciples to serve even beyond the call of duty by rewarding both routine monastic work and voluntary contributions to the Terāpanth order with merit points which could be used to "buy" personal services and to compensate for small penances. These could also be gifted to other mendicants. The introduction of a economy of merit-making into monastic life was predicated on the transformation of the qualitative distinction of *tapas* and *sevā* into a mere quantitative difference. This was largely accomplished by defining service as a form of atonement, and by introducing the principle of equality into the monastic economy. An important component of this restructuring process was an increased emphasis on the internal rather than external aspects of asceticism and the gradual elevation of the standard six inner forms of asceticism to the status of preferred atonements. However, the key element in the transformation of a traditional monastic status economy, based on the hierarchical values of asceticism and service, into an egalitarian economy of individual achievement and collective welfare was the invention of the individual merit account, presently called *kalyāṇaka patra,* that is a symbolic medium of bonus points to make the accounting and transfer of publicly recognised merit possible. This calculus of individual merit, originally reserved for the rites of atonement, permits the spiritual accounting of both 'good deeds' and 'bad deeds.' It is predicated on a distinction between 'karmic merit' and 'official merit.' The apparent contradition between the two types of merit, karmic and official merit, is bridged by the judgement of the *ācārya* and the periodic accounting of good and bad deeds with the help of the *kalyāṇaka patra,* which reflects the present monastic regime's attempt to integrate ontological purity and corporate welfare through the imposition of self-discipline.

Using Aristotle's terms,[135] one may say that whereas in the traditional monastic system of the Terāpanth rights and duties were

THE KALYĀṆAKA-PATRA FOR MUNI ṚṢABHKUMĀR, S.V. 2046-2052 (1989-1995)*

Kalyāṇak-patra	2046 pau.su. 15	2047 a.su. 14	2048 a.b. 14	2048 bha.su. 4	2048 phā.b. 6	2049 je.b. 2	2049 je.b. 12	2049 mt.b. 12	2049 ma.su. 5	2049 pha.b. 15	2050 ā.su. 11	2051 ā.b. 11	2051 ā.su. 15	2051 śra.b. 11	2052 ā.b. 12	2052 ā.su. 14	2052 śrā.su. 11	2052 kā.su. 12	2052 mā.su. 3/4	2052 ce.b. 8
ācārya śrī tulsī ko maiṃ tīrthaṅkar dev tulya mānatā hūṃ	mā.	mā.	mā.	mā.	mā.	mā.	mā.	mā.	mā.	mā.	mā.	mā.	mā.	mā.	mā.	mā.	mā.	mā.	mā.	mā.
amar-nidhi	102	100	98	84	75	70	65	63	72	73	69	67	59	54	52	50	49	48	79	78
cal-nidhi	0	2	2	14	9	5	5	2	0	0	4	2	9	5	2	2	1	1	0	1
anugrah	5	0	0	0	0	0	0	0	9	1	0	0	0	0	0	0	0	0	31	0
nigrah	0	2	2	14	9	5	5	2	0	0	4	2	9	5	2	2	1	1	0	1
dey	0	0	0	0	0	0	0	0	0	0	0	0	0	0	0	0	0	0	0	0
muni Ṛṣabhkumār	3	3	3	3	3	3	3	3	3	3	3	3	3	3	3	3	3	3	3	3

*b.=Badi/Kṛṣṇa (dark half), su.=Sudi/Śukla (bright half); ce.=Cait/Caitra (March-April), je=Jeṭh/Jyeṣṭh (May-June), ā.=Asāṛh/Āṣāḍh (June-July), śrā.=Śrāvaṇ (July-August), bhā.=Bhādoṃ/Bhādrapad (August-September), a.=Asoj/Āśvin (September-October), kā.=Kātik/Kārtik (October-November), mi.=Migasar/Mārgśīrṣ (November-December), pau.=Pauṣ (December-January), mā.=Māgh (January-February), phā.=Phāgun/Phālgun (February-March).

determined on the basis of the status of the parties involved, that is in terms of proportionate justice, they are now determined on the basis of equality, that is in terms of rectificatory justice. In the words of Durkheim,[136] the repressive rules of the canonical rites of atonement are in the process of being transformed into restitutive rules for the just distribution of community work. Max Weber has postulated similar developmental patterns in his analysis of the processes of rationalisation of charisma, and highlighted the significance of discipline as a rationalising factor. However, although the monastic economy of the Terāpanth is in the process of transformation, it is not yet systematically rationalised, because service as an atonement is not fully recognised as a functional equivalent of *tapas*. Severe violations of the fundamental ascetic rules still have to be expiated by compulsory fasting. Judging from the point of view of the legal treatises of Ācārya Jītmal and Ācārya Tulsī, the *kalyāṇaka patra* may, therefore, better be viewed as a preliminary, task-specific synthesis of incongruous classificatory and procedural patterns. In paraphrasing P.S. Jaini one might say, in conclusion, that the Terāpanth *ācāryas* attempted to raise service to a new status which incorporated both auspiciousness and supramundane purity. In this new scheme, anything which is defined by the *ācārya* as auspicious is considered to be pure: activities which are productive of salvation. However, as far as the atonements are concerned, monastic life is still divided into two incompatible spheres of action, asceticism and community work. Only the future can show to what extent Jītmal and Tulsī managed to turn the Jain ideal of world-renunciation not only into a monastic work-ethic but also into a motivating factor for world-transformation.

Bibliography

Texts and Translations

Āyāradasāo Sutta, Vavahāra Sutta, Nisīha Sutta (Daśāśrutaskandha Sūtra, Vyavahāra Sūtra, Niśītha Sūtra)

Tr. by W. Schubring & C. Caillat as *Drei Chedasūtras des Jaina Kanons. Āyārodasāo, Vavahāra Nisīha.* Alt- und Neuindische Studien 11. Hamburg: De Gruyter, 1966.

Āyāraṅga Sutta (Ācārāṅga Sūtra)

Tr. by H. Jacobi. *Sacred Books of the East* 22, 1-213. Oxford 1884.

Kappa Sutta (Kalpa Sūtra)

Tr. by W. Schubring as *Das Kalpa-sūtra. Die alte Sammlung jinistischer Mönchsvorschriften. Einleit, ung, Text Analysen, Übersetzung, Glossar.* Hrsg. Ernst Leumann. Leipzig 1905 (Tr. into English by J. Burgess as "The Kalpa-Sūtra. An Old Collection of Disciplinary Rules for Jaina Monks." *Indian Antiquary* 39 (1910): 257-267).

Nicomachean Ethics of Aristotle

Tr. by T. Irwin. Indianpolis: Hackett Publishing, 1985.

Sūyagaḍa Sutta (Sūtrakṛtāṅga Sūtra)

Tr. by H. Jacobi. *Sacred Books of the East* 45, 235-435. Oxford 1895.

Tattvārtha Sūtra of Umāsvāti

Tr. by Nathmal Tatia as *Tattvārtha Sūtra: That Which Is.* San Francisco & London: Harper Collins, 1994.

Uttarajjhāyā Sutta (Uttarādhyoyana Sūtra)

Tr. by H. Jacobi. *Sacred Books of the East* 45, 1-232. Oxford 1895.

Viyāhapannatti Sutta (Bhagavati Sūtra)

Tr. by K.C. Lalwani as *Sudharma Svāmī's Bhagavatī Sūtra.* Vol. I-IV. Prakrit Text with English Translation and Notes based on the Commentary of Abhayadeva Sūri. Calcutta: Jain Bhawan, 1973-1985. Analysis in Deleu 1970.

Modern Works

Akhil Bhāratvarṣīya Vardhamāṇa Sthānakavāsī Jaina Kānfrens

1987 *Akhil Bhāratvarṣīya Vardhamāṇa Sthānakavāsī Jaina Śramaṇa Saṅghīya Samācārī.* Dillī: Akhil Bhāratvarṣīya Vardhamāṇa Sthānakavāsī Jaina Kānfrens.

Balbir, Nalini

1993 *Āvaśyaka-Studien. Introduction Générale et Traductions.* Alt- und Neuindische Studien 45, 1. Stuttgart: Franz Steiner.

Bhāskara, Muni

1987 "Pūjyaśrī Ajrāmarjī Svāmī Nī Prarampară Bol Ko Ne Śuṃ Lābh Thāy?" *Sāmāyika Pratikramaṇa Sūtra Tathā Jaina Anuṣṭhāna Vidhi.* Rāpar/Kacch: Navalcandra Mahārāja Sārvajanika Pustakālaya, 166-168.

Bhikṣu, Ācārya

1960 *Bhikṣu-Granth Ratnākar. Khaṇḍ 1.* Sampādak: Ācārya Tulsī. Saṃgrāhakartā: Muni Cauthmal. Kalkattā: Jain Śvetāmbara Terāpanth Mahāsabhā.

1997 *Nav Padārtha.* Anuvādak-Vivecak: Śrīcand Rāmpuriyā. Lāḍnūn: Jain Viśva Bhāratī Sansthān (Prathamāvṛtti 1961).

Bronkhorst, Johannes

1986 *The Two Traditions of Meditation in Ancient India.* Stuttgart: Franz Steiner.

Bruhn, Klaus

1993 "Sectional Studies in Jainology II." *Berliner Indologische Studien* 7: 9-58.

1997-1998 "Five Vows and Six Avashyakas: The Fundamentals of Jaina Ethics." Ed. by C. Geerdes. *http://herenon4u.de/eng/spr/religion/ Brubn.html.*

Budhmal, Muni

1995 *Terāpanth Kā Ithihās. Pratham Khaṇḍ: Terāpanth Ke Pratham Cār Ācārya.* 4th Rev. Ed. (1st ed. 1964). Calcutta: Jain Śvetāmbara Terāpanth Mahāsabhā Prakāśan.

Caillat, Colette

1975 *Atonements in the Ancient Ritual of the Jaina Monks.* (Tr. from the French original, *Les expiations dans le rituel ancien des religienx Jaina,* by Mr. Jones, Mr. & Mrs. McKenna, and Mr. Whitehouse. Paris: Publications de l'Institute de Civilisation Indienne 25, 1965.) Ahmedabad: Lalbhai Dalpatbhai Institute of Indology.

Cort, John E.

2001 *Jains in the World: Religious* V*alues and Ideology in India.* New York: Oxford University Press.

Deleu, J.

1970 *Viyāhapannatti (Bhagavaī). The Fifth Anga of the Jaina Canon. Introduction, Critical Analysis, Commentary & Indexes.* Brugge: Rijksuniversiteit de Gent.

Devendramuni, Ācārya

1995 *The Jaina Conduct* (Tr. from the Hindi Original, *Jaina Ācāra: Siddhānta Aur Svarūpa,* by N.M. Sahal, 1982). Udaipur: Tarak Guru Jaina Granthalaya.

Dharmashila, Mahasati & Vora, Nilesh V.
1992 *Samayika Pratikramana Sutra.* Sthanakavasi Jaina Shravaka Sangha, Ghatkopar, Maharashtra. Adapted to American English and ed. by N. Sheth & S. Sheth. San Diego: Federation of Jain Associations in North America.

Douglas, Mary
1967 "Primitive Rationing: A Study in Controlled Exchange." *Themes in Economic Anthropology.* Ed. by R. Firth. London: Tavistock Publication, 119-147.

Dumont, Louis
1980 *Homo Hierarchicus: The Caste System and its Implications.* Complete Revised English Ed. Chicago: The University of Chicago Press.

Durkheim, Emile
1984 *The Division of Labour in Society.* (Tr. from the French Original, *De la division du travail social,* by W.D. Halls. Paris: Alcan, 1893). New York: Free Press.

Flügel, Peter
1994 *Askese und Devotion: Das rituelle System der Terapanth Svetambara Jains.* Doctoral Dissertation, Johannes Gutenberg-Universität Mainz.
1995 "The Ritual Circle of the Terāpanth Śvetāmbara Jains." *Bulletin D'Etudes Indiennes* 13: 117-176.
2000 "Protestantische und Post-Protestantische Jaina Reformbewegungen: Zur Geschichte und Organisation der Sthānakavāsī I." *Berliner Indologische Studien* 13-14: 37-103.
forth. "Atonements in the Rituals of the Terāpanth Śvetāmbara Jains." *Aspects of Jainism.* Ed. by M. Mejor & P. Balcerowicz. Delhi: Motilal Banarsidass.

Gombrich, Richard
1991 *Buddhist Precept and Practice: Traditional Buddhism in the Rural Highlands of Ceylon.* 2nd Ed. with minor Corrections. (1st Ed. Oxford University Press under the Title *Precept and Practice,* 1971). Delhi: Motilal Banarsidass.

Humphrey, Caroline

1992 "Fair Dealing, Just Rewards: the Ethics of Barter in North-East Nepal." *Barter, Exchange and Value: An Anthropological Approach*. Ed. by C. Humphrey & S. Hugh-Jones. Cambridge: Cambridge University Press, 107-141.

Jain, L.C.

1929 *Indigenous Banking in India*. London: Macmillan.

Jaini, Padmanabh S.

1979 *The Jaina Path of Purification*. Berkeley: University of California Press.

1985 "The Pure and the Auspicious in the Jaina Tradition." *Purity and Auspiciousness in Indian Society*. Ed. by J.B. Carman & F.A. Marglin. Leiden: E.J. Brill, 84-93.

Jītmal, Ācārya [Jayācārya]

1981 *Victory of Discipline*. Tr. of *Jay Anuśāsan* by S.K.L. Goswami. Compiled by Ācārya Tulsī & Yuvācārya Mahāprajña. Sampādak Muni Mahendra Kumar. Jayācārya Series, Vol. 1. Ladnun: Jain Vishva Bharati.

1983 *Terāpanth: Maryādā Aur Vyavasthā*. Compiled by Ācārya Tulsī & Yuvācārya Mahāprajña. Sampādak Muni Madhukar. Jayācārya Series Vol. 9. Lāḍnūn: Jain Viśva Bhārtī.

Krishan, Yuvraj

1991/1997 "Is There 'Balancing' of Karmas?" *The Doctrine of Karma. Its Development in Brāhmaṇical, Buddhist and Jaina Traditions*. Delhi: Motilal Banarsidass, 523-533.

Mahāprajña, Ācārya [once Muni Nathmal]

1968 *Acharya Bhikṣu: The Man and His Philosophy*. (Tr. of the Hindi original, *Bhikṣu Vicār Darśan,* by N. Sahal, 1959). Cūrū: Ādarś Sāhitya Saṅgh Prakāśan.

1989a *Preksha Dhyana: Self-Awareness by Relaxation*. 2nd ed. Tr. by Muni Mahendra Kumar & J.S. Zaveri. Ladnun: Tulsi Adhyatma Nidam.

1989b *Preksha Dhyana: Perception of Breathing*. 2nd Ed. Tr. by Muni Mahendra Kumar & J.S. Zaveri. Ladnun: Tulsi Adhyatma Nidam.

1994 *Steering the Wheel of Dhamma: A Biography of Acharya Tulsi*. (Tr. of the Hindi Original, *Dharma Cakra Kā*

Pravartan, by R.K. Seth, 1986). Ladnun: Jain Vishva Bharati.

Marx, Karl
1981 *Zur Kritik der Politischen Ökonomie.* (1st Ed. Berlin: Verlag Franz Duncker, 1859). Karl Marx, Friedrich Engels, Werke, Band 13. Berlin: Dietz Verlag, 3-160.

Polanyi, Karl
1968 "The Semantics of Money-Uses." *Primitive, Archaic and Modern Economics: Essays of Karl Polanyi.* (Reprint from *Explorations,* University of Toronto, October 1957). Ed. by G. Dalton. Boston: Beacon Press, 175-203.

Prasad, Nand Kishore
1972 *Studies in Buddhist and Jaina Monachism.* Vaishali: Research Institute of Prakrit, Jainology & Ahimsa.

Schopen, Gregory
1997 *Bones, Stones, and Buddhist Monks. Collected Papers on the Archaeology, Epigraphy, and Texts of Monastic Buddhism in India.* Honolulu: University of Hawai'i Press.

Schubring, Walther
1978 *The Doctrine of the Jainas.* (Tr. from the German Original, *Die Lehre der Jainas nach den alten Quellen dargestellt,* by W. Beurlen. Berlin und Leipzig: Walther De Gruyter, 1935). Delhi: Motilal Banarsidass.

Schubring & Caillat
1966 *See Āyāradasāo Sutta.*

Shāntā, N.
1997 *The Unknown Pilgrims. The Voice of the Sādhvīs: The History, Spirituality and Life of the Jaina Women Ascetics.* (Tr. from the French Original, *La Voie Jaina: Histoire, Spiritualité, Vie des ascètes pèlerines de l'Inde,* by M. Rogers. Paris: O.E.I.L., 1985). Delhi: Sri Satguru Publications.

Sumeramal, Muni (comp.)
1998 *Terāpanth Digdarśan 1996-97.* Kalkattā: Jain Śvetāmbara Terāpanth Mahāsabhā.

Suśīlkumār, Muni
1959 *Jaina Dharma Kā Itihās.* Kalkattā: Samyak Jñāna Mandir.

Tatia, Nathmal & Kumar, Muni Mahendra
1981 *Aspects of Jaina Monasticism*. Ladnun: Jain Vishva Bharati.

Tulsī, Ācārya
1962 *Prāyaścitt Vidhi: Prastāvit Jānkārī*. Lipikṛtā Muni Harṣcandra (Lāchuḍā), V.S. 2018 Phālgun Kṛṣṇa 10, Gaṅgāśahar (Ms.).
1989 [*Prāyaścitt Vidhi*]. Yuga Pradhān Ācārya Śrī Tulsī Dvārā Nirdhārit S. 2046 Bhādrav Kṛṣṇa 5, Jain Viśva Bhāratī (ms.) [Lāḍnūn].
1989 *Maryādāvalī*. 2nd ed. (1 ed. 1960). Lāḍnūn, V.S. 2046. Bhādrapad Kṛṣṇa 5 (typescript).
1995 *Illumination of Jaina Tenets (Jaina-Siddhānta-Dīpikā)*. Tr. with Notes by S. Mookerjee. Ed. with Notes and Introduction by N. Tatia & Muni Mahendra Kumar. 2nd ed. (1st ed. 1949, 1st Engl. ed. 1985). Ladnun: Jain Vishva Bharati.

Tulsī, Ācārya & Mahāprajña, Yuvācārya
1981 "Introduction to Jayāchārya." *Victory of Discipline*. Ācārya Jītmal. Ladnun: Jain Vishva Bharati, xi-xvii.
1981a "Jayācārya aur Marx." *Prajñāpuruṣ Jayācārya*. Ācārya Tulsī & Yuvācārya Mahāprajña. Sampādak Muni Dulharāj. Lāḍnūn: Jain Viśva Bhāratī, 111-124.

Weber, Max
1978 *Economy and Society: An Outline of Interpretive Sociology*. (Tr. from the German Original, *Wirtschaft und Gesellschaft: Grundriß de verstehenden Soziologie*. 4th rev. ed. by Johannes Winckelmann. Tübingen: J.C.B. Mohr (Paul Siebeck), 1964 by G. Roth & C. Wittich (1st ed. 1968). Berkeley: University of California Press.
1978a *Gesammelte Aufsätze zur Religionssoziologie*. Band II. Sechste Auflage (Erste Auflage 1921). Tübingen: J.C.B. Mohr (Paul Siebeck).

Williams, Raymond
1983 *Jaina Yoga: A Survey of the Medieval Śrāvakācāras*. (1st Ed. London: Oxford University Press, 1963). Delhi: Motilal Banarsidass.

Notes

1 I wish to thank Ācārya Tulsī and Ācārya Mahāprajña for their generous support of the research for this paper.

2 Jaini 1985: 90.

3 Ibid.

4 In the medieval *śrāvakācāra* literature of the image-worshipping traditions, *pūjā* is presented "as a mere aspect of *dāna*" (Williams 1983: 216).

5 *Tattvārtha Sūtra* (TS) 6.13.

6 TS 6.3-4.

7 Krishan (1997: 528f.) insists that this process does not involve a 'balancing' of *karmas*. Cf. Jaini 1979: 121.

8 TS 6.21-25, 8.26.

9 Cort 2001: 200.

10 Terāpanthīs regard *puṇya* as a mere side-effect of the elimination *(nirjarā)* of *karma* through 'truly' auspicious acts of self-restraint *(saṃyama)* and asceticism *(tapas): nirjarā neṃ punrī karaṇī ek ho* (Bhikṣu 1997: 196, cf. Tulsī 1995: 69f., 162-176). For them, the only acceptable, 'pure' form of *dāna* for laity is giving provisions to Jain mendicants (Tulsī 1995: 172f.): "No religious activity is meant for the achievement of any worldly end" (Note by Tatia & Kumar in Tulsī 1995: 158). The principal source for the nine forms *puṇya* resulting from *dāna* to ascetics only is *Ṭhāṇa (Sthānāṅga Sūtra)* (SthS) 9.3.676 (Bhikṣu 1997: 200).

11 For the history of the Terāpanth see Mahāprajña 1968, Budhmal 1995.

12 "Eventually, asceticism is completely re-interpreted into a means not primarily of attaining individual salvation in one's own way, but of preparing the monk for work on behalf of the hierocratic authority... Buttressed by its own charisma, such innerwordly asceticism always remained dubious to ecclesiastical authority, which relied solely on office charisma. But the advantages prevailed" (Weber 1978: 1167).

13 Weber 1978a: 207. See *Sūtrakṛtāṅga Sūtra* (SKS) 1.14.

14 Caillat 1975: 94f., 149ff.

15 There are two types of rules within organised Śvetāmbara Jain monastic orders, which might be called individual and organisation rules of conduct: the rules concerning the primary and secondary qualities of a Jain mendicant, as laid down in the Jain canon (both together are called *mūlottara)*, and the specific organisational rules *(maryādā)* and regulations *(vyavasthā)* of a particular monastic order (see n. 3, p. 186). It is unclear to what extent *jinakalpa* was practised in the early period. The term probably refers both to individual ascetics and losely organised groups without a disciplinary code.

16 Caillat 1975: 48, with reference to *Vyavahāra Sūtra* 4.26ff.

17 Caillat 1975: 59. See *Vyavahāra Sūtra* (VS) 10.3 and commentary (Schubring & Caillat 1966: 87); *Kalpa Sūtra* (KS) 3.21; Schubring 1978: 265, 283; Tatia & Kumar 1981: 6.

18 Service "is often the complementary observance to the rejection of karman *(nijjarā)*" (Caillat 1975: 59): "service... often appears as the necessary complement of mortification" (p. 115). See Schubring (1978: 283) and Tatia & Kumar (1981: 73), who refer to the canonical distinction between "self-service and service to the fellow monks" (p. 8).

19 Similarly, the most popular verse amongst the Jain laity: *parasparopagraho jīvānām* - "souls render services to one another" (TS 5.21).

20 See VS 5.20, and Schubring on Vav. 10.3 comm. in Schubring & Caillat 1966: 87. For *vaiyāvṛttya* (Pkt. *veyācaccā* or *veyāvaḍiyā)* see Caillat 1975: 112-115. Ten categories may claim services: 1. *ācārya:* teacher, 2. *upādhyāya:* preceptor, 3. *sthavira:* elder, 4. *tapasvī:* ascetic, 5. *glāna:* sick monk, 6. *śikṣa:* neophyte, 7. *sādharmika:* religious monk, 8. *kula:* sub-group of monks (lineage), 9. *gaṇa:* monastic group, 10. *saṅgha:* monastic community (VS 10.35, and UtS 30.33, cf. TS 9.24). Williams (1963) writes, "From this list it is clear that the scope of *vaiyāvṛttya* covers all reciprocal assistance within the community of monks and is not confined to services rendered by an inferior to a superior [which was nevertheless the rule]. It also includes services rendered by laymen"; *vaiyāvṛttya* "is the term used in the canonical texts for bodily services rendered to monks, in particular attendance on the sick" (p. 242); "Such actions bring their own reward both in this life and in succeeding lives" (p. 243).

21 Tatia & Kumar 1981: 8; SKS 1.13.18.

22 *Bhagavatī Sūtra* (BhS) 921a=UtS 30 *(=Aupapātika Sūtra* 30). See n. 4, p. 182, and on the "speculative" extension of the *tapas* concept to *vinaya* and *jñāna*, Bruhn 1993: 36.

23 The late canonical UtS 29.10 promises a better rebirth for those practising *vandanā.* See Tulsī 1995: 80.

24. Caillat (1975: 59) noticed that the contributions of the *ācāryas* to the "material and spiritual well-being" of their orders "simultaneously" increased their "own gains in these two spheres": "Their devotion brings them personal benefits; they hasten the elimination of their own karman; in addition, numerous honours fall to them - a secondary benefit, but one which seems to have been nonetheless much appreciated" (p. 55).

25 Asceticism was virtually identical with fasting and predominantly performed as an atonement of a particular sin, whereas 'voluntarily' service was seen as merely beneficial for the elimination of *karma* in general (Caillat 1975: 112ff.).

26 To date, I have only seen one printed merit book for the use of the Jain laity (of the *Botāḍ Sampradāy*).

27 Ācārya Bhikṣu (1997: 182-184) refers to UtS 29.43 for support of the view that service (as well as *vandanā* and listening to *dharma kathās*) produces both *puṇya* and *nirjarā*, i.e. simultaneously bondage and destruction of *karma*, while practising *tapas* produces only *nirjarā* (and *saṃvara*). But he maintains that the *vaiyāvṛttya tapa* can also lead an ascetic close to *mokṣa* (p. 602). Cf. p. 664f. on SthS 5.1.396f.; TS 9.3; Tulsī 1995: 80f.

28 The question, whether *sādhus* who privately own even a single sheet of paper are still proper mendicants was an important issue for Ācārya Bhikṣu (1960: Ch. 11.5).

29 1851:168 *sādhvīs* in total.

30 Budhmal 1995: 383f.

31 *Gāthā* here means "any kind of writing using 32 syllables" which is well enough executed to be acceptable to the *ācārya* (the standard of calligraphy was set by a copy of the *Bhagavatī Sūtra* in the possession of the *saṅgha*) (Budhmal 1995: 387). More precisely, one *gāthā* corresponds to one *anuṣṭubha śloka* consisting of 4 *pādas* of 8 syllables.

32 Whereas early canonical Jainism rejected writing altogether, traditional Jainism advocated the copying of manuscripts for the purpose of accumulating *puṇya*. The question, whether dictating texts to lay-scribes represents a form of *parigraha* or not is still contested within the Terāpanth .*śramaṇa saṅgha*.

33 Jayācārya gave the following recommendation to his successor: "O Master of the *Gaṇ*! If you wish the *Gaṇ* to grow, enjoin upon the leading *sādhu* in a group of three to compose about twenty-five *gāthās* (verses) every day. Thus should be done to keep in mind *dravya* (sub-stances), *kṣetra* (area), *kāla* (time), *bhāva* (mental states) etc." (Jitmal 1981: 94). Ācārya Hukmīcand (died 1860), the founder of the Sthānakavāsī Sādhumārgī tradition, the local competitors of the Terāpanth in Bīkāner, also introduced the copying of scriptures as a form of *"dāna"* to the *saṅgha* on his monks (Suśīlkumār 1959: 489).

34 Even today, while most *sādhvīs* are literate and produce their own writings, female *agraṇīs* are expected to present the *ācārya* with the 'tax' of one *rajoharaṇa* and one *pramārjanī* at the annual *maryādā mahotsava*.

35 *Ācārāṅga Sūtra* (AS) 2.5-6.

36 Mahāprajña 1994: 81. The term *dāna* refers only to laity, and *bhikṣā* to the ascetics.

37 Only the possessions of an individual mendicant are precisely delimited.

38 Shāntā 1995: 524.

39 Schubring 1978: 283.

40 Budhmal 1995: 394. In the first year of his rule, Jayācārya decreed that the procurement of water and food had to be allotted in turns in the sequence of monastic seniority, in order to reduce the overall workload and to prevent that every monk or nun had to do every task every day. This idea occurred to him after the initiation of an old man, Rāmadatta, who became too weak to perform all the daily duties of a junior monk and asked a senior monk who was much younger in age to do the work for him in exchange for receiving a massage of his feet.

41 In the words of his heirs, the *ācāryas* Tulsī and Mahāprajña "Jayācārya decided to lay the foundations of a disciplined religious organization.... He laid down the following guidelines: 1. Every male or female member of the organization will be the disciple of the *Acharya* only and of nobody else. 2. Nobody will be the owner of articles needed by the entire community. 3. There will be division of labour in the ascetic order. 4. Every ascetic will share his food with other ascetics. 5. There will be equal distribution of living space, clothes and articles needed by the ascetics. 6. It will be obligatory for every ascetic to offer his or her services to the ascetic community. 7. Ascetics will have to seek the permission of the *Acharya* in matters of their camps and migrations" (Tulsī & Mahāprajña 1981: xiii-xiv). According to current Terāpanth historiography, Jayācārya established a truly socialist organisation, not unlike the utopia of Karl Marx. However, in contrast to Marx, Jayācārya recognised the necessity of the state, and explained behaviour not only through contextual factors, but also in terms of psychological dispositions (ibid.; Tulsī & Mahāprajña 1981b; Budhmal 1995: 390).

42 Some of the oldest Jain scriptures unequivocally state that private property of certain essential objects is legitimate and that no ascetic may use the property of another without his or her permission (e.g. AS 2.5-2.7).

43 The works for the whole community were, at first, mostly associated with the centralised management of the daily food-supply (*āhār saṃvibhāg):* the task of keeping the records concerning food-distribution *(saṃvibhāg patra)* and dividing the collected food *(dhaṛe kā kām)* was done by one person *(dhaṛavāla);* counting, inspecting and distributing the food, and cleaning the ground after the distribution was done by four persons *(bānṭane kā kām);* collecting, carrying, straining, measuring and distributing water was done by several persons *(pānī kā kām).* All the works connected with the centralised distribution of food and water were stopped in 1949 by Ācārya Tulsī. He simplified the procedures and ordered that the collected food had to be shared informally within the *sājh* only (Budhmal 1995: 390-92; Tulsī & Mahāprajña 1981a: 120). Nevertheless, the food col-

lected during the almsround *(gocarī)* continues to be shown to the *ācārya* to assure the correct methods of procurement have been observed, and to enable the *ācārya* to select bits and pieces of the collected food for himself before it is redistributed (cf. AS 2.1.10.1-3, KS 1.39-42). The much reduced function of accountancy *(lekhakāra)* is today mainly performed by the *yuvācārya*. There are several discarding *(pariṣṭhāpana,* Mv. *paraṭhaṇā)* and cleaning-up tasks, called *cokī* (care-taking), such as washing-up *(dhonā kā kām),* doing the laundry *(vastra prakṣālan),* sweeping the abode *(sthān kā pramārjan),* inspecting the abode *(sthān pratilekhanā),* inspecting the books *(pustakoṃ kā pratilekhanā),* emptying and cleaning the chamber-pots *(pariṣṭhāpana* or *utsarga vyavasthā)* (Budhmal 1995: 387f.).

44 The *ācārya* is assisted by several senior monks and nuns, who are appointed to serve the throne *(bājoṭ).* They collect and serve food and water for the *ācārya,* look after his health and security, carry his *pātras,* do the *pratilekhanā* for him, etc. The menial and discarding work, such as cleaning-up, is done by several freshly initiated monks, who are under the personal supervision of the *ācārya.*

45 Budhmal 1995: 396-401. The members of each commensal group share a room within the abode of the *rāj*. Until recently, a basic division of labour operated within the *sājh* between those who inspected the books *(pustak pratilekhanā),* a task which was reserved for specially skilled ascetics in order to prevent the tearing of pages (each inspector was given two books to do), and less qualified ascetics who had to inspect and to clean the abode, the begging-bowls, the carrier-bags *(jholī),* etc., and to do the *gocarī*. The two types of tasks were seen as complementary and once governed by the rules of monastic seniority. However, Jayācārya and Ācārya Tulsī, in particular, decided that both functions should be reckoned to be of equivalent value in order to raise the respect for manual labour and to create the awareness that no work is low. However, even today the seniors tend to do the inspection work, while the cleaning jobs are done by the juniors.

46 Although stitching robes was not permitted by the oldest canonical scriptures, it was later allowed by the *Cheda Sūtras (Niśītha* 1.31, 1.49, in Prasad 1972: 133).

47 Tulsī & Mahāprajña 1981a: 119.

48 Budhmal 1995: 389. Compassionate help, "altruistic concerns" or "unselfishness" (Caillat 1975: 59f., 188) are not an issue here (p. 55).

49 Likhat 1795, in Jītmal 1983: 464, 468.

50 Effectively, different spheres of exchange exist within the Terāpanth monastic economy, one based on seniority and the other on equality. In accordance with scriptural precedence, fine clothes and all

other essential paraphernalia of a mendicant, which are held in private possession although ultimately belonging to the *saṅgha,* like the *rajoharaṇa, pramārjanī* and the *pātras,* are distributed according to monastic status (cf. KS 3.19-20); while food and drinking water is principally considered collective property and has to be shared equally, although the seniors enjoy precedence (cf. AS 2.1.5.5; UtS 11.9).

51 If, for instance, a *sādhvī* wants to give to her brother, who is also a mendicant within the community, some embroidery as a present, she will give it first to the *ācārya.*

52 A give and take of essential items like food and water between *sādhus* and *sādhvīs* can, if unavoidable, take place, but has to be recorded in the diaries *(vihāra vivaraṇa)* of the *agraṇīs* and reported to the *ācārya* at the end of the *vihāra.* It is neither conceived as exchange, nor as sharing, but as a exceptional form of compassionate and devoted service *(bhakti),* and is strictly regulated (Jītmal 1983: 368; cf. Williams 1963: 241).

53 Budhmal 1995: 412.

54 The total value of *gāthās* collected by each individual may have been entered into a central register which remained with the *ācārya.* But this is not the case today. The accountancy method of the traditional Indian money-lender involves two records: a cash book *(rokaṛ bahī)* or daily account book *(roznāmcā),* to record the daily transactions, and a ledger *(khātā bahī),* which contains the names of all customers with date references. See Jain 1929: 83, 90.

55 Bhikṣu in Jītmal 1983: 469.

56 Budhmal 1995: 385. The *sādhvī saṅgha's* property was overseen by the first *sādhvī pramukhā,* Sardārsatī (1808-1870), who was also the first *sādhvī* to copy a manuscript and, thus, to receive a bookstamp (ibid.).

57 Flügel 1994. For English translations of the text of the elementary *Āvaśyaka Sūtra,* which comprises only a small proportion of the entire text of the *āvaśyaka* ritual, see Williams 1983: 195f.; Bruhn 1997-1998.

58 The fact that almost one third of the annual *saṃvatsarī pratikramaṇa* is taken up by the *kāyotsarga āvaśyaka,* that is an act of compulsory internal asceticism *(abhyantara tapas)* (UtS 30.36, 29.12), underlines its importance. The *kāyotsarga* ritual itself has to be distinguished from the "low devotions" (Schubring 1978: 281) which are often associated with it, especially in the context of the *kāyotsarga āvaśyaka,* i.e. the recitation of hinduised devotional verses such as the *Logassa* as a "conjuration... to secure the favour of the divinity in the removal of all obstacles" (Caillat 1975: 146). The difference has been pointed out for instance by the Sthānakavāsī reformer Ācārya Dharmasiṃha, who devised a *kāyotsarga āvaśyaka* without the recitation of the *Logassa*

(Flügel 2001: 65). The *kāyotsarga,* with or without the *Logassa,* is also performed independently from the *pratikramaṇa* "there is a tendency to practise *kāussagga* before any enterprise - and, much more so, before an enterprise which is considered more difficult" (Caillat 1975: 147).

59 Cf. Caillat 1975: 90.

60 The first part of the first *gāthā (śloka)* is thus recited while breathing in: *logassa ujjoyagare,* "I shall praise those who have illuminated the world," and the second part while breathing out: *dhamma-titthayare jiṇe,* "the Jinas who proclaimed the sacred doctrine as a way across," etc. The number of breaths prescribed for the inner recitation of the *Caturviṃśatistava* does not coincide with the state of being of an average relaxed and healthy person, but requires a meditative slowing down of breathing or alternatively a speeding up of reciting in approximation of the meditative ideal.

61 Schubring (1978: 281f.), Williams (1963: 215) and Caillat (1975: 146) observed: "The duration of the *[kāyotsarga]* observance is measured in "breaths" *(ucchvāsa),* a unit defined by the time necessary for the mental recitation of a *pāda* of *śloka,* or, according to others, of a "homage," *namaskāra".* Although the *Caturviṃśatistava* comprises 8 *ślokas* or 16 *pādas* and should therefore be recited either in 8 breaths, 2x8=16 breaths, or 4x8=32 breaths, the Terāpanthīs generally recommend its recitation in no more than 25 breaths, because they equate the value of the recitation of one *Logassa* with 5 recitations of the *Namaskāra Mantra* in 5x5=25 breaths *(paccīs ucchvās).* Several Terāpanth mendicants informed me that the *pratikramaṇa* was recited in the past in "only 23 or 24 breaths" (instead of 25). Others believe that, because the *Logassa* contains 7 stanzas (colloquial: *gāthā),* it is equivalent to 7 *kāyotsargas.* Thus, 1 *Logassa* = 5 *Namaskāra Mantra* = 7 *kāyotsarga.* Many mendicants do not recite *ślokas,* but *"gāthās,"* that is they attempt to recite the *Logassa* not in 8, but in 7 single breaths, or in 2x7=14, or 4x7=28 breaths. When they recite the *Logassa* in public, they take conventionally 4x7=28 breaths, i.e. 4 times more than in meditation.

62 The performance of an entire morning or evening *pratikramaṇa* ritual lasts about 48 minutes amongst the Terāpanth, or one *muhūrta,* a time period which, according to BhS 274b, normally comprises 3773 breaths.

63 Devendramuni (1995: 278f.) cites other variants of this technique of recitation from Nemicandra's *Pravacanasāroddhāra* and from the writings of Amitigati and Aparājita. Many US-lay-Jains recite the *Logassa* only once (Dharmashila & Vora 1992: 1) and recommend the inner recitation in 25 breaths (pp. 9, 15). During a Mūrtipūjak *saṃvatsarī pratikramaṇa* which I witnessed in London 1990, 148 *Namaskāra Sūtras* were recited. Schubring (1978: 282) pointed out that such repeti-

tive recitations of the *Namaskāra Sūtra* in 8 to 1008 breaths are mentioned in the *Āvaśyaka Sūtra* (ĀvS) 19; SthS 212b and in Jinabhadra's *Jītakalpa Sūtra*. Balbir (1993: 74) quotes *Āvaśyaka Nirjukti* 1517-39 and Bh 232-5 for the practice of breath control during the *pratikramaṇa*.

64 Mahāprajña 1989a: 14.

65 Bronkhorst (1986: 37), who quotes the late-canonical UtS 29.72 as evidence for the interpretation that early Jainism pursued the telos of motionlessness, because it conceived the soul as a intrinsically passive substance. Schubring (1978: 127f., cf. 152) emphasised the intrinsically 'active quality of the soul' and the significance of 'right action' in canonical Jainism. The issue is contentious and has led to sectarian divisions within the Jain tradition. On the significance of insight and meditation in the context of the *kāyotsarga āvāśyaka* rites sec Caillat 1975: 108, 167.

66 Cf. AS 1.4.1.1. This is not the place to explore the history of these ideas.

67 "Breath and life are practically synonymous.... Vital energy itself is activated by the subtle body (*taijasa śarīra*). At the ultimate end of this chain is soul or consciousness. And hence perception of the vibrations of breath, body, vital energy and karmic energy is equivalent to cognition of the SELF - the conscious energy which animates all other energies including vital energy.... The deeper and slower is the breathing, the greater is the production and availability of energy. The soul, the conscious element of the psychic existence, possesses infinite vitality and power" (Mahāprajña 1989b: 1). Cf. Schubring 1978: 144f., 315. From a Aristotelian or a 'Tantric' perspective, a mendicant's exertions could be portrayed as a way of accumulating the 'vital breath.' Jain (1979) stresses (therefore) that there is in the "ancient texts no mention of yogic control over respiration *(prāṇāyāma)*" (p. 254); *pace* Caillat 1975: 145, n.; Bronkhorst 1986: 37.

68 UtS 12.44.

69 Usually, the text of the Terāpanth *pratikramaṇa* is recited by the *ācārya* or his representative. During the sections which require a regulation of breath, the ascetics accommodate their breathing to the rhythm of the recitation. However, this method, which is also used by the Sthānakavāsīs, is not consistently applied. Mūrtipūjak ascetics practice the *pratikramaṇa* individually and instead of the *Caturviṃśatistava* recite the *Namaskāra Sūtra*.

70 The ten forms of atonement of the standard list are arranged in a sequence of increasing severity in UtS 30.31=BhS 920a=SthS 484a: 1. *ālocanā:* confession, 2. *pratikramaṇa:* repentance, 3. *tadubhaya [mīsa]:* the combination of both ['mixed'], 4. *viveka:* restitution (to give up mixed things), 5. *vyutsarga [kāyotsarga]:* abandonment of the

body, 6. *tapas:* asceticism, 7. *cheda:* reduction of seniority, 8. *mūla:* complete reduction of seniority and re-initiation (as a mendicant), 9. *anavasthāpya:* temporary exclusion and re-initiation (as a householder), 10. *pārāñcita:* exclusion with or without the possibility of re-initiation after self-criticism (having remained a householder for 6 months). TS 9.22 lists only 9 atonements.

71 Cf. SKS 1.8.8, 2.2.23; BhS 754a.

72 The present Terāpanth *ācārya* Mahāprajña (1968) acknowledged the contradiction between forced punishment *(daṇḍa)* and voluntary atonement *(prāyaścitta):* "At times the Ācārya has to impose external limitations on an underdeveloped or little developed devotee when he lacks self-discipline. Whether external limitations should be imposed may be a matter well worth considering from the point of view of non-violence, but it cannot be helped in a group life. They may be useful for the organization as a whole, but they have little value from the devotional point of view. A sincere devotee finds only such limitations useful and necessary as are self-generated" (p. 113). Budhmal (1995) writes, in the spiritual world the believer 'takes' the punishment 'given' as an atonement, whereas the doubter 'takes' the atonement 'given' as a forced punishment: *daṇḍa aur prāyaścitta meṃ yahī to antar hai ki ek balāt thopā jātā hai aur dūsrā ātmaśuddhi ke lie svīkār kiyā jātā hai* (p. 407). See also Schubring 1978: 278; Caillat 1975: 70; Dumont 1980: 179.

73 Caillat 1975: 102, 111.

74 Caillat 1975: 95. In practice, only *cheda* and *tapas* are persistently treated as mutual substitutes. Today's Terāpanthīs use the equation: 1 *upavāsa*=1 day *cheda*.

75 External asceticism *(bāhya tapas)*: 1. *anaśana:* fasting (not-eating), 2. *avamaudarikā*: abstinences, 3. *bhikṣācaryā*: restraint in begging alms, 4. *rasa-parityāga*: renunciation of delicacy, 5. *kāya-kleṣa*: self-mortification, 6. *saṃlīnatā*: renunciation of temptations by retreating from the world. Internal asceticism *(abhyantara tapas)*: 1. *prāyaścitta*: penance, 2. *vinaya*: respect to the elders, 3. *vaiyāvṛttya*: service, 4. *svādhyāya*: study, 5. *dhyāna*: meditation, 6. *kāyotsarga*: abandonment of the body (UV 30=BhS 921a=UtS 30). It is widely recognised that there is "some confusion in this list" (Williams 1963: 238). Cf. TS 9.20, Schubring 1978: 312f., Caillat 1975: 93.

76 Malayagiri's 13th C. *Vyavahāra Sūtra* commentaries "sometimes" describe meditation, study, and compulsory service as forms of penance (Caillat 1975: 158, 83).

77 A 'voluntary' co-operative course of purification through service *(parihāra viśuddhi)* is outlined in the canonical literature as the third of the five stages of monastic conduct. See Tatia & Kumar 1981: 69ff.; TS 9.18; Caillat 1975: 41, 169.

78 Tulsī 1962.

79 Tatia & Kumar 1981: 6.

80 x karmas = 7 kāyotsarga = reciting 1 Logassa in 25 breaths: writing 25 gāthās = 1 day service = y goods. There is no evidence that the religious value of reciting 25 *'gāthās'* and of writing 25 *gāthās* was equated by Jayācārya, which would have been farcical.

81 Jayācārya excluded the possibility of a direct trade-off between obligatory services quapenances and obligatory services measured in *gāthās* by distinguishing different spheres of action.

82 Gombrich (1991: 279) quotes Buddhist texts where a fund of merit is treated "like a bank account... as a kind of spiritual money". Caillat (1975: 20) found similar statements in the Jain commentaries, where "The assessment of atonements offers convenient analogies with commercial transactions (Ṭ II49b-50a, ad 1, 7-12)." For a critique of the "western" idea of a balancing of good and bad types of karma, see Krishan 1997: 523f.

83 See Weber (1978: 1167). Gombrich (1991: 88) recalls Dickson's distinction between 'outward' and 'inward' merit in his remark that the word *pinkama (puṇya karma)* is in Sri Lanka only applied "to the outward manifestation of merit-earning - the public, not the private event."

84 Caillat (1975: 112) translates the word *guṇa* as monastic 'merit.'

85 Cf. Aristotle (1985: 126): "the judge is intended to be a sort of living embodiment of what is just" (1132a20-21) "the judge (dikastes) is a bisector (dichastes)" (1132a30).

86 The concept of transfer of merit via *anumodanā,* or consent, is not explicitly invoked.

87 Tulsī 1995: 69. Paradoxically, *'karma'* refers both to action and its result (p. 58).

88 Terāpanthīs distinguished "pure" *(lokottara)* and "impure" *(laukika)* or social forms of merit *(puṇya)*. From the *lokottara* perspective, impure merit equals demerit *(pāpa)*.

89 Cf. Tatia & Kumar, in Tulsī 1995: 158.

90 By definition, all activities of Terāpanth mendicants who act within the rules of the order are 'religious.' Collective work for the order can therefore be called 'socio-religious.'

91 "Discipline is necessary both for self-purification and group-organisation. One of them is the definite side and the other practical. A Muni accepts the five great vows for his life-time; this is the definite side of discipline" (Mahāprajña 1968: 118). For canonical sources on the difference between *tapas* and *saṃyama,* see Schubring 1978: 30, 310.

92 Weber 1978: 1149.

93 Ibid.

94 The *ācārya's* control over the coupon system and the principal arbitrariness of his judgements is the only barrier to this becoming reality. See Flügel 1995: 160.

95 Budhmal 1995: 389, n.1.

96 *ācārya tulsī ne saṃvat 2017 kārtik pūrṇimā ke avsār gāthā ko bhī use prapta karne kā sādhan sthir kiyā. ab 20 gāthā ke barābar 1 paraṭhaṇā mānā jāegā* (Tulsī 1962: 1f).

97 There are two types of transgressions: (1) transgressions of the primary qualities *(mūla guṇa)* and of the secondary qualities *(uttara guṇa)* of a Jain mendicant, as laid down in the Jain canon (both together are called *mūl'ottara guṇa)*, and (2) transgressions of the specific organisational rules and regulations *(vyavasthā* and *maryādā)* of a particular monastic order *(vyavasthā guṇa)*. Theoretically, transgressions of the first type can be rectified through the *prāyścittas* prescribed in the canonical scriptures, and transgressions of the second type through the *prāyaścittas* prescribed in the judicial literature of each sect. In practice, the sect-specific *prāyaścittas* are often based on selected canonical rules and administered to both types of transgressions.

98 Budhmal 1995: 398-400.

99 Tulsī carefully avoided the words *puṇya* and *pāpa.*

100 The opposite procedure is cited by Schopen (1997) from the *Upasampadakammavaca,* "where the candidate for ordination transfers his merit to the ordaining monk" (p. 54, n. 95).

101 Certain types of *bakhśiś (bhaksīs)* are also given for limited periods of up to several years; e.g. exemptions from: light fasting *(vigay bakhśiś),* carrying baggage *(bhāra bakhśiś),* serving old or sick ascetics *(sevā bakhśiś),* community work *(samūhik kā kām bakśiś)* such as preparing *rajoharaṇas,* etc. Shortly after his death, the accessories of the late Ācārya Tulsī have been honoured with 51 *kalyāṇaka* points each and/or certain annual or lifelong *bakhśiś;* for example, the exemption from collective work in the cold season *(śītakālīn samuccay ke kārya bhakśiś),* exemption from begging medicine or clothes, or the appointment of another mendicant for carrying their burden *(nijī bojhbhār)* (Sumeramal 1998: 142f.).

102 Tulsī 1989b: 11.

103 Flügel 1995-1996: 156.

104 Cf. Gombrich 1991: 88. Transactions within the monastic economy are not governed by the notion of putative karmic equivalencies, which Humphrey (1992: 132-4) observed amongst the Buddhist Lhomi in Nepal. See also Krishnan 1997: 531f.

105 The highest honours are titles which are not associated with material benefits.

106 Cf. Budhmal 1995: 398.

107 Lion-cloth=*colapaṭṭa,* inspection=*pratilekhanā,* hand-brush=*pramārjinī,* curtain=*cilmilī,* high-stool=*bājoṭ,* (medical) mortar made out of stone=*kharala,* broom=*rajoharaṇa,* collective work=*samuccaya kārya.* This list was communicated to me from Ācārya Mahāprajña, via letter from J.C. Jain, Lāḍnūn 22.5.1998. It is derived from Tulsī's (1962) list of 40 *paraṭhaṇās (=kalyāṇakas),* but does not mention the transgressions of the rules of excretion. In 1989, a shorter list of *prāyaścittas,* which puts even greater emphasis on forms of internal asceticism, was introduced by Tulsī (1989a). Today, only the killing of living beings is still punished with compulsory fasting. The principal *kalyāṇaka prāyaścittas* are left more or less unchanged. However, the introduction of meditation as a form of penance is a major innovation.

108 See Tulsī 1989b: 11f.

109 Most nuns have accumulated more than 1000 *kalyāṇaka* points, whereas no monk has more than 1000 at present (2001).

110 "Standard, or accounting, use of money is the equating of amounts of different goods either for the purpose of barter or in any other situation involving the need for accountancy. The sociological situation is that of bartering, or of administrative management of quantifiable objects. The 'operation' consists in attaching numerical values to the various objects so that their summations may be eventually equated" (Polanyi 1968: 192).

111 Because, for all practical purposes, both *karma* and *kalyāṇaka* are used as symbolic attributions, the term 'socio-religious capital' is preferred to Bourdieu's notion of 'symbolic capital.'

112 See *Nicomachean Ethics* 1133a19ff.; Marx 1981: 66-69; Polanyi 1968, and Mary Douglas (1967) on the delicate function of coupons in centralised bureaucratic economics "to reduce or eliminate competition in the interest of a fixed system of status" (p. 133).

113 Until recently, the Terāpanthīs distinguished between *pakkā upavāsa,* compulsory fasts, and *kaccā upavāsa,* optional fasts, which could be substituted by the study or recitation of an equivalent amount of *gāthās* or the deduction of *kalyāṇakas.* In 1989, *upavāsas, gāthās* and *kalyāṇakas* lost their status as preferred atonements to *prekṣā dhyāna.* But they are still practised.

114 Cf. Caillat 1975: 97ff. Similar processes are documented in the Dharmaśāstras.

115 This classification was ratified by Ācārya Tulsī in 1989.

116 For an analysis see Flügel (forth).

117 *śrāsocchvāsa* is now one of the favourite atonements-cum-punishments. For instance, leaving the abode once during the night is punished by 12 breaths (2x=18, 3x=25, 4x=30), inadvertently crushing one small insect is punished by 25 breaths, etc. (Tulsī 1989a).

118 1. *navkārsī (namaskāra sahitya)*: not to eat during the first 48 minutes after sunrise, 2. *prahara (pauruṣī)*: not to eat in the first 3 hours after sunrise, 3. *purimaḍḍha (dina pūrvārddha, purimārddha)*: not to eat until midday, 4. *ekāśana*: not to eat more than once a day, 5. *ekasthāna*: to eat only once a day within one hour, silently in only one position, 6. *nirrigya (vikṛti niṣedha)*: not to eat *vigaya* food, such as milk, yoghurt, butter, etc., 7. *vyambila (ācāmāmla)*: to eat only once a day one unsalted cereal, 8. *uparāsa (abhaktārtha)*: to fast for 24 hours, or to drink only water *(anuparāsa)*, 9. *divasa carima (carama)*: not to eat or drink one hour before sunset, 10. *abhigraha*: not to eat without prior fulfilment of the special vows one has accepted (ĀvS 6.1-10, in Williams 1983: 207-13).

119 The treatment of study and fast as alternative forms of penance or voluntary asceticism (some prefer fasting, others studying) seems to be a modern phenomenon. It has not been discussed by Schubring nor by Caillat. The manual of the Līmbḍī Sampradāya *muni* Bhāskar (1987: 167) and the Sthānakavāsī Śramaṇa Saṅgha *Samācārī* (AISJC 1987: 98) also state that reciting 2000 *gāthās* equals 1 *upavāsa*. The fact that the present penal code of the Terāpanth contains generally more lenient rules shows that, at present, a greater value is attributed to study and meditation than fast (cf. Tulsī 1962: 1; Tulsī 1989a).

120 Both forms of meditation fall outside Bronkhorst's (1986: 53) definition of 'mainstream meditation' in terms of the aim of 'absolute motionlessness.'

121 Cf. Caillat 1975: 91.

122 Ācārya Bhikṣu, Likhat from 1777 and 1795, in Jītmal 1983: 459-466; Tulsī 1989a: 1.

123 Ibid.

124 The merchant ethos has obviously permeated the monastic rites of atonement.

125 The administrative post of the *mahāśramaṇa*, great worker, was created by Ācārya Tulsī on the 9.9.1989 for Muni Mudikumār, who is now called Yuvācārya Mahāśramaṇa.

126 In the first column of the account, a credit of 5 points is recorded to bring the total account to 102. Six out of twenty entries were made on *pakkhī* days, the days of the obligatory fortnightly rites of repentance *(pākṣīk pratikramaṇa)* and forgiveness *(kṣamāpaṇā)*. Other entries in Ṛṣabhkumār's account were made on special days: Māgh Śukla 3/4, the day of the Indian Constitution, January 26; Māgh Śukla 5 *(basant pañcamī)*, the beginning of spring; Āṣāṛh Śukla 14 *(caumāsī caturdaśī)*, a fast day preceding the four-monthly monsoon retreat; Āṣāṛh Śukla 15, the day of the first *cāturmāsik pakkhī* and the foundation day of the Terāpanth *(terāpanth sthāpanā divas)*; Caitra

Kṛṣṇa 8, the birthday and initiation day of Tīrthaṅkara Ṛṣabha *(Ṛṣabh janm evaṃ dīkṣā divas)* and the beginning of the 'one year-fast' *(varṣītap prārambh)*.

127 The *kalyāṇaka patra* of Muni Kumārśramaṇ for the year 1999 also records credits on Māgh Śukla 5-8 (altogether 148) and deficits on *pakkhī* days (Vaiśākh Śukla 15 and Jyeṣṭh Śukla 14: 10 and 16 points respectively). Credits of 101 points were received by all mendicants on Ācārya Mahāprajña's birthday (Āṣāṛh Kṛṣṇa 13). See Photographs.

128 The *kalyāṇakas* are the five auspicious events in the life of a Tīrthaṅkara – conception *(garbha)*, birth *(janma)*, renunciation *(vairāgya)*, enlightenment *(kevala jñāna)*, and death *(nirvāṇa)* – which Jains celebrate as the paradigmatic markers of the ideal Jain life, and for merit and this-worldly welfare (Cort 2001: 179). The *kalyāṇaka* days and the *kalyāṇaka kṣetras* of the legendary twenty-four Tīrthaṅkaras constitute the backbone of the Jain religious year and their sacred geography. Terāpanthīs do not celebrate the *garbha kalyāṇakas*.

129 Cf. Flügel 1994, 1995-1996: 133, n. 33, 155, n. 65.

130 *ye sādhu (yā sādhviāṃ) aur pustakaṃ sab āp ke caraṇoṃ meṃ samarpit haiṃ. maiṃ bhī āp ke caraṇoṃ meṃ samarpit hūṃ. āp mujhe jahāṃ rakheṃ vahāṃ rahne kā bhāv hai* (Jītmal in Tulsī & Mahāprajña 1981a: 116). Non-redistributed items are deposited in the Sevā Kendra.

131 Cf. Budhmal 1995: 415.

132 Ācārya Tulsī's successor Ācārya Mahāprajña is addressed in the same manner: *ācārya śrī mahāprajña ko maiṃ tīrthaṅkar der tulya mānatā hūṃ*. The veneration of the *ācārya* as a godlike figure may come as a surprise, given the rationalistic tone of contemporary Terāpanth publications. However, a Jain *ācārya* has to appeal to a diverse audience. Numerous songs and prayers deify the head of the order in the manner of Hindu devotionalism. Cf. Caillat 1975: 59.

133 Letter, Jain Viśva Bhāratī 27.4.1998.

134 On 'Jain modernism' see Flügel 2000: 39. On the conflict between modernity *(navīntā)* and antiquity *(prācīntā)* amongst Terāpanth ascetics, see Budhmal 1995.

135 *Nicomachean Ethics* 1130b30-1131a9.

136 Durkheim 1984: 83ff.

10

Jain Monastic Life

A Quantitative Study of the Terāpanth Śvetāmbara Mendicant Order

One of the most neglected areas of research in Asian religions is the sociology of monastic orders.[1] This is surprising, given the pivotal importance of organised asceticism for contemporary Jain, Buddhist and Hindu traditions. Jain mendicant orders are the oldest surviving monastic traditions of the world. Today, they broadly refer to themselves as *śramaṇa saṅghas*, or ascetic communities. While information on the history and organisation of these itinerant groups is increasingly accessible, few studies inform us on their social and geographical dynamics. To remedy this situation regarding one centrally organised and tightly regulated Jain mendicant order in India, a combined socio-demographic and network-analytical survey was conducted by the present writer in 2001-2003 in Rājasthān, with the blessings of Ācārya Mahāprajña (born 1921), the current head of the Śvetāmbara Terāpanth mendicant order. The aim was to supplement previously collected qualitative data on the history, rules and regulations, monastic division of labour and religious life of the Terāpanth, and on general demographic trends in contemporary Jaina monasticism.

Muni Navaratnamal in Lāḍnūṃ 2000

The principal unit of investigation was the monastic order itself, which was treated as social system differentiating itself from the social environment through rules of membership, role-definitions, and emergent actions. The analysis of living social systems is predicated on third order observation, or observation of self-observation. While the Terāpanth order describes its own functioning in normative terms, resembling the model of rule-implementation of classical organisational sociology with a focus on values, norms, rules, commitment, hierarchy, lines of command, compliance, etc., the project aimed at an understanding of the social dynamics within a Jain monastic community which presents itself as a limiting case of perfect social self-regulation. Not the formal structure and the practice of rule-implication, but the conditions, functions and consequences of the process self-organisation were the main concern of the project.

The principal aim of this pilot study was to generate a clearer idea of the network structure of actual contacts within the mendicant order, ideally in form of a sociomatrix recording the internal transactions of all mendicants in selected media (name-recognition, communications, services, material transactions) within a defined time-frame and, to collect data for the study the spatial dynamics, measure group connectedness, statistically correlate the results with the newly generated demographic data, and to analyse outcomes in the light of the rules and regulations of the order and ethnographic background information collected over more than fifteen years. The project specified three main objectives:

1 To produce reliable statistical information on the demographic and social composition of the entire contemporary Terāpanth mendicant order, including psychological factors such as motivations for renunciation.

1 To produce a systematic analysis of the network structure within the order and the patterns of transactions in key media such as information and material support.

1 To learn more about the network analytic aspects of studying a trans-regionally organised group of itinerant mendicants.

The research was conducted in form of a survey amongst in 2003, 785 Terāpanth monks (19.6%), nuns (68.5%) and male (0.5%) and female novices (11.3%) using a two-part questionnaire in Hindi.

Data Collection

The first round of data collection took place between 1.8.2001–1.8.2002. After pre-tests, the distribution of the questionnaire amongst an exceptionally large group of some 450 monks and nuns attending the annual assembly, *maryādā mahotsava*, of the Terāpanth mendicant order held in January 2002 in the town Pacapadarā in Rājasthān proved to be a great success. With the help of a leading monk, Muni Sukhlāl (born 1930), and the junior monks under his guidance, research assistant Harshita Jain of Bikaner managed to get most of the locally distributed questionnaires returned in February 2002.

Because the response to the network analytical questions was insufficient for statistical investigation, additional questionnaires were distributed by mail with the help of Muni Sukhlāl and his associates. More than 100 questionnaires were returned in this way. Due to the geographical distances no interviewer could be used.

By August 2002, 477 mendicants completed the questionnaire, at least in part. The response rate of monks and *samaṇ/īs*, who are all well educated, was notably higher than of the nuns. Some mendicants were too old or sick to be involved in the project. Many older nuns did not answer the questionnaire because they could not read and write, though some asked younger nuns to help them.[2] A number of mendicants never received or did not return their questionnaire, and about 10-20% refused to answer or did not fill in the questionnaire properly for a variety of reasons, partly due to the mechanical and apparently meaningless nature of the exercise and the perceived "shallowness" of network-analytical questions geared towards quantitative analysis. The quality of the answers varied significantly from question to question.

Because of the not entirely unexpected difficulties encountered with the response rate and the quality of the data for network analysis, it was decided to initiate a second round of data collection with the help of interviewers during the period of residency of the mendicants during their annual rain retreat, or *cāturmāsa*, in July-November 2002, and to extend the project by six month until March 2003. During this period, the response rate was increased to 530 or 67.6%: 108 monks (14%), 362 nuns (46%), 4 male novices (0.5%), and 56 female novices (7%). For an additional 40 (5%) mendicants (13 monks, 12 nuns, 15 female novices) basic demographic information was extracted from mendicant biographies and group statistics published by Muni Navaratnamal (1981-2002). In this way, detailed demographic data were collected for 570 or 72.6% of all mendicants in the Terāpanth Jain order between August 2001 and

March 2003. However, for some items of Part I of the questionnaire the response rate was too low to form a representative sample, and in order to enable meaningful cross-tabulations, 74 of the 570 questionnaires had to be excluded from analysis.

The final sample of 496, 99 *sādhus* (20%), 341 *sādhvīs* (68.8%), 4 *samaṇs* (0.8%) and 52 *samaṇīs* (10.5%), is statistically representative of the population and forms one of the largest collections of demographic data on a South Asian mendicant order to date.

Social Background of the Mendicants

State of Origin:

The majority (78%) of the sample of Terāpanth mendicants came from a small number of districts in Rājasthān, in particular Churu (30%), Bikaner (20%) and Nagaur (10%), and from migrant families from these regions to Kalkatta (3.2%) and other commercial centres (where the majority of Terāpanth laity now live).

Birth Place:

Most mendicants were born and brought up in villages (52%) and small towns (36%), and only a minority in towns (4%) and cities (8%). The main recruitment areas were the small towns

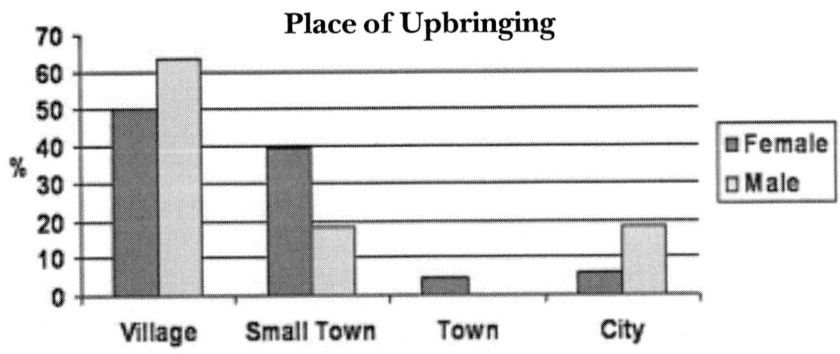

Sardarshahar (10%), Gangashahar (9%), Dungargarh (7%), Ladnun (9%) and the surrounding villages and adjacent small towns such as Sujangarh, as well as the area around Badmer and Kalkatta. The highest proportion of male renouncers came from villages. There is no significant evidence of (an impact of) family migration from villages to towns and cities or vice versa.

Caste:

The majority of the mendicants belonged to the Osvāl castes (85%) with a significant minority of Agravāls (12%) from the region of Hisar and Hansi in Hariyana (and Delhi and Orissa). Most respondents returned themselves as Bīsa Osvāl or emphasized that the status distinction between Bīsa- and Dasa Osvāl is not observed anymore.

Father's Occupation:

Generally, the data on father's occupation (in the majority of cases equivalent with family occupation) show that nearly all mendicants (87%) came from traditional self-employed lower middle class business families with a modest but relatively secure source of income. This seems to reflect the overall pattern amongst the Rājasthāni Osvāl castes. More than half of the business families from which Terāpanth mendicants emerged engaged in the traditional cloth (33%), jute (4%) and jewellery (5%) trades as well as in shop keeping (13%). Only 7% engaged in manufacturing, and 1% in finance. The rest were higher professionals and employees in government service and management etc. (11%), and a small number of (part time) farmers (0.8%).

The fact that wealthy metropolitan Terāpanth Osvāls families produced only few mendicants was explained by Terāpanth nuns with reference to the "greater freedom" and "more entertainment" and "opportunities for self-development" rich women enjoy. Women of "poor" middle class families in rural areas live in joint families. They have less time for themselves and are totally dependent on their husbands and their families. They have no independent income, cannot leave the house often, and, because the villages offer not much, enjoy few public entertainments. But they have more contact with mendicants than metropolitan families. The only entertainment and intellectual stimulation is often provided by religious contexts. Similar reasons have already been reported by Goonasekera (1986) for Terāpanth monks.

Family Name:

The mendicants were recruited from a small number of *gotras*, or exogamous family clans. Of altogether 114 family names mentioned by respondents, 17 names accounted for 33% of all mendicants.

Family Size:

Nuclear families (within the joint family) had a median size of 6 members (range of 1-14). This family size is not untypical for middle class Rājasthānī households, though firm data are a desideratum. It decreased slightly over the last 70 years. Most of the key families had more than one mendicant in the order (one nun could name 13 relatives inside the order).

Birth Order:

Previous studies on Buddhist (Spiro 1970) and Terāpanth Jain mendicants (Goonasekera 1986: 122) argued that the motivation for renunciation can be explained in terms of the emotional deprivation of middle children, i.e. Freud's theory that "middle children experience fluctuations of nurturing and affection from early childhood... especially girls." In contrast to Goonasekera's finding of a higher than statistically expected proportion of middle children amongst his sample of 75 Terāpanth "renouncers" (82%) - 65 females (86.6%) and 10 males (13.3%) - the present sample of 137 respondents - 56 *sādhus* (40.9%), 40 *sādhvīs* (29.9%), 41 *samaṇīs* (29.2%) - revealed only the expected percentage of 61% middle children (given an average family size of 6), as well as 26% youngest (Goonasekera: 10%), 11% eldest, and 2% only children. The overrepresentation of middle children in the earlier study may thus be a sampling effect. But both samples are not statistically representative. It is significant, though, that 10% more female than male middle children renounced. The high number of youngest male children reflects the economic and social importance of the eldest male child as the principal heir of the family business.

Initiation Age:

The data confirm the overall increase of the mean initiation age over time observed by Goonasekera, and substantiate trends, such as the impact of the aforementioned institutional factors on initiation patterns. The mean initiation age for the entire sample was 20 years. Generally, males (mean age: 18) were initiated earlier than females, nuns (20) earlier than female novices (*samaṇīs*) (24). However, during the period between 1931 and 1948 the mean initiation age of 15 years was identical for male and female mendicants. Gender differences developed with the creation of the first pre-monastic educational institution for girls in the town of

Ladnun in 1949, and in particular after the reforms of Ācārya Tulsī (1914-1997) in the 1980s which only permit male but not anymore female child-initiation (*bāla-dīkṣā*). Both the overall gender differential and the higher initiation age of female novices compared to nuns thus appear to be effects of institutional factors, especially the compulsory pre-monastic education for girls which also accounts for the increasing number of unmarried girls rather than widows in the monastic order (90% of the mendicants in the sample are unmarried). Social support for widows is nowadays provided by religious and social funds.

Initiation Year:

In 2001-2 the mean age of the Terāpanth mendicants was 52 (for monks it was slightly lower: mean 50, median 47) with peaks around 75 and 40, i.e. those born 1926 and 1961. This reflects the lower recruitment rate during the 1950s and 1960s compared to the 1940s and the 1980-1990s. The number of initiations increased

1 YEAR

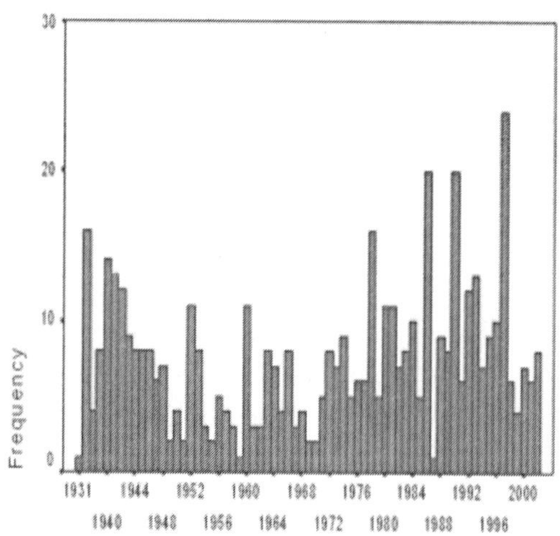

after the inaugurations of the last two *ācāryas* in 1937 and 1997, and during the decisive years of the Indian freedom struggle between 1940 and 1945, followed by a post-Independence low, and a peak after the establishment of two new institutions – the Jain Vishva Bharati centre in Ladnun in 1978 and the new Terāpanth novice order in 1980. Less than 50% of all initiations took place in the home-village/town of the mendicants.

Reasons for Renunciation

The two open questions concerning the causes informing the decision to renounce the world and the sources of inspiration identified push and pull factors. For statistical analysis, the spectrum of answers was coded into seven categories, after discussing the answers with Terāpanth *samaṇīs*:[3]

- SOCIAL REASONS (6%: male 4%, female 6%): social reasons, fear of marriage, the monastic environment, to live a meaningful life, to gain spiritual power, to gain the status of a mendicant.
- PSYCHOLOGICAL REASONS (27%: male 21%, female 28%): death of a family member or others, sight of suffering, illness, uncertainty of life.
- RELIGIOUS REASONS (7%: male 11%, female 6%): path of salvation, religious disposition, experience of meditation or ritual, experience of a natural event, religious literature, drama or film, inspired by a deity.
- INSPIRED BY A MONK OR A NUN (20%: male 33%, female 16%).
- SELF INSPIRED (34%: male 25%, female 37%).
- INSPIRED BY A RELATIVE (7%: male 6%, female 7%): inspired by a family member, inspired by the initiation ritual of a relative.
- OTHER (0.4%: male 0%, female 0.5%): unknown.

Statistical analysis demonstrated that religious experiences or doctrinal reasons were not the prime motivating factors. The fact that nevertheless relatively more men than women mentioned religious reasons may be explained by the perceived need of men to legitimize their interest in religion, since traditional role models cast them as 'less religious' than women.

A more detailed analysis of the responses revealed interesting gender differences. For males, especially young males, the personal influence of ascetics (sometimes but not necessarily relatives) was important, while for females (socio-) psychological factors were more significant. Personal interviews indicated that the most frequent answer of female mendicants in response to the question who inspired them to become initiated: 'self inspired' (*svataḥ preraṇā*) also served as a rationalization for a number of unspecified personal, spiritual, social and psychological reasons.[4]

Initiation as an alternative to marriage for women was not often explicitly mentioned (10 nuns and no monks), although in the ethnographic literature on Jain mendicants it is highlighted as the most important factor. However, this motive may also hide behind the answer 'self inspired' and co-varies with certain 'psychological reasons.' Interviews with Terāpanth nuns confirmed that relative poverty and family pressure only indirectly influence female renunciation "because the conflicts produce intense bitterness in the mind of the renouncer" (Goonasekera 1986: 224).

Widowhood (Boradiya 1975, Goonasekera 1986) could not be established as a dominant factor for renunciation anymore (15 widows, 2 widowers), since most initiation candidates are nowadays young and unmarried (Reynell 1985: 269). Within the Terāpanth this is not only a consequence of fewer numbers of child-widows and improvements in the social world of women (Cort 1991: 659f.), but also because of new rules regarding pre-monastic education of female candidates (Flügel 2006: 364f.).

For young women the 'experience of death' was an important explicit motive, but less so for young men, who more often mentioned 'religious disposition/inclination' (*dhārmik pravṛtti/ruci*) or the 'extreme attraction' (*atyadhik ākarṣaṇa*) of religious life as motives (despite the high number of fatherless male renouncers), which was rarely referred to by women. An explanation for this may be sought in the role patterns in Rājasthāni middle class and caste families, i.e. the strong family orientation that is imprinted more on women than on men, who are frequently on business travels away from home. Men have to legitimate their special interest in religion, which is taken for granted in the case of women, who described themselves as "more sensitive."

The analysis of the survey data showed that, in contrast to Buddhist societies (Spiro 1970), economic or status considerations were not directly important; nor are women forced to renounce by their families as is often suspected (see already Goonasekera 1986).

With regard to the factors 'own choice' and 'social' and 'psychological' reasons not much seems to have changed over the last 2000 years. Self-attributions of motives and intentions are, of course, constructions which are, more or less, informed by role expectations. Many of the returned reasons, especially extrinsic or psychological reasons, have already been enumerated in sections of the Jain canon "which, partly, give the impression of holding up a mirror to the monks" (Schubring 1935/2000 § 137). The ten principal reasons are listed in the *Couplets on Renunciation* (*Pavvajjā-padaṃ*) of Ṭhāṇa 10.15 [712a]: (1) one's own choice, (2) anger, (3) poverty, (4) dreams, (5) fulfilment of an earlier vow, (6) recollection of inspiration received in a former birth, (7) illness, (8) insult, (9) enlightenment by the gods, (10) affection for a son who is a *muni*. Ṭhāṇa 4.571-577 [276ab] lists additional this-worldly and other-worldly motives and methods for inducing the inclination for renunciation in another person. To put these empirical motives in perspective, Ṭhāṇa 4.577 distinguishes four types of renunciation on a scale beginning with renunciation free of fault and three progressively more faulty types. The leaders of Jain mendicant orders are compared with farmers who are interested in keeping only unsullied grain.

Reasons for Renunciation

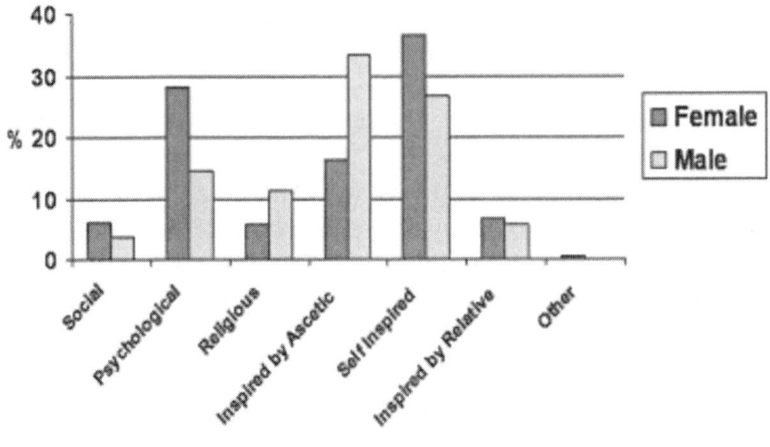

Division of Labour

The favourite activity of initiated monks (38%) and nuns (32%) is to study (*svādhyāya*), followed by service (*sevā*) to the order (16%) for monks, and needlework (*silāī*) (9%) and art work (*kalā*) (7%) for women, i.e. producing objects of daily use (begging bowls, etc.), drawing, and other crafts. This reflects the traditional sexual division of labour within the order which is perpetuated through a system of rewards (*kalyāṇaka* bonus points) (Flügel 2003b), though the quantity of items produced and transacted is low.

Statistically, needlework, study/research, and service to sick and old nuns and monks (it is obligatory for young monks and nuns to serve one year in one of the *sevā kendras* for old nuns and monks), but also artistic work, are more often than other 'good deeds' rewarded with bonus points by the present head of the order. Officially, *kalyāṇaka* bonus points should not be used as a medium of exchange within the order. However, for females the correlation of the length of time spent in the mendicant order with the number of bonus points collected for good work is statistically significant. Nuns accrued far more bonus points then monks. High scoring men and women tended to study and to write. By contrast, there is no statistically significant correlation with regard to males. This result furnishes indirect proof for the observed pattern that males used their bonus points as a medium of exchange and spent their *kalyāṇakas* on help offered by the nuns for mending clothes, etc., while nuns rarely received reciprocal services from monks. The rules of the order explicitly rule out the practice of equivalent exchange in favour of the ideal of service to the order.

Monastic Networks

The key questions for network analysis concerned the extent to which the order was socially integrated, which informal networks or groups ('cliques') existed, and how the monastic rules and regulations shaped the network structure.[5] The analysis of selected features of the monastic networks demonstrated: (a) that many mendicants do not know one another; (b) that older mendicants are better connected than younger mendicants; (c) that mendicants of the same category, gender, age group and kinship group are more connected than others; (d) that the members of the entourage of the head of the order, or *gurukula*, are more connected than others; and (e) that both novices (*samaṇ/ī*) and ex-novices who were promoted to the status of fully initiated mendicants are extremely well connected. There are three reasons for this: the *samaṇ/īs* lived and studied together for several years in religious boarding schools, they are allowed to travel and meet other monks and nuns, and they meet each other every year at the annual assembly of the mendicants. Thus, over time, the entire network structure of the order will be affected by the introduction of the novice category in 1980. Increased connectivity between the nuns is to be expected.

The data also showed that: (a) (with the exception of the members of the *gurukula*) fully initiated male and female ascetics hardly ever interact across the gender divide, since contact between male and female ascetics is strictly regulated and because there are few opportunities for itinerant mendicants to meet; (b) the networks are oriented towards the office holders of the centralised monastic hierarchy, who qua position know and interact with everyone; (c) family members of the same gender often live together in the same itinerant group, because in this way conflict within small groups is minimized; (d) family connections are maintained within the order through occasional "exchanges" of small gifts which have to be mediated by the group-leader and the head of the order; (e) group solidarity as a whole is strengthened through birth-day and initiation-day cards from the leadership of the order; (e) rotation of personnel does not often take place, except: in cases of conflict, to balance the educational and age profile of a group, and for specific collaborative projects; (f) due to the greater group size the rate of rotation is higher amongst nuns than amongst monks; (g) novices show a higher degree of mutual interaction than other mendicants for the said reasons.

Summary

On the basis of a sample of 496 mendicants of the Terāpanth Śvetāmbara Jain order in the years 2001-3, a number of ethnographic observations and theories on Jain ascetics could be tested, albeit only for few questions in a statistically representative way due to uneven response patterns. A socio-demographic analysis showed that the Terāpanth mendicants are largely recruited from lower middle class Osvāl business families in the villages and small towns of the Churu, Bikaner and Nagaur districts of Rājasthān. The pivotal families are long-term followers of the Terāpanth and often have more than one initiated family member in the order. Nowadays, the majority of the mendicants are unmarried females who renounce of their own accord, primarily because their conservative families do not offer them any other alternative to marriage, and because of their familiarity with Jain values and pre-established links with the well organised Terāpanth order which offers unique educational opportunities for women in a traditional social context. With regard to the rural background, the findings resonate with Spiro's (1970) observations on Theravāda Buddhist monks in Burma. However, the families of Terāpanth Jain renouncers are more urbanized and of higher social and economic standing than those of the Buddhist monks in Burma. There are no significant material reasons for renunciation, and no one is forced to enter mendicancy. Goonasekera (1986) offered a psychoanalytical interpretation of Terāpanth Jain patterns of renunciation, but overlooked the psychological significance of experiences of death and suffering for female renouncers in particular. By contrast, one of the main findings of this study is that social and organisational factors, such as the pre-monastic educational institutions of the Terāpanth founded in 1949 and 1980, have a strong influence on initiation patterns, gender relations, geographical spheres of influence, the division of labour and the social integration of the order.

References

Balbir, Nalini. "Recent Developments in a Jaina Tīrtha: Hastinapur (U.P.) - A Preliminary Report." *The History of the Sacred Places in India as Reflected in Traditional Literature.* Panels of the 7th World Sanskrit Conference Vol. II. Ed. H. Bakker. General Editor: Johannes Bronkhorst, 177 191. Leiden: E.J. Brill, 1990.

Boradiyā, Hīrābāī. *Jaina Dharma kī Sādhvīoṃ evaṃ Viduṣī Mahilāoṃ kā Itihās.* Ph.D. thesis, University of Indore, 1975.

Cort, John E. "The Śvetāmbar Mūrtipūjak Jain Mendicant." *Man* (N.S.) 26 (1991) 651 671.

Flügel, Peter. "Socio-Demographic Analysis of the Terāpanth Śvetāmbara Jain Monastic Order." *Final Report: British Academy Research Grant SG-32893.* London, 25.5.2003a.

Flügel, Peter. "Spiritual Accounting: The Role of the *kalyāṇaka patra* in the Religious Economy of the Terāpanth Śvetāmbara Ascetics." *Jainism and Early Buddhism. Essays in Honor of Padmanabh S. Jaini.* Ed. O. Qvarnström, 183-224. Fremont: Asian Humanities Press, 2003b. https://eprints.soas.ac.uk/965/

Flügel, Peter. "Demographic Trends in Jaina Monasticism." *Studies in Jaina History and Culture: Disputes and Dialogues.* Ed. P. Flügel, 312-398. London: Routledge, 2006. https://eprints.soas.ac.uk/6242/

Flügel, Peter. "Jain Monastic Life: A Socio-Demographic and Network Analysis of the Terāpanth Śvetāmbara Mendicant Order." *International Journal of Jaina Studies (Online)* (forthcoming)

Fohr, Sherry E. *Gender and Chastity: Female Jain Renouncers*. Ph.D. thesis, University of Virginia, 2001.

Goonasekera, R.S.A. *Renunciation and Monasticism among the Jainas of India*. Ph.D. Dissertation, San Diego, University of California, 1986.

Mitchell, Clyde. "The Concept and Use of Social Networks." *Social Networks in Urban Situations: Analyses of Personal Relationships in Central African Towns*. Ed. J.C. Mitchell, 1–50. Manchester: Manchester University Press, 1969.

Navaratnamal, Muni (comp.). *Śasana Samudra*. Vol. 1 18. Published by Uttamcand Sethia. Kalkattā: Śrī Jain Śvetāmbar Terāpanthi Mahāsabhā Prakāśan & Lāḍnūṃ: Jain Viśva Bhāratī, 1981-2002.

Reynell, Josephine. *Honour, Nurture and Festivity: Aspects of Female Religiosity amongst Jain Women in Jaipur*. Ph.D. thesis, University of Cambridge, 1985.

Schubring, Walther. *Die Lehre der Jaina. Nach den alten Quellen dargestellt*. Berlin: Walter DeGruyter, 1935 (*The Doctrine of the Jainas. Described after the Old Sources*. Translated by Wolfgang Beurlen. Third English Edition. With Three Indices Enlarged and Added by Willem Bollée & Jayandra Soni. Delhi: Motilal Banarsidass, 1962/2000).

Spiro, Melford E. *Buddhism and Society*. New York: Harper & Row, 1970.

Ṭhāṇaṃ (Sthānāṅga Sūtra). Mūla Pāṭha, Saṃskṛta Chāyā, Hindī Anuvāda tathā Ṭippaṇa. Vacana Pramukha: Ācārya Tulsī. Saṃpādaka-Vivecaka: Muni Nathmal. Lāḍnūṃ: Jaina Viśva Bhāratī, 1976.

Vallely, Anne. *Guardians of the Transcendent: An Ethnography of a Jain Ascetic Community*. Toronto: University of Toronto Press, 2003.

Notes

1. The project was funded by the British Academy Small Research Grant SG-32893. For a detailed account see Flügel Forthcoming.
2. Balbir 1990: 202-4, 223 reports similar experiences.
3. Boradiyā (1975: 265-80) interviewed 100 nuns "from various sects" and coded the stated reasons for renunciation in a similar way: 21 "personal reasons," 19 "inspired by particular nun", 17 "orphan," 14 "ambiance of ascetic community," 5 "outward appearance of ascetic

life," 59 "spiritually motivated," 17 "refuge," [? widows], 11 "increase of knowledge for specific religious end," 10 "service of the community," 3 "escape from marriage." The word 'reason' is ambiguous. Motives and intentions are rarely clearly distinguished.

4. "Within the order, desire to belong to the group, or attraction to a charismatic leader, is not treated as a 'social' motivation,stemming from worldliness. Instead, it too is seen as evidence of a spiritual purity" (Vallely 2002: 197).

5. The following characteristics of personal or ego-centred networks oriented the analysis in particular: (a) morphological: anchorage, reachability, connectedness (density), range, (b) interactional: directedness (symmetry/asymmetry), frequency, content. See Mitchell 1969.

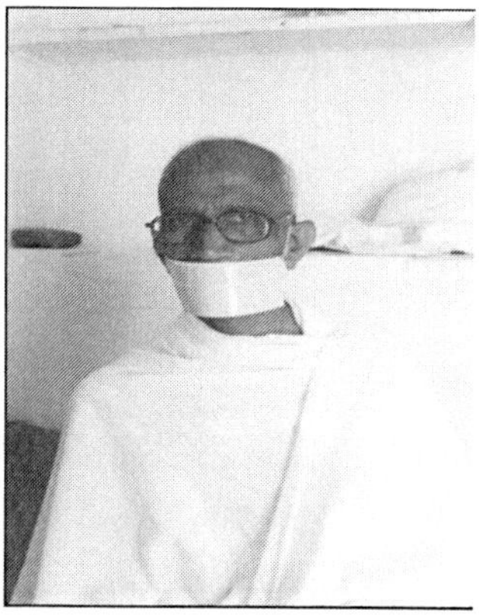

Muni Sukhlal in Pañcāvat 2001

11

Present Lord Sīmandhara Svāmī and the Akram Vijñān Movement

Introduction

Most textbooks present Jainism as a religion which survives in a pristine state virtually unchanged from the time of its last prophet, Mahāvīra, some two thousand and five hundred years ago. Walther Schubring, for instance, wrote in his classic work, *The Doctrine of the Jainas: Described after the Old Sources,* that the 'teaching proper' of Jainism, which propagates monastic asceticism as the principal means of salvation, was 'scarcely affected' by exterior changes: 'The new formations which developed to remain,' he writes, 'are nearly exclusively concerned with formalities.'[1] This view was reiterated by Robert Williams, in his book *Jaina Yoga,* which describes the textual prescriptions for the traditional rituals of lay Jainism, though he emphasised that the 'changelessness of Jainism is no more than a myth.'

> Admittedly there have been no spectacular changes in basic assumptions such as there were, for example, in Mahāyāna Buddhism. At most there have been variations in emphasis. Had Jainism, as at one time must have seemed possible, become a majority religion in southern India something akin to a Digambara Mahāyāna might, with continuing favourable circumstances, have emerged. But all that can be detected today are the traces of aborted developments.[2]

In his influential work *The Jaina Path of Purification,* P.S. Jaini detailed examples of the continual 'erosive' influence of Hindu devotionalism on almost every aspect of popular Jainism from the fifth century onwards, but restated Williams' view:

> No movement towards a more catholic viewpoint or liberalised discipline, no 'Jaina Mahāyāna' was ever allowed to develop among either the Digambaras or the Śvetāmbaras.[3]

In this essay I will present at least one case not only of a doctrine or isolated features but of a syncretistic religious movement which,

I would argue, can legitimately be called 'Jaina Mahāyāna,'[4] i.e. a primarily devotional form of Jainism, visibly different from the ascetic path outlined in the canonical and classical Jaina scriptures,[5] which congenially combines Kundakunda's 'Digambara Mahāyāna' soteriology (which is in many ways closer to Śaṃkara's Advaita Vedānta),[6] Sāṃkhya ontology and classical Jaina cosmology with a ritual idiom that is largely derived from popular Vaiṣṇava devotionalism and Tantric miracle cults?[7]

For practical purposes, I follow Heinz Bechert in defining Mahāyāna in the broadest sense through the concept of 'salvation through others,'[8] which is equally important in devotional Hinduism. In Buddhism, the concept has gained particular prominence in the so-called Pure Land *(Sukhāvatī)* school in East Asia and informs popular devotional practices which answer the religious needs of the Buddhist laity. The *Sukhāvatī* and similar schools offer temporary respites prepared by a *bodhisattva,* a Buddha-to-be, where the devotee prepares for one final rebirth in the presence of a Buddha after which *nirvāṇa* will be attained. In popular religion, these 'Buddha fields' *(Buddha kṣetra)* became soteriological ends in themselves, because they offer an easy and essentially non-monastic path to salvation which merely demands the recognition of the 'Buddha nature' within *(tathāgatagarbha),* that is, the true knowledge of the real self *(ātman)*. In other words, 'we are already fully enlightened Buddhas if we but recognise the face.'[9]

Instant Knowledge (Akram Vijñān)

The case I wish to present in favour of the argument that Mahāyāna-style forms of Jainism do exist — at least, on the margins of the five major traditions of the Bīsapanthī and Terāpanthī Digambara, on the one hand; and the Mūrtipūjaka and the Sthānakavāsī and Terāpanthī Śvetāmbara, on the other — is the Akram Vijñān Mārg in western India, literally the path of the stepless or instant acquisition of the knowledge (necessary for salvation). Because of its recent emergence, its lack of a scriptural 'great tradition' and its small size (quantity is not really an issue) the Akram Vijñān Mārg has not yet been studied, although it is highly interesting from a comparative perspective; not only because it combines Jaina and Vaiṣṇavite features in a unique way, but mainly because it offers its followers a method of purification which does not demand renunciation or difficult religious practices, such as asceticism *(tapas),* material offerings *(pūjā)* and gift-giving *(dāna),* or other ritual observances to annihilate *karma.* It therefore presents itself as an attractive option for anyone who seeks easy access to religious purity without the desire to renounce the world or to spend much money on such 'useless'[10] rituals. Moreover, the promise of instant access to salvific knowledge poses a fundamental threat to the traditional establishment of Hindu and Jaina religious functionaries, which are both dismissed as obsolete.

The Akram Vijñān Mārg is a lay movement which teaches that there are two paths in Jainism. The dominant *kramik,* step-by-step, Jaina path of purification is predicated on the cosmologically derived assumption that due to the current absence of the conditions for the existence of enlightened beings in our world, enlightenment and therefore final liberation is, at present, not possible anymore. By contrast, the *akramik,* stepless, path, offers a direct route to *mokṣa* through the grace *(kṛpā),* of the presently existing lord *(vartamāna tīrthaṅkara),* Sīmandhar Svāmī, one of twenty Jaina *tīrthaṅkaras* who according to classical Jaina mythology and cosmography presently lives in the mythical pure land of Mahāvideha Kṣetra, some 193,950,000 kilometres north of our continent Bhārata.[11] The Akram Vijñān movement offers 'instant salvation' to its followers by claiming that Sīmandhar can be accessed through magical means that is, through direct contact with a medium *(nimitta).* The principal medium, the late A.M. Paṭel, became a *bodhisattva*-like figure for his disciples by acting as an interlocutor between humans and the presently existing *tīrthaṅkaras* in the pure land of Mahāvideha.[12] The cosmological assumptions of this new method are not controversial, although they emerged relatively late in the history of Jainism,[13] and neither is the use of magical means of contact which, in this case, is probably inspired by the example of Kundakunda's yogic travels to these regions in search of inspiration from Sīmandhar.[14] However, nowhere has a separate path to salvation been offered explicitly in the Jaina tradition to date, though A.M. Paṭel claimed to follow the unique example of King Bhārata, the son of the first *tīrthaṅkara,* Ṛṣabha, and who, according to the Akram Vijñān version of the legend, was granted omniscience by an act of grace of Ṛṣabha.[15]

> There are two paths to liberation or freedom from all bondage. One is the royal road climbing the steps of [spiritual evolution] slowly

> [step by step]....It is a very arduous path. You have to climb up [rise] performing penance *(tap)*, renunciation, incantation of god's name *(jap);* and even then the sword of Damocles is dangling over your head. The second is the Akram Marg—the lift path. Here you have not to climb steps; you are to get into the lift–with wife and children, after getting sons and daughters happily married, after performing the worldly duties–for freedom from bondage. Performing all these mundane duties you do not lose your 'freedom' even for a second. This Akram Marg is also called an exceptionally 'rare' path. Once in a million years it manifests itself. Only king Bharat had got this 'knowledge' from his father, for Ṛṣabhadevji–Dādā Bhagawan bestowed this 'knowledge' only on Bharat out of his 100 sons.[16]

The principal doctrinal feature of the Akram Vijñān Mārg is the belief in the efficacy of the practice of *jñāna bhakti,* the magical acquisition of salvific knowledge through the devotional surrender *(samarpaṇa)* to its source—Sīmandhar Svāmī and his medium A.M. Paṭel. The main differences to traditional Jainism are: (a) indifference toward or rejection of scriptural knowledge *(śrutajñāna)* in favour of the direct experience of the soul *(ātmājñāna)*, (b) rejection of physical asceticism *(tapas)* in favour of spiritual knowledge *(ātmājñāna)* as the principal means of salvation, (c) rejection of monasticism and other institutionalised forms of religious practice, (d) the possibility of salvation for all through the grace *(kṛpā)* of Sīmandhar Svāmī, and (e) the acquisition of direct insight into the true nature of the self through devotion to a knower *(guru bhakti)*.

Self-enlightenment: A.M. Paṭel

The Akram Vijñān Mārg is a highly innovative religious movement. It originated in the 1960s in Bombay and is slowly spreading throughout western India and the Gujarati diaspora in East Africa, North America and the United Kingdom. The founder of the Akram Vijñān Mārg was Ambalāl Mūḷjībhaī Paṭel (7 November 1908–2 January 1988). His disciples called him *jñānī* or *jñānī puruṣa*–the enlightened being; *pratyakṣa ātmājñānī*—the presently living knower of the self; or simply *dādā bhagavān*—grandfather lord, because they recognised in him one who has realised his own inner ultimate self *(paramātmā)*. A.M. Paṭel was a contractor by profession. He was born into a Vaiṣṇava Pāṭidār family in Tarasālī, a village near Baroda (Vaḍodarā), and grew up in the village Bhadaran in the district of Kheda in central Gujarat. It is reported that when he was thirteen he once served a saint *(sant)* visiting his village, who blessed him with the words: 'May God gift you with liberation,' whereupon he replied:

> I don't want that liberation, if God is to give it to me. 'Given by him' means that 'he is my boss and he can take it back when he desires to do so.' Liberation itself means 'a state where there is no boss, no underhand.'[17]

In one of his published discourses he said, 'The lid of ignorance in my case was so thin (light) that at the age of thirteen, I had intimations of immortality' (ibid.: 8). In 1923, when he was fifteen, he married Hīrābā. Because she lost an eye at a young age, he was once asked whether he was interested in remarriage. But he stated that he had a happy marriage and would keep his marital vows. The couple remained childless, because both of their two young children (born in 1928 and 1931) died a few months after their birth. At this time A.M. Paṭel encountered the writings of Śrīmad Rājacandra and, through them, became interested in Jaina philosophy. Śrīmad Rājacandra (1867-1901) was a Gujarati Jaina householder and religious visionary who inspired new religious lay movements which represent the first predominantly devotional form of Jainism. A.M. Paṭel was particularly impressed by Rājacandra's teaching of *ātmādharma* and his rejection of *gurus* and of sectarianism.[18] He also began to practice temporary celibacy, or *brahmacarya,* and at the age of thirty, together with his wife, he took the vow of life-long *brahmacarya.*

Ambalāl Mūljībhaī Paṭel had only basic formal education and did not speak any English, except a few words, which he regularly interjected into his discourse. He moved to Bombay, where he stayed for most of his working life, and operated successfully as a contractor for the company Paṭel & Co. which was engaged in the construction and maintenance of the dry docks in the harbour of Bombay. It is said that notwithstanding his occupational commitments, throughout his life he was primarily interested in *mokṣa,* liberation and *jagat kalyāṇ,* welfare of the world, which for him, as for Rājacandra, meant offering salvation for the suffering humanity through freedom from passion, or *vītarāga*—detachment from the actions of mind, speech and body.[19] In July 1958, when he was fifty years old, he had what he later described as an experience of direct spontaneous enlightenment *(pratyakṣa jñāna),* which he attributed to the natural fruition of his good *karma.* The experience occurred suddenly while he was waiting for a train on a bench on the busy platform 3 of the railway station in Surat at about six o'clock in the evening and lasted '48 minutes.' The extraordinary feeling, which A.M. Paṭel himself called 'indescribable' and never put into words,[20] was characterised by his disciple Nīrubahen Amīn as follows:

> He had just finished his supper, and was waiting for a train. He was sitting on a railway platform bench in Surat, India, when the extraordinary event happened. The Lord became manifest in him. In one hour all the secrets of the world, life and universe opened up to him. He said later, that there are no words to describe what he experienced. Each and every *anu-paramanu* [atom] revealed his vision. He maintained that the external body of A.M. Paṭel is not God. The Lord who is manifest inside is revered by A.M. Paṭel. The experience of the Absolute established itself in him permanently. He became the Enlightened One. He became the first *Jnani Purush* to represent Akram Vijnan for modern times.[21]

Another description by Nīrubahen, which is corroborated by similar statements from other disciples, makes it clear that A.M. Paṭel had experienced what he believed to be the revelation or manifestation *(jñān pragaṭ)* of the god within, that is the pure self *(śuddhātmā)*, the vehicle of the fully realised supreme self *(paramātmā)*, which he called 'Dādā Bhagavān':[22]

> In the 'shrine' of the name of Ambalāl Mūḷjībhaī Paṭel, after infinite births, was manifested naturally: 'Dādā Bhagavān' in the form of Akram![23] In the span of one hour he had an experience of the entire universe! 'Who are we? Who is God? Who runs the world? What is karma? What is liberation? etc. All the world's spiritual questions were answered! In this way nature offered an unparalleled absolute vision to the world through the medium of Shree Ambalāl Mūḷjībhaī Paṭel, a Pāṭidār of the village of Bhadran, Charotar. Although a contractor by profession, he remained a *Vitarag Purush!*'[24]

Such an 'enlightenment' experience which reveals 'each and every atom of the world' is in Jainism technically known as *kevala jñāna*, or omniscience *(sarvajña)*,[25] though it is also held that A.M. Paṭel experienced only *samyak darśana* or *samyaktva*, right view—that is, spiritual insight into the true nature of the self being entirely separate from the *kārmik* body (as described by Jaina and Sāṃkhya doctrines).[26] The ambiguity is the result of Paṭel's attempt to quantify omniscience and to define *samyaktva*, which he calls *jñāna* or *prajñā*, as 'partial omniscience.'[27] The words most frequently used by him in this respect were *svarūpajñāna,* self-realisation, and *ātmājñāna,* self-knowledge (as opposed to *jagat-jñāna,* knowledge of the world, and *śāstrajñāna,* scriptural knowledge). The two terms refer to two processes which he, following Kundakunda,[28] regarded as intrinsically connected. Because he experienced his true self without the help of others, in Jaina technical terms, the event transformed him into a *svayaṃ sambuddha,* a being enlightened by itself. According to Nīrubahen Amīn, A.M. Paṭel explained that the revelation occurred after an experience of insult and humiliation, involving feelings based on great egotism. At the time of self-realisation, he became aware that it was not 'I', the pure self, or *śuddhātmā,* who experienced worldly insult, but only 'me,' that is the relative self, or *pratiṣṭhit ātmā,*[29] which is a superimposed, rather alien 'outward packing' in the form of Ambalāl Mūljībhaī Paṭel:

> What you see is Ambalāl Mūljībhaī Paṭel, a Pāṭidār of Bhadran, contractor by profession. But 'he' who is revealed within is a great wonder. He is 'Dādā Bhagwan.'...We haven't identified our 'self' with this Ambalāl Muljibhai even for a second. And ever since my self-realisation, I have been living with him as my first neighbour.[30]

After his enlightenment experience, A.M. Paṭel stopped working full time in order to concentrate fully on the permanent cultivation of this spiritual insight and left his contractor business to his partners, while living on the dividends of his company shares. However, he remained a householder and never stopped looking after his business throughout his life, because his soteriology demanded neither renunciation of the world nor asceticism. His followers proudly report that he 'never borrowed money from anyone in his life,' and lived by the principle: 'In business dharma will decrease, but in dharma, business will not decrease.'[31]

Insight through Grace: Kanu Paṭel

At first, A.M. Paṭel did not make his inner experience publicly known, except for a few relatives and close friends who noticed some changes in his demeanour and started asking questions. But already in 1962, he evoked for the first time the experience of *samyak darśana* in another person in his own rented house in Baroda. In the language of the Akram Vijñān Mārg this procedure is called 'transmitting the knowledge.' Why he thought this might be possible is not entirely clear, since he left few documents which could serve as a basis for a reconstruction of the development of his religious ideas. His brother's, now deceased, son Candrakānt Paṭel from Uganda (originally from Bhadaran, Gujarat), who called him reverently *dādā,* or grandfather, was very interested in his vision. Candrakānt was the first individual to experience a sudden insight into his own pure self in the presence of 'the *Dādā.*' The experience was triggered by a conversation. Candrakānt asked his *dādā:* '*Dādā* are you a Jñānī? How does one recognise a Jñānī?' A.M. Paṭel's answer opened his eyes. He said:

> Just slap me in my face, and look into my eyes, whether you see anything....Beat me up any way you like to make me human.[32]

This event, which involved nothing but the knower's words of truth *(āptavāṇī)*[33] and an informal blessing *(āśirvāda)* is remembered as the first performance of the *jñāna vidhi,* or rite of knowledge, the ritual for the evocation of the experience of *samyak darśana* through the destruction of all the obstructive *mohanīya,* or delusion producing *karmas.* In classical Jaina doctrine this is technically called *kṣāyaka samyaktva*[34] and is believed to be possible only in the presence of a Jina.[35]

The second person to be given the *jñān* was Kanubhāī K. Paṭel (born 1930) who became one of the two principal spiritual successors of A.M. Paṭel. He was the son of Kantilāl Paṭel, A.M. Paṭel's business partner, and worked until recently as a structural engineer. For fifteen years he lived together with A.M. Paṭel in the same house in Bombay. Later he married, but continued to work in the company Paṭel & Co. He prides himself that during these fifteen years he stayed with A.M. Paṭel round the clock and looked after his physical and mental well-being. This practice is called *sevā,* service, to the Dādā. In the late 1970s Kanubhāī took some business decisions against A.M. Paṭel's advice and lost a lot of money for the joint company. Thereupon, A.M. Paṭel left the partnership. Kanu Paṭel told me in 1999 about his experience of receiving 'the *jñān,*' that is *samyak-darśana,* from the Dādā. In 1963 he underwent a major crisis, which he characterised with the words 'to be or not to be.' One of his problems was that he could not sleep. However, one night the Dādā appeared in his dreams and after this he was able to sleep for the first time in a long while. The next day he went to A.M. Paṭel, put his head at his feet and asked: 'Who am I?' The Dada then gave him the knowledge. As in Candrakānt's case, no special ceremony was performed, just an informal conversation lasting five to ten minutes, which, Kanu Paṭel stressed, had changed his entire life. Everything turned 'upside down' for him during these few minutes.

The Rite of Knowledge (Jñāna Vidhi)

The once informal procedure of passing on spiritual energy for the separation of soul and non-soul in another person soon became more formalised. Between 1962 and 1968, A.M. Paṭel transmitted his spiritual powers only to select members of his circle of family and friends, but from 1968 onwards he offered to bestow with *samyak darśana (paramārtha samakit)* anyone who bowed to him and requested to be blessed by the *bheda jñāna,* the knowledge of separation. This was the origin of the devotional Dādā Bhagavān cult at the heart of the Akram Vijñān movement. In his discourses, A.M. Paṭel often said that the attribute *'Dādā Bhagavān'* was originally not of his own making, but introduced by his followers. Out of fear of public opinion, he said, he was initially not even sure whether he wanted to publicise his teaching beyond a small circle of friends, as had been the case with Śrīmad Rājacandra. But in response to public demand, he went to the Ṛṣabha temple in Khambhat near Vaḍodarā, where Rājacandra had stayed in 1893, to ask for Ṛṣabha's advice. Apparently, he was able to contact Ṛṣabha in *siddhaloka,* the realm of the liberated souls,[36] and to sit at his feet to receive the advice that he should convey 'the knowledge' to all strata of society, not merely to the select few. On request, the first public performance of the *jñāna vidhi* was held in 1968 in Bombay. In subsequent years the rite was performed at regular intervals and the procedure became more and more elaborate, until it attained its present form in 1983.[37]

Originally, A.M. Paṭel performed what was later called the *jñāna vidhi,* the rite of knowledge, only for individuals and under the seal of secrecy. Often, the rite was performed on remote mountain tops, because intense shouting came to be seen as a key ingredient for the removal of the obstructive *karmas,* as was the blessing *(prasādī)* performed by laying hands on the head of the bowing devotee (A.M. Paṭel did not like the term 'disciple') at the feet of the Dādā. With time, the *vidhi* became more elaborate and was performed in small groups. On request, the blessing was accompanied by a few firm knocks on the devotee's back with one of A.M. Paṭel's shoes or with a coconut, a symbol of auspiciousness which offered, as it were, a tangible equivalent to the imperceptible inner process of separation of self and non-self. All aspirants I interviewed insisted that they 'felt absolutely nothing' even at the severest blows. This divine blessing cum thrashing was called *alaukika prasādī,* otherworldly blessing, and apparently introduced 'only reluctantly' by A.M. Paṭel on 'request of the aspirants.' Additional blessings were sometimes given by showering the aspirants with rose petals.

In the beginning, the ritual was not informed by any explicit doctrine. However, from 1968 onwards A.M. Paṭel also started to teach his vision to others. On request, he held *satsaṅgs* or meetings for religious discourse in private houses, not unlike Śrīmad Rājacandra before him, and performed the *jñāna vidhi* regularly for groups of aspirants.[38] He now referred to himself as the *jñānī,* the self-realised knower who had directly experienced the difference between self *(puruṣa)* and non-self *(prakṛti),* and was thus qualified to act as a *sadguru* or a *satpuruṣa,* a good teacher or self-realised being, for the spiritual well-being of others, not unlike a *bodhisattva* in Mahāyāna Buddhism.[39]

A.M. Paṭel's religious terminology indicates that his teachings were strongly influenced by the Sāṃkhya view, both echoed and criticised by Kundakunda,[40] that all forms of action in mind, speech and body are merely material; that is, natural processes and thus entirely unconnected with the true self which is in essence a passive observer, not a doer.[41] For him, the illusion of a real connection between the essentially pure self and the action of mind, body and speech is a product of the conventional point of view *(vyavahāra naya),* whereas from the real point of view *(niścaya naya)* the pure self is essentially free and unbound.[42] Liberation can therefore be achieved through the mere acquisition of self-knowledge—the intuitive and strictly non-intellectual *(abudha)* immediate experience of the true nature of the self which exists in qualitatively identical form in all living beings.[43] A.M. Paṭel illustrated this fundamental insight for his audience with reference to the difference between the empirical self, the ego and the pure self:

> What you see here is not 'Dādā Bhagavān.' What you see is A.M. Paṭel.' I am *Jnani Purush* and He that is manifested within, is 'Dādā Bhagavān.' He is the Lord of the fourteen *lokas* (regions of the

> universe) and He is within you and everyone else. He is residing in an unmanifested form within you, whereas here (within me) he has completely manifested (manifested in an absolute form)! I myself am not the Dādā Bhagavān. I bow down to the Dādā Bhagavān that is manifested within me.[44]

In his later years, A.M. Paṭel explained his method of inducing liberating insight in others in his discourses. He described himself as a 'doctor of the mind' who uses his own miraculous powers *(siddhi)*[45] for performing painful surgery on the self of others[46] by squeezing their ego,[47] burning to ashes their sins from infinite cycles of births,[48] and finally separating their pure self *(śuddhātmā)* from their ego-centred mind *(manas)* in order to eliminate all sense of possessiveness and to make them understand the nature of *prakṛti*. He stated:

> 'We' are the exorcist *[bhūvo]* of the three ghosts of mind, speech and body that have possessed you. We can get you released from these three attachments.[49]

All that is needed is the blessing of the *jñānī,* who puts his hand on the head of the aspirant[50] and uses his faculty of speech in order to transmit his divine powers of intuitive knowledge to separate self and non-self:

> Suppose metals like copper, brass, silver got mixed up with gold, cannot a scientist separate them, examining their different qualities? He can do it easily. In the same way he who knows the qualities of the soul and the non-soul and who as an omniscient *Jnani* possesses infinite power, can separate these two substances after analysing them. 'We' are the greatest scientist of the world. Analysing every atom of the soul and the non-soul, separating both of them, 'We' give you the pure soul *(śuddhātmā)* in your hand in an hour.[51]

The destruction of the *mohanīya karmas* is thought to be achieved simply through the miraculous power of grace *(siddhi kṛpā)* of the god within, that is the all-compassionate Dādā Bhagavān as manifested within his 'boss' A.M. Paṭel:

> Ay, we are god's boss. Perfectly non-attached. God himself has given us the position of his superior.[52] He told us: 'We are in search of a worthy instrument and we discovered it in you. We are perfectly non-attached sitting in pure self-liberation. We cannot help anybody now. So you are the omnipotent manifest form. Though you live in a clay mould, you are perfectly non-attached. So we give you our

> superior power and accept you as our boss. And you do good to the world.' And therefore we have become even god's boss. We are the boss of the Lord of the fourteen worlds. With all his spiritual power has the incarnation of *Jnana* manifested itself. [53]

Like Śrīmad Rājacandra, A.M. Paṭel emphasised the impotence of scriptural or ritual knowledge for the liberation of the soul and pointed instead to the significance of direct contact with a living *jñānī*, since, in his view, the spiritual power *(siddhi)* that is necessary to separate self and non-self can only be transmitted through the direct speech *(pratyakṣa vāṇī)* and blessing of a true *jñāni*,[54] not through the indirect speech *(parokṣa vāṇī)* of the scriptures or an un-self-realised mendicant.[55] For him, the *jñānī* was the living embodiment of knowledge *(pratyakṣa sarasvatī)*. He therefore never tired of emphasising the unique opportunity of meeting a *jñānī* such as the Dādā Bhagavān:

> You ignoramus, a *Jnani* rarely visits the earth; and the *Jnani* of the Akram path (instant-liberation path) is born once in ten million years and that, too, in this present age of strange happenings, like the *kaliyug*. He lifts you up in a lift. You are not to gasp for breath after climbing the steps....Only *vitaraga vani* (speech free from any attachment) can lead to liberation. Our speech is sweet, melodious and unprecedented, unheard of before, direct. That speech [which is] contained in the scriptures is indirect. If one listens to the 'direct speech' one will have *'samakit'* Our speech is *syadvada*–not hurting anybody's view or standard–but acceptable to all views. It accepts all points of view because we are sitting at the centre. Our speech is impartial... *Vitaraga vani* is that which is replete with the feeling of complete spiritual well-being of others. Only *vitaraga vani* can do good to a person and lead him to liberation.[56]

Sīmandhar Svāmī

Although the matter is not entirely clear, it seems that at the beginning of his career as a religious virtuoso A.M. Paṭel did not refer much to Sīmandhar Svāmī, the Jaina *tīrthaṅkara* who is believed to be currently living in the mythical continent Mahāvideha. However, from the 1970s onwards, probably after a sustained reading of Jaina cosmological literature, he regularly invoked a special link to Sīmandhar Svāmī and distinguished three categories of enlightened beings: (a) the *siddhas*, or liberated beings living in *siddhaloka*, who do not speak and cannot be reached anymore; (b) the currently living *tīrthaṅkara* or *arhat* Sīmandhar Svāmī in Mahāvideha, who speaks to the Dādā within A.M. Paṭel, who contacts him through his 'astral body,' but does not instruct his followers; and (c) the Dādā, who speaks through A.M. Paṭel and instructs his disciples in this world. A.M. Paṭel claimed that he himself had not only experienced *samyak darśana,* but also '356 degrees' of total omniscience *(kevala jñāna)*. There was only a difference of '4 degrees' between himself and the *arhats* and the *siddhas.* Because of likeness of his own soul and the souls of the fully omniscient, he said, he was able to contact Sīmandhar Svāmī directly.[57] During the *jñāna vidhi,* he claimed, the voice of the Dādā, and through the Dādā, the voice of Sīmandhar Svāmī spoke directly through A.M. Paṭel, who acted as his medium in order to transmit 'the knowledge' to his devotees. Because he was accepted as a partially enlightened and passionless being, and was able to mediate in this way between his followers and Sīmandhar Svāmī, A.M. Paṭel was called *khaṭpaṭ vītarāga* by his followers, the passionless one who uses tricks to get things done.

In contrast to Rājacandra and the 'elitist' and 'decadent' Jaina mendicant traditions which follow the path of Mahāvīra, A.M. Paṭel held that the worship or past or future *tīrthaṅkaras* on the basis of scriptures and images can only function as a reminder of a distant ideal, whereas he himself has given his followers the opportunity to gain liberation themselves through direct contact with the present *tīrthaṅkara,* Sīmandhar. Unlike Rājacandra, who occasionally considered himself to be 'the second Mahāvīra,'[58] he did not present himself to be the source of possible liberation, but only an instrument, or *nimitta,* of Sīmandhar, although the distinction is often blurred in popular perception and sometimes Sīmandhar and the Dādā Bhagavān are deliberately identified.

This overview of the key differences between the teachings of Rājacandra and A.M. Paṭel points to an important shift of emphasis. The Akram Vijñān movement highlights the present possibility of salvation. It stresses the doctrinal fact that no past or future Jaina god *(tīrthaṅkara)* can grant any practical help to his present devotees, only a god living in the present *(pratyakṣa)* who is directly accessible to everyone – like Sīmandhar through his medium A.M. Paṭel – can do so. The followers of the Akram Vijñān Mārg believe that the fact that A.M. Paṭel has made his personal link to Sīmandhar available to his followers singles him out from the two other 'omniscient' *jñānīs,* Kundakunda and Rājacandra, as well as Kānjī Svāmī, the *brahmacārī* who is technically a Jaina layman, who provided vivid descriptions of their personal spiritual journeys to Sīmandhar without offering a direct link for everyone, as the Dādā did.

A comparison of the ways in which these three Gujarati Jaina laymen cognised the possibility of establishing contact with a living *tīrthaṅkara* under the conditions of the present time cycle shows variations along the dimensions of time, place and medium of communication. Rājacandra said he gained salvific knowledge through the memory *(jātisamaraṇa jñāna)* of an encounter with a Jina of the same continent (Bhārata) in a previous life. Kānjī Svāmī achieved this apparently through the memory of the encounter with a Jina of a different continent (Mahāvideha) in a previous life, while A.M. Paṭel maintained that he was in continuous contact with a Jina of a different continent in his present life. He was the only one who made this unique link available for everyone, while Rājacandra and Kānjī Svāmī projected themselves as *tīrthaṅkaras* of the future.[59]

Devotion and Self-effort

The mere participation in the rite of knowledge itself does, of course, not secure final *mokṣa*. But it is believed that it offers the possibility of achieving so-called living *mokṣa,*[60] and the prospect of being reborn 'at the feet' of the currently living *tīrthaṅkara,* Sīmandhar Svāmī in Mahāvideha Kṣetra, within not more than two lifetimes. According to Jaina doctrine, everyone has the opportunity of being enlightened in the presence of a living *tīrthaṅkara,* a process called *buddha-bodhita* that is attributed to his great compassion.[61] The question is how to get to Mahāvideha Kṣetra.[62] Classical Jainism teaches that a better rebirth can only be secured by reducing and purifying the *kārmik* burden of an individual.[63] A.M. Paṭel and his successors agree with this, but have a different opinion about the way in which this is achieved. Because they believe, like the Bhagavad Gītā,[64] that the soul is passive, not active, and that there is no real bondage between soul and body, and therefore there is no need for physical asceticism, their main concern is the continuous application of the liberating perspective of the pure soul to all aspects of life. The resulting non-attachment towards one's own actions secures both that no new *karmas* are accumulated and that old *karmas* come to fruition naturally. In addition, they also preach the principle of non-violence *(ahiṃsā)* and the abstinence from all intentional action in order to prevent the influx of new *karma*. If an act of violence nevertheless occurs and the ego is involved, fresh *karma* is produced. However, A.M. Paṭel taught how, through the technique of *anamnesis* of concrete violent actions from the point of view of the pure self *(niścaya naya)*, any such mistake can be neutralised by a devotee of the Dādā Bhagavān who has received the knowledge.[65] The Akram Vijñān Mārg thus teaches a mixture of devotion to the pure self and ethics. In this respect its soteriology differs from purely theistic or gnostic approaches.[66] A.M. Paṭel has made the importance of the role of self-effort – sandwiched between the initial gift of *bheda jñāna* by the grace of the *Jñānī* and the final gift of *sarvajñāna* by the grace of Sīmandhar Svāmī – explicit in the following statement:

> First I destroy all your blunders because by yourself it is impossible for you. How do I do it? By placing my hand on your head and letting Bhagvan (Dādā Bhagavān the Lord of the 14 worlds) give his divine grace *(kṛpa)*. Thereafter, you need to remove your mistakes yourself. You will be able to see your own mistakes. Daily you will be able to see 5, 50 or 100 faults of your own and thus these mistakes will go on their own. Your realisation of your self will increase as your mistakes (faults) decrease.[67]

The Dādā cannot purify. He can only give his knowledge and inspirational power to face own's own mistakes. Only the effort of maintaining a permanent awareness *(jāgṛti)* of one's real self can purify. In asking the Dādā for forgiveness for mistakes during devotional practices, the devotee is not assuming that the Dādā cleanses the soul by an act of pure grace, but in evoking the manifestation of the Dādā in his/her mind, the experience of his/her own pure soul is realised. It is only the awareness that this was not 'I' who has committed an act of violence, but 'me,' that is *prakṛti* or the accumulated *karmas* which come to fruition naturally, which reduces the burden of *karma*.[68]

Following

The Dādā Bhagavān cult developed first in Bombay and in A.M. Paṭel's hometown Baroda. In 1983, only twenty years after the first *jñāna vidhi* was performed, already forty of the fifty thousand followers[69] reportedly existed in southern Gujarat and Maharashtra. A.M. Paṭel's funeral in 1988 in Kelanpur near Baroda was attended by about 60,000 people, and for 1999 the figure of about 300,000 followers is mentioned by the magazine *Akram Vijñān*.[70] The followers of the Dādā were not recruited from any particular caste. But because of his own social and professional background, many of the leading adherents were middle-class Paṭels from Mumbai and Baroda. Even today, the chief personalities of the movement are engineers, merchants and medical doctors. However, most of the common followers of the Dādā are uneducated, often illiterate, members of the urban working classes, predominantly Paṭels, Mahetās and Śāhs from the Pāṭidār, Śrīmālī and Osvāl castes of Gujarat who traditonally practise Vaiṣṇavite and/or Jaina rituals often side by side.[71] A.M. Paṭel supplied their need for religious inspiration, and offered a path of salvation which was easy to understand and practise at the same time. The main reason for the popularity of the Dādā Bhagavān cult is its universal, non-intellectual and non-sectarian appeal. A.M. Paṭel was a simple, unassuming man with a good grasp of Jaina and Vaiṣṇava concepts. He spoke about subtle religio-philosophical ideas in an uncomplicated plain Gujarati language with interjected English terms which everybody could understand, and gave practical advice for the resolution of everyday problems from the point of view of 'absolute truth.'

Community Organisation

As a matter of principle, A.M. Paṭel rejected organised forms of religion, *gurus* and religious functionaries. He nevertheless 'agreed to' the creation of community associations. The main association of the Akram Vijñān Mārg is the Jay Saccidānanda Saṅgha in Mumbai. This organisation was founded under the auspices of A.M. Paṭel himself, who appointed Khetsī Narsī Śāh, the head of the local Dādā Bhagavān Vītarāga Trust, as the first *sakala saṅghapati,* or overall community leader, who acts as the chief coordinator of the activities of all local *saṅghs*. After the death of Khetsī Narsī Śāh, G.A. Śāh from Ahmedabad was appointed as the *saṅghapati*. His main duties are to organise the movements of the religious leader and his main disciples, the so-called *āptaputras* and *āptaputrīs,* a category of celibate laity who are invited by devotees all over the world, and to publish the community magazine *Akram Vijñān* which was first issued in 1979.[72] He also oversees the various building projects and looks after the community funds. Today, the organisation has important strongholds, led by local *saṅghapatis,* in Mumbai, Ahmedabad, Surat, London and in the U.S.

Ritualisation: Nīrubahen Amīn

The development of the Dādā Bhagavān worship from a charismatic family cult into an organised religious movement which refers to itself as the Akram Vijñān Mārg, the stepless path of knowledge, is to a large extent, though not entirely, the achievement of Nīrubahen Amīn (born 1944–2006), the second chief disciple of A.M. Paṭel. She was instrumental in publishing the discourses of A.M. Paṭel and effected the creation of an elaborate ritualism, including the formalisation of the *jñāna vidhi* which under her influence was developed into a public initiation ceremony lasting more than 48 minutes. She also composed a *pūjā* ritual and promoted the construction of temples for the veneration of Sīmandhar Svāmī.[73]

Nīrubahen Amīn is a gynaecologist by profession and the daughter of one of the oldest devotees of A.M. Paṭel, a multimillionaire from Aurangabad, whose family was traditionally Vaiṣṇavite. She was married, but later separated from her husband and took up medical studies in Bombay, when suddenly her husband died in 1968 under the suspicion of suicide. Shortly afterwards, her mother died as well. After these traumatic events, which left her heartbroken, she went to A.M. Paṭel, whom her father had asked to look after her in Bombay. 'With the Dādā's help,' she said, she finished her medical exams at the end of the year. On the same day her father died. Before the news reached her, 'the Dādā' told her about her father's death in great detail, although he had not yet received any report of the death himself. This confirmed to her his omniscience. When the official message was brought to her, she was prepared, fully detached and indifferent. The sad news could not harm her, because she had received the *jñāna* from 'the Dādā' A.M. Paṭel and knew that her father – as a dedicated follower of the Dādā – would be reborn as a higher incarnation: 'Life goes on, one just changes outer appearances.' From then on, she says, she became a devotee of the Dādā and was never again unaware of her pure self even for one moment.

Initially, Nīrubahen had no competence in the 'science' of the self *(ātmāvijñāna)*, but she was so impressed by the Dādā that she began to tape his religious discourses *(satsaṅgs)* from 1974 onwards. She collected in this way about four thousand tapes between 1974 and 1988, which are currently compiled, transcribed (in a few cases translated) and published under the title *Āptavāṇī,* or words of truth.

The currently twelve *Āptavāṇī* volumes represent the emerging doctrinal corpus of the Akram Vijñān Mārg.[74] The first one and a half volumes of the *Āptavāṇī* were compiled both by Kanubhāī Paṭel and Nīrubahen Amīn, and the first volume published in 1973 by the Jay Saccidānanda Saṅgha. Volumes published later than 1983 are based exclusively on Nīrubahen's tapes. The only other textual source for A.M. Paṭel's teachings is 'Vāsudev' Naṭubhāī Paṭel's collection of *satsaṅg* notes which were published in several volumes under the title *Svarūp Vijñān* in the 1980s.[75]

Except for the slightly modified, syncretistic version of the Jaina *Namaskāra Mantra,* called *Tri-Mantra,* or three-fold *mantra,* which includes references to the Jinas, Kṛṣṇa and Śiva and is recited at the beginning of every religious event of the Akram Vijñān Mārg,[76] none of the printed compilations used in the current ritual stems from A.M. Paṭel, who refused to write religious tracts. He only ever composed two short ritual texts, the *Namaskār Vidhi* in 1971–73,[77] a devotional hymn addressed to Sīmandhar Svāmī and to all other Indian saints and gods he considered worthy of worship, in descending order from the Pañca Parameṣṭhins of the Jaina *Namaskāra Mantra* down to Kṛṣṇa, the Dādā Bhagavān himself and the pure self of all living beings; and the *Nav Kalamo,* the Nine Precepts, in 1977, a prayer to the Dādā Bhagavān which is said to comprise 'the essence of all scriptures.'[78] The oldest ritual text of the Akram Vijñān Mārg which is the centrepiece of both the daily worship and the *jñāna vidhi,* the *Niścay-Vyavahār Caraṇ Vidhi,* or Absolute-Relative Foot Worship, was written by Vanubhāī Paṭel at the request of A.M. Paṭel and Nīrubahen Amīn in 1968.[79] The opening chants of today's formalised rite of knowledge were composed by a songwriter from Bombay, Navanit Paṭel, in 1970.[80]

In 1976 Nīrubahen had an ecstatic religious experience in A.M. Paṭel's presence which, in her words, also established a unique link between herself and Sīmandhar Svāmī, and inspired her to compose the text of an *āratī* ritual for the veneration of Sīmandhar. Her description of the event resembles the narration of the enlightenment experience of A.M. Paṭel. But it highlights the significance of the mediation of the Dādā and of a special *mantra* composed by him:

> Naturally, before I came into contact with Pujya Dadashree, I was not familiar even with the word 'Tirthaṅkar' in its real meaning. As such, how was I to have any information regarding Shree Simandhar

> Svami? It was 1971. We were in Vadva. At night, we were all sitting in a small room of Pujariji, Each one of us present there had to recite, one by one, the following mantra: 'In the very presence of Dada Bhagvan and through him, most devoutly do I bow in supplication unto *tirthankar* Bhagavan Shree Simandhar Svami, traversing at present Mahāvideha Kṣetra.'[81] First of all, Dadashri recited it to show us how it should be recited. Then he penned it on a piece of paper and gave it to me, asking me to make others recite it in turn. This was my first acquaintance with Shree Simandhar Svami. Then, in September 1972, there was one *shibir* of three days in Aurangabad. During the morning prayers, Dadashri reflected on something and told us all present there: 'One who recites this mantra forty times a day shall gain the fruit of offering one hundred and eight obeisance directly to Shree Simandhar Svami.' Thereafter everyone started reciting this mantra forty times a day. Dadashri had suggested that, time permitting, you should at least once a week, on a holiday, recite this matra forty times. As far as I am concerned, the rule of reciting the mantra, which was ingrained into my being then, has come down till today, uninterrupted and unbroken. In 1976, while Dadashri was staying in Mamani Pole, Baroda, I had the golden opportunity of serving him during his illness. It was 12.30 p.m. Having taken his dinner, he was, as usual, sitting on a bench. I was sitting on a sofa just opposite to him. On the wall facing me was a photograph of Shree Simandhar Svami. While conversing–I don't know how or why, be it some divine inspiration or be it ripe time to shower his infinite grace onto me–he attuned my being with Shree Simandhar Svami and set a unique link between us! I don't have adequate words to express my Ecstatic Experience and Great Bliss of that moment. Thenceforth, the moment my *chitta* [reflective mind] feels free and unoccupied, it gets lost in the lotus-feet of Shree Simandhar Svami. In those days, when Pujya Dadashri used to smoke a *hookah* [hubble-bubble], there sprung in me such an overflowing feeling of oneness with Shree Simandhar Svami that I was divined and inspired to compose His *aarti*. The *aarti* has in it all the mysteries of my unique union with Him.[82]

Nīrubahen Amīn continued to work in a small surgery in Bombay until 1978, when A.M. Paṭel suffered a fractured leg. From then on he needed constant medical care and Nīrubahen was asked to stay with him and to do *sevā* in the place of Kanu Paṭel. Her medical expertise was particularly valuable during A.M. Paṭel's missionary tours abroad between 1982 and 1987, which Kanu Paṭel, who had to look after the business of Paṭel & Co., could not join. Thus, for the last ten years of A.M. Paṭel's life Nīrubahen became the person closest to him, apart from his wife. Being the daughter of a multimillionaire, she was able, like her brothers, to live off her share in her father's business.

During the last years of A.M. Paṭel's life, the issue of how the movement could be perpetuated beyond his death was hotly debated. After some hesitation, A.M. Paṭel finally agreed in 1980 to the construction of a temple for the worship of the three images *(trimūrti)* of Sīmandhar, Kṛṣṇa and Śiva in order to spread the message of universal religion. But he spoke out against the worship of his own image and insisted that his method of liberation should only be spread by the lineages of his successors, which he called *jīvanmūrti*, or living idols:

> Don't we have the (paintings)of Mahavir and Kṛṣṇa? Keep them. Don't put our photograph. It won't be useful to you in any way. We'll leave behind us our successors and then the (chain) link of *Jnanis* will continue. Therefore find out a living idol. The puzzle won't be solved without his [sic!] guidance.[83]

In 1993 the impressive Tri-Mandir temple near Surat was inaugurated and a *dharmaśālā* was built nearby, both under the management of the Mahāvideha Tīrthadhām Trust. But, although the Tri-Mandir temple in Surat was constructed in such a way as to demonstrate that the same god (the pure soul) dwells within everyone – in Sīmandhar, Kṛṣṇa and Śiva – it also offers the chance to worship the photos of A.M. Paṭel and Kanu Paṭel in a separate chamber underneath the central Sīmandhar Svāmī Temple.[84]

Succession Dispute

Shortly after the death of A.M. Paṭel on 2 January 1988, the Akram Vijñān Movement split into two factions. The person who was close to him until 1978, Kanubhāī K. Paṭel, took over as the sole religious leader of the Akram Vijñān community with the institutional backing of the main community association, the Jay Saccidānanda Saṅgha in Bombay. Nīrubahen Amīn seceded and created a separate community on her own. There are two conflicting accounts of this split.

According to Nīrubahen, A.M. Paṭel decided near the end of his life to secure the continuation of the Akram Vijñān Mārg by passing on his powers *(siddhi)* of liberation *(mukti)*, knowledge *(jñāna)* and grace *(kṛpā)* to a number of successors. In 1987, he blessed

Nīrubahen 'in the presence of Sīmandhar' with a secret *mantra* through which she would be able to temporarily manifest the Dādā (the pure soul of A.M. Paṭel) within herself and thus be able to access him, and through him, Sīmandhar's spiritual power. In this way, a spiritual link would be maintained across the hiatus of physical death between the presently living *tīrthaṅkara* Sīmandhar Svāmī, the *jñānī puruṣa* Dādā Bhagavān and Nīrubahen who was called *satpuruṣa,* the divine being or the being of truth. A.M. Paṭel also gave her the authority to perform the *jñāna vidhi,* and trained her for five months, during which she learned the required words by repeating what he said.

After the death of A.M. Paṭel, Nīrubahen began to perform the *jñāna vidhi* on her own, claiming that the Dādā had given her the powers to do so and is actually speaking through her for a significant part of the ritual. Nīrubahen present herself as a medium *(nimitta)* of the Dādā. However, she says that she communicates with him even in her dreams, where she experiences how the Dādā passes her messages to Sīmandhar and Sīmandhar's answers on to her. This assertion was not acceptable to the leaders of the Jay Saccindānanda Saṅgha, who supported Kanu Paṭel as the successor of A.M. Paṭel, because they would not accept a female leader. However, Nīrubahen continued and left the community organisation to build up her own following. Like A.M. Paṭel, she officially rejects the notion of organised religion (in order to juxtapose herself against the followers of Kanu Paṭel), but nevertheless inspired the creation of organisations of her own supporters, first the Dādā Bhagavan Foundation Trust of Ajit Paṭel in Chennai and Ahmedabad, and more recently the Sīmandhar Svāmī Ārādhanā Trust in Ahmedabad and Nīrubahen Amīn's own Mahāvideha Foundation in Mumbai. At the moment, Nīrubahen Amīn is the most popular religious leader of the Akram Vijñān movement. She also frequently appears on Indian television. Since 1999 she is called Nīru-mā, 'Mother Nīru,' by her followers.

This version of events is contradicted by the account given by the followers of Kanubhāī Paṭel. They produced a tape of a private conversation between A.M. Paṭel and Nīrubahen, which was recorded by chance on their tour of the United States on 19 September 1987, to prove that the Dādā intended Kanu Paṭel and not Nīrubahen Amīn to be his successor.[85] At the beginning of the short conversation, conducted in a husky voice with long intervals between utterances, A.M. Paṭel gave her instructions for his funeral and then, using the formula *'Dādā Bhagavān bole che'* (Dādā Bhagavān says), he said that Nīrubahen should continue to perform six more *satsaṅgs* herself. After this, she should help Kanubhāī in the same way as she helped him to perform the *jñāna vidhi.* He then said: 'I have [already] passed the *vidhi mukeli* [rite of liberation] on to Kanubhāī.' This evidence seems to prove that A.M. Paṭel wanted his two main disciples to work together. He wanted Nīrubahen first to teach the performance of the ritual to Kanubhāī and then to assist him. At the time, Kanubhāī had no experience in performing the *jñāna vidhi* himself. He apparently received the powers to do so from A.M. Paṭel already in the early 1960s, but refused to perform the *vidhi* 'out of respect *(vinaya)* for the Dādā.' However, Nīrubahen performed the *jñāna vidhi* a few times herself. When she saw that it worked successfully, she simply continued and refused to step down and serve Kanubhāī.

The followers of Kanubhāī accept that Nīrubahen acquired many powers in her years in the presence of the Dādā, but emphasise that the power of liberating others has not been given to Nīrubahen, which she accepts herself. By contrast, the first two disciples of A.M. Paṭel, the late Candrakānt and Kanubhāī, are regarded by them as *jñānīs* in their own right who are entitled to perform the rite of knowledge on their own, without recourse to the Dādā. Many of Kanubhāī's devotees accept his claim that he will be reborn as one of the twenty-four *tīrthaṅkaras* of the next time cycle *(kalachakra)* and recite verse no. 10 of the *Namaskār Vidhi: 'Dādā Bhagavān na bhavi tīrthaṅkar sāhebo ne atyant bhakti pūrvak namaskār karuṃ chuṃ'*— 'With extreme devotion I offer my salutations to future *tīrthaṅkara* lords of Dādā Bhagavān.'[86] In other words, they see encounters with him as a possibility to establish a direct link *(ṛṇānubandha)* with a future *tīrthaṅkara.* 'Kanudādā' as he is sometimes called, is also recognised by the Jay Saccidānanda Saṅgha as the 'presently existing enlightened being' *(pravartamān pragaṭ jñānī puruṣa).*[87]

Two Approaches

Nīrubahen Amīn accepts that the Dādā passed the authority to perform the *jñāna vidhi* also to Kanu Paṭel (though not the *mantra).* But she does not agree with Kanu Paṭel's claim to spiritual leadership under the pretext that he is the currently living *jñānī puruṣa.*

Because, in her view, A.M. Paṭel was the only *jñānī,* she merely assumes the humble role as his spiritual medium *(nimitta)* for herself. Moreover, she accuses Kanu Paṭel of not distinguishing between *samyak darśana* and *mokṣa,* that is between the experience of the difference between body and soul, and salvation. Because he claims to be the self-realised one, she says, Kanu Paṭel has no religious aim, no transcendence to offer anymore, although his conduct hardly matches his claim to have reached salvation within the world. 'No-one owns this knowledge, only the *tīrthaṅkaras,'* she says, and only 'someone with sufficient purity can give the *bhed jñān* to others.'[88] Nīrubahen Amīn unequivocally states:

> The science of Akram Vijnan is transferable. Thousands became enlightened through the grace of Dadashree and thousands continue to experience instant living *moksh* even now provided they surrender their intellect and their beliefs to god, Dādā Bhagavān, the lord of the universe, who was fully manifest in A.M. Paṭel.[89]

It becomes obvious in the following quotation that Nīrubahen's interpretation of God comes close to what might be called the 'Jina-nature within,'[90] which is generally contrasted by her with the 'self-deification' practised by Kanu Paṭel:

> A very important message of note for all who are new to Pujya Dadashri's Science of Akram Vijnan is to be aware that the title of Dādā Bhagvan can never be given to any living being. Dādā Bhagvan is the name given to the Lord within. This was frequently asserted by the *Jnani Purush* Dadaśhri and now is being asserted by Pujya Nīrubahen and all who have received Jñān from her.[91]

Kanu Paṭel, on the other hand, insists that one cannot transfer spiritual experiences by performing ritual acts or by becoming a medium. Words themselves are not important, whether they are the exact utterances of the Dādā or not. The *vidhi* can be performed in any language, not only in Gujarati as Nīrubahen maintains.[92] For the *jñāna vidhi* to be efficacious it is of the utmost importance that the performer is enlightened himself. Everything must be based upon one's own experience, on mind *(manas),* not on action or speech:

> 'I cannot be out of my centre,' he said, 'my experience is individual, it has to be independent. There cannot be any hierarchy. The Dada did not give special powers to anyone. No person can make others experience the truth, neither can books nor any transfer of

intellectual knowledge. Grace is the only way to achieve self-realisation. And grace exists only when nothing is given and nothing received. I am neither the giver nor the receiver. I am totally free. I am not out of my centre. My own experience is more important than the word. The Dada's speech is fundamental in the *vidhi,* yet the potential for divine speech is essentially existing within everybody. Every human being can have the experience of liberation out of suffering in the present life Only animals and plants cannot have this experience. The *vidhi* itself does not cause any material changes.'[93]

Kanubhāī also claims to have experienced great intimacy with the Dādā, although Nīrubahen stayed with A.M. Paṭel during the last ten years of his life, and says that the Dādā was principally opposed to the development of any cult, and did not design any definite ritual, like Nīrubahen, because he thought that rituals and cere-monies develop naturally as a form of *vyavasthit śakti.*

However, there was another reason for the departure of Nīrubahen. Kanu Paṭel and the *saṅghapati* were simply not prepared to accept a female leader, although they offered Nīrubahen the opportunity to work for the *saṅgha.* They reported that the Dādā himself was opposed to women becoming *brahmacārīnīs,* 'just because they don't want to marry.' Apparently, A.M. Paṭel said: 'Women cannot observe my principles and better do more chanting,' although this is uncorroborated by the followers of Nīrubahen. He apparently also believed, like most Jainas (and Hindus), that women have an inferior *kārmik* constitution and that, therefore, few have higher spiritual experiences. It is widely held that women generally have more *mohanīya,* or mind-deluding, *karmas* and therefore cannot realise the effects of the *jñāna vidhi* as easily as men. Although the influx of new *karmas* will be stopped after undergoing the ritual, too many old *karmas* continue to discharge. Kanu Paṭel claims that this was the reason why A.M. Paṭel had initiated only *āptaputras* and no *āptaputrīs* at all [Kanu Paṭel has not initiated any *āptaputras* or *āptaputrīs*].

Kanubhāī's followers generally criticise Nīrubahen's 'desire for power' and her 'lack of humility' which they see confirmed by the fact that, in contrast to the Dādā and Kanudādā who continued to wear their everyday dress after their enlightenment, she (and her main disciples) changed her dress to pure white, thus getting involved in the 'relative world.' The Jay Saccidānanda Saṅgha officially rejected Nīrubahen Amīn's claim that she is medium of the Dādā, discouraged her following and frequently broke up her meetings. In 1993, at the consecration ceremony of the Akram Vijñān Sīmandhar temple near Surat, the asscociation produced a written document in which it renounced all responsibility for Nīrubahen Amīn's actions.

The aversion between the two sections of the Akram Vijñān movement is currently only concealed under a thin veil of silence publicly observed by the followers of both sides. Nīrubahen Amīn is said to have taken advantage of her position 'as a nurse' to claim greatest closeness to the Dādā out of greed and depression. And Kanu Paṭel is painted as a 'religious imposter' who claims *jñānī* status on no merit. Stories about the embezzlement of community funds to cover Kanu's business losses are also circulating. The religious leaders of both groups pressurise their followers to take sides or to risk losing the *jñāna,* 'because the turmoil of doubt caused in the mind will attract more *karmas,* if you support both sides, you lose your *jñāna.*'[94] Most followers understand this of course not in *kārmik,* but in personal terms, and fear to lose spiritual and social support. An atmosphere of supernatural angst therefore prevails in the Akram Vijñān community today.

Routinisation of Charisma

The developments shortly before and after the death of A.M. Paṭel correspond well to the pattern outlined in Max Weber's theory of the routinisation *(Veralltäglichung)* of charisma. In fact, the two solutions offered – the attempt to perpetuate the charismatic cult of the Dādā through a designated, similarly qualified successor, on the one hand, and the objectification of charisma in *mantras* and designated ritual acts with a magical link to the original charismatic source, on the other hand – are paradigmatic options of the model. The two groups also play the two sides of the ambiguous Dādā cult against each other: the Dādā as the medium of Sīmandhar, and the Dādā as a self-enlightened being. Since both groups tend to rely more and more on the creation of religious institutions and rituals, in particular the devotional worship of the Dādā image, it seems that Nīrubahen is better placed, because of the detachment of the source of charisma from her person to a *mantra* which can be transmitted from *guru* to *guru.* Therefore, (a) her future successors will not have to pretend to be self-enlightened, but will qualify for the performance of the *jñāna vidhi* by merely receiving the blessings of their predecessor and the Dādā's *mantra,* (b) the leadership and the *brahmacarya vrata* can be given by the spiritual leader, or *ātmajñānī,* of the movement to both men and women, and (c) the option of a pure image cult, entirely detached from a *guru* lineage, is maintained by the consecration of a new temple, the Mahāvideha Tīrthadhām, in Ahmedabad on 31 December 1999, to match the temple of Kanu Paṭel's followers in Surat. Ultimately, the anti-female position of the Jay Saccidānanda Saṅgha and the lack of a successor to Kanu Paṭel will probably turn the tide in favour of Nīrubahen Amīn, who is already more popular than Kanu Paṭel outside India, where she has founded the Jaya Saccidānanda U.K. and other community organisations in the U.S. However, it should be noted that some followers of the Dādā, most of them *mahātmās* associated with the Jay Saccidānanda Saṅgha, accept neither Nīrubahen nor Kanubhāī as their *gurus* but continue to venerate the Dādā and Sīmandhar Svāmī. Similar forms of routinisation of charisma can be found amongst the Śrīmad Rājacandra movement and the Kānjī Svāmī Panth.[95]

Conclusion

In contrast to the theistic Vaiṣṇava traditions, which propagate devotional religion *(bhakti mārga),* and to Śrīmad Rājacandra, who promulgated a *'kramik'* combination of devotion, asceticism and knowledge, with an emphasis on devotion, the new Akram Vijñān movement professes to follow the path of knowledge *(jñāna mārga).* However, a comparison with the Puṣṭimārgīs in Ujjain, for instance, who are aptly described in Peter Bennett's ethnography *The Path of Grace,* shows that the Dādā Bhagavān cult incorporated key elements of Vaiṣṇava forms of worship in their religious practices. Both traditions share the doctrinal rejection of asceticism and of strict rituals, and claim to offer a universalistic trans-religious vision open even to Muslims or Christians. However, the mediating role of the *guru* is pre-eminent and often no clear distinction is made between god and man. In practice, the professed doctrinal universalism therefore invariably turns into *guru* cults with exclusivist tendencies. The most visible resemblance between the Puṣṭimārgīs and the Akram Vijñān Mārg (as well as the Svāmīnarāyaṇ tradition) is the practice of symbolically surrendering all worldly attachments, that is *karmas,* including one's property, through a formal resolution *(saṅkalpa),* called *samarpaṇa,* at the point of initiation.[96]

In contrast to Jaina mendicants, the *sadgurus* of both the Rājacandra and the Akram Vijñān movement have in common with Hindu *gurus* that they often present themselves as *avatārs,* as manifestations of gods on earch, or as their mediums. However, in practice the distinction between incarnate god and medium is hard to maintain. Gombrich and Obeyesekere. who investigated the current urban resurgence of 'spirit cults' in Śrī Laṅkā, which combine elements of traditional Buddhism with influences of *bhakti* and Tantra, have observed:

> One can of course argue a difference between miracles, which a god produces by his grace to favour his devotees, and magic, a technique by which humans can coerce unseen powers. But when the miracle-working god takes human form, the distinction becomes blurred...[97]

Gombrich and obeyesekere interpret these spirit cults as imports from Hinduism, though the Buddhist *bodhisattva* worship takes similar forms. P.S. Jaini, who often acts as a defender of the classical view of Jainism, has also argued that similar popular forms of *bhakti* religiosity amongst Jains are forms of Hinduisation (though imported in a consciously Jainised form)[98]:

> For Jainas, in other words, no synthesis of the human and the supramundane was ever possible; hence the *tīrthaṅkaras* [and not the *bodhisattvas*] remained the highest models of spiritual development, and such tantric practices as identification of the self with the deity were simply out of the question.[99]

Although Jaini principally denies the existence of a 'Jain' cult of chosen deities *(iṣṭa-devatā),*[100] he does not fail to mention the frequent examples of Vaiṣṇava and Tantric influences on Jaina texts and practices such as the deification of the Jina, the visualisation of omniscience or the concentration on that which transcends form, mentioned for instance in Hemacandra's *Yogaśāstra,* which 'give the meditator a kind of experimental contact with the "ultimate Self" *(paramātmān),'* an experience which, Jaini hastens to add, is 'not equivalent to that of *siddhahood'* itself.[101] J.E. Cort also noticed that Mūrtipūjak Jains in Gujarat often blur 'the distinction between the Jinas and the living mendicants, in the same manner that Vaiṣṇavs oftentimes conflate Viṣṇu-Kṛṣṇa and their living gurus.'[102] However, 'the Śvetāmbar Mūrtipūjak guru remains much more a human being, albeit a special, powerful human being, whereas among the Hindu guru cults the guru tends to assume the status of a deity.'[103]

I would argue that the 'Digambara Mahāyāna' teachings of Kundakunda, which have greatly influenced a variety of Jaina lay movements, including the Śrīmad Rājacandra movement and the Akram Vijñān Mārg, cannot entirely be brought under the verdict of Hinduisation.[104] The fact that they could be easily reinterpreted by the layman A.M. Paṭel from 'theistic,' 'devotional' and 'Tantric' perspectives rather seems to reflect the fact that there is not one Jainism made up of a fixed set of discernable 'core beliefs'[105] promoted by identifiable individuals or groups but a plurality of doctrinal elements and practices that are compiled, combined and labelled in various ways.[106] What is certainly special about any self-consciously 'Jain' movement is the principal emphasis on the soteriological importance of non-injury and the soteriological goal of liberation preached by the Jinas, which is shared by both Kundakunda and the Akram Vijñān movement, although the latter adopts the Sāṃkhya ontology of the passive soul whereas Kundakunda retains the traditional Jaina interpretation of the soul as intrinsically active. In his analysis of Kundakunda's concept of self-realisation, William Johnson writes: 'one can only speculate on the effect of such ideas on the Jaina layperson,' arguing

> that any changes must have been largely in terms of expectation rather than practice... such theoretical possibilities as that of a 'Jina-nature' nevertheless make liberation *seem* closer. They are affectively satisfying...[107]

The logical, although not necessary, conclusion Johnson writes, for those who take Kundakunda's mystical philosophy seriously 'would seem to be abandonment of the external forms of Jaina ascetic life in favour of self-realisation, to be achieved by meditation on the pure self. It never quite comes to this.'[108]

This article has attempted to show that there is now a religious lay movement which works out the implications of Kundakunda's ideas from new angles. It can from different points of view, be interpreted as a form of 'Digambara Mahāyāna,' 'Jaina Sāṃkhya,' 'Jaina Vaiṣṇava syncretism' or 'Jaina Tantra.'[109] However, to the participant it does not merely represent an admixture of elements of Buddhist, Vaiṣṇava and canonical, classical or mystical Jaina sources, to the latter of which it is, nevertheless, closely related, but a new doctrinal synthesis, which offers salvation to everyone in the mythical pure land of Mahāvideha Kṣetra through the grace of Sīmandhar Svāmī. Because of the similarities in doctrinal structure, this synthesis can be legitimately labelled 'Jaina Mahāyāna.'

Notes

'This essay is based on intermittent field research in London, Ahmedabad, Surat and Mumbai between 1997 and 2001. If not indicated otherwise, all texts and translations have been cited verbatim from the literature of the Akram Vijñān Mārg.

1. Walther Schubring, *The Doctrine of the Jainas: Described after the Old Sources.* Translated from the original German by S.B. Shrotri, 2nd English Edition (New Delhi: Motilal Banarsidass, 1935/2000), 60f.
2. Robert Williams, *Jaina Yoga: A Survey of the Medieval Śrāvakācāras* (London: Oxford University Press, 1963/1983), xix.
3. Padmanabh S. Jaini, *The Jaina Path of Purification* (Berkeley: University of California Press, 1979), 88. See Chapter 9 on the issue of Hinduisation.
4. I will not attempt to trace the history of specific doctrinal imports from Mahāyāna Buddhism into Jainism but rather emphasise the general structural parallels to a new Jain religious movement.
5. If anyone should prefer the label 'Jaina Sāṃkhya' or 'Jaina–Vaiṣṇava syncretism' for the characterisation of the Akram Vijñān Marg, I would not object, since the thrust of my main argument is not affected by this.
6. The Digambara *ācārya,* Kundakunda, lived in South India sometime between the first and the eighth century CE.
7. The 'import' of elements of Mahāyāna, Sāṃkhya and Vedānta philosophies, especially by authors such as Kundakunda who are associated with the Digambara Jain *'mystical'* tradition, has been discussed in particular by Helmuth von Glasenapp, *Jainism: An Indian Religion of Salvation.* Translated from the original German by Shridhar B. Shroti (New Delhi: Motilal Banarsidass, 1925/1999), 504; A. Chakravarti, 'Introduction,' in *Ācārya Kundakunda's Samayasāra, with English Translation and Commentary based upon Amritacandra's Atmakyat:* 3rd Edition, edited by A. Chakravarti (New Delhi: Bhartiya Jñānpith, 1925/1989), 103ff; Adinath Neminath Upadhye, 'Introduction,' in *Śrī Yogīndudeva's Paramātmaprakāśa (Paramappapayāsu): An Apabhraṃśa Work on Jaina Mysticism* (Bombay: Sheth Manilal Revashankar Jhaveri, 1937), 29ff; Walther Schubring, 'Kundakunda echt und unecht,' in *Zeitschrift der Deutschen Morgenländischem Gesellschaft* 107 (1957) 568–74; Ram Jee Singh, *The Jaina Concept of Onniscience* (Ahmedabad: L.D. Institute of Indology, 1974), 54–57, n. 25; Bansidhar Bhatt, 'Vyavahāra-Naya and Niścaya-Naya in Kundakunda's Works,' in *Zeitschrift der Deutschen Morgenländischen Gesellschaft, Supplement II* (1974) 283; Bansidhar Bhatt, 'On the Epithet: *nāṭaka* for the *Samayasāra* of Kundakunda,' in *Jainism and Prakrit in Ancient and Medieval India,* edited by N.N. Bhattacharya (New Delhi: Manohar, 1994), 432, 455; William J. Johnson, *Harmless Souls: Karmic*

Bondage and Religious Change in Early Jainism with Special Reference to Umāsvāti and Kundakunda (New Delhi: Motilal Banarsidass, 1995), 45, 180ff, 281-87; Nalini Balbir and Colette Caillat, 'Introduction,' in *Yogīndu: Lumière de l'Absolu,* traduit de l'apabhraṃśa et présenté par Nalini Balbir et Colette Caillat, Préface de Bernard Sergent (Paris: Éditions Payot & Rivages, 1999), 40ff.

8. Heinz Bechert, 'Buddhist Modernism: Present Situation and Current Trends,' in *Buddhismus, Staat und Gesellschaft in den Ländern des Theravada-Buddhismus. Band II. Burma, Kambodscha, Laos, Thailand.* Neuausgabe mit Supplementen sowie Personen-und Sachregister (Göttingen: Seminar für Indologie and Buddhismuskunde, 2000), xxxii.

9. The student of Mahāyāna Buddhism will find numerous structural similarities in the following description of the Akram Vijñān Mārg, although I refrained from pointing them out one by one, to mention only the significance of wisdom, compassion, devotion and magic in the cult of the *bodhisattva* and the concepts of *Buddha kṣetra* and *tathāgatagarbha.* There are equally important parallels to Vaiṣṇavism.

10. Statement of a male devotee of the Akram Vijñān Mārg in London.

11. On Sīmandhar Svāmī and Mahāvideha see Mohanlal Mehta and K. Rishabh Chandra, compilers, *Prakrit Proper Names, Part II* (Ahmedabad: L.D. Institute of Indology, 1972), 799; and Paul Dundas, *The Jains* (London: Routledge, 1992), 255f, n. 65. Sīmandhar is not only worshipped by the Akram Vijñān Mārg. The Mūrtipūjaka Tapāgaccha tradition of the *ācāryas* Buddhisāgarsūri, Kailāśsāgarsūri, Kalyāṇsāgar and Subodhsāgar, inspired the construction of the first modern Sīmandhar temple in Mahesana in north Gujarat. Sīmandhar is also worshipped by the Digambar followers of Kānjī Svāmī. References to Sīmandhar abound in the post-canonical literature, but until recently he never became the focus of the religions cult, like Mahāvīra.

12. It seems that the Jaina *tīrthaṅkaras* in Mahāvideha play a similar role to the Buddhas in the pure lands of Mahāyāna Buddhism, while A.M. Paṭel, the Dādā Bhagavān, resembles the *bodhisattvas* in Buddhism, who are able to communicate with the Buddhas in the Buddha fields with supernatural means. Although outwardly human, he acts as a self-awakened enlightened being, and thus as a god on earth, for the benefit of others. However, this is not yet recognised in the scholarly literature. See Suzuko Ohira, *Study,* 204f.

13. For conceivable reasons for its creation see. Ohira, *Study,* 33, 168. The possibility of visiting the Mahāvidehas, where always 4–24 (the number varies from text to text) Jinas live due to the absence of the time cycle, is discussed already in the canon. See *Viyāhapannatti (Bhagavati)* 25.6.11 (=895b). On Mahāvideha and its *arhats* see in particular *Ṭhāṇa (Sthānāṅga)* 3.390, 4.137, 4.315, *Uvavāiya*

(Aupapātika) 101–116, *Viyāhapannatti* 20.8 (=791b); Willibald Kirfel, *Die Kosmographie der Inder nach Quellen dargestellt* (Hildesheim: Georg Olms, 1920/1967), 229–42; Schubring, *Doctrine,* 220, 222. The possibility of achieving liberation in Mahāvideha is described in canonical narrative texts such as the *Nāyādhammakahāo (Jñātṛdharmakathā)* I. 1, 19, 13, 16, 19, etc. and the *Uvāsagadasāo (Upāsakadaśāḥ)* 2, 7, etc.

14. See the commentary on the *Pravacanasāra* 1.3–5 by the twelfth century *ācārya,* Amṛtacandra, in Ācārya Kundakunda, *Pravacanasāra together with the Commentary, Tattva-dīpikā by Amṛtacandra Sūri* (=PS). Vol. I. Jain Literature Society Series. English translation by Barend Faddegon, edited with an Introduction by F.W. Thomas (Cambridge: Cambridge University Press 1935), 3–4; Dundas, *The Jains,* 230.

15. Late-canonical mythological and cosmological texts such as the *Jambūdvīpaprajñāpti* do not refer to the conveyance of omniscience to Bhārata through an act of grace. Bhārata is invariably characterised as a *pratyeka buddha,* a self-enlightened being. He is however the only householder mentioned in the canon who gained omniscience spontaneously, without first having been initiated as a monk. See Schubring, *Doctrine,* 22, 225; Ācārya Hemacandra, *Triṣaṣṭiśalākā-puruṣa-caritra* (=TSPC), translated by Helen M. Johnson as *The Lives of Sixty-three Illustrious Persons,* Vol. 1, Verse 715–45 (Baroda: Oriental Institute, 1931), 376–78.

16. A.M. Paṭel, *Āptavāṇī I,* edited by Khetsī Narsī Śāh, translated by V. Pathak and G. Śāh (Bombay: Saccidānanda Saṅgha, 1983), 11, cf. 70. Compare the original Gujarati text, *Āptavāṇī* (=AV), Vol. 1–12, compiled and edited by Nīrubahen Amīn (Amadāvād: Dādā Bhagavān Foundation, 1995–1999), Vol. 1, pp. 9, 57 (the first edition of Vol. 1 was compiled by Kanu Paṭel and Niru Amīn and published on 15 July 1973 by the Jay Saccidānanda Saṅgha in Bombay).

17. A.M. Paṭel, in Khetsī Narsī Śāh, 'Foreword,' in A.M. Paṭel, *Science of Liberation,* compiled by Āptaputra Dr. Shailesh P. Mehta, edited by K.N. Śāh (Bombay: Saccidānanda Saṅgha, 1995), iv. See the original passage AV I, 6f, and its English rendition in A.M. Paṭel, *Āptavāṇī I,* 7f.

18. Rājacandra's original name was Lakṣmīnandan Mahetā. Although he rejected traditional *gurus* and his contemporary Jaina mendicants who acquired their charisma only *qua* position, he taught *bhakti* towards a truly enlightened *guru* as the principal path towards salvation. (See Emma Salter, 'Unity and Diversity amongst the followers of Śrīmad Rājacandra,' in *Jinamañjari* 23, 1 (2001): 32–51.) His emphasis on *ātmadharma* derives from the tradition of Kundakunda.

19. Another word that he often used was *muktabhāva,* or freedom from the effects of feelings. See Nīrubahen Amīn, 'Who is Dādā Bhagavān?' in *Dādāvāṇī* (Ahmedabad: Dādā Bhagwan Foundation, n.d.), 30.

20. The only self-description I found was in a short discourse (translated?) in Hindi in A.M. Paṭel, *Āptavāṇī I,* 2nd edition, edited by Nīrubahen Amīn (Madras: Dādā Bhagavān Foundation, 1973/1995):

    Prashna: Ap jnani *kaise hue?*

    Dādā: Yah but natural *ho gaya hai. 1958 mem Surat steshan par lakri ki bench par sham ko suryastakal ke samay andar achanak jnan prakash ho gaya. Sare brahmand ko ham ne dar asal vastu ke rup meim dekha. Tab se vah* 'jnan' *nirantar prakash deta hi rahata hai. Yah* natural production *hai. Khud prayatna karke prapta karna bahut hi mushkil hai.* (215)

21. Amin, 'Who is Dādā Bhagavān?'30.
22. A.M. Paṭel utilises the terminology of Digambara mysticism, which has parallels in the Vedantic tradition, in order to explain the relationship between soul and body; in particular, Kundakunda's distinction between three aspects of the soul: *jīva* (life), *ātmā* (individual self-consciousness), and *paramātmā* (supreme self or God), which is frequently equated with *śuddhātmā*. Instead of *ātmā,* he often uses the term *pratiṣṭhit ātmā* to mark the difference between ego-centred erroneous *(vikalpa)* self-consciousness and the pure self. For *jīva* he often uses the word *bhāna,* or consciousness, stating: 'A *"Jīva"* does not know "who am I"' (A.M. Paṭel, *Āptavāṇī I,* 115, cf. AV I, 94).
23. That is, a stepless or instant experience, not generated through specific religious practices.
24. See Nīrubahen Amīn, 'Who is "Dādā Bhagwan",' in A.M. Paṭel, *The Essence of All Religion,* edited by Nīrubahen Amīn (Ahmedabad: Dādā Bhagwan Foundation, 2000), iv, cf. Niṣpakṣpati Trimandir Saṅkul Mahāvideh Tīrthadhām (=NTS), editor, *Trimandir Paricay* (Surat: Mahāvideh Tīrthadhām, n.d.), 15.
25. Padmanabh, S. Jaini, 'On the *Sarvajñatva* (Omniscience) of Mahāvīra and the Buddha,' *Buddhist Studies in the Honour of I.B. Horner,* edited by L. Cousins et al. (Dordrecht: D. Reidel Publishing Company, 1974), 71f; and R.J. Singh, *Jaina Concept of Omniscience,* identified two different interpretations of 'omniscience' in the Jaina tradition, 'namely, omniscience as knowledge of essentials [the eternal self, P.F.] and omniscience as universal knowledge' (56). Kundakunda *(Niyamasāra* 158, in ibid., 53) tried to combine both views. Consistent with Kundakunda's views, A.M. Paṭel claimed to know 'every atom of the soul and the non-soul, separating both of them' (*Āptavāṇī* I, 20, cf. AV I, 16).
26. The best discussion of *samyak darśana* is chapter 5 of Jaini's *Path of Purification,* 134–56.
27. 'Even a degree of *Keval Gyana,* "we" call *Pragna*...Absolute Omni-Science of *Keval Gyana* is at the completion of 360° full' (A.M. Paṭel, *Āptavāṇī* I, 272).

'A circle has 360°. The English are on 110°, the Muslims on 120°, the Paris on 140° and the Hindus on 220°; and all of them look at reality from their own points of view...But "We" are sitting at the centre-completing full circle of reality and so our vision is perfect. A Gnani [a realised soul] sitting at the centre has the right [true] perception of reality...But... "We" also could not digest 4° more and hence "we" are poised on 356°' (ibid., 207).

28. 'Knowing here means realising' (Singh, *Jaina Concept of Omniscience*, 51). See also Johnson, *Harmless Souls*, 238.

29. A.M. Paṭel sees the 'superimposed' or embodied self as a mixture of ego (I) and attachment (me): *ahaṃkāra (hūṃ) ane mamatā (marūṃ)* (AV I, 109, cf. A.M. Paṭel, *Āptavāṇī* I, 134f).

30. A.M. Paṭel, *Āptavāṇī I*, 7, 6. Compare the following analysis of A.M. Paṭel which uses techniques of reversal that are frequently found in Tantric literature. It is a good example of the way in which 'the knowledge (sans intellect)' is applied: 'Nobody likes to be insulted. But "We" say that it is very "helping." Respect and insult are the sweet-bitter juice of the ego. Let me tell you, he who insults you has come to squeeze the bitter taste out of you. When somebody said, "You are a fool", he drew away that juice from you. The ego gets broken in proportion to the amount of juice extracted from it and this is done, without our labour, by someone else...We *"Gnani Puruṣa"* are *"Abuddha"* (sans intellect); but know that the *"Gnani"* possesses so many powers that he can easily squeeze all the juice of the ego. But you don't have such powers' (A.M. Paṭel, *Āptavāṇī* I, 119, cf. AVI, 97).

31. Amin, 'Who is "Dādā Bhagavān",' v.

32. Interview with Kanu Paṭel, 1999.

33. The word *āpta* means also trustworthy, reliable, authoritative. For its use in Jainism, see Jayandra Soni, *The Notion of Āpta in Jaina Philosophy: The 1995 Roop Lal Jain Lecture* (University of Toronto, 1996).

34. Only the *mohanīya*, or delusion-producing *karmas* can be destroyed by the *Jñānī*. Thereafter, the aspirants are said to be able to prevent the influx of new *karmas* through the practice of passionlessness. However, the already accumulated *karmas* need to come to fruition naturally. If they are acted out dispassionately they will not bind new *karmas*.

35. It is believed that in the presence of a Jina or his immediate disciples, arhatship can be achieved within a few births through the annihilation of the *mohanīya karmas* via *kṣāyaka samyaktva*, insight through destruction, in the eighth *guṇasthāna*, or stage of purification (Jaini, *Path of Purification*, 146).

36. A doctrinal impossibility, which devotees explain was made possible by the intervention of the gods.

37. For a detailed description and analysis of the rite, see Peter Flügel, 'Beyond the Hindu Frontier: Jaina-Vaiṣṇava Syncretisṃ in the Gujarātī Diaspora I-II, *International Journal of Tantrik Studies* 7', 1-2 (2005), Forthcoming.

38. Śrīmad Rājacandra, *Śrīmad Rājacandra,* edited by Manubhai B. Modi, 7th Edition (Agās: Śrīmad Rājacandra Āśram, 1951/1995), 679. Translated in U.K. Pungaliya, *Philosophy and Spirituality of Śrīmad Rājacandra* (Jaipur: Prakrit Bharati Academy, 1996), 204. For affirmative references to the example of Rājacandra, who is popularly called Kripalu Deva, or merciful god, see A.M. Paṭel, *Āptavāṇī* I, 207f. (cf. AV I, 97) and *Generation Gap,* 62: 'If you pray to Kripalu Dev (another *Gnani Purush)* or Dādā Bhagavān, it will be the same, because they both are the same in the sense of *Atma.* They are physically different in appearance, but in essence the same. Even if you invoke Lord Mahavir, it is one and the same.'

39. A.M. Paṭel declared that only three *jñānīs* ever existed in Bhārata (India) since the *nirvana* of the last *tīrthaṅkara:* Ācārya Kundakunda, Śrīmad Rājacandra and himself. He did not regard the neo-Digambara *brahmacārī,* Kānjī Svāmī (1889–1980), as a *jñānī.* For Kānjī Svāmī, see Dundas, *The Jains,* 227–32.

40. Kundakunda maintained the principle that the soul is active, though it can only transform itself. See Ācārya Kundakunda, *Samayasāra, with English Translation and Commentary based upon Amṛtacandra's Atmakyati* (=SS), 3rd Edition, edited by A. Chakravarti (New Delhi: Bharatiya Jñānpith, 1925/1989), verse 340–41, 202f. See also A. Chakravarti, 'Introduction' 108, 157f; and Johnson, *Harmless Souls,* 292–95, on Sāṃkhya and Vedānta influences on Kundakunda's philosophy.

41. Like Rājacandra (SR 238), A.M. Paṭel was strongly influenced by the Bhagavad Gītā, in which, in the words of J.A.B. van Buitenen, *The Bhagavad Gītā in the Mahābhārata: Text and Translation* (=BG) (Chicago: The University of Chicago Press, 1981), at least in certain passages, 'a three-order universe (God, *jīvas, prakṛti)* is superinposed on a Sāṃkhya two-order universe *(puruṣas, prakṛti)* with the implications not wholly thought through' (169, n. 2, commentary on BG 37).

42. The two-truth theory in a mature form was introduced into Jainism by Kundakunda, *Samayasāra,* Verse, 7, 14f.

43. Rājacandra writes in his famous text on the six principles *(ṣaṭpada),* that it is the activity of the soul itself that binds *karma: 'ātmā che,' 'te nitya che,' 'che kartā nijakarma,' 'che bhoktā,' 'vaḷī mokṣa che,' 'mokṣa upāya sudharma' (Ātmasiddhi* 43, in Rājacandra, *Śrīmad Rājacandra,* 538). In other words, 'the soul is the doer *(karta).'* A.M. Paṭel, on the other hand, insists that 'the soul is not the doer,' it is 'only the knower.' Accordingly, Rājacandra teaches a more traditional interpretation of Jainism, although he also writes: *'kartā bhoktā karmano, vibhāva varte jyāṃya; vṛtti vahī nijabhāvamāṃ, thayo akartā*

tyāṃya' (*Ātmasiddhi,* 121, 554): 'In delusion one does the deeds, receives the fruits; bur non-doer he is, when he sows the knowledge-seeds, and constantly remains the knower' (*The Self-Realisation, Being a Translation of Atma-Siddhi of Śrīmad Rājacandra by Brahmacārī Govardhanadasajira,* Agas: Śrīmad Rājacandra Ashram, 1985/1994, 87). The principal difference between the teachings of Rājacandra and A.M. Paṭel is that the latter emphasises exclusively the religious value of the *niścaya* perspective, whereas Rājacandra combines, often in an unexplicated way, *niścaya naya* and *vyavahāra naya.* The classical Jaina view is that without taking into account the *vyavahāra* perspective, religion remains ethically impotent and salvation impossible. For Rājacandra, world-renunciation is ultimately indispensable. On this point, see Pungaliya, *Philosophy and Spirituality of Śrīmad Rājacandra,* 285f.

44. A.M. Paṭel, in N. Amin's 'Introduction' to A.M. Paṭel, *Generation Gap,* ii.

45. These powers include mind-reading, *manaḥparyāya jñāna.* See A.M. Paṭel, *Āptavāṇī I,* 90, cf. AV I, 75.

46. Ibid., 204, cf. AV I, 185.

47. Ibid., 119, cf. AV I, 96f.

48. Ibid., 55, cf. AV I, 45f.

49. Ibid., 27, cf. AV I, 21f.

50. Ibid., 58, cf. AV I, 47: *'Jyāre akram mārg maṃ jñānī puruṣ mathe hath muke to pote puruṣ thai akhi prakṛti ne samaji jay.'*

51. Ibid., 21f, cf. AV I, 15f.

52. God is, here, the soul and the boss is A.M. Paṭel, though the statement is deliberately ambiguous.

53. A.M. Paṭel, *Āptavāṇī I,* 71, cf. AV I, 59.

54. Kundakunda also devaluates scriptural knowledge in favour of self-realisation, but he does not mention the possibility of a transfer of self-knowledge.

55. Kṛṣṇa Kumar Dixit, *Jaina Ontology* (Ahmedabad: L.D. Institute of Indology, 1971), 133, and Jaini, *Path of Purification,* explained that the common sense use of the term *pratyakṣa* for 'ordinary, sense-mediated cognition' is a specific historically development (ibid., 122, n. 44).

56. A.M. Paṭel, *Āptavāṇī* I, 72f, cf. AV I, 59f.

57. Although the term 'astral body' is occasionally used, this is apparently achieved without even utilising the so-called communication body, or *āhāraka śarīra.* See Schubring, *Doctrine,* 137–39, on the Jaina doctrine of the five bodies. A.M. Paṭel, *Vartamān Tīrthaṅkar Śrī Sīmandhar Svāmī,* edited by Nīrubahen Amīn (Chennai: Dādā Bhagavān Phaundeshan, 1994), said elsewhere that the grace of Sīmandhar operates only indirectly through *anumodana,* his empathy (13).

58. *Huṃ bījo mahāvīra chuṃ, em mane ātmika śakti vaḍe jaṇāyuṃ che* (SR 27, 165f).

59. Also Kanu Paṭel. Paul Dundas, 'Somnolent Sūtras: Scriptural Commentary in Śvetāmbar Jainism,' *Journal of Indian Philosophy* 24 (1996): 82f., also interprets Sīmandhar as a *tīrthaṅkara* of the future, comparable to the future Buddha Maitreya: 'Śvetāmbara sources suggest that...only goddesses could have immediate access to Sīmandhar.'

60. The Akram Vijñān Mārg distinguishes between final *mokṣa* and living *mokṣa*. See Sharadaprasad Ramadevanahalli. See page 2 of http://www.geocities.com/Atens/Acropolois/7591/gnani.html. Two other websites contain useful conformation on the Akram Vijñān Mārg are: http://www.dadabhagawan.org and http://www.dadashri.org.

61. See Jaini, *Path of Purification,* 142f.

62. In other sources, rebirth after a strict monastic life is presented as the standard method for reaching Mahāvideha. See the story of Ambada in the *Uvavāiya Suttam (Aupapātika Sūtra)* 101–116, which presents Mahāvideha without reference to Sīmandhar Svāmī, who seems to be a historically later invention.

63. The problem is that the realisation of old *karma* automatically binds new *karmas* of the same type. It is therefore assumed that the cycle of bondage cannot be interrupted merely by assuming 'a good state of mind' and waiting for the natural maturation *(udaya)* of *karma,* but only through a slow and painful process of purification of one's old *karmas (apūrva karaṇa)* through a logical sequence of stages of asceticism and meditation which cause the premature maturation *(udīraṇa)* of *karma* in a controlled way. See Helmuth von Glasenapp, *Die Lehre vom Karma in der Philosophie der Jainas* (Leipzig: Otto Harrassowitz, 1915) 81; and Schubring, *Doctrine,* 325, cf. 178f.

64. The Bhagavad Gītā follows the Sāṃkhya view. The following well-known passage must have influenced A.M. Paṭel: 'At any rate, actions are performed by the three forces of nature, but deluded by self-attribution, one thinks: "I did it!" But he who knows the principles that govern the distribution of those forces and their actions knows that the forces are operating on the forces, and he takes no interest in actions' (BG 3.27–3.33, 83f).

65. This technique is a major improvement over the schematic rites of repentance *(pratikramaṇa)* which are obligatory for Jaina mendicants. For a detailed analysis of the ethical principles and the rites of purification of the Akram Vijñān Mārg, see Flügel, *'Beyond the Hindu Frontier: Jaina-Vaiṣṇava Syncretisṃ in the Gujarātī Diaspora'.*

66. Johnson, *Harmless Souls,* 271, 281f, 293, etc. notes a similar 'eclectic' combination of gnosis and ethics in Kundakunda's *Samayasāra,* and argues—*pace* Schubring, *Kundakunda,* 574, but with B. Bhatt,

Vyavahāra-Naya and Niścaya-Naya in Kundakunda's Works, 288, who attributes only the gnostic sections to Kundakunda—that the text, whose content appears to be inherently 'contradictory,' must be the product of more than one author and compiled with a social purpose in mind (265, 307). A similar theory could obviously not explain A.M. Paṭel's views.

67. A.M. Paṭel, *Who Am I,* edited by Amin, 34.

68. The idea that self-knowledge is the true form of renunciation, not the renunciation of physical objects, had been stated by Kundakunda (SS 34, translated by Johnson, *Harmless Souls,* 288).

69. Nīrubahen Amīn, compiler, *Tirthankar of Today Shree Sīmandhar Swami,* translated by G.A. Shah (Bombay: Shri Dada Bhagvan Vitarag Trust, 1983), 22.

70. *Akram Vijñān* 20, August 1999, 35.

71. The great majority are Pāṭīdārs, the dominant agricultural caste of Gujarat, who traditionally practice some form of Vaiṣṇavism. Most of them perform the emotive *Kṛṣṇa bhakti* worship of Vallabhācārya's *Puṣṭimārga,* the path seeking the grace of God, or the Svāmīnarāyaṇ tradition of Sahajānanda Svāmī (1781–1830). An excellent ethnography of the *Puṣṭimārga* is Peter Bennett's *The Path of Grace: Social Organisation and Temple Worship in a Vaiṣṇava Sect* (New Delhi: Hindustan Publications, 1993).

72. Both wings of the Akram Vijñān Mārg distinguish today three religious statuses: (1) The spiritual leader, Kanu Paṭel on Nīrubahen Amīn, who carries the title *pūjya ātmājñānī,* venerable knower of the soul, and who alone can perform initiations and the rite of knowledge, (2) the group of approximately fifty male and seven to ten female celibate disciples *(brahmacārī* or *brahmacāriṇī),* called *āptaputras* or *āptaputrīs,* or true spiritual sons or daughters of the Dādā, the one with the speech of truth *(āptavāṇī),* and (3) the common believers, who, after their initiation, are either called *mumukṣus,* seekers for salvation, like the followers of Rājacandra, or *mahātmās,* great souls. The leaders of the local or all-embracing lay associations are distinguished with the title *saṅghapati.*

73. The reason for this is that rebirth in Mahāvideha Kṣetra is believed to be achievable through the creation of a link of mutual indebtedness *(ṛṇānubandha)* with Sīmandhar generated by devotional practices (A.M. Paṭel, in Amin, *Tirthankar of Today,* 29f). Because Sīmandhar is a living *tīrthaṅkara* he can indeed, if accessible, enter relationships of reciprocity, in contrast to the liberated 24 Jinas of our world. Sīmandhar thus plays a similar role in the religious imagination of his devotees as miracle-working Jaina ascetics or the deceased *dādā guru devas* of the Kharataragaccha described by Caroline Humphrey and James Laidlaw in their book *The Archetypal Actions of Ritual: A Theory of Ritual Illustrated by the Jain Rite of Worship* (Oxford: Oxford University Press, 1994), 50, etc.

74. See AV (1995–1999). In contrast to Rājacandra, who explained his teachings mainly in his letters to his closest friends, collected in the volume *Śrīmad Rājacandra,* A.M. Paṭel did not write tracts or letters on religious subjects. His discourses were informal conversations in Gujarati with the participants of his *satsaṅg.* Although he has not attempted to produce a work of systematic theology, his teachings are logically coherent. Only the first volume of his published discourses is available in translation. See A.M. Paṭel, *Āptavāṇī* I.

75. Naṭubhāī B. Paṭel, editor, *Svarūp Vijñān: Pūjya Dādā Bhagavān nī Jagatkalyāṇ nī Vāṇī Emnā Ja Śabdo maṃ,* Shreni 2-3 (Mumbai: Shri Dādā Bhagavān Vitarag Trust, 1989). Initially, A.M. Paṭel did not permit the taking of notes of his discourses, but Naṭubhāī Paṭel convinced him that otherwise he could not remember much.

76. Apart from the first sentence of part I, '(1) I bow before the unattached ones *(vītarāga),*' the first part of the text is identical with the (Mūrtipūjaka) Jaina *Namaskāra Mantra.* However, part 2-3 is idiosyncratic: '(2) Om. I bow before Lord Vāsudeva [Kṛṣṇa]. (3) Om. I bow before Śiva. Hail to the eternal truth, knowledge and bliss [of the pure soul].' In the original: (1) *namo vītarāgāya,...* (2) *om namo bhagavate vāsudevāya.* (3) *om namo śivāya, jay saccidānanda* (Nīrubahen Amīn, compiler, *Caran Vidhi).* 2nd Edition (Chennai: Dādā Bhagavān Phaundeshan, 1998).

77. A.M. Paṭel, in *Dādāvāṇī,* n.d., 13–16. For a rendering into English, see A.M. Paṭel, *Ultimate Knowledge,* edited by Rakesh M. Paṭel (London, 1994), 68–70. The key verse is no. 13: 'The real self is god and therefore I see god in all living beings' (70).

78. A.M. Paṭel, in *Dādāvāṇī,* 18–22. For a rendition into English, see A.M. Paṭel, *Ultimate Knowledge,* 73–76. The text is a variation on the theme of the five great vows *(mahāvrata)* of the Jainas: '(1) He Dādā Bhavagan! Give me the infinite inner strength not to hurt, cause someone to hurt, nor instigate anyone to hurt the ego of any living being, even in the slightest extent...' (73).

79. See N. Amin, *Caran Vidhi.*

80. The devotional form of this rite which aims at the creation of a union between the worshipper and the worshipped was almost certainly inspired by Amṛtacandra's depiction of Kundakunda's legendary yogic travels to Mahāvideha in search for inspiration from Sīmandhar. See Amṛtacandra, *Tattva-dīpikā,* 3–4.

81. The original Gujarati text of the *mantra* is identical with the first verse of the *Namaskār Vidhi* text as reproduced in footnote 81. Cf. A.M. Paṭel, *Vartamān Tīrthankar Śrī Sīmandhar Svāmī,* 11.

82. N. Amin, in: N. Amin, *Tīrthankar of Today,* 24f.

83. A.M. Paṭel, *Aptavani* I, 73, cf. AV I, 60.

84. A similar arrangement – the image of the *sadguru* placed in another room underneath the Jina image – can be found at the temple in Agas, the main centre of the Rājacandra cult.

85. Both Nīrubahen and Mīnā (Paṭel) taped all *satsaṅgs* of this tour, and Mīna's tape-recorder went on recording the conversation which took place the *satsaṅg.* it was later discovered and excerpts printed in the magazine *Akram Vijñān,* June-July 1999, 5. (I had the opportunity to listen to a copy of the tape.)

86. In A.M. Paṭel, *Essence of All Religion,* 51.

87. NTS, 16.

88. These statements have been compiled from the author's interviews with Nīrubahen Amīn.

89. N. Amin, 'What is your spiritual state after "Gnan Ceremony"?,' 30.

90. Johnson, *Harmless Souls,* 282f has introduced this term.

91. www. 7.1.1999 (the website does not exist anymore).

92. The followers of Nīrubahen always insist on the special status of Gujarati as the religious language of the Dādā.

93. Author's interview in 1999. However, the following critical report of a participant indicates that Kanu Paṭel's performance is not much different from Nīrubahens: '*Samyak darśan* cannot be achieved through magical means, but only through self effort. I met Kanubhāī Paṭel and went through one of his sessions. Before shouting *"Huṃ śuddhātmā chuṃ"* everyone was touching Kanubhāī's toe to get the power of enlightenment transferred from Sīmandhar while Kanubhāī, who was in touch with Sīmandhar through *ātmasākṣātkar,* was muttering a *mantra.* It is impossible to get *samyak darśan* transferred this way. Even asceticism only prepares the ground. Important is only *ātmasākṣātkar,* experiencing one's own soul' (Interview with Anupam R. Śāh, Mumbai).

94. Comment of an *āptaputra.*

95. Salter, *Unity and Diversity,* 44–49, observed three methods of tradition-building amongst the followers of Śrīmad Rājacandra which she analysed in terms of two types of 'true gurus': (1) present/living *gurus (pratyakṣa guru):* (a) *guru* lineages, (b) independent *gurus;* and (2) absent/dead *gurus (parokṣa guru)*—Rājacandra and his immediate disciples. Both the veneration of the independent *gurus* and the absent *gurus,* she writes, are based on Rājacandra's writings and, at least in the latter case, also on his image. As in the case of the Akram Vijñān movement, there are at least two types of *guru* lineages: (a) the line of Rājacandra's personal disciples which terminated with the death of his last disciple (direct contact with the founder: lineage of Agās), and (b) a lineage based on the transmission of a secret *mantra* authenticated by Rājacandra (indirect contact with the founder: lineage of Sāylā). On the Kānjī Panth see W.J. Johnson, forthcoming.

96. Bennett, *Path of Grace,* 35, sees the initiation *mantra* as the 'lifeblood' of the segmentary lineage structure of the Puṣṭimārgīs.

97. Richard Gombrich and Gananath Obeyesekere, *Buddhism Transformed: Religious Change in Śrī Laṅkā* (Princeton University Press, 1988), 55. The authors define Tantra 'by the doctrine that the same observances may yield either material benefits *(bhukti)*–notably power–or salvation *(mukti)*' (56).

98. Schubring, *Doctrine,* emphasised that already Umasvati, the principal author of classical Jain doctrine, managed to 'incorporate the magical faculties' *(iḍḍhi, laddhi, siddhi)* frequently mentioned in the Canon into the system (316). He interprets this as a 'concession made to the popular belief' (ibid).

99. P.S. Jaini, 'The Disappearance of Buddhism and the Survival of Jainism: A Study in Contrast,' in *Studies in the History of Buddhism,* edited by A.K. Narain (New Delhi: BR Publications, 1980), 88.

100. Jaini, *Path of Purification,* 254. The analytical literature on Jain *bhakti* is still sparse. Lawrence A. Babb, *Absent Lord: Ascetics and Kings in a Jain Ritual Culture* (Berkeley: University of California Press, 1996), 177, *pace, 93,* tends to regard all types of Jaina Bhakti as variations of a 'common South Asian theme'; while Jaini, *Path of Purification,* writes that even though 'the Hindu concept of *iṣṭa* has exerted a certain amount of influence... Jain devotionalism is oriented not towards a chosen deity *(iṣṭa-devatā)* but toward an ideal, the attainment of *kevala jñāna;* thus reverence is given to all beings who have been or are actively engaged in pursuit of that ideal' (163, cf. 194f). John E. Cort, *Jains in the World: Religions Values and Ideology in India* (New York: Oxford University Press, 2001), has emphasised the non-derivative nature of Jaina *bhakti* and proposed 'to conceive of *bhakti* as a style of religiosity, one that can be applied to almost any religons content' and suggested the 'term *enthusiasm*...as an alternative gloss' (John E. Cort, 'Singing the Glory of Asceticism: Devotion of Asceticism in Jainism,' in *Journal of the American Academy of Religion* 70.4 (2002): 738; while M. Whitney Kelting, *Singing to the Jinas: Jain Laywomen, Mandal Singing and the Negotiation of Jain Devotion* (Oxford: Oxford University Press, 2001) 113, emphasises the commitment to 'the right sentiment' and that in fact appeals to the 'grace and compassion of the Jinas are not seen as "un-Jain"' (13). The issue of the absence of the divine in Jainism has been extensively (and controversially) discussed by Sinclair Stevenson, *The Heart of Jainism* (New Delhi: Manohar, 1915/1984), 289–98.

101. Jaini, *Path of Purification,* 256.

102. John E. Cort, *Jains in the World,* 114.

103. Ibid., 116. For a similar verdict see Jaini, *Path of Purification,* 254.

104. Cf. Schubring, *Kundakunda,* 569, on SS 141–44.

105. Cf. the *tattvas,* or truths, of classical Jainism.

106. See the work of Klaus Bruhn on Jaina texts.

107. Johnson, *Harmless Souls,* 282f. They are certainly also cognitively satisfying for the believer.

108. Johnson, "The Religious Function of Jaina Philosophy: *Anekāntavāda* Reconsidered", in *Religion* 25 (1995): 47.

109. References to the scant literature on Tantric practices in Jainism can be found in the David G. White (ed.) *Tantra in Practice* (Princeton: Princeton University Press, 2000).

Beyond The Hindu Frontier Jaina-Vaiṣṇava Syncretism in The Gujarātī Diaspora

Article 51A(f) of the Indian Constitution recognises what many politicians and anthropologists still fail to do: India does not represent a civilisational whole[1] but has a "composite culture."[2] That this statement does not merely reflect the wishful thinking of the constituent assembly but historical fact is no more evident than in the continued presence of the ancient traditions of Buddhism and Jainism in India,[3] which contemporary religious nationalists have for decades unsuccessfully tried to incorporate into the indefinable 'Hindu' mould; not to speak of the presence of Christianity, Islam, Judaism, Sikhism, Zoroastrianism, and diverse tribal communities. This article tries to demonstrate through the analysis of the unique conversion ritual of the Akram Vijñān Mārg, a new religious movement in the Gujarātī-speaking world, that the supposition of a civilisational unity of India or of South Asia is a theoretical abstraction which obstructs rather than illuminates the understanding of the cultural and religious history of the Indian subcontinent. Heterogeneity and processes of bricolage, mixture, syncretism or hybridisation are not merely the consequence of external cultural interaction, migration and travel, that is the advance or retreat of a well-defined cultural frontier,[4] but situated at the very heart of religious and cultural life beyond the homogenising cultural politics of the state[5] and organised religion.[6] The article is based on intermittent fieldwork between 1997-2004 in Amadāvād/Ahmedabad, London, Mumbaī/Bombay, Surat, and Vaḍodarā/Baroda.

દાદા આપે દીકરીને 'સિદ્ધિ'ના આશિર્વાદ,
જ્ઞાનવિધિ કરાવી ફેલાવો વિશ્વે અક્રમ-ના સાદ.

The Akram Vijñān Movement

The Akram Vijñān Mārg, or the Stepless Path to Soteriological Knowledge, has currently approximately 300,000 followers amongst the Gujarātī-speaking diaspora in India, East Africa, Great Britain, Fiji and the U.S.A. The movement was started in 1962 in Baroda by the religious visionary Ambalāl Mūljībhāī Paṭel (7.11.1908 - 2.1.1988), a businessman with only basic formal education who belonged to a Vaiṣṇava Pāṭidār family from Tarsālī, a suburb of Baroda. He spent most of his life as a married householder without children in Bombay where he worked as a contractor for the company Paṭel & Co. which specialised in the construction and maintenance of the dry docks in the harbour. In 1958, while waiting for a train at the railway station of Surat, he had reportedly a forty-eight minutes long 'enlightenment' experience. It is said that he was able to contact Sīmandhara Svāmī, the Jain *tīrthaṅkara* who presently lives on the mythical continent of Mahāvideha,[7] and due to Sīmandhar's grace (*kṛpā*) was able to achieve the state of permanent self-realisation, or *ātmajñāna*.[8] Suddenly, he understood the solution to all spiritual conundrums: "God is your real self";[9] "All you need to know is to understand your real nature."[10] He understood at once that through this insight he had gained *jīvanamukti*, or liberation in this life, since he was from now on able to directly experience the difference between the inner 'real self,' which he later called Dādā Bhagavān, Grandfather Lord, and the outer 'relative self,' that is A.M. Paṭel, and his actions which appeared to be nothing but *karman* accumulated in previous lives that come to fruition (*karmaphala*), without any involvement of the real self.

From 1962 onwards, A.M. Paṭel, the *jñānī*, or knower, taught his insights, first to family members and friends and later, on popular demand, in public meetings (*satsaṅga*) to anyone who was interested. He used the ontological categories of the Sāṁkhya tradition to describe the disjunction between pure consciousness (*puruṣa*) and the activities of the body-mind complex (*prakṛti*) which a self-realised being merely observes from the outside without identifying with them. However, most of the recognisable cosmological, soteriological and ritual concepts of his idiosyncratic teachings (which were only orally transmitted and via tape recordings)[11] stem from the Jain tradition. Like Sāṁkhya ontology, Jaina ontology is dualistic. It distinguishes between soul (*jīva*), or pure consciousness, and non-soul (*ajīva*), or matter, but characterises pure consciousness not as a passive but as an active force. In addition to right knowledge Jainism stresses the soteriological importance of non-violent action, because the karmic bondage of the soul is perceived to be real, not just an illusion based on ignorance.

The principal text of classical Jainism, Ācārya Umāsvāti/Umāsvāmī's 5th century *Tattvārtha Sūtra*, propagates a threefold path to liberation: through right vision, right knowledge, and right conduct.[12] According to this view, salvation can only be achieved if non-violent conduct is informed by the knowledge and the belief in seven fundamental truths (*tattva*), which describe the mechanism of karmic bondage and the traditional path of liberation through the stepwise purification of the soul.[13] The combination of the three aspects of the path of liberation is still regarded as the essential feature of what later came to be known as *jaina dharma*, the doctrine of the Jinas, or victors, i.e. the twenty-four fordmakers (*tīrthaṅkara*) which showed the way out of the eternal cycle of death and rebirth.[14] However, in practice, many Jain traditions have stressed one aspect more than others. As a consequence, contemporary Jainism presents at least three different Jain paths to salvation:[15] asceticism (canonical and classical monastic Jainism), devotion (classical lay Jainism)[16], and knowledge (Digambara mysticism). I have suggested elsewhere[17] that the Akram Vijñān Mārg is the only religious movement which has developed the anti-ascetic implications of Kundakunda's Digambara mysticism, with its emphasis on self-realisation and salvific knowledge, into a Mahāyāna-style alternative to the classical path of purification. The emphasis on knowledge and devotion certainly proved to be of interest for many lay Gujarātīs, because it offers the option of a stepless (*akrama*) or instant 'enlightenment' (*vijñāna*) for everyone 'through the grace of Dādā Bhagavān,' that is the self-realised soul of A.M. Paṭel.

The movement,[18] which crystallised around A.M. Paṭel from 1962 onwards, cannot be easily located within any pre-existing religious tradition, although it clearly draws upon ritual and doctrinal elements of Vaiṣṇavism and Jainism whose classical conception of *siddhaloka*, the realm of the liberated souls, serves as the ultimate goal of the spiritual journey. It is argued here that the process of formation of this new religious movement is typical for many similar movements, probably since time eternal, by not being a product of cultural diffusion through travel or conquest, but a creative synthesis of elements that are cumulatively selected from the universe of known ideas and practices under conditions of positive feedback.[19] The resulting syncretism is difficult to classify, because the Akram Vijñān movement explicitly rejects the conventional attributes 'religion,' 'sect,' 'cult,' 'movement,' 'scripture,' 'doctrine,' 'ritual,' 'guru' and 'disciple,' which it regards as worldly and particularistic. It favours a universal 'non-sectarian' path (*mārga*) to salvation through introspection and the mystical experience of individual self-realisation which is beyond words and not accessible through the intellect. This direct experience of the transcendental truth – which provides a shortcut to salvation[20] and marks the end of conventional religion – is offered to the followers of all religions, including Islam, Christianity, Zoroastrianism, etc. This article analyses the method which A.M. Paṭel, the Dādā Bhagavān, invented to transmit his self-knowledge directly and unconditionally to all interested aspirants.

Worldwide Mission

Although A.M. Paṭel rejected organised forms of religion, he invented a ritual technique for the 'transmission' of his experience of self-realisation to others. This unique procedure was called *jñān vidhi*, or the rite of knowledge, and became the focus of a new organised 'guru-cult' which spread quickly throughout the Gujarātī-speaking world, especially amongst urban working class and lower middle class professionals with limited formal education from Vaiṣṇava and Jain families.[21] In 1973, A.M. Paṭel gave his blessings to the creation of a community organisation, the *Jay Sacchidānand Saṅgh* in Mumbaī, for the financial and organisational support of his missionary tours in India and abroad, and for publishing and construction projects. The first leader of this nation-wide organisation was the head of the *Dādā Bhagavān Vītarāga Trust* in Bombay, Khetsī Narsī Śāh, who after his death was succeeded by G.A. Śāh from Ahmedabad. Important local *Sacchidānand Saṅghas* in India are located in Vaḍodarā, Surat, Amadāvād and Mumbaī. Amongst the Gujarātīs in East Africa, including several relatives of A.M. Paṭel, the community of Kampala (Uganda) has the greatest number of followers. In 1982, A.M. Paṭel was invited for the first time to the U.S.A. by the family of Vasant Paṭel in Oak Ridge Tennessee, the U.S. community leader, and returned to the U.S.A. every year until his death in Baroda on the 2.1.1988, which was mourned, amongst others, by more than 10,000 U.S. Gujarātīs.[22] The number of followers has continuously increased ever since.

Schism And Continuity

In the last decade of his life A.M. Paṭel became almost a full-time preacher, due to popular demand. Until 1978, when he had an accident which left him with a fractured leg, A.M. Paṭel and his wife lived together with the family of Kanubhāī Paṭel (born 1930), a structural engineer who worked for his company and who became his most dedicated follower. However, from 1978 onwards he severed his business connections with Kanubhāī and concentrated entirely on his religious work. He was accompanied on all his missionary tours by the medical doctor Nīrubahen Amīn (born 1944–2006) from Auraṅgābād, the widowed daughter of one of his earliest devotees, from the Carotar Paṭel *jñāti* of the village Vaso in Gujarāt, and herself a devoted follower who committed herself entirely to his service (*sevā*).

After the death of A.M. Paṭel in 1988 a succession dispute flared up between Kanubhāī Paṭel and Nīrubahen Amīn, which in 1993 – the year in which the first of three Tri-Mandira shrines of the Akram Vijñān movement dedicated to Sīmandhara Svāmī, Kṛṣṇa and Śiva was completed in Surat[23] – led to the split of the movement into two factions. At present, the oldest community organisation, the *Jay Saccidānand Saṅgh*, still supports Kanubhāī Paṭel, but the majority

of the believers follow Nīrubahen Amīn. The ongoing dispute between the factions focuses on the charismatic qualification of Nīrubahen Amīn, the person which was closest to A.M. Paṭel during the last decade of his life, to act as a religious leader. Nīrubahen Amīn claims that, in 1987, A.M. Paṭel (who publicly did not determine any successor since he rejected organised religion) had given her a secret *mantra* which allows her to temporarily invoke the spiritual power (*siddhi*) of the Dādā within herself and to act as a medium for the performance of the rite of knowledge, the principal focus of the Akram Vijñān movement, after his death.[24] Kanubhāī Paṭel, on the other hand, points out that he was the person closest to A.M. Paṭel before 1978 and received from him the powers to perform the *jñān vidhi* already in 1960. His followers preserved a clandestine tape recording of a private conversation between A.M. Paṭel and Nīrubahen Amīn on the 19.9.1987 which seems to prove that he wanted Nīrubahen to work together with Kanubhāī and to assist him in the performance of the *jñān vidhi*. In contrast to Nīrubahen Amīn who does not claim to be enlightened herself but acts merely as a spirit medium (*nimitta*) of A.M. Paṭel, who in her view was the only *jñānī* of this age, Kanubhāī Paṭel asserts that he is a *jñānī* in his own right, and the only presently existing enlightened being/man (*pravartamān pragaṭ jñānī puruṣ*).[25] One of the main objections of the *Jay Saccidānand Saṅgh* to Nīrubahen's succession is that she is a woman.[26]

Religious Hierarchy

Both wings of the Akram Vijñān Mārg distinguish today three religious statuses: (1) The spiritual leader, Kanubhāī Paṭel or Nīrubahen Amīn, who carries the title *pūjya ātmājñānī*, venerable knower of the soul, and who alone can perform initiations and the rite of knowledge, (2) the category of presently ca. fifty male and seven-to-ten female celibate disciples (*brahmacārī* or *brahmacāriṇī*), called *āptaputras* or *āptaputrīs*, or true spiritual sons or daughters of the Dādā, "the one with the speech of truth (*āptavāṇī*),"[27] and (3) the common believers, which, after their initiation, are either called *mumukṣus*, seekers for salvation (like the followers of Rājacandra), or *mahātmās*, great souls or great beings. The social leaders of the local or the all-embracing lay associations are distinguished by the title *saṅghapati* or *sakal saṅghapati*.

Ātmājñānī

The spiritual leader, who alone can perform the *jñān vidhi*, is evidently the most important individual of the Akram Vijñān movement. As a matter of principle, there is only one spiritual leader in each of the two present groups, qualified either by personal charisma or through the possession of a special *mantra*, i.e. objectified charisma, and the ritual competence learned in the presence of

A.M. Paṭel.[28] Since the Akram Vijñān Mārg is an egalitarian and rather informal lay movement, without rules and regulations or institutionalised hierarchies of command, the most important structuring device is the relationship between the *ātmājñānī*, the knower, and the *mahātmā*s, the great souls which have received 'the knowledge' from him or her. This relationship was originally purely emotive.[29] The first '*jñān vidhi*,' i.e. the transmission of the experience of *samyak darśana* to another individual, was performed by A.M. Paṭel in 1962 in his rented house in Baroda for his nephew Candrakānt Paṭel from Uganda through an informal discourse (*āptavāṇī*) followed by a personal blessing (*āśīrvāda*). Since 1983, the relationship was cemented by a formal initiation ritual which precedes the *jñān vidhi* and which requires the devotee's symbolic surrender (*samarpaṇa*) of 'mind, speech, and body' to Sīmandhar Svāmī in the presence of the *ātmājñānī* (thus effectively to both). Since, in principle, the hierarchical relationship depends on nothing but the bond of a shared religious experience of 'the pure soul' and the mutual recognition of 'knowers,' the initiation does not involve any definition of mutual rights and duties or expectations of material or immaterial services. The designations *guru* and *śiṣya* are therefore deliberately avoided.

Āptaputra/Āptaputrī

The *āptaputras* and *āptaputrīs* are *mahātmās* who practise celibacy in order to enhance their spiritual purity. They do not expressly claim the formal status of religious virtuosi, but many of them act as charismatically qualified preachers under the instruction of the respective *ātmājñānī*.

Brahmacarya, or celibacy, is the only commitment which was taken over by the Akram Vijñān movement from the lists of the five principal Jain vows (*mahāvrata*): non-violence (*ahiṁsā*), truthfulness (*satya*), not stealing (*asteya*), non-possessiveness (*aparigraha*), and celibacy (*brahmacarya*) (AS 2.15.29f.). A.M. Paṭel himself rejected world renunciation and monasticism, because in his view leaving the family behind to rely on other people's work creates violence itself. In accordance with his overall philosophy, he also did not share the Jain concern with the subtle physical violence accompanying every sexual act as a major argument for celibacy.[30] However, he recommended *brahmacarya,* because he regarded sexual desire as the greatest distraction from the concentration on the pure soul, the source of real happiness, particularly in this "sexy age," to use Nīrubahen's words, but also because it generates the willpower (*ātmaśakti*) that is necessary for the incessant application of *bhed jñān* in everyday life.

The Jain lay vow of *brahmacarya* demands the observation of a great number of ritualistic rules and regulations, such as observing fast-days (*poṣadha*) four times a month and not eating at night (*rātri bhojana tyāga*), although permitting work and other aspects of householder life.[31] From the point of view of A.M. Paṭel, observing such vows and fasts may be helpful, but is not necessary. In his opinion, asceticism (*tapasyā*) cannot destroy *karman*, which can only come to fruition naturally.[32] Only the stoppage (*saṃvara*) of the influx of new *karman* through non-attachment and the constant awareness of the pure self combined with the process of automatic fruition of the already accumulated *karman* can liberate. He rejected therefore all the physical exertions and ritualistic formulae associated with the Jain practice of *brahmacarya* and emphasised that, like Kṛṣṇa, ideally, a true *jñānī* practices *brahmacarya* spontaneously in his everyday life.[33]

A.M. Paṭel initiated nevertheless twenty-seven celibate male disciples (*brahmacārī*) which he called *āptaputras*, true spiritual sons of the one with the speech of truth (*āptavāṇī*). Later, an *āśram*, called *Saṃyamdhām*, abode of restraint, was constructed for the *āptaputra*s in Sīṅgod, some 40 km away from Surat. At present, ten *āptaputra*s who have vowed to practice celibacy for the rest of their lives live there to practise constant awareness of the soul. They are provided with all material necessities by the local *Āptaputra Trust* and undertake long journeys to the U.S.A., Canada, Great Britain, East Africa and Oceania (Fiji, New Zealand, Australia) to preach the teachings of the Dādā to their Gujarātī-speaking followers at *cāturmās*, the four month period of the traditional Jain monsoon retreat, during which most of the important religious festivals are celebrated.[34] However, during most of the year they continue to work in their chosen professions.[35] All of the presently twenty-two surviving *āptaputra*s were initiated by the Dādā in their early twenties. Another twelve *āptaputra*s which were initiated by A.M. Paṭel himself live with their families which have not yet given them permission to leave for the *āśram*. Some of the *āptaputra*s told me that in future no more *brahmacārī*s will be initiated, because only the Dādā was able to do that. These conceptions are obviously designed to enhance the status of the remaining *āptaputras* of A.M. Paṭel. But they also prevent Kanubhāī Paṭel from initiating his own celibate disciples.[36]

Nīrubahen Amīn, by contrast, initiated some thirty-five male and female *āptaputras* up to the year 2001. She permits them to take the vow of *brahmacarya* either lifelong or only for a limited period. Before the proper initiation of a lifelong *brahmacārīī* or *brahmacārinī* a five-year probation period is customarily observed. If someone comes to Nīrubahen and asks her to accept him or her as a lifelong *brahmacārī* or *brahmacārinī*, she will ask the individual first to attempt to live for five years "as if" being a *brahmacārī*. Only after the successful completion of the probation is the initiation conducted with a small informal ritual. The candidate first touches the feet of a statue of Sīmandhar Svāmī, then states the intention to become a *brahmacārī or brahmacārinī*, whereupon Nīrubahen utters several times "*śuddhātmā*," pure soul/self, and then transmits to the candidate her inner strength by silently reciting the secret *mantra* that was given to her by the Dādā and by blessing the freshly initiated candidate, who bows down to touch her feet. Formally initiated *brahmacārīs* of A.M. Paṭel and Nīrubahen give up tailored clothing and permanently wear a simple white cotton garment which is nowadays the only outward characteristic of a Akram Vijñān *brahmacārī*, white being the colour of purity. The *brahmacārinīs*, however, continue to wear normal clothes, as did the Dādā himself.

The first *brahmacārī* of Nīrubahen was Dipakbhāī Ghardas Desāī (born 1954), a softly-spoken textile engineer from Vavāniyā, the home town of Śrīmat Rājcandra, who was attracted to A.M. Paṭel's teachings in 1971 by Nīrubahen and "given the *jñān*" by "the Dādā" in 1977. Dipakbhāī became the first *āptaputra* initiated by Nīrubahen and is recognised as her dedicated successor "by the Dādā's word." It is said that in future he may become self-realised himself. He masters great influence amongst the predominantly male *brahmacārī* community which once resided in his apartment in Ahmedabad.

Most temporary *brahmacārīs* live a normal life with their families. However, the majority of the ca. thirty lifelong *āptaputras* and *āptaputrīs* have never married and lived "like a family" together with Dīpakbhāī Desāī and Nīrubahen Amīn in their apartments in Ahmedabad and Mumbaī. Recently, Nīrubahen's core following of celibate males and females has moved together into a new apartment block in Ahmedabad, which also houses a newly consecrated temple. All of them either work during the day, or live on the interest of their personal wealth to devote all their time to the propagation of the Dādā's message. There is no practice of begging alms or giving donations in order to accumulate merit in the Akram Vijñān Mārg. The *āptaputras* and *āptaputrīs* work for their own spiritual progress, by individually performing a number of religious practices based on idiosyncratic reinterpretations of Jain rituals such as the forty-eight minutes meditative introspection (*sāmāyika*) and the rite of repentance (*pratikramaṇa*), or they simply read the edited discourses of the Dādā alone or collectively after dinner for one to two hours (ca. 20.30-21.30). Their main religious exercise is, however, the attempt to maintain a constant awareness (*jāgrati*) of the soul for twenty-four hours a day, a practice which is also conceived as a form of internal asceticism (*bhāva tapas*).

In addition, they do "the Dādā's work" for the religious community as a whole by organising *śibirs*, which are informal meetings of ca. 1000 devotees that are held in the evenings from ca. 18.00-24.00 four or five times per month, where videos of A.M. Paṭel's discourses are shown and discussed, *satsaṅgas* or question-and-answer sessions, and *yātrās*, or pilgrimages, which are effectively sightseeing tours with Nīrubahen or Dīpakbhāī which allow their followers to bond with them. They also edit, transcribe and translate the Dādā's taped discourses for publication, publish the community journal *Dādāvāṇī*, organise communications, maintain websites and generally organise the infrastructure of the still rather informally organised community.

Apart from Nīrubahen, only seven *āptaputras* currently hold *satsaṅgs* on their own, and four to five work full time for the *Dādā Bhagvān Foundation Trust.* Because the parents of interested girls often do not allow their daughters to live a communal life "without protection," there are only seven *āptaputrīs* at the moment. Some of the *āptaputrīs* also left the group after one year to marry. The *āptaputrīs* supervise the cooking of the communal vegetarian meals by ca. thirty-five Brāhmiṇ girls, who do the menial work, and generally look after the communal household, which is also called religious service (*sevā*). The living arrangements are rather informal, although men and women live of course in different rooms, since the Akram Vijñān Mārg doesn't believe in rules and regulations, which "only create transgressions."

In 1999, the new *Mahāvideha Tīrthadhāma* in Ahmedabad became the main centre for communal living and worship. Similar '*āśrams*' exist today in five places: Vaḍodarā (4), Rājkoṭ, Surat, Valsaḍ and New Delhi. Other members of the cult also live temporarily together with the celibate disciples of Nīrubahen. The desire to be close to her and the ideal of a communal living currently inspires large building projects such as the enclosed Akram Vijñān Mārg compound of a Tri-Mandir temple (consecrated on the 29.12.2002), apartments and service facilities for communal living in Adalaj 18 miles north of Ahmedabad, called *Sīmandhar City*, which is under construction. It will be used not only by the *brahmacārīs* and pilgrims but also as retirement accommodation by expatriate Gujarātī *mahātmās* from America, Great Britain and East Africa. For financing this project a special *Sīmandhar Svāmī Ārādhanā Trust* has been established.

Mahātmā

Individuals who have been graced by the Dādā with the experience of the pure self (*śuddhātmā*) are called *mahātmās*. This experience is 'received' through the participation in the collective *jñān vidhi*, the ritual of knowledge, which is nowadays preceded by an initiation ritual, called *samarpaṇ*, or surrender. Anyone who is eighteen years of age, vegetarian, abstinent from alcohol, and who practises sexual continence (exclusive commitment to wife or husband) qualifies for the ritual transformation into a *mahātmā*, irrespective of sex, caste, race, nationality, or religion.[37] Since the Akram Vijñān movement emphasises its spiritual and non-institutional character, it rejects the term initiation (*dīkṣā*), which implies the existence of an organisation. Rather than establishing membership in an institution, the *jñān vidhi* aims at the spiritual transformation of the candidates from the state of ignorance to the state of intuitive knowledge of the true self. However, a closer look at the two crucial elements of the ritual as performed by Nīrubahen Amīn, the vow of surrender in the presence of a *jñānī* or his medium and the active participation in the subsequent *jñān vidhi*, show all the hallmarks of a classical initiation or conversion ritual. Nīrubahen Amīn says that without the formal vow of surrender, which is preceded by the enlistment of the name and address of the candidate, no spiritual energy and moral instruction can be transmitted and received, because it is predicated on the correct devotional attitude. Moreover, whoever has been initiated by Nīrubahen will lose the knowledge if he or she participates in the rite of Kanubhāī Paṭel and *vice versa*. The *samarpaṇ* ceremony is clearly regarded as the formal condition for the success of the rite and effectively functions as an initiation into a more or less exclusive cult community. Until the year 2001, Nīrubahen Amīn has initiated ca 50,000 *mahātmās* world-wide, 5000 in Britain alone. However, she concedes that "of course not all are practising, in Britain maybe 100-500."[38] The precise number of initiations performed by A.M. Paṭel and Kanubhāī Paṭel is not known.

The Ritual of Knowledge

The *jñān vidhi* can only be performed by *ātmājñānīs* or by a specially qualified medium such as Nīrubahen Amīn who has also been honoured with the title *ātmājñānī*. The rite in the present form is an expanded and formalised version of the first public performances of the ritual by A.M. Paṭel in 1968. Between 1970-1983 the initially unstructured ritual *séance* was rationalised and augmented through the incorporation of preparatory songs and prayers, composed by the poet Navnīt Paṭel from Bombay and by Nīrubahen Amīn, and by explanatory lectures. Today, the schematic structure of the entire ritual, in which I participated myself three times between 1997-1999,[39] involves four stages, including the registration of newcomers, the opening lecture, and a concluding communal meal, called *prasād*. The ritual of knowledge as such, the third stage, comprises again four parts, with the original *jñān vidhi*, here called *bhed jñān vidhi*, sandwiched between an extensive prelude followed by the initiation rituals (*samarpaṇa*), and the concluding explanation of the five basic precepts (*pāñca ājñā*) for the attainment of salvation to the new *mahātmās*. The structure of the ritual as a whole corresponds well to the famed tripartite analytical scheme of Hubert and Mauss (1898/1981) which inspired van Gennep and Turner: entry-consecration-exit, which is replicated within the middle section again. The key ritual, the *bhed jñān vidhi*, lasts about forty-eight minutes, or one *muhūrta*, while the entire ritual takes about four hours:[40]

A. registration of new candidates

B. lecture on the meaning and effect of the *jñān vidhi*

C. *jñān vidhi*: rite of knowledge
   1. prelude (ca. 10 minutes)
      a. everything of mine is surrendered (song)
      b. invitation to the Gods to come (song)
      c. invitation to the Dādā and Sīmandhar Svāmī to speak through Nīrubahen
      d. request to the Dādā for strength
   2. *samarpaṇ*: initiation of new candidates (ca. 20 minutes)
   3. *bhed jñān vidhi*: ritual separation of soul and body (48 minutes)
   4. *pāñc ājñā*: explanation of the five precepts (ca. 45 minutes)

D. *prasād*: communal meal

(A) Registration

The *jñān vidhi* is a collective public ritual for the transformation of newcomers into *mahātmās*, which can only be performed in the presence of an *ātmājñānī*. However, the entire congregation of local *mahātmās* following Nīrubahen Amīn (or Kanubhāī Paṭel: the two groups never mix) actively takes part in the ceremony. The underlying idea is that the more often a *mahātmā* participates in the ritual the stronger and longer-lasting will be its effects. For any local congregation, the visit of the *ātmājñānī* is rare, and the *jñān vidhi* is always a special event of his/her schedule (during each visit only one or two *jñān vidhis* are performed). The participation in the ritual is therefore seen as a unique chance to directly experience an intuitive insight into the inner pure soul.

The event usually takes place between 2-6 p.m. on a Saturday or Sunday and is advertised through e-mail lists, leaflets and small announcements in local Gujarātī newspapers. The venue is either a rented public hall or – if the congregation is small – a living room in the house of dedicated *mahātmās*. The hall is usually not decorated at all, except for an improvised shrine for the Dādā with a flower-rimmed photograph of A.M. Paṭel at the centre beneath a depiction of Sīmandhar Svāmī, flanked by images of Śiva and Kṛṣṇa. In front of this shrine, a small marble statue of Sīmandhar Svāmī is placed, usually on a table with a chair next to it; and on the left side, somewhat removed from the shrine, is a divan or a sofa chair covered with white cloth next to a microphone. In front of this ritual 'stage' separate seating areas are demarcated with sheets of white cloth for men on the right side and for women on the left side of the central passage to the shrine. Placed at the back of the room and along the walls are chairs for the elderly, and for officials and guests of honour.

The ritual infrastructure and the material arrangements of the ritual are prepared by the principal local male *mahātmās* who usually wear a plain white cotton dress on the day to indicate their special role. At the point of entering the hall or the house in which the ceremony is held, they request new candidates for initiation to write their name and address on a list which is later used to individually call them for the *samarpaṇ* ritual. This list represents the only documentary evidence of discipleship or membership and also functions as a mailing list. The majority of the participants of the *jñān vidhi* are *mahātmās* who have already undergone the initiation ceremony and do not need to repeat it. Many families with children attend and the atmosphere is informal, warm and welcoming and permeated by an egalitarian spirit. The only requirement for joining the congregation is the removal of the shoes. The ceremony is open to non-participating observers as well.

(B) Lecture

Nīrubahen Amīn conducts all her engagements with the support of her personal attendant Brahmacārī Dimple Maheta, an ex-stock broker from Mumbaī in his late 20s who serves her in the same way as she once served the Dādā A.M. Paṭel. Dimple orchestrates the ritual performance with a second microphone. Once the majority of the congregation has assembled he is the first to enter the stage to give a short lecture to the newcomers on the structure and the aim of the ritual.

At the outset, he explains that the rite as such consists of three parts: (1) the initiation of new candidates through the surrender (*samarpaṇ*) of all worldly possessions to "the Dādā," that is the pure soul; (2) the forty-eight minute long *bhed jñān vidhi,* a collective meditation on the qualities of the soul, wherein "the Dādā" says a sentence and everyone else repeats *unisono* what he said in order to generate the conscious or unconscious experience of the separateness of the pure soul from the body (*bhed jñān*) or right insight (*samyak darśan*); and (3) the explanation of the five precepts (*pāñc ājñā*) which, if applied correctly in everyday life, can lead to salvation at the feet of Sīmandhar Svāmī after only one more rebirth.

Dimple emphasises that, despite the enlisting of names and the ensuing vow of allegiance to Sīmadhar Svāmī, the rite is not an initiation – not even a ritual – because the Dādā did not crave for disciples nor for the creation of a cult, but simply offered his assistance for the evocation of the immediate experience of the soul in everyone through the direct transmission of his unique spiritual energy.[41] It is a necessary precondition that those who desire to be graced with *samyak darśan* by him have to assume an attitude of devotion to him and Sīmandhar Svāmī and surrender all worldly attachments.

After the short overview of the structure of the rite, Dimple indicates the page numbers of the texts which will be recited during the first part of the ritual from a small booklet with the title *Caraṇ Vidhi*, foot worship, which had been distributed among the congregation. This booklet is the main ritual manual of the Akram Vijñān movement and owned by every dedicated follower. It contains a collection of ritual texts, such as the '*Jñān Sākṣātkār' Pāmelāo Māṭenī Niścay-Vyavahār Caraṇ Vidhi*, the Real-Relative Worship of the Feet (of the Dādā) for obtaining a 'Clear Vision of the Knowledge,' which gave the compilation its name.[42] The exact words of this text in particular should be recited daily by all *mahātmās* as a means of concentration on the pure self.

Parts of the text, called *Ātmā Sāmāyik*, are also recited by the medium Nīrubahen Amīn in the crucial *bhed jñān* section of the *jñān vidhi* during which she utters isolated sentences or whole sections of the text which the assembly then repeats *unisono*. The selection, sequence and number of sentences vary from performance to performance. However, almost all sentences can be found in the *Jñān Sākṣātkār* text, and certain sections at the beginning and the end are usually recited entirely as printed in the book. The text is never recited exactly in its printed form, because the words of Nīrubahen Amīn are supposed to come directly from "the Dādā" and not from a book. Dimple Mahetā sometimes points out in his introductory lecture that, in order to safeguard the immediacy of the experience, the *jñān vidhi* itself should not be taped nor photographed, in contrast to the *satsaṅgs*, the congregational question-and-answer sessions for the discursive clarification of doubts, which are nowadays always filmed on video. Regular participants of the *jñān vidhi* are familiar with most of the sentences they encounter during the *bhed jñān* ritual. But beginners find it difficult to remember everything they hear. The increasing familiarisation with the procedures and texts of the rituals is regarded as part of the long-term process of induction.

(C) Jñān Vidhi

The ritual proper is conducted by Nīrubahen Amīn herself, with support from Dimple. At some stage during Dimple's speech she suddenly appears without any formalities and climbs on her divan.[43] Often she is greeted by dedicated female devotees who bow to her feet and adorn her with flower garlands in order to receive her blessings.

Prelude

(1) The rite begins with the invocation of the Dādā and the Gods. The opening sequence has a fixed form. It consists of four elements: First, the congregation requests, through the collective chanting of devotional songs and *mantras*, the Gods to be present, and then invites the Dādā and Sīmandhar, who are invariably perceived as an inseparable unit, to reside in Nīrubahen and to speak through her and to transfer to everyone present the direct knowledge of the pure soul.

(a) First, the members of the congregation bow to A.M. Paṭel, the manifest supreme God, and announce their heartfelt desire to surrender all their worldly attachments and possession to the 'omniscient'[44] Dādā Bhagavān with the song *Sarvasva Amārūṁ Arpaṇ Che* - Everything of Mine is Surrendered:[45]

> Everything of mine is surrendered,
> surrendered to you almighty, to your holy feet;
> for spiritual bliss supreme bliss,
> as a devotee of this realised soul, to his holy feet.
> The shadowy illusions of mind, speech, and body,
> of internal actions, habitual actions, and material actions;
> accept these childlike delusions,
> allow me to surrender this battlefield of life
> to none other but you.
> Everything of mine is surrendered.

The pearls of the nectar of knowledge,
are picked by the swan in the lake of pride;
in the light of this 'divine eye,'
of truth, bliss, and beauty.
Everything of mine is surrendered.

What an offering of the sun this is!
In the cool rays of the moon;
with a 'balanced mind' dispose of,
the conflicts arising within.
Everything of mine is surrendered.

Day and night, dawn and dusk,
how wonderful is their regularity!
The ebb and tide of the ocean of the mind,
is determined by 'natural law' and 'order.'
Everything of mine is surrendered.

Let life be one 'vision,'
but the 'soul' is the eternal mirror;
'transactions' may be with millions,
but 'absolute determination' be only in the almighty.
Everything of mine is surrendered.

For the liberation of the 'unenlightened soul,' the 'pure soul' is awakened;
extraordinary, 'beyond the reach of the senses'
and full of joy,
bright light in body and mind.
Everything of mine is surrendered.

Who opens the gate of liberation,
'the path of immediate understanding' never seen before;
O realised supreme soul in visible form,
'you' are my 'pure soul.'
Everything of mine is surrendered.

The song recalls the basic principles of the Akram Vijñān doctrine and expresses the longing of the worshippers to identify with the manifest self-realised soul of A.M. Paṭel.

(b) Now the Gods, that is the twenty-four Jain tīrthaṅkaras, are invited to come and to listen to the Omniscient one with the song *Devone Āvāhan* - Invitation to the Gods to come:

There is darkness of a million years, but it will disperse in a moment of sixty seconds, this insoluble unbreakable knowledge, will reveal itself in the form of light. Thirty-three million Goddesses and Gods,[46] will come for peace, for the equanimity of the pure soul, which the extraordinary "knower" will bring.

To the voice of 'Dādā Bhagavān,' the Tīrthaṅkaras are listening, at the holy feet of the Omniscient, the soul will find peace. I am surrounded by the flames of the forest fire, the whole universe is ablaze, an underground spring full of compassion, sprinkles cool water. The nectar-like speech of Bhagavān, will extinguish (the fire) by becoming cool water, the perfect twenty-four all together, 'truth, consciousness and bliss' is 'that' knower. Oṃ hṛṃ I go to the omniscient Dādā Bhagavān to take refuge.

These words are not really sung but recited in a peculiar sing-song which stretches each word and puts great emphasis on certain words by rising pitch, volume and melody. The words *devī-devatā*, or gods and goddesses, are chanted particularly loud and at a high pitch, and the singing is performed deliberately off-key. It is at this moment that Nīrubahen, who participates in the incantations of the first song with her hands folded, begins to turn inward and to recite a special *mantra*, only known to her, while looking around in a slightly agitated way. When the words *devī-devatā* are mentioned, she holds her folded hands up and, for a short moment only, moves them in a dance-like circular motion over her head, a very slow controlled expression of ecstasy, while occasionally rolling her eyes until a single hiccup invariably indicates that a connection has been established. The following Sanskrit *mantra* is then collectively recited several times:

"Oṃ hṛṃ Dādā bhagavān sarvajña śaraṇaṃ gacchāmi."

"*Oṃ hṛṃ*, I go to the omniscient Dādā Bhagavān to take refuge."

(c) After the two opening songs, both the Dādā and Sīmandhar Svāmī are requested by Nīrubahen and the congregation together to come and to reside in Nīrubahen, by reciting the following sentence once:

he dādā bhagavān, he śrī sīmandhar svāmī prabhu, āp ahīṁ padhāro, nīrū bolnā kaṇṭhe virājo. āp bolāvo ane hamo badhā bolīśuṁ.

> O Dādā Bhagavān, O Śrī Sīmandhar Svāmī Lord, come here and place your voice in Nīru's throat. You cause us to speak and we will all speak.

The Dādā is now assumed to be present within Nīrubahen. However, outwardly Nīrubahen acts normal, and no-one could tell that she is, or acts, at this very moment, as a medium of the Dādā, the incarnate pure self-realised soul.

In many ways, the invocation of the Dādā is the most crucial element of the entire ritual because without his presence it is bound to be ineffective. The use of the word Nīru instead of the respectful Nīrubahen indicates that, in the first place, Nīrubahen herself invites Sīmandhar Svāmī and the Dādā to manifest themselves within her. The capacity of the medium Nīrubahen to become temporarily 'possessed' by the Dādā, or rather of becoming his incarnation (*avatāra*), and thus endowed with his energy,[47] is said to be predicated on her knowledge of a secret *mantra* which A.M. Paṭel gave her before he died. 'Dādā' Kanubhāī Paṭel, on the other hand, claims to be a *jñānī* in his own right.

(d) The opening phase of the rite of knowledge terminates with the collective request to the Dādā to evoke the direct experience of the soul in everyone present and to give the strength to all *mahātmās* to perpetually maintain the experiential state of being a pure soul. This request is expressed in form of a self-suggestive formula which is uttered several times, first by Nīrubahen herself, and then repeated with great vigour by the whole congregation:

> *huṁ niścay nirṇaythī keval śuddhātmā chuṁ.*
>
> With absolute resolve and determination I am only a pure soul.

The end of the prelude to the rite is marked by the twofold recitation of a long drawn out *oṃ* and consecutive shouts of "*jay saccidānand*" - "victory to truth, consciousness and bliss."

Surrender

(2) At this point, Dimple takes the candidate list and calls the neophytes up to dedicate themselves to the Dādā and Sīmandhar Svāmī formally in the presence of Nīrubahen, who now descends from her divan to place herself on the chair next to the small Sīmandhar Svāmī statue on the table in the centre of the room,

holding a copy of the list with the names of the new candidates for initiation. The candidates then form a queue and wait to be invited by Dimple to step up to the statue, either one after the other or in pairs. Nīrubahen sits now with folded hands next to the statue, sometimes rolling her eyes in a strange way to indicate that she is, at this moment, in direct spiritual contact with the Dādā and with Sīmandhar Svāmī. While the rest of the congregation chants devotional songs with hands folded, the first one or two candidates step to the statue, take off their glasses if they wear any (the contact with the *jñānī* should be non-mediated), and decorate the statue with flowers, or necklaces, which are at hand. Then they bow to Sīmandhar with folded hands and put their heads on the table. Ideally, the closed eyes of the initiate should touch the toe of Sīmandhar to enable the direct transmission of his knowledge-revealing power. However, to facilitate the procedures, this practice is omitted. Nīrubahen and her attendant only make sure that the heads of the candidates firmly touch the tabletop. Often they press the candidates' heads down with their hands. Then the text of the *samarpaṇ,* or self-offering, dedicated to the Dādā and Sīmandhar, is read out by the *āptaputra* in a business-like tone and repeated, sentence by sentence, by the candidates. Nīrubahen looks on, smilingly, with folded hands, making sure, that the direct link to Sīmandhar is maintained:

> O Dādā Bhagvān, O Śrī Sīmandhar Svāmī Lord![48] Whatever I _________ [insert your name] call mine, my thought, speech, and body, is all illusion (māyā) [I am a pure soul].
>
> I surrender all my inner actions, outward actions, and reflex actions[49] at your holy feet, you are the revealed God in the form of the supreme soul.

After repeating these words, which are sometimes recited in English if the candidate does not speak Gujarātī, each neophyte receives a rose with a very strong scent. With the rose in the hands he or she returns to the floor and sits with eyes closed, silently repeating "*śuddhātmā, śuddhātmā* ...," "pure self, pure self ..."

The initiations are witnessed by the whole congregation which participates in the ceremony by singing devotional songs. Already initiated *mahātmās* are instructed to silently repeat the dedication themselves to reconfirm their commitment. The ritualised public surrender represents obviously not just a form of inner devotion, but also a formal initiation into the cult of the Dādā, despite all exclamations to the contrary by Nīrubahen and Kanubhāī. The most obvious proof of this evident fact is the list of addresses, which effectively functions as a membership list, and enables the leaders of the community to circulate leaflets and e-mails with updates on the travels of Nīrubahen Amīn and her dedicated successor Dīpakbhāī Desāī.

Knowledge of Separation

(3) The main part of the *jñān vidhi*, the induction of the experience of the distinctness of soul and body (*bheda jñāna*), now begins. While Nīrubahen climbs back on her divan, Dimple explains that the following main part of the ritual, the forty-eight-minutes-long *bhed jñān* ritual is a 'scientific experiment' that is conceived as an attempt to separate body and soul in the experience of the participants, and to empower them to directly realise their own self with the help of the spiritual energy of the Dādā which is transmitted through his words, which have to be repeated exactly in the same way as they are uttered. Dimple stresses the crucial importance of non-mediated experience for the success of the experiment. Any interference by the intellect will preclude the mind from the requisite emotional experience 'of the heart' which is the real key to religious understanding. In this respect, the *bhed jñān vidhi* consciously departs from all other, officially less important, parts of the *jñān vidhi*, especially from the framing lectures, which emphasise the significance of cognitive understanding of the meaning of the ritual and of the complex Jain, Vaiṣṇava and to a lesser extent Śaivaite philosophical terminology employed therein, which not everyone will immediately understand.

Paradoxically, it is emphasised by the Akram Vijñān movement that the Dādā's 'pure speech,' i.e. words charged with spiritual energy which should be repeated but not reflected upon, should always be in his native Gujarātī; which automatically limits the circle of potential followers. This is somewhat awkward, because many young expatriate Gujarātīs in East Africa, Great Britain and the U.S.A. understand English better than Gujarātī. This is another reason why emotional understanding is privileged over cognitive understanding. However, the official explanations of the meaning of the ritual before and after the *bhed jñān vidhi* are given - according to the audience - either in Gujarātī, Hindī, or English.

Social Anthropologists such as Victor Turner (1986) emphasised that the experiences of others can only be understood through their expressions.[50] A.M. Paṭel similarly stressed that transcendental experience is only transmittable from one person to another through language. However, he argued that only the 'pure language' of the Unattached One (*vītarāgī*) can function as a medium for the transmission of the subtle emotions and energies that are required for the realisation of direct insight (*saṃjñā*) without the interference of the intellect, not the conventional 'relative language' of everyday life. Not the communication of symbolic meanings, but the transmission of living energy produces the intended transformation.[51] However, to create the effect of insight, the structure of the *jñān vidhi* systematically combines songs and repetitions of suggestive phrases with reflective discourse, and alternates between 'relative language' and 'transcendental language' and the corresponding 'absolute point of view' (*niścaya naya*) and 'relative point of view' (*vyavahāra naya*).[52] It can be analysed as a ritual which transforms the amorphous lived experience (*Erlebnis*) of the participants of the *bhed jñān vidhi* into a reflected experience (*Erfahrung*), that is in an object of conscious reflection and self-interpretation in the light of the presented teachings of A.M. Paṭel.[53] The *bhed jñān* ritual can, if at all, only be effective if it is embedded in a context of framed antecedent preconceptions and subsequent reflections. It is merely the central or liminal phase of the *bhed jñān vidhi*, where the Dādā by speaking directly through Nīrubahen 'transmits his knowledge' and graces all those in the congregation who resolved to surrender their worldly existence to the inner God, with the awakening of the experiential knowledge of the self. The psychological precondition for the perceived efficacy of this rite is the attitude of surrender and the assumption of an undisturbed steady state of equanimity (*sāmāyika*), open for a direct inner experience, not mediated by the intellect or by written words. Some effects of relaxation are already produced through the twenty minutes of chanting during the *samarpaṇ* rite. Others are produced through the participation in the performance itself.

At the beginning of the forty-eight minutes long *bhed jñān* ritual Nīrubahen asks the participants to close their eyes and to repeat, as good as they can, what will be said without attempting to understand its meaning: "the meaning is not important, no intellect should become between the words of the Dādā and the receptive souls of the congregation." Then she closes her eyes and suddenly begins to raise her voice, saying: "*huṁ śuddhātmā chuṁ*" – "I am a pure soul." The whole congregation repeats: "*huṁ śuddhātmā chuṁ*" – "I am a pure soul. "After a few repetitions of the same sentence, which often marks the beginning of the *bhed jñān* ritual, she switches to another, similar sentence, such as: "*huṁ param jyoti svarūp siddha bhagavān chuṁ*" – "I am the supreme light, the self-realised Lord," and so on. Although most sentences can be found in the *Ātmā Sāmāyik* text of the ritual manual *Caraṇ Vidhi*, the sequencing of these sentences is different at every occasion, and while some sentences of this text are not uttered at all, new sentences are included. Many of the sentences that are not printed in the ritual manual contain the suggestion of being liberated from one's sins (*pāpa*), and particularly from the obstinate *mohanīya karmans*, the delusion-inducing *karmans*, which, according to Jain doctrine, prevent the true perception of reality and the soul. Most sentences are shouted out more than once by Nīrubahen, who uses a microphone, to be repeated in exactly the same way by the congregation. The entire forty-eight minutes long *séance* consists of a frenetic dialogic repetition of such auto-suggestive utterances.

The intensity of Nīrubahen's delivery varies. The pitch, volume, speed, rhythm, and melody of her manner of speaking are imitated by the congregation. Most sentences are pronounced in an unusual way and often shouted in a fast, hypnotic rhythm which leaves little time for taking breath or thought. This exhaustive technique induces hyperventilation and heavy breathing, which on its own can lead to experiences of relaxation. Some elderly devotees invariably fall asleep. Dimple Mahetā, who does not participate in the rite himself, therefore regularly patrols between the rows of the devotees and scans the congregation with his eyes to make sure that everyone has the eyes closed and that no one is asleep. Sometimes he wakes someone up or orders others to close their eyes.

The rapid and often changing rhythms and noise levels create what Lévi-Strauss (1982 I: 31) would call a 'pure physiological time of hearing.' They destroy the awareness of both diachronic time and of discernible semantic meaning by forcing the participants, on one level, to concentrate only on their breathing and the proper mechanical repetition of the phrases in an extended present, while, at the same time, stimulating the self to observe itself observing the ritual mechanics from the outside.[54] After a while, the utterances of the language of truth (*āptavāṇī*) which supposedly 'communicate' the experience of direct insight (*samyaktva*)[55] are not perceived as semantically meaningful elements anymore but as *mantra*-like vehicles of meditation.[56] In fact, the word *mantra* is used for certain phrases by Nīrubahen Amīn herself, although the sequential changes of her delivery do not conform to the formulaic format of *mantras*.[57] Maybe the best comparison is with the experience of music[58] which, in the words of Lévi-Strauss (1982 I: 31, 51), is coexistent with the emotive function and 'transcends the dimension of the articulate language.' This is here achieved not through the regression to the phonemic dimension of language but through the meta-linguistic perception of morphemes, units of signification, as phonemes,[59] that is as intrinsically non-significant (but not arbitrary) elements of transcendental ritual communication, which Frits Staal (1993: 267) called "language used in a pre-language fashion."[60]

In the case of Nīrubahen, the pre-linguistic use of language is predicated on a deliberate state of possession. Dumont (1980: 270) highlighted the "importance of institutionalized possession of a man by a god (or several gods)" in popular Hinduism, and in *bhakti* religiosity in particular, where he observes the phenomenon of *entasis*:

> It is true that 'meditation' also recalls the ritual identification of the priest with the god ..., and also that the *bhakta* does not prophesy as does the possessed. Yet it remains that both possession, a functional feature of folk religion, and *bhakti*, a characteristic of many sects, rest upon a common psychological condition, and that bhakti takes up in more or less sublimated form an aspect of common religion ignored by Brahmanic orthodoxy. We must remember that possession by a god is in popular religion one of the circumstances in which the divine resolves itself into an individuality. Even though it underwent a thorough intellectual elaboration, identification with a god was given in immediate experience (p. 283f.).

During the entire *bhed jñān vidhi* Nīrubahen speaks with the voice of the Dādā, which outwardly manifests itself in the strange oscillation of the pitch in her voice. It is said that she does not know where she is at the time, but she would not confirm this herself, but merely say that the Dādā is always with her. Nīrubahen admits that it is difficult to maintain the experience of being a pure soul continuously for forty-eight minutes, and that the Dādā does not always directly speak through her during the entire rite. She says, sometimes he comes only for a few moments, but this is enough. Nīrubahen says she is only an instrument (*nimitta*). The words she utters are the actual words of the Dādā, who speaks through her.

These very words were apparently heard for the first time by A.M. Paṭel during his enlightenment experience. They are the words of the pure soul whose effect cannot be explained but only experienced. However, it is the power transmitted by these words, not the words themselves, through which the knowledge of separation (*bhed jñān*) is mysteriously transferred to the initiates.[61] It is said that many have tried to perform the *jñān vidhi* themselves, by memorising and repeating the phrases that were recurrently used by the Dādā and Nīrubahen, yet they remained unsuccessful, because the authoritative power (*śakti*) is missing, which only a person who has already experienced the *jñān* itself can have.[62] According to Jaina and Saṁkhyā-inspired interpretations, all speech is "totally material," that is a manifestation of *karman*. However, the speech of the Dādā is special because it is the unattached speech (*vitarāga vāṇī*) of a self-realised pure soul: "our speech articulates after touching the conscious-manifested (chetan-pragat) paramatman and therefore it is spiritual (living)," "Our speech is real and living Saraswati. It burns to ashes others' sins of infinite (cycles of) births. Our speech is absolutely free from attachment" (A.M. Paṭel, in Shah 1983: 71).

Though many *mahātmās* insist that it is Sīmandhar himself who speaks through the Dādā and now through Nīrubahen, the doctrinally-trained *brahmacārīs* insist that it is not Sīmandhar who speaks, but that he is only present through our belief, devotion, and surrender. However, they all assume that it was possible for the Dādā to communicate with Sīmandhar through a subtle body (*sukṣma śarīra*), technically called conveyance body (*āhāraka śarīra*),[63] which he detached from his body in his dreams to ask questions, sometimes returning with surprising answers.

The last part of the rite is fixed and the wording of the final section identical with the last section of the published *Ātmā Sāmāyik* text:

> O universally adored and fully manifested śuddhātmā Bhagavān! Let your enlightened congregation constantly dwell in me (repeated 3x). Let your enlightened right knowledge keep me aware of the

> pure self at every moment (3x). Instil in my heart the knowledge that all gross circumstances, subtle circumstances, and circumstances of speech, are (separate from me and) dependent on external factors. Give me the strength not to interfere or quarrel (with the natural order of things) (3x). Give me the strength to perform only observation (3x). I only desire your grace (3x). Let your lotus feet dwell in my heart (3x). I am a pure soul (25x). With absolute resolve and determination I am only a pure soul! (2x). Victory to truth, consciousness and bliss (5x).

The repeated collective shouts of "*huṁ śuddhātmā chuṁ*" - "I am a pure soul" - and "*jay saccidānand*" - "Victory to truth, consciousness and bliss" - which mark the end of the rite of separation are followed by the extremely slow, trance-like recitation of the words: "'*huṁ Vijñān svarūp chuṁ*" - "I am by nature pure experiential knowledge," which formally state that the aim of the rite - the transmission of the knowledge - has now been achieved. After the subsequent recitation of the *Tri-mantra* - the Akram Vijñān version of the Jain *Namaskāra Mantra* with additional references to Kṛṣṇa and Śiva and the phrase *jay saccidānand* - the whole congregation ecstatically chants the words "*Dādā bhagavānanā asīm jay jaykār ho*" - "Infinite glory to Dādā Bhagavān" - which are also said to destroy sins - faster and faster, and the last time very slowly, for up to ten minutes. This is the devotional praise (*kīrtan bhakti*) of the now 'directly accessible supreme self' (*pratyakṣa paramātmā*) (A.M. Paṭel, in R.M. Paṭel 1994: 77): "When one sings it for a minimum of eight minutes onwards and an optimum of forty-eight minutes, one starts feeling a taste of nectarlike happiness within. It heals old wounds of insults, assaults and sorrows of the worldly life. By doing it layers around the pure soul get destroyed" (Shah 1995: 45).

'Actual experience'

Some people get quite agitated during the forty-eight minutes of meditative shouting. Some ecstatically shake their upper bodies. Others fall into a kind of trance with a strong tendency to fall asleep. I asked about fifty participants at various performances about their experiences during and after the rite. Everyone said that it is difficult to describe the feelings experienced during 'the separation.' Most respondents, even stern believers, told me that - apart from physical exhaustion caused by the intense shouting - they felt, like myself, 'nothing' or 'absolutely nothing.' An educated Jain sceptic told me, he experienced the rite as a form of 'brainwashing.' Some people said, they experienced relaxation; some, that they perceived lights; others, that the Dādā actually appeared and spoke to them; or, generally, that they vaguely perceive things differently afterwards. One man in his thirties told me: "I felt as if I was floating, forgetting everything, thoughts, worries about money, relatives, etc." He also felt empowered by the transfer of the Dādā's energy through the rite: "When she says '*śakti*'," he said, "then inspiring energy is released for whatever you do." Another man of similar age said, he felt absolutely nothing during the process, but for two or three days afterwards he felt incredibly light, and was truly able to see the pure soul in everyone. Most respondents confessed their ignorance, and merely repeated what Nīrubahen has said: "Don't listen to the words [that are uttered during the course of the ritual]. Their meaning is not intelligible at first, but understanding will develop later, with more practice. No miracle happens [during the rite]."

Several explanations are readily offered by the participants for discrepancies between the promised insight into the true nature of reality and actual experience. Most explanations cite the doctrine of *karman* and of the hierarchy of karmically-inherited sensibilities as the cause of different experiences. The three reasons that were quoted most often to me were: (1) Differential karmic constitution: people that are born with good *karman*, are more likely to consciously experience the effect of Dādā's transmission of energy.[64] (2) Failed performance: the words have not been accurately repeated, or/ and the required inner devotional attitude was not realised. (3) Latent efficacy: even those who are not consciously aware of any experience have unconsciously gained the benefit of the separation and will realise its effects later in their life.[65] Whatever their individual experience was, all participants were acutely aware of A.M. Paṭel's promise that whoever performs the rite secures for him/herself the possibility of salvation within not more than two more lives. Even those who were sceptical about the doctrine of the Akram Vijñān movement wanted to make sure that they don't miss out and took advantage of this opportunity as part of their spiritual insurance policy.

The discourse on the presumed effects of the *jñān vidhi* is an important part of the religious culture of the Akram Vijñān movement. The individual self-exploration of the promised changes in the days and weeks after the ritual and the mutual communication and interactive validation of (usually affirmative) self-observations produces a self-confirming discourse amongst the believers which forms the bedrock of the religious movement. It is based on the preliminary acceptance of the premise that participation in the ritual indeed produces conscious or unconscious effects. An interesting, evidently well rehearsed, written account is available from Juan C. Garcia from Spain, now a committed devotee, who participated in a *jñān vidhi* in London in May 2002, following the suggestion of an internet contact. He reports that he experienced tremendous perceptual changes afterwards, although he could not understand a word of what was said in the 'Hindu' congregation. He was, however, offered a short version of the *vidhi* in English during a one-to-one encounter with Nīrubahen immediately after the public programme:

> In the beginning I didn't feel anything special not to mention the normal feeling of relaxation after one hour meditation (with closed eyes). I took the underground back to my hotel and when coming out of the station I started to feel a sort of an unexpected euphoria and joy coming from within. It was no longer a feeling of relaxation due to meditation. I started to think that may be it could work for me. On the way to the hotel I noticed that my whole awareness of space and time was being changed, not being changed but more like being destroyed. It was the first time in my life that I was no longer sure that "that" called "Juan" which was walking in the hotel was me. This time it was not at all a play of intellectual concepts borrowed from somebody else, it was a real experience happening within me. ... Even sleeping I felt the touch of this Bliss which seemed to sprout from the heart area. It was as if my heart was full of light spreading this light all around me. I noticed that even my thoughts were no longer so important and that they took the form of visualisations which I could observe before [they were] effecting me at all. ... When I looked at my hands I could observe them as being separated from my real "I." The same happened with the thoughts, and with all this "doll" called Juan was doing. You could even observe your words as coming out of your mouth automatically (Garcia 2002).

Similar self-conscious, rationalised experiences are expressed more informally in the form of oral autobiographical narratives that are at various occasions shared and discussed by *mahātmās* in the light of the doctrines of A.M. Paṭel. These are learned, step-by-step, through the repeated contact with Nīrubahen (or Kanu Paṭel) and their *brahmacārīs*, and by reading the published transcriptions of the oral discourses of A.M. Paṭel.[66] The collectively-shared esoteric experience of receiving the *jñān*, real or putative, and the accepting egalitarian atmosphere of the community clearly lift the spirits of the *mahātmās* and trigger their magico-religious imagination, as the following narrative of a dream experience by S. Paṭel, an approximately fifty-five year old man from Gujarāt who lives London, illustrates:

> A couple of weeks ago I had a dream that I was travelling to Sīmandhar Svāmī in Mahāvideha Kṣetra together with the Dādā. There I was sitting at the giant feet of Sīmandhar. He was huge, dressed with a crown and sitting cross-legged, just like the statue in Ahmedabad. After a while, Sīmandhar slaps my front once with his fingers just like this [he hits me gently on my front to demonstrate what he felt] and I instantly gained *kevaljñān* (omniscience). The feeling was indescribable and I cannot put it into words, since I also cannot remember everything. But the dream experience is still very vivid with me. For three days afterwards I felt extremely good. Of course, this was just a dream. I have certainly not gained omniscience. But only few people have such dreams."[67]

In order to underline the last point he told me about a similar dream soon thereafter:

> Later, I dreamt I was again at the feet of Sīmandhar Svāmī together with Nīrumā. I asked him when Nīrumā was to become omniscient. Sīmandhar answered that she will not yet receive omniscience since Sīmandhar wants her first to continue her religious work in Bhāratkṣetra.

He said, he discussed this dream with Nīrumā and she said that he must have had an experience of *jātismaraṇjñān* that is he was experiencing an event that happened in a previous life. In this way, she put his claim to be able to communicate with Sīmandhara directly (which would be the next step in doctrinal evolution) into perspective, by implicitly contrasting it with the well-known belief that only A.M. Paṭel had the unique capability of contacting Sīmandhar Svāmī in this life.[68] That the message from Sīmandhar was nevertheless correct was evidently the case because she had the Dādā's assurance that she would ascent to Mahāvideha after this life and gain omniscience.

The mutual reinforcement of belief within the hothouse of the closely monitored cultic atmosphere surrounding Nīrubahen Amīn and similarly Kanu Paṭel is achieved through narratives such as this which contribute to a discourse of mutual recognition of charismatically qualified individuals with extraordinary religious experiences. Through the catalyst of Nīrubahen and her entourage of *āptaputras* the most unlikely claims can gain acceptability if they accord with the doctrines of the movement. Nīrubahen Amīn, whose opinion is, qua status, always more respected than others, effectively exercises a monopoly of interpretation. Her recognition of narrated experiential claims can officially validate the reported magico-religious messages that are received in dreams and visions. This two-step procedure corresponds well to the pattern of transmission of charisma through a *guru* which is superimposed upon the initial processes of interactive validation of religious charisma between institutionally unconstrained individuals who meet as equals.[69]

Five precepts

(4) The main part of the rite has now been completed. The experience of the separation, which nominally transforms every devotee into a *mahātmā*, that is someone who has received the *jñān* directly from the Dādā, has been imparted to the congregation. What remains to be answered is the question how to live a religious life leading to salvation without renouncing the world. One of the main attractions of the stepless path is that the *mahātmā*s continue to live a normal householder life without being asked to renounce anything. Although their self-perception should have changed, outwardly they remain indistinguishable from anyone else. Only during religious ceremonies some male *mahātmā*s, usually the local community leaders, distinguish themselves from the rest of the congregation by wearing the same white clothes as the *brahmacārī*s to indicate their dedication. When *mahātmā*s meet or talk on the phone they also recognise each other by saying "*jay saccidānand*," just as Vaiṣṇavaites say "*jay śrī kṛṣṇa*" and traditional Jains "*jay jinendra.*"

The mere participation in the rite itself does, of course, not secure final *mokṣa*. But it is believed that by creating the condition of a non-attached way of life it offers the real possibility of achieving so-called living *mokṣa*, or *jīvanmukti*, and the prospect of being reborn at the feet of the currently living *tīrthaṅkara* Sīmandhara Svāmī in Mahāvideha Kṣetra within no more than one or two lifetimes. According to Jain doctrine, everyone has the opportunity of being enlightened in the presence of a living *tīrthaṅkara,* a process called *buddha-bodhita* that is attributed to his/her[70] great compassion, and to achieve liberation thereafter. The question is how to get to Mahāvideha Kṣetra? Classical Jainism teaches that a better rebirth can only be secured by reducing the *karmic* burden of an individuaL.A.M. Paṭel and his successors agree with this, but have a different opinion about the way in which this is achieved. Not asceticism or devotion, but the application of spiritual knowledge and passionlessness in everyday life is the key. In this respect the soteriology of the Akram Vijñān differs from the Vaiṣṇava approach.

A.M. Paṭel has made the importance of the role of self-effort, sandwiched between the initial gift of *bhed jñān* by the grace of the *jñānī* and the final gift of *sarvajñān* by the grace of Sīmandhar Svāmī, explicit in the following statement:

> First I destroy all your blunders because by yourself it is impossible for you. How do I do it? By placing my hand on your head and letting Bhagawan (Dada Bhagawan the Lord of the 14 worlds) give his divine grace (kripa). There after, you need to remove your mistakes yourself. You will be able to see your own mistakes. Daily you will be able to see 5, 50 or 100 faults of your own and thus these mistakes will go on their own. Your realization of your self will increase as your mistakes (faults) decrease" (A.M. Paṭel, in Amīn 1994: 34).

In order to provide an easy answer to the question of how to remove one's own mistakes, A.M. Paṭel drafted a list of five precepts (*pāñca ājñā*) which, if observed correctly in everyday life, would inevitably lead to salvation, ideally within only two rebirths. The precepts are explained immediately after the *bhed jñān* ritual. They are formulated in colloquial language, but their meaning is cryptic and unintelligible without supplementary explanations, which is not uncommon for mystical cultic milieus:[71]

1. From the 'relative' point of view 'I am Candulāl' (substitute 'Candulāl' with your own name).
2. From the 'real' point of view 'I am a pure soul.'
3. This world is ruled by scientific circumstantial evidence.
4. Clear your files with equanimity.
5. Enter credit into the account book of the pure soul.

Do not look at the outer wrappings ('packing')[72] but look with divine sight at the pure soul.

These five precepts summarise the method of liberation propagated by the Akram Vijñān Mārg. They are not formally accepted like the five great vows (*mahāvrata*) of the Jain ascetics or the twelve vows (*barah vrata*) of the Jain laity in traditional Jainism, but serve as regulative ideals for those who wish to progress towards salvation, like the seven truths (*tattva*) of classical Jainism. Their meaning is explained in detail by Nīrubahen for up to an hour immediately after each *bhed jñān* performance. Strictly speaking, the *pāñc ājñās* are only revealed to initiated *mahātmās*,[73] but any bystander can eavesdrop on the public discourse as well.

The phrasing of these five precepts, which, if properly observed, are believed to lead to certain salvation, betrays the ethos of the Gujarātī business culture within which the Akram Vijñān Mārg thrives. They are composed in a popular language which an average Gujarātī businessman can easily identify with. Nevertheless, most of my informants, apart from Nīrubahen and the *āptaputras*, found it very difficult to explain what precisely is meant in particular by the enigmatic precepts 3 and 4.

Precepts 1-2

The first two precepts are self-explanatory: From a common sense perspective we appear to be differently named individual personalities, but from the ultimate point of view we are all pure souls. The name 'Candulāl' should be substituted by the name of anyone who tries to apply these precepts. 'Relative' and 'real point of view' is a translation of the philosophical distinction between *vyavahāra naya* and *niścaya naya*,[74] which may well have been introduced by Buddhist philosophers such as Nāgārjuna (ca. 2nd century CE) and then incorporated into Jainism by the Digambara Jain *ācārya* Kundakunda, who lived in Southern India sometime between the 1st and 8th century CE; though many Digambaras reverse the chronology, while the Śvetāmbaras point to the 'implicit' application of this distinction already in the canonical *Viyāhapannatti*. The soteriological use of the two-truth theory by A.M. Paṭel overlaps with the oppositions of *puruṣa* and *prakṛti*, soul and matter, essence and appearance, knower and devotee, observer and actor, etc. In practical terms, the aim is to perceive everyone as a pure soul, and not as a mortal individual with all its natural, or rather 'karmic,' deficiencies, which is one of the cardinal mistakes of the beginner. "If we see the *prakṛti* of others we have missed the five *ājñās*. So *ājñā*

1, 2 are very important. Irritation also means you have missed the *ājñās*" (Nīrubahen Amīn, lecture). Hence, one should only perceive one's own mistakes.[75]

Precept 3

The difficulty of rule three, "This world is ruled by scientific circumstantial evidence," is to understand the philosophical implications of the English expression 'scientific circumstantial evidence' which A.M. Paṭel often preferred to the original expression *niyamtā-vyavasthit śakti*, which can be translated as 'the power of natural law.' What is meant are the combined effects of nature and the law of *karman* that are signified by the term *prakṛti*.[76] The precept expresses the conviction that the experienced world is neither governed by human intentions, nor by the laws of physics, but by circumstantial combinations (*saṃyoga*) which emerge through the co-occurrence of *karmans* which come to fruition under certain conditions.[77] In other words, what happens to the individual during one life, its actions and thoughts, is happening as the unintended consequence of inherited dispositions which were acquired in previous lives. There is nothing one can do about this, since human intentions, let alone habits, feelings or the biological metabolism, are merely *karmic* effects: "Everything that happens to you is destiny! [*prārabdha*]."[78] From the perspective of the pure soul, human action and life in general appear as a series of events which unfold through the interaction of *karmic* dispositions, which can only be observed but not be influenced or controlled by the pure self, because it is entirely distinct from the material and mental world, as *puruṣa* is from *prakṛti*. In accordance with Sāṁkhya doctrine, A.M. Paṭel does not conceive the soul as active, as in classical Jainism,[79] but as inactive. Therefore, the only choice that is left is to switch from the perspective of the relative self to the perspective of the real self. Once the soul realises that it is not a doer, and does not identify with the actions of the body and mind, then the charge, or bondage, of new *karman* is stopped (*saṃvara*), and an improved rebirth in the next life ensured. According to A.M. Paṭel, *karman* never comes to fruition in the same life in which it was accumulated:[80] "Everything you do in this life won't change your present life, but it will have a considerable effect in your next life. ... In the present life we are only the masters of charge [*pūraṇa*],[81] not discharge [*gālana*]."[82]

Precept 4

This leads to the next question: How shall we act?[83] This question is answered by precept four: "Clear your files with equanimity." The term 'file' is here used as a synonym for the different types of *karman* which are generated through the interaction of the relative self (*jīvātmā* or *pratiṣṭhit ātmā*)[84] with lifeless matter (*ajīva*).[85] The sum of an individual's *karmans* is pictured as a filing cabinet: file 1 contains the acts of the egotistic mind, file 2 relates to the body, file 3 to marriage, file 4 to neighbours, etc. In order to clear the files, the *karmans* have to realise themselves naturally, without any attempt of active intervention by the soul. This can be achieved by avoiding worldly presumptions and intentions (*saṅkalpa*) altogether in favour of the, ideally, permanent orientation towards the pure soul. The pure soul is not a doer, it is an observer. From the absolute point of view, actions should therefore be perceived as *karmic* results (or 'happenings around one-self') not as conditions for the fulfilment of a goal, that is from a retrospective point of view, not from a prospective point of view. Active interventions such as world renunciation, vow-taking, ritual observances, or fasting, as practised for instance by Jain mendicants, do not make much sense from the perspective of the pure soul, because they involve the relative self, the ego, and only create new attachments. For clearing their 'files' the followers of the Akram Vijñān Mārg do not need to change their life at all. It is not necessary for them to impose painful restrictions upon themselves or to follow rigid rules. They only need to perform a change of perspective or attitude towards the actions by assuming the passive and unattached stance of a pure observer towards anything that happens in the world. Everything else follows naturally, without coercion and self-torture. The pure self is not responsible for the actions of the ego if it merely observes its deeds with detachment and equanimity. In this way, it prevents the bondage of new *karmans* and at the same time discharges the *karmans* of all the actions which it merely observes without identifying with them: "there is no need to give up anything except your wrong beliefs."[86]

Precept 5

In the same way, past mistakes (*karman*) can be neutralised by the practice of *sāmāyik*, or meditation, and other methods of self-purification. Precept five says: "Enter credit in the account book of the pure soul." This means that spiritual 'credits' should be accumulated by stopping the influx of both *pāpa karman* and *puṇya karman* and by discharging the *karmans* that have already been accrued. Crucially, credits are not defined as *puṇya*, or good *karman*, but as the freedom from the effect of all types of *karman*. There are four basic methods of doing this: (a) applying the five precepts to all aspects of one's life,[87] (b) studying A.M. Paṭel's discourses, (c) visiting Nīrubahen Amīn's *satsaṅgs*, and (d) trying to minimise violence by recognising other living beings also as pure souls. All useful practical advice is said to be condensed in the only written religious text that A.M. Paṭel himself ever composed – the short *Nav Kalamo*, or Nine Laws – which, as stated in its subtitle, comprises 'the essence of all scriptures' and 'of all religion.'[88] The core message of this text – non-violence – has been adopted from Jainism and is summarised in the following 'golden rule':

> Try your best not to give any living being unhappiness. If you do (as a result of your previous lives), then ask for forgiveness immediately."[89]

If nevertheless *karman*-charging acts of violence occur, then rituals of purification should be performed immediately to destroy the fresh *karmans*. The Akram Vijñān teaches that, after receiving the *jñān*, the *mahātmās* can purify themselves from newly committed mistakes simply through confessing and repenting their misdeeds, and promising not to commit them again. Giving gifts (*dāna*), fasting (*tapasya*), worship (*pūjā*), and other traditional Jain rituals are explicitly rejected, since the Akram Vijñān movement believes that inherited *karman* can only be discarded by acting it out, while newly acquired *karman* can be dissolved immediately,[90] if recognised, through processes of meditative recollection *cum* repentance and apology 'to the pure self.'

Rites of repentance

Four ritual forms of 'apology,' of 'asking for forgiveness,' or 'saying sorry' (*kṣamā*) are recommended for the purification of the soul:

1. absolute-relative foot worship (*niścay-vyavahār caraṇ vidhi*)
2. prayer to the pure self (*śuddhātmā pratye prārthanā*)
3. repentance (*pratikramaṇ*)
4. rite of restoring equanimity (*sāmāyik pūrvenī vidhi*)

The first two of the four rituals, which cannot be analysed in detail here, the 'absolute-relative foot worship' and the 'prayer to the pure self,' are part of the recommended daily routine of worship. They are not considered to be obligatory, and are practised variably according to individual preference. The multi-purpose *niścay-vyavahār caraṇ vidhi*, or absolute-relative foot worship, consists of the recitation of the published *Ātmā Sāmāyik* text (the same text that provides the foundation of the *bhed jñān vidhi*) which should be performed daily for the purpose of 'remembering one's true self' and for 'asking the Dādā for forgiveness' for the fresh mistakes that were committed. The *śuddhātmā pratye prārthanā*, or prayer to the pure self, fulfils the same purpose.

The most common rite of purification is the third ritual, the *pratikramaṇa*, or repentance. It is not performed periodically in a ritualised form, as it is by traditional Jains, but immediately after recognising an error (*doṣa*) or as soon as possible thereafter in order to prevent the *karman* leaving a durable imprint on the soul. It consists of a simple formula, a 'divine apology,' that is modelled on the Jain *Sāmāyika Sūtra*, and of a subsequent ca. fifteen-minute-long meditation on the freshly committed mistakes. Interestingly, asking forgiveness (*kṣamā*) does not necessarily require the presence of an interlocutor, because *karman* can only be dissolved by the perpetrator itself.[91] It is enough to ask one's own pure soul for forgiveness, since "the good vibrations of one's own pure soul, once they are activated, automatically reach the other soul and clear the *karmas* from the mind of the injured person as well" (Nīrubahen Amīn, lecture). Wrongdoing can be confessed to one's self (*śuddhātmā*), to the person concerned, to the Dādā, to the Gods, to the assembly of the believers (*satsaṅga*), or to Nīrubahen. Sometimes a list with the names of the injured parties and the mistakes committed is drawn up on a piece of paper which is read out aloud first. Then the *pratikramaṇ* rite is performed, i.e. the mistakes are formally confessed, repented, and resolved to be never committed again.

The fourth ritual, the *sāmāyik*, is the preferred method of purification of the Akram Vijñān Mārg. The Jain term *sāmāyika* (Prakrit *sāmāiya*) is here used as a designation for the retrospective *anamnesis* and confession of all past acts of violence that can be remembered. The *sāmāyik* thus incorporates features of the traditional Jain rituals of confession (*ālocanā*) and repentance (*pratikramaṇa*). In contrast to the *pratikramaṇa* rites which are performed to cancel out short-term karmas, the *sāmāyika* procedure is used in the Akram Vijñān Mārg to cancel the effects of mistakes committed a long time back, as far as one can remember, and to restore former purity. It is therefore the functional equivalent of asceticism in traditional Jainism, since the Jain rites of atonement (*prāyaścitta*) are not performed as a matter of principle.[92] The *sāmāyik* is the most innovative purification ritual of the Akram Vijñān Mārg, because it demands from the *mahātmās* the concrete analysis and insight into their own behavioural patterns,[93] which should be remembered and observed from the point of view of the pure soul 'like a film,' rather than the formulaic recitation of schematic lists of mistakes (*aticāra*) in the traditional Jain *pratikramaṇ* ritual.[94] Traditional Jain laity practice *sāmāyik* either individually or collectively in the form of forty-eight-minute-long meditations during which they study religious texts (*svādhyāya*), perform repetitions (*japa*) of the *Namaskāra Mantra*, or other purifying practices. Usually, the followers of the Akram Vijñān Mārg perform the *sāmāyik* collectively, preferably in the presence of Nīrubahen or one of the *āptaputras*, though, in principle, the *sāmāyik* can be practised individually at any time.

The perceived effectiveness of the four purification 'rituals' (*vidhi*) is predicated on the prior acquisition of *samyak darśan* during the *bhed jñān vidhi*, and on the formal renunciation of the faults committed by the 'relative self' through self-confession (*ālocanā*), repentance (*pratikramaṇa*), the promise not to relapse (*pratyākhyāna*), and the request for forgiveness (*kṣamā*). It is stressed that not the ritual procedures purify, but the insight that the pure soul itself has not committed any mistake, only the *karmans* which came to fruition. Thus, the four methods of purification of the Akram Vijñān Mārg are all based on the identification of specific individual mistakes in terms of the Jain *karman* theory, and on the 'reviewing of the video' of these mistakes from the point of view of the pure self. The salient feature of this method is the insight into the illusory character of the common sense notion that 'I have done this.' That is, the key for the purification of the soul from sin is the understanding of the false notion of agency: "it is not the karmas that obstruct our liberation; it is our ignorance."[95] Only the direct intuitive realisation that it was not 'I' who has committed the mistakes, but the '*karmans*' that were accumulated in previous lives, can purify. 'I' was not the doer, but 'me.' As soon as the awareness of the pure soul emerges, the mind and the conscience are clear.

The dissolution of *karman* through repentance, in the wider sense, is thus predicated on a process of inner distanciation and objectification which Dumont (1980: 282) has called the internalisation of renunciation, and which A.M. Paṭel called self-knowledge. William Johnson (1995: 260) has characterised Kundakunda's[96] exposition of the philosophical bedrock of such techniques in the tradition of Digambara mysticism (as well as Vaiṣṇava and Śaiva philosophy) as follows: "it is not the physical objects which make up the *ajīva* world themselves which are to be renounced, but the attitude towards these objects."[97] The Self "does not have to do anything to renounce since, having no other states and being in contact with no other states, there is nothing to renounce" (ibid., p. 288f.), except the attitude of desire and identification with the ego.

Knowledge and Conduct

The pending question to what extent God's grace is evoked in the act of purification is interesting, since the rejection of this possibility is widely regarded as a main difference between Jainism and Hinduism.[98] In asking the Dādā for forgiveness the devotee is not assuming that A.M. Paṭel cleanses the soul by an act of pure grace, but by evoking the manifestation of the Dādā in his/her mind, the *mahātmā* can experience again his/her own self and systematically reduce the karmic load through the method outlined in the five *ājñās*. It is only the awareness that is was not "I" who has committed the mistakes but the discharge of my outer *karmic* fetters, the body-mind-speech complex called *prakṛti*, that can purify. In contrast to the 'Hindu' devotional traditions, it is believed that neither the god-like figures of Sīmandhar Svāmī nor the Dādā can purify. The Dādā can only give his knowledge and inspirational power to face one's own mistakes. Only the instantaneous awareness of one's real self can purify.[99]

Whereas principle four of the *pañc ājñā* resembles more or less the teaching of the *Bhagavadgītā*,[100] to remain unattached towards the fruits of one's actions, violent or non-violent, principle five implicitly refers to the Jain ethics of non-violence as the measure of good and bad actions. These ethical presuppositions are not always clearly expressed since the mystical philosophy of the pure soul has been put in the centre, but without them the movement could hardly be linked to Jainism, despite its orientation towards Sīmandhar Svāmī and the goal of *mokṣa*. The question is whether violent action can function as a form of discharge without the bondage of further *karman* if it is performed in a non-attached way, as recommended by the *Bhagavadgītā,* or not? If this is the case, then non-violence should not be a necessary condition of salvation.

A.M. Paṭel's answer is unanimous: non-violence is an absolute condition of salvation, because it is the only form of action which is not only an effect of *karman* but, inevitably, also the cause of new *karman*. Why this should be the case is not immediately transparent. It seems, A.M. Paṭel assumes that violent or injurious actions cannot merely be observed but involve necessarily a sense of agency which by definition causes the inflow of *karman,* whereas the mere observation of one's other forms of action from the outside causes the dissolution of *karman*: "To support the action with the belief 'I am the doer' is called binding the karma";[101] "If you relinquish the doership, you are free of karma."[102] In an attempt to clarify the issue, A.M. Paṭel distinguishes 'cause karma' and 'effect karma.' Interestingly, effect karma is usually discussed by him in terms of the suffering experienced due to the actions of others, and cause karma in terms of one's 'own' actions causing suffering in others.[103] Yet, in practice the line between effect karma and cause karma is difficult to draw, as the tape-recorded and transcribed discussions of the *satsaṅgs* of A.M. Paṭel show. After all, "Everything you encounter is your own design. Nobody else is responsible for it"; even the co-occurrence of one's own actions with the actions of others is karmically determined.[104] That is, the suffering experienced through the actions of others is interpreted as self-created. If someone is inflicting pain on you, then for you the other is merely acting as the instrument of your own *karman* (apart from his/her own). The golden rule is that "The fault lies within the one who suffers."[105] From the point of view of the pure soul, suffering is a form of discharge of *karman* and therefore to be welcomed. This is one of key insights of A.M. Paṭel. But new *karman* will be bound if one reacts violently to such external or internal experiences. Ultimately, A.M. Paṭel takes recourse to psychological factors such as intention, attitude and perspective of doer/observer to draw the line between action and reaction somewhere:[106] "It is this inner reaction that will bind karma. ... While experiencing the effects one creates new causes."[107] It is simply assumed that subjectively violent action can only occur if the ego is involved, but not if the individual is oriented towards the pure self. If violence occurs, it should be repented immediately.

Discriminative knowledge alone is clearly not considered sufficient for realising the pure self, as William Johnson (1995: 282f., 285) expected from any movement based purely on Kundakunda's concept of self-realisation. A.M. Paṭel insists on the importance of practising non-violence and mental detachment while acting out one's *karman*, whose discharge cannot be accelerated by asceticism, only slowed down. That is, despite offering 'instant salvation' to everyone, he holds on to a stepwise path of purification qua karmic discharge. In other words, it is not – as Johnson predicted – the practice of meditation as an internalised activity (*ātmabhāvanā*), set apart from everyday life, which is important, but the unattached reflection on every form of action or conduct, as it unfolds. If the action/behaviour is violent, then it should be repented immediately, to prevent its bondage.[108]

(D) Communal Meal

Nīrubahen's explanation of the basic implications of the five precepts, which in contrast to a *satsaṅg* is predominantly monological, takes up the rest of the afternoon until the time has come for the congregational evening meal which is, fittingly, called *prasād* (lunch is called *mahāprasāda*) – a term which can designate both the food offered to gods and the sacramental leftovers.[109] The shared meal must therefore be regarded as the final part of the rite of knowledge itself. The smell of the Gujarātī vegetarian food that is being prepared by female *mahātmā*s in a separate room pervades the congregation hall during last part of Nīrubahen's lecture. The meal itself is taken informally. There is no seating arrangement or order of precedence in the process of food distribution, but a simple queue. In fact, even Nīrubahen, who is usually quite exhausted at this stage, and Dimple often eat together with everyone else, which is typical for the highly emotive and egalitarian family atmosphere amongst the followers of the Akram Vijñān Mārg.[110] The informal get-together over a meal gives everyone, male and female and old and young, the chance to discuss the effects of the *jñān vidhi* and to socially integrate new *mahātmā*s into the circle of regular participants in the congregation.

Relative And Absolute Religion

The Akram Vijñān Mārg presents itself as the very opposite of organised religion. It is, in the words of A.M. Paṭel, not a cult but a method to directly experience the ultimate truth. Anyone, whether Hindu, Jain, Muslim or Christian, is therefore invited to follow the stepless path and to realise that all living beings are essentially pure souls:

> All religions of the world are correct by their own view point. But the religion which investigates, 'Who am I?' and 'Who is the doer?' is the final path. The absolute religion is the one that gives us the one and final understanding of 'Who is the knower and the seer?.'"[111]

The acceptance of the doctrines of all religions as partially but not absolutely true is informed, on the one hand, by the Jain distinction between the practical point of view (*vyavahāra naya*) and the transcendental point of view (*niścaya naya*) and, on the other hand, by the Jain doctrine of qualified assertion (*syādvāda*) which is predicated on the belief in the omniscience of the Jaina *tīrthaṅkaras* and of permanently self-realised beings such as the Dādā, who alone are able to see the absolute truth, while unenlightened beings or members of organised religions such as Jainism have to remain satisfied with the manifest plurality of partial truths:[112]

> All these religions are true but they are relative religions. They are religions based on different view points. But if you want totality, you'll have to be in the centre. True (Real) religion is at the centre which includes all aspects of reality, integrates all fragments of reality. That is the religion of the soul (Atmadharma) for it leads to self-realisation. He, who sits at the centre, comprehends the view points of all and hence he has no cause for quarrel with any religion. That is why 'we' say that 'we' are 'Mahaveer' of the Jains, 'Krishna' of the Vaishnavas, 'Sahajanand' of the Swaminarayans, 'Christ' of the Christians, 'Zarathustra' of the Parsis and 'Allah (Khuda)' of the Muslims. Ask anything you love and it shall be given (A.M. Paṭel, in Shah 1983: 9f.).[113]

Of course only few, if any, Muslims or Christians etc. accept this argument which may, on the contrary, be perceived as a hegemonic device. But many Jains and Vaiṣṇava and Śaivaite Hindus, particularly those who live outside India, are currently attracted by the individualist and universal trans-sectarian message.

Before A.M. Paṭel, a similar message was preached by his Gujarātī compatriot Śrīmat Rājacandra whose philosophy was somewhat closer to classical Jain ontology, and to the concept of the path purification through acts of asceticism and renunciation, but also influenced by Vaiṣṇava *bhakti* movements going back to the *Bhagavadgīta*.[114] It is evidently not the hierarchical idiom of purity and pollution but the individualistic, egalitarian spirit of *bhakti* which colours many forms of religious expression in Western India and the Indian diaspora today. These devotional movements can not be easily accommodated within conventional models of Indian religion and culture, neither within 'orthodox Brāhmaṇism' or so-called 'popular Hinduism,' nor within 'heterodox Jainism,' since both the path of grace (*bhaktimārga*) and the path of knowledge (*jñānamārga*), as advocated by the *Akram Vjñān* movement, is invariably characterised by its adherents as superior to the traditional paths of merit (*puṇyamārga*) and of asceticism (*taptamārga*), etc., which are explicitly rejected.[115]

Almost all Jain and Non-Jain devotional movements developed institutions, which betray their characteristic ideological rejection of organised religion – in particular lineages of charismatically qualified virtuosi and initiation rituals. These features are typical for routinised forms of charismatic religion, as outlined by Max Weber. The principal organisational features of the Akram Vijñān Mārg, the officially denied *guru-śiṣya* relationship and the egalitarian cultic milieu, are in this form not present in the typical dualistic organisation of the mainstream 'fourfold' Jain sect, the *caturvidha saṅgha*, as analyzed by Weber (1951: 196) and Dumont (1980: 186), whose definition of 'the Indian sect' as "a religious grouping constituted primarily by renouncers" proves insufficient in this respect.[116] Not only bows the individual follower of the Akram Vijñān Mārg to his own pure soul, and to the knower, but the knower also bows to the *mahātmās*. Although Dādā Bhagavān was recognised as a spiritually superior, A.M. Paṭel himself and his successors Nīrubahen and Kanubhāī are regarded as human beings of equal status. Yet, despite the outwardly egalitarianism, no detailed religious instruction on the *pañc ājñā* is imparted by Nīrubahen to anyone who has not performed the *jñān vidhi*, and she also creates a strong sense that it is only by her grace – as the medium of the Dādā and Sīmandhar – that the initiation is given, as it were, as a personal favour.

In this respect, many similarities exist to the practices of the Vaiṣṇava Puṣṭimārga and other Vaiṣṇava and Śaiva devotional movements. In his exemplary study of the religious practices of the Puṣṭimārg, Peter Bennett (1993: 35), for instance,[117]also highlighted that the *mantra* of initiation is the "lifeblood" of the segmentary lineage structure of the Puṣṭimārg, and that "the Maharaja [guru] is at liberty to refuse a request for initiation, though I heard of no specific instances of this kind."[118] Moreover, the purification of the self through the formal dedication of all possessions to Kṛṣṇa[119] and the emphasis on his grace (as opposed to *karman* and *jñāna* in early Vaiṣṇavism), is one of the principal components of the *śuddhādvaita* Puṣṭimārgī initiation, the *brahma sambandha*, which shares many features with the initiation of the Akram Vijñān movement, amongst others.

The attitude of devotion and surrender expected by the devotee is the same in both traditions, although the Akram Vijñān Mārg does not propagate the worship of a transcendent God, but the veneration of one's own pure self through the mediation of Dādā-Sīmandhar as a quasi-personal God. Like the Puṣṭimārg *mahārājās*,[120] both the *ātmajñānīs* and the *āptaputras* visit family homes, which are thereby turned into temporary temples (*ghārasevā*), where they sit on an improvised throne (*gaḍḍi*), are garlanded and venerated through toe worship, and the *āptaputras* even receive gifts of money in return for their religious instruction and, sometimes, for the consecration of small house shrines (which a *jñānī* never does). However, in contrast to the Puṣṭimārgīs, the leftover food of the *ātmajñānīs* and *āptaputras* are not regarded as *prasāda* or *āhāra amṛta*, since the religious virtuosi of the Akram Vijñān Mārg eat together with their hosts.[121] The communication between the godlike *jñānī* and the *mahātmās* are characterised by great intimacy – hugging, for instance, is quite common – and couched in a discourse of love and transcendental unity, which is usually not found in Jainism, but in the Vaiṣṇava and the Śaiva Siddhānta traditions.[122] In fact, the accessibility of the religious functionaries and the closeness between them and their followers is one on the most attractive feature of the cult for its devotees, which, like the Puṣṭimārg, makes no caste distinctions, and rejects brāhmaṇic discourses of purity and pollution[123] in favour of a purely spiritual experience of the pure soul. These attributes are also manifest in the ritual offerings of both movements.[124] Yet, in contrast to the Puṣṭimārgī, the followers of the Akram Vijñān path do not perform elaborate material *pūjās*, but only *ārati* to the images of Sīmandhar Svāmī, Kṛṣṇa and Śiva and to the photograph of Dādā Bhagavān in their temples. They also do not display the same concern about food at all,[125] nor about charity,[126] or asceticism, which are all perceived as mere preoccupations of relative religion.

"Who Am I?"

The question how the Akram Vijñān Mārg as an organised religious movement succeeds in transcending reified Jain, Vaiṣṇava and Śaiva etc. identities seems to lie in a particular variant of the proverbial dance (*nāṭaka*) of the mind which serves as a metaphor for the relationship of the dancer *prakṛti* and the spectator *puruṣa* in the Sāṁkhya inspired religious movements.[127] Because the inner self of the devotee and of the *jñānī*, the self-realised God, are essentially identical in the Akram Vijñān doctrine, paradoxical shifting identities are created:

> Basically, you should play two different roles. With your external eyes you see by relative view-point and with your internal eyes you are the soul (pure-self). ... We should also remember that we too are playing two roles; the human being and the soul."[128]

The question of how the alternating of perspectives is practiced by the *mahātmās* who, at best, can only temporarily realise their pure self, can be answered through a comparison of the phenomenology of religious experience of the Puṣṭimārgīs, for instance, and of the Akram Vijñān Mārg. Bennett observed that the initiation into the Puṣṭimārg resembles a consecration (*prāṇa pratiṣṭhā*) of a statue, because in both cases the *guru* makes the identity of the divine qualities of both the image (*mūrti*) and the real nature or *svarūpa* of the soul of the devotee manifest.[129] The word *svarūpa* is similarly used by the Akram Vijñān to describe the manifestation of Sīmandhar-Dādā's real form, as opposed to his outward appearance or figurative representation, in the inner experience (*bhāva*) of the *mahātmā* who is contemplating the Dādā by means of songs, *darśan* or *pūjā* to an image of Sīmandhar or the Dādā, the pure soul (*śuddhātmā*) is ideally felt as being actually present. There are no rules for the performance of *darśan* by an initiated *mahātmā*, since the knowledge and the devotional attitude towards the pure self alone is crucial for the realisation of the God within through the medium of an image, be it a statue, a photograph, or a living manifestation, such as the Dādā himself, and his words:[130]

> These our *mahatmas* can perceive the god residing in you and have 'his' darshana, because 'we' have blessed them with divine eyes (divya chakshu). These eyes of yours are physical ones which can see only transient things. The indestructible Bhagavan can be perceived with divine eyes only. ... But (this) wonderful Gnana (knowledge) is naturally revealed. It is a natural adjustment and therefore divine eyes are so effortlessly available in an hour. This, our word, your soul must accept because I am seated within you; but you must not be intransigent. We do not find any difference either in you or in us."[131]

The presence of Kṛṣṇa is experienced by the Puṣṭimārgīs as a momentary revelation in form of a sudden and brief change of consciousness, called *sākṣāta darśana*, or face-to-face vision.[132] Similarly, through the vision and voice of Dādā-Sīmandhar, the *mahātmās* suddenly temporarily realise the presence of their own pure soul, which is also characterised by the word *saccidānanda*, or truth, consciousness and bliss, which is used by Vaiṣṇavas to designate Viṣṇu and by the Śaivaites to designate Śiva, who are identified with the ultimate self-existing spirit (*brahma*).[133] Sīmandhar Svāmī, like Kṛṣṇa amongst the Puṣṭimārgī, "is both mediated by and manifested in the figure of the guru."[134] Although the soul of the worshipper is conceived in Jain terms as an individual entity and not as a reflection of the one and only soul of God, during the veneration of the Dādā in the experience of the worshipper the soul of Dādā-Sīmandhar and his/ her own soul almost unnoticeable tend to merge into one. Momentarily, at least, all souls seem to be an integral part of Sīmandhar Svāmī and the Dādā as his medium, in the same way as Kṛṣṇa is worshipped by the Puṣṭimārgīs and Śiva by the Śaiva Siddhāntins as the only real self.[135]

It is an interesting question whether and how the doctrinally prescribed difference between the similarity and the identity of souls can actually be experienced in religious performances. The ritual texts of the Akram Vijñān are, it seems, at times deliberately ambiguous. They indistinctively use phrases such as "'*āp' ja cho mārā 'śuddhātmā'*" - "'you' only are my 'pure soul'"[136] or "*āpnuṁ svarūp te ja mārūṁ svarūp che*" - "only your natural form is my real form,"[137] instead of "you are like my soul" as in the phrase "*huṁ 'dādā bhagavān' jevo śuddhātmā chuṁ*" - "I am a pure soul like 'Dādā Bhagavān.'"[138] The semantic shift in expressions such as this from comparison to identification, from 'your soul is *like* my soul' to 'you *are* my soul' and back again, shows that the Jain and Vaiṣṇavite or Śaivaite perspectives are still discernible, and have not yet been melted completely into a new syncretic synthesis which the theology of the Akram Vijñān Mārg generally represents.[139] Rather they are transformed into one another through subtle shifts in perspective produced both by the ritual dynamic itself and by the deliberately ambiguous composition of the ritual texts.[140]

If pressed, the *ātmajñānī*s of the Akram Vijñān movement prove to be clearly aware of the difference between themselves and Sīmandhar Svāmī, since they do not consistently claim to have already achieved complete omniscience themselves. Although they never cite any texts, they are also conscious of the differences between the Jain and Sāṁkhya ontologies, which both in their non-theistic emphasis on *karman* and (internalised) renunciation share an individualistic orientation[141] which probably accounts for the 'trans-sectarian' outlook and the contextual adaptability of movements such as this. In future, the Akram Vijñān movement may gain even more influence well beyond the Indian or Gujarātī diaspora if only it could detach itself from the infrastructure of spiritual lineages and temples which it shares with other religious movements of Indian origin. Typically, most *gurus* of such modern devotional movements developed a 'Western' following,[142] and the Akram Vijñān Mārg is no exception, though there seems to be limited influence beyond the Indian diaspora in Africa or the Middle East.

Conclusion

The ways in which we imagine our world is part of the world and influences our individual and collective behaviour. In the past, Anthropologists have privileged a culturalist group-focused mode of imagination based on the dominant modern western utopia of the nation state with a homogenous population and culture and clear cut boundaries between one culture and the next. In the more diverse cultural universes of Africa and Asia plural ways of existence do still find more acceptance. The analysis of ritual dynamic of the conversion ritual of the Akram Vijñān Mārg casts some light on the ultimately dogmatic or political question whether this syncretic movement can be categorised as 'Jain' or not. In his book *Absent Lord: Ascetics and Kings in a Jain Ritual Culture,* L.A. Babb (1996: 44) identified the conundrum of the absence of the divine as the defining problematic of the Jain tradition:

> The ultimate locus of the sacred for the Jains, the Tīrthaṅkar as a generic figure, is no longer present in the world. In the aftermath of their era, therefore, the task is to maintain some kind of contact with their presence as it once was."[143]

P.S. Jaini (1985: 104), on the other hand, emphasised the soteriological conundrum of self-liberation and criticised theistic interpretations of Jainism for ignoring the fact that orthodox Jainism locates the principle of sacrality not within a transcendent God but in man (*jīva*) itself: "It is the contention of the Jainas that a person becomes an Arhat not by the grace of any Higher Being, but by dint of his own insights *(darśan)* and exertions *(caritra).*" Jaini (1979: 88ff., 134-41, 312) argues that these 'core beliefs' clearly demarcate 'the Jainas' from their theistic (Hindu) and fatalistic (Ājīvika) rivals. I would argue that the Akram Vijñān Mārg can be regarded as a 'Jaina' tradition, although its leaders claim to transcend all organised 'religions,' because it shares at least three of its key features. What is special about any self-consciously 'Jain' movement is the principal emphasis on the soteriological importance of non-injury and the soteriological goal of liberation preached by the 'Jinas.' It is the orientation toward the Jinas as the sources of the soteriological knowledge which defines the movement as 'Jain.'

However, the real significance of the sudden insight of A.M. Paṭel at the railway station in Surat did not concern questions of group identity or philosophical doctrine, but the experience of the individual. It was that suffering is the consequence of one's own *karman,* and that every insult suffered from someone else without reaction causes the discharge of one's own *karman* (and simultaneously a charge of the other's *karman*). If one realises this, then the other is doing oneself a favour: "the ego is melting away with every insult suffered happily."[144] This theodicy seems perfectly suited for the lower classes, transforming social suffering and anger into an experience of bliss. But the sociological question remains, whether the control of anger, celebrated as a personal triumph rather than as a humiliation, is functioning predominantly as a 'weapon of the weak' (Scott), a device for the 'pacification of the powerless' (Weber), or indeed a universal answer to the experience of suffering.

Bibliography

Amīn, J.P. (comp.). *Pragaṭ Anubhav Jñān Sūtro*. Śreṇī 1-14. Amadāvād: Jay Sacchidānand Saṅgh, 1997-2003.

Amīn, Nīrubahen. "Foreword." *Aptavani* I. Ed. K.N. Shah [no pagination]. Bombay: Sachchidananda Saṅgha, 1983.

———. "What is your Spiritual State after "Gnan Ceremony"?" *Dādāvāṇī*. Ahmedabad: Dada Bhagwan Foundation, n.d.

Amīn, Nīrubahen (comp.). *Who Am I*. Ahmedabad: Dada Bhagwan Foundation, (1986) 1994.

———. (comp.). *Caraṇ Vidhi*. 2nd Edition. Madrās: Dādā Bhagavān Phāunḍeśan, 1998.

———. (comp.). *The Essence of All Religion (Intentions Improve Life After Life)*. Ahmedabad: Dada Bhagwan Foundation, 2000a.

———. (comp.). *Generation Gap*. Ahmedabad: Dada Bhagwan Foundation, 2000b.

———. (comp.). *The Science of Karma*. Ahmedabad: Dada Bhagwan Foundation, 2003a.

———. (comp.). *Freedom Through Apology & Repentance: Pratikraman*. Ahmedabad: Dada Bhagwan Foundation, 2003b.

———. (comp.). *Brahmacarya. Celibacy attained with Understanding*. www.dadashri.org, 2005.

AS = *Ācārāṅga Sūtra*. Tr. H. Jacobi. *Sacred Books of the East* 22 (1884) 1980.

AV = *Āptavāṇī*. Vol. 1-12. Sampādak: Dr. Nīrubahen Amīn. Amadāvād: Dādā Bhagavān Founḍeśan, 1995-1999 [the original Edition of the first Volume of A.M. Paṭel's Discourses was compiled by Kanu Paṭel and Nīru Amīn and published on the 15.7.1973 by the Jay Sacchidānand Saṅgh].

Babb, Lawrence A. *Absent Lord: Ascetics and Kings in a Jain Ritual Culture*. Berkeley: University of California Press, 1996.

Bennett, Peter. *The Path of Grace. Social Organization and Temple Worship in a Vaishnava Sect*. Delhi: Hindustan Publications, 1993.

BG = *The Bhagavadgītā in the Mahābhārata*. Tr. J.A.B. van Buitenen. Chicago: The University of Chicago Press, 1981.

Bhatt, Bansidhar. "On the Epithet: *nāṭaka* for the *Samayasāra* of Kundakunda." *Jainism and Prakrit in Ancient and Medieval India.* Ed. N.N. Bhattacharyya, 431-462. New Delhi: Manohar, 1994.

Bronkhorst, Johannes. "Ājīvika Doctrine Reconsidered." *Caturaranayacakram: Essays in Jaina Philosophy and Religion.* Ed. P. Balcerowicz, 153-178. Delhi: Motilal Banarsidass, 2003.

Bruhn, Klaus. "Soteriology in Early Jainism." *Hinduismus und Buddhismus.* Ulrich Schneider Felicitation Volume, 61-86. Freiburg, 1987.

———."Five Vows and Six Avashyakas: The Fundamentals of Jaina Ethics." Ed. C. Geerdes, 1997-1998. http://here-now4u.de/eng/spr/religion/Bruhn.html

Caillat, Colette. *Atonements in the Ancient Ritual of the Jaina Monks.* L.D. Series 49. Ahmedabad: L.D. Institute of Indology, (1965) 1975.

Chakravarti, A. "Introduction." *Āchārya Kundakunda's Samayasāra.* With English Translation and Commentary based upon Amṛtacandra's Ātmakhyāta. 3rd Edition. Ed. A. Chakravarti, 1-110. New Delhi: Bharatiya Jnanpith, (1925) 1989.

Cort, John E. *Jains in the World: Religious Values and Ideology in India.* New York: Oxford University Press, 2001.

Dalmia, Vasudha, Angelika Malinar & Martin Christof (eds.). *Charisma & Canon: Essays on the Religious History of the Indian Subcontinent.* New Delhi: Oxford University Press, (2001) 2003.

Daniels, R. Cathey. "Spiritual Mission to U.S. begins in OR." *Akram Vijñān* 20.1 (1999) 34f. (first published in *The Oak Ridger* 8.6.1999, Oak Ridge, Tennessee).

Dikshit, Sudhakar S. (ed.). *I Am That. Talks with Sri Nisargadatta Maharaj.* Translated from the Marathi Tape Recordings by Maurice Frydman. Bombay: Chetana, (1973) 1999.

Dumont, Louis. *Homo Hierarchicus: The Caste System and its Implications.* Complete Revised English Edition. Chicago and London: The University of Chicago Press, 1980.

Dundas, Paul. "Becoming Gautama: Mantra and History in Śvetāmbara Jainism." *Open Boundaries: Jain Communities and Culture in Indian History.* Ed. J. Cort, 31-52. Albany: SUNY, 1998.

Flügel, Peter. "Power and Insight in Jain Discourse." *Paper presented at the Jains in Indian History and Culture Workshop.* Amherst College, 26.6.1993 (Published 2010).

———. "Present Lord: Sīmandhar Svāmī and the Akram Vijñān Movement." *The Intimate Other: Love Divine in Indic Religions.* Eds. Anna S. King and John Brockington, 194-242. Delhi: Orient Longman, 2005.

Fuchs, Martin. *Kampf um Differenz. Repräsentation, Subjektivität und soziale Bewegungen. Das Beispiel Indien.* Frankfurt am Main: Suhrkamp, 1999.

Fuller, Christopher John. *The Camphor Flame. Popular Hinduism and Society in India.* Cambridge: Cambridge University Press, 1992.

Garcia, Juan Carlos. "'My' Experience after the Gnan Vidhi Given by Atma Gnani Dr. Nirubahen in London, May 2002." *www.realizaciondadashri.com*

Glasenapp, Helmuth von. *Die Lehre vom Karma in der Philosophie der Jainas.* Leipzig: Otto Harrassowitz, 1915 (Translated from the original German by B. Gifford and revised by the Author as *The Doctrine of Karman in Jain Philosophy.* Ed. H.R. Kapadia. Bombay: Bai Vijibai Jivanlal Panalal Charity Fund, 1942).

Heesterman, Jan C. "The 'Hindu Frontier.'" *India and Indonesia: General Perspectives.* Ed. J.C. Heesterman et. al., 1-15. Leiden: E.J. Brill, 1989.

Hubert, Henri & Marcel Mauss. *Sacrifice: Its Nature and Functions.* Chicago: The University of Chicago Press, (1898) 1981.

Humphrey, Caroline & James Laidlaw. *The Archetypal Actions of Ritual: A theory of ritual illustrated by the Jain rite of worship.* Oxford: Clarendon Press, 1994.

Jaini, Padmanabh S. *The Jaina Path of Purification.* Berkeley: University of California Press, 1979.

———. "The Jaina Concept of the Sacred." *Perspectives in Jaina Philosophy and Culture.* Ed. S.S. Kumar & K.C. Sogani, 102-105. New Delhi: Ahimsa International, 1985.

Jaiswal, Suvira. *The Origin and Development of Vaiṣṇavism. Vaiṣṇavism from 200 B.C. to A.D. 500.* Delhi: Munshiram Manoharlal, 1967.

Johnson, William. J. *Harmless Souls. Karmic Bondage and Religious Change in Early Jainism with Special Reference to Umāsvati and Kundakunda.* Delhi: Motilal Banarsidass, 1995.

———. "Knowledge and Practice in the Jaina Religious Tradition." *Jain Doctrines and Practice: Academic Perspectives.* Ed. J.T.O' Connell, 18-49. University of Toronto: Center for South Asian Studies, 2000.

Lévi-Strauss, Claude. *The Raw and the Cooked.* Translated from the original French by John and Doreen Weightman. London: Cape, (1964) 1982.

Monier Williams, Monier. *Sanskrit-English Dictionary.* Revised Edition. Oxford (1899) 1986.

Parry, Jonathan P. "The Gift, the Indian Gift and the 'Indian Gift.'" *Man (N.S.)* 21, 3 (1986) 453-73.

Patel, Ajit (ed.). *Charan Vidhi.* Ahmedabad: Dada Bhagwan Foundation, n.d.

Patel, Rakesh M. (comp.). *Ultimate Knowledge.* 2nd Edition. London, 1994.

Pocock, David. *Mind, Body and Wealth: A Study of Belief and Practice in an Indian Village.* Oxford, 1973.

Pungaliya, U.K. *Philosophy and Spirituality of Śrīmad Rajchandra.* Jaipur: Prakrit Bharati Academy, 1996.

Ramadevanahalli, Sharadaprasad. *Akram Vignan... Instant Moksha.* http://www.geocities.com/Athens/Acropolis/7591 gnani.html

Ryan, James. "Erotic Excess and Sexual Danger in the *Cīvakacintāmaṇi.*" *Open Boundaries: Jain Communities and Cultures in Indian History.* Ed. J.E. Cort, 67-83. New York: SUNY, 1998.

Salter, Emma. "Unity and Diversity amongst the Followers of Śrīmad Rājacandra." *Jinamañjari* 23, 1 (2001) 32-51.

Schubring, Walther. *The Doctrine of the Jainas. Described after the Old Sources.* Translation from the original German by Wolfgang Beurlen. 2nd English Edition. Delhi: Motilal Banarsidass, (1935) 2000.

———. "Kundakunda echt und unecht." *ZDMG* 107 (1957) 537-574.

Shah, Khetsi Narsi (ed.). *Aptavani I.* Tr. V. Pathak & G. Shah. Bombay: Sachchidananda Sangha, 1983.

Shah, G.A. *"Dada Bhagavan's Akram Vignan." Way to Blissful Living.* Oak Ridge: Jai Sacchidanand Sangh USA, 2003.

Smith, Wilfred Cantwell. *The Meaning and End of Religion.* Minneapolis: Fortress Press, (1962) 1991.

Soni, Jayandra. *The Notion of Āpta in Jaina Philosophy.* The 1995 Roop Lal Jain Lecture. University of Toronto, 1996.

Sontheimer, G.D. "Hinduism: The Five Components and their Interaction." *Hinduism Reconsidered.* Ed. by G.D. Sontheimer & H. Kulke, 197-212. New Delhi: Manohar, (1989) 1991.

SS = *Samayasāra* of Kundakunda. With English Translation and Commentary based upon Amṛtacandra's Ātmakhyāt by A. Chakravarti. 3rd Edition. Ed. A. Chakravarti. New Delhi: Bharatiya Jnanpith, (1925) 1989.

Staal, Frits. *Rules Without Meaning: Ritual, Mantras and the Human Sciences.* New York: Peter Lang Verlag, (1990) 1993.

Stevenson, Sinclair. *The Heart of Jainism.* Delhi: Manohar, (1915) 1984.

Tambs-Lyche, Harald. *London Patidars: A Study in Urban Ethnicity.* London: Routledge, 1980.

Todarmal, Pandit. *Moksha Marg Prakashak (The Illuminator of the Path of Liberation).* Tr. H. Jain. Bombay: Shri Kund-Kund Kahan Digambar Jain Tirtha Suraksha Trust, 1992.

TS = *Tattvārtha Sūtra.* Tr. N. Tatia. The Sacred Literature Series of the International Sacred Literature Trust. San Francisco: Harper Collins, 1994.

Turner, Victor W. "Dewey, Dilthey, and Drama." *The Anthropology of Experience.* Eds. Victor W. Turner & Edward M. Bruner, 33-44. Urbana and Chicago: University of Illinois Press, 1986.

Upadhye, Adinath Neminath. "Introduction." *Śrī Kundakundācārya's Pravacanasāra (Pavayanasāra). A Pro-Canonical Text of the Jainas (2nd Ed.),* i-cxxvi. Bombay: Sheth Manilal Revashankar Jhaveri (Rāyacandra-Jaina-Śāstra-Mālā 9), (1930) 1935.

UtS = Uttarajjhāyā (Uttarādhyayana Sūtra). Translated by Herman Jacobi. *Jaina Sūtras. Part II. Sacred Books of the East 45,* 1-232. Oxford: Clarendon Press, 1895.

Viy. = Deleu, Jozef. *Viyāhapannatti (Bhagavaī). The Fifth Anga of the Jaina Canon. Introduction, Critical Analysis, Commentary & Indexes.* Brugge: Rijksuniversiteit de Gent, 1970.

Williams, Robert. *Jaina Yoga.* London: Luzac, 1963.

Websites

www.dadabhagawan.org

www.dadashri.org

www.realizaciondadashri.com

Appendix

Sequence of Texts Used in the Jñān Vidhi

Original Gujarātī Texts[145]

(1a)

sarvasva amārūṁ arpaṇ che

sarvasva amārūṁ arpaṇ che,
bhagavān tamārā śaraṇomāṁ, su-caraṇomāṁ;
ādhyātmik ānand paramānand,
ā param-haṃsnāṁ satsaṅgmāṁ, su-caraṇomāṁ.

man-vacan-kāyā chāyā, māyānā, bhāv-no-dravya karma;
svīkāro bhrāṁti bāḷaknī, ananya śaraṇ dhyo bhavaraṇmāṁ.
- sarvasva amārūṁ arpaṇ che.

jñānāmṛtnāṁ motī cūge, haṃsā mān sarovarmāṁ;
satyam śivam ne sundaramnī, ā 'divya-cakṣu'nī jyotimāṁ.
- sarvasva amārūṁ arpaṇ che.

sūrajnuṁ kevuṁ tarpaṇ che! candānāṁ śītaḷ kiraṇomāṁ;
'sambhāve' nikāl karo, ghaṭmāḷ ūṭhe je antarmāṁ.
- sarvasva amārūṁ arpaṇ che.

rāt-divas, sandhyā-uṣā, kevāṁ adbhut che niyammāṁ!
bharatī-oṭ man sāgarnī, 'niścit' ne 'vyavasthit'māṁ.
- sarvasva amārūṁ arpaṇ che.

jīvan bhale ek 'darśan' ho, paṇ 'ātmā' śāśvat darpaṇ che;
'vyavahār' bhale ho koṭi saṅg, paṇ 'niścay' kevaḷ bhagvānmāṁ -
sarvasva amārūṁ arpaṇ che.

'mūḍh-ātmā' no uddhār karī, je 'śuddhātmā' ne jagāe che;
apūrva 'agocar' ne ullasit, jhaḷhaḷ jyoti tan-manmāṁ.
- sarvasva amārūṁ arpaṇ che.

'akram' nī aṇadīṭh keḍīthī, je mokṣadvār ughāḍe che;
paramātma-svarūp he pragaṭ puruṣ, 'āp' ja cho mārā 'śuddhātmā.'
-sarvasva amārūṁ arpaṇ che.

(1b)

devone āvāhan[146]

andhārā koṭi varṣnā, paḷ sāṭhmāṁ ulecaśe,
ṭaṅkotkīrṇ jñān abhed-nā jyoti svarūpe pragaṭaśe.

tetrīs koṭi devī-devatā, śānti kāje āvajo,
sāmāyik śuddha-ātmānī, "jñānī" apūrva lāvaśe.

vāṇī 'dādā bhagavān' nī, tīrthaṅkaro sāmbhaḷe,
sarvajñanāṁ su-caraṇo mahīṁ, ātmā śātā pāmaśe.

dāvānaḷnī jvāḷā mahīṁ, brahmāṇḍ paṇ bhaḍake baḷe,
pātāḷī jharaṇ karūṇā bharyāṁ, jaḷ-śītaḷ chaṇṭakāraśe.

amṛt-vāṇī bhagavānnī, jaḷ-śītaḷ thaī ṭhārśe,
caram covīśī sāmaṭī, 'jay saccidānand' jñānī 'te.'

oṃ hṛiṃ dādā bhagavān sarvajña śaraṇaṃ gacchāmi.

(1c)

he dādā bhagavān, he śrī sīmandhar svāmī prabhu,
āp ahīṁ padhāro, nīrū bolnā
kaṇṭhe virājo. āp bolāvo ane hamo badhā bolīśuṁ.

(1d)

huṁ niścay nirṇaythī kevaḷ śuddhātmā chuṁ.

(2)

samarpaṇ

he dādā bhagvān, he srī sīmandhar svāmī prabhu! [huṁ] man, vacan, kāyā .... nā nāmnī sarva māyā [huṁ śuddhātmā chuṁ]. bhāv karma, dravya karma, no karma, āp pragaṭ paramātmā svarūp prabhunā su-caraṇomāṁ samarpaṇ karuṁ chuṁ.

he dādā bhagavān
oṃ śuddhātmā che

(3)

ātmā sāmāyik

'jñān sākṣātkār' pāmelāo māṭenī niścay-vyavahār caraṇ vidhi

dādā bhagavānne trikāḷ namaskār, namaskār, namaskār. he nirāgī, nirvikārī, saccidānand svarūp, sahajānandī, anantjñānī, anantdarśī, trailokya prakāśak, śuddha, buddha, caitanyaghan svarūp, param jyoti sukhdhām evā he vītarāgī paramātmā! huṁ niścay nirṇaythī kevaḷ śuddhātmā chuṁ (3x). mane āpnī apūrva śakti āpo, śakti āpo, śakti āpo. mane śuddhātmānuṁ satat smaraṇ āpo.

āpnuṁ akhaṇḍ nididhyāsan āpo. āpnuṁ akhaṇḍ sānnidhya āpo. āpnā sarvotkṛṣṭ sadguṇo mārāmāṁ utkṛṣṭapaṇe sphurāymān thāo, sphurāymān thāo, sphurāymān thāo.

he viśvavaṃdhya evā pragaṭ śuddhātmā svarūp prabhu! āp ā kāḷne viśe bījā rām ke mahāvīr ja cho. āp ja mārā pragaṭ śuddhātmā cho. āpnā māṁ jevo ātmā varte che, tevo ja ātmā mārā māṁ vartāvo. māruṁ man ane buddhi sarvathā āpne vaś vartyā karo. samasta viśvanī vismṛti ane kevaḷ ek āpnī ja smṛti mane prāpta thāo. bhāve karīne kevaḷ śuddhātmānubhav sivāy ā jagatnī koī paṇ vināśī

cīj māre joītī nathī. huṁ kṣaṇe kṣaṇe sadāy sarvathā svasattā māṁ rahī svasattāno ja upabhog karuṁ, tem ja parasattā māṁ kadī ja praveś na karuṁ,

e māro dṛḍh nirṇay niścay pūro pāo.

he viśvavaṃdhya evā pragaṭ śuddhātmā svarūp prabhu! mārā sarva prakārnā sarva doṣonī mane kṣamā āpo, kṣamā āpo, kṣamā āpo. dayā āpo, śānti āpo, samatā āpo, satya āpo, tyāg āpo, vairāgya āpo.

sansār bhajavavānā ārambh kāḷthī āj dinnī adhyakṣaṇ paryaṁt, ā jagatnā jīvonī

kaṁī paṇ śaṅkā-kuśaṅkā karī, karī, karāvī ke anumodī hoy, kaṁī paṇ āparādh karyā, karāvyā ke anumodhyā hoy, kaṁī paṇ virādhanāo karī, karāvī ke anumodī hoy, kaṁī paṇ antarāyo karyā, karāvyā ke kartā pratye anumodhyā hoy, cha mahāvratonā bhaṅge karī aḍhār pāpasthānakoe karīne kaṁī paṇ avinay, avivek,

abhakti, apakārya ke doṣ, jāṇye-ajāṇye karyā, karāvyā ke kartā pratye anumodhyā hoy, to te sarva doṣonī huṁ kṣamā māguṁ chuṁ, ālocanā, pratikramaṇ, pratyākhyān karuṁ chuṁ. mane kṣamā karo, kṣamā karo, kṣamā karo.

he viśvavaṁdya evā pragaṭ śuddhātmā svarūp prabhu! āp nirāgī, nirvikārī, saccidānand svarūp, sahajānandī, ānantajñānī, ānantadarśī, trailokya prakāśak cho. hūṁ bhāv karma, dravya karma, no karma, man, vacan, kāyā .... nā nāmnī sarva māyā, āp pragaṭ paramātmā svarūp prabhunā sucaraṇomāṁ samarpaṇ karuṁ chuṁ. (3x)

huṁ caitanyaghan svarūpī evo śuddhātmā chuṁ (3x). huṁ arūpī chuṁ (3x). huṁ asaṅg chuṁ (3x). huṁ akṣay chuṁ (3x). huṁ amūrta chuṁ (3x). huṁ acyut

chuṁ (3x). huṁ ajanma chuṁ (3x). huṁ amar chuṁ (3x). huṁ janma-maraṇthī mukta evo śuddhātmā chuṁ (3x). huṁ avyābādh svarūp chuṁ (3x). huṁ paramānand sukh svarūpavāḷo chuṁ (3x). huṁ ṭaṅkotkīrṇavat evo śuddhātmā chuṁ (3x). huṁ sva-par prakāśak evo śuddhātmā chuṁ (3x).

huṁ 'dādā bhagvān' jevo śuddhātmā chuṁ (3x). huṁ 'ṛṣabhadev dādā bhagavān' jevo śuddhātmā chuṁ (3x). huṁ 'mahāvīr bhagavān' jevo śuddhātmā

chuṁ (3x). huṁ śrī 'sīmandhar svāmī bhagavān' jevo śuddhātmā chuṁ (3x). huṁ śrī kṛṣṇa bhagavān'jevo śuddhātmā chuṁ (3x).

huṁ jñātaputra chuṁ. ane āp mārā jñātapitā cho (3x). huṁ param jyoti svarūp siddha bhagavān chuṁ (3x).

huṁ anant jñānavāḷo chuṁ (3x). huṁ anant darśanavāḷo chuṁ (3x). huṁ anant

śaktivāḷo chuṁ (3x). huṁ anant sukhnuṁ dhām chuṁ (3x). huṁ aguru-laghu svabhāvavāḷo chuṁ (3x). krodh-mān-māyā-lobh, e laghu-guru svabhāvnā ja che (3x).

dravye karīne huṁ sampūrṇ śuddha chuṁ, sarvāṁg śuddha chuṁ (3x). jñān-darśanādi anantā guṇo thakī huṁ sampūrṇ śuddha chuṁ, sarvāṁg śuddha chuṁ (3x). anantā jñeyone jāṇavāmāṁ pariṇamelī anantī avasthāomāṁ huṁ sampūrṇ śuddha chuṁ,

sarvāṁg śuddha chuṁ (3x).

huṁ avināśī chuṁ (3x). huṁ avyay chuṁ (3x). huṁ sūkṣma chuṁ (3x). huṁ keval nirvikalpa vītarāg kṣān mātra chuṁ (3x). huṁ nirmaḷ akhūṭ paramānand svarūpī chuṁ (3x). huṁ sarva paradravyothī sarvathā udāsīn ja chuṁ (3x).

sūrya samān tejasvī ane candra samān śītaḷ evā he vītarāgī paramātmā! tamām

lepāyamān bhāvothī huṁ sarvathā nirlep evo śuddhātmā chuṁ (3x). man-vacan-kāyānī tamām saṅgī kriyāothī huṁ tadna asaṅg ja chuṁ (3x). man-vacan-

kāyānī ṭevo ane tenā svabhāvne huṁ jāṇuṁ chuṁ ane mārā sva-svabhāvne paṇ huṁ jāṇu chuṁ (3x). man-vacan-kāyāthī tadna bhinn evo huṁ śuddhātmā chuṁ (3x). sthūḷatamthī sūkṣmatam sudhīnī tamām samsārī avasthāono huṁ jñātā dṛṣṭā mātra chuṁ, ṭaṅkotkīrṇ chuṁ, ānand svarūp chuṁ (3x). āhārī āhār kare che ane huṁ nirāhārī mātra tene jāṇuṁ chuṁ (3x). avasthā mātra kudartī racanā che, jeno koī bāpo ya racanār nathī ane te 'vyavasthit' che (3x).

man-vacan-kāyānī āpnā jevī sahajtā mane prāpta ṭhāo (3x). āpnī vṛtti e ja mārī

vṛtti raho (3x). āpnī dṛṣṭi e ja mārī dṛṣṭi raho (3x). āpno svabhāv te ja māro svabhāv raho (3x). āpnuṁ jñān, darśan, cāritra ane sukh te ja māruṁ jñān darśan, cāritra ane sukh raho (3x).

he viśvavaṁdya evā pragaṭ śuddhātmā svarūp prabhu! mane ane sarva kalyāṇamūrtī, samakitadhārī mahātmāone tīvra jñān daśā prāpta thāo, sampūrṇ arpaṇtā prāpta thāo, sampūrṇ abhedatā prāpta thāo, sampūrṇ vītarāgatā prāpta thāo, prabaḷ puruṣārtha prāpta thāo.

sarva kalyāṇamūrtī samakitadhārī mahātmāonā śuddhātmāne atyant bhaktithī
abhedabhāve vāraṁvār trikāḷ namaskār, namaskār, namaskār karī eṭluṁ māṁgu chuṁ, ke samatābhāve meṁ je dṛḍh

nirṇay niścay karyo che, ke mane śuddhātmānubhav prāpta thāo, ane te prāpta thavāmāṁ sarva kalyāṇamūrtī samakitadhārī mahātmāonā sarvotkr̥ṣṭa sadguṇo mārāmāṁ utkr̥ṣṭapaṇe sphurāyamān thaī mane śaktivaṁt banāvo, śaktivaṁt banāvo, śaktivaṁt banāvo. samasta viśvanuṁ kalyāṇ karo, kalyāṇ karo, kalyāṇ karo ane kalyāṇ karavānī mane param śakti āpo. samasta viśvanā jīvo sukh ane śāntine pāmo. samasta viśvanā jīvo mokṣane pāmo.

he viśvavaṁdhya evā pragaṭ śuddhātmā svarūp prabhu! huṁ kadī paṇ āp gurudev thakī, jñānavādthī, syādvādthī, paramajñānthī, paramadhyānthī, śuddhātmāthī, śuddhātmānī upāsanā karanārāo sarve kalyāṇmūrtī samakitadhārī mahātmāonā śuddhātmāthī, sarva siddhothī, santothī, mahantothī, jagatnā jīvamātrathī kadī ja paṇ śaṅkit, vañcit, ke bāḍo na banuṁ tevī śakti, bhakti, dr̥ṣṭi, jñān, vivek, vinay, cāritra ane prajñā āpo.

ekaniṣṭhāpūrvak kevaḷ ek āpnī ja ājñāmāṁ ja vartavānī mārī je dr̥ḍh abhilāṣā che

ane pratijñā che, te pūrī karavānī śaktio mane prāpta thāo, prāpta thāo, prāpta thāo. āj dinnī adhyakṣaṇ paryaṁt āpnī je koī ājñā mārāthī pāḷī śakāī nathī, te sarvanī huṁ kṣamā māṁgu chuṁ; ālocanā - pratikramaṇ - pratyākhyān karuṁ chuṁ. mane kṣamā karo, kṣamā karo, kṣamā karo.

he viśvavaṁdhya evā pragaṭ śuddhātmā svarūp prabhu! āpno bodhelo satsaṅg
mārāmāṁ nirantar thāo, nirantar thāo, nirantar thāo. āpnuṁ bodheluṁ samyak jñān mane kṣane kṣane jāgr̥ti arpo, jāgr̥ti arpo, jāgr̥ti arpo. sthūl saṃyogo, sūkṣma saṃyogo, vāṇīnā saṃyogo par che ne parādhīn che, e jñān mārā hr̥dayne viśe sansthāpit raho, sansthāpit raho, sansthāpit raho. ḍakhoḍakhal karuṁ nahi tevī śakti āpo. (3x) kevaḷ dekhbhāḷ karvānī mane śakti āpo. (3) kevaḷ ek āpnī ja kr̥pāno abhilāṣī chuṁ. (3x) āpnāṁ caraṇārvid mārā hr̥daymāṁ sthān pāmo. (3) huṁ śuddhātmā chuṁ, śuddhātmā chuṁ (25x) huṁ niścay nirṇaythī kevaḷ śuddhātmā ja chuṁ! (2x) jay saccidānand (5x).

'huṁ vijñān svarūp chuṁ'

(4)

pāñc ājñā

1. *'rileṭīv' vyu poinmthī 'huṁ candulāl chuṁ.'*

2. *'riyal' vyu poinmthī 'huṁ śuddhātmā chuṁ.'*

3. *jagat niyamtā-vyavasthit śakti.*

4. *phāiḷono sambhāve nikāl karvo.*

5. *śuddhātmānā copaḍāmāṁ rakam jame karvī.*

pekiṅgne na jotāṁ enā śuddhātmāne divyadṛṣṭithī jovo.

English Translation

The rite of knowledge
1. Prelude

(1a)

Everything of mine is surrendered (song)

Everything of mine is surrendered,

surrendered to you almighty, to your holy feet;
for spiritual bliss supreme bliss,
as a devotee of this realised soul, to his holy feet. The shadowy illusions of mind, speech, and body, of internal actions,[147] habitual actions,[148] and material actions;[149] accept these childlike delusions,
allow me to surrender this battle-field of life to none other but you.
- Everything of mine is surrendered.

The pearls of the nectar of knowledge, are picked by the swan in the lake of pride; in the light of this 'divine eye,' of truth, bliss, and beauty.
- Everything of mine is surrendered.

What an offering of the sun this is!
In the cool rays of the moon;
with a 'balanced mind'[150] dispose of,
the conflicts arising within.
- Everything of mine is surrendered.

Day and night, dawn and dusk,
how wonderful is their regularity!
The ebb and tide of the ocean of the mind,[151]
is determined by 'natural law'[152] and 'order.'[153]
- Everything of mine is surrendered.

Let life be one 'vision,'[154]
but the 'soul'[155] is the eternal mirror;
'transactions'[156] may be with millions,
but 'absolute determination'[157] be only in the almighty.
- Everything of mine is surrendered.

For the liberation of the 'unenlightened soul,' the 'pure soul' is awakened; extraordinary, 'beyond the reach of the senses'[158] and full of joy,
bright light in body and mind.
- Everything of mine is surrendered.

Who opens the gate of liberation, 'the path of immediate understanding'[159] never seen before; O realised supreme soul in visible form, 'you' are my 'pure soul.' - (To you) Everything of mine is surrendered.

(1b)

Invitation for the Gods to come (song)

There is darkness of a million years, but it will disperse in a moment of sixty seconds, this insoluble unbreakable knowledge, will reveal itself in the form of light.

Thirty-three million Goddesses and Gods,[160] come for peace, for the equanimity of the pure soul, which the extraordinary "knower" will bring.

To the voice of 'Dādā Bhagavān,' the Tīrthaṅkaras are listening, at the holy feet of the Omniscient, the soul will find peace.

I am surrounded by the flames of the forest fire, the whole universe is ablaze, an underground spring full of compassion, sprinkles cool water.

The nectar-like speech of Bhagavān, will extinguish (the fire) by becoming cool water, the perfect twenty-four all together, 'truth, consciousness and bliss'[161] is 'that' knower.

Oṃ hṛṃ I go to the omniscient Dādā Bhagavān to take refuge.

(1c)

Invitation for Dādā Bhagavān and Sīmandhar Svāmī to come and to reside in Nirūbahen

O Dādā Bhagavān, O Śrī Sīmandhar Svāmī Lord, come here and place your voice in Nīru's throat. You cause us to speak and we will all speak.

(1d)

Asking the Dādā for strength

With absolute resolve and determination I am only a pure soul.

(2)

Dedication

O Dādā Bhagvān, O Śrī Sīmandhar Svāmī Lord! Whatever I ________ [insert your name] call mine, my thought, speech, and body, is all illusion[162] [I am a pure soul]. I surrender all my inner actions,[163] outward actions,[164] and reflex actions[165] at your holy feet, you are the revealed God in the form of the supreme soul.

(3)

Self-meditation[166]

(Absolute-relative foot worship for obtaining 'the direct vision of the knowledge')

Humble obeisance (3x) to Dādā Bhagavān at all three times (through past, present, and future). O unattached Lord within; you are free from passions;[167] of the natural form of truth, consciousness and bliss; innate joy;[168] infinite knowledge; infinite vision; illuminating the three worlds;[169] pure; wise; in the form of knowledge; the abode of infinite joy and the supreme light (of knowledge). O unattached One! With absolute resolve and determination I am only a pure soul (3x). Bestow upon me your unprecedented strength (3x). Bless me with the perpetual awareness of the pure soul.

Bless me with the perpetual visual contemplation of your formless attributes.[170] Comfort me with your perpetual proximity. May all your magnificent attributes become instilled within me, instilled within me, instilled within me.

O universally adored and fully manifested Śuddhātmā Bhagavān! You are another Rām or Mahāvīr of this age. You are my own manifest pure soul. Let me experience the same soul that you experience. May my mind and my intellect be completely absorbed in you. Let me become oblivious to the entire universe and keep only you in my mind. From the bottom of my heart, I do not desire any perishable worldly things. I only want the perpetual experience of the pure soul. Let me remain every second and in all ways in the realm of the self and enjoy the realm of the self, and never transgress into the domain of the non-self. I supply this resolve with my firm determination.

O universally adored and fully manifested Śuddhātmā Bhagavān! Please grant me forgiveness for all my mistakes, forgive me, forgive me. Give me compassion, give me peace, give me equanimity, give me truth, give me renunciation, give me detachment.

From the beginning of this world's drama until this very moment; for all the times that I – through my own actions, through the actions of others acting on my behalf, or through my approval of the actions of others – have doubted or been suspicious of any living being in this world; for any hostility towards another living being; for criticising any living being;

for obstructing another living being; for knowingly or unknowingly doing, causing to be done, or approving of others doing[171] the slightest discourtesy, indiscretion, non-devotion, or harm to any living being, and for all the times I have committed any of the eighteen states of sin[172] or broken any of the six great vows[173] – I criticise myself,[174] and repent all these wrongdoings, and resolve not to commit such mistakes again, and ask to be forgiven. Please grant me your forgiveness (3x).[175]

O universally adored and fully manifested Śuddhātmā Bhagavān! You are detached; passionless; of the natural form of truth, consciousness and bliss; innate joy; infinite knowledge; infinite vision; illuminating the three worlds. Whatever I ________ [insert your name] call mine, my thought, speech, and body, is all illusion, I surrender all my inner actions, outward actions, and reflex actions at your holy feet, you are the revealed god in the form of the supreme soul. (3x)

I am a pure soul by nature knowledge incarnate (3x). I am formless (3x). I am detached (3x). I am imperishable (3x). I am intangible (3x). I am eternal (3x). I am without birth (3x). I am immortal (3x). I am a pure soul free from birth and death (3x). I am by nature imperishable (3x).[176] I am by nature supreme infinite bliss (3x). I am a (permanent) pure soul like (something) inscribed with a chisel (on a rock) (3x).[177] I am a pure soul that illuminates the difference between the self and non-self (3x).[178]

I am a pure soul like 'Dādā Bhagavān' (3x). I am a pure soul like 'Øṣabhdev Dādā Bhagavān' (3x). I am a pure soul like 'Mahāvīr Bhagavān' (3x). I am a pure soul like Śrī 'Sīmandhar Svāmī Bhagavān' (3x). I am a pure soul like Śrī 'Kṛṣṇa Bhagavān' (3x). I am your knowledge child.[179] And you are my knowledge father[180] (3x). I am the liberated God (Siddha Bhagavān) in the form of divine light (3x).

I possess infinite knowledge (3x). I possess infinite vision (3x). I possess infinite energy (3x). I am the abode of infinite bliss (3x). I am, by my very nature constant, without highs and lows. Anger-pride-deceit-greed, these highs and lows are by their very nature unstable (3x).

My substance is such that I am completely and totally pure (3x). Because of my absolute knowledge, absolute vision, and infinite other qualities, I am completely and totally pure (3x). In knowing infinite objects that give rise to infinite situations, I am completely and totally pure (3x). I am indestructible (3x). I am immutable (3x). I am subtle (3x). I am only absolute, changeless, detached knowledge (3x). I am pure, inexhaustible supreme bliss (3x). I am entirely indifferent to all other substances (3x).

O dispassionate supreme soul, you are as radiant as the sun and as soothing as the cool moon! Amidst all the worldly desires and wishes, I am a completely detached pure soul (3x). I am absolutely separate from all attached actions of mind, speech and body (3x). I know of the bad habits of the mind, speech and body and of their nature, and I also know of my own (soul's) nature (3x). I am a pure soul, completely separate from the mind, speech and body (3x). I am knower and seer of but completely separate from the gross and subtle circumstances of the world, I am inscribed with a chisel.[181] I am full of bliss (3x). The eater eats, and I, the 'non-eater,' know (3x). All the phases of life are created by nature, of which there is no creator, and they are '*vyavasthit*' (systematically arranged)[182] (3x).

Please bless me with the same innate state of mind, speech, and body that you possess (3x). Let your dispositions also be my dispositions (3x). Let your vision also be my vision (3x). Let your nature also be my nature (3x). Let your knowledge, vision, conduct, and bliss also be my knowledge, vision, conduct, and bliss (3x).

O universally adored and fully manifested Śuddhātmā Bhagavān! Bless me and all other virtuous,[183] self-realised[184] great beings[185] with the acute condition of knowledge (of the pure self), with total surrender (to you), in a state of complete oneness with all, with complete detachment, and strengthen our endeavour.

I bow down,[186] I bow down, I bow down to the pure souls of all great beings[187] who are the living embodiment of auspiciousness and self-realisation,[188] with extreme devotion, unreservedly,[189] repeatedly, three times (through past, present, and future)[190] and request, what I firmly resolved with the feeling of equanimity,[191] that I may be granted the experience of the pure soul, and, in obtaining it, that the best qualities of all the auspicious and self-realised great beings may come into me[192] in the best possible manner and make me strong, make me strong, make me strong. May you bestow spiritual welfare[193] upon the entire universe, and give me supreme strength to be an instrument for its welfare. May all living beings of the universe attain peace and happiness. May all living beings of the universe attain liberation.[194]

O universally adored and fully manifested Śuddhātmā Bhagavān! Give me strength, devotion, vision, knowledge, discrimination, humility, right conduct and wisdom, so that because of you O Gurudev I may never doubt, be left out, or become blind towards the path of knowledge, the many-pointedness of existence,[195] the supreme knowledge, the supreme contemplation, the pure soul, the worshippers of the pure soul,[196] of the pure souls of all the auspicious self-realised great beings, of all liberated souls, saints, religious superiors,[197] and all living beings of the world.

Please give me (3x) the full strength to fulfil my intense hope and determination to loyally remain in your commandments[198] alone. Until this very day, for whichever commandments I have failed to follow, I ask your forgiveness; I confess, and repent, and resolve not to commit such mistakes again. Forgive me (3x).

O universally adored and fully manifested Śuddhātmā Bhagavān! Let your enlightened[199] congregation[200] constantly dwell in me (3x). Let your enlightened right knowledge[201] keep me aware of the pure self[202] at every moment (3x). Instil in my heart the knowledge that all gross circumstances, subtle circumstances, and circumstances of speech, are (separate from me and) dependent on external factors. Give me the strength not to interfere or quarrel (with the natural order of things) (3x). Give me the strength to only perform observation[203] (3x). I only desire your grace (3x). Let your lotus feet dwell in my heart (3x). I am a pure soul (25x). With absolute resolve and determination I am only a pure soul! (2x). Victory to truth, consciousness and bliss (5x).[204]

I am by nature experiential knowledge.[205]

(4)

The five commandments

1. From the 'relative' viewpoint 'I am Candulāl' (substitute 'Candulāl' with your own name).
2. From the 'real' viewpoint 'I am a pure soul.'
3. This world is ruled by scientific circumstantial evidence.[206]
4. Clear your files with equanimity.[207]
5. Enter credit in the account book of the pure soul.

Do not look at the outer wrappings ('packing') but look with divine sight at the pure soul.

Endnotes

1 See particularly Dumont's 1980 still influential variant of methodological holism.

2 *The Constitution of India.* 24th Edition. Lucknow: Eastern Book Company, 2003, p. 30.

3 In a footnote, even Louis Dumont 1980: 427, n. 6 emphasises that Hinduism does not encompass these religions: "'Hinduism' is used here in the habitual sense to mean the present religion of those Indians which are not Muslims, Christians, Parsis, Sikhs, and with these exceptions, the religion of the caste society." At the same time, he favours a "unitary definition of Hinduism and even of Buddhist and Jain religions" because, despite their philosophical differences, within India all these groups "have castes" (p. 46, cf. p. 269). 'Hinduism' (the term is missing in the index of *Homo Hierarchicus*) is for him "the religion of caste and of renunciation" (p. 285, cf. p. 428, n. 10): "belief in gods does not transcend this fundamental opposition of caste [i.e. 'pure and impure']" (p. 270). Fuller 1992: 91 criticises this approach as "sociological reductionism," though reverting to it himself elsewhere (p. 157f., etc.).

4 See Heesterman's 1989 influential article "The 'Hindu Frontier'" which utilises Redfield's term 'great tradition,' Srinivas' concept of Sanskritisation, and Dumont's insights on the 'complementary opposition of power and authority' to delimit the 'sharp edge' of 'Indianisation.' In his view, Buddhism "can mark the 'Hindu frontier' as well" (p. 11). For similar generalisations see for instance Parry's 1986 article on 'the Indian gift,' which is exclusively based on brāhmaṇical conceptions.

5 The, ultimately divisive, politics of cultural homogenisation is primarily a project of the modern nation state. In India, the ancient hierarchical ideologies, the cultural pluralism on the ground, and the secular constitution have, thus far, put a break on the supremacist 'Hindu' religious nationalism which, however, turns out to be difficult to contain.

6 Reified definitions of 'religion' and of religions such as 'Hinduism' or 'Jainism' are a modern, highly-politicised preoccupation. On the term 'religion' see for instance Smith 1991 and for 'Hinduism' Sontheimer 1991.

7 Mahāvideha plays an important role in Jain cosmology and cosmography. See Schubring 2000 ī 102ff.

8 The Jain terms *samyak darśana* (right insight) or *kevalajñāna* (omniscience) are rarely used in this context, presumably to avoid unnecessary debate. See A.M. Paṭel, in Amīn 1994: 77.

9 A.M. Paṭel, in Amīn 1994: 32.

10 Ibid., p. 72. With the exception of the Appendix, I follow throughout the text the official English renditions of the original Gujarātī that are offered in the Pamphlet literature of the Akram Vijñān Mārg.

11 Orally transmitted practical philosophy of a similar style was also practised by the Marāṭhī-speaking householder Guru Nisargadatta Mahārāj (1897-1981), a petty shopkeeper in Mumbaī whose birth name was Māruti before he was initiated into the Advaita Vedānta Navnāth Sampradāy in 1930. See Dikshit 1999. Within the Jain tradition, the teachings of the Gujarātī *brahmacārī* Kānjī Svāmī (1889-1980) are also transmitted in this form. The only direct influences cited by A.M. Paṭel himself was the Gujarātī Jain householder Śrīmat Rājacandra (1867-1901) and the Digambara Ācārya Kundakunda (ca. 1st-8th century CE).

12 *samyag-darśana-jñāna-cāritrāṇi mokṣamārgaḥ* (TS 1.1).

13 Soul (*jīva*), non-soul (*ajīva*), inflow of karmic particles (*āsrava*), bondage of karmic particles (*bandha*), stoppage of the inflow of karman (*saṃvara*), annihilation of karman (*nirjarā*), liberation from karman (*mokṣa*) (TS 1.4).

14 On the principal features of canonical (and classical) Jainism see Schubring 2000.

15 See Johnson 2000.

16 Devotion here means merit making through *pūja*, *dāna*, *vandanā*, etc., in combination with asceticism. A Jain version of *bhakti* religiosity without the necessity of asceticism and study can be found amongst the followers of Śrīmat Rājacandra (Salter 2001).

17 Flügel 2005: 195.

18 The term 'movement' is theoretically uninformative, as Luhmann 1984: 543 rightly stressed, and is here only used for convenience for non-institutionalised collective behaviour. Luhmann suggests to rather talk about 'the production of effects through unintended self-amplifying effect-cumulation,' i.e. self-referential processes which initially emerge through the accidental coincidence of events which generate a series of unintended consequences, until they are stabilised when the notion 'movement' is used as a self-description (p. 544). A functional theory such as this comes somewhat closer to the self-interpretation of the Akram Vijñān 'movement' in terms of the contingent discharge of various individual *karmans* which come to fruition through natural processes or 'scientific circumstantial evidence' (*vyavasthita śakti*), rather than the reference to a common ideology (Salter 2001: 49) or political interests (Fuchs 1999: 59).

19 The aggregative, syncretic nature of 'Brāhmaṇism' and 'Hinduism' (and its 'tolerance' of heterodox sects) was highlighted by Dumont 1980: 269, 284, etc. But he denied this very feature to the religious 'sects' which, he argued, are "inclusive as regards the subjects, the faithful, but strict and exclusive as regards the god or belief, the object of religion" (ibid.).

20 "This is a short cut a diversion path (marg) a different (akram lift - "stepless" elevator). You don't have to do any effort" (A.M. Paṭel, in Amīn 1994: 81f.).

21 For further details on the history, doctrine and following of the Akram Vijñān Mārg see Flügel 2005. Most followers are Gujarātī Pāṭīdars on which see Pocock 1973 and Tambs-Lyche 1980.

22 Daniels 1999: 34f.

23 The two other temple complexes are near Baroda and near Ahmedabad. The latter is the only Tri-Mandir temple of the followers of Nīrubahen to date..

24 Recent publications edited by her contain the following quotation of 'Dada Bhagavan' under the heading 'Current link for attaining the knowledge of Self-Realization (Atma Gnan)': "I am personally going to impart siddhis (special spiritual powers) to a few people. After I leave, will there not be a need for them? People of future generations will need this path, will they not?"

25 The word *puruṣa* means either human being or man. The following characterisation of the 'Vatsalyamūrti Kanubhāī Dādā' is given by the president of the Jay Saccidānand Saṅgh, G.A. Shah 2003: 23: "In Him is the divine love of God personified. ... Today, DADA BHAGAVAN manifests in full spiritual splendour in Revered KANU DADAJI with all the spiritual might of conducting 'Gnan Vidhi,' separating 'I' from 'My' – Eternal DADA BHAGAVAN – The Formless 'Pure Soul' (Paramatma) is experienced in physical form and frame of KANU DADAJI. As the Liberator and Saviour of all aspiring Souls he is moving all over the world."

26 For further details on the reasons for the split and the processes of the 'routinisation of charisma' within the movement see Flügel 2005: 218-225.

27 The word *āpta* means also trustworthy, reliable, authoritative. For its use in the Jain tradition see Soni 1996.

28 For a similar structural divide see the Śrīmat Rājacandra movement which has been studied by Salter 2001.

29 See Flügel 2005: 202ff.

30 Cf. Williams 1963: 91.

31 ibid., pp. 84ff., 172ff.

32 Bronkhorst 2003 argued that similar conceptions must have prevailed amongst the Ājīvikas.

33 A.M. Paṭel in Amin 2005. In the words of Kanubhāī Paṭel (in J.P. Amīn Vol. 11 1997-2003: 10): "Real 'Penance' - 'Tap' is spontaneous and borne with equanimity within, not from any activity." *Brahmacarya* does not involve taking a public vow of celibacy, but merely the inner belief "that 'I am a Brahmachari'" (p. 20): "'Renouncement' is not of things, house, wife or children. No, it is the 'attaching force' that is to be renounced and in present times that is only possible after Self Realisation first, through the grace of Atma-Gnani the Self-Realized One" (p. 18).

34 In the U.S., apart from Oak Ridge, they travel to dedicated followers in Chicago, Houston, Los Angeles and Montreal. In 1994, a conference of 700 followers was held in Oak Ridge (Daniels 1999: 34f.).

35 The names of 17 of the 27 *āptaputras* initiated by A.M. Paṭel himself are: Pareś Aṇākhīvālā (from Surat, working in Mumbaī as a computer engineer), Bihārī Bhagat, Kantilal Bhagat, Navin Bhagat, Bharat Mahetā, Kamleś Mahetā, Mineś Mahetā, Dr. Śaileṣ Mahetā, Yogeś Mistrī, Aśok Mocī (a chemist), Pradīp Parekh, Maheś Paṭel, Pulin Punātar, Jaymeś Śāh, Kamleś Śāh, Mahendra Śāh, Nimeś Sakhīdās.

36 I do not know more about the relationship between Kanubhāī Paṭel and the *āptaputras*, nor his personal views on this point. Kanubhāī Paṭel regularly travels to the U.S.A., Great Britain and East Africa. He toured West Africa in 1996 where he created a following amongst the small Indian diaspora in Lagos (Nigeria) (G.A. Shah 2003: 1).

37 Amīn 1983: 89.

38 Personal communication, 1999.

39 Dudden Hill Community Centre, London NW10, 11.5.1997, 14.30-19.00; Madhanta Youth and Community Centre, London HA9 7EE, 16.5.1999, 15.00-18.00, and 8.8.1999 15.30-19.30. I attended two other ceremonies in London for a limited period of time and was assured that exactly the same format is applied in India and elsewhere in the

world. I have only participated in the rites of knowledge *cum* initiations conducted by Nīrubahen Amīn who officially initiated me. Kanubhāī Paṭel apparently performs the ritual in exactly the same way (personal communication, November 2003), and I saw a video which seemed to confirm this.

40 Cf. Amīn 1983: 82f. For the Digambara Jain concepts of *bheda jñāna, jñānī, śuddha-upayoga*, etc., see the writings of Ācārya Kundakunda, and Upadhye 1935.

41 The paradox of mediated immediacy is not explained.

42 Amīn 1998: 30-43.

43 This technique of turning up "unexpectedly and suddenly" apparently out of nothing is utilised by many modern saints such as Sai Baba. See Swallow, in Fuller 1992: 178.

44 The term omniscience (*sarvajñāna*) is here used in the narrower mystical understanding that: "When 'knower' is 'known,' everything is known in the universe," i.e. everything that matters (Kanu Paṭel: Aphorism 101 in J.P. Amīn Vol. 11 1997-2003: 16).

45 For full texts and translations of the texts cited in this section see Appendix.

46 The *tīrthaṅkaras* are included here.

47 Cf. BG 10.49, cited in Jaiswal 1967: 119.

48 I have not seen the Gujarātī original of a more elaborate English version of the first part of this offering which is often cited in the pamphlet literature: "O universally adored and fully manifested Śuddhātmā Bhagavān! O Dādā Bhagvān, O Śrī Sīmandhar Svāmī! You are detached, free from passions, blissful, natural, full of infinite knowledge, infinite vision, illuminator of the three worlds (the entire universe)."

49 The characterisation of the relative self in terms of the expression *huṁ bhāv karma, dravya karma, no-karma*, here translated as 'my inner actions, material actions and reflex actions,' requires some explanation. A.M. Paṭel equated these three types of actions with 'charging, discharging, and neutral action,' i.e. the mechanism of the acquisition of *karman* through the inner feelings or passions, the discharge of *karman* through action, and reflex behaviour. According to canonical Jainism, *no karma* is produced by reflex actions caused by *no-kaṣāya*, or subsidiary passions of the four principal passions anger, pride, deceit and greed. The following nine *no-kaṣāyas* are habitual in everyday life, but decrease with spiritual advancement: laughter (*hāsya*), enjoyment (*rati*), apathy (*arati*), grief (*śoka*), fear (*bhaya*), disgust (*jugupsā*), and sexual cravings for the male, female, and hermaphrodite (*strī-veda, puṃveda*, and *napuṃsakaveda*) (UtS 32.102, 33.10-11). On *no-karma* see Schubring 2000: 87, Jaini 1979: 120, Bruhn 1987: 69. See also Chakravarti's 1989: 129, 75 commentary on SS 190-192, and SS 87, and Johnson 1995: 287.

50 See also Geertz 1986: 373.

51 See Cort 2001: 153 for similar 'magico-religious' assumptions underlying the rather mechanical *Kalpa Sūtra* recitations of Mūrtipūjaka Jains during *paryuṣaṇa*. For examples from 'Hindu' contexts see the contributions in Dalmia et.al. 2003.

52 The distinction was introduced by the Digambara *Ācārya* Kundakunda (SS 7) into Jain discourse. On the shock of insight created by the reversal of perspectives in Jain conversion stories see Ryan 1998: 77 and Flügel 1993. In the present case, the shock of insight is explained as the product of non-cognitive ritual action.

53 Turner 1986: 35 translates Dilthey's terms *Erlebnis* and *Erfahrung*, which have no equivalent in English, as '*mere* experience' and '*an* experience.'

54 This formally resembles the separation of ritual and meaning postulated by Humphrey and Laidlaw 1994, following Frits Staal 1993, but can hardly be interpreted as a universal condition of ritual action, as proposed by the authors.

55 "If one listens to the 'Direct Speech,' one will have 'Samakita'" (A.M. Paṭel in Shah 1983: 72).

56 A more differentiated analytic terminology is needed to make further distinctions.

57 E.g., Amīn 1983: 33. See Staal 1993: Ch. 3 and p. 192 on the 'power of inspiration' associated with words, derived from the Sanskrit (S.) root *dhī-* (e.g. *dhyāna*), and its manifestation in language, especially verses, chants, and formulae, called *mantra*, which were at an early state distinguished from ritual itself: "Mantras [sacred formulae] are always the elements that are recited or chanted; they are neither the ritual acts themselves, nor the glosses or meanings ..."

58 In contrast to the 'absolute,' that is instrumental, music (Dahlhaus 1978: 13), 'pure speech' is not intended as a 'pure structure' without object or function, but has a strong 'conative function,' i.e. it is intended to direct the gestures of the participants (Lévi-Strauss 1982 I: 49). See also Staal 1993: 221 for the similarity between *mantras* and music.

59 Cf. Staal 1993: 233f. on Buddhist 'meaning(ful)-memorization' (*artha-dhāraṇī*) and on the Jain *Namokār Mantra* etc. (p. 223): "Many mantras [whether meaningful or meaningless] are constructed from language, but in their ritual use, which is their proper use, they do not conform to any of the normal uses of language" (p. 265). Staal argues "that language derived from mantras in the course of the evolution" but also describes the opposite phenomenon of "the musicalisation of language" (ibid.) under the same term (cf. Lévi-Strauss 1982 I: 42f. remarks on the differences between structuralism and serialism). The ritual communication of the *bhed jñān vidhi* is an example of the latter, since it clearly presupposes language.

60 "The mystical state is a state of awareness that can be reached or produced with the aid of mantras, a state of consciousness that is 'beyond language' or 'ineffable'" (Staal 1993: 274).

61 "'Understanding' is not the function of language" (Kanu Paṭel: Aphorism No. 46, in J.P. Amīn Vol. 11 1997-2003: 8).

62 The emphasis on *śakti* reveals Śaivaite influence. Compare Staal 1993: 242 on the eligibility of using mantras.

63 Classical Jainism distinguishes five types of bodies: gross body (*audārika śarīra*), transformation body (*vaikriya śarīra*), communication body (*āhāraka śarīra*), fiery body (*taijasa śarīra*), and karmic body (*karma śarīra*). The *āhāraka śarīra* is said to be an attribute of ascetics with the knowledge of the lost fourteen *Pūrva* texts only. See TS 2.37 for details.

64 Garcia 2002 writes for instance: "This combination: one guru and a heavy load of karma made it impossible for me to experience anything within. Even when I experienced something, now I know it was due to the power of my own mind concentration and not necessarily due to the power of the guru."

65 Compare the somewhat similar Mimāṃsā concept of the invisible (*adṛṣṭa*) effects of ritual (*apūrva*).

66 See www.dadabhagawan.org. To dispel doubts about the efficacy of the rite, Nīrubahen Amīn n.d. published also an explanatory article: "What is your spiritual state after the 'Gnan Ceremony'?" which is often consulted.

67 The dream was related to me in 2001. On the significance of dreams see A.M. Paṭel, in K.N. Shah 1983: 168: "A dream is the complete effect. There, ego being inactive, causes do not get implanted. ... You gain profusely more by seeing 'Dada' in a dream and seeking his assistance, than by seeing Him in person. This Dada is capable of doing everything in a dream! Yes, you must know what you want to ask for. Some of our Mahatmas see Dada in dream everyday. As the scriptures sing: Even in a dream who has 'Darshan,' Not shall his mind seek another vision. The 'Darshan' of the Gyani Purush even in the dream will put an end to all the other rovings of the mind."

68 Śrīmat Rājacandra claimed to have met a Jina in a previous life. See Flügel 2005: 210.

69 Salter 2001: 46-47 reported similar processes amongst the followers of Śrīmat Rājacandra: "It is believed that one self-realised person can accurately recognise another ... If they reach the belief that the *guru* is authentic they go on to become a disciple and hence enforce the *guru*'s status." See also Dumont's 1980: 282 statement that "in order to conceive of a personal Lord there must also be a believer who sees himself as an individual."

70 The Śvetāmbaras believe the *tīrthaṅkara* Mallinātha was female.

71 See Gombrich & Obeyesekere 1988: 61.

72 That is the body (A.M. Paṭel, in R.M. Patel 1994: 4f.).

73 The precepts are only printed in a single small booklet (Amīn 1998) which contains all important ritual texts in Gujarātī. It is only given to *mahātmās*.

74 In the ritual literature of the Akram Vijñān Mārg the word *niścaya* is sometimes interpreted literally, as resolve or decision, i.e. the intention of completely surrendering the relative self to the real self (not philosophically, in terms of *niścaya naya*). Shifting interpretations such as this offer escape clauses against the arguments of sceptics. It is argued that the *jñān vidhi* merely conveys the energy or spiritual power for the resolve, not access towards transcendental perception itself.

75 See Schubring 1957: 569 for critical reflections on the possibility of the apocryphal interpretations of SS 141 which identify the *niścaya* point of view with the view of a spiritually advanced believer.

76 "Prakriti means Circumstantial Evidence. This, that goes on, is nothing but the puppet show of Prakriti. One dances or does anything as it makes him to, and yet he brags: 'See, I dance! I renounce!' Renunciation is possible, only if it is in one's Prakriti" (A.M. Paṭel, in K.N. Shah 1983: 257). On the use of the metaphor of dance, well-known in Vaiṣṇavism, for the ambiguities generated by the two-truth theory in Digambara Jain literature see Bhatt 1994.

77 On complementary *karman* see for instance A.M. Paṭel, in Amīn 2003a: 20.

78 A.M. Paṭel, in R.M. Paṭel 1994: 50.

79 Cf. SS 332-344.

80 In classical Jainism, the technical terms for bondage and stoppage are *bandha* and *saṃvara*. A.M. Paṭel occasionally employed these terms, but usually used Gujarātī equivalents.

81 Literally 'filling.'

82 A.M. Paṭel, in R.M. Patel 1994: 11. Bronkhorst 2003: 169 has shown that already the Ājīvikas must have believed that the real self does not act, and that karmic changes can only occur through rebirth. Yet, the Ājīvikas did not – like A.M. Paṭel's 'moderate fatalism' (which rejects the concept of 'untimely death,' see N. Amīn, in R.M. Patel 1994: 54f.) – consider the possibility of changes and shortcuts in the karmically predetermined course of rebirths through 'the path of introspection' (*antaramukhī mārga*) (A.M. Paṭel, in N. Amin 2000a: 7).

83 Cf. Todarmal's 1992: 174-76, 203f. critique of the Sāṁkhya view: "nothing is achieved by mere knowing. ... So long as one believes Prakruti to be the doer (of attachment, etc.) and the self as non-doer, why would then he try to reduce attachment, etc.?" (p. 176).

84 A.M. Paṭel, in K.N. Shah 1983: 230.

85 Classical Jainism categorises the different types of *karman* according to effect (*prakṛti*), duration (*stithi*), intensity (*rasa*) and quantity of space points occupied (*pradeśa*). Four principal types of bondage (*bandha*) of *karman* are distinguished: wrong belief (*mithyātva*), non-restraint (*avirati*), passion (*kaṣāya*), and activity (*yoga*). Starting with wrong belief, they should be eliminated one after the other to prevent further bondage. The effects of *karman* are of three types: (1) *bandha* - bondage, (2) *sattā* (*ābāhā*) - latency, (3) *udaya* (*prārabdha*) - realisation: (a) *udīranā* - premature fruition, (b) *saṃkrama* - transformation of one type of *karman* into another (Viy. 57b; TS 8.2): "Of one's own accord one makes [karman] effective (*udīrei*) and one repents (*garahai*), checks (*saṃvarai*), suppresses (*uvasāmei*), experiences (*veei*) and annihilates (*nijjarei*) it by an effort of one's own will (*vīriya*)" (Vij. 1.3.6 (56b), in Deleu 1970: 78). See also Glasenapp 1915: 20ff., 35-38, 42, 75.

86 N. Amīn, in R.M. Patel 1994: 56.

87 Practical rules that are given orally, for instance: "to look at everything only as a karmic result," to "accept everything that happens," "never misuse the power acquired through the *jñān vidhi* for worldly ends," "never resolve to do anything intentionally (*saṅkalpa*)," "don't be presumptuous of the form 'if I ____'," etc. For lists of practical advice see also A.M. Paṭel, in N. Amin 2000a: 17, 36.

88 A.M. Paṭel, in R.M. Patel 1994: 73-6.

89 Ibid., p. 62.

90 At least 'seventy-five percent' of it (A.M. Paṭel, in Amīn 2003a: 74).

91 Cf. A.M. Paṭel, in Amīn 2003b: 107f.

92 On the Jain rites of atonement see Caillat 1975.

93 The Akram Vijñān movement often uses popular metaphors such as 'video-rewinding' or 'the cinema approach' to *karman*, i.e. life as a film (A.M. Paṭel, in N. Amin 2000a: 33f.), for the reflective *anamnesis* as the following summary of Nīrubahen Amīn's Telesatsang on the 23.7.2000 illustrates: "Every 15 to 30 minutes rewind and fast forward your inner video and if you miss this, then at the end of the day rewind the entire day's video for 10 to 15 minutes. Our Godown is stuffed full. Let us resolve to clear it with the phenomenal Grace of Dada and all His Gnan material. Remove all vyavahaar aagrahs and the rest is all nikaal. ... Observance with awareness is the essence of Time and the state of the Self. Day's events and agenda: Set in advance the 5 agnas and then proceed. Thereafter rewind and set review and reset. ... When you get engrossed ... get unentangled by video rewind and review. When you are reviewing you are the observer and therefore free. To rewind and reset is your Purusharth. To forget your Self is what you have brought with you. Observe this in samayik

am till eve ... watch whether your upayog was of the Self or not. Set 5 Agnas. Set your Self: I am Shuddhatma. Observe all events of File 1. Observe all events of food intake situations. Observe all events of speech, thoughts, acts of the whole day. Observe and separate acts of chit buddhi and discharge ego. Observe all work done for mahatmas and dada versus your selfish self. Observe your upayog during charan vidhi. ... . Is the reading merely an act or is there an upayoga? Observe the nature of this neighbour of yours. ..." (now defunct website).

94 Bruhn 1998: V.1 has argued that even in classical Jainism "– there is no distinct meditation technique (leading to concrete experiences or insights). 'Meditation' in Jainism means realization and internalization of important dogmatic subjects but even that is more implied than expressly stated." Cf. Schubring 2000: 314.

95 A.M. Paṭel, in Amīn 2003a: 77.

96 Some of the statements in Kundakunda's *Samayasāra* are clearly the source of inspiration of A.M. Paṭel's teachings: "That ignorant Self which makes non-self, self, and the Self non-Self, becomes *Kartā* or causal agent of those various *Karmas*. - That knowing Self which does not make non-self, self, and the Self, non-self, does not become the *Kartā* or causal agent of those various *Karmas*" (SS 92f., tr. Chakravarti 1989: 78f.; cf. Johnson 1995: 280). "The scripture is not knowledge, because scripture knows not anything. Therefore, the Jinas said that knowledge is entirely different from scripture" (SS 390, tr. Chakravarti 1989: 226; cf. Johnson 1995: 275). See also SS 152, 404, etc.

97 "As (self-) knowledge renounces all (mental) states (bhāva), knowing them to be other (than the self), so (self-) knowledge should be considered to be the real/definitive form of renunciation [*pratyākhyana*]" (SS 34, tr. Johnson 1995: 288). Cf. the translation by Chakravarti 1989: 37f.

98 See Jaini 1979: 89, and Beck 1997: 91: "Overall, the developing Hindu devotional tradition strikes one with the forceful theme of utter dependence on grace alone for remission of sin, leaving aside completely all self-restorative rituals and penances."

99 The *brāhmaṇical* practice of transacting *karman* or pollution to others, as recently discussed by authors such as Parry and others, is rejected as an impossibility by Jainism, Buddhism, and Hindu devotionalism. See Cort 2001: 111.

100 The Gītā is cited explicitly on the official website: www.dadabhagwan.org/new/introduction/akaram-intro/eng/akaram-intro.html

101 A.M. Paṭel, in Amīn 2003a: 2.

102 Ibid., p. 7.

103 "If your wife who is normal and intelligent becomes insane all of a sudden, whom can we blame? She turns insane as the result of the timing for your own karma coming into fruition. So you should realize this and accept that it is your account. ... You have no choice but to experience them" (A.M. Paṭel, in Amīn 2003a: 39).

104 A.M. Paṭel, in Amīn 2003a: 3. There are, therefore, no accidents in life, there is not even the possibility of an accidental death.

105 A.M. Paṭel, in R.M. Patel 1994: 48.

106 A.M. Paṭel, in Amīn 2003a: 31f. It is asserted for instance, on apparently purely casuistic grounds, that: "discord does not occur because of effect karma. It arises because of ignorance" (ibid., p. 47). See similar discussions in the same volume.

107 A.M. Paṭel, in Amīn 2003a: 13.

108 "The process of killing is a karma effect and it has to be suffered [by the killer, P.F.]. One must accept the fruit of the karma, but if repentance is done whole-heartedly, then the new karma will become light" (A.M. Paṭel, in Amīn 2003a: 72f.).

109 Sometimes, after *ārati* rituals, one plate (*thāḷī*) is placed in front of the picture of 'Dādā Bhagavān.'

110 This has also been noted by Garcia 2002.

111 A.M. Paṭel, in R.M. Patel 1994: 63.

112 "An Enlightened Guru like Dada Bhagwan accepts all view-points, all of these are included in his vision. A Guru can be said to be sitting at the centre, while all the other religions are in the surroundings in search of the truth" (A.M. Paṭel, in N. Amin 2000a: 30).

113 "The Germans are in search for 'Absolutism.' They have carried away our sacred books and they have dedicated themselves to the search of 'Absolutism.' But it is not easy to find it. ... When 'we' go to Germany 'we' shall tell them we are the horn of plenty (kalpa vriksha), ask anything of us and you shall have it, because 'we' have personally come before you" (A.M. Paṭel, in Shah 1983: 10f.).

114 For an overview of modern variants, see Fuller 1992: 174-77.

115 See for instance Bennett's 1993: 136f. critique. Dumont 1980: 282ff. and Fuller 1992: 157f. acknowledge the antinomian character of devotionalism. But both argue that though it may be antithetical to 'Hinduism' on the level of ideas (Dumont characterises devotion as an internalisation of renunciation though), it is not on the level of social practice, since it accommodates itself to 'the caste system.'

116 Dumont 1980: 187, but see his earlier and more flexible formulation on p. 284 in the light of the theory of *bhakti* as a form of internalised renunciation.

117 For further evidence see the majority of the contributions in Dalmia et. al. 2003.

118 Bennett 1993: 66.

119 "Possessions" is the English translation used for *dravya karma* here.

120 Bennett 1993: 60.

121 Ibid., p. 43.

122 Love "that is constant is paramatma's love (God's love). It will subdue anyone. I for myself do not wish to subdue anyone, but they surrender to my love. It is revealed in the presence of *Gnani Purush.* This love is absolute and unconditional. The Gnani's love is God's love" (A.M. Paṭel, in Amīn 2000b: 25).

123 Bennett 1993: 89.

124 Ibid., p. 124.

125 Ibid., p. 196ff.

126 Ibid., p. 254.

127 For imports into Digambara Jain mysticism see Bhatt 1994: 447.

128 A.M. Paṭel, in R.M. Paṭel 1994: 49.

129 Bennett 1993: 90.

130 Bennett 1980: 97, cf. 87 analysed similar processes amongst the Puṣṭimārgīs in psychological terms: "Those who experience *bhava* are by definition divine souls *(daivijiva)* aware of their innate identity as fragments of Brahman. Their divinity is not a quality received from Krishna, rather this is through Krishna's grace that inner divine qualities are made manifest." "The *svarup* becomes an actual manifestation of Lord Krishna through the combined efforts of the guru and the devotee. Although the guru initiates the process of the transformation of a murti into a *svarup,* the full identity of the *svarup* is revealed only through the efforts of the *sevak.* .. the *sevak* projects emotions into the *svarup* with the result that the *svarup* develops a lively personality" (ibid., p. 89).

131 A.M. Paṭel, in K.N. Shah 1983: 21f. In the original Gujarātī, the phrasing of the last sentence is: *ā amārī vāt to tamāro ātmā ja kalūb kare. kāraṇ ke tamārī mahiṁ huṁ ja beṭhlo chuṁ, tame jo āḍāī nahīṁ karo to! amne tamārā māṁ ne amārā māṁ bhed na hoy* (AV I: 16f.).

132 Bennett 1993: 85.

133 Monier Williams 1986: 1135. The meaning of *saccidānanda* is interpreted slightly different in various traditions. Vallabhācārya wrote: "From the joy-form of God came out the in-dwelling spirits which have in them all the three attributes of God, being (*sat*), consciousness (*citta*) and joy (*anand*). The *jīva* (individual souls) are without joy, and matter is without joy and consciousness" (in Pocock 1973: 110f.). The classical Jain tradition defines: *sat* = the six 'eternal' categories of being: *caitanya* (consciousness), *pudgala* (matter), *kāla* (time), *ākāśa* (space), *dharmāstikaya* (medium of movement), *adharmāstikaya* (medium of rest); *citta* = *jñān* (knowledge) + *darśana* (perception); *ānanda* = happiness or bliss (cf. Jaini 1979: 97, 122).

134 Bennett 1993: 60, cf. 41. Another example of this dynamic of devotional worship is the following line from a poem of Devacandrasvāmī that was quoted by Rājacandra in letter 753: *jina pūjā re te nijapūjana.* "It means 'worshipping the Jina (the conqueror) is worshipping yourself (your own pure soul).' What he means is that by nature the soul of a Jina (or a siddha) and that of the aspirant are equal" (Pungaliya 1996: 290f.).

135 Cf. Bennett 1993: 67.

136 Amīn 1998: 7.

137 Ibid., p. 23.

138 Ibid., p. 35.

139 See also Dundas' 1998: 43-46 comment on the putative ritual function of the Tantric Mūrtipūjaka *sūrimantra* which is meditated upon so that, according to one Mūrtipūjaka interpretation, "the meditating *sūri* [is] becoming Gautama" (ibid., p. 44), although others insist that the meditator merely becomes "'like' or 'equal to' (*tulya*) Gautama" (ibid.). For general observations of the conflation of *guru* and god in Jainism see Jaini 1979: 256 and Cort 2001: 114.

140 Ultimately, a pure soul may only be conceived as a separate entity if the term *ātmaśuddhi* figures prominently as well, as Richard Davis has argued in his study on the Śaiva Siddhānta (in Babb 1996: 182f.).

141 Dumont 1980: 282.

142 Nīrubahen Amīn is now targeting this audience. Two hundred and fifty Europeans participated in a *satsaṅg* in Spain in May 2004.

143 The issue of the absence of the divine in Jainism has been extensively (and controversially) discussed by Stevenson 1915/1984: 289-98.

144 A.M. Paṭel, in Amīn 2003a: 32.

145 Most of the ritual texts, with the exception of 1c, have been published in the pamphlet literature of the Akram Vijñān Mārg. The principal ritual manual and the main source for this appendix is N. Amīn 1998. The texts are here presented in the sequence of their ritual performance, not as printed. Section numbering and sub-headings have been inserted by the translator (P.F.). Section three, the 'meditation on the self' cum 'foot worship,' is a ritual text which should be read out every day. However, it is not exactly recited in its printed form during the *jñān vidhi.* The translation has been informed by English renditions published by the tradition itself.

146 The song was composed in 1970 by Candrakhand Navnīt, a singer from Mumbaī.

147 *bhāv karma.*

148 *no-karma.*

149 *dravya karma.*

150 *sambhāv.*

151 I.e., of the waves of desire.

152 *niścit.*

153 *vyavasthit.*

154 *darśan.*

155 *ātmā.*

156 *vyavahār.*

157 *niścay.*

158 *agocar.*

159 *akram.*

160 Jain Tīrthaṅkaras are included here in the category 'God.'

161 *saccidānand.*

162 *māyā.*

163 *bhāv karma.*

164 *dravya karma.*

165 *no-karma.*

166 The translation of is based on A. Patel's n.d.: 13-22 rendition of the *Nishchay Vyavahar Charan Vidhi* text.

167 Or: 'changeless' (*nirvikārī*).

168 *sahajānand.*

169 That is, the entire universe.

170 The Vedāntic term *nididhyāsana,* profound and repeated meditation (Monier Williams 1986: 549), is explained by Kanu Paṭel's Aphorism No. 89, in J.P. Amīn Vol. 11 2003: 14: "To see the formless within the aspectral forms of a Live Liberated State is called *Nididhyasan,* and when you see that, that seeing function is again formless because it is divine vision."

171 This famous formula of the Jain vow of renouncing violence (*sāmāyika*) is applied to all the listed misdeeds.

172 In classical Jainism, the eighteen states of sin (*pāpa sthāna*) are: 1. killing (*prāṇātipāta*), 2. lying (*mṛṣāvāda*), 3. thieving (*adattādāna*), 4. unchastity (*maithuna*), 5. acquisitiveness (*parigraha*), 6. anger (*krodha*), 7. pride (*māna*), 8. deceit (*māyā*), 9. greed (*lobha*), 10. attachment (*rāga*), 11. hatred (*dveṣa*), 12. disputation (*kalaha*), 13. false accusation (*abhyākhyāna*), 14. backbiting (*paiśunya*), 15. denigration (*par-parivāda*), 16. elation and depression (*rati arati*), 17. deceitful speech (*māyā mṛṣā*), 18. false belief (*mithyā darśana śalya*). The first five sources of sin refer to the five Jain *aṇuvratas*, or small vows, and the next six to the principal passions, or *kaṣāyas*.

173 The classical Jain *mahāvratas* are: 1. non-injury (*ahiṁsā*), 2. truthfulness (*satya*), 3. not taking what is not given (*asteya*), 4. non-possession (*aparigraha*), 5. celibacy (*brahmacarya*). Only in the DVS 4.17 a sixth *mahāvrata* is mentioned: not eating after sunset (*rātri bhojana tyāga*). It is surprising that these Jain categories are mentioned in the text, because such vows are not regarded as important by the Akram Vijñān.

174 *ālocanā*, or confession.

175 The terminology and the phrasing of this section is derived from the formulae of the canonical *Āvaśyaka Sūtra* (*Āvaśyaka Nirjukti*) and the Jain *Pratikramaṇa Vidhi* texts.

176 The word *avyābādha* (from S. *a-vyava*) was explained by A. Paṭel n.d. as "I can never be hurt nor can I hurt others."

177 *ṭaṅkotkīrṇ* (S. *ṭaṅka-ut-kīrṇa*), lit. 'chisel-inscribed,' here means 'unerasable.'

178 Patel n.d. translates: "between the real and the relative."

179 *jñānaputra.*

180 *jñānapitā.*

181 *ṭaṅkotkīrṇ.*

182 Patel n.d. translates "governed by an impartial precise energy called 'vyavasthit.'"

183 *kalyāṇamūrti.*

184 *samakitadhārī*; *samakit* is a colloquial expression for S. *samyaktva.*

185 *mahātmā.*

186 *namaskār.*

187 *mahātmā.*

188 *samyak darśan*, right insight.

189 *abhedabhāv.*

190 The explanation in brackets has been given by A. Patel n.d., though 'morning, midday, and evening' could also have been intended.

191 *samatābhāv.*

192 *sphurāymān*, from S. *sphur*, to sping, burst, manifest, etc.

193 The word *kalyāṇ*, welfare, means is here understood as 'spiritual welfare.'

194 *mokṣa.*

195 *syādvād.* Inserted by A. Paṭel n.d.: "(not to hurt another's viewpoint)."

196 *upāsanā.*

197 *mahant.* This term is uncommon in Jain literature but frequently used in Hindu contexts.

198 *ājñā.*

199 *bodhelo.*

200 *satsaṅg.*

201 *samyak jñān.*

202 *jāgṛti.*

203 *dekhabhāḷ.* Translated by Patel n.d. as "stay the 'Knower' and 'Seer.'"

204 *jay saccidānand.* The following instruction at the end of the printed text explains why the ritual is also called "foot worship" outside the context of the *jñān vidhi*: "(touch yourself with the big toes of your feet on your forehead connect the wire with the inner God in the form of infinite knowledge and say at least five times)" (Amīn 1998: 43).

205 The word *vijñāna* is usually translated as "scientific" by the followers of the Akram Vijñān Mārga.

206 A.M. Paṭel often used the English expression, though *niyamtā-vyavasthit śakti* can also be translated as "power of the systematic-regulator (god)," i.e. here "the power of natural law," the law of *karman.*

207 The official translation is reproduced here because it is often cited in the congregation. An alternative translation would be: "Settle your accounts with impartiality."

Index

A

B

E

F

G

H

I

J

K

M

N

O

P

R

S

W

Y